F

ALLEN

THE BUSINESS OF LOVING

THE BUSINESS OF LOVING

A NOVEL

by

GODFREY SMITH

LONDON
VICTOR GOLLANCZ LTD
1961

PR 6037 . M4 B8

First published May 1961
Second impression May 1961

Printed in Great Britain by
The Camelot Press Ltd., London and Southampton

FOR
MISS CHARLIE SMITH

What will happen will happen
The whore and buffoon will come off best;
No dreamers, they cannot lose their dream.
Louis Macneice

I

"Felix! It is you, isn't it?"

"Of course it is, Benny. But what a surprise. How are you?"

"I'm fine. But how extraordinary. What an odd place to meet. Are you a member here?"

"Yes. Well, I thought it would be an amusing place to bring people, though I doubt if I'll ever be called. Don't tell me you're reading for the Bar too?"

"Good heavens no. I came in with Jeremy Grumman. Do you know him?"

"Not yet I'm afraid. I hardly know anyone. Which is he, the old boy with glasses sitting on your left?"

"Yes, that's him. He's not so old. But what a coincidence. I can't get over it. How many years is it since we met? Twelve years?"

"Twelve or thirteen. You haven't changed much. A bit plumper perhaps."

"I recognised you at once. You look thinner."

"Even thinner?"

"Well, you always were a bit scraggy, Felix. But tell me about yourself. What are you doing beside reading law? Are you married? Where are you living?"

"I'm in the export business. I expect you remember."

"Yes of course I do. What's it like?"

"So so."

"And your father?"

"Oh fine. Taking it a bit more easily now. Writing fewer pamphlets than he used to. He's had a spot of blood pressure you know. Nothing to worry about, but he snoozes in a big chair every day for an hour after lunch."

"That's good. But what are you doing Benny? You look disgustingly prosperous."

"I've got my own business. I make gramophone records."

"You don't say! Gramophone records! I remember you always used to be a keen collector. That confounded club of yours . . . but how did you ever come to be in the business?"

"It's a long story. I'd like to tell you. Couldn't we meet for lunch or something?"

"Love to. One day next week?"

"Yes. Let me look at my diary. Tuesday?"

"Yes, I can make Tuesday. Have lunch with me. Come down to Pimm's in Threadneedle Street. Do you know it?"

"Yes I do; but I'd like you to have lunch with me."

"Oh but let me——"

"No really. To tell you the truth, I have to follow a strict régime."

"A diet? Surely not ulcers already, Benny?"

"Good Lord no. I mean—I have a sort of routine I keep to. I have lunch in my office. Don't worry, it's quite nice. I have a good chef."

"A *chef*? Benny you're not serious?"

"I'm afraid it must sound a bit extravagant. But after a lot of trial and error, I decided it was much cheaper than taking people to the Mirab—to restaurants. You know how it is."

"I wish I did! Well, you intrigue me. O.K., I'll come to you. Now what's the address?"

"It's Diskon House in Curzon Street."

"Diskon? Surely that's not your company? Why, I've got some Diskon records at home!"

"Yes. We're Diskon all right. It's quite a small company you know."

"Benny you astound me. Imagine you in big business! But how exciting!"

"Look, I must get back to poor old Grumman, Felix. He seems a bit put out. But before I go—you didn't say whether you were married or not."

"No. No I'm not married. Are you?"

"No. I'm not either."

"Oh. Neither of us. How strange. Must be something wrong with us. I mean, all our old friends . . ."

"Have you heard anything of Laura?"

"Laura? No I haven't seen her since—well, when I last saw you. Don't you know either?"

"Oh a little. Nothing really. But you're sure—I mean you haven't seen anyone from Aylsbourn who would have known her?"

"My dear chap, I haven't been near Aylsbourn for thirteen

years either. Oh, I believe I went through on my way to the coast one day. But no, I haven't heard a word of Laura for thirteen years. She might be dead for all I know."

"No. She's not dead."

"You've heard from her then?"

"In a way. I know she's not dead."

"How——?"

"Felix, I really must go. Poor old Grumman. I'll see you at Diskon next Tuesday then. A quarter past one all right?"

"Yes. Yes that's fine, Benny. Goodbye. I'll see you then. Awfully nice to see you again."

"Goodbye, Felix."

Jeremy Grumman watched them as they talked. Before him lay the slice of cold beef and the pickles, the cold potatoes and the beetroot he had chosen from the exiguous menu. The two tankards of beer stood untouched. There were not many people in; a handful of benchers and some black men. It was not the ideal place to bring Benedict, but on the other hand it saved a lot of expense. It was unlikely to cost him more than fifteen shillings for the pair of them. Really, he should have taken Benedict somewhere else, somewhere more lavish. No, it wouldn't do to try too hard. In any case, Benedict hadn't seemed to mind.

He sighed and took a swig of cold bitter beer. The need to get out of this soul-destroying occupation had grown to an obsession with him. It was too bloody ironic: he came from a celebrated legal family and was himself one of the most respected men at the Bar. People said he made fifteen thousand a year. Really, it was a good laugh. Last year he had in fact nearly killed himself with overwork and had cleared about two and a quarter thousand. In his twenty-five years at the Bar he had saved about two thousand; his wife had four hundred a year on trust. Even so, with three sons to educate, it was getting ridiculous. None of them was particularly bright, and their education was going to take a big bite out of his savings. He came in by tube from Moor Park every morning, and caught a bus from Baker Street. He worked like a dog, but the truth was, the majority of his time was still taken up with trifling cases. Yet he had what they called a first-class financial brain. His work on Company Law was supposed to be the best. Maybe: at the moment it had only one possible use in his mind. It might help him get a job with Benedict.

11

Perhaps even a directorship! It was a hell of a big business for any one man to carry on his shoulders.

He was reliably informed that the Diskon turnover was already £460,000 a year, and a good slice of the labour was unskilled. It would be no real hardship to pay him a regular three thousand out of that. And he would be able to put his feet up and watch the television play when he got home in the evening.

Benedict needed new blood! It would be a fine career and he'd be out of the treadmill for good.

There should be a pension at the end of it; perhaps an expense account even! It all depended on Benedict. A slight sense of antipathy ran through him, a glancing shiver of resentment. He watched Benedict talking; he seemed unusually animated. He was a cool customer normally, but sometimes you couldn't help wondering . . .

No doubt about it, though, a big man. One of the quickest new capital formations since the war. Now there might be a question of forming a public company, of floating a lot of shares. Well, Grumman was the boy for *that*.

A good man, Benedict. A very sane man indeed.

Weston was thinking as they talked: I wonder if he has forgiven me? I wonder if there is anything to forgive? I wonder if he is altogether sane? I wonder if it's possible that she *was* responsible for his failure? Because all this crap about Diskon doesn't make sense. At least, it makes all too excellent sense. Diskon is a monument to his failure; it's a by-product of all the spilled-over love, all the years of useless and wasted longing. What waste there is in romantic love! What a waste, oh what a bloody waste! Because we were friends once, good friends; and it's not as if I even took her away from him. What did I do that was wrong then? Was it merely that on that very still night thirteen years ago when we sat on the jet-black rock, unreal in the moonlight, with the lukewarm sea lapping at our feet, I told him the truth about love? Or did I tell him just the truth about *her*? Or the truth about himself? Or the truth about me? And isn't it true that nothing's gone right since that day on the jet-black rock? Because he may have a chef to save him bothering to go to the Mirabelle, but has he got anyone who can look after his mind and heart? Why does he stare at me so as we are talking now; with fear and sadness in his eyes? And it's all so long ago now anyway and I truly don't know what happened to Laura. But it is absolutely typical of Benny the lover and the dreamer that he should know something of Laura even now; even if it's only that she isn't dead. I sometimes wish I could believe in love as he does; because what else is there? Yet what has it brought him but pain and emptiness? And what has not believing in it brought me? And what is there common to our condition but the knowledge of Laura? And why do I keep thinking of Laura, turning her name over and over in my mind like an amulet? Why do I, if I don't believe in her, or in love, as Benny does?

Benny is a nice fellow, only stark, stone bonkers. How he stares!

"I'm terribly sorry about that, Jeremy. It's a very old friend of mine—a school friend in fact. Felix Weston. He's a member of your Inn."

"Oh really? I don't recognise him."

"He's new here. Do you know it's thirteen years since I last saw him?"

"Really? It looked as if you were making up for lost time."

"Yes, I suppose so. I'm sorry. But I've arranged to meet him for lunch next week. Then we can go back over all those old times. A terrible mistake, but hard to resist."

"Oh, it's nice to meet an old friend."

"Yes. But the funny thing is, I've always hated his guts."

"Always . . . ?"

"No, not always. For a long time. I'm glad I've met him. You can't go on hating someone like that."

Benedict paused and for a moment seemed at a loss.

"It would be good—it would be a good thing if we could be friends again."

Benedict left Grumman cordially at about ten-thirty. They shook hands outside the Inn and went their separate ways: the one to the underground, Moor Park, his semi-detached house, his anxious wife, his next day's brief, and his tremulous hopes; the other on foot to his flat in Upper Brook Street near the business he had built; profoundly troubled by the chance that had brought him face to face with his own past.

He walked because he loved to go on foot through London at night, because the air was cold and crisp, the shop windows laden and glowing, the coffee bars jangling with youth and excitement, the old men loitering in the streets, just ejected warm and protesting from their snug boozers; Long Acre, Leicester Square, Lisle Street—he floated with the tide, past the hamburger stores and the hygienic stores, his tall, slightly stooping figure encased in a heavy black overcoat, his hands in his pockets, no hat on his head, and his head cast down as he sauntered along; oblivious to the oyster bars and the hell-fire preachers and the buskers and the whores, the news-vendors, the shoe-shine boys, and the narrow plush-carpeted pink-lit doorways leading down to hell. He was thinking about Felix Weston.

"Good old Felix! Well hit, Weston! Come on, Benny! You've got time for another!"

The voices carried over the years clear and fresh and the sunlight was quicksilver again. It was the old hot nineteen-thirties sun; the sun, Benedict reflected, that had shone down on Hitler at Berchtesgarden, on the men going out to die in the Thetis, on Jesse Owens's flashing legs, on the matinée theatre-goers blinking as they came out of *French Without Tears*, on his heroes McCorkell and Arnold as they batted all afternoon for Hampshire.

On this day though, he and Weston were merely giving a lusty impersonation of their idols. Valhalla Preparatory School needed a mere six runs to beat their old enemies Locks Priory with six wickets still standing; it was really only a question of who was going to make the winning hit. They took two runs and Felix Weston faced up to the bowling again. Benedict leaned on his bat and wiped the sweat off his face, glancing at the mighty Margrave Brewery scoreboard. He could hardly believe his eyes, yet there it was. Opposite batsman number one (that was Felix, he always opened for Valhalla) stood the figure 53. Batsman number six—Benedict—was credited with the incredible, the perfectly fantastic total of 48 runs. Valhalla had scored 112 runs altogether; he and Felix must have made a stand of getting on for 90. He couldn't quite believe it.

The snub-nosed, sandy-haired Locks Priory bowler began his run and Benedict crammed his handkerchief hurriedly away. His bat trailing, he took two or three steps in consonance with the bowler as he had often watched McCorkell do, so that he would be already on the move if there was the chance of a run.

And there was. Weston cut the ball stylishly out towards point, and they took a quick single. Now Benedict faced the bowling. He was unconcerned; he had thoroughly played himself in and the ball was looking about the size of a pumpkin. He thumped a new centre and took guard.

The ball pitched short and Benedict had plenty of time to get his bat to it. He hit it with a rather ugly cow-shot but well in the centre. He felt that strong sensual pleasure as the spring took the shock, and then he heard applause run round the roped boundary. He wiped the sweat off his face again and self-consciously banged the end of his bat at an imaginary spot in the pitch, his head down. The applause continued, and he realised the Locks Priory boys were clapping too. With shyness, he raised his cap, as he had been taught to do, in acknowledgement of the applause. It was the first triumph of his life; he was thirteen and a half years old.

Felix Weston came half-way down the pitch for a conference (just as McCorkell and Arnold used to). He was a dark, good-looking boy, with curious black rings already forming under his eyes, as if he were an embryo debauchee. He grinned as Benedict approached.

"Good show, Benny," he said, "a lovely half century. Now don't do anything rash. You don't want to get bowled now. If you're not out it'll do your average a power of good."

"O.K., Felix. I'll block the rest of the over."

"O.K."

They separated to their respective ends.

The sandy-haired boy ran up again, and pitched up a fast, straight one. Benedict blocked it with respect and it began trickling down the pitch back towards the bowler.

Suddenly Weston shouted: "Come *on*, Benny!" and began to run hard. Benedict took three steps, realised his mistake, and yelled, "No!" He was too late. The bowler scooped up the ball and flung it hard at his wicket. His heart sank as he heard the clatter behind him.

Weston ran up as he began his dejected walk back to the pavilion. "Benny," he said, "how can I apologise? It was just an impulse. For goodness sake, forgive me."

"That's all right, Felix," Benedict said. "We're going to win. That's all that really matters."

Benedict's father was standing up as he came into the pavilion. He was clapping dementedly.

He was a tall, stooping, ruddy, excitable man, lean, his hair grey but his face still young and full of enthusiasm. He was forty years old. A fervent patriot, he had enlisted in the Hampshires in the first world war. This had not embittered him; on the contrary he had noticed only the courage, the comradeship, the *nobility* of war. He had many good war stories. Keith Margrave,

heir to the great brewery business, had been his platoon commander, and after the Armistice he had asked Mr. Benedict to
come in as a traveller. This Mr. Benedict had agreed to do with
his usual enthusiasm, and he had done very decently at the job.
He had a wide territory—Hampshire, part of Sussex and Surrey,
and he rattled cheerfully from one pub to the other in his brewery
van. Where the publican was a Margarve licensee, his task was
relatively simple: to encourage and incite, to note shortages and
rectify complaints, to keep the supply of Margrave's celebrated
bitter flowing freely to all who desired it. The hard selling came
in on the soft drinks side. It was Mr. Benedict's duty to build up
the sale of Marfrute in restaurants and groceries throughout his
territory. He did this loyally, but without conviction. He had
only three great loves that ruled his life. They were his beer, his
cricket, and his son. He was a widower. He lived in a small house
adjoining the "Thorn and Sceptre", a Margrave inn which served
the inhabitants of Ashdale, a village just outside Aylsbourn. Mrs.
Sampson, the landlady of the "Thorn and Sceptre", provided
father and son with their evening meal and Kate, one of the
barmaids, cleaned and laundered for them. The boy had lunch at
Valhalla during term time and in the Margrave staff canteen
during the holidays. Mr. Benedict made breakfast for them both
himself. It was a pleasant life that the two had made for themselves.

Mr. Benedict had few outside interests. He enjoyed his job and
indeed was an authority on the beer for thirty miles around. He was
a keen cricketer and turned out regularly for the Brewery second
eleven. He did little serious reading, though he studied the sports
pages of the *Daily Mail* each morning. He read an occasional
Cronin novel, but his evenings were generally spent drinking
bitter at the "Thorn and Sceptre", in reminiscing about the
curious people he had come upon in his thousands of miles as a
traveller, and in entering for crossword competitions. He had
been doing these for nineteen years now, and save for a guinea
postal order one Christmas, he had met with little success. He
was sure he would win one day.

"We'll go to Switzerland," he used to say to his son, "and stay
at the Chalet Bisque in Lausanne, where your mother and I went
for our honeymoon. Marvellous hot croissants we used to have
for breakfast every morning. Monsieur Blanchisseur—he is the
patron—will serve us personally. Great big jolly fellow, he was,

red face and walrus moustache; we were favourites of his; he couldn't do enough for us. And we'll have some Chocolat Meunier with the croissants; marvellous stuff, like black honey. We can't make chocolate here, you know. The Swiss beer's not up to much of course; like gnat's pee, to put it vulgarly. That's the only thing I'll miss, the beer. But we'll go one day, son, you can bet your life on that."

Then beaming and enthused with nostalgia, he would bend his attention to the simple linguistic permutations that by a perennial hairsbreadth eluded him. He would never give up trying. And he would never give up loving his son.

"Well done, well done!" he cried embarrassingly, as the boy approached from the wicket. He shook his hand in an access of paternal pride.

Mr. V. V. Varley, headmaster of Valhalla, joined them. A large florid man of sixty, he stood six feet one inch and (as he was fond of telling his boys) swung the scales to just on eighteen stone.

No one knew exactly where Mr. Varley came from. He was called "Colonel" in the "Thorn and Sceptre", where he drank port and lemon each night, but malicious people in the town said he had promoted himself. It was even rumoured that he had been a sergeant-major. There was no way of confirming or denying this, for no one dared to ask Mr. Varley himself.

He had come to Aylsbourn in 1922, and bought Valhalla, a large ramshackle Victorian house, for what he jocularly called "a hundred down and chase me for the rest". It had once been a prosperous brewer's residence: basement, spacious ground floor, two floors above, maids' rooms, box rooms; the whole thing highly impractical to run even in the comparatively spacious nineteen-twenties.

At first people had been wary of the preparatory school which Mr. Varley had opened there. He seemed to have few academic qualifications, and the mauve and gold school uniform which he designed himself struck the population as flamboyant. On the other hand, he soon gathered round himself a legend for discipline. In consequence, he soon had an impressive row of successes in the Common Entrance examination. In the seventeen years of its existence Valhalla had prospered, till now it could boast a hundred and twenty boys, each of whose parents willingly paid fifteen guineas a term for the privilege of wearing the hideous mauve and gold cap. Mr. Varley was a great man, an institution in Aylsbourn.

He had black hair, still thick and wavy, which he brushed back severely. In the winter he wore a heavy black raglan coat with a white silk scarf, and carried a swordstick. For cricket, however, he wore a loud regimental blazer over crisply-laundered white flannels, with a white silk scarf knotted and tucked jauntily in at the throat.

"Well done, Benedict," he boomed. Then, turning to his father, he observed: "You must be a very happy man, sir."

"I most certainly am, I most certainly am." Mr. Benedict nodded several times with emphasis. They beamed down at the boy, who swung his bat awkwardly and stared at the floor. He was struggling with an unfamiliar problem: how to succeed gracefully. It was for this kind of skill that parents paid the fifteen guineas a term.

"What about a drink, eh?" Mr. Varley suggested.

"Never say no," Mr. Benedict claimed.

They turned into the pavilion, redolent still with the aroma of sawdust and oil lamps. The boy bashfully followed them.

"Lucky there's a club licence, what, Mr. Benedict?" chaffed Mr. Varley. "What's it to be—a pint of that excellent Margrave Ale of yours?"

"No better beer made," Mr. Benedict affirmed seriously.

"Right," said Mr. Varley. "And what about our hero— lemonade or ginger beer?"

"Lemonade please, sir."

"Rightyho. Two pints of Margrave Best Bitter and a pint of lemonade," roared Mr. Varley to the barmaid.

It was the best lemonade in the world, Benedict thought as he raised the pint tumbler to his lips; a cold acid-drop yellow liquid made with a liberal base of crystals that left a sharp citric flavour on the tongue; there could never be a drink in the world to match it. Not even Margrave beer, which was his father's livelihood. He drank half a pint of lemonade without pausing, while the two men watched benignly.

"Good lad," said Mr. Varley as Benedict lowered his glass with a gasp. "Chip off the old block, eh, Mr. Benedict?"

"He certainly is," Benedict senior confirmed with a beam of universal euphoria. "Your very good health, Mr. Varley."

"And yours, sir."

19

Just then an extra-long burst of applause told them that the game had ended in victory for Valhalla. In a moment the pitch was clouded over with small boys in white.

Mr. Varley frowned out of the window and finished his beer at a gulp. "Discipline," he said firmly. "Excuse me, please."

As he strode across the grass, the boys divided before him. He took a silver whistle from his blazer pocket and blew spiritedly on it. The chatter died away. "*To me, Valhalla,*" he called.

"Excuse me, Dad" Benedict said, and trotted briskly towards the throng of small boys who were scrumming tightly round the centripetal figure of Mr. V. V. Varley. The Locks Priory boys watched gobstruck.

"Valhalla," Mr. Varley boomed, "have just won a fine victory. It was a good clean game, with plenty of give and take, and a thoroughly sporting occasion from start to finish. Now then, I want you to show your appreciation of the gallant show put up by our old rivals. School, three cheers for Locks Priory. Hip hip . . ."

The cheers rang crisply in the warm summer air. Like garish targets in a shooting range, the violet and gold caps bobbed up and down as if on invisible currents of air.

"As you know," Mr. Varley continued, "it is not the Valhalla custom to pick out boys for individual approbation. We believe here in the team spirit first, last, and always. But I will break a rule today. Weston and Benedict made a magnificent stand. Without my reference books I cannot say if it is a school record, but whether it is or not, it was an achievement of which every Valhallian can be proud. School—three cheers for Weston and Benedict. Hip hip . . ."

And again the shrill cheers echoed over the brewery pavilion.

"Once again, we near the end of the summer term," Mr. Varley continued. "I shall expect every boy punctually on parade for nine o'clock drill as usual on Monday. If you behave, you should be away for your summer hols, reports signed, by twelve. But you know me well enough to remember that I am quite capable of flogging the whole school at the slightest sign of indiscipline, last day of term or no. Bear this well in mind. Happy weekend, boys."

"Happy weekend, sir," came back the crisply-drilled chorus, and the caps bobbed once more into the air. It was the valedictory at the end of each Friday afternoon. The tight concentric circles of violet and gold split and sundered in all directions. The boys walked smartly in groups of two or three, exemplars of decorum, at any rate till they were out of Mr. Varley's sight.

Mr. Benedict came over and put his hand on his son's shoulder. He smelt faintly—and pleasantly—of beer.

"I must get along, son," he said. "Have to deliver twelve dozen Marfrute bottles over at Little Welcaster. I'll be back by six. Are you having tea at school?"

"Not today, Dad. Felix has asked me home."

"Oh." Mr. Benedict frowned. "Bloody young fool, getting you run out like that."

"It was just over-keenness."

"I suppose so. Anyway, you got your fifty. Ah here's the rascal now."

Felix Weston raised his cap politely as he approached them. He still looked crestfallen. With his jet black hair and his black eyes set in the dark face, he looked like a small Spanish pirate.

"Good afternoon, sir," he ventured deferentially. Then in a rush: "You must think me an awful tick, running Benny out like that. I just seemed to lose my head."

"Never mind, Felix." Mr. Benedict was in a forgiving mood. "It was a historic partnership. You'll both be playing for Hampshire, I'll take money on it."

Not only did Mr. Benedict believe this with every fibre of his uncomplicated and affectionate soul; he could envisage no higher ambition for either of them.

The boys grinned and exchanged glances. Fathers could be a blasted embarrassment.

"Anyway," Mr. Benedict added, "I'm off. Back at six, son."

"O.K., Dad." Benedict found it hard to conceal his relief.

The boys sauntered over to the railings, mounted their bicycles, and pedalled slowly out of the Margrave Brewery ground. A few minutes later, a small Margrave Brewery van, driven by Mr. Benedict, rattled by them. He honked his farewell and disappeared.

The two boys cycled slowly down the main road until it began to merge into Aylsbourn High Street. They did not speak. It was a moment of peace between them. They floated in a slight interregnum between the past and the future; this moment was the end of childhood, the overture of youth. They had played their last game for Valhalla, taken their last cold bath and—subject to good behaviour on Monday morning—been beaten for the last time. It was Weston who broke the silence first:

"You know, Benny, I'm going to miss you terribly."

"But I haven't got into Shallerton yet."

"You will. Easily."

The next morning Benedict was to sit for his scholarship to Shallerton Oaks, the nearest public school. The fees, £150 a year, were far beyond Mr. Benedict's slender resources. Indeed he felt that he had had a good year when he made £500 with commission and expenses. It paid, in 1939, for a fortnight at Brighton for both of them, covered the rent of the house, met the upkeep on the Morris Eight, enabled him to buy a round of Aylsbourn bitter at the local, to give his son a new cricket bat on his birthday, to clothe him in grey flannel suits and even fork out the fifteen guineas a term for Valhalla. Quite evidently, though, it would not run to the £150 a year that Shallerton would cost.

But there was a scholarship; a benefaction of Margrave's Brewery worth at the moment about £135 a year. There was only one of these scholarships, and it was awarded on an examination, together with an interview. Mr. Benedict knew Ross-Tayfield, the headmaster of Shallerton, well, and consequently had no doubt that his son was going to win the scholarship. His evidence for this was in fact rather thin. He had button-holed Ross-Tayfield at the Margrave Sports, where the latter was an unwilling guest. Ross-Tayfield was a tall, gaunt, gloomy Scot, whose leisure was devoted entirely to ornithology. His idea of a treat was to give the school a lantern lecture with his latest slides of rare birds. Mr. Benedict had persuaded Ross-Tayfield to drink a pint of Margrave bitter with him, and had sung his son's praises. This would have entirely ruined the boy's chances, had not Ross-Tayfield already heard from Mr. V. V. Varley that the young Benedict had the makings of a really useful stand-off half. The only ambition in Ross-Tayfield's life was to see his school trounce Wargrave Castle. Since Ross-Tayfield had become headmaster of Shallerton, his school had in fact drawn twice with the Castle and lost four times, the last occasion forty-seven nil. He had sacked his rugby master and redoubled his efforts. Hence if this Benedict boy made any sort of show with the papers, he would have Ross-Tayfield's active support at the interview. Of course there was competition. Half a dozen boys a year went in for it, but luckily it was restricted to the sons of Margrave employees, and Benedict, beside being the best footballer of his year, was reliable, if not brilliant at English. So, if only his maths paper were not too bad . . .

Weston sighed. His father hated public schools, even small ones like Shallerton Oaks. This was especially annoying, because he could quite easily have afforded to send Felix there. The Weston money came from a Midland chain store business. Weston's grandfather had begun life as a grocer, and built up his trade until he had thirty shops. He had made the mistake of sending his only son, Gerard Weston, to Cambridge. Here Gerard had fallen in with a group of left-wing intellectuals, and, to his family's horror, had become an ardent communist. He had retired from the business, though prudently retaining his share in it. The stores were now run by a small consortium of managers, and Weston, since he had come back from Spain, had retired to the country to write a history of the civil war, to donate large sums to his party, to inflame the local peasantry with speeches and posters, and, perhaps pre-eminently, to brood. His first wife, Felix's mother, had died, and his second wife, a stunning artist's model, still only nineteen, now lived in the elegant Georgian house in the High Street which unflaggingly displayed communist slogans at by-elections.

So there was no question of Felix going in for the entrance examination, let alone the scholarship. He was going to Aylsbourn Grammar School. It was incongruous, Benedict thought; Felix belongs naturally at Shallerton; I belong to Aylsbourn. For once, he reflected, I have the edge on Felix; poor old Felix.

He turned impulsively towards him. "I could always fail tomorrow Felix. You know I can't go unless I get the scholarship."

Weston pulled up sharply and grabbed Benedict's bicycle by the saddle, hauling him to a halt too. He stared at Benedict hard, then his Mediterranean-dark face broke into a generous grin.

"Benny," he said, "you know you're nuts, don't you?"

"I don't really care about Shallerton Oaks. It's a good school, but—well I feel I belong here."

"You mean you think you're too bloody humble to go there?"

"Good Lord no. But I like it here. Don't you? I—I think I'll be a bit lost at Shallerton."

Weston stared at him again in affectionate disbelief.

"You really like this one-eyed hole? I'm longing to get out of it."

"I don't understand you, Felix. Do you know, I'd like to settle down and live here."

"Whatever for?"

"Well—it sounds silly I suppose, but I love the smell of the place."

"The smell?"

"Yes. It's a mixture of the Welcaster pond smell, and the dusty smell of the chalk in the air at Valhalla, and the glossy smell on the new books at Strether's shop, and the warm smell of the fresh doughnuts in Miller's bakery and—even the grass has a sort of——"

He looked at Weston shamefacedly.

"I suppose it sounds screwy."

Weston nodded solemnly. "Benny," he said. "You really are nuts. Anywhere—or anyone—can smell like that if you want them to. For heaven's sake remember that or you'll come a terrible cropper one day. But look here. Promise me one thing. Promise me you'll do your damndest on Monday."

Benedict grinned.

"O.K.," he said. "I'll do my damndest. After all, Shallerton is only eight miles away. I can cycle over to see you in half an hour."

Weston shoved Benedict's bicycle forward in a gesture of affectionate despair and they pedalled on dreamily again, each lost in his own thoughts. They turned down Brewer's Lane, which ran parallel to the High Street and just behind it, and banged the back door in Mr. Weston's garden wall noisily open. It was a small garden, but it had run to seed. In the kitchen window they saw the large, beneficent features of Mrs. Duncher, the Westons' housekeeper. She beamed when she saw them.

"Come along you boys," she called. "I expect you're hungry and thirsty."

In the drawing-room it was cool; the venetian blind was still down. For all his progressive thinking Mr. Weston was not a particularly sociable man. He and his wife had gone on one of their periodical day-trips to London. He would be attending a communist committee meeting in the East End while she went shopping at Harrod's; they would meet for lunch at the Savoy Grill and part again for the afternoon. She would go to the hairdresser's, he to the London Library. At six they would meet for a drink at the Fitzroy, and they would generally go to the theatre in the evening. They caught the last train, the 10.55 from Waterloo, back to Aylsbourn, and took a taxi up the hill home again. They would be indoors by a quarter to one. The Aylsbourn stationmaster said that Mr. Weston was often drunk when the train drew in.

At any rate, the house was now empty and cool. The sober works of Hegel and Marx fought for space on the bookshelves with the Hemingway novels, Gollancz yellow jackets, and the latest copies of the new magazine *Picture Post*.

It was (as Mrs. Duncher knew) Benedict's favourite high tea: veal and ham pie set in a huge dish of green salad, lettuce, cucumber, radishes, tomatoes, and cold potatoes. There was a thick, dark fruit cake and a monster pot of tea. The boys sat at each end of the long table and ate with gigantic zest. Benedict had six cups of tea, Weston five. They spoke little. The warmth and torpor of the summer day enveloped them. At thirteen it seemed hard to think about the past: even harder to cast the mind forward into the future. At length Weston said: "Come up to my room, Benny. I've got something I think will interest you."

Weston's room was at the top of the house, in what had once been a maid's room. His bookshelves provided an interesting comparison with his father's. There were Neville Cardus's *Cricket*, C. B. Fry's *Batsmanship*, and W. W. Wakefield's *Rugger*. There was a book by J. N. George called *English Pistols and Revolvers*. There was Auden and Isherwood's *The Ascent of F.6* and Macneice's first volume of poetry. There was a book by a man called Malinowski entitled *The Sexual Life of Savages*. But it was not books that Weston had brought Benedict to see. On the table under the gable window stood a small table, and under it a stack of records.

"I've got a new one, Benny." Weston grinned like a pirate returned to treasure trove. "And I know you're going to like it."

Gently he placed the shiny black disc on the turntable, wound the clockwork motor, and lowered the steel needle on to the track. There was a loud hiss and then the melancholy strains of the Basin Street Blues filled the little room.

Benedict listened entranced. Though the music was tinny and distorted, he thought he had never heard anything more moving in his life. He had only a remote idea where Basin Street was, yet he felt as if he had walked its pavements. They would be drowsy and sun-sluiced and the hot, rich, boozy, jazz would

25

float up from the tenement basements as you wandered along them. . . . He closed his eyes and drowned his senses in the music. He had never met an American, let alone a negro; but he felt he understood instinctively what the singer was trying to say.

"Play it again, Felix," he said. "It's superb."

They played it a dozen times, then some of their other favourites. So far Weston had only a score of records; the vogue had only just begun to filter down to them from the nineteen-year-old layer of English society that year. They had the Benny Goodman Trio playing "Avalon", and the Quartet playing "Moonglow"; they had Bob Crosby's "Royal Garden Blues" and Louis Armstrong's "Save It, Pretty Mama"; they had Muggsy Spanier's "Big Butter and Egg Man", and King Oliver's "Dippermouth Blues".

Already the earlier records were looking grey and old. But it seemed they would never tire of them.

Benedict watched his friend with anxious affection. Weston lay curled up in a basket chair, his feet tucked under him. His eyes were closed in concentration, his lips pursed to an imaginary trombone, his left hand holding its valve to his lips, his right executing elegant glissandos on the slide. Dear old Felix, the imperturbable! But Benedict had something on his mind now which he felt Weston simply had to know.

The record ended and Felix began to re-wind the motor. It creaked as he ground away energetically. Benedict half opened his mouth to speak, drew in his breath sharply, and said nothing. Felix looked up, grinned and said: "Bloody marvellous the first four or five times. Then it gets tiring. Have you heard Goodman's 'Lonesome Road'?"

Benedict shook his head.

"It's great. I'll play it next." He put it on, set the needle down, released the catch; there was the familiar excitement of the little hiss and the kick of the opening bars.

Benedict decided to speak over the sound: perhaps it would be easier.

"Felix," he said.

He had not spoken loud enough. Felix had closed his black-ringed eyes once more. Ecstatically, he accompanied the great Goodman on an invisible bass violin, plucking huge chords from its vibrating strings.

"Felix," he said again.

26

Weston opened his eyes. "Yeah, man?" he asked flippantly. To all intents and purposes he was in New Orleans.

"Felix, I've something important to tell you."

"Speak on, friend."

It was a little difficult above the strident jazz, but Benedict plunged manfully on.

"It's about Arabella. She's going to have a baby."

Weston opened one eye, but showed no further interest. Arabella was his father's second wife.

Benedict felt a sense of anti-climax at his friend's apathy. Felix was a damnably cool cove! He waited with exasperated affection till the last bar of the record had faded away. Then Weston carefully took the record off, dusted it with his handkerchief, and put it away.

"Who told you?" he asked casually. A shade too casually; he was deeply interested.

"My old man of course. He heard it from Keith Margrave. I suppose your old man must have told him. What do you say, Felix?"

Felix pondered. His face was set in an expression of almost comical gravity.

"When's it due?" he asked.

"Not till February."

Felix did a quick calculation with his fingers. "Seven months. He hasn't wasted much time spreading the glad tidings."

"It'll be odd, won't it, Felix? I mean to have a brother or sister and you old enough to be its father. Well almost I mean."

Felix reflected. "It'll be a damn nuisance," he observed tetchily.

"Why?"

"Well, the old man gets quite broody enough over her as it is. Imagine the state he'll be in for the next seven months. He'll be even more under her thumb than he is now. You know she has him twisted round her little finger."

His young face was dark and clouded with complex and private griefs.

Benedict had a question he had wanted to ask for a long time.

"How did they meet, Felix?"

"Oh at that bloody old fool Bantinglow."

"But Bantinglow is one of our most distinguished painters."

27

"That's as may be. He's certainly a slavering old lecher. Arabella was his model."

"A *model*. Crikey!" It was the world before the war, and in Aylsbourn, which was fifty years behind the times anyway, the word could have only one connotation: free love!

"Yes, his model. And his mistress of course." Weston flung the intelligence off lightly, but he knew the effect it would have on his romantic and idealistic friend.

"Felix, you don't mean Arabella and that old reptile of eighty . . ."

"Sure I do. Nothing the old swine likes more. I can't blame him though. Arabella must be pretty hot stuff in bed."

"Yes, but surely, Felix, you don't think your father married Arabella just for *that*? I mean quite frankly I find it hard to imagine him and Arabella . . ."

"Do you? I find it the easiest thing in the world. What do you think they go down to the caravan every weekend for?" This was a particular source of irritation to Felix. Already he was developing sophisticated tastes. The idea of weekending at Torquay was mysteriously delightful to him. But a fat chance he stood of making up a threesome with his father and Arabella! He didn't know which of the two he resented more. He picked up a pencil and began to chew the end savagely.

Benedict sat struggling to order his jumbled emotions. He shook his head.

"Felix, I just can't understand you. First of all, I don't believe what you say about Arabella and Bantinglow. She's so—so *young* and, well, beautiful."

"Neither," replied Weston drily, "has yet been thought to disqualify one from lechery."

"But what would *she* get out of it?"

"The same as him. That's why I shall have a middle-aged mistress as soon as I'm old enough. They say you can play some good tunes on an old fiddle."

"I know they do, Felix, but that's just folklore. I don't believe that's *all* there is between people like your father and Arabella; not an *intellectual* like your father." The word intellectual figured frequently in Benedict's conversation: it was the greatest compliment he could convey.

"My dear old boy," Weston explained superciliously, "intellectuals are the biggest rams of all. Haven't you ever heard my

28

father talk about the orgies at Cambridge when he was an under-. . . ."

"Arabella married your father because she loved him," Benedict blurted out. It was his entire confession of faith; the gospel and the apostles.

"Because she loved him," echoed Felix, mocking Benedict's reverent voice. "Look, Benny, my father's worth a hundred thousand. That's point number one. Secondly, he's a randy old goat, with lots of experience gained in all the brothels south of the Pyrenees. Don't you think he's a better bet for Arabella than some doomy young bearded penniless painter from the Slade? Anyway," he added thoughtfully, "she can always pick up someone like that when he's dead."

"But your father isn't all that old, Felix."

"He's forty-five if he's a day."

"Yes, I suppose he is pretty old."

"And remember my mother is already dead."

"They didn't get on, did they?"

"No. She used to drink. Can't say I blame her. Always at the gin bottle, even before breakfast. There used to be some really gorgeous rows between them. Of course it was useful from my point of view."

"Why was that?"

"Well, as you know, I want to be a writer one day. I'm already keeping a journal. I've never told a soul this before, Benny"— and here Felix gave his most appealing smile—"so keep my secret for me, please. I know I can trust you."

"Of course you can, Felix. But what do you put in it?"

"Anything. Everything. Snatches of conversation, ideas, sketches, tram tickets. But the stuff between mother and father was the best. Boy, it was fruity!"

Weston closed his eyes and beamed to remember.

"Wasn't your mother very famous?"

"She was a chorus girl in the nineteen-twenties. God, she didn't half use some ripe language when she felt like it. She was a slut, you have to face the fact."

"But she was your *mother*, Felix."

"Yes. And a slut. But tell me, Benny, why do you look so shocked at the idea that my father and his gorgeous model should live together in lust? Isn't that what everybody else does?"

"No. At least I don't think so. My father was terribly in love with my mother."

"Was he? He gets maudlin about her when he's got four pints of Margrave Best inside him. What were they like when she was alive? Didn't they row like all other married couples? Weren't there moments when they wished they hadn't set eyes on each other?"

Benedict hated his friend at that moment. Weston was a cynical swine. There was more to life than that, he was certain.

"Maybe they didn't row," Weston went on meditatively. "Maybe they had just grown into vegetables. That, I suppose, is what most of the peasants in this town do."

Benedict got to his feet. Weston looked up in surprise. "Off so soon, Benny? Why don't you stay to supper and see the radiant pair come home tonight? I can see them already: him with that shifty look in his eyes he always has when he's made a quick tax-free thousand on the Stock Exchange; her with that cow-like look they all get as soon as they're in the family way. Ugh!" He made a terrifying face, full of hate and renunciation.

Benedict had recovered himself; he smiled affectionately down on his friend.

"When did your mother die, Felix?"

"Three years ago. Nearly four. Of course *he* didn't bother to see her; hadn't seen her for years. It was just me and Mama and the nursing home."

"Felix, you'll get over it. It's your mother dying that's upset you, I'm sure of that."

"You think I shall grow used to the little trollop?" He sighed resignedly. "I suppose we grow used to everything in the end."

"One day, you'll fall in love, Felix, and then you'll understand and forgive."

Weston made an impatient movement. "Benny, unless you destroy this romance in you you'll destroy yourself. There is desire. There is conquest. There's comfort. There's resignation, dislike, and in the end quiet desperation. That's all love is!"

"Beside all these thing," Benedict said softly, "there is love."

"How do you know? Have you ever been in love?"

"No. But when I do it will be with everything I've got: heart and mind and guts. . . ."

"Haven't you left something out?" enquired Weston drily.

Benedict laughed. "Yes and that too. But that's only the

beginning. If you never get any more than that, you've only got dust and ashes."

Felix uncurled from his chair. He grinned at Benedict, his young black eyes glistening with affection and pleasure at what he saw. "Oh my poor Benny," he said. "What awful pain lies ahead for you."

The clock was striking seven in the hall as they passed through. Benedict put his head round the kitchen door and thanked Mrs. Duncher for his tea.

"Do you think the old battle-axe knows?" Felix asked.

"No. She'd be—sort of agog. You know how women are."

Felix dug his hand deep in his pockets as Benedict mounted his bicycle.

"I know what women are," he said solemnly. "The only question is, Benny, do you? And will you ever learn?"

"We'll see which of us is right," Benedict said good-naturedly. "Good night, Felix."

"Good night, Benny. And good luck in the examination to-morrow. I really mean that."

"I know you do, Felix. I'll do my best."

"That, unfortunately, Benny, is what you'll always do."

The High Street ran through the town from west to east, and he lived right at the eastern end, down Hop Field Lane. The simplest way home was along the High Street. But this evening something made him turn right and climb towards the long ridge of the Hampshire Downs which ran along the southern boundary of Aylsbourn. It was called Windmill Hill at its western end, and Cromwell Hill at the eastern end. A narrow lane ran along the top of the hill, serving the well-fed houses on the top which looked down the Cressbrook valley. He could get home this way; it was longer, but it was quieter. For some reason he did not understand, he wanted to go this way. It was a tiny decision, but his own choice; and it altered the course of his whole life.

Windmill Hill was steep—as much as one in six in places. For much of its way it was bounded by a high privet hedge; then the hedge divided for the gates of the Grammar School. It lay back in a hollow, built in 1582 and extended in the eighteenth and nineteenth centuries. It was a small school, with hardly more than two hundred and eighty pupils, girls and boys. It was impossible to see very much of it from the road. Benedict had never had cause to go inside.

31

The school was just over the brow of the hill, and Benedict was going to coast down the other side; he was no longer pedalling, still drifting in the warm emollient wash of the evening air, drifting with the mood, with the day. As he was about to pass the school gates, two cyclists were emerging, and he pulled up to let them go by.

They were a boy and a girl; the boy was about sixteen, the girl looked a little less. The boy wore a pair of heavy-lensed glasses. He had a curious, wedge-shaped face; strong yet with humour in it. He wore a green blazer over white tennis clothes, and there was gold lettering under the breast pocket badge.

The girl wore a lime-green summer dress, open at the throat. Her arms were bare, and she carried a tennis racquet: she wore no hat and her fair hair was combed down to her shoulders.

They wheeled right as he drew up to let them by, and as they did so she half-turned and smiled to thank him. She had wide-apart green eyes and a pale skin; perhaps a few freckles. Then they sped down the hill and the boy said something which made the girl laugh. Then they were gone.

Benedict cycled on for a while, but he was in a trance. He had never seen anything so—perfect. That fellow—he was an intellectual of course!—anyone could tell. But, an athlete too. And that girl—she must have been *his* girl! These two, each perfect, each suspended at this moment in time, he had surprised in their happiness. *Perhaps they were in love!* He stopped altogether and stared down the long lane that wound down the other side of Windmill Hill. *They must be in love*, he thought. How could any other emotion between them be possible? Benedict tingled with pure, unentangled happiness. He was happy because they so evidently were happy too. He had no wish to intervene. He was grateful merely to have been there. There would be no coming back to this moment, but equally no taking it away. It was his moment and theirs. Nothing could ever alter that.

A voice calling in a ripe Hampshire burr recalled him; it was a labourer telling his children to come in to their tea. He pedalled on again, but was in no mood yet to speak to anyone. A little lower down the lane there was a stile on the right, below a green notice-board which said simply "To Westaker Farm". Benedict threw his bicycle down, vaulted over the stile, and followed the path along the edge of the field.

32

There was a high fence on his right, behind which lay the little bungalows of the Sir Jonathan Rexcoth Hospital; the Aylsbourn air was so good that there were several famous hospitals built on its hills. Then the path turned right, and began to climb again; and as he came over the brow he knew he would see his secret view.

It was a wonderful view by any standards; yet no one had noticed it but Benedict. Six miles to the south-east he could see the great beech range of Oakhanger, where Garnett had written his famous natural history. From that side, the view was famous; there had been a half-page picture in *The Times* of it once.

This side, though, nobody knew; and Benedict thought it was a better view. He was looking down the Cressbrook valley; it was not particularly deep, but it lay like a long saucer down to Oakhanger and beyond; and the little hills of the Hampshire Downs cupped it in so gently that it was impossible to see the hard-limned horizon. The most distant woods lay in a haze of purple turning lime under the declining sun; in the middle distance the ploughed earth stretched away, biscuit-coloured and dry as meal.

There were no more than three buildings in the whole huge saucer; he was looking down on ten thousand acres of pure farming land. There were half a dozen cottage-loaf haystacks at Westaker, and beyond the grey slate roofs of the outhouse he could count the white windows in the side of the orange brick farmhouse. There was no sign of another living thing; only fields beyond number tilting at crazy angles and sewn together by the little hedges; yellow-green fields, then pea-green and then a sudden splash of coffee-brown soil. And some of the ploughed fields were bone white.

Not all the buildings were old; he could just see the silver glint on a modern metal granary in Oakhanger village.

He lay on his back and stared up, his hands behind his head, a straw in the mouth, feeling the hard, dry earth cradle him against the shoulder blades and hips; and he stared up into the sky.

There was no cloud; only a hard blue infinite lid over this bone-dry saucer which was his favourite and secret piece of earth. He allowed his mind to drown in the sky's empty and timeless and pitiless enormity.

They must have been in love, he said out loud; and the loudness of his own voice frightened him.

He lay there a long time, until the Aylsbourn mist began to gather. Then he scrambled up and ran down the path till he got back to the stile. Here he halted, and putting his hand on the crossbeam he said very quietly, but with the greatest possible solemnity: "I shall never forget today."

Then he vaulted over the stile, jumped on his bicycle and pedalled swiftly home.

Mr. Benedict peered at his son over his glasses as he came in; he was reading the *Daily Mail* sports page in the yellow light; a pot of tea under a cosy and two mugs stood at his elbow. He had taken off his shoes and put on felt carpet slippers through which his toes protruded; he had taken off his jacket and hung it behind the door. Blue pipe smoke filled the little room; he needed only his son.

"Hello, boy!" He greeted Benedict with his accustomed enthusiasm, throwing down the paper in a gesture of renunciation. "Here, I've just made another pot of tea, have some with me."

"Thanks, Dad." Benedict sank into the armchair opposite his father.

"Well," said Mr. Benedict, pouring with care, "that was some innings, son. If you go on like that you'll be playing for Shallerton first eleven in two or three years."

"I haven't passed the scholarship yet, Dad."

"You'll get it, don't worry, boy. Mr. Varley is prepared to take money on it. He knows a good thing when he sees one."

Benedict grinned. "Varley would bet on the date of his grandmother's funeral." Then he went on more seriously: "But tell me, Dad, why does it matter so much that I should get in to Shallerton?"

"Because it's a fine school!" cried Mr. Benedict. He passed over the mug of tea and began to pace up and down the room. "A *public* school. You'll be a public school man, Benny, think of that!"

"But isn't it going to cost you an awful lot of money?"

"Not if you get the scholarship."

"But the incidentals—clothes, books, pocket money...."

Mr. Benedict dismissed them all with an impatient wave. "Worth every penny!" he cried.

"The other boys will be much better off than me."

"Don't worry about that. A gentleman never worries about your means. The main thing is to play the game and not be afraid to take your punishment like a man. They'll like you, Benny. A man who can bat like you today has nothing to fear at Shallerton."

"But is that the only advantage of being good at cricket? I play for fun, not so that people will like me."

Mr. Benedict seemed for a second to be losing his usual tolerance. Then he checked himself and went on patiently: "Benny, I'm hoping you'll go on to Oxford. You've got the brain, I know. You could be a blue: think of that—a cricket blue. Maybe even a double blue!"

"Sure, that would be nice, Dad. But it's not an end in itself, is it?"

"Of course not. Let me tell you son"—he leaned forward confidentially—"an Oxford blue can go anywhere in the world. He is welcome in any club; and take it from me—he never wants for a job. Why, the City will give a blue a job any time! And do you know there are three Blues on the board of Margrave Brewery at this very minute?"

"Yes, but two of them are members of the family, and the other married into it."

"But don't you see, son"—Mr. Benedict seemed genuinely pained—"*it all goes together*. A man with a blue is a man with a passport. He's a gentleman, and a scholar and a sportsman. What more can you want?"

"Why a scholar? Don't a lot of Blues fail their degrees and get sent down?"

Mr. Benedict paused as he filled his pipe and winked broadly. "Where there's a will there's a way. The varsity has never lost a good man yet. There's always the pass degree. You've got to be an imbecile to fail that."

Benedict decided to change his tack.

"So I'm to go to Shallerton to get a Blue. Surely I could get by going through the Grammar School?"

Mr. Benedict frowned.

"It's a question of contacts you see, son—friendships and connections. If you look through the history of Shallerton you'll be astounded at the great men it has turned out. Soldiers, statesmen, company directors—all united by this one bond." Mr. Benedict was lyrical now. "You'll love it. And I shall be proud to think a son of mine is there. It's—it's a question of *tradition* you see. You can't beat tradition."

Benedict pulled a large book called *Aylsbourn Antiquities* from the shelf, consulted the index, and turned the pages.

"Do you know when Shallerton was founded, Dad?" he enquired.

"Oh heaven knows. Hundreds of years ago."

"It was founded in 1841. And Aylsbourn Grammar School"— he flipped the pages again—"was founded in 1582. Robin Lazenby, the Elizabethan poet, went to school there; so did John Garnett, whose natural history is probably one of the hundred greatest books in the world; so did Benjamin West, the man behind the Reform Law agitation"—but he stopped as he saw Mr. Benedict's evident distress.

"I've nothing *against* the Grammar School, son," he said quietly. "I just want the best for you. I want you to get on, to be a success. I want you"—he hesitated in embarrassment, then plunged on desperately—"to have the best this country can give you; and I want you to learn how to give it back again. That's all."

There was a silence between them. At length Benedict closed the book with a bang and grinned.

"All right, Dad," he said. "I'll get that ruddy scholarship."

"That's the boy. You're not swotting tonight, I hope?"

"Good Lord, no." Mr. Varley was a crafty examination tactician and it was a cardinal rule in his campaign that the boys should relax completely the night before. "No—I think I'll read for a bit. Something really good." He glanced along the book-shelves, past the collected Caxton Shakespeare, the set of Dickens collected with three hundred newspaper coupons, the A. J. Cronins in their yellow jackets, the crossword companions and the standard works on brewing. No, there was nothing there. He pulled his small case on to his lap and rummaged inside it till he found what he wanted.

"I think I'll read H. G. Wells," he said.

"Ah that Red," observed Mr. Benedict without passion. "Wells and Shaw. As bad as one another. You'll get past that stage."

"I'm reading him for fun," Benedict explained. "You've no idea how exhilarating he can be. It's one I haven't read before— *The Food of the Gods*. It's terrific."

36

"Well, if it takes your mind off the exam tomorrow, I shan't complain."

Benedict read for an hour, while his father sat with his feet up and smoked his pipe. Not another word was spoken till, at half-past nine, Benedict got up and bade his father good night.

As he undressed he realised how stiff he would be in the morning; already there was a pleasing ache as he moved his hips. He picked up his bat and stroked the oily yellow wood, then swung it a few times, feeling again the lovely springing thump of the ball as it whined away to the boundary, and he heard in his imagination the indolent ripple of applause again for his fifty runs. Then he knelt on the bed and looked out of the window. There was no moon, but there was no wind either; the Aylsbourn earth lay breathless and expectant beneath him; and every star was in the sky.

There was a good smell in the air as if wood was burning; it was the rich, special, unmistakable smell of Aylsbourn. "One day," thought Benedict, "I really must find out what that smell is." As his eyes grew accustomed to the dark he picked out the low line of the Hampshire Downs, lying like a fat black porker against a backdrop-blue skyline.

Then Benedict remembered the encounter on the hill, and he said to himself out loud: "This is the happiest day of my life."

Then he jumped into bed, and opened his book by H. G. Wells and read till it slid from his hands; and so ended his happiest day.

Saturday

He awoke to find himself a prisoner in a platinum-tinted cage of light. He jumped out of bed and ran to the window, gulping in the air in case he had forgotten how good it was. But the smell was still there: heavy, rich and—now he thought about it—saddening, because there was in it an element of decay.

His legs were now full of their sensual, athletic ache, and he squeezed the calf muscles voluptuously to loosen them again, one leg after the other, his left hand still holding the window sill. Perhaps he could find some mushrooms!

It took hardly thirty seconds to dress: shirt, trousers, a pair of running shoes. He straightened up from tying the shoes and caught his reflection in the old-fashioned oval windows of his dressing-table. He saw a rather tall boy, with a long, pink, serious face, and solemn caramel brown eyes. How odd, he thought. What an odd fish I am! And how can such an odd fish know eternity? For he thought he smelt eternity in the Aylsbourn air: no less.

He picked up a towel, stole silently down the stairs and ran to the end of their garden, vaulting the rhubarb pots and the low hedge which separated them from Twenty Acre field. There was dew still on the ground, marvellous, giving back the silver morning light, and the grass was fresh, still, and pure under his scurrying feet. His ankles were wet with dew; he ran without seeming to touch the ground.

The Cressbrook stream ran across the bottom of Twenty Acre, limpid, clinking and muttering. There were always three boulders he crossed it by and he leaped over them—one, two, three—without hesitation. After that the ground began to rise sharply towards that part of the Downs called Cromwell's Hill, where a skirmish was fought in the Civil War.

This hill flanked the farther side of the Cressbrook stream and was thickly wooded; but you could get over the fence easily and climb up through the undergrowth, seeing the sky above you only here and there through the thickets. Here the chalk had been thrown up nearly to the surface; you trod on pieces as you climbed and there were great white vertical cliffs in the hillside where the sparse earth had been washed entirely away by the rain.

He climbed up through Cromwell's Hill, taking a well-known path, picking at creepers till his hands were smeared a vivid green, brushing the soft morning cobwebs from his eyes.

Once over the top of the hill the wood ended abruptly and the land ran down again to Bailey's Farm. Here he thought there would be mushrooms.

He trod carefully over the springy field, avoiding the cowpats as he went, and then he saw his first mushroom, its white bulbous head peeping shyly through the grass. He tested it (as he thought) to make sure it wasn't a toadstool; but it peeled quite easily, it was all right. And what a whopper! There ought to be some more. Then he saw a little crop all together, and no sooner had he snapped them off by their spongy white stalks than he saw another three or four of the little white domes, dotted about like Maginot entrenchments in the grass.

Soon he had as many as he could carry. "Marvellous!" he said out loud.

It took only two minutes to scramble down again through the wood. At the edge of the Cressbrook he paused, glanced casually round and, assured that he was alone, threw off his clothes and dived cleanly in at the part where the stream opened out into a wide running lake. He slid through the green water, naked between the reeds, and only a line of silver bubbles showed his progress; then he broke the surface noisily, splashing and shaking his head like a dog, and struck out in a lazy crawl to the other bank. He touched it and turned, rolled on his back and threshed his legs in the air, blew water from his mouth and nostrils and gulped in the cold morning air. The sun shone on him through a filagree of fine branches.

He pulled himself ashore and rubbed himself down roughly till his young pink body glowed and steam rose from the bare flesh. He dressed again in thirty seconds, towelled his hair carelessly, scooped up his precious mushrooms, leaped his three boulders and in another minute was home again.

His father was up now, moving about the kitchen in his shirt-sleeves, his collar not yet put on, a front stud hanging carelessly in the button hole. He hummed as he made the tea.

"Hello, son!" he said. "What a load of mushrooms! Oh ho! We are in luck!"

Benedict laid the mushrooms on the kitchen table for his father to see. "Masses of them, Pop!"

"Not half bad," said Benedict senior appraisingly. Then he turned his attention back to the teapot. "But let's have a cuppa first. We can brew a fresh lot for breakfast."

They sat at either end of the kitchen table over the ritual, sipping the strong, hot sweet tea with little gasps of appreciation. Mr. Benedict had the *Daily Mail*, as usual, in front of him. There was a lot of unpleasant war news on the front, but he ignored it, and turned at once to the cricket scores.

"McCorkell 66!" he cried triumphantly. "What a hell of a grand bat he is, Benny! I hope he's in form on Sunday."

"Gosh, yes," Benedict agreed. "I'm longing to see McCorkell play again."

Margrave Brewery promoted a special gala cricket match for charity once a year. Many Hampshire cricketers came down for it, and there were always some celebrities; people like the Western

39

Brothers, and a sporting columnist or two. The crowd came in their thousands, so many that beer crates were pressed into service for them to sit on; and the sun always seemed to shine. Benedict and his father were regulars at the game.

"Well," said Mr. Benedict, "this will never do. Let's get down to the mushrooms."

He cooked them with particular care, peeling them meticulously and frying them gently in butter. Soon the whole house was full of their unmistakable and delicate aroma.

It was the first sophisticated smell Benedict had ever known.

Then Mr. Benedict picked up some brown eggs, still mottled with little pieces of straw, and broke them into the pan. Benedict made the second pot of tea. Within five minutes they were sitting down to what Benedict and his father believed to be the best breakfast in the world.

It was still only ten past eight when they had finished and Benedict was due at Valhalla by nine sharp. He went up to his room, peeled off his old clothes, chose a new white shirt and his best grey suit, tied his mauve and gold Valhalla tie with care, polished his shoes and brushed his damp hair down into place. His father met him at the foot of the stairs and held out his hand.

"Good luck, boy."

"Thanks, Pop. It'll be all right, you'll see."

In the back yard of Valhalla School, the boys who were taking entrance and scholarship examinations to Shallerton Oaks that day were already arriving. Some were usually quiet, others boisterous. Benedict leaned against the fence, his hands in his pockets, watching the little groups of boys, at peace with the world.

Today he thought, *I shall win the scholarship. It's my day.*

Suddenly the bulking figure of Mr. V. V. Varley materialised at the top of the ironwork steps leading into the big classroom. He, too, seemed specially polished for the occasion. His black wavy hair was freshly brilliantined and his huge, red, knobbly, terrifying face shone in the morning sun. He wore a grey chalk-stripe suit, cut cleverly to accommodate his great belly. His boots (for he never wore shoes) glistened like black glass. He took out his whistle and blew a loud blast on it. Every boy in the yard stiffened to attention. As a second blast they doubled into lines, right arms stiffly extended, heads at the eyes right, shoes shuffling expertly as they formed two straight ranks, tallest boys at each end, shortest in the middle. At a third blast from the whistle they came to the eyes front. They drilled like guardsmen, and rather enjoyed it.

Mr. Varley passed slowly along the ranks. As he came abreast Benedict could smell the mysterious adult male aroma of lather, tobacco, and alcohol, so close was Mr. Varley to him. The knobbly face had been newly cut by a razor, he now saw, and a fresh piece of white cotton wool hung from the massive chin. Then his headmaster was by, and Benedict sighed under his breath. Mr. Varley was not easily satisfied. Two boys were sent inside to polish their shoes again, and another boy was set to work frantically cleaning a spot out of his tie. But in ten minutes the solemn little platoon was ready and Mr. Varley addressed them again.

"Valhalla," he boomed. "Right turn. Forward—*march.*"

They swung along, arms moving briskly, and Benedict allowed himself to sink mentally into Varley's world. He was all right, the old bounder, as long as you jumped to it; as long as you played the game. But Benedict played *that* game, as well as other games, easily and well.

They swung into the station yard and marked time till Mr. Varley brought them to the halt and gave them permission to fall out. Each boy bought a return ticket to Shallerton and they streamed on to the platform to await the train. Still Benedict was in a dream. He sat alone on a station seat, the hum of the railway telegraph lulling him into an endless, mindless euphoria.

"Well, Benedict." The boy started and jumped to attention. "At ease, Benedict." Mr. Varley was in a relaxed mood this morning. He had drilled his boys ruthlessly the whole of this last vital year, but he knew when to take the pace off. "Going to get that scholarship today?" he enquired genially.

"I very much hope so, sir."

"I'm sure you will. And I know your father shares my view. Remember, don't rush at the questions. Read them right through, even the ones that you don't think you can do. Spend a couple of minutes thinking about each one if you like. Make notes on your rough paper. Be orderly. Don't ramble. Don't try to show off. Come to the point quickly, say what you have to say, and finish. Remember the examiner is only human. Make his job as simple as you can. And write legibly, Benedict!"

"Yes, sir."

"And another thing—when you come out at one, go to Dickins, the newsagent in the High Street. I have an account there. Order what you like in the way of chocolate and tell them to charge it to me."

"Oh *thank* you, sir." Benedict was deeply impressed with this evidence of a wider, adult world; he was intoxicated with the conception of credit *carte blanche*. Suppose he and the other boys *went off their heads* and bought the whole stock? What a scandal! And would Mr. Varley go bankrupt? Or was he limitlessly rich?

His dream-line was broken by the far-away thrum of the electric train. It was their train, coming to take them to Shallerton, to the future, to the unknown. Nothing could stop it now. He leaped aboard with his friends, bagged a corner seat, noted with relief that Mr. Varley was two doors down, and dozed in the cradling rhythm of the carriage wheels all the way to Shallerton.

Shallerton was a bigger and altogether smarter town than Aylsbourn. It was only fifty-nine minutes from Waterloo by fast train, and was therefore popular with men making between two and five thousand a year in the City. A hundred and fifty years ago it had been the central market for the English corn trade; the Georgian farmhouses built then had been snapped up and tarted over with white paint. Running water, central heating, electricity and telephones had been installed and the drives freshly gravelled to accommodate the big tyres of Bentley saloons.

But there was plenty of indigenous money in Shallerton too; although an economic spasm had carried the market away, it had not taken the rich farming land with it. There were squat, comfortable shops down Shallerton High Street that still catered for the local farmers; shops selling guns, saddles, stoves and boots. There were lending libraries for the farmers' wives, and small scented dress-shops selling tweed suits and twin-sets; there were three or four coaching inns, some estate agents and accountants, four banks, a solicitor, and one mysterious window behind which sat an old gentleman called the Commissioner for Oaths. There was a garage which sold bright red tractors and one reasonably good teashop which sold home-made shortbread.

It was a warm, friendly town that always gave Benedict the impression of self-indulgence. It was a town that seemed to do itself pretty well. It was a worldly and sophisticated place compared with Aylsbourn, whose air always seemed keener and thinner, yet somehow more pure and exhilarating.

Benedict felt content in Shallerton; but he felt alive in Aylesbourn. He loved both towns unaffectedly.

The boys tumbled out of Shallerton station and fell in again under Mr. Varley's booming orders. "Valhalla," he thundered. "Fall *in*." People stopped and stared at the tiny drill-parade in the station yard with amusement, and one or two local urchins shouted rude remarks; but the Valhalla boys were used to that and ignored it.

"Right *turn*. Forward *march*."

They swung up Station Road with Mr. Varley at their head. At the junction with the High Street he stepped out into the middle, raising both arms like a policeman, and imperiously halted the coast-bound traffic. Benedict was always deeply impressed by this; it was either enormous cheek on Mr. Varley's part or great moral courage; either way, it was admirable. Secure under his billowing black gown, they marched solemnly across the High Street, impervious to the frenzied honkings from the column of cars they had so brazenly halted. They wheeled left, and marched up the High Street, then right and climbed the hill towards Shallerton Oaks School.

Here was their severest test. For as they marched up the school drive, they could see little knots of boys from other schools standing about informally. Every eye turned on the brave little column from Valhalla as it swung along. Benedict gritted his teeth and kept his eyes to the front. What did it matter what these other bastards thought? Perhaps they thought Valhalla soft. In that case, they should come and try one of Varley's cold baths some freezing morning. That would teach them.

"Valhalla *halt*. Left *turn*. Stand at *ease*. Stand *easy*."

Mr. Varley then marched forward and almost, but not quite, saluted Mr. Ross-Tayfield, who had watched the whole farcical scene with scarcely concealed contempt. No doubt, he reflected, all these blasted Valhalla boys would pass the entrance exam as usual. It was extraordinarily hard to fail the little swine. As for the scholarship—his eyes lingered on the languid, dreamy figure of Benedict—well, that had its compensations. The boy's father was dreadful, and so was his headmaster. The boy himself seemed half asleep most of the time and painfully gauche the rest. Against this, he was going to be a really beautiful scrum-half. . . .

Mr. Ross-Tayfield smiled thinly as he recalled the day he had surreptitiously come over to watch Benedict play for Valhalla the previous autumn; he recalled the long stride and the wriggle in the boy's hips and the ghostly dummy he had sold to six opponents in a row; and Mr. Ross-Tayfield smiled at this. Yes, he could put up with Benedict.

He clapped his hands sharply. "Scholarship boys, this way," he called.

Half a dozen boys detached themselves from the groups and followed Mr. Ross-Tayfield. Benedict joined them. They were led into a classroom full of chalk-dust and sunlight.

A young assistant master rose as his headmaster entered. He was reading a novel.

"Here you are, Johnson," said Mr. Ross-Tayfield. "The six Margrave scholarship candidates. I leave them in your care."

"Right, sir. Sit where you like, boys. You'll find writing paper on each desk." They scattered over the empty seats. Benedict chose a seat right at the back.

The young master strolled round with the printed examination papers, one of which he placed face down on each boy's desk. Benedict stared down at it. He was feeling drowsy after his early-morning swim; the morning sun was tempting him to close his eyes. He pulled his fountain pen mechanically from his breast pocket, tested it to be sure it was full, and wrote: BENEDICT: VALHALLA in the top right corner.

"Now then, chaps," said the young master. "It's two minutes to half past. I'll tell you to turn over at half past precisely. It's a three-hour paper on English Language. No talking, of course; and if any boy wants to go out he must raise his hand and I'll ring for someone to escort him. Don't rush at the questions, think them over for a few minutes; I think you'll find it pays. Well, good luck, everyone. Begin."

In a daze, Benedict turned his paper over. The words swam at first and he could not focus on them. Then they cleared and leapt up from the page with the dramatic super-reality of obscenity or news of death.

The minutes ticked away, and a boy dipped his pen into the ink with a sigh and began to write. Then another followed; and another; within six minutes each head was bent over the work—except Benedict's. He floated in the appalling enormity of the occasion. *This* was the moment that he had been trained for all his life, *this* was the moment when his future must be decided, *this* was the moment when his destiny must be hammered out. He

44

had only to reach out now and take success by the throat; his stars were high in the sky; even Ross-Tayfield had smiled on him.

Yet just *because* he was free to choose, some entrenched perversity made him delay while the minutes ticked away. He was still in a trauma of delight from his encounter the night before on Windmill Hill: over and over he repeated to himself: it was my happiest day.

He sat staring out of the sun-slotted window, impassive, motionless.

It was fifty minutes before the young master noticed that Benedict was not writing. He watched him for some minutes then softly closed his book and tiptoed up.

"What's the matter, old boy?" he enquired kindly. "Not feeling well?"

Benedict jumped at the sudden voice. "No thank you, sir. I'm fine. I was just thinking."

"Oh. Well, don't leave it too long. You've just over two hours left."

He tiptoed away and Benedict looked down at his paper. The first question asked candidates to discuss a stanza of poetry:

> *You say there is no substance here,*
> *One vast reality above;*
> *Back from that brink I shrink in fear*
> *And childlike hide myself in love.*

Benedict stared at the lines desperately. At length he wrote on his answer paper:

"*The poet is right. There is only love.*"

Then he methodically screwed up his fountain pen and walked out. It was a few minutes after eleven. The school drive was deserted. All the other boys had gone into their classrooms for the entrance exam. Mr. Varley was on his way back to Aylsbourn, where he was looking forward to his first port of the day in the "Thorn and Sceptre".

Benedict walked down the drive, each step in the gravel magnified by dry-mouthed fear. He passed between the iron gates and said to himself: I shall never go to Shallerton now. Then another thought struck him; I shall spend the rest of my schooldays in Aylsbourn.

He lifted his dream-racked head and gulped in the rich air. Then he sauntered along to Dickins and bought himself a two-penny bar of milk chocolate. He drifted along the High Street, munching it absent-mindedly as he went. He felt no fear or shame, only a great lightness under him, as if he were exempted from the cares of gravity. Now I shall see them both again, he thought.

Sunday

There was a fine mist over the fields next morning. Mr. Benedict sang as he made the early-morning tea; this was one of the great days of their year and the sun was going to shine for them both once again. His son read the *Sunday Dispatch* in bed. Fortunately, no hint of the examination débâcle had penetrated; he had come in at six as if he had completed both papers, answered Mr. Benedict's eager questions non-committally, and gone to bed early with a book. Still he felt no remorse for what he had done. Indeed, he was not quite sure if he remembered properly what had happened the day before. Was it possible that he had written only eight words altogether? Surely not: it must be a trick of the imagination: he had been too tense, too over-wrought. Of *course* he had answered all the questions!

The game did not start until two; so father and son could go to church as usual in the morning. Mr. Benedict was not a religious man, but he felt, like many Englishmen of that generation, that he ought to go to church before he went into the "Thorn and Sceptre" for a pint of bitter. "It always seems to go down better after a service," he used to say. "I suppose it's all that singing; it gives you a real urge to wet your whistle."

Mr. Benedict was no drunkard. But he loved drink. "I often wonder what the vintners buy," he would declaim each evening in the "Thorn and Sceptre", "one half so precious as the goods they sell."

By the time the last hymn was announced that morning, Mr. Benedict was clearly very thirsty indeed. He sang loudly and with a good grace, but he fingered his stiff white collar nervously. That always meant, Benedict knew, that it was time his father had a beer.

All the same, the hymn seemed to have an added poignancy that morning, singing as it did of simple human endeavour:

> *There's no discouragement*
> *Shall make him once relent*
> *His first avowed intent*
> *To be a pilgrim.*

"Let us pray," intoned the Rector, and as he delivered the final blessing: *Oh God*, Benedict prayed, *don't let it be true that I wrote only eight words. I don't care for myself, but it would hurt my father so much.*

Mr. Benedict hummed a tenor accompaniment to the organ as they filed out past the Rector. "Good morning, Mr. Benedict," he said. "No doubt we shall meet at the game this afternoon?"

"We certainly shall, Rector."

"There you are," added Mr. Benedict as soon as they were out of earshot. "That's what I call a really sporting parson. I bet he wouldn't mind a beer after preaching all that time. I've half a mind to go back and ask him."

"You can't do that, Pop." The boy was terrified that his father would be rebuffed.

"No, I suppose not." Mr. Benedict was for the moment downcast. Then he cheered up again. "But I know what I can do. I can buy you a shandy."

"What exactly *is* a shandy, Pop?"

"A shandy is a mixture of beer and ginger beer generally; sometimes beer and lemonade. A marvellous thirst-quencher. We used to drink it on route marches during the war."

"But I can't drink *beer*, can I Pop?"

"Why ever not? Got to start sooner or later. And I wanted to celebrate that fifty of yours on Friday too, son. Oh yes, this is definitely the day for you to have a shandy."

"O.K., Pop. Whatever you say." The boy sat on the bench outside the "Thorn and Sceptre" as he always did. His father reappeared with a pint of bitter and a pint of ginger beer.

"Now then, son; drink a bit of that up and I'll pour in some real beer for you. That's it. That'll do for a start."

The boy had drunk some two inches, and this Mr. Benedict gravely refilled with Margrave bitter. The boy took a deep breath. He wasn't sure if he would like it. Suppose he was sick—how disgraced his father would be!

"Cheers, Pop."

"Cheers, lad."

That first taste—how it still lingered; bitter and clean through the fizz!

"Well?"

"Not bad at all, Pop. Let's have another."

"Another!" Mr. Benedict was greatly amused. "Another. My

goodness, we'll make a drinker of you yet. All right, just this once."

He went inside and the boy leaned back against the whitewashed wall. So this was beer; this mysterious elixir on which his father's whole philosophy floated!

They drank two pints each, then went round to the back door for their Sunday dinner. A new linen cloth was laid in the parlour because it was Sunday.

They ate, as they always did, roast beef, roast potatoes and green peas, with apple tart, sugar and cream to follow. Then came two very big cups of strong sweet tea, which they dispatched very much more quickly than usual.

"Right son!" said Mr. Benedict, putting down his cup with a clatter. "The cricket match!"

The Margrave Brewery cricket ground was already crowded as they clocked in through the turnstiles. Inside was the scene that never failed to thrill them both.

The pitch, newly rolled and watered, stretched away, emerald and silk-smooth before them. The celebrated Margrave beer crates lined the boundary, forming an extra row of seats. A large white marquee had been erected beside the pavilion, and already gave off that unmistakable, English smell of canvas, grass, watercress and light ale. The Brewery Silver Band had been playing a selection from Gilbert and Sullivan to entertain the crowds, and was marching off just as the Benedicts arrived. They were just in time to get two of the crates to sit on side by side. They took off their jackets and rolled up their sleeves. They bought a scorecard each and took out their pencils. An avuncular sun beamed down on them from a cobalt sky.

There was a small spatter of claps as the captains came out to toss. Hampshire won and decided to bat first. Two minutes later, Arnold and McCorkell appeared side-by-side from the pavilion and began their slow gossiping amble to the wicket. The Brewery field fanned out further for Arnold, five men curved in a tight crescent behind the wicket.

Arnold took guard and Benedict took in a quick quarterlungful of air to help his heart cope with the delight.

It was spectacular cricket to watch, for the Hampshire men were unconcerned with championship points and opened their shoulders like Guinness-full coal-heavers. Fours and sixes fell like mortar-fire among the spectators. Wickets began to fall quickly as the county players took wilder and wilder risks, and soon the tail of film and radio celebrities had to be winkled out of the Brewery pavilion bar. The crowd guffawed at the droll contrast between the lusty professional hitting and the wild daisy-cutting antics of the amateurs, and there was a general susurrus of approval when Hampshire were all out in two and a half hours for 123 runs. Everyone then stopped for the tea interval, and Mr. Benedict led the way into the marquee.

It was always the tea of the year: soft white sandwiches filled with cucumber and egg, boxes of strawberries and cream, and thick white cups of strong tea, with plenty of beer for those who preferred it. Benedict ate two boxes of strawberries, dipping each red and luscious fruit first in the cream and then in the sugar. His father had two bottles of beer and a number of sandwiches, then strawberries and finally a large cup of tea. It was a delicious ritual which everybody in Aylsbourn loved. It was cornucopia; there were so many boxes of strawberries that stacks of them still stood unopened at the end of tea. Margrave Brewery never stinted its guests at the annual cricket match.

They settled back on their crates at five and waited for the Brewery to bat. "Sir Keith is opening again this year," Mr. Benedict said. "He'll be good for a few runs. What a sportsman he is! And a brave man: I'll never forget him in the trenches. A major was watching the enemy from an observation post with a pair of binoculars and was shot through the head by a sniper. Died at once, poor devil. Keith Margrave stepped straight into his place without hesitation. He was nineteen then, a second lieutenant. That's real courage for you. Cool as ice, he was."

"A bit reckless, wasn't it, Dad?"

"You can call it that if you like. But where does courage end and recklessness begin? Ah, here he comes now."

Keith Margrave was coming out to bat. He was putting on weight, and his blond hair was thinning a little on top. But he still looked like a rather plump and overgrown sixth former. He wore an I Zingari cap. Benedict strained to see who it was accompanying Margrave to the crease as the other opening bat. The slim shape and the thick spectacles seemed familiar. Then the batsman lifted his cap for a moment to wipe his glasses, and Benedict saw that it was the Aylsbourn boy he had seen last night. He glanced eagerly down at his programme. Yes, that must be him, No. 2: HAMMOND, A. R. D. He flipped the pages to the notes on the two teams:

"HAMMOND, A. R. D. Tony Hammond at sixteen is one of the most outstanding schoolboy athletes of his generation. He is already in Aylsbourn Grammar School's First XI and First XV and has been given several games this season already by the Hampshire Colts. We understand the County Cricket Club are also taking an interest in his progress. He will be representing his county again this year in the AAA Southern Junior Championships and is much fancied to win. He is the son of that famous Hampshire athlete of yesteryear, the late Colonel John 'Stingo' Hammond."

Benedict read with hypnotised excitement. So this was Hammond! He had of course heard of his feats even at Valhalla. But still, it was an honour to open for the Brewery with Sir Keith, even if you were Tony Hammond!

The two batsmen held a parley in the middle of the pitch, a slightly comic contrast in silhouettes, then returned to their separate ends. Margrave was to take first knock and he faced up to the bowling professionally. He had a nice stance and though obviously a little out of training had no difficulty in presenting a plumb-straight bat to the first three balls from the Hampshire opening bowler, who was putting them down with a lot of zip. Then Margrave cut a loose ball through the slips and they took two runs. Mr. Benedict applauded. "Good old Keith," he cried. "He's away."

Soon after this Margrave was dropped. It was a fairly simple catch and it was impossible to say whether the Hampshire fielder had missed it deliberately by way of courtesy to such a generous host or whether he had genuinely muffed it. At any rate, Margrave made no more mistakes and hit a clean and solid forty-four runs before he was bowled, trying to lift a ball over the pavilion. He raised his cap modestly to the applause as he trotted into the pavilion, evidently well pleased with his day's work.

Meanwhile Hammond had been playing with cool elegance at the other end and had quietly collected thirty-one. With two extras, the Brewery needed forty-seven to win. Hampshire crouched ferociously: the game had suddenly taken on a piquant note of challenge.

Unfortunately the rest of the Brewery side seemed overawed. Two of the best wickets fell with only another six added, then a stalwart bottler blocked heroically for half an hour before finally snicking one up to the wicketkeeper. With six wickets to fall and fifty-five minutes left to play, the Brewery still needed thirty-one runs to win. Benedict sat on the edge of his beer crate, biting his knuckles with suspense.

Hampshire now had entirely woken up. The skylarking was discarded and even the comedians in the outfield trained their eyes ferociously on each ball. Number five just managed to survive to the end of the over.

Now Hammond had the bowling. He glanced round the field nonchalantly, then squared up to the Hampshire fast bowler, who had come back on after a rest. His first ball was a trifle short, and Hammond cut it imperiously for four. The ball rattled up against the crates only a few yards away from where the Benedicts sat.

"A very useful bat, this young fellow," said Mr. Benedict.

The next ball was very fast and straight and Hammond blocked it respectfully. He turned the next stylishly to fine leg and they took two. The next ball kicked high and smashed his spectacles into pieces. Little pieces of glass lay glinting in the sun.

Benedict half rose in his seat, breathlessly with anxiety. But miraculously Hammond had not been hurt. He handed the remains of his glasses to the square leg umpire and boldly took stance again. But hardly before the ball had left the bowler's hand he was running down the pitch to meet it with a most uncharacteristic swipe.

"Probably can't see an inch in front of his face," said Mr. Benedict. "But what guts!"

The ball rose in a very high parabola and fell with neat certainty into the hands of mid-on. Hammond had not stopped running and he wheeled to trot into the pavilion, raising his bat to acknowledge the hero's ovation he received. He had made forty-eight and the Brewery needed only twelve to win. It was too much for them: whether the heat or the beer or the occasion was responsible no one knew. But in the upshot Hampshire won by nine runs.

By now it was half-past six. The spectators rose and stretched themselves pleasurably. Then they began to move towards the pavilion, where it was the custom for Sir Keith Margrave to make a short speech. He appeared on the balcony in a blazer and Old Hanovarian tie and raised his hand to end the cheers.

"Ladies and gentlemen," he said when the noise had died down. (He had a pleasant voice with no trace of Hampshire in it, but on the other hand with little class affection either. It was not what Mr. Benedict would have called a "posh" voice. On the other hand, it was clearly different from the way his employees spoke.)

"Ladies and gentlemen," he said, "thank you all so much for coming along today to this game." ("Hear hear," said Mr. Benedict.) "It's been enormous fun, and how we managed to get as many as we did against Hampshire I shall never know." ("You got forty-four, sir!" called Mr. Benedict. His son blushed and looked down in case anyone noticed his connection.) "May I say once again how very much we appreciate the way these splendid Hampshire players give up their Sunday each year to make this match possible." ("Hear hear!" again from Mr. Benedict, but not so loud. He had noticed his son's embarrassment.)

"And now—let's get down to the dancing. I want you all to stay right to the end and remember—all the beer is on me to-night." ("Hear hear!" from everybody.) "I want you all to enjoy yourselves as much as I know Lady Margrave and I will. And don't go before the fireworks! We've got some quite sensational ones for you this year. On with the dance!"

There was another round of applause, and the strains of "Blue Skies" could be heard floating out from inside the pavilion. The young Brewery men and their girls began to move inside, hand in hand, humming as they went.

Mr. Benedict began to push his way through the crowd. "Come along, son!" he cried. "We must meet Keith Margrave."

But the boy hung back, overcome with awe and embarrassment. "No, please don't, Pop," he pleaded. "I'm sure he's busy."

"Nonsense! I often speak to him about you. He'd love to see you again!"

The boy followed with immense reluctance. His father jostled eagerly through the crowd which had now gathered round the Chairman and his wife, trying to catch his employer's eye.

At close quarters Keith Margrave was larger and older and pinker. His cheeks were already mottled a bonhomous red through over-indulgence and drops of sweat stood on his face. But there were kindly wrinkles round his eyes. Yet still the boy

52

prayed: *Oh God, don't let me have to talk to him. Let him not notice my father.*

"Sir Keith!" called Mr. Benedict, over several heads. "Sir Keith!"

"Oh hello, Benedict," said Margrave with easy upper-class charm. It had cost many thousands of pounds to teach him that particular kind of graciousness; but he had learned the trick well.

"Good evening, Sir Keith. Do you remember my son? I've often told you about him."

"Hello young Benedict." The kind blue eyes stared down at him with mild and amused interest. "I hear you're quite a useful man with a bat. You'll have to play for us next year."

"He scored fifty on Friday for Valhalla against Locks Priory," Mr. Benedict said proudly.

"Jolly good show! So you're at Valhalla, are you?"

"Yes, sir."

"Jolly good. A splendid chap, old Varley. And where are you going when you leave Valhalla?"

"To Shallerton, sir, on a Margrave Scholarship," Mr. Benedict put in with a beam. "He took the exam yesterday."

"Shallerton, eh? Good school. And on our Scholarship? Capital. When d'you know the results?"

"In about a fortnight, sir," said the boy. What would Sir Keith Margrave say if he knew what that answer paper contained? There is only love—but of course he was dreaming; he must have written more than that!

"Well, cheerio, Benedict," Margrave was saying. "I must get in to the dance. See you both there, eh?"

"You certainly will, sir," said Mr. Benedict. "You certainly will." Then, when the great man was out of earshot: "There! It wasn't so terrible, was it?"

"No, Pop." But he still wished his father hadn't done it.

They began to move into the clubhouse with the high-spirited shoals of Margrave employees. "This way, son," called Mr. Benedict. He pulled open a side door marked "Changing Rooms", and they both slid in through it. Immediately Benedict was assailed by the warm adult male smell of sweat and embrocation. There was a huge communal bath in which seven or eight young men were splashing noisily. They had a sort of phallic splendour: majestic in their hirsute nakedness, lordly and insouciant. Benedict remembered this bitter-sweet moment always; it lay

53

complex in his memory, a touch of happiness for its insolent carelessness, a tang of sadness for its haunting reminder that all men, however noble they may seem, are merely animals that must suffer, procreate, decline and die.

But that was only a moment; then they were through the changing rooms and into the clubroom. Mr. Benedict fought his way to the bar, jocularly exchanging wisecracks with his many friends and amiably introducing his son: "This is my boy. Scored fifty for Valhalla against the Priory yesterday. Play for the Brewery? He's going to play for *Hampshire*." Then at last, when he had reached his haven, he turned, beaming with pleasure and pink from the sun, to ask: "What's it to be, son? Another shandy?"

"Yes please, Pop." The boy was caught up in the mood, exhilarated by the infectious happiness of the great Margrave clubroom. Like his father, he was gregarious by inclination.

Mr. Benedict ordered his customary Margrave Bitter and handed the boy the long, tan-coloured, fizzing shandy. "Well, cheers, son. Here's to the future."

"Cheers, Pop. And thank you."

Through the great noisy gusts of bonhomie, like cream running over Gaelic coffee, there slid the soft seduction of saxophones playing "Sweet Lorraine". The young men glanced up, looked at their wrist-watches, straightened their ties, and finished their drinks.

"The dance is beginning, Dad."

Mr. Benedict looked down at his son, and for a second there was a trace of fear in his benignant eyes.

"The dance? You're a bit young for dancing, aren't you, son?"

"Oh, I don't want to *dance*. I just wanted to watch and listen. I've never seen a dance before."

"All right. Let's go into the dance." Mr. Benedict could refuse his son very little.

The dining-room in the Margrave clubhouse had been cleared, and at one end the Margrave Serenaders, an ensemble recruited for the occasion from the personnel of the Silver Band, played dreamy, inoffensive dance music. After "I'm For Ever Blowing Bubbles" came "Red Sails in the Sunset", and then "Little Man You've Had a Busy Day". The couples shuffled round languorously, cheek to cheek, the young men in Brewery cricket blazers, the girls in summery print dresses. Sir Keith Margrave was dancing with Miss Maddocks, his secretary. She was forty, and had been harmlessly in love with him for nearly twenty years. Everyone knew, nobody cared, except possibly Miss Maddocks herself. She had a lean, noble face and grey hair drawn severely back. Few people knew that she had taken a good degree in economics at London University, and could have been earning six times as much in retail business by now had she wanted.

The boy did not know the story; but he thought Miss Maddocks was enchanting. Indeed, to be fair, he thought every girl there enchanting that night.

His father went off to get another round, was detained and away gossiping for twenty-five minutes. Benedict did not care. He sat in a corner, mesmerised. He was outside time and dimension, floating on the deep content that had settled over the room.

Then the M.C. stepped forward, and took the microphone. "Ladies and Gentlemen," he said. "Tonight we have a very special attraction for you. You may be surprised to hear that Mr. Tony Hammond, hero of today's game, is also a jazz trumpeter of no mean ability. He has recently formed his own jazz band—the first ever formed, I believe, in Aylsbourn. Ladies and Gentlemen—Tony Hammond and his Original Dixieland Jazz Band!"

The curtains swung back, to reveal Tony Hammond still in white cricket flannels and shirt, but wearing too his green first eleven blazer. He now wore an old pair of glasses held together by sticky tape. Behind him were a trombonist and clarinet player, both of whom Benedict recognised as having played in the game that day, a boy of sixteen or so with a banjo, a bearded man of thirty on the drums, and a young negro bass-player. There was a whistle of surprise from the Brewery employees. No one had seen such a bizarre assortment of people gathered together in captivity before.

Tony Hammond raised a yellow, much-battered trumpet to his lips and struck his left foot smartly flat on the floor twice, then four times at twice the speed: one, two—*one-two-three-four*. And so, as they swung into "The Jazz Band Ball", the sleepy Hampshire town of Aylsbourn heard the music of New Orleans for the first time.

Benedict was transfixed. Though he had heard Felix's records, the music on them seemed to be coming from thousands of miles away. Now it was in the room with him: urgent, driving, and full of joy.

Benedict knew that only one thing was necessary to complete his happiness: the girl. His eyes wandered over the room; she was nowhere to be seen.

Tony Hammond played with his eyes closed, his head tilted slightly back, his glasses glinting in the light, his strong brown fingers moving expertly over the valves. He played with a tearing, gay virility that took Benedict's breath away. At the end of his solo the clarinet took over, pure and liquid after the rasping brass, and after that the sonorous trombone caught up the melody and worked long improvisations into it. Then they were playing gloriously together, while the bass thumped sonorously behind them and the drums limned their music in a tight rhythmic framework.

As the sound died away everyone applauded. Benedict jumped to his feet and clapped for all he was worth.

Now Tony Hammond led his band into a slow, melancholy tune; like the first they had played, it was famous, a cliché of jazz, but Benedict, on that summer day in 1939, had heard it only once before in his life, the previous day, in Felix Weston's house. It was the Basin Street Blues, slow, sad, haunting. . . .

> *Where all the dark and white folk meet*
> *In Basin Street, land of dreams,*
> *You'll never know how nice it seems*
> *Or just how much it really means.*

Benedict let his attention wander once more over the crowded floor. This tune—could it have significance for them too?

Then he saw her; perhaps in answer to the incantation of the blues, perhaps by the merest chance, she had slipped into the room while the music was playing, and now she stood watching as Tony Hammond took up the story on his trumpet again where the negro had left it.

She was wearing a white dress and her hair was still combed down to her shoulders. She was smiling to herself as she watched Hammond play, a little private smile, and Benedict was able to confirm now that her eyes in truth were green and that there were one or two little freckles on her face; her nose was small and turned up at the end with a tiny arrogant gesture. She was a little above the normal height for a girl of her age and she conveyed a

56

marvellous sense of coolness and grace. Benedict was only a dozen feet away from her. He was bewitched; he could not have moved if he had tried.

After the second chorus Tony Hammond laid his trumpet gently on a chair and strolled across the floor, threading his way between the shuffling couples in the crooning haze with certainty to where she stood watching. She smiled at him; he held his arms out, and in a moment they were drifting on the floor, melting into the mood and the moment. Benny was spellbound. Her small left hand lay, not decorously against Hammond's shoulder blade, but round his neck, and her fingers moved gently in the short hair just behind his ears. Benny felt for the first time in his life, a small stab of sensual longing; but his principal emotion was one of simple excitement and delight. The rhythm section, holding the fort while the brass and reeds had a quick drink, now changed their style again, and broke into a quick one. Benny hummed the melody—it was one of those Fred Astaire things—what was it . now? Ah yes, "Cheek to Cheek"—and how apt! How beautifully they danced, he reflected wistfully; they moved on the floor with the ease and sophistication of very old and bored lovers.

They passed out of view in the swirl of the dance and another, much larger couple swam into range. Benny started: it was his headmaster! Yes, it was Mr. Varley all right, in his well-pressed cricket flannels and blazer, swinging along in a brisk, business-like quickstep. And the woman in his arms was—surely not!—yes, it was Madam.

Benny had never listened to the stories about Mr. Varley and Madam. As far as he was concerned, Mr. Varley was the fountain of all honour. Why, each morning he addressed the whole school, drawing some moral instruction from a story in the morning paper. His code was simple and rigorous; the Ten Commandments covered it pretty adequately. There was nothing in the Commandments about not drinking port and lemon. Apart from this one, and in Benny's world, quite forgivable lapse, Mr. Varley was decorum personified. "Listen to the story of this wretched little worm, boys," he would declaim from his high stool. "He was only a chandler's clerk, but some designing woman got her claws into him. Result? He steals twenty thousand from his employer over a decade; but is eventually and inevitably apprehended. Now he is doing seven years' hard labour in Wormwood Scrubs—and never were they more richly deserved.

Mark that well, boys. Lust is the root of all evil." He would then rake the little room with his liquorice-black eyes while the boys sat rigid with terror. Did the headmaster know about *them*? Would he one day find them out? And if he did, what unimaginable punishment would follow?

Yet here was Mr. Varley, nimble as many another fat man on his twinkling, well-polished toes, steering Madam round the floor; more than that, holding Madam in his arms!

Madam was the housekeeper at Valhalla. None of the boys knew what her real name was. She was a big, terrifying woman of about fifty-five, with a jutting bosom and iron-grey hair swept straight back in a severe bun. She smoked Balkan Sobranie cigarettes and drank pink gins. Her voice was loud, clear, rasping, and "posh". According to one story, Madam was the daughter of a famous county family who had employed Mr. Varley in his youth as a butler. It was Lady Chatterley's Lover all over again. According to another version, Madam had been a mistress at a famous girl's public school. Mr. Varley, stationed nearby as a regimental sergeant-major, had won her heart and spirited her away. Now she was Mr. Varley's mistre—— But Benny could never bring himself to pronounce the word, heavy as it was with cabalistic undertones of adulthood, corruption and experience. Dash it all, the stories might have been true; but if Mr. Varley had fallen in love with Madam, why had he never married her? This, for Benny, solved the whole conundrum. The stories were untrue and Mr. Varley was a man of honour.

However, it could not be denied that he was now circling the dance floor with Madam in his arms; and they both seemed to be enjoying themselves.

Madam wore a red brocade dress and three rows of choker pearls. She wore no wedding ring but several others; they were all large, ornate and, it was thought locally, genuine. Her face was pink with excitement and perhaps one or two gins and she threw back her head, laughing alarmingly in her massive contralto at one of Mr. Varley's sallies. They both looked—thought Benedict—though it was faintly ridiculous to use the term of two such very old and formidable people—they both looked *radiant*. Then Benny had a flash of insight. He saw the whole thing. *They had just fallen in love!* After all those dull and wasted lonely middle-aged years, each a stranger to the other in the musty schoolroom world, heavy with chalk-dust and the smell of old plimsolls, they had found each other. Suddenly perhaps, meeting in a corridor at dusk, when the day-boys had gone and the emaciated boarders were settling to sleep in their hard narrow beds, Madam and Mr. Varley had passed in the corridor and their eyes had met. Mr. Varley would have stopped dead in his tracks and she would have paused, a little timorous for once, and asked if he wanted her for anything. And he would have said no, unsure of himself for half a historic moment, and then he must have said, in a rush of confidence, "Madam, may I escort you to the 'Thorn and Sceptre' for a nocturnal pink gin?" And she, her upper-class training showing at once, would have taken the invitation in her well-bred stride: "But how kind, Mr. Varley. I should be enchanted."

That was it all right, thought Benny; and it's only happened a day or two ago; that's for certain. They are in love too.

They passed out of sight, and for a little he saw no one who was close to him; though he knew everyone at the dance by sight at least. But a few minutes later, he saw, with a leap of the heart, Felix's father and stepmother dancing an elegant tango.

Mr. Weston was a short, dapper man, with well-groomed black hair and a small, neatly-trimmed black beard. He wore heavy spectacles. His political beliefs had not noticeably affected his weakness for clothes. Tonight he wore a white tuxedo; in his breast pocket was a red display handkerchief, and he wore a pair of black suède shoes. These last particularly offended Benny's father. "Bloody brothel-creepers," he used to murmur, whenever he saw them.

Arabella Weston had certainly not grown tired of her husband yet, despite Felix's gloomy forecasts. She was quite a little girl, with her hair parted down the middle and simply brushed; she was brown and wholesome as a new-laid egg. She wore a simple rust-coloured dress and danced very close to her husband. Benedict tried hard to master the reality of the news; these two who now embraced on the dance floor, moving with practised ease over the polished floor, were also consummated lovers whose congress had been sanctified by the rites of the local Register Office. At one anonymous moment some eight weeks ago this experienced middle-aged intellectual and this fresh young girl had, in the endorsed privacy of their marriage bed, conceived a child, which, even as they circled the floor in a gay beguine, she

59

carried for him in her womb. What enormous joys they must know! And what extra edge was given to the excitement by the notion that she was almost a child herself; not all that much older than he was! And yet at some moment unknown, she had crossed over from innocence into knowledge. How this legislated adult happiness beckoned him on! How wonderful it must be to long for love and find it!

"Another shandy, son?" Benedict came back from his long reverie with a click of guilt. His father had returned at last, bearing the best peace-offering he knew. The moment of dissonance between them, his father's first hint of fear at parting and his own answering resentment, had gone. They were friends again.

"Oh hello, Pop. Thanks very much. Cheers. Tell me, what sort of chap is Tony Hammond?"

"A really fine lad. I don't know him well, but of course I knew his father, old Stingo. Charming chap; such a damned pity he took to the bottle."

"What actually happened, Pop?"

"Well, like so many of these athletes, he made the mistake of going into the wine trade, into one of Keith's subsidiaries in fact. Everything went fine for a while; he was one of the most popular men in the county I suppose, and whoever went to see him had to stay for a drink. Well that was all right, but one day Hammond found he couldn't do without a drink, even if it meant lifting the wherewithal from the till. Keith had no choice, really, but he just had to sack him. There was no question of calling the police. The D.T.s did the rest."

"What happened to the mother?"

"She went off to South Africa and married again."

"So who looks after Tony Hammond?"

"An old clergyman over at Bales Whitney. There's no money left at all; I think Keith contributes a bit."

"Then why didn't Hammond go to Shallerton?"

"He's a very stubborn boy and he refused. Said he was going to repay Keith Margrave anyway, and the less it cost to educate him the sooner the debt would be paid. He's an extremely independent young man."

"What'll he do when he leaves school?"

"Why, go to Cambridge of course. He's a dead cert for a Double Blue and a good job in the City."

That, as far as his father was concerned, was the ultimate satisfaction a business career could offer.

"What a sad story, Pop."

"Life is full of sad stories. But what's so very terrible about Tony Hammond's life? The world is at his feet."

And the girl was in his arms; they danced by, deep in conversation, and Benedict's father seemed not to notice or to comprehend the wonder and excitement of it. Soon Mr. Benedict was gossiping with Brewery friends again and the boy slipped gently away. Quietly he edged his way through the bar and out into the open. He strolled across the cricket pitch, his hands deep in his pockets, content. It was quite dark now, and moonless, but the stars gave back to the earth a strange luminosity. It was, in the literal sense, very silent, and yet the pitch on which he walked, scuffed from the heroics of the great day, seemed to contain the faint echoes of the cheers and laughter. It was as if he was walking along the soft floor of some mighty sea-mollusc, hearing all round the murmurs it had trapped over the centuries. The air was warm and—yes, there it was once more—the mysterious and bitter-sweet Aylsbourn smell. I shall remember the smell, he thought to to himself, when every other memory has gone.

He didn't recall how long he stayed out alone in the darkness; it seemed a very great time, but it was probably not more than half an hour. He was disturbed by the doors of the clubhouse balcony being thrown suddenly open, and by the sudden burst of noise and laughter from the revellers. People came pouring out on to the balcony and Benedict realised it must be time for the firework display. This was the climax of the Cricket Match; Keith Margrave loved fireworks in a secret way and was said to spend five hundred pounds on them each year.

Benny hurried back and joined his father. Soon there was the huge whoosh of the first rocket, the exploding radiance of its green stars in the sky, and for a moment every upward-turning face, caught in its glow, was battle-pale. The boy felt a sharp snatch of pity for this plangent reminder of their common humanity. Then the crowd gave a great "Ah!" as it burned away and a great "Oh!" for the next rocket with its crimson stars and soon the whole horizon was stained the long gamut of the spectrum as Catherine Wheels spun in their silver spirals and the Golden Rain cascaded into the gunpowdered air. They were all children again; the pyrotechnical magic seemed to renew their forgotten innocence. Benedict wanted the delight never to end, but for the shadowy Margrave employees crouched behind the set-pieces to fill the sky with multi-coloured light till dawn. But all too soon it was time for the great finale, the illuminated set-piece of the King and Queen, with GOD BLESS THEIR MAJESTIES in letters of fire beneath, and as George the Sixth and his consort sputtered and glowed in effigy, they all rose to sing the National Anthem. Benedict noticed, in the weird refulgence, that Tony Hammond stood just in front of him and that the girl was still beside him and that her hand was in his.

Monday

Each day at Valhalla—even the last day of all—began with prayers. At nine-fifteen precisely the whole school assembled in the main hall (it was in point of fact the drawing-room of the old house, its many layers of chocolate paint kicked bare by hundreds of boys' shoes) and Mr. Varley himself conducted the service. He swept in that Monday morning, Benny remembered, fearful as ever, his great black gown billowing behind him, his enormous red face shiny and knobbly and perennially terrifying.

Mr. Varley's views on religion were so eccentric, and the phrasing of his prayers so idiosyncratic, that many parents simply did not believe what their sons reported on the subject. Those who did might well have been tempted to take their sons away, had not Mr. Varley attained such a reputation as the best crammer in a fifty miles radius. Those boys who simply could not make their parents believe that they were telling the truth about the shape and content of Mr. Varley's morning service often got cuffed for blasphemy. Mr. Varley's service was certainly unique. One distinctive feature was the movements that accompanied it.

Mr. Varley closed his eyes that last morning as usual and said: "Let us pray." A hundred boys bowed their heads and closed their eyes. To have been caught with them open would have been inviting Mr. Varley to fling an inkpot across the room at the offender. More than once a boy had been carried out unconscious after being struck on the head.

Having got through the Lord's Prayer at drill-ground speed, Mr. Varley launched into his own prayer:

"Oh Lord, help us to remember the sufferings of thy son Jesus Christ. Get those arms up in the air," he barked in a military aside. A hundred small pairs of arms rose to a horizontal position. The room seemed to be suddenly filled with little scarecrows. "Now just keep them up. Keep them *up*, Weston, if you want to get away on your last day without a beating. See how it hurts. Now think how our Lord must have felt. Keep them up!"

The boys gritted their teeth. It was not a bad game, a sort of battle with your own will, and you gradually got used to the pain.

"Right! Lower them."

The arms thudded gratefully down.

"Help all doctors and nurses," Mr. Varley continued, his eyes still tight shut. "And guide thou the surgeon's knife."

A mighty crash shook the room as a hundred small hands came down on the desks in front of them. With the expertise of long practice, the hundred fists slid down the desk lids, performing an imaginary incision with a scalpel.

"Bless all cashiers"—the boys doled out imaginary cash across a putative counter—"with their special temptations. Bless all sailors and those in peril on the sea"—the boys paid out imaginary anchors—"Bless all teachers and parents" [no action for this] "and bring us all in thy good time to thine abode. Amen."

Mr. Varley then instructed the boys to sit. This was usually the moment for his little homily. Today was no exception.

"Today," he began with great solemnity, "you are about to break up for the long vac. Many of you are saying goodbye to Valahalla for the last time. Many of you, indeed, thanks to my coaching methods, are going on to fresh fields and pastures new. As you know, Varley of Valhalla is not given to idle boasting. But you can all be proud of the fact that this school is sending one of its number on next term to one of England's most famous public schools; in fact to Sedbergh."

There was a murmur of approval at this. Most Valhallians were died-in-the-wool snobs. In the past Varley had sent very nearly all his boys to Shallerton Oaks, which was known to be a fourth-rate public school. But Sedbergh, that was something!

"Some of you are going to Dartmouth and so will at once be faced with all the manifold temptations the world has to offer. I need not specify. Some of you, after a brief apprenticeship, will be entering your fathers' businesses. To these I say a special word: remember that other people's money is sacred, even your fathers'. Remember the parable of the talents. That talent I have tried to make you live, eat, and breathe in this school."

He's done that all right, thought Benny. He quite liked old Varley at that moment.

"But to every boy leaving Valhalla this term," Varley continued, "I have this special, final word to say." He inclined confidentially over the desk.

"What I want to talk to you about," Mr. Varley continued, "is constipation." There was a little murmur of relief round the room.

"No boy should tolerate constipation," Varley continued, "for a moment. In a fit, active youth, the motions should be as regular as clockwork. Once, twice, or even three times a day."

He paused, and frowned.

"However, even on the most conscientious of us constipation may lay its dread hand. If it does, it must be rooted out at once." He leaned forward. "Take a laxative boys. Never be afraid to take a laxative. As you know, here at Valhalla we believe in Epsom Salts for normal cases, and castor oil for the obstinate ones. Whatever your predicament, boys, never shirk your duty. Take your medicine like men! And the stronger, the better."

He paused again, and looked round the room.

"Never fear the consequences of being taken short in the street. If it happens, approach the first respectable door you see, raise your cap, and ask to see the lady of the house. When she appears, raise your cap again and state your business briefly but succinctly. Once the matter is over, thank the lady of the house, leave sixpence for the maid, and take your leave."

Benny had heard this speech five times now, at the end of each school year, but it never failed to fascinate him. He was sure that it would be etched into his brain when he died.

Mr. Varley then appended his valediction.

"For those of you," he said, "going on and out into the world, this is a moment of joy and sorrow mixed. Temptations as well as opportunities await you.

"Some of you, I do not doubt, will climb the Ladder of Success. Some of you will slide down into the Slough of Despond. Some will falter, some will founder. But remember this. You are always welcome at Valhalla. Varley of Valhalla is always good for a loan. No Old Valhallian need ever go hungry. Many a Valhallian have I helped over the style. Many an old boy has come to me penniless, and not one has ever been turned empty away. Many a temptation has laid an Old Valhallian low. Sometimes it has been drink, sometimes gambling; sometimes"—and here Mr. Varley fixed the school with his black, glassy eyes—"it has been a woman who has brought an old Valhallian down to perdition. But whoever has come to me, I have in no wise cast out. The price of a dinner, a glass of decent wine, a cigar—these no old Valhallian has ever asked of me in vain. Nor ever will. To paraphrase Belloc's beautiful lines:

> *Valhalla made me*
> *Valhalla fed me*
> *Whatever I had, it gave me again.*
> *And the best of Valhalla loved and led me——*

Mr. Varley paused, then in a voice resonant with emotion concluded:

God be with you—Valhalla men.

At this there was a spontaneous applause, but Mr. Varley quickly checked it with uplifted hand. He nodded to Madam, who sat rigid and unmoved at the upright piano in the corner. She lifted her heavily beringed fingers and the school stood to sing the traditional valedictory hymn: "Lord, Dismiss Us with Thy Blessing."

Benedict sang, as always, with gusto. It was a solemn moment, for, despite the appalling rigour of Varley's régime, he had quite enjoyed being at Valhalla. In a way it was a little disquieting to realise that he would never come back to face those liquorice-black eyes again. He could, of course, come back as an Old Boy to enjoy a port and lemon with his old headmaster at the "Thorn and Sceptre" one day. Only—would Mr. Varley have forgiven him, even after the lapse of years, for the disgrace he was about to bring on the school? There is only love . . . He still couldn't believe he had done it.

The hymn ended and the boys resumed their seats. Now came the prize-giving. The boys leaned back pleasurably. It was an enjoyable ritual, for Varley always concealed the names of the winners until this moment.

There were a number of prizes at Valhalla.. Varley had a liking for honour, and he had created a number of his own decorations. There were bronze and silver medals for the best performances in each sport, and silver cups for the victorious houses. There were four houses at Valhalla—Foch, Kitchener, Pershing, and Hindenberg—and Benedict, as Captain of Kitchener, went up proudly twice to pick up the trophies his boys had won. But the supreme prize at Valhalla was the Varley Award for Endeavour. It was won on an elaborate points system, kept by the headmaster himself, with marks allotted for industry, honesty, courage, and a number of other virtues. Benedict had always secretly hoped he would win it, and now his chances seemed high. His academic work had been sound, and his house was in good shape. That fifty last Friday might just tip the balance!

The Award for Endeavour took the form of a small golden Ganymede, naked on a plinth. One or two parents of boys who had won it had sent it back as unsuitable for display in their drawing-rooms. However, there it stood again this year, glistening on the headmaster's desk.

Mr. Varley cleared his throat. "We now come," he said portentously, "to the principal award. As you know, this is the greatest honour our school can bestow. I make my selection each year only after the most careful thought. This year the choice has been particularly difficult. Two boys have been outstanding and there is virtually nothing to choose between them. Their names are Weston and Benedict."

Many eyes turned curiously to regard the two friends, now thrown into an unexpected antagonism, and Benedict felt cold with suspense. Weston leaned back, unconcerned.

"Unfortunately," Varley continued, "there is only one trophy. So in the end I came to a very simple decision. I tossed a coin—heads for Benedict, tails for Weston." He paused and gave the two boys one of his rare and formidable smiles.

"It came down tails. Come up, Weston."

Felix uncoiled lazily from his desk and strolled up to the front, loudly applauded on all sides. His sophistication and cynicism had endeared him to his contemporaries.

Benedict felt ill with shock and disappointment. What a way to decide! Trust Felix to come off best! Would life alreays treat him as the runner-up?

Weston lounged back to his seat, looking thoroughly bored. He placed the little golden Ganymede on the desk in front of them. "I don't know where the hell I'm going to put it," he muttered to Benedict. "It's too damned vulgar for my study. What do you think it'll fetch melted down?"

But before Benedict could answer, Mr. Varley raised his hand for silence.

"The coin's decision was swift, but entirely arbitrary. So of course I have not forgotten the runner-up. Benedict, come up. I have a little consolation prize for you."

He rose and went forward. What on earth had the headmaster got up his sleeve now?

Mr. Varley picked up a small white box that lay before him. "Well done, Benedict." He beamed down at the boy and suddenly the great face was no longer terrifying. "I'm sorry you couldn't have the Ganymede, but I went to the jeweller specially to get you this." He handed over the box; Benedict opened it, and saw that a half-hunter watch lay in the cotton-wool. It was gold. He couldn't believe it.

"Turn it over, Benedict."

He turned it. On the back there was an inscription. In flowing italic, two words had been etched out of the polished metal: *Honoris Causa*.

"What does it mean, Benedict?"

"It means for the sake of honour, sir."

"Yes, as a mark of honour. I hope you'll keep it always."

"I will, sir."

Benedict went back to his seat. Felix looked at the watch without interest.

"Second-hand I imagine," he said. "What's the scribble on the back?"

Benedict showed him and Felix snorted. "Bloody rot! That proves it's second-hand. I mean not even Varley would write crap like that on the back of a watch."

Benedict never discovered whether Mr. Varley had put the words on or not. He looked at the watch several times more during the course of the morning.

At twelve-thirty the bell rang for their last school lunch. They queued up down the stairs leading into the basement. In this dingy and subterranean area, Madam cooked food of frightening inedibility; frightening, because no boy was allowed to leave a mouthful. Small boys were sometimes seen chewing on with agonised determination a quarter of an hour after the plates had been cleared away. Boys had smuggled out pieces of meat and subjected them to scientific tests; seeing if they could be melted in hydrochloric acid or severed with a hammer and chisel.

Mr. Varley stood at the door of the dining-room with a large hairbrush in his hand. The boys waited docilely to have their hair brushed unceremoniously before they went in. As his face was pressed for the last time into Mr. Varley's waistcoat and he felt the rough motion over his scalp, Benedict felt another pang of loss and nostalgia. It would never happen again.

Madam had turned up trumps for their last day: it was cottage pie and beetroot followed by sago pudding. The boys ate in silence at a long gloomy table. Mr. Varley sat at their head eating a hot and nourishing stew. He never tired of telling his boys that as a grown man, he needed more calories than they did; a lot more.

But at last it was done, and they were released up into the sunlight. They cleared out their desks, returned their books to the store, and shook hands one by one, a solemn little file, with Mr. Varley at the front door. "Goodbye, Benedict," said Mr. Varley when his turn came. "Or rather, *au revoir*. I'm sure we'll see a good deal of you when you're at Shallerton. You'll play for the Valhalla Old Boys of course?"

"Of course, sir."

He sighed as he pedalled away with Weston. "You know, Felix," he said, "I shall miss that old scoundrel."

"Of course you will, Benny," said Felix sardonically.

"Won't you?"

"I hope I never set eyes on him again. And with a bit of luck I won't have to, judging by the state of his blood pressure right now."

Benedict laughed. How cold and refreshing Felix's cynicism was! What a healthy corrective to his own optimism!

They cycled lazily out of Aylesbourn towards Welcaster. Felix had been given five shillings. Despite his misanthropic pose he was generous-natured and had suggested a celebration tea in Miller's cake shop.

To get there, they had to leave their bicycles by a fence and cut across a meadow. As they were crossing it, they saw two boys approaching from the other side. Both were wearing the yellow and green blazers of the Grammar School.

When they were clearly within earshot Felix said offensively: "I suppose these are the sort of peasants I shall be living with next term."

The two boys obviously had heard, for they halted, blocking the pathway. Neither was much of a beauty: one boy was tall and gangling, with jug-handle ears and a strangely bent nose. The other was short and square, with a homely potato face. He carried a cricket bat.

The taller one spoke. His voice still had a trace of Hampshire in it, but he spoke with authority and precision.

"Would you kindly repeat that?"

"I said," Felix repeated clearly, "that you were the sort of peasants I should be living with next term."

"We look forward to the pleasure of your company," said the taller boy levelly. "Obviously Mr. Varley has not been able to teach his young gentlemen very good manners. However, we have ways of knocking them into shape."

"We're getting an extra supply of Lifebuoy soap in at home," Felix informed him. "My people are anxious that I shouldn't catch anything infectious from the lice-ridden proletariat."

The two grammar school boys exchanged glances. "I wonder if it would be any help if we gave him a preliminary doing now," said the small, square boy reflectively.

"No, Ken," said the other, shaking his head regretfully. "This problem must be tackled at leisure. Let them by."

He stood to one side with elaborate courtesy and made a small bow.

Felix went to walk by, but the tall boy's long leg shot out like an adder's tongue and tripped him. Trying to save himself, Feliz grabbed at him as he fell, and in a moment they were rolling on the grass, locked together and punching each other savagely.

Benedict sprang forward to pull them apart and saw too late that the potato-faced boy had swung back his cricket bat. It was as if somehow he had always known what was going to happen. He tried to duck, but there was no time. Even as he saw the bat scythe through the air he felt in anticipation the horror of the moment. He never quite got rid of it.

And then the bat hit him, with all the boys' force behind it, right across the face; across the bridge of the nose and the right eye. For another second it seemed as if his body simply could not believe it; then the pain scooped him up and encapsulated him. As the light died away there was a sound in the back of his head like a great gong being struck somewhere deep beneath the level of consciousness. He sank slowly to his knees and the last thing he remembered was the hot, wet blood running down his face.

He was out for probably no more than fifteen seconds, but when he came round he saw three anxious faces staring down at him. His nose was swelling and unreal; he could see it mushrooming from his left eye. But—oh the terror if it—he could not see at all from his right eye. He opened and closed the bruised eye-lid, but there was only a red haze, whichever he did.

He sat with his head bowed, holding both hands to the injured eye. "Felix!" he cried. "Oh Felix! I can't see!"

All anger had melted away. The boy who had hit him knelt down beside him. "Let me see," he said quietly. He moved Benedict's hands gently away and Benny always afterwards remembered his grave face, white with shock, close to his, studying the grisly damage with solemn concentration.

At length he got to his feet.

"We've got to get him to a doctor," he said. "Where's the nearest?"

"Mackay," Felix put in. "That's his house over there."

"Anderson is my doctor," Benedict said mechanically.

"Too far. We can't take you all that way. This may be urgent."

The three boys stared down at Benny in concern. There was blood all down his shirt now and the eye was coated with a red film.

"Benny," Felix said. "You've got to get over to Mackay's. Come on, we'll help you."

They helped him gently to his feet. His legs trembled, but he could walk, supported on each side.

It seemed a long way to Mackay's house.

Felix rang the bell and stood back. The three of them were crestfallen and awed by the enormity of what they had done.

There was a long silence. "Oh my God," said Felix. "Don't say they're not in."

He rang the bell again; and at last they heard footsteps.

"Thank goodness," whispered Felix. His precocious assurance had melted away.

The door opened. It was the girl; she was wearing the same lime-green dress as when he had first seen her. Even in his misery, though, he felt a quick thrust of disappointment that she should be as tall as he was; even in low heels her eyes looked straight into his.

Her eyes were the same colour green, her skin pale and a little

70

freckled as he so vividly remembered, her blonde hair drawn back and cascading luxuriantly in a pony-tail. On her arms was golden down and her young figure was sweetly full; she was, in nature, a woman already, and despite his stricken condition, Benedict was desperately and poignantly aware of it.

He was a horrifying sight. Already a huge aubergine-tinted bruise was spreading, while the blood ran without stint down his chin and his shirt was blotched crimson. His hands were red as a butcher's and trembling.

But she had evidently seen blood before and she did not hesitate.

"My father and mother are out," she said. "But if you'll come into the surgery I'll do what I can until they get back. You boys can wait in here."

She indicated the waiting-room, and led Benedict by the arm into her father's surgery.

Benedict always hated surgeries; especially he hated the display of steel instruments in glass cases. But today, for all his distress, he didn't mind.

She quickly took out a sponge, gauze, and bandages, and held the sponge under a cold tap. She glanced over her shoulder and saw that he was still standing.

"Sit in that chair, please," she said briskly. He sat heavily; his knees were trembling too.

She was ready. For a moment she studied the battered face, frowning seriously. "It won't hurt," she said. "It'll just be cold." And she placed the sponge gently on his face.

After the first shock, it was very comforting. The cold water seemed to draw the aching bruise right from the bone. He gave a little sigh.

"Does it hurt?" she asked quietly.

"Oh no, thank you. It feels wonderful now." And having said that he suddenly found himself shaking and sobbing violently. The tears poured down his face, mingling with the blood. "I'm sorry," he gasped between sobs, "terribly sorry."

She bit her lips. "It's all right," she said. "Don't worry about it. You've got shock, that's all. It's quite natural. It always happens. Here; come and lie down."

She lifted him from the chair and gently led him to the couch. "Lie down," she commanded him. She tucked a blanket over him and he felt suddenly warm and protected. But as she resumed the sponging, he began to shake even more and his teeth chattered alarmingly. She came to a quick decision: she sat down herself on the couch and lifted his head on to her lap. He turned and lay with his face against the cool lime-green cotton of her summer dress and was at peace.

It seemed a very long time before Dr. Mackay came home. But at last the surgery door opened.

"Hello, Laura. What have you got here?"

Laura: it was the first time he had ever heard her name.

"This boy has been hit in the eye, Daddy. I've just sponged the blood and covered him up. He's got shock."

"Dear, oh dear." Benedict detected, in the articulation of those three words, a faint but attractive remnant of Scottish, and it was strangely comforting.

Mackay went to the sink and meticulously scrubbed his hands. Then he came over and said: "Let's have a look, young man."

Benedict always remembered the doctor's face staring intently into his injured eye, the tiny tufts of beard where he had not quite shaved thoroughly in the morning, the odd lines of grey in his black hair, the St. Thomas's Hospital tie, and the gold signet ring on the little finger of the hand that gently held the damaged eye open.

Finally he stood up. "You're very lucky, young fellow," he said. "It's just a bruise. In twenty-four hours you'll see as well as ever. I'll bandage it up for you and give you something for the shock. Now what's your name?"

"Benedict, sir. Peregrine John Benedict."

Mackay laughed at this. "Bit of a mouthful, isn't it?"

"Yes, sir. It was my mother's idea, that Christian name. Everyone calls me Benny."

"Any relation to John Benedict at the Brewery?"

"He's my father, sir."

"Is he now?" The doctor beamed with pleasure and Benedict felt an enormous surge of relief. It was nice to have people smile when they heard your father's name. With all the old boy's faults, he was really quite a charmer.

"Then you must be the young Benedict who hit fifty for Valhalla on Friday."

"Yes, sir." How on earth did he know that?

"Quite a famous young man, Laura," the doctor observed as he worked on the eye. "Mr. Varley was telling me all about him.

72

A pity he's going on to Shallerton, or Tony would have been interested to meet him."

"Oh, sir, but I'm not going to Shallerton," Benedict blurted out. "I've failed the examination. I'm going to the Grammar School."

"Good gracious, you're a little pessimistic, aren't you? The examination was only this weekend, wasn't it?"

The doctor was evidently well informed on all local affairs.

"Yes, sir, but I know I've failed."

"Nonsense. You've just had a nasty sock in the eye and it's upset you. You'll be right as rain in the morning and ready to hit your first century."

Father and daughter smiled down at him.

"Now where do you live, Benny?"

"At the other end of the town, next door to the 'Thorn and Sceptre'."

"Yes of course you do. I'll run you home."

The three boys rose in crestfallen silence as Doctor Mackay and his daughter gently shepherded Benedict through the surgery door.

"Is he all right, Doctor?" asked Felix anziously.

"Oh, it's you is it, Felix? He's bruised the eye, but he'll see again in the morning."

"Thank God for that," said the potato-faced boy. "I'm afraid it was my fault, sir."

"No," said Felix. "I was to blame."

"We all were," said the tall boy with jug-handle ears.

"Well I'm glad to hear that. You must all be good friends, eh, Benny?"

"No, sir, not exactly; at least——"

"We've never met I'm afraid," said the potato-faced boy. "I'm Kenneth Heppel and my friend is Milo Johnston."

"Ah." They were now at the car. The doctor settled Benny in beside him and Laura sat on Benny's left. "Well, you'd better jump in too and explain yourselves to Benny's father."

They scrambled into the back and the doctor's Railton moved smoothly off.

"If you're Milo Johnston" remarked the doctor, to the jug-eared boy, "I imagine you're a relation of Johnston the Physics master?"

"Yes, sir, he's my father."

73

"And you" (to the potato-faced one) "must be a relation of Will Heppel at the garage?"

"He's my father, sir."

"Well, well, it's a small world. And you say you're not friends?"

"We didn't know each other before," said Benedict. "But I think we are friends now."

III

T HAT WAS THE end of that long summer weekend in 1939; four days whose every minute he seemed to recall with perfect clarity. Then it all became confused again, and he remembered only in snatches and fragments, irrationally, as most people do. He remembered:

One afternoon in the summer of 1939

Kenneth Heppel and Milo Johnston called to see Benedict. He was in his favourite place, suspended in a hammock strung up between an iron hook in the wall of his father's cottage, and a branch of their greengage tree. Lazily he dipped into a bag of greengages while he ploughed steadily through a library copy of *Those Barren Leaves*. This, as far as Benedict was concerned, was the nearest he would ever get to heaven. It had been a warm day again; there had been that delicious ankle-deep mist on Twenty Acre when he first looked out of his window that morning; and now the great warm patriarchal sun was descending slowly over the elms. Soon it would be time for his evening glass of shandy, carried foaming to him by Kate from the back door of the "Thorn and Sceptre". He lay, at peace with the world, transported in his imagination from the gentle market town of Aylsbourn to Mrs. Aldwinkle's sunbaked castle above the glittering Tyrrhenian Sea.

He was disturbed by the rap of the front door knocker. Sighing, he laid down the novel; it was physical distress to him to be recalled nowadays to the real world.

The two boys stood sheepishly in the front porch.

"Oh hello," said Benedict.

"Hello," said Kenneth Heppel. "We just came round to ask about your eye."

"Oh. That's very good of you. It's all right now thanks. I can see just as well out of it as ever."

The battered eye had now indeed receded very nearly to its normal size, and only the faint lingering discoloration of the gargantuan bruise remained.

75

There was an uncertain pause. Then Benedict said: "Why don't you both come in? There's no one here; my father's still out and I'm just reading."

He led them through into the little kitchen garden at the back, found them deck chairs and brought one out from the woodshed for himself.

"What we wanted to do," said Milo, choosing his words carefully, "was to talk to you about your friend Felix Weston. We had a few words with him after we saw you home the other day, and we decided that he wasn't quite such a creep as we thought. Still, it was really his fault, you know, that you got that sock in the eye."

Benedict grinned. "I nearly always carry the can for old Felix," he explained. "But you know, really he's a very amusing fellow. And he has some family troubles which make him act like a screwball."

The two visitors exchanged glances.

"You mean," asked Heppel, "Arabella?"

Benedict was startled.

"You mean you know Mrs. Weston too?"

The two visitors grinned. "Of course," Milo said. "After all, it was in all the papers, wasn't it? I mean about her being Bantinglow's model and all that."

"In fact," said Benedict, "I don't think it's Arabella that really worries Felix. It's his father."

"It's two halves of the same problem," said Kenneth. "But we wanted to tell you that whatever he's suffering from he'd better watch out when he gets to Aylsbourn in September. We've agreed to leave him alone; but we can't guarantee the behaviour of all the others if he comes out with any more of that offensive class-war stuff."

"He doesn't mean it, you know. It's only a reaction because his father's a communist."

"The last time we had a boy from Valhalla," Milo said, with a little relish in his voice, "he was carried home the first day with five stitches in his head."

"What on earth did he do?"

"He asked the fellows when lunch would be served."

"I'm sorry. I don't follow."

The two boys smiled grimly at each other.

"It's just as well you're not coming to Aylsbourn," said Kenneth. "You'd get carved up too. Midday, we eat dinner."

76

"That's a bit fierce, isn't it? I mean to belt a boy just for saying that?"

"If Weston calls the chaps peasants," said Kenneth, "we can't be responsible for his safety."

Benedict laughed. "It was a bit much. But I'll be there to look after him."

"Surely you're going to Shallerton?" asked Milo.

"I think you'll find I've failed to win the scholarship."

"Well, won't your father pay for you?"

"Good Lord, no! He's not a millionaire."

"Isn't he? We thought all those Brewery executives made a fortune."

"I don't suppose he makes any more than your father."

"Well," said Heppel, "he certainly makes more than mine."

"I think we ought not to quibble about this," said Benedict. "There's only one man in Aylsbourn who makes any money, and that's Margrave. What does it matter whether your father makes eight pounds a week or ten pounds a week? Margrave is worth a hundred thousand."

"I think you'll find," said Heppel, "that Weston isn't worth much less."

"Look," said Benedict. "I've got an idea. Why don't we go up and see Felix now? He's really very amusing company."

They looked at each other. "All right," said Heppel. "Perhaps we can see the gorgeous Arabella at the same time."

But there was no sign of Felix or Mrs. Weston when they rang the back bell of Felix's house ten minutes later. Mrs. Duncher opened the door.

Perhaps, Benedict thought, she's been admitted to Arabella's secret. Her mild blue eyes seemed to have an unusual gleam in them and she showed unaccustomed animation. It was as if someone had just passed a high electric current through her dumpy body.

"Felix isn't back yet," she told them. "He's gone out shopping with Mrs. Weston."

"The lucky sod," muttered Milo Johnston.

"Tell you what though," said Mrs. Duncher. "They'll be back for tea soon. I expect I can find you boys a cup if you'd like to wait."

"Thanks very much, Mrs. Duncher," said Benedict quickly. "It is rather important that we see Felix."

Over the fireplace in the drawing-room was a creamy nude by Bantinglow. The model had her back to the artist, but there was something in the delicious flow of her back and buttocks that seemed familiar.

"Christopher!" exclaimed Milo. "It can't be!"

"It is," said Benedict.

"Fancy letting that old lecher see you starkers!"

"Nothing to it," Benedict said casually. "Bantinglow—even at eighty is a man of the world. He would be far more exciting to a girl like Arabella than some doomy poet."

"Yes," said Milo. "He might have more small talk. But just imagine . . ."

"Ah," said Kenneth, who had been peering out of the window, bored by this exchange. "Here they come."

The three boys jammed themselves into the window-seat and stared down. Arabella was coming along the High Street arm in arm with Felix. He was carrying her shopping bag and they were deep in conversation.

"Just look at that lucky sod!" breathed Milo.

Benedict knew as soon as he set eyes on them what had happened. Arabella had told Felix her news. That was why she was going out of her way to be nice to him. They made, Benedict reflected, a rather charming couple; Felix was already the same height as she. They looked happy and insulated, like young lovers.

In another moment they heard the key in the latch, the sound of their voices, the answering voice of Mrs. Duncher, and then the drawing-room door opened. The boys rose to their feet awkwardly.

Arabella came in first. She seemed to Benedict to be in bloom, like an early-morning rose. Her face was a little flushed and her eyes shone. She wore, Benedict always remembered, an olive green corduroy suit, and a russet-coloured blouse. Felix followed. When he saw the visitors, he tried hard to wipe the expression of serenity from his face. He was too late; Benedict, for one, noticed.

"Well, boys," said Arabella. "This is a nice surprise."

"I don't think you've met Milo and Ken before," Felix said to Arabella rather ungraciously. And then, to the boys a little grudgingly: "This is my—— This is Arabella."

Good God, thought Benedict, he's actually shy about her.

"You must all stay," said Arabella, "and have some tea. I'll ask Mrs. Duncher to lay it here in the drawing-room."

"Look," said Felix, "why don't you all come up to my room? I've got some marvellous new jazz records. My father bought them for me in London yesterday."

"Does Mrs. Weston like jazz?" asked Benedict doubtfully.

"Heavens yes," said Arabella. "But I don't know much about it. When I was rushing about in London we always used to go crazy about Harry Roy."

She realised from the boys' faces that this could not be right. Felix explained to her. "Harry Roy is not exactly *jazz*, Arabella," he said. "I'll play you some real New Orleans music and you'll soon see the difference."

"I'll go and see what Mrs. Duncher can cook up," said Arabella. "You boys go on up and get something really hot for me to hear. I want to learn."

It was mysteriously delightful to all four of them, the thought of this little assignation with Arabella in Felix's room.

Gerard Weston had certainly turned up trumps. A keen believer in the sentimental, folklore aspect of jazz, he had gone to town and bought Felix some treasures. He had got some Parlophone Black Labels and some of the Brunswick Sepia series. There was Jimmy Noone's "Way Down Yonder" and Gene Krupa's "Three Little Words"; Louis Armstrong's "Muskat Ramble" and Johnny Dodd's "Bucktown Stomp".

In ten minutes Arabella was back with Mrs. Duncher. Both women carried large trays; they had made a splendid high tea. There were scrambled eggs on toast and Devonshire splits and toast and strawberry jam, and a plate of Huntley and Palmer's chocolate biscuits.

Mrs. Duncher withdrew, and Arabella sat at the top of Felix's table and poured out large cups of tea. Felix turned the gramophone off till after they had eaten, so that they could concentrate on the music later.

"Well, now," said Arabella, "I hope I'm not inhibiting your conversation. I'd like you to treat me as one of the gang."

"The trouble is, Arabella," said Felix, "that normally we talk about only sport, which wouldn't interest you, and sex, which you know all about anyway."

"That's not fair, Felix," Arabella reprimanded him. "I'm madly interested in cricket at the moment. I adored that game on Sunday. And as for sex: truly, I'm a complete beginner."

Benedict stared at her, mesmerised. He had never heard a woman say such a thing in his life.

"You can't," said Milo, "be quite such beginners as we are."

Arabella gave a little chuckle at this. It was a sound which riveted Benedict in his chair. "Now boys," she teased them, "this is too modest of you. I've heard of all the affairs between the boys and girls that take place under dear old Sandy Macpherson's unwitting nose. You all spend your time falling in and out of love with each other. You don't know how lucky you are. I was brought up in a convent. I didn't kiss a young man until I was seventeen."

The boys stared at her with respect. She had certainly made up for lost time!

"Could you tell us, Mrs. Weston——" began Benedict. But she gently interrupted him. "Please call me Arabella. After all, I'm not very much older than you. And I'm certainly not old enough to be your Mum."

She was clearly enjoying her little flirtation with them. Benedict cleared his throat and began again rather shyly: "Could you tell us, Arabella"—it was delectable, the unwonted, the previously forbidden pleasure of using her Christian name—"what it is like to be a girl?"

They all laughed at this one, uproariously. "Oh Benny," cried Felix, "you really are priceless."

"No,' said Arabella smiling gently at Benedict when they had subsided, "it's a perfectly good question. But it's a jolly difficult one to answer. I mean, I have no comparative experience. How does it feel to be a boy?"

"Awful, quite often," said Milo, unexpectedly. "I mean, you're so unsure of what you can do."

"But," said Arabella in mock surprise, "that's just what it's like when you're a girl. Truly. You're full of strange dreams and fears and hints of future delights and little shiverings and portents of romance. You're so—*vulnerable*."

"Did you ever want to be a boy?" asked Kenneth Heppel boldly.

"Oh passionately, especially when I was small and I couldn't do the things my brothers could do. It's hateful to be told that you're soft and delicate"—here a shadow of vestigial resentment flitted across her face—"when you want to be out climbing trees. You feel—sort of second class. But eventually, when you get to about fifteen—when you become conscious that you're a woman—then it has its compensations."

Benedict was fascinated. He had never heard any woman speak so—frankly—before.

"What sort of compensations?" he asked. His voice sounded odd to him: it was an almost histrionic whisper.

Arabella looked at him for a second and then said: "The usual things; the fun of wearing a new dress. Colours, sights, smells; being given flowers. Having men look at you in the street in a certain way."

"You mean you *enjoy* that?" asked Benedict incredulously.

"Yes. Why ever not?"

"It doesn't strike you as—crude?"

"No. It is part of life. My dears: this is my philosophy. All people can be divided into two great categories. They are the life-diminishers and the life-enhancers. Now, as for me, I'm pro-life, one hundred per cent. So if a man looks at me in the street and his look says I like you—then I'm glad. It's as simple as that."

The boys digested this novel intelligence in silence.

"Suppose," said Milo, "I saw you in the street. In London one day; suppose we passed in Charing Cross Road. Suppose I looked at you and realised that you were the only girl there could possibly be for me——"

"You'd be wrong," Arabella interrupted him drily. "There are lots of girls for all of you. Maybe in this town, maybe on the other side of the world; maybe they're hardly toddling about yet; maybe they're already dreaming about you; but believe me; there is no one and only girl."

"But suppose——"

"Ah yes; in Charing Cross Road. To me, as a member of the Pro-Life Party, it would be a shame—no, much worse—a scandal and a crime—if you allowed her to pass you by."

All the boys began to speak at once. "Oh, I know," she conceded, "there are the big conventional forces against you. But they're only inside you. The girl wouldn't mind. On the contrary, she'd be delighted. Isn't that what a girl is waiting for all her life? If you don't speak, you may be cruelly wasting that girl's life—taking away her one real chance of happiness."

"I'll tell you all something now which I've never told anyone," said Milo with unusual animation. "One day I was going up to London in the train. And there was a girl in the compartment with me. She got in at Shallerton. She was truly beautiful. As beautiful as you Arabella"—a strange nearness had fallen over the little attic room as though the people in it had been friends or lovers for years—"and you know I did the most reckless thing."

"Milo," said Kenneth with mock concern, "think carefully before you speak."

"I suddenly said to her," Milo blurted out, "I said—'I bet you wouldn't kiss me.' And she did."

"All the way to *London*?" asked Benedict.

"Yes. She wouldn't tell me her name, and of course I've never met her again. She ran away from me at Waterloo and disappeared in the crowd. I've never forgotten that," he concluded sadly.

"And she won't forget you," Arabella comforted him. "You know, Milo, that kind of thing happens all the time. Even in jolly old England, where it's not supposed to. It even happens here in Aylsbourn."

Great heavens, Benedict thought. Who would dare suggest a thing like that to *Arabella*?

"Yes," Arabella went on, evidently enjoying the little scandal she was creating. "There's at least one distinguished gentleman in this sleepy old town who makes passes at other people's wives— and quite a distinguished citizen too."

Great heavens, thought Benedict. Surely not Macpherson? Or Sir Keith Margrave? Surely not Doctor Mackay? Not— perhaps—*my own father*? But Arabella wasn't saying. "Boys," she went on, with a touch of remorse, "I've already been frightfully indiscreet. Let's keep it within these four walls, shall we?"

They all nodded. "But," Milo persisted, "Arabella, how *could* you meet a girl you just passed in the street?"

"Good heavens," Arabella chided him. "That's up to you, Milo. Pity the poor girl. She can't very well waylay a man she likes in the street. Not in this civilisation, in this century, anyway. Of course, she can make it pretty plain in all sorts of ways that she's not averse to being approached."

"A glance would do?" asked Benedict.

"A glance would do," said Arabella seriously. "Or better, you should see to it that your fingertips touch as you pass."

"What do you look for in a man?" enquired Kenneth Heppel.

Arabella considered this question. The boys waited in a torture of uncertainly. What on earth would she say now?

"I think first," said Arabella slowly, "arrogance. Yes, I definitely put arrogance first."

The boys listened in respectful and awestruck silence.

"Then I look for something a little indefinable. I think I shall have to call it—appetite. Not in the literal sense of course; I mean appetite for life; joy in being alive." She paused. "You must think me a very wicked woman. I mean what about kindness, generosity, patience, tolerance—all those things you read about in women's magazines? Well, I've nothing against them except that I don't believe in them and they bore me. I'd never *look* for them."

"What else?" asked Benedict.

"Oh," said Arabella casually, "the right smell. A man can be an angel, but if he doesn't smell right it's no good."

She laughed. "If you boys could see your faces! But now, this is rather unfair. What do you boys look for in a girl? Come, Benny, you are the only true romantic here. What do you look for?"

Benedict realised that everybody was watching him curiously. He racked his brains. The answer seemed to come up from a long way down in his sub-conscious memory. It was as if he had always really known what he was going to say, but had never dared admit it to himself. He cleared his throat nervously.

"Magic," he said.

Once again they all collapsed, as if knifed through with laughter. Even Benedict joined in this time. At length Arabella took out a little handkerchief and dried her eyes. "Oh Benny," she said, "you have such delicious miseries ahead of you!"

"Tell us one more thing, Arabella," pleaded Felix. "Benny and I have often argued about this. Is there really such a thing as love?"

There was a silence again in the attic room; not an absence of sound but a taut stillness, like the interval between a sliver of lightning and a clap of thunder. Benedict noticed that now Arabella had gone very pale. Even her lips had lost their usual vivid colour. The question had evidently distressed her.

"I think," she answered thoughtfully at length, "that love is possible between two people; just as I believe that it has occasionally been possible in history for mystics to communicate directly with God. It's of that order of probability—and that order of importance."

"But for most of us," urged Felix, "there is only flattery, sex, habit, despair?"

"Oh, but besides all these things, Felix," said Arabella, but she was speaking to herself, "there is love."

Benedict often found himself wondering why, at that moment, she looked so pale.

That awful day

When his father heard about the scholarship. They hadn't had the grace just to say he'd failed; no, there had to be a consultation between Mr. Ross-Tayfield and Mr. Varley, and then another consultation (in the relative comfort of the "Thorn and Sceptre") between Mr. Varley and Mr. Benedict, and then that excruciatingly embarrassing interview with his father when neither quite liked to look at the other.

"They seem to think, son," his father had begun shiftily, "that there may have been some mental—er, some nervous trouble. Let's see now, when did you get that sock in the eye?"

"Two days after the exam." It was no good trying to give his father that easy let-out.

"Yes. Well, they seem to think it would be a good idea son, if" —and here his father's face was in an agony of self-consciousness —"you went and had a chat to the doctor. I mean, they feel you must have been definitely ill on that day. Would you mind doing that for me, old chap?"

"No. Not a bit. But I'm afraid you'll find there's nothing wrong."

There had in fact been nothing wrong—nothing that the doctors could put their fingers on, anyway. Anderson had called in Mackay, and they had both sent him up to see a specialist in London, who had asked him several hundred questions and hit his nerve-centres with a small rubber hammer; but it all came to nothing in the end. Later there was another harrowing conversation with his father about taking the Shallerton scholarship again; the boy had been adamant and his father had finally given in. But he had been mystified and hurt: clearly there was more to his son than met the eye. And any variety of off-centre behaviour made Mr. Benedict instinctively uncomfortable.

84

Benedict was desperately sorry about his father's distress and often racked his brains for an explanation. But his own behaviour was as big a mystery to him as it was to the doctors. The night he had heard the news first, Benedict always remembered, his father had got drunk at the "Thorn and Sceptre", a thing he had never done before. Four pints of Margrave best bitter had always been his father's mellow limit; but that awful night he had gone on to neat whisky, and been sick in the kitchen. They both had tried to forget about it, but the memory was still there between them.

Mr. Varley had taken it in quite an unexpected way. He had asked Benedict to come and see him one evening soon after. The boy had found his old headmaster sitting in the high chair in his study. The room was illuminated only by one small reading-lamp, and there were long shadows on the walls, casting an eerie glow on the groups of cricket and rugger teams and the long line of silver cups.

"Benedict," Mr. Varley had said with surprising gentleness, "I am very sorry indeed to hear what has happened. I understand and I sympathise. I know how you must be feeling. You see, I have had the experience of mental trouble in my own family. My poor younger sister was a stranger to us for many years, and they finally had to take the dear creature away. There are moments in all our lives, I sometimes think, when sanity seems to hang by a thin thread. I know that has been my own experience. If that ever happens to you again, you must go to your best friend at once and pour your troubles out. Never bottle it up inside you. The brains, my dear Benny, are only like rather complicated bowels. They must never be allowed to clog."

"Thank you, sir. I'm truly sorry to have let you down."

"Don't ever worry about it, Benny." He noticed that his headmaster had used the affectionate diminutive. "I'm still convinced you'll be a credit to me. You're still only a very young fellow. There'll be plenty more chances in your life. You've lost a battle, you haven't lost the war. Oh yes, Valhalla will be proud of you one day."

"I wish I could believe that, sir."

"You've got to believe in yourself, Benny. Until you do, nobody else will believe in you."

"I'm afraid no one else will ever believe in me, sir."

Mr. Varley smiled. "I'm not much of a betting man, Benny, but I'd take money on you."

"That's very good of you, sir. I'll try not to let you down again."

"You haven't let me down, Benny. You don't think all this"—he indicated the roll of honour behind him, on which his boys' successes were inscribed in gilt—"means a thing to me, do you? That's only for the parents' benefit! It's the boys themselves that matter. You know"—and here his voice took on a slightly dreamy quality—"it's sometimes the biggest rascals one's most fond of. Yes, the biggest rascals." He was smiling to himself. "You know," he added, "I used to be a bit of a rascal myself."

They parted good friends that night; friends in a way they would never have been if he had won his scholarship.

But that was Mr. Varley's reaction; his father was made of very different stuff and he would never really get over it.

September 3rd 1939

The Rector had rigged up a wireless in the church, so they knew it was pretty serious. God, what a beautiful day it was! The leaves were pancake yellow and toffee brown, the sun spun gold in the branches, and the air so crisp and thin that it made you want to run, your feet never properly touching the ground.

The Rector turned on the wireless after the Magnificat and they sat listening to that flat, gentlemanly voice. Years afterwards, one saw this moment recalled by the movie camera, captured from a thousand different angles: the crowds in London, somehow shabby and old-fashioned, the women with their embarrassingly short skirts, and even the men somehow skimped in their suits and ludicrous, not moving jerkily as they did in the first world war films, yet unmistakably out of date, belonging firmly to another age.

". . . I have to tell you that this country is at war with Germany."

Benedict gazed down from the choir-stall at the rows of stolid English faces. War with Germany, war with Germany. It was tautologous: whoever else would one be at war with? Benedict had never known war at first hand, but he had read about it in the encyclopaedias and he had seen the ghastly frieze in the War Museum which showed blinded soldiers groping along patiently, one behind the other; he had seen all the boys' books and worshipped all the normal heroes; and all this vicarious experience

86

had left him with one over-riding notion: war and Germany were one and indivisible.

Yet he felt no hatred of Germany at that moment; only a love for his own people so ferocious and proud that the tears came and he cursed himself. He looked at the faces again, but more carefully now, trying to see not one large friendly blur but sharp individual portraits. There was his father of course, wriggling in his stiff white collar and best blue suit and already eyeing his watch carefully to see how long it was to drinking time. There was Mr. Varley, vermilion-faced and gigantic, bulging from his check suit, both big hairy hands on his stick, leaning forward intently to hear Chamberlain's words. There was Keith Margrave, mottled and patriarchal and upper-class in his Old Harrovian tie, and next to him poor patient Lady Margrave in a navy blue suit and sensible shoes. And then there were the Mackays. Laura's father and mother did not normally go to church and presumably had come today merely to convey a sense of solidarity. Benedict studied them with interest. Dr. MacKay, he estimated, was about forty. He wore a tweed suit and suède shoes, and a red woollen tie with a large knot. He looked like an economics lecturer at a small provincial university. But to Benedict he was an intellectual, a man of reason, and hence almost beyond criticism. He had never seen Mrs. Mackay before. She wore her blonde hair like Laura's, though a little darker, drawn severely back over the ears, emphasising, to Benedict, the *spirituality* of her face. She was small, with little well-scrubbed hands and a plain gold wedding-ring. Benedict stared down at her with awe: she was Laura's mother.

Laura wore a biscuit-coloured coat with a high collar, and a yellow silk scarf, and she had snuggled down into it like a squirrel; her hair was brushed down to her shoulders and held in place by an Alice band. Occasionally she turned the pages of the Prayer Book absent-mindedly, and the thin gold bangles on her wrist glistened in the sun. Once she turned and looked quickly behind her at the solemn rows of parishioners, as if she were looking for somebody.

What did war mean to Laura? A succession of absurdly romantic cameos flowed through his imagination. If the Germans ever got to this church, he would fight them right the way back to the pulpit, just as, in the Civil War, a Cavalier Officer had fought off a dozen Roundheads from it till finally one of the swine had got behind and run him through. He would give his life gladly for Laura, he reflected; if this new war needed justifying, then for him Laura was its complete justification. And then, just then, Laura saw him, and remembered, and smiled. And to his amazement, she put her hand up to one of her marvellous green eyes, made a face, and dropped it down again into her lap, as if to indicate that she remembered that terrible, blood-soaked summer's day. Then she looked seriously down at her Prayer Book again.

The broadcast ended, and there was a sighing and stirring in the little church. "Let us pray," said the Rector. He prayed that Britain would win; and after that Benedict remembered that they had sung a beautiful anthem: *God is a spirit, and they that worship him must worship him in spirit and truth.* Benedict was never deeply religious, yet this music and these words seemed to him always afterwards to represent the quick of the mystery; for if there *were* a God, then he must, Benedict reflected, be infinitely mysterious and unknowable. Why should a God who was omniscient and omnipresent, eternal and infinite, be also loving? For loving was a human condition, in altogether a different bracket from all the divine attributes. It was like one of those exam papers in logic. Pick out the word which does not belong: beauty, truth, justice, pudding; omniscient, omnipresent, eternal, infinite, loving; *that* was about how different it was. The lines rang in Benedict's head, mocking him as they often did, but never more ironically than now: "Back from that void I shrink in fear, and childlike hide myself in . . ."

Only a mysterious God would do then, one infinitely incomprehensible, unclutchable, unknowable, unheeding. And what point was there in worshipping a God like that? Yet how tranquil and liberating was the old Judaic invocation at the end of the service: *this* God, whom the Jews had invented and the Christians had borrowed, *this* family patriarch was *somebody*: "The Lord bless you and keep you; the Lord lift up the light of His countenance upon you, and give you His peace."

Then the Rector rose and said rather self-consciously: "Today I am sure we would like to conclude by singing our National Anthem together." The organ pounded out the simple and sad little tune and everyone rose to sing it. But today the odd thing was, they *did* sing it, even the mumblers like his father opened their mouths and their chests, proclaiming for all they were worth the naïve and jingoistic sentiments with unusual gusto:

Send him victorious,
Happy and glorious,
Long to reign . . .

Benedict stopped singing in the middle of the line, and gripped the carved wooden choir stall to steady himself. He closed his eyes in disbelief, then opened them again. It was true; it was no nightmare. Tony Hammond was in the congregation; right in the back, and he had noticed him merely because, while everyone else stood, Hammond remained in his place. Benedict already knew that Hammond was an unbeliever. Why then was he in church that morning? Was it God or Laura he wanted to be near? And now, had he found God or—— Benedict could not bear to formulate the question, even to himself. For as they all sang together, with such wonderful and unwonted gusto, calling God the infinite and unknowable spirit to their country's aid, Tony Hammond remained seated in his place.

Christmas 1939

Or rather a few days before Christmas; the last day of term at Aylsbourn Grammar School. For that was where he now belonged. There was no snow, but ice, and a hard frost. Benedict walked to school with a long gold and green woollen scarf swung round his neck and woollen gloves; but no overcoat. In those days he never seemed to need one. He hummed as he strode along. It had been a happy term. He had never touched the ecstasy of the summer again, but he had been content. He had been disconcerted at first by the teaching at his new school. Before, he had been crammed with information; now he found he was expected to have ideas. He was expected to argue and think for himself. Before, he had been drilled with machine-tool precision; Mr. Varley asked no higher virtue than obedience. Benedict had picked up the new technique quickly; in the green exercise book which he carried under his arm there were already several A minuses. He had worked hard, responding eagerly, and now it was the last day of term, and three weeks of delicious idleness stretched ahead.

The whole school was to assemble in the Old Hall. This was a long low room, part of the original Elizabethan building, into which the whole school could cram if necessary. Normally the girls occupied the new building on the other side of the road. Today they filled the whole of the right-hand side of the Hall and, perhaps because they were girls, they were there first, row upon row of them in green woollen sweaters, white blouses and grey skirts. They were chattering among themselves, then as the boys hurried in, eyes met across the room. There was a curious tension in the room as it filled; it was full of love. Yes thought Benedict, this room is full of love. The chatter increased, and the laughter; the room was gaily decked with winter flowers and paper chains; there was a sense of holiday in the air.

Abruptly the common-room door in the extreme right opened and the staff filed in. First came the Headmaster, old Macpherson. He was Scottish, a fisherman's son, a tall, bald man in pince-nez with a rich deep voice full of good round vowels. Boys from the Cressbrook Valley, whose train was sometimes so late in the morning that they missed prayers, would congregate of their own will outside the middle door of the Old Hall, which was just behind his dais, so that they could hear his beautiful bass voice rise and fall in sonorous melody with the hymn. He built Latin and Greek into his boys' minds with the expertness and solidity of a craftsman, so that they never forgot: *Quiss multa gracilis te puer in rosa perfusus liquidis urget odoribus grato, Pyrrha, sub antro?* The lines would run through Benedict's brain all his life, rooted there for good; and all the grammatical apparatus of the languages stayed with him too, like Government debentures, faithfully bearing interest, but rendered ridiculous by inflation. He was destined to remember all his life the gracious feel of his blue book of Horace's Odes, the forbidding shiny green of the Livy, the fat, friendly red of the Tacitus. It was all part of Benedict, useless as the memory of a broken romance; but cherished perhaps for that very reason.

Macpherson was a scholar, a dry kindly old man whose wife was an invalid and whose only son had died in infancy. He gave all his considerable gifts to his school without question and without stint. He did not understand politics, but wanted only to conserve things as they were. He read minor Latin poets for fun and had published an edition of Catullus. He kept a pet tortoise in his garden. He went once or twice a year to London to attend meetings of the Horace Society and would attend a Bach concert in the evening if he could. He lived in the School house, which was part of the original Elizabethan structure, and, to Benedict, the most gracious building he had ever seen. No one ever knew for sure whether Macpherson believed in God or not. Certainly he sang the morning hymn in his beautiful bass voice every day, and read the prayers with resonant piety: "Lord of the seedtime and the harvest, grant thy blessing we beseech thee to this thy school. May there be from these human hearts an abundant ingathering. . . ." But he did not go to church, and read Voltaire for pleasure. He was the most serious man Benedict had ever met, and the most considerable. There had been one memorable morning when, because the master concerned was ill, Macpherson had taken them for English.

"Now boys and girls" he enquired amiably that day: "which poem shall we read this morning?"

No one had any ideas, so Macpherson made a proposal. "Have you ever read Milton's sonnet On His Blindness? No. Then we shall study that today."

They read it first straight through, then line by line, Macpherson interpolating and explaining as they went along: " 'Ere half my days', boys and girls. Can ye imagine what it meant to the poet to be blind before he was thirty-five? . . . 'Fondly.' Now that doesn't mean lovingly, as it would today. It means foolishly. 'I fondly ask'—he sees that it is foolish to question God's will even as he does so. 'Thousands at his bidding speed and post . . .' Now that doesn't mean they post letters, boys and girls. It means that they travelled by post-carriage, the fastest there was in that time. So post means to ride at express speed. And so to the great affirmation of the final line: 'They also serve who only stand and wait.' Now, that doesn't mean to stand and loiter. It means to wait at the Lord's table. A perfect line of poetry and deservedly part of everyday English usage. Now boys and girls, let us say the poem again out loud, but this time trying to give every word its true meaning." And together, accompanying their headmaster, they began again:

When I consider how my light is spent
Ere half my days in this dark world and wide
And that one talent which is death to hide
Lodged with me useless, though my soul more bent
To serve therewith my Maker, and present. . . .

91

Always the lines came back to Benedict without effort, and the sound of the chanting voices, Macphersons grave and deep beneath, and the calmness in the room, as if the spirit of Milton himself had filled it. Benedict had never consciously learned the poem; after that hour with Macpherson it was his for ever. Now another such moment was about to be born.

Macpherson mounted his dais, his firm old face illuminated in the buttery light of the December sun, his ragged gown lending him mysterious dignity; the rest of the staff filed along and stood to each side of him. The whole school rose and there was exhilaration in the air, a sense of occasion. It was the end of the year; the old exercise books, replete with errors and blots and crossings out, would be thrown away, and new ones started next term. It was a moment of lightness and hope.

"Today," Macpherson's Scottish voice rang round the room, "as is our custom, we sing a Latin Christmas hymn. 'Adeste Fideles—O Come All Ye Faithful'." The piano banged out the first few lines, paused, then began again, the whole school singing at the top of its voice:

Adeste fideles, laeti triumphantes,
Venite, venite, ad Bethlehem.

The tears came into Benedict's eyes at the beauty of the hymn. Already he had lost his precarious faith; but he was too full of the world's awe ever to lose the overwhelming emotion the melody conjured up in him. Always, whenever after he heard it, the crowded school-room came back, and all the voices singing:

Natum videte, regem angelorum.

And then there was the simple but, to Benedict, quite marvellous choral device: at the next line the girls stopped singing and the boys' voices were heard alone:

Venite adoremus . . .

And then the girls alone:

Venite adoremus . . .

Benedict looked along the rows of girls, until he saw the only one who mattered; and he saw with joy that Laura sang with the best of them.

Then together again, with the basses and tenors among the

masters and senior boys weaving a joyful counter-melody into
the climactic final line. And Benny saw that even Tony Hammond
was singing:

> *Venite adoremus,*
> *Dominum.*

Then the next verse, and the next: the singing was glorious;
Benedict wanted it never to end.

The afternoon of the Christmas Party

It was the custom at Aylsbourn that each House had a party
on the last day of the Christmas term. Benedict was in Johnston's
House, so called after Milo's father, and to his great delight he
quickly discovered that both Laura and Tony Hammond were in
Johnston's too. Milo was in Johnston's for family reasons, and
Kenneth Heppel was in the house as well, though only by chance.
Felix was in Parkinson's House—they had decided it was not
fair to put two of Valhalla's most talented athletes together—
so he was the only member of the group who could not be present
at the Johnston's party. He claimed not to care tuppence: "I'm
only interested," he told his friends, "in women of forty."

Looking back on it later from the adult world, Benedict often
thought what an enlightened little society it was. It was accepted
that everyone would want to have a partner at the house party,
and for days beforehand there was a heightened excitement in
the air. It was always known that Mr. Johnston had a list of
every boy and girl in his house and would do his best to see that
each went with the partner he or she wanted. The intrigues, the
whisperings in corners, the notes to and fro, the heartaches this
modest list entailed each year! Yet in the end everyone was
paired, and the few broken hearts were soon mended.

Benny decided he would ask Constance Pickering. Though he
still worshipped Laura from a distance, he realised in his more
rational moments that she was nearly two years older than he; an
enormous gap at their age—and in any case he knew she would
be going with Tony Hammond. But Constance; she was within
the ambit of what was just possible; indeed she sat only five feet
away from him each day. She was a curiously proud girl, and
she customarily held her head very high; she walked with great
grace even though her dress always seemed rather racily short.

Anyway, her legs were worth looking at, Benedict always thought. She spoke rather softly and had a slightly cynical sense of humour. She was exceedingly bright, and the boys often had some difficulty in keeping ahead of her. By long and unwritten convention at Aylsbourn, the boys did as little work as they could—until a girl got to the top in a particular subject. Then the boy who was thought to be best in that field would have to set to and work until he had got to the top again. Constance was unnervingly good at unlikely subjects like mathematics and physics: Milo was thought to be the expert in these subjects and he often used to curse at the way she made him sweat to stay ahead. However, it probably did him a lot of good.

Constance lived at Welcaster, a hamlet just down the main road from Benedict's own village of Ashdale. She had no parents, but was looked after by a rather elderly and strict couple called the Hayleys. It was thought that her parents had been split up by the war. Constance had little time for flirtation; she worked hard and took a noticeably cool view about romantic attachments. Benedict, however, was undeterred by this rather unpromising set of facts; since they had talked to Arabella, he and his friends had developed a new confidence. To have called it arrogance would have been exaggerating; but Benedict was certainly less easily diverted by thoughts of his own inadequacy than before. He decided to sit down and write Constance a letter asking her to be his partner. All the same it took him nearly a week before he could both work up his courage and write exactly what he meant to say. During this period, he kept glancing at her across the room; but there was never a hint of her intentions on her proud and beautiful face.

In the end he wrote the note: "Dear Constance, Would you please come to the Christmas party with me?" It was not a very complex communication; but it was his sixth shot.

He sent it across to her in the Larousse dictionary. This was the way all amorous communications were exchanged at Aylsbourn; the convention was so prevalent that the staff must surely have known about it. But nothing was done to prevent it. Indeed, the whole school lived all the year round in a higher octave of excitement because it was mixed. It was normal, as Arabella had suggested, for each boy to fall in love with most of the girls of his generation in turn before he was eighteen. Indeed, romance was not unknown in the common-room. It was said that Mr.

Parkinson, the squat, dark Welshman who had taught himself chemistry in between shifts at the mines to get out of his native valley, had been seen with Miss Aliss, the faintly soignée if now grey-haired geography mistress on his knee one afternoon. It was rumoured that Miss Collins, the biology mistress, though at least fifty and no oil-painting, had a crush on Mr. Johnston, despite his married status and jug-ears. It was even known that old Macpherson himself had been seen walking arm-in-arm with Miss Dindale, breathless and fresh from Somerville with her good second in English. . . . But it seemed to be pretty innocent; and in all his time at Aylsbourn, Benedict heard of only one scandal. That, though, on the afternoon of the party, was still a long way into the future.

"Please pass on to Constance," he had written on his note. "Private." No one had been known to break the strict conventions of the game, and Constance was the first to read his private message.

She read it, then without hesitation took out a sheet of paper and wrote carefully on it. He watched the Larousse come back across the room with suspense and longing.

The note was neatly folded. On the outside she had written: "Please pass to Benny. Private." He opened it in sharp and delicious terror.

"Dear Benny," she had written, "it is sweet of you to ask me. I don't quite know yet what my plans are. Someone else has asked me but I may say no. Can you dance? I don't mean are you an expert, but can you get round the floor without the usual excruciating flounderings?"

Benedict was in despair. He deliberated for a long time before replying. At length, though, the ponderous Larousse went back across the room with his reply in it.

"Dear Constance," he wrote, "I have to tell you the truth. I can't dance. And yet I sometimes feel as if I'm almost dancing. This is especially so when I'm listening to jazz. I feel I could learn quite quickly. I wonder—is there the slightest chance that you'd teach me? Just enough, I mean, to get by without disgracing you."

He watched for some hint of emotion on her face. There was none. She wrote busily:

"Dear Benny. Yes, I'll teach you. I'm not sure if I'll go with you yet. It rather depends how you get on. Love Constance."

It was the first time any woman had ever sent him her love. He was transported. And whenever he looked back to this little exchange over the years, he reflected that, though he had forgotten every damned word in the Larousse, he had learned something far more useful: that no woman ever says yes; at least not just like that.

It was arranged that the first lesson should be in the library that same evening. There was a radiogram there, and after the librarian had finished dispensing books it was tacitly understood that the room could be used for social purposes. Benny looked round nervously as he hurried in; fortunately, however, none of his friends was to be seen. He had made a weak excuse about having to check some points in the reference section and the others had gone off unsuspectingly to gossip in Miller's teashop. He opened the door gingerly and saw with a thumping heart that Constance was already there. She sat in a corner, legs demurely crossed, reading the *Oxford Book of French Verse* with somewhat studied detachment.

"Hello, Constance," he said. "How nice of you to come."

"Hello, Benny. Don't be silly. Every boy should be able to dance. Did you bring any records?"

His spirits sank. "No. I'm afraid not. Aren't there any here?"

"Not really. I've had a look and there only seems to be a rather cracked recording of the New World Symphony."

"Oh hell." He rummaged about anxiously.

"Ah, what's this. 'Dinah.' Will that do?"

"Yes. It's a quickstep. Aren't there any more?"

"Don't seem to be."

"O.K. Put it on then."

His fingers shook rather badly as he placed the needle on the well-worn disc. The music brayed suddenly and with unnerving volume.

"Isn't it a bit loud?"

"Sorry." He turned the volume down. "Dinah" became a whisper.

"Now I can't hear anything."

"Sorry." He fiddled nervously with the knob.

"That's better. Come on then."

So the actual moment had arrived when he had to take the delectable Constance in his arms. Surely she couldn't be *serious* about this?

But she was; she stood in the middle of the library floor, waiting for him. It was quite dark outside, and inside the library the reading lamps in their amber shades cast a discreet light. Her face was half in shadow. She noticed him hesitate, and smiled. He could hardly believe it. Suddenly she didn't look quite so proud and unattainable.

"Come on, Benny," she said. "Don't be shy."

He placed his left arm diffidently round her waist. It was a slim waist and the manœuvre presented no difficulty. Now that it was done, it seemed the most natural thing in the world. He took her hand in his. It was a small hand, and a little less warm than his own. Her fingers closed gently but deliberately round his. Now it was her turn to hesitate.

"You know, Benny," she said, "we shall never be able to dance unless you hold me a bit closer."

"Closer?"

"Yes. It should be possible for us to dance holding a record flat between us."

"You're not serious?"

"Of course. You are a duffer, aren't you? Didn't you know that?"

"I'm afraid not. But there isn't another record, except that Dvorak. . . ."

"She laughed. "I don't think we need to put it to the test. Hold me a bit closer. I'll tell you when you're close enough."

He tightened his hold a minuscule.

"A bit tighter. I won't bite you."

He held her, as it seemed to him, recklessly tight.

"That's better. Now we can dance."

"Well tell me what the steps are."

"Just move your feet after mine. It's a bit difficult because I'm supposed to follow you. But just follow."

They began to move round the floor in a simple geometrical progression. After six or seven steps, he nearly tripped.

"Sorry."

"It's all right. Now then—'Dinah, is there anybody finer, in the State of Carolina . . .' "

The minutes passed in a mindless flow of unimagined delight. Constance danced lightly, and soon he fell in to her rhythm. They played the record again and again. Benny wanted the lesson never to end. Finally, however, she stopped, her cheeks a little flushed with the exertion—or perhaps even with a little of his communicated excitement—and said: "I think that'll do, Benny. You can dance—enough for the party anyhow."

"But what about the tango and the slow foxtrot and all that?"

"Oh you'll pick those up easily enough now. Anyway, they only play quicksteps."

She stowed the *Oxford Book of French Verse* away with some other books and papers in an old string bag.

"Then we can go together to the party?"

She didn't look up. "Yes, I think so."

"Your other arrangement has fallen through?"

"Benny, why are you so tiresome? I said I'd go with you."

"I'm sorry, Constance. It's just that I've never been to a thing like this before."

"Oh well you'll enjoy it. Now are you going to see me home?"

He could hardly believe his ears. "*May* I?"

"It would be more polite if you had offered first."

"I'm sorry. Of course—I mean there's nothing I'd like more."

"Come along then."

Once they were out in the dark road, to his terror and delight she slipped an arm through his. They walked in silence. It was a marvellous Aylsbourn evening, with that unmistakable sharp tang of decay in the cool air.

"Tell me about yourself, Benny. You're rather an odd boy you know. I can't make you out."

"Why ever not? I'm extremely ordinary."

"No, you're not. You're very dreamy. Often you look as if you're miles away. And you're dreadfully sensitive too. If anyone says anything unkind to you, you look as if you're about to burst into tears."

"It's because," said Benedict in a sudden mad access of confidence, "I really *feel* like crying. I wish I were as tough as my friends; I mean people like Felix."

"Oh, but you're much more interesting than they are."

They walked on in silence.

"Tell me, Benny," she asked after a while, "what do you want to do when you leave school?"

"I've never given it a thought. I'm so—sort of intoxicated —with being alive that I can't think ahead. I can't imagine that anybody would ever *pay* me. I mean I'm so hopeless at all practical things. I'm sure I shall be very poor when I'm old. But—what about you, Constance?"

"Oh I'm quite certain. I'm going to be a biologist. I'm fascinated by it. I shall go to Southampton University College —maybe even Cambridge if I work hard enough—and when I've got my degree I shall do research. I'm positive about it."

"Will you ever—marry?" It was an impertinent question; he wished had hadn't asked it even as he said it.

"I expect so, Benny. People usually do, don't they? Probably some excruciatingly dull chemist."

"You don't believe in love, then?"

"Not really. I am a biologist you see; and once you've studied biology at all thoroughly, romantic love seems rather ludicrous."

"I dare say it does." Unhappily they had arrived at her guardian's house. There seemed no good reason for prolonging the delectable conversation any longer.

He remembered, though, that as she said "Goodnight, Benny" they seemed suddenly to be shaking hands in a rather formal way. Yet she had squeezed his hand with what seemed like affection. Only he must have imagined it.

And now it was the day of the party.

Milo's mother had asked him to bring home one or two friends to lunch first. The fact that later in the afternoon she would have to feed fifty starving adolescents seemed not to deter her. Possibly the experience she had gained over the years in trying to quell Milo's gargantuan appetite had inured her. He was without question the hungriest boy in Aylsbourn. He had grown six inches in the last two years and it seemed that he would never have enough to eat. He was badly spoiled by his mother and two sisters; if he wanted something he usually got it.

It must, Benedict always thought wistfully, be fabulous to live surrounded by women as Milo did. Mrs. Johnston was a plump brisk woman of forty and a bit, who seemed to revel and thrive on the many cares of her young family. She made, Benedict always thought, the best home-made jam in the world: plum jam, apricot jam, strawberry jam, blackcurrant and apple jam, melon and ginger—there were always fifty gleaming jars of the stuff standing on the big shelf in her larder, each with a neat white label and white paper cap. She also made home-made wines with a kick like neat Scotch—Milo had already surreptitiously, as an experiment, drunk himself into a stupor on them. All through his life, Benedict remembered the vivid taste of the vegetables from the Johnston's garden—the new potatoes, sweet and fresh from the earth, the smooth broad beans, the soft green peas, the pure green-edged-with-white of the crisp young lettuces. As far as Benedict was concerned, Mrs. Johnston was the best cook the world had ever known. And even when, in later life, he had eaten at the Mirabelle, he didn't really change his mind.

Milo had an older sister called Joanna, and a twin sister called Tessa. Neither daughter, unfortunately, had much natural beauty. Mr. Johnston's spectacular jug-ears had been heedlessly transmitted by the life-force to all his children. Joanna was a mysterious girl, who said very little, but was thought to be unusually clever at mathematics. Mr. Johnston planned to send her one day to London University. A very tall, leggy creature, she was naturally gifted at games, and was the best runner in the school. Because Johnston's already had so much athletic talent, she had been put in Parkinson's House. In her bedroom, so Milo reported, there were several dozen photographs of Cary Grant. She was quite uninterested in boys of her own age, and had accepted with amused contempt an invitation from Felix to go with him to Parkinson's Christmas party. Her acceptance had secretly delighted Felix: "I don't know what it is," he had confided to his friends, "but I can only take an interest in women older than myself." Joanna was some fifteen months his senior.

Tessa was quite different. She wore her hair in a page-boy cut and had an appealing gentleness. She seemed incapable of expressing an opinion or finishing a sentence. Benedict thought her a trifle boring, but luckily Kenneth Heppel had asked her to come with him. Milo himself had invited a round-faced little girl from London called Doreen Pepper. She was wildly unpopular with the other girls because of her relatively sophisticated London point of view and her precocity at languages. Even the boys found her snatches of French—"Quel ennui" and "Espèce de merde" were her two favourite expressions—a little overpowering.

All the Johnston children and their partners were at lunch that day, and so were Benedict and Constance. With Mr. and

Mrs. Johnston, that meant that there were ten people seated round the long farmhouse table in the kitchen. This seemed positively to inspire Mrs. Johnston; Benedict always remembered the huge dish of steak and kidney pudding she made for them that day, and the blackberry tart which Tessa had made, and the sarcasm which Milo had levelled at it, pretending that he was unaware of the tart's authorship.

"Good Lord, Mum," he said after the first mouthful. "This tart is a bit heavy, isn't it? Not like yours at all."

"Don't be so unkind, Milo," said his mother. "You know perfectly well that Tess made it."

"I certainly didn't," cried Milo, "or I'd have had some of the apple dumplings instead."

Tessa blushed and looked as if she might cry.

"You do talk rot, Milo," Benedict put in. "It's the most delicious tart I've ever tasted."

"Trust Benny," said Felix sarcastically, "gallant as always."

"Strangely enough," said Kenneth, "I'm sure he means it."

"Of course I mean it," Benedict said indignantly.

"You mean to say," asked Milo incredulously, "that as a matter of scientific fact, it's the best tart you've ever tasted in your life?"

"Certainly."

"Benny, you see," said Constance, "is a special kind of maniac. What he wants to believe, his senses make him believe."

"A psycho-somatic," put in Mr. Johnston.

"Oh, is that what he is?" said Felix with mild interest. "I always knew he was a screwball."

"I think Benny was just being polite," said Mrs. Johnston.

"A virtue we don't hear too much about in this day and age," added her husband.

"I wasn't being polite," Benny insisted with some heat. "I mean it as a cold, sober fact."

"You may take it as a cold sober fact," Joanna Johnston echoed sardonically to her younger sister, "that your tart is the finest Benny has yet tasted in his journey through this vale of tears."

"Quel espèce de bavard," interposed Doreen Pepper. The others looked at her with distaste.

Tess had not spoken. She still seemed on the brink of tears. Instinctively Benedict reached across and put his hand on hers.

"Don't you worry what they say, Tess," he reassured her. "I'll still maintain it's so till my dying day."

The table rocked with laughter. Benedict blushed and bowed his head quickly, concentrating with unnatural ferocity on the disputed tart. Then Tess really did cry. She jumped up from the table and ran out of the room. Benedict half rose in his chair to go after her, but Mrs. Johnston motioned him to sit down. "I'll go," she said.

"God, what a milksop I have for a sister," grieved Milo. "Can't even take a little honest criticism."

"One day," said his father, "you'll discover that it's very hard to take."

"But I take it every day," expostulated Milo. "From you, from my friends . . ."

"But never," said his father, "about anything which has meant the slightest heart-ache to you. You've never done anything that meant as much to you as that tart did to Tess."

"Good Lord, Daddy," said Joanna. "What nonsense you do talk! Such a fuss about such a little thing!"

"Not such a little thing," her father insisted. "The great proportion of mankind are concerned with things as small. The luxury of leisure for abstract thought is the prerogative of only a fraction of one per cent of those who live on the earth's crust."

Benedict looked at him with new interest. He had never quite understood what Mr. Johnston remained in Aylsbourn for: He had got a first in physics at London; he could have gone into research or industry; why had he buried himself in this somnolent Hampshire backwater? There was nothing in his outward appearance to explain it; he was a gangling, skinny man with a round head perched on the end of a long neck. The remarkable jug-ears lent him the curious appearance of a human water-pitcher. He wore old sports jackets with leather patches in the sleeves and corduroy trousers. There was no doubt though in Benedict's mind that he was an *intellectual*. That, for Benedict, excused almost everything.

Tessa and her mother came back into the room.

"I'm sorry, everybody," Tessa said.

"We're the ones who should be sorry," corrected Kenneth. His responsibility as her partner at the party later that afternoon had dawned on him rather late in the day.

"Yes," said Milo. "I'm sorry I ever tasted your confounded tart."

"It was all a storm in a teacup," said Mrs. Johnston comfortingly. "Really we should be ashamed of ourselves. After all, we've all got so much to be grateful for."

Yes, thought Benedict looking round the room, she's right. Shall we ever be so happy again? He let his gaze slide slowly round the room. All his friends were here: Kenneth Heppel the tough boy from the poor side of town, Milo Johnston the thinking machine, Felix the precocious man of the world: his closest friends. And although the only girl who would ever matter in his life was not there, well, he would see her later in the day, and in the meantime it was comforting to have the proud and cynical Constance sitting next to him: so close indeed that their legs seemed to touch under the table; and the odd thing was, Constance didn't move her leg away. Come to think of it, they'd been sitting like that for ten minutes. But Constance showed no sign of concern or indeed excitement; she ate her blackcurrant tart with nonchalance. That, thought Benedict to himself, is what biology must do for you. However, he didn't move his leg either.

And now, at last, it was time for the Christmas party. They walked down from the Johnston's house to the school in the early December twilight; Constance had a scarf over her head, Benny always remembered, and she wore a cherry red coat over her party dress; and as they walked along he remembered her saying how idotic such parties were: "You know, Benny," she said, "while we are bursting balloons people will be dying."

"Where?"

"In the war, you moron."

"But there's precious little war going on."

"Oh, but there will be, Benny. You'll see."

"Do you think we'll win, Constance?"

"No."

"No?"

"That's what I think. We're so hopeless. We're so amateur. We only just won last time, didn't we? And we haven't got America this time. Look what Hitler has done in Poland. Did you read what happened to Warsaw?"

"Yes, but they were stabbed in the back by the Russians."

"Who's to say that's the end of the Russians in this war?"

"You mean they might try to carve us up too?"

"I don't know. But I should like to know what Felix's father feels about Russia now."

"I don't think he takes the pact very seriously. If doing a deal with the Germans will help communism, then it must be done. The end always justifies the means."

They walked a few yards more in silence. Then Benedict said: "What do you think will happen to us if we lose the war?"

"You'll be shot," said Constance with what sounded suspiciously like relish. "And I will become the mistress of a lieutenant-colonel in the SS."

"Will you mind that?"

"Not as much as you'll mind being shot."

They were at the gates of the school. Members of Johnston's House were arriving in little knots, gossiping, laughing. Benedict felt the communicated excitement in the air. Perhaps they were doomed; if so, all the more reason to be happy while they could!

The tables were already laid for tea, with small white cards at each place. Benny and Constance found themselves at the head table. The other names, he saw with a catch at the heart, were Mr. Johnston himself and Miss Dindale, Tony Hammond and Laura.

The room began to fill up. There was a pleased buzz of anticipation as each couple worked out where they were to sit. Mr. Johnston and Miss Dindale threaded their way through the tables to their place. Miss Dindale shone with enthusiasm and what appeared to be Lifebuoy soap. Mr. Johnston, now that he had changed into a suit, looked almost respectable. He greeted Benedict, though they had only just been together, with kindness. "I thought you'd like to sit at my table, Benny," he said, "as this is your very first term with us."

The minutes passed. "Trust Tony Hammond," said Mr. Johnston good-naturedly, "Late as ever."

"Oh but he has other virtues," said Miss Dindale rather dashingly. She had a soft spot for Hammond too.

"Ah," said Benedict, "here they are."

Hammond and Laura stood in the doorway, looking for their table. He was wearing his characteristically off-hand clothes— a pair of corduroy trousers, a red shirt, an old cable-stitch fisherman's sweater, suède shoes. Laura, as if in sympathy, wore a black sweater and red check skirt. She still wore her Alice band and her honey-coloured hair was as usual combed down to her shoulders. By Aylsbourn standards they looked pretty avant-garde. Mr. Johnston waved, Laura saw him and touched Hammond's arm. Then they both smiled and began to make their way across the room. They made a pleasing pair.

"Here come the young Marxists," said Constance.

"Who isn't a Marxist these days?" Benedict said, half to himself. He couldn't take his eyes off Laura.

Tony Hammond was in a genial frame of mind. "Good afternoon, sir," he said to Mr. Johnston, squeezing his shoulder amiably before sitting down. What splendid arrogance! thought Benedict. Arrogance had become a key-word in his vocabulary. "Hello, Benny," he added, swinging into the seat beside him. "Mind if I sit here?"

"Not a bit, Hammond." They had spoken only two or three times altogether—imagine Hammond remembering his name!

"And I'll sit on Benny's other side," said Laura.

He could hardly believe his good luck. Now, for the first time, since that terrible day in the surgery, he would have a chance to talk to her.

"What have you got for us today, sir?" Hammond asked politely.

"We've a couple of one act plays, then a few carols, then tea, and then dancing."

"Quite a programme. Who's doing the plays?"

"Oh, it's the Cressbrook Gang."

The Cressbrook Gang was an institution at Aylsbourn. The river meandered some twenty-five miles down the valley before debouching into the Southampton Estuary. Along its banks there were one or two scattered villages which were almost unbelievably secluded from the twentieth century. Often for days on end they would be cut off altogether by floods or snow. The people who lived in the Cressbrook villages tended to be dark and volatile; so much so that one local historian had even advanced the theory that they were still pure Celts. They were a clannish and talented people: musical, eloquent and extravert. The Cressbrook children came up to Aylsbourn each morning on a branch line, and stuck very much to each other. One of the Cressbrook Gang, a very poor boy called Aelfric Gates (and where the devil, Benedict used to think, had he got *that* name from, if there was nothing in the Celtic theory?) was thought to be potentially the most brilliant in the school. Though he was only a few months older than Benedict, he already understood differential calculus. He had written and was producing the two short plays. As the lights went down, Benedict leaned back with a sigh of sheer content.

Aelfric Gates certainly knew his stuff. Both plays were a riot. Benedict rocked with laughter at a most palpable imitation of Milo's father. When the lights went up even Mr. Johnston was wiping his eyes. "Well," he said philosophically, "it's a sort of fame."

Next Miss Dindale went to the piano and they plunged with whole-hearted pleasure into the carols. Benny sang with gusto, and was pleased to notice that Tony Hammond and Laura both sang too. Hammond supplied a bass melody while Laura had a light, pleasing contralto voice.

At last it was time for tea. "My goodness," said Mr. Johnston, "that was thirsty work!"

"Not so thirsty as playing a trumpet," said Hammond.

"Tell me about this jazz," said Miss Dindale. "Is it just a passing phase? Or is it here to stay?"

"Miss Dindale," said Hammond with mock seriousness. "Once we've had you out there swinging on the floor you'll never look back. You'll *know* that jazz is here to stay."

"Are there any special steps you have to learn?"

"You can do a quickstep to it. But there's a new sort of dancing just beginning in America. It's called the jitterbug. Rather a vulgar title I'm afraid—they'll think of something neater soon— and this new dancing goes perfectly with jazz. It's quick, intricate, elegant—a kind of galvanised gavotte."

"Can you do it?" enquired Constance.

"Yes," said Laura. "Tony and I can do it. We can show you when the dancing starts." Then to Miss Dindale. "If you have no objection."

"Good heavens, no," said Miss Dindale. "I'm fascinated. But have we got any suitable records?"

"Yes," said Benny. "I've brought a lot of Felix Weston's. They don't have any dancing at Parkinson's party."

"Good gracious," said Miss Dindale. "Then how do they pass the time?"

"Oh," said Constance, "a lot of adolescent games. You know."

Laura suddenly turned to Benedict. "Well, Benny," she said with affection and mischief in her voice. "And how's that poor old eye? I've never seen a sight like it in all my years as my father's unpaid nurse. You know, I felt quite faint myself."

"Well you certainly didn't show it." But Benedict's voice sounded unreal to him—thick and high in his throat. He was talking—at last—to Laura!

"Yes," said Hammond with sudden interest, "that reminds me. Benny, I've watched you play a couple of times this term and I'd like you to come and practise with the School Colts next term."

Benedict could hardly believe his ears. The Aylsbourn Colts! This was success beyond his most extravagant dreams.

"Now there's something else I just don't understand," complained Miss Dindale. "Can anyone explain the point of this rugby football to me?"

"Yes," said Laura, "I can. It's one of the biggest kicks I know in life, watching the boys play. That, and jazz."

"Is it?" Miss Dindale looked a little taken back by this frank revelation. "Do you often watch, Laura?"

"I never miss watching Tony play," Laura said simply. But she was not looking at Hammond; she seemed to be staring into the middle distance.

"We're not just thugs you know, Miss Dindale," said Mr. Johnston. "Benedict is an Aldous Huxley fan, so I hear."

"*Are* you now?" said Hammond with new interest. "What have you read, Benny?"

"Oh," said Benny, embarrassed, "not much I'm afraid. Things like *Those Barren Leaves* and *Eyeless in Gaza*."

"Haven't you read *Brave New World* yet?"

"I'm afraid not."

"Then I must lend you my copy. It's one of the great books of the twentieth century. And what about *Point Counter Point*?"

"Afraid not."

"You shall have that too."

"Aren't you," asked Laura with mock concern, "putting rather advanced ideas into young Benny's head?"

"Impossible," said Constance, "Benny will never be a cynic. He is a romantic."

"And what," asked Mr. Johnston, "do you mean exactly by

107

that? I mean, is he a romantic in the purely literary sense—or does this romanticism permeate his everyday life?"

"In every sense," said Constance with a trace of contempt.

"Only in the sense," Benny heard himself saying, "that I believe in love."

Laura and Hammond exchanged a glance. Then Laura smiled at him. "Benny," she said, "there's more to you than meets the eyes."

"There's more to all of us than meets the eye."

"Leave him alone," said Hammond. He was interested. "What about Evelyn Waugh, Benny? Read any?

"Sorry, no."

"Oh. Then you must have my copy of *Decline and Fall*. You haven't lived till you've read that. What about Hemingway?"

"Sorry. . . ."

"He's an American writer. Superb. You must read *Death in the Afternoon* and *The Sun Also Rises*. Here"—he took out his diary—"I'll make a note to look them out for you."

"That's awfully kind, Hammond."

He studied Hammond surreptitiously as they talked. He had never been quite so close; now he could analyse his appearance in some detail.

It was a curiously wedge-shaped face; very strong, with a sharply defined cleft in the chin. The eyes were a mild bluish-grey; his hair the colour of straw and very thick. He wore a pair of heavy horn-rimmed glasses with thick lenses; he was known to be as blind as a bat without them. He had a pleasing, if slightly derisive, smile. His voice was deep and musical. There was a scar across the bridge of his nose from an old football injury. He talked in a natural and relaxed manner, which did not change whether he was in conversation with Mr. Johnston or Benedict or indeed Laura. There was nothing gallant about him; he didn't go out of the way to pay compliments. He was a trifle under six feet tall, but very slim in the waist. The most surprising thing about him were his hands. They were rather terrifyingly big; square and very strong.

To Benedict, Hammond was the epitome of the complete man. He had played stand-off half for the Hampshire Colts, and was quite certain, Benedict thought, to win an Open Scholarship to Cambridge. He read authors like Huxley and Hemingway, and had written three, to Benedict, exquisite short stories about the

Spanish Civil War, which had been published in the *Cressbrook Review*, a highbrow Hampshire magazine. He had had a poem published in the *Poetry Quarterly*. He played a swinging jazz trumpet. Over and above all these things, though, he had won the love of Laura.

By shifting his position slightly, and pretending to be engrossed in the conversation, Benedict could study Laura too. It was her green eyes, he decided, that were the most riveting thing about her; he had never seen anything quite so startling. Her skin too was striking in its paleness; she looked as if she might be Scandinavian.

Her hands—the hands he remembered so well—were small and the nails neatly kept; squarely cut without fuss or adornment. She still wore the thin gold bangles she had worn in church the day war began. Her wrists were almost touchingly thin. She listened a good deal and laughed quite a lot. Her favourite expression, he noticed, was "Gee *whiz!*"—with all the emphasis, used ironically, on the whiz.

"Now for the dance!" decided Mr. Johnston. Quickly the chairs and tables were stacked and soon they were launched into a set of old-fashioned dances, beginning with the Sir Roger de Coverley. Benedict trembled with anticipatory pleasure each time it was his turn to link arms with Laura. She danced so deftly that those moments passed all too soon.

When they had tired of traditional dancing, Mr. Johnston decided they could play some quicksteps. The school radiogram bounced out the naïve melody of "Dinah", and the young couples launched themselves tentatively on to the floor. Benny found himself opposite Constance. They smiled at each other, remembering their travail in the library in preparation for this moment.

"Come along, Benny," said Constance. "And don't forget what I told you about the gramophone record."

In a moment they were moving round the floor, looking quite expert against some of the others.

"Look at Hammond and Laura," said Constance. "It will interest you."

Benedict glanced round and saw that Laura had one arm twined affectionately round Tony Hammond's neck. She was not behaving in quite the uninhibited way she had at the Margrave dance; still it was, to Benedict, a novel spatial relationship.

"That," said the knowledgeable Constance, "is called the college clutch."

"It looks quite fun."

"You think so? Let me try it on you."

Benedict was horrified. "Don't be so outrageous, Constance. People might see us."

"They can see Laura."

"Yes. But she——"

It was too late. Constance was bent on experimenting with the college clutch and he was part of the essential apparatus for the experiment. To his surprise, he found himself enjoying it. His sense of decorum soon ceased to trouble him.

"You know, Constance," he said, "I've never met a girl quite like you before."

"I bet you say that to all the girls."

"I've never talked to any other girl. Except Arabella Weston."

"I expect she told you a thing or two."

"She certainly did. You know she said a most extraordinary thing."

"What?"

"Well, I really can't repeat it here. It will interest you though. As a biologist, I mean."

"I can hardly wait to hear."

"Oh look, Constance. That must be the jitterbug."

Tony Hammond and Laura were jiving with relaxed elegance in the centre of the floor. They looked insouciant and beautiful. Benedict and Constance stopped to watch.

"You know," said Benedict, "it must be marvellous to be in love like that."

"They're not in love," said Constance definitely.

"How on earth do you know?"

"I know."

"Well, how on earth . . .?"

"Don't be tiresome, Benny. I'll tell you why some other time. When you tell me what Arabella said."

"I don't know if I could repeat——"

"Benny, some day a woman will have to take you in hand."

"Perhaps you."

"No. It won't be me."

"How can you be so sure?"

"It's a question of chemistry. Valencies and all that stuff. You're too nice to appeal to me."

"I suppose it's no secret to you that———"

"You dote on Laura? No secret at all."

Benny swallowed. "Do you think it's obvious to other people?"

"No. You see I'm the only one who's bothered to make a proper study of you, Benny. You're a very interesting psychological specimen. In fact, one day, I shall probably win my Ph.D for a thesis on you. I can imagine it now: 'P. J. Benedict—A casebook in romantic psychopathology.' "

"I shall be pretty flattered. I mean, it's my only chance to become famous."

"Nonsense, Benny! People who are as nuts as you generally end up in the headlines."

"You think I'm nuts too?"

"No. I think society is nuts."

A few minutes later, Mr. Johnston called for silence. "Before we conclude tonight's most enjoyable party," he said, "I'm going to call, by general consent, for a Ladies' Excuse Me."

Constance rose. "I shall be back, Benny," she said.

"Who are you going to ask?"

"Mr. Johnston. I'm ambitious, you see."

Benedict sat bemused. What an astonishing girl! And what on earth did she mean by saying that Laura and Tony weren't in love? If that wasn't love, then what in the name of heaven . . .

He was disturbed by a shy voice. It was Tessa Johnston. "Benny," she said, "would you like . . .? I mean . . ."

"Tessa, I'd love to dance with you." To his shame he had forgotten all about her. She seemed to tremble slightly as he put his arm round her waist, but she followed very easily as he launched into his newly acquired steps.

"Thank you, Benny," she said. "for what you said today."

"I meant it, Tessa; truly I did."

"I know you did. That's why I shall never forget it."

In the summer of 1941

Old Macpherson retired. He had not been well for some time, and now his heart was showing definite signs of weariness. He was in any case sixty-seven and his normal retirement date had been postponed by the war. He told the school he was going without fuss on the last day of the summer term. No one could quite believe it. Macpherson and Aylsbourn had become interchangeable symbols. But he said he would continue to live in the town and he hoped they would all keep coming to see him. Then came even more startling news.

"You may well be wondering, boys and girls," he said carefully, "who is to take my place here. Our governors have gone into the matter very carefully, for as you know, they always have your welfare very much at heart. I think they have found you a new headmaster who will give you the very greatest intellectual stimulus." He paused. It was not easy for him. "Your new head, boys and girls, is to be Mr. Chrisopher Ilex."

There was an audible stir among the senior school. Ilex the poet, spokesman of the left and ardent educational reformer! Coming to Aylsbourn of all places!

"This," muttered Felix, "is my father's work."

Gerard Weston had been appointed a governor of the school before his extreme political views had become well known locally. The fact was that, like all communists, he was extremely conscientious in public service, and had probably done more good than harm to the school over the years. But Ilex . . . this indeed was a *coup de théâtre* that Weston had engineered.

Ilex in 1941 was still only twenty-eight. The son of an Anglican bishop ("Always a bad start," as Felix remarked), he had had a remarkable academic career at Winchester and Oxford. He got a crashing first in history, won the Newdigate Prize, was President of OUDS, and had been offered a Fellowship. Just then the Spanish Civil War broke out and Ilex immediately went out to join the Republicans. He published a long volume of poetry which became a rallying-point for his generation, was badly wounded, returned to England in 1939, resigned from the communist party over Poland, though maintaining his Marxist views, worked in a publisher's for six months, then got a job as an assistant master at Eton. His second book of poetry had been published that spring and showed even greater achievement than the first. And now he was coming to Aylsbourn.

"You should be a happy man today, Benny," said Ken Heppel with affectionate irony. "Aylsbourn has acquired another intellectual."

"Maybe even Stephen Spender will come down to talk to us,"

Felix mocked him. Ilex was known to be friendly with the Auden/Isherwood/Spender/Warner axis.

"As long as he doesn't scrub science altogether," Milo Johnston said. Ilex was an ardent defender of the humanities.

"But what does he want to come *here* for?" Benny asked.

"That's obvious. Because he can be the boss. He couldn't treat a big public school quite so radically. But us! We're perfect material. Peasants' sons, noble savages; you can imagine how his dim idealistic mind works."

"Tell you something else," said Milo. "It'll be the first homosexual Aylsbourn has ever known."

"Well," said Felix, "*vive le sport*. Only you'd better watch out, Benny. Those liquid brown eyes of yours will probably appeal to him."

"Maybe," said Benedict absent-mindedly, "he'll write some poetry about Aylsbourn."

"I can just imagine it," said Ken Heppel. He thought hard, screwing up his homely features in concentration. "It'll start:

'Enriched with Aylsbourn dung my peasant mind . . .
'Swings on its rusty hinges glory's gate.' "

"The trouble is," said Benedict, "that you're all secretly jealous. I can't help it if I have an ambivalent appeal, can I?"

This canard about Benedict was based on the slimmest possible evidence. He had that February received a Valentine card couched in clearly homosexual terms. Felix, however, was thought to be its anonymous author.

The scandal received powerful support when it was heard that Ilex was bringing with him Martin Hennessy, also a poet member of the new left. The word ran round that Hennessy was Ilex's boy-friend. Then the scandal-mongers had a set-back. It was discovered that Hennessy had just married a rich American woman, whom he had met during a research year at Princeton. It was said that she was old enough to be his mother, and was a close friend of Ezra Pound.

"You have to admit," Benedict told his friends, "that the old place is looking up."

Ilex's first public appearance was something of a disappointment. When he emerged from the common-room door into the Old Hall on the first day of the new term, he looked rather unimpressive. He was a small man, no more than five feet three, but he had a very large head, rather like a tadpole's He wore a very well-cut dark grey worsted suit and sandals. When he spoke, however, his voice came as a shock. It was enormously deep and fruity and not in the slightest bit revolutionary. The girls looked at him with especial interest. "If he's what you say he is," said Constance later, "I think it's a cruel waste."

"I've already decided on my plans," said Joanna. "I'm going to seduce Martin Hennessy from that rich American wife of his."

"You'll never succeed," Tessa said firmly. "Anyone can see that he's incorruptible."

Incorruptible perhaps he was; but beyond a doubt he was inexhaustible. The first morning he was to teach them, he came bounding into the room in his dinner jacket, stretching his arms over his head. "I've been up all night at a party in London," he told his mesmerised audience. "There was a perfectly ghastly air-raid, so we all moved down into the cellar. I went for a row on the Cressbrook at six a.m., then had some bacon and eggs at the 'Wheatsheaf', and now I'm bursting to do some Roman History with you. Anyone here ever read a book by Robert Graves called *I Claudius*? No. Well I'll start by telling you about that. . . ."

"You know," said Felix afterwards, "you sat through that as if you were in a trance."

"It's just," said Benedict, "that I've never seen anyone wear a red bow-tie with a dinner-jacket before."

"I've got a feeling," said Ken Heppel, "that we haven't seen anything yet."

One day in January 1942

Mr. Benedict received his call-up papers. He opened the official envelope at breakfast with evident excitement. Benny knew—or divined—what it contained and he was afraid. Why did his father have to go? He was getting on for fifty and he had more than done his bit in the last war. It would leave him entirely alone in the world. Something like panic seized him. Then the emotion passed away; he couldn't resist the pleasure so obviously written in his father's face. For Mr. Benedict, war meant life with the throttle wide open; he was never a hundred per cent alive in peacetime. And the Army was the best club he knew.

114

"It's a training battalion, Benny," he said excitedly. "Just the thing I wanted to do."

There had been an element of estrangement between them ever since that awful day when his father had heard about the scholarship. This made it seem all the more intolerably poignant to Benedict that his father should be leaving him now. It was all very well to talk of a training battalion; but just suppose his father were posted overseas and killed before he had had a chance to make it up! He felt the tears not far away. This was terrible; he couldn't disgrace his father further by crying in front of him.

"That's wonderful, Pop," he made himself say. "When do you go?"

"In four days. Not very long. But I've one nice surprise for you, Benny. I've arranged for you to go and live with Milo. His father and mother are both very fond of you, and they've agreed to look after you for the rest of the war. We'll keep the cottage on and of course you'll be able to come back here so that we can spend my leaves together. Keith Margrave is being very generous and making up my pay, so don't worry about the financial side. I'll pay Mr. Johnston for your keep."

"But they're such a large family already. . . ."

"You know how it is in life, Benny. To them that hath shall be given. There's nothing they like better than young people in the house. Won't you enjoy being there?"

"Oh yes of course—if you're quite sure——"

"You'll see, old chap. They'll love having you."

It'll be odd, thought Benedict, to live in a house where there are women again. It softened the thought of his father going more than he would have thought possible.

One night in February 1942

Benedict was awakened from his sleep by a very gentle tapping on the wall. He had been living with the Johnston's for a month, and was happy in a way he had never known possible. The family, as his father had promised, had received him with open arms, and he relished all his life their long rambling discussions round the big kitchen table: what dress Tessa ought to buy, whether Joanna ought to go to Cambridge, what was wrong with Milo's football; religion, politics, gossip; it was all grist to their mill. He had an attic room at the top of the house, divided by only a thin plaster and lath partition from Tessa's room; they could—and did—talk to each other through it.

At first Benedict thought he was dreaming, but as he opened his eyes he heard the sound again—a very gentle but persistent knocking on the partition. He sat up.

"Is that you, Tess?"

"Yes. I—I'm sorry, Benny. I feel frightened. Can I come and talk to you?"

"Yes of course."

There was full moon, the colour of Wensleydale, throwing its pallid light across his room. There was a little knock at his door and then Tessa came in. She was wearing an old red flannel dressing-gown over her striped pyjamas. Both had been handed down from her elder sister. Her hair was pulled back in a knot, emphasing her large, saucer-like eyes, and odd little ears. She was trembling slightly.

"Oh, Benny, you must think me dreadful."

"Of course I don't, Tess. Come and sit down."

She sat on the edge of the bed.

"Now tell me what the trouble is."

"I shall feel such a fool in the morning. Suddenly the whole world seems terrifying. It's so—big and somehow indifferent to us."

"It is big—but you're one of the luckiest people in it. Very few girls in the world have the sort of family you've got—I mean so much security and fun and affection."

"I know. I know it sounds ungrateful but—well, they won't always be there. Won't it be terrible when we're on our own?"

"There'll be other people. After all, your father and mother didn't always have each other."

"I know I shan't ever be as happy as they are."

"That's a pretty sweeping statement. Why on earth shouldn't you be?"

"I seem to make such a mess of my life. You know Ken Heppel is very fond of me?"

"No, I hadn't realised."

"He's written me letters. One every day. They're so sweet. And I feel dreadful because I can't feel the same way about him."

"Don't worry about it, Tess. You're too young to feel like that about any boy."

"That's not true, Benny, you know that."

"Well, of course sometimes we *think* we feel . . ."

"You're in love with Laura, aren't you?"

"How did you know that?"

"I know."

"I don't think we ought to use this word. It's such a big word, and we're so young to use it."

"But tell me truthfully, Benny, will you ever feel about any other girl the way you do about Laura?"

"I can't imagine it. No, I can't think what it would be like. You see, basically, Tess, I'm a one-girl sort of person. I'm very romantic. I put this one girl on a pedestal. . . ."

"Poor Laura!"

"Yes, but she doesn't know." A frightening possibility crossed his mind. "She *can't* know, can she?"

"I don't think so, Benny. I think she's far too wrapped up with Tony Hammond to notice anyone else."

"That's the funny thing, you see. I'm happy for her to be with him. It seems so right for them both. Don't you agree?"

"Of course I admire him. But I couldn't feel about him the way Laura does."

"Tell me, as a girl, do you find Laura beautiful?"

"Of course I do. She's the most beautiful girl in Aylsbourn, everyone knows that."

"Do you remember when she fell off her horse and broke her arm? And then went out riding again when it was still in plaster? That's when she really looked superb. It was such an—an arrogant thing to do. It really seemed to knock all the breath out of me when I saw her ride up our lane that day, very straight, one arm in a sling, but still sort of—disdainfully in command, if you know what I mean."

"One thing about you, Benny—you do appreciate a girl."

"But isn't being alive so exciting that you've got to be crazy about it? That's how I feel. I get so excited sometimes I can hardly speak, and when I run my feet don't touch the ground."

"Aren't you ever afraid?"

"Of course I am."

"You never seem to be. I'm afraid most of the time."

"Whatever of?"

"Oh, everything. Of death, for instance."

"Well, everyone's a bit afraid of that, Tess."

"But not as much as I am."

117

"Have you ever read the *Life and Death of Socrates*?"

"No. You know I'm not very clever."

"You don't have to be clever to read that. It's beautifully simple writing. I think I've never felt really afraid since I read it."

"I don't think reading would help me, Benny. It's just a feeling in my case."

"Yes, I understand. Then the only answer to that is that you must have someone whose hand you can reach out and touch—not necessarily in the literal sense. That's why all our little jealousies and rivalries and pushing and struggling for power always strike me as so tragic. There's only one real enemy and that's death; just as there's only one great sin, and that is waste of life. We're all on the same side in this battle, and death plays a confidence trick on us when he pretends he's an ally."

"Will you be a conscientious objector?"

"I don't know."

"Ken will be. He's a complete pacifist. He says he won't take a life under any circumstances, whatever they do to him."

"You know, Tess, if you travel all over the earth you'll never find anyone who has more goodness than Kenneth."

"I realise that, and that's why I feel so dreadful that I can't return his love. Because that's what it is, isn't it?"

"Yes, I think it is. To tell you what I honestly feel, I think we can love now in a way we shall never be able to again."

"Then why don't older people understand? I mean, they'd think we were absolutely crazy if they could hear us."

"Perhaps they do understand. Perhaps they're just trying to protect us."

"But you said we only had each other."

"That's what I believe, Tess. Look, you have me, for example. I'll always be your friend."

"Will you, Benny?"

"I promise you. And you know I never break a promise."

"I believe you, Benny. I shall be able to go back to sleep now. But, please, never tell anyone I've been here will you? It sounds so—brazen."

"You, Tess? Never!"

"One day I might be."

"Tess, don't try to shock me!"

"Does it shock you?"

"Of course it does. You know I put all my girls on a pedestal."

"But you said you were a one-girl man."

"I can't always live in a dream, Tess. Perhaps it's just as well that the ideal thing should always be out of reach. I'll have to find another girl one day, a real flesh-and-blood one, not a dream-girl like Laura."

"I hope you do, Benny."

"And you'll find somebody too, I know you will. Then you won't be afraid any more."

"I'm not afraid now."

"That's good. I'll see you in the morning."

"And when we meet at breakfast . . ."

"No one will ever know, I give you my promise."

"I believe you, Benny."

The day of the first great rugby game

Christopher Ilex lost no time in stamping his personality on the school. Felix reported that Ilex had confided his secret ambition to his father: it was to take an ordinary grammar school and, with the ordinary material available, by sheer dint of personality make it so good that parents would actually hesitate between sending their sons there or to one of the big public schools. Soon distinguished poets, actors, writers were staying in the school house, organising concerts, speaking, lecturing, arguing, debating. It was intoxicating: but there was something hothouse about it. "I sometimes get the impression," grumbled Milo, "that we're just his bloody guinea-pigs."

However, everybody began to respond. Ilex had so much energy and so much fire in his own teaching that it was hard not to catch his enthusiasm. He gave them a series of lectures on Greece and another on modern architecture; he formed a small dining club from the senior school and actually got a cabinet minister down to it that first winter as well as an air marshal, a trade union leader and the head of an Oxford college. The squeeze was on: Aylsbourn was going to get its name into the Open Scholarship list or bust.

Ilex also showed an unexpected interest in sport. He was sufficient of a realist to know that athletic achievement still counted in England and he was determined therefore that Aylsbourn should triumph in sport too. Martin Hennessy had played wing forward for Cambridge and he was put in charge of the school fifteen. Four nights of the week they went out running and this secretly to Benedict was one of the sharpest pleasures life could afford. There was the long trot through the thick November leaves down to Welcaster pond, with the air coming into his lungs in great rasping gulps that seemed to make him drunk; then the long climb up Cromwell ridge with the calves aching and the ribs tightening; then the glorious run along the top of the Downs, with all Aylsbourn lying in soft silhouette beneath; then the final agonising sprint down the Brewery Hill and into the school's hot baths. All the four friends played for Aylsbourn: Felix and Ken affected to despise the game, Milo and Benny openly loved it. Milo, in fact, was already playing full back for the school; with his dangling arms and meat-plate hands he was a natural for the job. "Besides," as Felix pointed out, "it doesn't matter how much he gets kicked in the face. It can't get any worse than it is."

This was Tony Hammond's last season; he had been playing for the school for four years now and he would soon be nineteen. He had only one remaining ambition: to trounce Shallerton before he went. The trouble was to persuade them to play; when Hammond had written challenging them to a game they had sent an offensive note back offering to send their second fifteen. Ilex quickly changed all that. He and Ross-Tayfield belonged to the same London club, and one telephone call quickly clinched the matter. Shallerton said they had of course a full fixture list, but, seeing that Ilex was now in charge, they would be glad to send over their first fifteen for a trial of strength on the first Saturday in December.

This was Tony Hammond's great challenge. It seemed to matter more to him than even his newly-won place at Cambridge. He soon became fast friends with Martin Hennessy and together they trained the school relentlessly evening after evening.

Hammond had always played stand-off half himself; he was a thrusting, ruthless player and Benedict could make himself almost sick with excitement to see Hammond carve his way through an opposing pack, leaving them sprawled on the grass like a row of ninepins. But now Hammond had a better idea. He brought Ken and Benny up from the second fifteen as a pair of halves. Ken was a natural scrum-half ("It's his working class background," Felix used to say. "He's used to being trodden on.")

and he and Benny had developed a remarkable understanding. Kenneth would sling the ball out time after time without so much as a glance behind, and somehow Benny always managed to be there to scoop it up. They played mock games at enormous pressure, stopping every quarter of an hour for a breather and a talk. Hennessy played too; Benny felt a faint sense of lèse-majesté the first time he brought him down, but Hennessy didn't seem to mind. They all grew hard and fit, keyed and tuned to a pitch they had never before experienced. The tension as the fateful Saturday grew nearer set their teeth on edge.

Even the girls caught the sense of excitement. Tessa became an expert with the embrocation bottle; even her brother thought she might find her life's work as a masseuse. With her gentle hands she had an instinctive knack for easing all the bruises and aches out of them. Joanna, an instinctive athlete, probably understood what they were trying to achieve best; night after night they used to sit round the fire planning their tactics and drawing diagrams. Sometimes Hammond himself would join them; then, when they grew tired of football, they would all sit round the big kitchen table and the talk would go on into the small hours. Hammond talked of the books he was reading, of the Cambridge college to which he was going next autumn, of jazz, of his hopes and plans for the future. (He had swung round completely in the previous two years about the war; and now he badly wanted to fight. But his eyesight was hopeless, and he was turned down on medical grounds.)

Constance claimed to hate all violent sports; but she said she would come to the game to see what it was they all got so excited about. All the Mackays were coming and Felix's parents, and Sir Keith Margrave would be there for sure.

On the great Saturday the Shallerton coach rolled through the school gates and Benedict felt his nerves contract in the pit of the stomach as they got out. They wore chocolate and cream jerseys and looked thoroughly bored.

Hammond went up to meet their captain, Gervase-Jones. He was a very dark, offensive young man of eighteen, with black wavy hair and thick lips, who tried hard not to look as if the whole outing was a most appalling chore. He knew Hammond; they had played for the Hampshire Colts together many times. Hammond disliked him cordially.

"So this is your little place," Gervase-Jones began with

monumental diplomacy. "Amazing what you can get for nothing these days, isn't it?"

When Shallerton came out on to the Margrave Brewery ground they faced a wall of hate you could almost reach out and touch. Benny looked round and felt a quick stab of simple happiness to see all the people he loved best lined up together for the fight: Milo, at full back, looked almost comically grim, but Benny knew that no one from Shallerton could get by him while he remained on his feet; Ken Heppel, small, bouncing and tough, like a rubber ball, was just in front of him; Hammond was on his right, his curious wedge-shaped face serious but very calm; Felix out on the wing, lean, very fast and nonchalant and somehow extremely comforting; Aelfric Gates out on the other wing, pawing the ground like a long, delicate hare. These were his friends and his people, and those bastards from Shallerton would cross their line over his dead body.

It was a perfectly crisp late autumn day and the air was absolutely still; chimney-smoke rose straight into a Gillette-blue sky and the grass had a deliciously rough spring in it. The last thing Benny remembered clearly before Gervase-Jones kicked off was Laura standing on the touchline, her hands deep in the pockets of her coat and he bit his knuckles to restrain his joy.

It was a perfect kick; the ball climbed slowly up into the crisp air, turning lazily over and over then plummeting down into Hammond's safe hands. He swung the ball out clean and true to Felix, who dropped it. They scrummed and Shallerton got it out. Gervase-Jones gave it a mighty punt and with an upper-class cry of "Follow up, School", headed at full speed for the point where Milo was waiting to receive it. The three met at the same spot together and went down in a heap. Only Gervase-Jones got up. Milo lay where he was. Only one leg rose and fell to show he was conscious.

Hammond turned him over. Milo's ugly and battered face was pumice coloured. It did not take long to diagnose the trouble. "I'm afraid, old chap," said Hammond, "that you've bust a collar-bone."

They carried Milo off and Hammond dropped back to take his place. In the next forward rush he went down on the ball in the absolutely lion-hearted way he always did, and was kicked very hard on the head. He lay on the grass, still, with the untroubled expression of death on his strong face. It took him half a minute to come round and Dr. Mackay ordered him to be taken off. "No more football for him today," he said firmly. After that it was a shambles. Shallerton won by forty-four points to nil, and at tea afterwards Gervase-Jones talked quite openly about cancelling the return game.

The day of the second great game

After that Hammond lived for nothing else but the return game. He had willing allies. Even Felix had taken the strongest exception to Gervase-Jones. The contest between the two schools had in it the hard bitterness of class war. They drove themselves remorselessly all through the next three months. Ilex himself referred to the return game the day before it was due to be played. "As you know," he told them, "we had appallingly bad luck last time with accidents. But Johnston, I'm glad to say, is absolutely fit again, and Hammond is none the worse for wear. I shall be present myself tomorrow and I expect every single person in this school to be there too." He looked down the serried rows and repeated carefully: "Everybody."

When they got over to Shallerton their hearts sank. It was a big, ugly, Victorian building, but imposing, and all their five hundred boys were there to see the slaughter. The Aylsbourn supporters—boys and girls—stood along the other side and Benny couldn't help thinking how much more decorative they looked.

They kicked off into a cold wind and for the first half they were seldom out of their own twenty-five. It was desperate defence; tackle, loose scrum, kick for touch, line-out, tight scrum and then the same again. Every time Hammond fell on the ball Benny's heart was in his mouth. But though he was kicked black and blue he somehow stayed on his feet. He lent them all a super-addition of courage.

As the minutes passed Benedict felt his spirits rising. The truth was, man for man, fifteen men for fifteen men, they were as good as Shallerton; neither side could make an impression. And it might be that the Shallerton men would tire first.

As they sucked their crescents of orange greedily at half-time Hammond grinned at them. "You lovely bastards," he said. "You know something? Today we're going to win."

Gervase-Jones kicked off for the second half and the roar

from the crowd took on the ugly baying sound which the audience at a big fight make when they want to see a kill: a high fluting noise like a wind in tall trees. Only a minute later came the chance Aylsbourn had been waiting for; Ken Heppel got out a very hard clean straight one to Benny who took it at full tilt, then had the absolute satisfaction of handing off Gervase-Jones with a thump that might have been heard a mile away. The ball went down the three-quarter line like a hot potato to Aelfric Gates. He made for the right corner with the entire Shallerton pack after him, then just as it seemed he must go down, Hammond whipped across behind him, at an angle of ninety degrees, snapping up the ball in a beautiful scissors movement that they had practised a thousand times. Felix was coming down the blind side sly and jet-quick and he took the ball from Hammond absolutely flat out; and nothing, Benny was sure, on God's earth could have stopped him then. He streaked over the Shallerton line, but not satisfied with that, cut into the centre and put the ball down right between their goal posts, ending up with four men on top of him and all the wind knocked out of his body. But the shout of pure joy from the Aylsbourn line made it all worth while. Hammond converted and Shallerton came back as if berserk. But it was no good now; Aylsbourn were not going to give an inch. Hardly one of them escaped without some sort of injury, but when the final whistle went their line was still unviolated.

The Shallerton boys were quite nice afterwards. They showed their guests round the school, which now seemed even more ugly and cold than before and stank of carbolic soap. On the way home in the school bus they sang their hearts out.

When they got to Aylsbourn High Street and the bus had stopped, Ilex got up and announced: "Gentlemen, I am proud of you. It has been one of the happiest days in my life."

"Do you know," said Felix later in disbelief, "old Ilex was actually blubbing when he said that? I was right next to him and as he sat down he took out his red silk handkerchief and wiped his eyes."

One day in late February 1942

—he could never think which, he was going up to Shallerton in the train, and he had forgotten why he was on his own. He had wandered on to the platform and saw that Hammond and Laura were already there. Hammond was wearing a dark lounge suit and looked as if he might be going to a party. She on the other hand, was rather casually dressed in a sweater and skirt. It was a mild morning, with just a hint of spring in the air. He tried to avoid them, but they both saw him and looked pleased.

"Hello, Benny," called Hammond. "Are you coming to Shallerton with us?"

"Well—I was going. But I don't want to inter——"

"Nonsense. We'd like you to come with us. Wouldn't we?"

Laura nodded. They both looked relaxed and happy, yet somehow—conspiratorial.

They got into a third-class coach. "What are you going for, Benny?" Hammond asked.

"Oh, just to get some books."

"Very sensible. There's a much better selection up there. Laura's going shopping; why don't you go together?"

Benedict could hardly believe his ears. "But what about you, Hammond? Aren't you——?"

"I'm visiting some friends. We're only travelling on the train together, aren't we?"

Laura nodded seriously. "Do keep me company, Benny," she said.

Benedict swallowed back his astonishment. Here was a thing! He looked from one to the other. No, there was definitely more in this than met the eye. But what? It was utterly baffling. Perhaps they wanted people not to know they were together. But if so, why *set off* from Aylsbourn and then part company at Shallerton? It didn't make sense.

Hammond talked easily all the way to Shallerton. He seemed to bubble with high spirits. He had got a place at Cambridge for September, he had defeated Gervase-Jones; ahead of him lay one more carefree term's cricket and perhaps a trial for Hampshire. He had received an encouraging letter from the Editor of *Penguin New Writing*. Everything was coming easily to him. Benedict studied the strong, wedge-shaped face with awe; there was no limit to what Hammond might achieve. He might even be Prime Minister one day! After the war there might be a communist government. Or he might be the Auden of the nine-teen-fifties, or England's answer to Hemingway. . . .

Laura listened. But now that he watched her intently she

125

seemed not to be listening properly. Her thoughts were miles away. Where?

Outside Shallerton station Hammond waved them a cheerful goodbye and made off with long energetic strides up the Castle Hill. They watched him disappear. Then Laura turned to Benedict. She looked at him for a moment as if she had only just realised he was there.

"Well, Benny," she said, "let's go shopping."

"Where do you want to go, Laura?"

She gave a little shrug. "Oh, I only wanted some stockings. We can get those anywhere."

Then why come to Shallerton for them, thought Benedict.

They spent a blissful hour together buying books, and then they went to buy her stockings, and there was still time for them to catch the 12.57 back to Aylsbourn. Laura said nothing all the way home. She sat in a corner and stared out at the hedges and fields racing by the window. And as he watched her beautiful face a sudden thought came to Benedict: maybe Constance is right after all. Maybe they aren't in love. But if they're not . . .

He turned the problem over often in his mind after that; but there was no solution.

One day in April 1942

Benedict was sitting reading a book in front of the kitchen fire. He had a bad cold, and Mrs. Johnston had told him to stay in for the day. The family had gone out; it was a perfect spring day and Mr. Johnston had taken them all for a drive to visit relatives at Winchester. Joanna, however, had asked to be excused.

She came into the kitchen and sat down in the rocking chair. "Hello, Benny," she said.

He glanced up. "Hello, Joanna. Didn't you want to go with the others?"

"No. I feel—rather upset."

Benedict put down his book with new interest. Joanna was usually such a withdrawn girl—she must have something important on her mind.

"Whatever is the trouble, Joanna? It takes a lot to upset you."

"I discovered today that Tony Hammond is leaving."

126

"Yes, that's right—at the end of the summer term." An alarming thought crossed his mind. "What; not *now* . . . ?"

"Right now. To tell you the truth, he's been given the push."

"*What?*"

"Ilex has told him to go. He's going to take a temporary job in London until September."

"But whatever for? I mean he's the most brilliant chap we've ever had. . . ."

"I don't know. It's a scandal of some sort. It may even be political. Your guess is as good as mine."

"Is it——?"

"No." Joanna shook her head and permitted herself a little smile. "No, it's not your beloved Laura. I'm sure of that."

"How do you know?"

"I heard Daddy talking on the telephone. I couldn't help it— I picked up the extension upstairs when he was in the middle of a telephone conversation with Ilex. He realised I'd heard them talking and made me promise not to tell a soul."

"Then . . ."

"Why am I telling you? Because I must tell somebody. You see I was rather fond of him myself."

"Well we all were. But how do you know Laura wasn't involved?"

"Because I asked Daddy. He looked rather embarrassed and said it was nothing like that at all. I know he wouldn't lie to me."

"Then what on earth can it be?"

"I haven't the slightest idea. He left this morning, so we can't ask him. All I know is that he's gone. Perhaps"—and there was a sadness and loss in her voice that Benedict never forgot—"we shall never see him again."

In early September 1942

Milo went up to Cambridge to try his hand at a scholarship paper. He was not yet seventeen and there was really no chance of his winning anything for another year; still, Ilex wanted him to have the experience. His three friends took him to the station and put him on to the train.

"And don't forget," Benedict shouted as the train drew out, "to write and tell us how it's going." Milo was the first of them to try his strength in the outside world.

Milo beamed out of the window. "You'll get the first gripping instalment tomorrow," he assured them.

Nothing, however, appeared in the next morning's post; nor Wednesday's. On Thursday, however, Benedict came down in the morning to find a letter in mauve ink and in Milo's familiar flowing hand awaiting him. It was his usual inimitable style:

Dear Chums:

As it is my custom to commence with the most important item, I'll give you a list of what I've eaten to date. I arrived at Cambridge station and reached Trinity College at about 3.20. I was shown my rooms and mooched about until dinner came up at 7-0 p.m. We all sat down in a huge hall very much like Westminster Abbey and numerous waiters passed round: (1) tomato soup (2) stewed meat (assorted) and dumplings, potatoes and parsnips. Coffee cream followed.

For breakfast this morning we had porridge, fish, toast, butter, jam, coffee, plenty of sugar etc. For "luncheon" at 12.15:— Bacon and eggs on toast, with potatoes and leeks, followed by chocolate cream and wafers. (Of course new bread and water are always present.) For dinner tonight:— oxtail soup, roast beef, Yorkshire pudding, roast spuds, and spinach, suet pudding etc.

All the waiters are in evening dress at dinner but wear shoddy (e.g. tweed suits) at other times.

A woman wakes us up at 7.45 with hot water, cleans our shoes, lays the fire and makes our beds.

The college is like Windsor Castle and Hampton Court rolled into one. Physics this morning was the easiest scholarship paper I have seen but even so I could only do one question.

The crackling from the neighbouring women's colleges— Girton and Newnham—is terrific but unfortunately Cambridge abounds in R.A.F. aircrew and Americans.

About 300 blokes are sitting for Natural Science Schols alone; however a week here is worth the 9/- a day they charge any time.

Tuesday 7.30 I got some matches and we've lit the huge fire. I discovered some more of Trinity: huge masses of cloisters and courtyards etc. on the other side of the road. Two of the courtyards over there are known as the billiard table and the spittoon.

I hear there is a roof-climbing society which operates during term nights.

Needless to say the paper was awful again this afternoon (I did one question in Chemistry—the wrong way). Still there's worse to come—tomorrow is pure maths.

Around the dining hall are pictures of the great men of Trinity—Isaac Newton, Francis Bacon etc. Pity Milo Johnston will never adorn the wall.

Wednesday 7.30 I've just seen that bastard Gervase-Jones. It seems he's coming up this year and has come up a few days early to do some rugby practice. He recognised me at once, but pretended not to. Dinner tonight was celestine soup, fried fillet of haddock, parsnips, potatoes, blackberry slice. Our written exams finished at 12 noon and after "luncheon" (savoury pastie, greens, potatoes and bread pudding) I went to see Eric Portman in "Escape to Danger". Afterwards I had tea in Lyons (sausage, egg and baked beans on toast, tea, cake etc. etc.).

The tutor gave me another interview tonight and said that if I win anything he'll send me a telegram and if not he'll write to say why not.

Our physics practical is to be held in the Cavendish Laboratory of all places and for this I have to stay till Monday mid-day. I'll be home about eleven, and Benny, please ask Mum to have something ready because I shall be bloody ravenous.

Till then chums,
Your old pal,
Milo.

Milo failed to get a scholarship, but Ilex's strategy worked, for the next year he won himself a place at Trinity—provided the county would support him, which they quickly said they would—for September 1944. Benedict secretly believed that one day Milo's portrait really would hang in the Trinity hall.

New Year's Eve 1942

Ilex was giving a dinner party for his staff; Mr. Johnston unwillingly struggled into his old-fashioned dinner jacket with its high wing collar and drove off with his wife at seven o'clock.

His wife was not really looking forward to the occasion any more than her husband; she would have preferred to be at home with her family and in any case found Ilex rather trying company. To make it up to her children, she suggested that they ask one or two friends in for the evening. "I'll make you some mulled claret," she promised, "and a cold supper, and you can see the New Year in and enjoy yourselves."

"Which is more than we shall do," grumbled her husband.

The Weston and Mackay families were going away together to Torquay for Christmas. Benedict felt ill with jealousy, but Felix reassured him. "You may take it as read," he said, "that I have got my eye on one of the maids at our hotel. There's nothing I like better than a bit of low life. But I'll keep my eye on your lovely, languorous Laura for you. There's always some keen young R.A.F. officers down there. Now surely you'd rather me than them?"

Benedict reluctantly agreed that this was so. "But promise me," he begged, "that you'll write to me if she falls for anyone else. Don't keep it from me. I must know."

"If the worst comes to the worst, you shall be told," Felix promised solemnly. So far, however, there had been no word from Torquay and Benedict—who knew Felix could never resist the opportunity to transmit a little scandal—began to breathe more easily.

Though the New Year's Eve party would lose some of its spice without Laura and Felix, it was still fun to work out whom they should invite. Ken would come of course, and Constance; and they decided they would ask Aelfric Gates, of whom they were increasingly fond.

That made seven. For even numbers, they needed one more girl. Milo had a suggestion. "Why not," he asked, innocently, "Doreen Pepper?"

"Oh really, Milo," said Joanna. "Is that the best you can do? She's such a common child."

"Yeah, but sexy," said Milo with deliberate vulgarity, rolling his eyes saucily.

"I'm surprised that you haven't got better taste, Milo," said Benny, "but if you have this *nostalgie de la boue*, I suppose it's got to be satisfied."

"You said it, man."

"I think," said Tessa, "that Milo doesn't give a jot about the

Pepperpot. I don't think he cares tuppence about any girl. He's just doing it for a joke."

"Oh *ask* her," said Joanna, who was technically in charge. "We'll see who gets tired of her first. Us or Milo."

"I am insatiable," said Milo greedily. The others looked at him with interest. Was Milo joking after all? One never knew for sure.

Benny was up in his room shaving as the Johnstons' majestic old bull-nosed Morris rolled down the drive. He hummed as he worked. Shaving was a new experience in his life and was still hardly necessary to him more than once a week. But for a special evening like this, a special toilet was required. He was disturbed by the now familiar tapping on the wall.

"Hello, Tess."

"Hello, Benny. I say, Benny."

"Yes."

"Could you zip me up?"

"Of course."

He wiped his face clean, and went into Tessa's room, knocking carefully on the door first. Tessa was wearing a charming dress of primrose yellow which was especially flattering to her dark complexion. From the front it looked complete, but when she turned her back towards him he saw that it was unzipped down to her waist. She lifted both hands in a movement of instinctive shyness to her face and said:

"I don't know what I'd do without you here, Benny."

"I expect you'd have to zip it yourself."

"Don't be beastly, Benny. You know perfectly well that's pretty well impossible."

"I'm glad to hear it. It makes a very agreeable duty. There— is that right?"

"Thank you, Benny." She leaned slightly backwards, and to his surprise he found he had to hold on to her so that they both kept their equilibrium. His hands joined quite naturally round her waist. Looking into the mirror, he thought they made a slightly idiotic couple—she with her hauntingly large eyes and painfully thin body, he with his intense and liquid brown eyes and excessively earnest expression.

"Benny," she said. "I'm going to wear scent tonight for the first time in my life. The scent you gave me for Christmas."

"It was a very small bottle. Are you sure you want to waste it on an occasion like this?"

131

"What better? Benny, it was kind of you. It must have cost the earth."

"It cost six and six as a matter of fact. I bought it from the money I got for fire-watching."

"Benny, you must learn never to tell a woman exactly how much a present cost. Then she can always delude herself that it was much, much more. Not that it matters in my case. I thought it was sweet, whatever it cost. But tell me, why did you buy me *scent* of all things?"

"I just thought you'd—enjoy having it."

"It's a very *special* present for a man to give to a girl."

"You're a very special girl."

"Do you think the scent will attract Ken Heppel?"

"I don't think it will exactly restrain him."

"Have you tried it yet?"

"I sniffed it vaguely in the shop."

"I'll put some on and you tell me what you think?"

She dabbed some on to the back of her hand and proffered it.

"I think Ken Heppel will go berserk."

"You know, I like him a little better. At least, I always liked him. But now . . ."

"Now you feel maybe . . ."

"Yes." She dabbed the scent behind her ears.

"You know, Benny," she said, "tonight for the first time I feel like a woman."

"To me you are a woman. The one I know best in the whole world."

"Is that really so, Benny?"

"Who better? Laura bewitches me and Constance——"

"You're sure you haven't got a soft spot for Constance?"

"No—not exactly. I don't feel—close to her, the way I do towards you."

"She's a very sophisticated girl."

"You mean you don't like her?"

"Certainly not. I do like her. But she's rather frighteningly intelligent."

"I agree. Also she's slightly—well outrageous."

"You mean—fast?"

"I don't know. All I know is, she does this college clutch in a rather embarrassing way."

"But I could do that, Benny."

132

"Yes, but you wouldn't."

"I might."

"Well try it on Ken Heppel and see what happens."

"Oh I wouldn't do it to Ken."

"Why ever not?"

"It might encourage him."

"Tessa, I shall never understand women."

"There's nothing to understand."

"Listen. There's the bell. Someone's arrived. The party's beginning."

Mrs. Johnston had excelled herself: her cold supper was delicious and the mulled claret very quickly had its effect; they sat round the kitchen fire drowsily, talking in small groups of two or three. Benedict found himself unexpectedly next to Aelfric Gates, and in half an hour had found out more about him than ever before.

By now Gates was very nearly six feet tall, alarmingly slim, but built like a thoroughbred greyhound. His shy faun's eyes lent credence to the idea that he was some gentle animal that would scamper away when you stepped on a twig in the forest. It turned out that his father was in fact a forester.

"So what do you want to do when you leave Aylsbourn?" Benny asked him.

"I don't care. As long as I can read philosophy."

"Philosophy?"

"Yes. Whitehead. And Russell. Have you ever read *Principia Mathematica*?"

"Can't say I have."

"It's a fabulous book. Intoxicating."

Benny studied Aelfric with interest. He thought he could almost see what Ilex got out of his new job; what Felix called his "intellectual orgasm from watching raw intelligence spawn out of the earth". Aelfric was now far and away the cleverest boy in the school; he churned his way through all the books in the library with contemptuous ease; he soaked up languages like a piece of blotting paper, and he ripped through mathematics papers like a child tearing newspapers.

"But if you want to be a philosopher, why are you specialising in history?"

"Because Ilex talked me into it. You see, most annoyingly, my highest marks in the Cambridge exams this summer were in history. Ilex said I might be the first boy to win an Open to Oxford or Cambridge from Aylsbourn. And he made the point that in Hennessy we have one of the best modern historians in the country."

"But it meant giving up mathematics."

"Well, he advised me to. It hurts me to remember it sometimes. I read on my own. But mathematics is a funny thing. Unless you keep in top gear, you can go rusty quite easily. And a lot of the big schools have real assault courses on the Open Scholarships in Maths and Science. Ilex is a bit contemptuous of our science teaching here."

"But Milo's father is quite good at teaching maths, isn't he?"

"Ilex doesn't think he's up to teaching scholarship stuff. He may be right."

Benedict turned this conversation over many times in his mind afterwards. He had suffered a similar disappointment. His own marks in the Cambridge that summer had shown a strong bias towards science. This, he was convinced, was due simply to his friendship with Milo and the specially good teaching of Mr. Johnston. As it happened he was most keen to take English. But Ilex had been against this.

"Frankly, Benny," he said on the day they discussed his future (Ilex had latched on to all his boys' nicknames very quickly), "I don't see you as a prospect for an Open. But you might well win a County Major or one of those local awards. Only you must be sensible about it."

"But I like English best, sir."

"It's not a question of what you *like* best, Benny. It's a question of what's going to get you furthest. In two years' time when your age group leaves here, I want a dozen scholarships at Oxford and Cambridge. You're part of that plan. Now tell me—would you rather read physics at Cambridge or Eng. Lit. at some grubby provincial university college?"

It was on the tip of Benedict's tongue to say the latter; but he stopped himself; it wasn't true. For one thing, he wanted desperately to stay with his friends, and Ilex had already launched Milo at Cambridge. Ken Heppel and Felix Weston were both hopeless at science, and would have to take an Arts course. But in any event, they were not going to end up in a grubby provincial university college. So Benedict had acquiesced. He was quite

134

enjoying science, but now and again he had a sharp stab of regret that he would not read English.

The time passed pleasantly, but by half-past nine Milo became restive. He looked at his watch and realised that his parents would be back in roughly ninety minutes' time. He had a clear notion now he wanted to fill in the intervening period.

"Well now, folks," he announced, "I think the time has come for a game of Murder."

"Haven't you got over those childish games yet?" Joanna asked.

"It's not childish the way I play it."

"Who wants to play Murder?" asked Joanna.

"I do," said Kenneth promptly. He looked at Tessa shame-facedly out of the corner of his eye. The only advantage of the game as far as he was concerned was that it would provide a legitimate opportunity to be alone with her.

"I'm all for it," said the Pepperpot. The other girls looked at her. They had not been in any doubt about *her* views.

"I'd rather go on talking," said Aelfric.

"Benny?" asked Constance.

"I'm happy. Whatever the others want."

"Constance?"

"Yes. Why not?"

"Tessa?"

"I don't know. At least I think——"

"That's it then," said Milo unceremoniously. He got out a pack of cards and shuffled them expertly. "Now you all know the rules. Ace of Spades is the murderer. Keep quiet if you get it. A gentle squeeze round the throat means you've committed the crime. The victim must count ten before screaming to let the murderer escape. Everyone must stay where they were when they hear the scream. Jack of Spades is the detective. He can ask any number of questions but only accuse one person of being mur-derer. O.K.?"

He doled out the cards. "Oh," said Joanna. "I'm the detec-tive."

"All right. Stay here and put your feet up. You'll have work to do later. Everyone else scatter over the house. I'll turn the lights off at the main switch."

Benedict felt his heart begin to thump harder as the whole house was suddenly drowned in darkness. He had played this game too often not to know its curious and minuscule tactile pleasures. He moved quietly through the darkness and began to creep up the stairs. On the landing he tripped over what felt like a sack of runner beans on the floor. He reached out a hand and felt to see what it was.

"Go away," said the sack. His hand encountered a well-shaved male neck, and a female hand round the neck. It was Milo; and unless he was much mistaken, the Pepperpot. He prowled on up the second, narrower flight towards his own room. Near the top of the stairs he stopped. Someone was in the way, he was sure. Again he groped. His hand closed on a bare arm. He slid his fingers down to the wrist, seeking identification. Still there was no move or word from the darkness. Then the problem was solved for him. A light scent, which had cost him six and six a few days ago, was in the air.

"Is that you, Tess?" he whispered.

"Yes. We're not supposed to talk are we?"

"No. Are you the murderer?"

"No. Are you?"

"No. Let's hide from the others. I hate being murdered."

"Where?"

"Your room is nearest."

They tiptoed in and closed the door gently behind them. Benedict steered her gently towards the bed. She resisted a little.

"Benny, do you think we ought? I mean, won't people talk?"

"I'll go when they scream."

They sat side by side on her bed. Only their hands touched. They heard a bump and laughter downstairs.

"Do you know who the murderer is, Benny?"

"Yes. Milo."

"How do you know?"

"I've seen him do it before. He gives himself the ace so that he can control the length of the game. No one can turn the lights on till he's done the murder. It may take anything up to half an hour."

"Do you think he's really a sort of Casanova?"

"I think he thinks he is."

"You're not a bit like that, Benny."

"Only because I'm too nervous."

"Even of me?"

"Yes."

136

"What do you think of my Tropical Sin."

"Your *what*?"

"The scent you gave me, you idiot."

"Oh. Pretty good. That's how I knew it was you."

"You recognised me by the scent?"

"Yes. You know, according to Aldous Huxley, there are some very disgusting things in scent. For instance——"

"Don't, Benny. You're spoiling it for me. Tell me, does this scent tempt you at all?"

"Yes. As a matter of fact it does."

"But you're too shy to do anything about it."

"No I'm not."

"Obviously you are."

Even Benedict realised that this was an open invitation. He slid his left arm round Tessa's waist and put his right hand gently on her neck, turning her face in the pitch darkness nearer to his. He could feel the large vein in her throat bumping under his little finger.

"What are you waiting for, Benny?"

"Nothing." The next moment their lips met, slightly asymmetrically, but with unhurried gentleness. He never forgot the innocence of that kiss. It seemed to go on for a long time.

Tessa put both her arms round his neck and very slowly slid her lips away. "Oh Benny," she whispered. "That was the very first time."

"It was for me too."

They kissed again. Benedict's mouth was as dry as if he had just escaped death and his heart pumped recklessly. It was as if he had just finished a five mile race. To his great surprise, he found he was shivering. And so was Tessa.

She took her mouth reluctantly away from his.

"Benny," she said. "This is awful."

"Why?"

"Well I mean, we live next door to each other. Where will it stop?"

"Don't be ridiculous, Tess. There's nothing immoral in a kiss."

"Yes, but suppose my mother discovered we were making love right under her nose?"

"I could ask to move into Milo's room."

"Oh no. I couldn't bear that."

"Then we'll just have to be strong."

They kissed again and she ran her thin fingers through his hair.

"Where did you learn to do that?"

"In a film."

"I wonder what people did before films. I suppose they just taught each other. Do you realise that the knowledge of love is the one subject that's passed on from generation to generation with almost nothing being written down?"

"Benny, why are you so serious? Kiss me again."

During their fourth kiss there was a horrifying scream from below.

"That's that awful little bitch Doreen Pepper. She's been murdered. I'd know her voice anywhere."

Tessa jumped up, turned on the light, and began to arrange her hair in the mirror.

"Quick, Benny," she whispered.

He tiptoed out, slipped quickly into his room, and was lying on the bed reading a Penguin when Joanna came in on her tour of inspection.

"Well," she said sarcastically. "Here's a new talent. Reading in the dark."

"It was only while I was waiting."

"I've seen enough, thank you. Here," she handed him a handkerchief from a pile of newly laundered linen on his dressing-table.

He sat up and looked in the mirror. There was a large red smear on his face and another on his collar.

"Good heavens!" he said feebly. "How on earth did that get there?"

"That's what I'm going to find out," Joanna said with mock iciness. "Come downstairs."

It took her only thirty seconds to discover that Milo, a poor liar, was the murderer. He shuffled the cards enthusiastically again. As he did so the boys and girls eyed each other with heightened interest. He dealt the cards out.

"Oh!" said Tessa, and the disappointment was sharp in her voice. "I'm the detective."

Benedict's eyes met hers across the room and said: Don't be sad. There'll be plenty of other times. She recovered herself, smiled, and said, "Off you go then. And behave yourselves."

Benedict decided to follow the same strategic plan as before.

He would make his way stealthily up to his room and sit in the darkness there, away from everyone, trying to re-create the delight he had just experienced.

He edged his way cautiously up in the darkness, each sense needle-sharp, aware that other lives were expanding near his in response to the beauty of sharp new tactile sensations. He reached his room at last, and softly opened the door. He tiptoed across the little room and reached out to discover exactly where his bed was. But all his groping hand encountered was something warm, curving and silky. He withdrew his hand sharply. It was a girl's leg!

"Hello, Benny," said a languid voice. He recognised it at once.

"Hello, Constance."

"Is this your room?"

"Yes."

"I thought it must be. Am I taking all the space?"

"No. Oh thanks."

He sat on the edge of his bed. Somewhere beside him in the darkness Constance was delectably stretched out, apparently entirely at her ease. It was enough to give a chap the creeps!

"Are you the murderer?" he whispered.

"No. Are you?"

"No. And it can't be Milo again. He wouldn't give himself the same card twice, would he?"

"Oh so it's fixed, is it? I thought it might be. Why doesn't he take the Pepperpot out into Twenty Acre if he wants to smooch with her?"

"I think he doesn't quite know how to set about it. But in the dark, everyone seems to lose their inhibitions. Have you ever noticed that?"

"No."

"No?"

"Not in your case anyway, Benny. You must be the slowest male in the county of Hampshire, unless you count that old tortoise in Macpherson's garden."

"I'm nothing of the sort. I'm just not—er—promiscuous."

"Oh is that what it is? There is only one overwhelming passion in your life?"

"You know there is."

"It must be a bit boring though. Will you be able to live on Platonic love for ever, Benny? Rather in the way some inventors thought they could find an engine that ran entirely on air?"

139

"Of course not."

"The funny thing is, you would make a good lover. You're so absurdly pure."

Benny felt a slow sense of shame rising inside him.

"I'm not all that damned pure!"

"Oh really? You surprise me!"

To his mortification he heard her give an overt and rather theatrical yawn. Suddenly he felt wildly angry. He half-turned, and swung his legs up on to the bed beside Constance. He put his arm right round her waist and pulled her roughly until she was tight up against him. Their faces were now side by side on the counterpane. He could feel her quick breathing.

"Say that again."

"What?" She sounded a little frightened, or perhaps excited.

"What you just said."

"I said you surprised me."

"Before that."

"I forget. Benny you're hurting me."

He hadn't noticed that he had dug his fingers hard into her arm. He relaxed them as if he was going to get up and leave her and then changed his mind and kissed her quite viciously. She stiffened for a second with the shock, then relaxed completely and put both arms round his neck. She half opened her mouth and, to his astonishment, bit his lower lip, though quite gently. He took his mouth away, more in surprise than anything, and to his further surprise she slapped his face quite hard. The sound rang out in the darkness and or a moment he felt slightly stunned.

"What in hell's name did you do that for?"

"Because you asked for it."

"Why do you talk such nonsense? I can't make you out at all. First you ask me to kiss you and then——"

"I didn't ask you."

"Well you invited me to."

"The trouble with you, Benny, is that you're so inexperienced. You've probably never kissed a girl before in your life."

"Oh yes I have," Benedict said confidently, secretly thanking his lucky stars that he had lived through the last half hour.

"How many?"

"Plenty."

"That's a likely story. I can tell that you're a beginner from the way you kiss."

"I wouldn't like to say what I can tell from the way *you* kiss."

"I expect you've never been kissed properly before."

"Who taught you to kiss like that, Constance?"

"My priest."

"*What?*"

"My priest. You know I'm a lapsed Catholic?"

"No I didn't."

"Well that's what made me give it up. I told my confessor that a boy had kissed me, and he asked whether it was with the mouth open or shut."

"And that put the idea into your head?"

"Yes. Don't you find it pretty exciting?"

"Yes."

"I must say you don't show it."

"I'll show you."

They kissed again. Benedict found it an intoxicating, though alarming experience. He had never been in such proximity to a girl in his life. There seemed no part of Constance that was not pressed very hard against him. An extremely naïve thought passed through his head: if there were a Creator, then what artifice he had shown, what divine imagination in shaping men and women in such a deliciously complementary way! How marvellous, for instance, that a woman's hips were made so invitingly wide, so that——

Just then all the lights went on.

"Cave, everybody!" They heard Milo calling. And then there was the sound of the Johnston's bull-nosed Morris coming slowly up the drive.

They stared at each other, not quite believing that they had just been locked so impetuously together. Constance took a small handkerchief from her bag and carefully wiped Benedict's face clean. Then she nonchalantly put on some lipstick, and straightened her hair in the mirror. Next, she put her arm through Benedict's.

"I'll tell you a secret, Benny," she said. "It was the first time for me. The first proper time the way the priest said. I'll always be grateful to that priest."

"So will I" said Benny.

That night it was his turn to tap on the wall. Tessa was awake.

"Yes, Benny."

"Tess, I must see you."

"Come in, Benny."

He pulled on his dressing-gown and tiptoed through. It was a moonless night; he couldn't see her face.

"Come and sit down, Benny. What's the matter?"

"I can't sleep."

"Why not?"

"I feel such a—so unfaithful to you, Tess."

"Why? What did you do?"

"I—I kissed Constance."

"But I don't mind, Benny. After all, why shouldn't you?"

"I wanted to remember this evening as something special between us. Completely innocent and yet—memorable. And then I have to spoil it by misbehaving with Constance."

"But you didn't *misbehave*, did you?"

"Oh no of course not. But she's a very passionate girl."

"I like her. She's different from any other girl I know. Do you like her very much, Benny?"

"She frightens me a bit. She's fascinating and tough and very nice all at the same time."

"Maybe she has reasons for being tough we don't know about."

There was a silence.

"Tessa, do you think your parents realised what was going on?"

"Of course they did."

"They didn't mind?"

"No—they know we wouldn't do anything really bad."

"Why did the game go on so long? It seemed hours, that second time."

"Because Milo took the Ace of Spades out of the pack. I saw him. If there's no Ace there can be no murderer and no murder. So the game goes on indefinitely."

"Trust Milo! And is that why he made you detective?"

"I think he thought I was not likely to like that sort of thing."

"Well, he was wrong, wasn't he?"

"Not really. It was only because it was you, Benny. I wouldn't with just any boy."

"That's why I feel so awful. I mean first you and then——"

"Oh don't worry about it, Benny. All men are like that."

"Are they?"

142

"Yes. Men are naturally polygamous; women are monogamous."

"Well I'm not. Not really. I was just——"

"Led astray? But that's always the trouble, Benny. Everyone sets out with the best intentions."

"Tessa, do you think I'll always be like this? I mean unable to resist temptations? I do so want to love only one person."

"If it's Laura, I think you'll be all right."

"But she's right out of reach."

"Not any more—not since Tony Hammond went away."

"But I'm sure they're still in love."

"No they're not."

"How can you be sure?"

"Something. I don't quite know. Anyway, he's in Cambridge now; probably he's met all sorts of exciting girl undergraduates. You know what, Benny? You ought to ask Laura out. She's awfully lonely, anyone can see that."

"Oh, but I couldn't Tess."

"Why ever not?"

"First, it would be so dishonest. It would look as if I was trying to steal her behind his back."

"You won't steal her unless she wants to be stolen."

"And anyway, she'd never go out with *me*."

"Why ever not?"

"Well, she's a year older for one thing."

"But you're both in the senior school now."

"I'm sorry, Tess. Of course I'd like to, more than anything in life. But I won't—not while she belongs to Hammond."

"Poor old Benny! You are faithful. No—not faithful—honourable."

"That's almost an insult these days. Do you know what Constance called me?"

"No."

"Pure."

"And you were upset at that? But it's the nicest thing anyone could say about you, Benny."

"I'm not pure. I'm only human, Tess."

There was a long silence. At length she said:

"Benny?"

"Yes?"

"Have you ever thought what it would be like to kiss Laura?"

"No. At least—not in any clear way. You see it's such an unlikely thing. . . ."

"But suppose it happened. What do you think it would be like?"

"I just can't imagine. It would be indescribable."

"Shall I tell you something, Benny?"

"Yes, please."

"It would be just like kissing Constance or me."

"But——" He paused. He couldn't hurt her by saying how infinitely separate those two experiences were. And yet—perhaps she was right. Perhaps she would combine all the sweetness of Tessa with all the passion of Constance!

"What is it, Benny?"

"Oh nothing. Just that everything is so baffling. And wonderful. Do you honestly forgive me, Tess"?

"There was nothing to forgive, Benny."

"And we're still friends?"

"We'll always be friends."

January 4th, 1943

was the day Felix was due back from Torquay. Anxious to see his old friend again—and in particular anxious to know what news there was of Laura—Benedict set off early along the High Street to call at the Westons' house and ask Mrs. Duncher what time the family were expected. To his surprise, however, he saw Felix walking down the High Street towards him. He was surprised on two counts: that Felix was back so early, and that he should bother to start walking towards Welcaster to call on Benny— for there was nowhere else he was likely to walk. As Felix drew near, Benedict realised that Felix had some news for him. His dark face gleamed with unusual excitement.

"Benny," he said as soon as they had greeted each other. "I've got news for you."

"What is it?"

"Not here. Let's go into Miller's."

They settled themselves in their favourite corner, well out of earshot, and ordered coffee. Benedict watched his friend's face anxiously.

"Well, how was Torquay?"

Felix made an impatient gesture of dismissal.

144

"All right. Benny, I've discovered why Hammond left in such a hurry. But you must give me your word of honour never to tell a soul. I found out through reading something I shouldn't, and no one must ever know."

"I give you my solemn promise."

Felix waited till the waitress had brought the two coffees and withdrawn. Then he leaned across the table and said, very slowly and distinctly: "Because he was having a love-affair with Arabella."

IV

B<small>UT ALL THAT</small>, thought Benedict as he let himself into his flat had been a long time ago; seventeen years ago, to be precise; he had lived as much life again since that astonishing January morning. He was just twice as old as that boy whose heart had seemed to stop when Felix broke the news to him. For a dream had been destroyed in that moment, and another planted in its place. He would never admire Hammond in quite the same way again; but suddenly, as the mystery of Laura's relationship with him had become clear, a long avenue into the future had seemed to open. He had not known whether to cry or laugh that morning; he had been born into a new world. The moment of truth over the coffee cups in Miller's had sliced his life neatly in two. And what could he say of the seventeen years that had followed after?

He crossed his drawing-room and went out slowly on to the balcony. As he breathed the London air, he remembered suddenly that he had not been really alive since the day he left Aylsbourn, for the simple reason that always afterwards he had felt sub-consciously as if he were choking a little. It would be good, he thought, to breathe that marvellous air again. It had been—what?—thirteen years now since then, and a good deal of it he did not care to remember.

And yet—was he so very different from the Benny his friends remembered? Let's see, who was he today? Did a different personality entirely inhabit that same mortal shell? Today he was P. J. Benedict, Managing Director of the Diskon Company, a Fellow of the Institute of Directors, with seventy-five thousand five shilling shares in his own company. What would Benedict, the boy, the dreamer, the lover, say to *that* lot?

What would he say to P. J. Benedict, proprietor of two paintings by Kokoschka, a drawing by Picasso, a nude carved by Butler, a first edition of *The Masters*, signed by the author? Not much; it was too damned studied, the front he presented to the polite world. What, then, of the *Collected Poems of Auden* and the *Journals* of Stendhal that he kept—and conscientiously read—in the lavatory? Still pretty suspect.

What would he say to P. J. Benedict, tenant of an eight-room apartment off Upper Brook Street, weekender at a cottage in Rye, skipper of a Dragon Class yacht, proprietor of a 110 m.p.h. Bristol 406 costing £4,500? Mm—not much.

And what about P. J. Benedict, shopper at Fortnum's, connoisseur of château-bottled claret, whose shirts were made in Jermyn Street for five guineas each and whose suits were made in Dover Street at fifty? What would he say of Benedict, habitué of the Ecu de France, the Caprice, the Mirabelle? Thumbs down, for sure.

Finally then, what would he say to P. J. Benedict, member of the Reform Club, earnest Liberal voter at election times, aficionado of the *New Statesman*, donor of a hundred guineas a year to Christian Action? So-so; he'd think it pretty standard, a sterotype do-gooder set of reflexes.

No, Benny the boy, the lover, the dreamer, would have had one hard, unnerving question for his yet unknown older self, a question that P. J. Benedict did not like to face, even in his imagination. You seem to have done pretty well, Benny would have said; you've been lucky and you've got quite a lot. *But what have you given back? What in God's name have you given back?*

V

How on earth could one have explained to Benny at seventeen, except by transporting him forward through time? It was all so unimaginably different, and all so long ago. Benedict went over to his writing desk and opened it with a key from the heavy bunch on his chain; stigmata of the capitalist through the generations. Under the photograph albums and the account books there was a thick volume bound in good green leather: it had been his Christmas present from Tessa. He had begun writing in it a few days after Felix broke his news; it had taken a few days for him to assimilate the shock; he had begun to write on—he opened the book—ah yes:

Friday, January 15, 1943

Today—my seventeenth birthday—I start to write this chronicle of my thoughts and experiences. I do so with very mixed feelings. It will never seem anything but naïve when I look back on it one day; yet it is the only way I know for a man to look at himself objectively.

I hope it will teach me something about myself. Above all, I hope it will help me to come to terms with the strange and troubling new turn my life has taken—which makes me tremble even now as I try to write about it. I shall really go stone bonkers if I try to contain my emotions any longer. Better by far to lay them out and dissect them; to do the job thoroughly with a sharp surgeon's knife.

It's Laura, of course. Where else but here would I dare to confess that I haven't really had a quiet moment since I first saw her more than three years ago? And how, Benny, people would say, can anyone of *your* age possibly know what it's all about? Well, I wish the people who say those things could be put through the torture I've been through. Then they'd know. I know now as certainly as I sit here that I shall never love anyone else quite as I love Laura. I don't have the experience, unfortunately, to cope with a situation quite so alarming.

I suppose I was a fool not to have guessed about Tony Hammond. After all, Gerard Weston has always been his great mentor in politics; the two of them as far as I know, form the entire communist cell in Aylsbourn. (Ilex? Who knows?) I remember so vividly in retrospect those long evenings *chez* Weston, the marvellous and incongruous vintage port circulating round the table (Gerard Weston was too sensible ever to have thrown away *that* bourgeois bequest of his father's), Felix and I spellbound by our elders, G. W. and Hammond always talking and arguing, setting the world to rights on Marxist principles, while Arabella sat watching them at the end of the table, her lovely eyes resting gently first on one, then the other. And I remember one evening as we were listening to the Mozart Clarinet Quintet round the fire that I saw a look pass between Tony and Arabella, just a glance, but they smiled at each other and I ought to have guessed.

Felix says that according to the letter he found—a recent one—his father seems to have forgiven Arabella and they are going to carry on; Hammond has promised never to come back to Aylsbourn; Gerard took it pretty well—a man of reason and all that crap—but of course he was smashed by the shock. It was his self-esteem which took the worst beating. I asked Felix why she didn't run off with Tony if she loved him; he says he doesn't know how serious it was on Tony's part and there's also Felix's little half-brother Timothy to consider. He'll be three in a few days, and though it nearly killed her having him she dotes on the dribbly little wretch. In common sense, how could she go off with Tony? Would she live in digs in ecstatic poverty just to be with him while he was still just a student? How would he react to that kind of responsibility? No, obviously, she has to stay where she is. I feel so sorry for all three of them. Felix says the only surprise to him is that Arabella stuck his father for so long.

It's now clear that Laura was merely acting as an extremely decorative and efficient decoy for this affair; a strange and not very pleasing role for her. But she did it beautifully, as she does everything.

So Tony Hammond has passed out of all our lives—presumably for good. I confess to myself that the world is just that bit greyer without him. I shall always be grateful to him for teaching me as no one else could how sweet it is to be alive. I shall remember him best the night of the great game, after we beat Shallerton.

149

Hennessy gave a party for us at his place—the Tithe House, about a mile down the Cressbrook. It's an old Queen Anne sergeant's mess of all things, but done up, of course, and one odd feature is the threshing barn, a long low building which the previous owner meant to convert into an annexe for a married couple to look after him. But he never did, so it's still in its original state. It's immensely old, and big, but still just a barn. By the time we got there Hennessy had got the place rigged up like a night club—as I *imagine* a night club—with tables and trestles and candles stuck in bottles. Mrs. H. had just got a splendid food parcel from America. She cooked us some southern fried chicken and there was a barrel of Margrave bitter which some of us drank straight for the first time. We got there at about eight-thirty after changing and having a hot bath and a shave to coax out all the aches and bruises. There were about twenty-five of us altogether. The band was already there and just as we got there Tony Hammond got up and led them into their opening number, The Original Dixieland Onestep. And whenever I hear that old tune now I feel a sense of joy so fierce that it seems to be strangling me. It crystallised the miracle of the day.

I wish it had been possible to record him that night. No, strictly I don't, because of course it would have been dreadful in retrospect; ragged I dare say, and naïve. But at the time it sounded out of this world. Tony plays with that hard, low, driving snarl that you hear when Spanier blows, and I suppose he's learnt a lot from the Spanier classics. The beauty of jazz is that it's never the same two nights in a row; each occasion is unique. That night, to me at least, he seemed to play as if it were his last night on earth.

All the girls looked enchanting that night—to me anyway—even Tess had somehow made herself look touchingly pretty—but I was waiting for Laura. She arrived at about ten, wearing that biscuit-coloured coat which always makes her look a bit like some delicious squirrel, and when she took off her coat she was wearing a dress of black and gold that seemed to glow in the candlelight. Hennessy asked her jokingly if she'd like some beer and I always remember the special little grimace with which she refused, and then, damn Hennessy, he asked her to dance and I was gibbering with jealousy.

It took me four beers to get up the courage to ask Laura to dance. I don't know how I got up or went over or what the hell

I said or how I said it, but I know she smiled and said of course, and the next thing I knew we were dancing.

She's nearly as tall as me and as I looked at her I realised once again that those astonishing green eyes are her secret; they're quite wide apart; I once read that if a woman's truly beautiful, you can put another eye between her two eyes, and absurd and mechanical though this explanation sounds, it does apply in her case. It gives a quality of serenity. I don't know. We talked about the great game and she said it was the most super thing she'd ever seen in her life. I know this sounds ridiculous in cold print, but she uses schoolboy words and somehow succeeds in making them sound madly sexy. Of course she's being ironical; just in the way that she says Gee *whiz* when anybody says something particularly pompous.

She danced with Tony Hammond when he was taking a breather between tunes and I danced with Tess and Constance. It was a fabulous party and they didn't play "The Saints" till about one—and then he took about nine extra choruses till we all went wild. It was the most un-English thing that ever happened in Aylsbourn.

That very night I ought to have realised about Tony, or seen that something was wrong, because he said he had to drive over to Shallerton to stay with friends. Why he should want to do so at that hour of the morning never occurred to us; in fact he and Arabella were borrowing a flat over there which belonged to a friend of hers, an artist. She was supposed to be in London. So Tony Hammond asked me if I'd see Laura home. Would I!

There was a monstrous moon, orange in the Aylsbourn mist, and an iron frost; the frozen puddles crackled and clouded as we stepped on them. The Cressbrook Valley was wallowing in a calm, Wellsian, lunar radiance. If the Martians had come that night, I don't think any of us would have turned a hair. The earth seemed specially blessed. You could see for many miles. Laura took my arm.

I can't record what we said. I can't remember what we talked about and if I could I wouldn't. It would break the spell.

Saturday sixteenth

I had to stop then, partly because I was so damned tired, partly because I couldn't think how to circumscribe in words the strange thing that has happened to Laura and me. I can't now.

Last Thursday evening—it was a soft, caressing, January day, with already a faint murmur of spring in the earth—the kind when Aylsbourn always looks its haunting best—I happened to have to go back to the library to get a book. It was about seven-thirty. As I walked along the High Street I realised through a chink in the blackout that the light was on and I couldn't help wondering if perhaps somebody hadn't broken in. I let myself in (Ilex has given us all a key to the front door) and tiptoed up. I confess I was pretty damn scared and there was no saliva left in my mouth by the time I got to the top of the stairs. I pushed the door slowly open. Laura was sitting there all alone, her head buried in her arms at the long table where we all work. She was crying.

I tried to mutter some excuse, but she said it didn't matter. "Please come in, Benny," she said—how can I ever forget it? —"you're the only one I could stand seeing just now."

So I sat down and said nothing for a long time, and then after a bit she dried her eyes. I thought I should be horrified to see her cry—after all no girl looks her best with red eyes—but oddly, it only accentuated her desperate wistfulness and for once I didn't feel she was unattainable at all. I felt only that I'd like somehow to protect her—whatever it was that she needed protecting from.

"Oh Benny," she said at last, "you must think me an awful idiot. It would be more sensible if I could offer you some explanation. But I can't. I'm just crying because life is so intolerably sad."

"Is it?" I said. "Usually I can hardly stop myself jumping in the air because I'm so doomy and glad to be alive."

Then she smiled at me and said: "Good old Benny. You know, I'd trust you to the ends of the earth."

"Well then," I said, "trust me to the end of the High Street; let me see you home."

She looked at me for quite a minute, and then she said, rather under her breath, yes. It was as if she'd seen me for the first time, and I truly believe that was the explanation of her strange expression.

We walked very slowly and after a while she put her arm through mine as she had that night in the Cressbrook Valley and we didn't say anything. Dr. Mackay and his wife were playing bridge with some friends. She asked me to come in—odd I'd never been back there since that terrible day in 1939—but I said I wouldn't. Instead I asked her if we couldn't perhaps meet the next day and to my astonishment she said: "Oh that would be particularly nice; I'd so much like to talk to you."

I still don't know for sure why she was crying.

Sunday 17th

Yesterday Laura and I went to London. My father had sent me a pound for my birthday; I've never had so much money in my life. Ilex and Hennessy have made us ravenous to catch up with all the books we've never read. In Charing Cross Road we searched all the small shops for anything by D. H. L. or Havelock Ellis or a new Huxley. We finished up with the Penguin *Psychopathology of Everyday Life* and also *Totem and Taboo*. Then we went into Soho and had lunch together. "Isn't it wonderful," she said, "to feel we're really grown up?"

We came back on the fast corridor train and walked up to her house from the station.

Now here is a strange thing: from that haunting encounter in the library till last night there had been no *physical* relation between us even of the most innocent sort. Yet, last night, at her gate, she suddenly put her arms round me and began to cry again. That was all that happened; nothing more; not one kiss. She is a most mysterious and enchanting creature.

There was a terrible air-raid down in the Portsmouth area tonight. Owing to the odd shape of the Downs we can see all the way there on a good night, and hear the guns and see the fires. It was unearthly and hellish, but it had a perverse beauty. It seems to heighten the intensity of each passing emotion between Laura and me.

Monday 18th January

For a year and three months now Milo and I have been committed to science—he gladly and I with dragging feet. I hope Ilex is right. We have Constance with us and little Tess, who's not very bright but is trying her damnedest to keep up with her brother. Ken and Felix are on the Arts side with Laura—who is of course a year ahead of us—and this fellow Aelfric Gates who's been shooting up through the school ever since Ilex took over.

Aelfric, it's now definite, is to be our very first guinea-pig for an Open Scholarship; he's very tall and shy, a bit like a rabbit. The fact that his father is a forester, says Felix, gives the project added piquancy for Ilex, an ardent socialist and cousin of a lord.

However, the significant thing is that, though Laura and I read different subjects, we can meet every day in the library, which is reserved now strictly as a sort of common room for the senior school. We sit there playing records and talking. Laura is now nearly eighteen and she still doesn't know what to do with her life. Sometimes she thinks she'll read medicine like her father, other days she wants to work in an antique shop. It hurts me to see this beautiful creature so lost, and there's nothing—not yet anyway—that I can do to help.

Yet this is the difference she had made to me: my actual perceptions seem keener and stronger, and sometimes I quite genuinely have difficulty to stop myself jumping in the air with excitement. I'm on a new level of experience, I seem to live in a sharper, clearer air.

Tuesday 19th January

Walking home tonight Laura said suddenly: "I'm sure my life will be very unhappy." It was quite comical, like the girl in *The Seagull* whose first remark is that she's in mourning for her life. But Laura really believes it. I said, what about her own parents; they were perfectly happy, why couldn't she be? She said no, although they looked so solid and cosy together, they hadn't always got on, and for a period when she was quite a child they'd lived apart. This was news to me. Then she made a very simple declaration of faith; I suppose any woman could subscribe to it; yet it was quite moving. She just said: "I love beautiful things; trees, water, flowers, scents, sounds, colours; I hate ugly things."

I wouldn't bother to record what appears such a banal statement, except that I am sure in her sub-conscious mind she was referring to Tony Hammond, and very deep down she doesn't think that what he did was ugly.

Wednesday 20th January

Laura came this evening to my Gramophone Society for the first time. It was, I'm afraid, not a very distinguished programme, but I shall always remember Laura curled up in the armchair. She looks so serene sometimes that I can hardly bear to look at her. Holberg Suite good. Greensleeves always drives me almost nuts with happiness; that arcadia in the dawn of everything before corruption and lust and jealousy got hold of us.

Thursday, 21st January

I find myself surprisingly attached to physics despite everything. It's entirely due to working with Milo. He's my catalyst. It sounds ridiculous (all this journal will one day) but it's true.

He *looks* like a piece of lab equipment. Maybe it's because his father teaches us physics. Milo is the thinnest man I've ever seen and his ears are at right angles to his head. He is also the funniest man I've ever met and, come to think of it, the hungriest. He eats like a bloody horse. I've seen him eat three lunches one after the other at school, including the rice pudding, and anyone who can do that has a worm.

Milo doesn't have emotions; he just works and eats. I only have to come within his magnetic field and I start working too, like a bloody fiend. He's a Jesuit among scientists. I'm sure he'll be a great scientist one day.

About being an instrument. When there's a German bomber going over, he turns his head from side to side, using those big bat-like ears like home-made radar. Then he stops with his funny bent nose pointing at a certain angle and says: "That's where the bastard is coming from."

He gets up at six every morning to work.

A really shameful incident this evening. It's one of the strangest things that has ever happened to me. I was coming out of the library when I saw Felix talking to Laura. Though I desperately wanted to stay and talk I saw the Shallerton bus coming and jumped on it without saying hello. I had the curious premonition that if I did stay there would be some bitter consequence one day. It must have seemed extremely ill-mannered. I didn't even appear to recognise Laura.

Friday 22nd January

I went with Kenneth Heppel to see *In Which We Serve*. It helped me sort out the curious and very mixed feelings I always have when condemning England to my friends. I now see that I do love England even though I object to the principles and policy of its government. This should really have dawned on me before. How could I, loving the Cressbrook Valley as I do, ever hate the country of which it's a part?

Afterwards Ken and I went into the coffee bar in the High Street. Mrs. Duncher, the Westons' daily woman, was in there and she told us that a German plane had come down low that afternoon over Bales Whitney (her village) and machine-gunned the children. No one was hurt, luckily, though there are deep grooves from its cannon shells right across the road. Mrs. Duncher said that if she were an R.A.F. pilot she would go over Germany and shoot every German man, woman, and child on sight. Neither of us agreed with her, though for rather different reasons.

Ken Heppel is a pacifist, but a real hundred per cent one. He will never fight and never change his mind. I suppose he's the nicest chap I've ever met. He's small and rather knobbly, with a working-class face. This sounds a pretty offensive thing to say, but he'd laugh.

Class is a strange business. I don't think we know much about it here in the Cressbrook Valley. We have enormous local rivalries, such as our hatred of Shallerton. The fact is that in this small community, we range through just about every social class. Tony Hammond's mother is related to the original family who built our school and who were given a peerage under George the Third. The present Lord A. is a pasty little snurdge of fourteen. However, they're authentically upper-class all right; there are members of Hammond's family buried in the churchyard four hundred years back.

Laura is upper-middle class. One of her grandparents, she says, was a famous Edwardian surgeon, another was some relation of Tennyson. Felix's father is upper-middle class, communist sub-division. Milo, I think, is middle middle.

I am lower middle, and Ken seems to be in the upper slice of the working class. His father is a mechanic, a trade unionist, militant Labour man, skilled, who spent a long time on the dole and took part in the General Strike. Mr. Heppel works at the Aylsbourn Garage; goes in each day in overalls and comes home each day covered in oil.

The Heppels live in a council house on the poor side of town up by the graveyard.

There are also people at school whose fathers are unskilled labourers. Aelfric is the cleverest; how wonderful it would be for us all if he did win an Open. I wonder what will become of us all?

But this all started because of the German machine-gunning. Ken flatly disagreed with Mrs. Duncher on straight Lansburyan grounds. I disagreed too, yet I fully accept that we can't have any squeamishness if we are to win the war. But against this, if we use their methods we lose our own ideals and become no better than they are. We have already lost. It's an appalling dilemma.

It was such a lovely night that I walked home with Ken. He asked me about Tess, and I said I thought her quite enchanting. He then said something very reckless: that he would never love anyone else quite as he loved her. He asked me if she ever talked about him. I said yes, sometimes, and always with affection. I hope that wasn't too encouraging.

We were talking so hard, and so intoxicated with our talk, that he then walked back with me, and then I walked half-way back with him. God, though, it was fun. Bed at 1.30 absolutely exhausted.

Monday 25th

We went to Miller's as usual. We always order a dozen cakes and a large pot of tea; then we can sit there from four to five-thirty. When Laura poured tea for us, still flushed from the cold air outside, her tongue between her lips in concentration, she looked suddenly very young. I felt a ridiculous tenderness for her.

She says that the bracelets she wears are a hundred years old. I watch her quick fingers as she pours the tea with fascination and awe.

This afternoon I went to hear Ilex taking them for Greek. They work in the library. It was marvellously snug up there; the fire was piled high with wood and the wind whistling outside only accentuated the sense of safety. I listened spellbound. They're reading *The Frogs*. I can't understand much but I enjoy the sound of the Greek, especially when Ilex reads a bit. We are indeed lucky to have him. Perhaps in Ilex we see the dawn of the new era in education. In his two years here he has opened our lives to the world outside the Cressbrook Valley.

After the incessant rain the Cressbrook flooded today in a way I've never seen before. The water rose to within six inches of the archtop under the Watermill and great waves were rolling across Twenty Acre. The wind, I estimate, was gale force. Laura and I stood on the parapet of the Watermill and watched the water froth and boil in the weir. Truly it was exhilarating to feel the force of that strangely warm wind in the face and to be sprayed by the fine rain.

We went to see one of the most plainly told screen stories I've ever come across: *Wake Island*. We got talking about films afterwards and decided to put this in our gallery of great pictures: *Fantasia, Gone With The Wind, In Which We Serve,* and *Citizen Kane.*

Thinking of these films for which I have a special affection reminded me of many other things which I shall always hold as beautiful. First, always, the day when I first saw Laura. Then, two poems by de la Mare: "The Listeners" and "I Sit Alone". Then, the memory of the first concert I ever heard; even though it was only the New World Symphony in Shallerton Town Hall, a thing you can always sell to a semi-literate audience.

Today I add two more things to my list. The first is a poem by D. H. Lawrence called "Snake". The other was the sky tonight as we walked home along the top of the Downs. Though it's so early and the nights are still long, it had a premonition of Spring and this despite the cold; a smoky duck-egg blue with that curious and special tang in the air; you gulp it down and it makes you feel tipsy.

A baffling experience today: Keith Margrave asked me to lunch at the Brewery. I've grown up with the smell of it. I know it will one day be Proustian in its power, wherever I am, to throw me back in my imagination to Aylsbourn. He showed me over and I saw the entire operation. They use enormous copper vats and the yeast on the top is thick and frothy, the colour of milky coffee whipped up. The one thing they fear like the plague is what they call ropey beer—it means some bug has got into the system and it can take two years to get out. When this last happened to a brewer, Margrave told me, all the others rallied round to help him out. There are still quite a lot of craftsmen working there, especially the coopers who make the barrels; but I noticed they're using electric tools now and to hell with the old hand craftsmanship. When there's a really good froth on the beer they call it a rocky head. Margrave gave me some Russian stout to try; they bottled it originally for the Czar of Russia and my God it's strong. Frankly too strong for me. We had an excellent plain lunch in the boardroom—roast beef and apple tart. There were just the two of us. He asked me how my father was and I said he seemed to be enjoying life enormously down at Salisbury. He asked me a lot of questions about my work and hopes and I told him I had no clear ideas yet.

I told Laura about it this evening and she said I am a clot; obviously Margrave wants me to come into the Brewery. I think he was just trying to be kind to the son of one of his favourite men. It is true that he has no children of his own.

Friday 29th

Ilex came into the library today when we all were sitting about. He looked upset and with reason: poor old Macpherson had had a mild stroke. Worse, though: apparently some small arteries behind his eyes are hardening and his sight is rapidly going; what little there is left mustn't be taxed. We would be able to imagine, Ilex said, better than he, what it would mean to the old fellow not to be able to read, for it is his greatest pleasure in life. Would any of us, he asked, volunteer to read to him? Needless to say every one of us, even Felix, volunteered at once. I remembered that day when we read Milton's sonnet "On His Blindness" with Macpherson. As soon as I could I got out and walked for half an hour trying to get used to the cruelty of it, but it was no good.

Monday 1st February

Tonight we had the first evening this year of the Eccentrics, a club that Hennessy formed when he first arrived. Since then we've had some intoxicating discussions: free will, free love, and this evening communism. It was the most riveting evening I've known, the intellectual excitement of it was indescribable.

The conversation turned to the civil war in Spain. Hennessy was out there, on the Republican side of course, but an ambulance driver because he's also a pacifist. He read us some short stories he wrote during that period. One or two seemed good to me. One especially was haunting: about a young wounded soldier lying in a shell-hole and whistling "Frankie and Johnny" to keep his courage up.

The news from Russia has been marvellous. Last week the German Sixth Army, commanded by von Paulus, surrendered at Stalingrad. Mr. Johnston says that one day we shall see that their scientists are every bit as good as ours. One or two of our best scientists went there before the war and came back saying this, but weren't believed. I find it hard to believe myself.

I could swallow communism more easily if it didn't mean disloyalty to England.

Later we got talking about dreams and I was fascinated to see what Laura would say about hers. But they turned out to be fairly conventional: dancing by a moonlit sea (with whom?), being chased (by whom?), falling over a cliff, and getting married (we asked her to whom but she could never see). Later I asked Ken Heppel if he thought she really didn't know and he said she certainly wasn't telling us the whole truth. I can't be sure. But this I do know: there is a lot about her I don't understand properly yet.

Then we got talking about extra-sensory perception and taboo. Mr. Johnston said there was a rational explanation for all the strange phenomena one reads about—the Versailles apparitions and Borley Rectory.

I wish there were a little more magic in the world.

Tuesday 2nd

Laura took me home this evening and we had supper with her parents. I don't know quite what they make of me; on the whole I imagine they think I'm harmless, and on the whole they're right. Dr. Mackay knows Auden; he has books all the way up the stairs of the house. He and Laura's mother used to leave every summer and travel for two months before the war; sometimes Spain or Yugoslavia or Greece, but they've been as far as North

Africa. To me they look perfectly happy; but Laura insists they parted once. Moreover, she says all married people do, metaphorically at least unless they've become complete vegetables with no feelings left. I can't accept this. My own parents were perfectly happy, I'm sure, though of course I only have my father's evidence.

The Mackays accept that there was nothing between Laura and Tony but a curious hero-disciple relationship; she has talked to me about it now. She says that Tony was often at their house because his father and the Mackays were once good friends; that Tony always treated her as a favourite younger sister, taught her tennis and all that, but there was nothing else. He used to tell her all his secrets and she got a vicarious sense of adventure from his relationship with Arabella. When I asked her what she thought about him sleeping with Arabella, she made a typical wisecrack: "Who *wouldn't?*"

Wednesday 3rd

Laura took me out riding with her this afternoon. I'm a complete peasant in this, but she's an expert. I'm bound to say it's quite agreeable when we're just moving at a very slow walk, but anything faster puts the wind up me. She has a mare, a bright chestnut, which stands just over fifteen hands and is seven years old. She's fairly well built to my layman's eye, part Welsh cob, part thoroughbred. Laura's been schooling her for two years now and jumping in local and novice competitions and small shows. She's won several prizes, though not as many as she'd have liked because Rosie (that's her mare) refuses at walls painted red. Laura has even—and this I don't like to mention too much in front of my friends—hunted.

Everything about Laura—even her bloody horse or mare or whatever it is—fascinates me. I can never hear enough.

Monday 8th February

Laura and I went to the Classic to see Jack Benny and Ann Sheridan in *George Washington Slept Here*. It was one of the funniest films we've seen in years. We walked home; there was a gibbous moon and a little mist. But again, there was an enticing touch of spring in the night air; how odd that you can feel it so early in England. I wonder what sort of summer we shall have and where we shall all be eighteen months from now? Soon it will have been four years of war. I'm unable to believe in the war in one sense. I know those poor sods are dying by the thousands in Russia, and I know all about North Africa. But here it's so damned peaceful; we're cradled in this valley and in a way the horror we see in the sky over Portsmouth only seems to accentuate our own womb-like safety. Of course it's an illusion. Once or twice already bombs have dropped in the Cressbrook Valley; usually because the pilot's lost his way; but on one famous occasion because the German captain was a Wykehamist and couldn't bear to drop his cargo—or so the papers would have us believe—on his old *alma mater*. The Germans could do with a few more Wykehamists.

Tonight nothing happened; it was utterly still and moonshot and the whole town seemed to be only just breathing. There's hardly any traffic ever now even on the main road to London. We often walk down it four abreast. I long sometimes for the day when it'll be full of old Fords bumper to bumper and heading for the sea, the families disgorging their empty packets of Smith's Crisps and Tizer bottles on us. This just shows how bad the ache for peace can be and how hallucinatory this false peace in which we're all so seductively lulled. It's often said but it's true: war brings happiness to many people, just as it brings misery and pain and death to many more. One day soon it will take us all out of the Cressbrook Valley. I go for my medical this April. I shall be seventeen and a quarter then, the minimum age to volunteer for aircrew. I've never had any doubts or misgivings about this.

Tuesday 9th

We went to the market at lunch-time today; Laura wanted to buy a rabbit for a small male cousin of hers. I'm bound to admit here privately that though I should hate to work on the land I do get a kick from the bucolic dung-imbued ambience of the place. We went into the "Wheatsheaf" for lunch and bumped into Mr. Varley. He's looking almost mauve now—much worse than the small veins on Margrave's face—and really not terribly healthy. Also, I noticed that there are some grey streaks in his glossy black hair. I introduced him to Laura and he treated her with almost exaggerated gallantry. He insisted on buying us both a shandy. Afterwards I asked Laura what she thought of him. She said he had the particular enticement that all former criminals had. I asked her what on earth she meant and she said that she had no evidence that he'd been inside at all, it was just a hunch. How astonishing if she were right! She usually is.

Afterwards we strolled through the market again, inspecting the porkers, the cutters, the baconers, the capons, the cockerels and rough-plucked hens. Laura found two charming little rabbits.

This afternoon I did my best afternoon's work in chemistry this term: two whole volumetrics (oxalic and H_2O_2 with $KMNO_4$) and preparation for a third (iron in ferric alum).

Wednesday 10th

Today chemistry was dull, so in the afternoon I eaves-dropped on Hennessy's class in American History. I truly believe he could make any damned subject on earth interesting. He has a long lean face, thick lips, slightly protruding blue eyes and a bow tie. There are still occasional suggestions that he and Ilex have a homosexual relationship. It may be that they do but only, I think, a Platonic one.

I looked over Laura's shoulder and saw that he had given her an alpha minus query minus. I've never heard of such a complicated mark before. I don't quite know what it means but sometimes I wish science were amenable to that sort of imprecision.

Hennessy came to the Gramophone Society tonight—"Love of Three Oranges" was best—and stayed on afterwards telling us about the Fabians and particularly the Wells-Belloc literary battle (Mr. Belloc objects and Mr. Belloc still objects). Also the Chesterton-Shaw debate, G.K.'s weekly, and the Belloc-Selfridge debate. All this was new and fascinating to us. We got on to Freud and H. said Freud was over-inclined to attribute everything to sex; recommended us to read Adler as a corrective, but warned us that he went to the other extreme and attributed everything to desire for power. I'm pretty sure F. is right in saying that this lust for power is basically sexual.

Laura says her father takes a cool view of Freud. He says that his case histories give an exceptionally biased view because many of his clients were bourgeois Jewish women brought up in a rigid and conventional framework—hence all the neuroses and repressions.

Pretty well an ideal day. My leg is still painful from last week's football injury so they told me not to play today. Instead I went alone to London on the fast train to Waterloo. I walked—or rather sped—up Villiers Street and Charing Cross Road and bought a Pelican by Waddington called *The Scientific Attitude*. In Foyles I made two fairly routine purchases: *Opera*, a Pelican, and Joad's *Guide to Modern Wickedness*. I walked for half an hour trying to find this new gramophone exchange place, but no luck. I cursed myself for not making a note of the address. In Villiers Street on my way back I was disturbed by what I thought was the slow, dull beat of dive-bombers; it turned out to be just the air-conditioning plant of the underground.

I got home at seven and found to my great delight that my father would be here tomorrow on his way north to a new posting.

After supper Tessa, Joanna, Milo and I played Louis Armstrong records. T. and J. find his voice coarse and a little shocking, but we tried to explain to them the feeling he puts into even the most corny little piece. I really believe we have no right to run down negro music; especially not right now, when you look at what white civilisation has achieved in central Europe.

I looked at Joanna while the music was playing and thought to myself that though she will never be a beauty she will appeal to somebody. When you're not talking to her and she doesn't realise you're looking, she looks sometimes dreadfully wistful. How our faces give us away if we don't keep our guard up! She has a pleasing shape too. Milo is rather coarse about her pectoral development; she pretends to resent it, but I think secretly she quite enjoys it. Poor little Tess will have to wait another year or two before we start making fun of her on that score.

My father came in time for lunch. He looked marvellous; absurdly young and good-looking in his second-lieutenant's uniform. There's no doubt that he's one of the men who blossom in war. To him it's just a rather good game, with strict rules of conduct to be adhered to on both sides. However, he is not such an idealist that he has any illusions about the Germans—how could he after spending three years as a prisoner in their hands? He talked amusingly about the Army and the astonishing people he meets. We put him on the train at five with several jars of home-made jam in his bag. Tessa said this evening that as he was so attractive it was a shame he didn't marry again. I had never thought about this before, and now she's raised the possibility I find it distressing.

Today Milo nearly killed himself. He added thio-cyanate to hot dilute acid and collapsed from HCN fumes.

Although Ilex doesn't understand science he realises its importance. He's badgered the county into converting some old workshops into a new laboratory. Considering it's wartime, this is an achievement; but I'm sure they're right. One day it will pay dividends. We move in next week—quick work considering they began work only a month ago.

Frankly the leg is all right, but I played truant from football because Laura wanted to go to London. We got there early and booked seats for the evening performance at the Saville. Then went to the Shaftesbury Avenue Gram. Exchange and bought the Italian Symphony. But we couldn't get "Bach Goes to Town"—our new favourite. We lunched in Glasshouse Street on Spaghetti Bolognese and half a carafe of ordinaire. It cost six and two. Laura went halves.

When we came out it was foggy. It was strange to walk across Waterloo Bridge and hear the rumbling of the engines without being able to see them. Laura said Limbo would be just like that.

When I'd said good night to Laura I waited under her window until her light came on. She sat at her dressing-table and brushed her hair for about ten minutes. Then she did her nails or something. Then she got up and drew the curtains and I waited for another ten minutes before the light went out. I wasn't—at least I hope I'm not—becoming a voyeur: but I just can't take my eyes off her.

Milo wanted to go down to the High Street this afternoon so I said I'd go too. He didn't look very pleased and I couldn't understand why, for he was only going to buy chocolate with his sisters' ration cards—the hungry-gutted bastard. Afterwards he wanted to go into the library to hear some records. He's an odd fish. He seems cold sometimes, yet he was moved almost to tears by "Slaughter on Tenth Avenue". We jawed about jazz and philosophy. I told him about Louis Macneice, whom I've just discovered, and he threw bits of Whitehead at me.

At about six-thirty all became clear: the Pepperpot appeared wearing a lot too much lipstick and eyeshadow. She wore a tight blouse and a skirt with a slit of about four inches in the side. I don't know what Milo sees in her and nor do his sisters. I decided to beat it, but they said to stay a bit and play a few more records. This gave me a good chance to gauge her mentality. I put on a Goodman record and she said it was terrific—whose record was it? I said it was hers. She was quite gobstruck; apparently there's a favourite of hers on the other side and she had never turned it over. Soon after that I left them to it.

Milo came in at about ten-thirty looking sheepish and gave Tess his handkerchief to wash. It was covered with the Pepperpot's vile lipstick. However, if it makes him happy.

Working late in the lab tonight I did a colorimetric (Lovibond comparator) for iron which Constance checked. We got exactly the same result. This shows that, by co-incidence, we have the same red colour sensitivity. It sounds incongruous, but I felt in the lab this evening as if I belonged there, and was not just an intruder.

On the way home Constance asked me about Laura; was she missing Tony? I said I thought so; she had a card at Christmas, otherwise the only news we've had came when Ilex told us he'd had a university trial. He didn't make it this year, but he's almost bound to next. I asked C. what she thought of Laura. Constance made a very odd reply. She said: "Laura has a greater capacity for disaster than any other girl I know."

Tuesday 23rd

I'm liking calculus a lot lately. Milo is more persistent than I am at it though. If he doesn't understand something he goes on and on asking until he's got it right. He has an absolute fixation about space flight. He spends all his spare time designing rockets. They frighten me. I am sure they will kill a lot of people before we eventually hit the moon; but Milo's the sort of moonstruck fool who would volunteer to go the first time. In a weird way, I think he would like to die in outer space.

Saturday 27th

Went into Shallerton early this morning to buy Felix a present for his seventeenth birthday; finally settled on John Buchan's *Augustus*. I think Felix and Augustus have this in common at least: neither would ever let any woman deflect him. This evening there was a little party *chez* Weston. Arabella is looking perceptibly older, her adventure seems to have coarsened her face slightly and she smokes about forty cigarettes a day; there is a nicotine stain on her charming little fingers which I hate to see. But she is terrific fun still and the most outspoken woman for sure in the Cressbrook. She sat next to me in a corner and talked about her son, Timothy. She seemed to glow with the excitement of having made him; in fact she said several times: "He's very well *made*—all legs at the moment but the head is very fine"— rather as though he were a piece of sculpture.

We discovered an astonishing thing tonight—she is only *twenty-four*. Constance said rather coarsely that this was no doubt the reason for Tony Hammond; that Gerard was getting past it. He looked old tonight, though he's only just fifty. He drank a lot and got very excited about Russia. Now we could see, he exclaimed, whether they were serfs or not; would serfs have defended Stalingrad like that? He and Arabella appear to get on, but if you watch carefully you do notice little asperities between them sometimes. That sort of thing must leave its mark, even on men of reason.

Felix was in fine form. He said he would fight in this war, but only because it's the safest thing to do. The best plan, he explained to us, is to be a staff officer fifty miles behind the front lines billeted in a château well stocked with Veuve Cliquot and a lonely châtelaine. Gerard enjoyed this; he's proud of Felix.

Everything comes easily to Felix. He should get a Classical Open to Oxford. He's the most *mature* friend I have. He doesn't carve me up quite the way he once did, though, I've got used to him and can carry on the debate with him on more or less equal terms. Constance says he will come to a sticky end. She is a profoundly pessimistic girl. In this way, she and Felix have a lot in common, but they don't get on well.

Later in the evening Arabella took me up to show me her son. He lay sleeping peacefully and I must say it was comical to see how like Felix he was, and yet not so at the same time; there were hints of Arabella in his little face. Arabella said something significant: "He makes it all worth while." All what?

Sunday 28th

I'm on edge, my nerves seem to be stretched taut like violin strings. For instance, I went into the lab to do some ferric reduction titrations this evening; it was very peaceful and I could work really fast, completing six titrations. Yet the hissing of the acid down the sink made my skin crawl, I don't know why. I feel as if something enormous is going to happen any moment. The tension is about as much as I can take.

Thursday 4th March

We went to the Classic tonight and saw the Glenn Miller film *Orchestra Wives*. Though of course many of my friends say Miller is corn, I suspect his music will give us all a Proustian throwback one day, and some of the corn—"At Last", "Perfidia", "American Patrol"—is charming in a light way. All sorts of dance tunes are threading themselves through our lives. I don't think I'll ever forget dancing with Laura to Artie Shaw's "Begin the Beguine"; it's a tune that seems to have been playing all through my young life. The same can be said of "That Old Black Magic". Very occasionally, as in "Smoke Gets In Your Eyes", the words rise above the usually abysmal level of banality. I dare say some earnest young American graduate will write a thesis about this in 2043.

At the Eccentrics tonight we discussed what education should be like after the war. Afterwards we played records till midnight. Felix had a good story for us: apparently a girl who was at school a few years ahead of us, called Nancy Foster, got married in Aylsbourn on Saturday. She's twenty and was a shorthand-typist in Shallerton; she left school at fifteen. Everything went well till the reception when her boss, who was giving her away, made a very complimentary speech about her. She then burst into tears and said she really loved him! (That is, the boss.) Confusion all round. Her friends managed to calm her down and finally she went off rather tearfully with her groom.

Laura then made a very curious remark. She said she was sure that many girls had similar ambiguities in their emotions when they married; the only difference about this girl was her appalling frankness. Constance said it was stories like this which convinced her she would never marry. Yet how strange women are: before the evening was out she said quite distinctly: "*When I'm married* I shall expect my husband to have a horse and a car." What sort of sense is that?

Felix remarked that forty was the perfect age for a man to marry. When pressed to tell us how old he thought his wife would then be he replied cryptically: "Either seventeen or forty-three."

I remarked how dreadful it must have been for the groom. Ken said what about the boss—he wouldn't feel too comfortable. Constance said on the contrary: for the boss it must have been a delightful experience—a public declaration of undying love from a woman and absolutely no obligation to do anything about it.

Milo, of course, brought the conversation down to earth by enquiring how they would have got on during their wedding night. Constance drily remarked: "Probably as well as most people." A very interesting discussion then developed about whether one ought to sleep with one's fiancée before marriage. Every single person there said yes, including Hennessy. Felix tried to pull my leg. He said he was disappointed—how could I seriously claim to be a romantic if I took this view? I said I thought far too much about the real importance of sex ever to entrust a delicate and important initiation of that sort to the hazards and leering, back-slapping, boozy heartiness of the wedding day.

I got some very heartening support from Laura. She said she found the ritual of a traditional marriage service nauseating—all that white, symbol of virginity, and fertility-rite stuff with the rice and the shoes. She said that when she wanted to be deflowered no one would know about it. Tess said what a terrible waste; Laura would look terrific in white. Then, exasperatingly, Laura added absent-mindedly that she might get married in white after all if she had a really fabulous dress. How the devil can one keep pace with a woman's mind from one moment to the next?

Thursday 25th March

A fabulous film at the Classic, *The Magnificent Ambersons*, produced by the one and only Orson Welles. I said to Laura afterwards that it must be both marvellous and terrifying to have to struggle with a talent as Welles did; it would be a bit like having a Rolls-Royce engine in an Austin Seven, the enormous power of the talent would almost shake itself out of one's body with impatience. Then I asked her if she thought anyone we'd ever met had a touch of original creativeness, might, in fact, come to anything in the outside world. I was thinking of Tony of course. I shouldn't have asked her, because she could only give an evasive reply. But I wasn't expecting what she did say: "You're the only one we shall ever hear of again." For once, she's wrong.

Friday 9th April

I've got back from my R.A.F. medical. Everything went fine on the first day—I held up the mercury in the barometer and all that; but during the eyesight tests I could see they were worried about something. Finally the M.O. asked if I'd had a bash in the eye. I said yes—what else could I do? He said that though it was only very slight, one of my muscles didn't respond properly and I could never therefore be passed as a pilot. I could be a navigator—what about it? I was desperately disappointed for a moment; but even in the middle of my despair I remembered thinking that I must never tell anyone why I'd failed in case it ever got back to Ken Heppel—who would never forgive himself.

And then something Ken had said came back to me and made it easier to bear. He had been talking only a few days before about the emotive propaganda effect of R.A.F. uniform. Suppose, Ken said, we were a really adult society, and that we had decided that for survival's sake we had to fight. Then the actual killers should be chosen by lot and dressed in a drab prison-grey uniform which buttoned up tight at the neck, rather like a Chinese peasant's; and this would be a perpetual reminder to them and anyone else of the evil thing they were being forced to do. For what is the reality of the matter? These glamorous R.A.F. bomber boys with their wings and gongs *are* killers, when all is said; their job necessarily involves eviscerating women, ripping little children limb from limb (how horrible even to write it down—but they actually have to do it). But by the accidental separation of cause and effect—you can't actually see your bombs gouge people's entrails out down below—you can maintain the illusion of romance. Of course that's why some men prefer being fighter pilots. But whether it's really any better morally to fill another pilot with cannon shells—rather than some German down below—I don't know. Anyway, I suddenly saw how little it mattered what I did in the war.

The difference between Ken and me is that I, while acknowledging the horror, believe it must be done to defeat a worse horror. He won't have anything to do with it. He is in for a rough time, I'm afraid.

I said yes to being a navigator, and already I'm rationalising my disappointment. After all, the pilot is only the bloody driver. The navigator is the real brains of the outfit. But the moral responsibility is exactly the same.

Mr. Varley died this week, after a heart attack, and I went to his funeral this morning. I don't really know why. I wore a rose in my buttonhole—one of the yellow ones that came from his garden and which he wore every day through the summer. It was just a little hopeless gesture of defiance from life to death. The most harrowing moment came when the earth was thrown into the open grave; Madam (her name I've discovered is Mrs. Fitzherbert and she's a widow; there's not much doubt what she was to Varley) cried pitifully. There were a lot of O.V.'s there.

Most of them looked like car salesmen, but there was a fair sprinkling of offensive-looking R.A.S.C. subalterns.

Varley was in many ways a ridiculous person and yet I had a lot of affection for him. The world is a little bit greyer without him.

There was a fascinating obituary notice in the *Cressbrook Journal* today. It turns out that he *was* a regimental sergeant-major. He came out after the 1914-1918 war and got a job as a physical training instructor in a Borstal, before buying Valhalla on the never-never. Laura—as usual—was astonishingly prescient about him. He wasn't of course, a criminal, but he had lived with naughty boys. It's as if she's got a crystal ball she can nearly, but not quite, read.

Saturday 24th July 1943

Laura and I went to London to see the ballet at the Lyric. We were early so we walked across Hungerford Bridge. *Twelfth Night* was superb; in fact I'm afraid that in the terrific heat *Les Sylphides* was a bit of an anti-climax. Afterwards we went into the Coventry Street Corner House and ate waffles. Then a most astonishing thing happened. Suddenly Laura put her hand on mine. I looked up—needless to say I was just taking a mouthful of waffle—and saw her looking at me as if she'd never seen me before. "Benny," she said, "why are you so sweet to me?" I muttered something. "No," she insisted gently. "Tell me. Why are you always so good to me when I never give you any affection in return?" I began to say I didn't want anything, that to be with her was all I needed. But I couldn't express myself. And then the words came tumbling out and I told her all about that first time I'd seen her and how I'd loved her ever since and would never love anyone else in quite the same way.

All this in Lyon's Corner House—of all the places in the world to choose!

She didn't answer, but kept staring at me with a sort of gentle astonishment; she seemed to be searching every line in my face to see if I was joking. I don't think she could take it in at first. Then she put both her hands on mine as it lay on the table and said softly: "Hello, Benny." With those absolutely typical yet quite unexpected words, she committed herself to me. I think we have a love affair on our hands.

This morning we met early and went for a walk. I wanted to show her the exact route I'd taken that day, which changed my life. As we walked I even told her about the examination fiasco, a thing I thought I'd never tell another soul. At last we got to my secret view. It was a marvellous summer morning, and we sat in the grass looking out towards Oakhanger. It was absolutely still. Then she said: "Benny, why have you never kissed me?" And I said: "Because I never thought you wanted me to." Then she said: "Kiss me now." I could hardly believe it wasn't a dream. For a moment or two I couldn't have obeyed if I'd tried; my mind seemed to have ceased to relay messages to my body, so great was my surprise. Then I half turned and I remembered her face was very grave, just as Hammond's was at the beginning of that game, and in an absurd way the analogy is real, for to her it was the beginning of a more serious adventure. And then— how else can I put it down, except in plain words?—I found that I was kissing her, and her bare arms came slowly round my neck and drew me softly down into the grass.

It was quite different from anything I've ever experienced; neither quite innocent like Tess, nor wild like Constance. Instead, with unhurried gentleness, she let her kisses wander all over my face, as if she were on a voyage of exploration: she kissed my eyes, my throat, even my hair. In a little while I began to respond and in a few moments we were both trembling with the unspoken promises made by our silent lips.

Soon we drew apart and lay staring up into the sky, only our hands touching, for inexperienced as we both were, we could read the message in those kisses and we were both reluctant that we should in any way be hurried. We talked drowsily, like exhausted lovers instead of two young innocents brushed by the finger-tips of desire, and we had no wish for any other expression of our love. For that was what it was. If Laura never loves me again, I know she loved me just then.

I won't try to describe the rest of the day; as far as the world is concerned we passed it in a quite ordinary way; but every word and every look between us was on two levels of meaning: the world's and our own. We parted quite early because we were both incapable of any more emotion, and besides, by doing so, we will make the next day seem to come more quickly.

173

We're into our last year. Most of our futures seem fixed. Milo has his place at Cambridge next autumn, Felix at Oxford, though he will go into the Army first, Ken Heppel will almost certainly get into Southampton when he comes out of the mines. I'm definitely fixed at Imperial College, London. Laura is going to Art School next autumn, probably in Shallerton; Joanna is going to King's College, London, and Tess is doing a secretarial course. Poor little sweetheart, even Ilex couldn't win her a scholarship. Constance, cleverest of all our girls, has got into Somerville. Our great triumph is Aelfric Gates, who won an Open at Oxford right on schedule. Next summer Ilex will have fourteen university places, eleven at Oxford and Cambridge. You can't begrudge the man his triumph; already they're calling it The Aylsbourn Experiment and odd-looking men from the Ministry of Education are coming down to give us the once-over.

Wednesday 9th February

The snow's been falling steadily in the Cressbrook Valley for two days and tonight we were out tobogganing. Milo has a sledge and we took it in turns to whiz down the side of the Downs in it two at a time. I took Laura down with me; she lay on top of me and with her arms round my neck was quite safe as we streaked to the bottom. We all felt like children again.

Thursday 10th February

Poor little Tess was rushed to hospital for an emergency operation today; how quickly happiness can go sour. It was acute appendicitis. However, thank God, it seems tonight she's going to be all right. The thing that touches me most, though, is that she asked for me first when she came round. The fact that she was so near death brought the old enemy into perspective for me again; it would be so bloody *annoying* to die now. By way of an amulet, I think I should make a note now of the people to whom I owe thanks; for since I can pay no allegiance to God I must offer my gratitude to my fellow-men and women. First then, to Laura, for the gift of love; next to my father, for showing me what is good; then my friends—Felix for shattering my dreams; Milo for giving me so many laughs; Ken for understanding me better than anyone else in the world; Tess for her tenderness; Joanna for her wistfulness; Constance for kissing me the way she did; Macpherson for teaching me what language is; Ilex for making me reach further than I thought I could; Hennessy for making me think; Arabella for showing me what a woman is; poor old Varley for teaching me how to put up with the world as it is; Mrs. Johnston for feeding me; Miller's teashop for harbouring me; the Cressbrook Valley for filling my lungs every day with its good air; Hammond for teaching me how sweet it is to be alive.

Wednesday 17th May 1944

Each day I grow more disillusioned with this course of science I so recklessly embarked on. It's all my own fault, I quite concede that; but I shall never be better than mediocre at it. The day of reckoning is very close now.

Friday 23rd June 1944

Mr. and Mrs. Johnston have gone to Bournemouth for a few days. Needless to say, this suggested to Milo that we ought to have what he calls an uninhibited party. It's to be tomorrow night; the girls are making some food and we're laying in a barrel of best Margrave bitter. How delightful to be eighteen, free, idle and in love on a summer's day!

Sunday 25th June, 1944

Well, it was quite a party. We played a lot of records and danced to them: innocuous tunes like Tommy Dorsey's "I'll Be Seeing You", Glenn Miller's "Perfidia", Artie Shaw's "Begin the Beguine". Then we had some supper and sat around talking. Later, Milo put some Beethoven sonatas on the radiogram and turned the sound up to full bore. It's amazing how we never really listen to music when it's played as a sort of teashop noise; just as coffee is best strong, so good music is best loud. Then we turned off the lights and drew back the curtains. The garden was drenched in moonlight. The girls curled up on our laps. We drowned in the music. It seemed to lift one's imagination right out of its physical mountings, to use a rather crude analogy, and

175

sent it floating away over the Cressbrook Valley. It was the kind of evening where when you wanted to speak you couldn't because the music had been quietly strangling you. Later we played the Brahms First Quartet—the thing it took him four years to write—and what an impact that has! You feel him carrying you along with absolute certainty. You feel that the music has been chiselled and hammered and polished till it has a hard glowing brilliant perfection. I can't imagine that life has any keener pleasure to offer.

No one noticed the time until suddenly Ken said, "Look—it's dawn" and we saw that very delicate, pale hint of light in the sky. Then we stretched ourselves and went out into the garden where it was very cool. There was a light dew on, the grass and Laura cut a yellow rose off one of Mr. Johnston's trees with a pair of sewing scissors and put it in my button-hole. She knows I love them—a trait I picked up from old Varley. It was a very young bud and still closed, and there were little drops of dew glistening on it. I don't think there will ever be another night quite like it.

Sunday 17th July

I've not tried to write down everything that's happened between Laura and me because I don't happen to have the necessary intellectual equipment to crystallise it in words; the dream is corrupted as the pen touches the paper. Also, I've no wish to record all the moods and subtleties and complexions and shadows of our love-affair because one day it may make bitter reading; I mean that everything else must seem an anti-climax. What I will do is transcribe in this journal one of her many notes to me; I am tearing all the rest in little pieces. They would never be understood by anybody else, and might not even be understood even by me one day; there is a lively possibility that the man who would read them in twenty years would be a stranger to me.

But I can't resist the temptation to transcribe just one note. The sight of her handwiting is the keenest pleasure I know. *My* name in *her* writing—P. J. Benedict Esquire indeed! And inside I found a casual prose sonnet:

Benny my dear:

I called to see you but found no one in. You were with the

boys up in Felix's room. The light was on as we walked up from the station and I heard music. Needless to say, you were playing one of those very old Armstrong's. I felt warm and safe to think of you there. But, unexpectedly, I was too shy to knock. I should have wanted you to myself. London was awful without you. It was one of those female days: shopping and the hairdresser. My father was at a medical conference at the War Office; mama and I went to a place in Soho called Le Jardin des Gourmets; apparently papa used to take her there when they were, to use that blushmaking old word, courting. I looked at it with astonishment and a sort of prenatal recognition. I can't imagine them holding hands there any more than I can imagine—but you know what I'm trying to say. Benny, dear, I'm in bed now, in a demure white cotton night-dress (what a provoking little bitch I am) and I love you. Please take one special kiss to bed with you from me.

Laura.

Friday 21st July

Ilex called us all into his study—it was the last day of term and our last day there—and gave us all a glass of sherry. He then made a very touching little speech—that is to say he was touched, indeed near to tears. He said it had been the happiest three years of his life, that we had all done him proud (he didn't put it like that of course), and that he couldn't imagine life ever offering him any greater reward. Then came the usual drill about keeping in touch and coming to see him which old Varley gave. He didn't offer to pay our debts, but he did give the impression he'd be only too pleased to act as our Father Confessor. There've been hints for some time that he's going over to Rome.

Ilex is a man whose faults are written large all over his face, but he is a remarkable man all the same and we're lucky to have known him. Hennessy is leaving this term and going to America. He's the one I shall miss most of all.

And now we have three months left—three delicious months with nothing to do, no responsibilities, no duties, twenty-four hours in each day our own—before the world scoops us up and takes us out of the Cressbrook Valley.

VI

THE SUMMER of 1944 was, then, the last that Benedict and
his friends were to spend together. It was unique for this alone,
but it was memorable in several other senses. It was, first, a
beautiful summer; not as good as 1940 but full of warmth and a
new quality—hope. There was a sense of excitement in the world
which had permeated even Aylsbourn. The allied armies had
invaded Europe early that June and each day the boys would
work out the advances on a large map with pins and coloured
string. It was a timeless summer; they had absolutely nothing
to do but wait. For its differing reasons the world did not require
them till autumn; there was a formless vista of weeks stretching
ahead of them without care. No one expected anything of them
till then. They had little money, but they had something far more
precious: freedom.

The routine for each day, therefore, was exactly like the one
before. Benedict and Milo would get up at about eight, and
read the morning papers over a long lazy breakfast. Then they
would stroll round to fetch Ken Heppel from the council estate
near the cemetery, and on down to the High Street to collect
Felix, who was generally still in his dressing-gown. Then they
would move on at a leisurely pace to Miller's where Joanna and
Tess, Laura and Constance, would be having coffee. They would
sit and talk idly for an hour and a half. Then they would drift
down the High Street, stopping to buy a record or two, the ante-
diluvian shiny black heavy ones which used to spin at seventy-
eight revolutions per minute.

Then they would meander on up to the market square and
into the "Wheatsheaf" for bitter beer. They all drank this, girls
as well. Even Laura had grown to like it. Then they would eat
lunch in the "Wheatsheaf's" back room. It cost in those days one
and ninepence: meat and two veg. and a roly-poly pudding.
After that they would walk out of Aylsbourn, each day by a
different footpath. Usually they followed the Cressbrook. There
was a compelling quality about its crystalline clarity and pure-
ness; it was hypnotic to lie by it and let one's hand trail in the

cold, clean water. The pebbles were smooth and golden and the cress rippled in the tide. Sometimes they would swim where the Cressbrook widened out into the Mill Pond. Then they would lie on the bank, read the latest Koestler novel or a bit of Auden, gossip, lie on their backs, chase each other, sleep.

Sometimes they would take a portable gramophone up into the Aylsbourn Downs and play the latest Frank Sinatra or Glenn Miller records—never anything more complicated. Somehow, the one tune which seemed to emerge for Benedict as the theme song of that interlude was Tommy Dorsey's "I'll Be Seeing You". Though the lyric was naïve, it seemed to sum up their subcutaneous emotions, and the tune, though simple, was hard to forget. Often Benedict found himself humming it, as he strolled along the sun-poached pavements on those idle days of interregnum. It seemed to carry overtones of their own transitory situation:

> In a small café,
> The park across the way,
> The children's carousel,
> The chestnut tree,
> The wishing well.

And time without number, he danced to that hissing old record with Laura.

In the evenings they would go to the Classic, hoping always to see another *Citizen Kane* or *Le Jour Se Lève*, and even if—as nearly always happened—they were disappointed, it was part of the ritual of their life. After that, they would go to Felix's room and play poker tirelessly till one in the morning.

There was only one troubling interlude during those three months: Constance left suddenly to get a job at Portsmouth. No one ever got to the bottom of it; true, her guardian, Mr. Hayley, had become ill and had been obliged to retire from the Post Office; what puzzled her friends was that her parents, wherever they were, seemed to take no interest. Ilex was known to be furious. His cleverest girl not taking up a place at Somerville! There were angry exchanges between him and the Hayleys and it was still not quite clear what was to happen when she departed abruptly for Portsmouth one day in September.

They all went to see her off at the station. She looked adult and soignée in a tweed suit and appeared quite unaffected. They stood about not knowing quite what to say while the train made its preparations to go. Benedict began to feel a sense of sadness, bitterness and waste welling up inside him. He took Constance by the arm and walked a few paces with her.

"Constance, please, isn't there anything we can do?"

"Nothing, Benny."

"But you can't just give up a chance like that."

"I have no choice."

"But you had such great dreams—to be a new Madame Curie!"

"All dreams have to end, Benny, as you'll find out one day."

"Promise at any rate you'll keep in touch. Write to us."

"I can't promise. I may."

The guard's whistle blew. Her three pathetically small suitcases were stowed aboard. They all kissed her goodbye. As the train drew out, she didn't wave; in fact she turned her face away from them.

"You know," said Laura as they walked home, "it's a funny thing, but I never saw Constance cry before."

Mr. Benedict came home for a short leave late in September and stayed for forty-eight hours at the "Wheatsheaf." He still looked full of beans. Benedict took Laura to meet him at tea-time on Sunday. He seemed painfully shy at first, then realised she was on his side and talked too much, but was full of gaiety and hope. His cadets, he claimed, were the finest in England, far finer even than the young officers in the first war—fitter and more articulate and less snobbish. His mild blue eyes sparkled as he talked; Benedict found himself hoping, to his shame, that no bloody woman would snap him up; his father was too precious to share.

Laura came to the station with them. On the platform father and son disappeared into the Gentlemen's; it was not a very private place but it had to do. They stood side by side.

"Do you like her, Pop?"

"Of course I do. She's a sweet girl. Is it serious?"

"Yes."

A fleeting expression of loss and pain passed over his father's usually untroubled outdoor face. Then it cleared and he smiled.

"She'll be a credit to you, son. You have my blessing."

He waved vigorously till his train was out of view. Then Laura said: "What a poppet. If you ever desert me, there'll always be your father."

The dates fell close together: Ken Heppel had to leave for Durham on October fourth, Benedict went to his Aircrew Receiving Centre on the sixth, Felix reported to Aldershot on the seventh, Milo went to Cambridge on the ninth. They decided, therefore, that they would spend their final evening, October third, together.

They began to drink punctually at six in the "Thorn and Sceptre". The Margrave bitter seemed never to have tasted better. It was limpid and full of life. They sat on wooden trestles down each side of one of the pub's wooden tables, talking and laughing uproariously between long swigs. By eight o'clock they had finished four pints each. But they felt no effect whatsoever, until they went outside. Then the Aylsbourn air took its sudden, heady effect, and they were drunk.

It was a moonless night, but every star was in the sky. Benedict gulped in some deep breaths. "Tell me," he asked them, "what is it about this air?"

"It's the manure that excites you," explained Felix. "A simple case of coprophilia."

"It's the malt from the brewery," suggested Milo.

"It's the hay," Ken suggested. "Or maybe it's the Cressbrook. All rivers have their own smell."

"I think it's the wood," Benedict said absently. "All trees breathe. They give off a sort of sweetness when they're heavy with fruit."

"Or maybe," said Ken, "it's all these things."

"Whatever it is," Benedict said, "I shall never find it again."

"Any small country town could smell like this," Felix said.

"But not to me," Benedict replied.

"Hey," said Milo, "I want to show you all something. Have you ever tried spinning a dustbin lid? I've discovered quite by chance that if you throw one with a really good flick it'll spin for miles. It's something to do with its aerodynamic shape. Watch this."

He lifted the lid quietly off the dustbin outside the "Thorn and Sceptre". He leaned back, like a young Greek athlete, then whipped it away from his body with a quick horizontal movement. He was quite right. The lid rose, as if carried by a gust of warm rising air, and sailed away into the dusk, and out of sight. They waited for what seemed a month. At last there came a far off crash and tinkle of glass.

Doubled up with laughter, they trotted away. They worked their way steadily from one end of Aylsbourn to the other, drinking half a pint of beer in each pub, and skimming dustbin lids away into the night between drinks. By ten o'clock they were gloriously and uproariously tight, with the sort of euphoria which only very young men, with untried livers as clean as a whistle, could hope to achieve. Finally they found themselves marching out of Aylsbourn with a dustbin lid apiece, held in front like a breastplate, singing *Il Toreador* rather incongruously at the top of their voices. After half a mile a workmen's hut came into view. The road was up and the excavation was protected by a cluster of red lanterns. "Hey!" said Milo. "I've got a better idea. Bring one of these lamps each."

He picked up one of the red lamps in his long ape-like arms and trotted over the grass with it. The others followed. They were past caring. Milo led the way down to the edge of the Cressbrook. It flowed sweetly under them in the dark, chinking and muttering as it always did.

Milo leaned over and gently lowered the lid horizontally on to the water so that it floated like a shallow boat. Then he stood the red lamp on it and pushed the little home-made lightship out into the middle of the stream. It twirled once or twice, then set off downstream in the current, the lamp borne along erect on its float. The others followed suit. Soon the four red lamps were bobbing down the Cressbrook in line astern. They made a curious and beautiful sight.

The friends followed, stopping now and then to double up with laughter at Milo's bizarre device. In half a mile the Cressbrook flowed out into a much larger river and as they saw their brave red lamps swept out into the stronger current they became silent. They watched without speaking until the little pools of light faded from sight.

"By morning," said Milo at last, "they'll be out to sea."

It was Benedict's turn to tap on the wall.
"Is that you, Benny?"
"Yes. I'm drunk. Can I talk to you?"
"Of course."

He stumbled and nearly fell over as he came in.

"Oh sod it!"

"How much have you had, Benny?"

"I don't know. About eight pints I suppose."

"How can you hold so much?"

"You can't. We were all sick. Except Felix, and he was looking pretty green when we left him."

"Is Milo all right?"

"He was when we'd put his head in the horse trough. By the way, Tess, if you ever see the Pepperpot again, say it was all our fault."

"What was?"

"Well really it was Milo's idea. We posted sixpennorth of fish and chips through her parent's letter box."

"Oh Benny!"

"And we—oh Tess, never mind what we did. The room's spinning round and I can't see you."

"Lie back then."

She held him gently and felt his forehead with her hand. "Gosh you're hot!"

"Lay your sleeping head my love," murmured Benedict, "human on my faithless arm."

"I'll never be faithless to you, Benny. You'll always be someone special in my life. No one will ever quite replace you."

"I know that, Tess. Tess—I can only tell you this because I'm drunk and I can't see your face. . . ."

"Tell me, Benny."

"I'm afraid. Afraid to leave you and your parents and my friends. And to leave Laura. Tess, I'm afraid of leaving the Cressbrook Valley. I'm afraid I shall lose you all. And what else will there be? I don't believe in God. I believe only in men and women. We only have each other."

"You'll always have me, Benny. I'll write to you all the time you're away."

"Will you promise? You know I'm going abroad—probably to America or South Africa to start my training? Will you write to me wherever I am and tell me everything that's going on here?"

"Yes. I'll tell you everything I can. You know I shall only be home at the weekends—but I'll find out what's happened and write to you."

"Thank you, Tess. That will make all the difference. You promise?"

"I promise, Benny."

He had arranged to say goodbye to Milo and Felix the night before so that he could be alone with Laura at the station. It was an exquisite Aylsbourn autumn morning, with that characteristic catch in the early air. The autumn, thought Benedict, is the best season; it never lets you down. It makes no promises; it is beautiful but inexorable. As you get older it must become more and more the best season of all; rich, sad, elegiac. A season to say goodbye in.

Laura wore her old coat and scarf thrown loosely round her neck. She seemed to want to look as casual as possible. When the signal plonked down to announce that the train was due and the rails began to thrum quietly under its approaching wheels, she put her arms round his neck, despite the handful of early-morning passengers, and put her mouth very close to his ear.

"Benny," she whispered. "I'm sorry I've never slept with you because then I'd have a part of you that no one could ever take away. But please promise me, when you come home, that you'll take me away—maybe to that old pub at the source of the Cressbrook—remember?—where you can hear the water running underneath the window. And then we shall be able to make love properly, as no two people ever did before. I know we're young and don't understand very much about it, but we can teach each other. Will you promise?"

"Yes."

He loaded his cases, full of his life's belongings and Mrs. Johnston's home-made jam, into the rack and held her hands until the whistle blew. The train began to move very slowly and she walked beside him as long as she could, until at last their hands had to part, and he watched her until she vanished in a jumble of signal gantries. Then, no longer a boy but a man called by his country to fight for the Cressbrook Valley, he went and shut himself in the lavatory and wept all the way to London.

1764305 2nd/Lt. Weston F
GHQ SEALF
SINGAPORE
May 16 1945

Sᴡᴇᴇᴛ sʟᴏʙ:

How bloody pleased I was to receive a letter from you today.
I was lucky to get it, for everything's had to be re-addressed twice.
I must say I'm enjoying Singapore. First it is green. Second it
looks like our accepted idea of a city—shop window-dressing is
an art. Every variety of entertainment exists except dog-racing
and even the tarts are mechanised. They follow one around the
streets in what we call tri-shaws (a bicycle with a small carriage
attached) and if you feel like it you can hop in beside them and
are whisked off to the nearest knocking-shop.

The only trouble is that everything is so expensive. A cinema
seat costs seven shillings. Fortunately alchohol is duty-free.
Chinese girls are most attractive and, I am told, quite splendid in
bed. I will write to you in more detail about this later. They wear
a very seductive two-piece costume in a very thin material
and I am curious to know what, if anything, they wear
underneath.

It is ironic that whereas during my brief stay in India I left the
women alone because they were so repulsive and pox-ridden,
though I could well have afforded it, here the cost is so high that
one simply has to save up—and I'm still afraid of catching pox.
The 85% pox rate here is a legacy from the Japanese occupation.

You may be surprised to hear that I am commanding a
company. The reason is simple: the real company commander is
on a week's course, and I am holding the fort till he gets back.
Of course I am only a figure-head who signs chits. However, it is
comforting to think that, in principle at least, I hold the power of
life and death over 147 men—up to seven days' CB or three
extra guards or forfeiture of leave.

To tell you the truth, Benny, I have a notion that I may stay on in the Army. It is an ideally lazy life and there is no question of taking decisions. Moreover, I find the people very amusing. I am bound to say that I had a signal success at a concert the other night, when I sang our old song "Please don't burn our shithouse down" to an audience of three hundred men and twelve officers. You'd have been proud if you'd heard the applause. It just shows what the old alma mater can do for you. Oh, and I brought the roof down in the mess the other night with "There was a young girl of Antrim"—remember how Milo recited it to us that day in the library early in 1944? At last I see the benefits of a classical education.

Sorry this is such a short letter but I'm on duty as I told you. I send you my love you old slob and don't let the bastards grind you down.

Yours ever,
Felix.

Trin Coll Camb
June 28 1945

Dear old butch,

Thanks a lot for your last letter. I was glad to hear you're enjoying life out there and doing plenty of flying; don't get too homesick; the weather is appalling and there's a mood of frustration and bloody-mindedness in the air.

You're quite wrong in assuming that I'm just living it up in Cambridge. Didn't you realise that I had to face the Preliminary Examination of the Natural Science Tripos at the end of this term?

I started my revision just two and a half weeks before the great day. Two weeks before the first examination the Ministry sent round a charming little note to all tutors saying that the number of scientists at Cambridge must be reduced by at least 20%. These unfortunates were to be extracted from those in the age group born between April 1925 and September 1926 which as you know includes yours truly. My hair turned a touching birch-grey. I asked my tutor if he thought a second would do. He said that if the government wanted these boys they'd take them if they had starred firsts.

That night I did twelve hours work and went to bed at 4.30

a.m. and was up early enough to do an hour's work before breakfast. A second year man kept me going with benzadrene. Believe me those two weeks were a hideous nightmare. I even gave up my place in the college tennis team; I couldn't have held the racquet. When I saw the Electronics paper my grey hair turned to a beautiful silvery white. The chemistry wasn't too bad and for physics I had revised the right things. For maths just the wrong.

By the end of it all I was convinced I had got a third and would shortly be on the way to join Felix in Singapore. To crown all, the college tennis matches against Girton and Newnham cancelled. Never in all my life did I need your moony old face so much to cheer me. However, my tutor has just written to me. . . . "Dear Johnston. Congratulations on your second class which was not at all far from being a first. Your marks were etc." So I have scraped my way back into Cambridge for another year.

Thanks for your queries about my sisters; Joanna is working hard at London and Tess seems to like her shorthand. Ken Heppel seems to spend all his spare time seeing her; I can't think what they see in each other. I saw Laura walking down the High Street when I was at home last vac. She looked terrific. We stopped and exchanged thoughts about the weather, the state of the world, Felix, and (did you guess?) you, you, and you again. I don't know what it is about your pixilated old mug that inspires this devotion in her. But I confess I'd love to set my eyes on it too. My parents send their love to you.

Your old pard
Milo

Miners Hostel
Blackhill
County-Durham.
July 23 1945

Darling boy,

I just wanted you to know that I'm going to marry Tess. You will throw up your hands in horror I know but we're both quite sure about it. Of course I'm not twenty yet so it won't happen for two years at least, but we shall probably get engaged officially this Christmas.

Please don't ask me why. We just think we have an enormous chance of being happy. Also, between us, I'm afraid if I don't grab her someone else will. I know she's not a great beauty but she is the gentlest creature I've ever met or ever will.

Please send us your blessing.

Yours always
Ken

Fourth Training Group
"L" Divisional Headquarters,
Sebastopol Lines
Salisbury
August 2 1945

Dear Cadet Benedict,

It is indeed a most unhappy duty for me to confirm the telegram despatched yesterday. Your father had established himself as one of our most valued training officers, and his death is a severe blow to us all.

You may care for a slightly fuller explanation of how the tragedy occurred. As far as I can gather, Lieutenant Benedict had led his men on a training exercise over rough country some fifteen miles from here, and, as laid down in his orders, was instructing them in negotiating water at night. One of the cadets got into trouble when out of his depth, and your father immediately dived in to rescue him. I understand from the medical report that heart failure—probably caused by the shock of the cold water—was responsible for his death. The cadet in question managed to struggle ashore.

In view of the gallant nature of his act, formalities have been opened to make him a posthumous award. Though I do appreciate that this can be of little solace to you at this juncture, we all feel here that it is the smallest gesture we can pay to his memory. We are, all, believe me, mostly deeply grieved at this tragic waste of such a valuable life and at the loss of such a congenial and well-liked brother-officer.

Yours very truly,
J. P. R. O'Creasy
Commanding Officer

Fourth Training Group
"L" Divisional Headquarters,
Sebastopol Lines
Salisbury
August 2 1945

Dear Mr. Benedict,

I am writing on behalf of the cadets in "B" platoon who were under your father's care to tell you how terribly sorry we are about his death. Lieutenant Benedict was not just an officer as far as we were concerned; he was like a father to us. If I may give you just two small examples; before our rooms were inspected he used to go round secretly putting an extra polish on our shoes in case we were charged with slackness. He always used to give us his sweet ration. These are very small matters, and perhaps, objectively, slightly ridiculous. I can only tell you that we did not look at them in that light. We are all more upset than I can adequately say. The fact that the man he gave his life for lived makes it all the harder to bear. Please accept our most heartfelt sympathy.

Yours faithfully,
F. J. Dean
Officer Cadet

The Brewery
Aylsbourn
August 3 1945

From the Chairman's Office

My dear Benny,

We are all most dreadfully grieved at the tragic loss of your father. He was one of my oldest friends, and in the Brewery and this part of Hampshire he will never be replaced. A part of the old world has died. I do wish he could have lived just a few more days to see the end of this terrible war.

I'm not going to write you a long testimonial to the memory of your father; it would be an impertinence to someone who knew and loved him as you did. I do want to say just this: that if when you come out of the forces you want to join us here there will always be a place for you. It would be a delight and a consolation to me to have a Benedict with us once more. And I need hardly tell you that this is a business with a very solid future; I believe you could go a very long way in it.

As you know, I am your father's executor. You may be surprised to hear that he had never at any time cashed the Margrave shares which we pay to our executive staff at the end of each financial year. In consequence, he has left you some £700 of Margrave stock which I strongly advise you to keep. The brewery are going to double that for you.

He left all his books to me—as he rather touchingly put it, they were all too lowbrow for you! But after that you are of course the sole beneficiary.

The cottage, as you know, is Margrave property. It is yours, and we shall not let it to anyone unless you quite definitely do not intend to return and settle here.

It is very much my hope—and Betty's—that you will, though. She joins me in sending you her love and sympathy.

Believe me Benny,
Your old friend,
Keith Margrave.

GHQ SEALF
SINGAPORE
August 9, 1945

Dear Benny:

I've only just heard about your father's death and I'm writing at once. You won't expect—or get—a lot of maudlin clap-trap from me about it. But it did occur to me that perhaps you would be in a state of pointless remorse because you didn't fulfil the image he'd made for you. You could masochistically make out a case to show you had disappointed him. You didn't go to Shallerton and you never played for Hampshire and you didn't get a Blue and you haven't even got a commission yet (nor will you, if the war packs up in the next few days). You haven't fallen into his mould of "gentleman". And yet I am quite sure that the day you hit that thumping fifty for Valhalla (and I like a fool ran you out) made him as happy as he was ever likely to be. It's ironic what trifles will make some people happy.

I thought this might stop you moping. If not, please forgive your cynical old pal for interfering.

Yours ever,
Felix.

The Mill House
Aylsbourn
August 6 1945

Benny my darling,

I'm sitting down now to write to you because we all needed you so terribly today and I can only begin to imagine how you must be feeling. Why they couldn't have flown you home I don't know. I suppose six thousand miles is a long way in wartime. All the same, it must have broken your heart not to have been here when your father was buried.

I won't distress you with a long account of the service; strange, though, like you, I haven't a vestige of faith left, yet there's still that odd emotive comfort in the words of the Prayer Book. It was a beautiful Aylsbourn morning; still quite cold, but with a sense of summer in the air. Everyone was there; Keith Margrave, and Lady M, my parents of course, the Westons even (the first time he's been in church in thirty years so they say) all the Johnstons (Milo came from Cambridge) all the Heppels—yes even Kenneth had come down from Durham, and Ilex. I was glad there were no women members of your family—when the earth is thrown down into the open grave it is truly a terrible moment for believers and non-believers alike and I don't think I've ever seen a woman who could stand up to the horror and hopelessness and futility of it.

The Rector was on his best form and spoke quite touchingly about your father; it wasn't even hypocritical as these speeches usually are. For he *was* a good man, in any reasonable definition of that over-worked term. He had no enemies and such a lot of friends.

I remembered what you always say about the life-diminishers; I always feel they come into their own at a funeral. So to show I was a member of the Pro-Life-Party I wore my gayest dress and I was delighted to see quite a few eyebrows raised. I know if you'd been there you'd have worn an Aylsbourn rose in your button-hole, which is your special and wonderful arrogance.

After the service we all came out feeling dry and somehow a little lighter in heart—odd, that lifting of the spirit you get afterwards—and some of us went into the Thorn and Sceptre to have drinks—which—to coin the old cliché—is what he'd have wanted, and as God is our judge, exactly what he'd have done himself. Then my parents went off to London and I shut myself in my bedroom and sobbed my heart out, for I felt as if I'd lost a little bit of you. Forgive this, Benny darling, I'm thinking of you continually and come safely home soon.

Laura.

VIII

(a)

Benedict sat in the sun and waited. His aircraft had landed him at Salisbury airport at the uncivilised hour of five-thirty a.m. and he had no idea when he would be collected. He had already been sitting there two hours. He didn't care. It was pleasant to bask in the sunshine and meditate. The great point about this life, he reflected, and the thing that must endear it to Felix so much, was that there was absolutely no decision to be taken, no responsibility. He unfolded for the twentieth time a worn piece of paper containing his orders. It was headed "Confidential" and said simply:

"You will proceed to Salisbury in Southern Rhodesia, flying by BOAC flight 162 on the night of January 6/7, 1947. You will wait at the airport where you will be contacted by Squadron Leader Rupert Ripley D.S.O., D.F.C. You will be under his personal command from then onwards."

Benedict had been in some odd situations since that day he had left Aylsbourn, but none stranger than this. The letter had emanated from a section of the Air Ministry with an ominous and indeed phony-sounding title: "Department of Psychological Research."

However, who was he to worry? As long as it made the time pass more quickly till he saw Laura. . . .

A Humber shooting brake swung through the station gates. It pulled up sharply right where Benedict sat, and a scruffy young R.A.F. pilot leaped out. With his battle dress he wore a bow tie and a pair of flying boots. However, he wore the ribbon of the D.S.O. and D.F.C. Benedict jumped up and saluted.

"Good morning," said the pilot pleasantly. "I take it you're Benedict?"

"Yes, sir."

"Fine. I'm Ripley. Jump in."

He took one of Benedict's bags and swung it aboard. Benedict scrambled into the Humber and Ripley made as if to let in the clutch. Then he stopped and said: "What's your other name?"

"Other name, sir?"

"Yes. Christian names?"

"Oh. Peregrine John."

"Christ! What a mouthful. What do people call you?"

"Benny, sir."

"Benny. That's fine. My name is Rupert. For God's sake call me that and drop this sir crap."

"Right." He couldn't quite get the Rupert out the first time.

He watched his new commanding officer as he drove. He was very tall and at close quarters not so young as all that—at any rate not as young as Benedict. Twenty-eight? His limbs were loosely articulated and he wore a revolver in a holster, which, in Rhodesia, seemed a little eccentric. He had a humorous hawk nose, bushy eyebrows and black eyes. He was good-looking in a desperate sort of way. Benedict tried to recall what this particular variety of slightly piratical good looks reminded him of. Then he remembered: Felix.

"Well, Benny," said Rupert after a long silence. "This is the craziest one I've ever been in to date, and I've been in some pretty Fred Karno jobs in my time."

"I'm afraid I haven't a clue what we're supposed to be doing."

"Nor have I. Here." He swung the Humber into the kerb. "Let's have some breakfast. I imagine you haven't eaten yet. Then we can talk."

They sat down and ordered bacon and eggs and coffee.

"Now," said Rupert, "I suggest we start by exchanging brief biographies. Tell me yours first."

"There's not much to it. I volunteered for aircrew when I was seventeen and a quarter——"

"When was that?"

"April 1943. I was called up in October 1944 and came straight out here as a u/t navigator. I was within forty-eight hours of passing out and getting my commission when the Japanese war ended. Then they said either we had to sign on for three years or it was too bad. I didn't want to sign. So they made me redundant."

"And since then?"

"Absolutely nothing. I've made tea, swept out hangars, all that kind of thing. Then I suddenly got posted down here."

"How old are you?"

"I'll be twenty-one in a few days."

194

"So you hadn't done anything before you joined up?"

"I was at school."

"What are you going to do when you do get out?"

"I'm going to read physics at Imperial College, London, specialising in electronics."

"Where are you from?"

"A small place in Hampshire. You wouldn't know it."

"I might. Tell me the name."

"Aylsbourn. It's a little brewery town in the Cressbrook Valley. About seventy miles from London."

"I know it. I've been through it on the way to sail at Buckler's Hard, haven't I?"

"You might have done, yes. Very few people recall it, I find."

"Sleepy little place with a nice High Street. Smells of malt if the wind's in the right direction?"

"That's it." He found himself warming to Rupert. A perceptive chap! He hadn't met anybody else in the entire Air Force who knew anything about his town.

"Right. Now I'll tell you mine. I got expelled from my public school at sixteen for laying one of the maids. My father, a stiff-necked old sod, a Presbyterian, a Scotsman, and a chartered accountant—if you can imagine a more diabolical combination —threw me out."

"What—out into the street?"

"Right. Bags and baggage. I didn't mind a bit. I never got on with the old bugger. So I made straight for Soho."

"You went to live in Soho at sixteen?"

"Yep. Why not?"

"Must have been pretty interesting. But what did you do for a living?"

"I got a job with an outfit called Crackerjack Films. I got £2 a week. My room was eleven and six so it wasn't as bad as it sounds." He smiled to remember. "The film industry before the war was a romantic place in a mad, broke way. I always remember the first day I went there. There were three Hungarians in the studio. They were singing "Funiculi, Funicula". I always remember the scene-painters. They used to fill themselves up with beer and work all bloody day and night. They got three to four quid a week. It was slave labour really. There were no unions, you see. It was pitiful. Anyway, the boss, Captain Yodel, took a fancy to me. It was my clean white collar that did the trick. He used to send me down to the City every Friday to get the cheque to pay the wages. I had instructions not to come back till I'd got it. I used to plead with them until they gave in. Then I'd dash back with it in a taxi and we'd pay it in at the back door of the bank."

"Sounds an unstable sort of business."

"It was. The people in it were so odd you see. We had a bloke called Llewellyn Williams. He had played rugby for Wales. He was mad as a hatter. He used to advertise a special device in the small ads which he said was certain to kill flies. You sent in sixpence and he sent you back two wooden blocks. I remember he used to take a sack of sixpences in to the Gerard Street post office every Saturday, laughing fit to bust."

"But wasn't that fraud?"

"People were simpler then than they are now. He had another one. Football pools were just starting and he had an ad which said: 'Why face odds of a million to one when with our permutation you can reduce it to fifty-six to one?' "

"And could you?"

"Yes—for a stake of £1,984. But our creditors were the best value. At first when they called they used to send me out and I'd say that Captain Yodel was out and wouldn't be back. Finally they got wise to that and brought a mattress round. They used to sleep in our front office."

"You're not serious."

"My dear Benny, I am telling you the solemn truth. You have no idea what life was like in the hysterical thirties."

"Did you make any films?"

"Heavens yes. We had a vaudeville thing—Windmill type—and a serial. People liked half-hour instalments in those days. One of our salesmen had a bright idea. He joined twelve together and flogged it as the longest film on earth. It was too. It sold like hot cakes. The only trouble was, every so often the heroine would appear to be run over by a train only to be miraculously rescued the next second."

"What were the actors like?"

"Quite awful. But I and another boy used to have a lot of fun. We used to ring up bit-part actresses and say we were doing a film test that evening. Then we'd buy a one and sixpenny bottle of cocktail mixture from the Regent Wine Company and shoot them

196

some line about the camera breaking down and throw a party. You never knew your luck."

"But surely this didn't go on for ever? I mean what about the creditors?"

"Yes—all good things have to come to an end. It folded. Next day I answered an ad for a presentable, well-educated young gentleman who would earn £8 a week selling textiles. I turned up and was interviewed by a Wing-Commander Maxwell. He had two brothers, Lieutenant Commander de Winter and Brigadier Hazelwood."

"How on earth could they be brothers then?"

"Their real name was Alhambra. They were Egyptians. The ranks were equally phony; but it seemed to help in business before the war. Anyway, they took me on and the next morning I reported for work. I was shown into a room with about thirty other young men in it. De Winter was standing at a blackboard with two words written on it. One was BOXES and the other was WAKAZOO."

"I don't follow."

"Neither did I. We had to spell them out in a unified chant, like an American football crowd: B-O-X-E-S and W-A-K-A-Z-O-O. Boxes, it appeared, were what we sold—three pairs of silk stockings in each. We had to sell eight to ten boxes a day. Anyone who got over ten was called a hot-shot."

"What was Wakazoo?"

"That was just their war-cry. We had a song too. It went:

" 'Psycho Silks are just the greatest, WAKAZOO,
   'Psycho Silks are up-to-datest, WAKAZOO.'

and so on."

"But that surely wasn't taken seriously?"

"Believe me, Benny, it was taken dead seriously. It was that or not eating. I remember I once lived for four days on a sample of dog biscuits I found in Norfolk Square. I've slept on Brighton beach several times."

"How much were the stockings?"

"Five and eleven and six and eleven. We got a shilling a pair on one lot, one and three on the other."

"What kind of people did this job?"

"We were an astonishing collection. There were defrocked priests, remittance men, Malayan tea-planters who'd come home

197

to start a farm and lost everything, and public school wasters like myself. There were also one or two very amusing and talented people among them."

"Any women?"

"Oh Lord, yes. We had one old dear of eighty. She used to swoon on people's doorsteps and say she hadn't eaten all day. She made a packet. She used to sing us songs in a frail, genteel little voice. One, I think, used to go:

> *"What wonderful fish the sole is*
> *What wonderful fish are soles."*

He paused to light a small cigar. "One had the odd impression," he went on, "going round middle-class Britain in those days, that the place was loaded with neurotic and sex-hungry women. Sometimes a salesman would disappear for a week at a time. My greatest *coup* was in Bath. I was passed on from salon to salon for days on end."

"I suppose it all ended with the war."

Rupert sighed. "Yes. That was the end of it. I joined up, figuring it was the safest course, did half a tour, and then had the good fortune to get shot down. I bust a leg and got grounded. And so—here we are."

Benedict took a deep breath. "Well, Rupert," he said, "I'm afraid my story is pretty tame compared with yours."

"Nonsense! Everyone has a fascinating story to tell."

They got up. Rupert paid the bill. He grinned at Benedict.

"I've got a feeling we're going to get on, Benny," he said.

"Thanks," said Benedict. He wondered what his friends at home would say to all this. He was not sure how much to believe. On the whole he had already learned that there was no circumstance too bizarre for reality; it was only fiction that had to draw the line. He estimated that Rupert's story was about eighty-five per cent on the level.

When Benedict had changed he called at Rupert's office. He found his commanding officer smoking another cigar with his feet, still encased in flying boots, on the table in front of him. There were pictures of Betty Grable and Ann Sheridan on the wall.

"Ah there you are, Benny," cried Rupert. "Now sit down and I'll tell you all about our secret mission. It's this. We have to travel throughout the whole of the MEDME area, lecturing the troops on 'The World of Tomorrow' and answering their questions."

"*What?*"

"That's it. That's my brief direct from the Air Ministry. Here —you can read the letter if you like." He passed over a document headed "Most Secret". Benedict read it. Rupert was telling the precise truth.

"But what on earth do we know about the World of Tomorrow, Rupert?"

"I don't know what your information is Benny, but I know sweet F.A. about it. No, don't worry, we'll tour the stations, get the chaps together, then I shall tell them a few of my better yarns and a few flying adventures and we'll push on to the next place."

"But what am I supposed to do?"

"Make a note of their questions and send them back to the A.M. They're trying to find out what's on the average service-man's mind. I could tell them: one sharp short four-letter Anglo-Saxon word; however, if they're prepared to finance this Cook's tour for us, who are we to grumble? So don't be an awkward young cuss, Benny; help me draw up an itinerary. . . ."

That was Monday. Within a few days Benny had become enchanted with Rupert. His commanding officer was a man who had never heard of Angst. His motto was *carpe diem*, and he seized each day with an exhilarating zest. Benny began to unwind in his company, became less tense, moonstruck, dreamy and with-drawn. As their first weekend drew near, however, Rupert became broody.

"Benny," he said, "we have got to get ourselves organised with some crackling. Do you care for girls?"

"Of course, Rupert. I was brought up with them you see, and I've missed their company dreadfully."

"You can say that again. So do I; every bloody minute. But I've been doing a little groundwork in the two weeks I was here ahead of you. I've got a sweeet little number lined up for Sunday called Mimi Chimes. If you have no objection I'll ring and ask her to bring a friend so that we can make up a foursome. You'd like that?"

"Yes."

"It's as good as fixed then."

On the Sunday morning they were both ready at nine. Two large American cars rolled up to the door of their camp.

"Bit extravagant—two cars—isn't it?" Asked Benny innocently.

Rupert stared at him in disbelief. "My dear old fellow, you don't believe in that *menage à quatre* lark do you?"

"Oh no; I just forgot how well-off people were here."

Benny's date was a fluffy blonde called Tootsie. She was nineteen and said she worked as a secretary. Her accent fascinated him; it was just as he imagined someone from Deep South in America would talk. She prattled away about her parents: ("Mah Deard and Mah Merm") told him about the time she thought she saw a ghost ("Ah was so skeered ah was paralahsed") and said how much she hated black men. However, it was certainly fun to be with any girl after so long. Soon she was questioning him about his own life: did he have a girl friend back in England?

"Oh yes," said Benny. "Her name's Laura. She's twenty-two, an art student. I'm afraid that doesn't convey very much. But I'm longing to see her again. It's been nearly two and a half years."

"You're lucky," said Tootsie. "Ah hev an unhappy lerv lahf. You see, Benny, ah'm in lerv with a married man."

Here we go again, thought Benny. But it was such a marvellous day, and the air so rich that he could almost imagine he was home again. They stopped at a place called Mermaid's Pool and picknicked there. The girls had brought a splendid cold lunch—cold meats, asparagus, amacunda pears, cream and bottled beer. It was poignantly nostalgic. Afterwards they lay in the sun and Tootsie volunteered to read his fortune from the palm of his hand.

"Ah'm afraid, Benny," she said, after a close study, "ah see a terrible ernhappiness in yoh lahf. But you hev good kahnd friends and yoh'll never be pohr."

When they drove back into town Tootsie invited him to stop at her parents' house for a glass of whisky. "Mah Merm and Deard hev gone away to Durban," she said, "so ah hev the place to mahself, which is kahnd of cosy."

"Thank you very much, Tootsie, but really I have to get back into camp by twelve." (He didn't, but it was the only excuse he could think of.) Tootsie seemed surprised. "Well, Benny," she said, "if yoh quite sure, ah'll understand. But ah will say this. They're aren't so many boys like yoh left. But yoh can kiss me good night, ah trust?"

"Oh yes," said Benedict. "I can do that."

Rupert beat his head against the wall in despair when he heard about it. "Handed to you on a plate," he kept moaning, "and you drop it through your butter-fingers. Oh Benny, I'm so ashamed for you. Please promise never to mention it again. I don't know what my friends would say."

"I'm sorry to be such a prune, Rupert. But I shall be going home in a few months and—well, Laura and I have got something special planned."

"She must be a dish if you can wait that long."

"She is, Rupert."

Early in March Felix wrote to say he was sailing for home. Was there any chance of seeing his pixilated old friend en route? Benedict took the letter to Rupert. He had told him much about Felix and he was curious to see how the two would get on. "I just wondered, Rupert," he said, "whether we might fly up to Malta next and meet Felix there. His ship stops there for a couple of days."

"No sooner said than done," said Rupert decisively. "There's a little piece of Maltese crackling pining her heart out for me in Valetta. Benny, my boy, arrange the tickets."

(b)

Odd, thought Benedict, how offensive a lieutenant's uniform can make a man. He studied Felix's appearance with disfavour. His cynical friend had grown almost nut-brown in the sun; he looked more Spanish than ever. The three sat drinking Chianti and exchanging reminiscences of their lives. Felix's researches into the social mores of the Chinese girl had been thorough; he and Rupert were soon busy exchanging notes. Benedict sat moodily. He felt left out of it; and Laura was still such a long way away. He blocked out each passing day in his diary; it was only a matter of weeks now and they would be together; they would go to that pub at the source of the Cressbrook. . . .

"Snap out of it, you moonstruck old prune," cried Felix at last seeing his friend's reverie. "You're missing the fiesta."

They had crossed to the Island of Gozo with a barrel organ playing in the little ferry boat and a Mediterranean sun beating down on them. It was one of the most peaceful places Benedict had ever seen. One day, he thought, Laura and I will come here.

The fiesta was charming in its innocence: procession, fireworks, and music. When it had passed by the three friends began to drink again. Then Rupert suggested that they should take a new bottle of Chianti and go and sit on the rocks looking over the sea. There was an enormous Mediterranean moon and they could sit with the warm water lapping round their bare feet. They drank steadily, passing the bottle backwards and forwards between them. It was their third bottle of the evening. The conversation was drowsy and desultory; Benedict was half asleep. Suddenly Rupert prodded him.

"Wake up, Benny," he cried jovially, "stop thinking about that dream girl back home."

"Dream girl?" enquired Felix thickly. He was very drunk.

"Yes," said Rupert, "Laura."

"Oh dear old Laura," said Felix. "The constant nympho."

Benedict sat up.

"What did you say, Felix?"

"I said the constant nympho."

"What do you mean by that?"

"Well, Christ, Benny, surely I don't have to tell you. Everyone knows she's the hottest little bitch in the Cressbrook Valley."

"That's right," said Rupert, not entirely understanding, "Benny's been living a life of monastic purity out here, dreaming of the day when he gets back to her. Must be some dish to be worth that kind of wait."

"I wonder how much waiting *she's* doing," Felix said.

"Felix I'm warning you . . ." Benedict was angry now.

"Everyone knows she's been sleeping around since she was about fifteen. First there was dear old Tony Hammond, then of course she had to make that pass at me down at Torquay. . . ."

"That's a lie, Felix."

"Is it, my dear innocent Benny? And how the devil do you know?"

"Because I know Laura."

"Because I know Laura." Felix mimicked him. "Benny, you'll learn one day that no woman is worth waiting for. Love 'em and leave 'em. Especially when it's only a randy little whore like Laura. *Hey, Benny!*"

Benedict never quite knew what made him do it; it frightened him always afterwards to remember, for he had never lost his temper before. He recalled nothing for some thirty seconds, and then through a deep darkness, laced with exploding rockets, he heard Rupert shouting: "Let go, Benny! For God's sake let go. You're killing him!"

He opened his eyes. He was sitting on top of Felix with both hands round his throat. Felix's tongue was swollen and protruding from his lips. His face, in the unearthly moonlight, looked a brownish-purple. He was holding Benedict off with all his strength, and Rupert had both arms round him from behind. But it was several minutes before with their combined efforts they could prise Benedict off. Felix sat doubled over, getting his breath back in long sobbing lungfuls.

"For Christ's sake," Rupert said. "You nearly killed him, Benny. No girl is worth that much."

"This one is," Benedict said. He turned and walked back to the hotel, still shaking. He and Felix did not speak to each other again that night; and they parted company in the morning without saying goodbye.

Before he went, Felix said to Rupert privately: "For God's sake keep an eye on that manic fool. He'll do himself serious harm one day."

January 9th 1947

BENNY MY DARLING

... It's just two years and a quarter since you've been away;
I remember as if it were yesterday walking home from the
station and—because I badly needed something to occupy me—
doing the washing up. There was a pile of brown string in our
kitchen which you produced at the last minute—remember?—
to tie up some of your things. In a way I'm glad we've had this
long separation and the chance to carry on our unending conversations in this way, it can't have done anything but good. ...

January 23rd 1947

Benny my darling,

... I've just washed my hair and done some much overdue
darning—romantic pastimes both—and now I'm sitting down to
write to you. I am sending today's Observer off to you and you'll
see from it that Hampshire walloped Cambridge but I don't
know whether to be glad or sorry, what with Milo and everyone
going there. Incidentally, it appears that Joanna is having some
fearfully torrid love affair with a married man in London . . .
they're all awfully worried about it, but what on earth can they
do? I did tell you, didn't I, that she got a jolly good degree in
June, not quite a first but an upper second, and now she's
working with the American Air Force on some complicated
problems to do with rockets. All those Johnstons go the same way.
No one knows anything about this man but I'm glad to say he's
NOT an American. Not that I'm anti-American but the distance
would be an added factor against it, if there were any hope of
their marrying. Benny it must be dreadful to see one's children
growing up and having to go out into the world defenceless
against being hurt; yet what can one do to help? I think we can
only tell them how to live and then leave it to them. I suppose our
children will give us the same heartaches. I find it hard to
imagine exactly how it will feel to have your children. . . .

I'm following your journeys on a map. You do get around

don't you? I hope Rupert is looking after you; he seems old enough to be your father from what you say about him in your letters. And I do hope Transport Command is looking after you.

One of the students here asked me out to an oyster supper at some place in Soho, but I said I'd rather not. I couldn't bear Soho without you.

You are a darling to say you want to buy me some things; really you shouldn't bother, but since you so sweetly insist on checking my measurements, it's shoes five and a half, stockings nine and a half, and—maidenly modesty on one side for the moment—vital statistics, 34-25½-34. (The waist is the true figure —I could squeeze into something a little smaller, but it wouldn't be very comfortable.) One thing I *have* been looking for for ages is a pair of sandals with wedge heels, medium height, heelless and toeless, but you're only to buy them for me if they're cheap and *you* like them. . . .

February 19th 1947

Benny my darling,

. . . I was so thrilled to get your long letter and the photographs. As you say, the camera didn't seem to be quite in focus but they are a joy to have all the same. Rupert looks quite harmless, now that I've seen what he looks like. Benny, I'm so worried about your lip. I love you to play rugger, you know that, but I do wish you didn't always have to be the one to be bounced . . . it must be awful trying to eat and drink. Do be more careful next time you play. I know that's pointless advice but I do worry about you.

We went to London last night, just my parents and I, to celebrate—you'll never guess—their *twenty-fifth* wedding anniversary. We went to Manetta's for a dinner dance and met some friends of theirs, a doctor who'd been a student with Daddy, and wife and a son of about our age. Let me tell you at once that he was an utter prune, a snurdge of the first water. I didn't feel like dancing without you—I kept remembering that unforgettable summer in 1944 which seemed as though it would never end, when it seemed we danced to Glenn Miller night after night after night. . . . Benny, I'm sure you'll be madly famous one day and that some ghastly little man will sit in the British Museum editing our love letters. I'm afraid mine will look so unintelligent to his fish-like eyes; I wish I were as clever as you . . . never mind him though, let's always write just for each other. You know I often wish I could post myself to you in one of these dull Forces parcels. One day I suppose we'll look back on this time and smile about it from our cosy, sanctified married state.

The snow's coming down deep and crisp and even and I ache unbearably to recall how we used to whizz down the side of the Hampshire Downs in Milo's toboggan, me hanging on round your neck like grim death and you always steering with what Felix so rightly called your "dexterous ferocity". You know, mention of my parents' celebration of their quarter century of (so-called) connubial felicity reminds me; I'm afraid the Westons' marriage is breaking up. According to that old gossip Mrs. Duncher, they're throwing plates at each other and it's pretty established he has a little piece of nonsense down in Southampton. Poor things . . . can you imagine us ever throwing plates, Benny?

March 19 1947

Benny my darling . . .

 . . . Felix came home today and insisted on taking me out to supper at the Shallerton Arms. It's a new place, they've converted an old disused mill, and between you and me it's rather nasty. You get a lot of chaps there with Jaguars who've made a fortune out of plastic handbags and the wine tastes like vinegar . . . however, Felix obviously meant well; this was part of his disguise as the perfect *homme du monde* as you always call him. . . . He's a little plumper and quite good-looking in a spivvy sort of way but I'm bound to say he was the perfect "gentleman". . . . We talked a lot about you and though he didn't want to mention it I gathered there had been some enormous row between you. Anyway, he's quite forgiven you he says; I wonder if you've forgiven him? He wouldn't say what it was all about. I think under that cynical exterior he's really very fond of you. Shall I tell you a funny thing? I believe he's really very frightened of women. None of us know what effect it must have had on him to see his mother die when he was so young and on his own; and nice as Arabella is, no child can adjust easily to have his father marry again. . . .

206

Benny my darling:

    . . . I've just come back from Milo's twenty-first birthday party.
It was enormous fun, but I did miss you. Everybody was there
and you know I had a strong impression of how we're all growing
up . . . there were four or five *couples* there, that is people going
steady and pretty well engaged. Tess and Ken have fixed to
marry in June; how wonderful if you could be back by then.
The weather has been bitter; it's the worst winter in living
memory and poor old England is just about at rock-bottom; we
had all the electric fires turned off at art school the other day,
you can imagine what it was like trying to paint. Oh and what
do you think, one of the boys here who is studying photography
has asked me to act as his model . . . if you don't think it too
unrespectable I think I'll do it so that you can have a new
photograph. He shot me a lot of stuff about my being very
photogenic. I went to the hairdresser this morning and had my
hair done in a new way for the party—I can't exactly describe it
to you but it was piled up on top . . . but I felt sad because you
weren't there to approve or disapprove. Milo was full of beans;
he's a little more serious now and working hard for his degree in
June; then it seems he will have to go into the army. He's in
the university tennis team, did I tell you? And they'll be out
practising as soon as this dreadful winter shows signs of breaking up.

    Tess and Ken look completely out of this world and you know
she is looking prettier every day. She's got a job with a solicitor
in Shallerton which she'll keep after they're married; meanwhile
they're looking for somewhere to live here. But as you know flats
are pretty hard to find these days. Oh Benny, seeing all their
plans and preparations makes me think such a lot about us. . . .
You know sometimes I'm frightened; we will have changed and
we musn't be surprised if it takes a little time for us to get
used to each other again. Ken has a marvellous plan. He's
buying an old M.G. on the never never—one of those four-seater
ones, and he suggests that he and Tess and you and I should go
on a tour of England in it this summer; wouldn't that be heaven?
I send you thousands of unplatonic kisses. . . .

Benny my darling:

    . . . The most astonishing thing: Constance came back to
Aylsbourn today. We had a long talk in Millers and I'm delighted

to say she's going to live here again. But my dear, can you imagine—she's been married and divorced since we last saw her. Apparently only a few months after getting to Portsmouth she married an American naval officer. It seems he was a nice guy, but very young and they lasted six weeks. Six weeks . . . imagine Benny. I tried to get out of her why she rushed into marriage like that, she just shrugged her shoulders and said it was one of those things; but I'm convinced it was a bitter reaction from the disappointment of not going to Somerville. I still can't get to the bottom of why she didn't go. Can you imagine what she did in Portsmouth? She worked in a department store. Can you imagine Constance selling dresses??? She said it was the best way to earn money quickly, she was on wages plus commission and I imagine she could sell quite well if she put her mind to it. I asked her how it felt to be married, and she said she had never felt so imprisoned in her life. Oh I should have said that this naval officer, though a nice guy, was rather addicted to what Constance calls hitting the bottle; she said it was disconcerting to wake up in the morning and find that your husband couldn't stop shaking until he'd had a shot of Scotch from a bottle by the bed. I said hadn't she noticed that before she married him? She said no, they all drank a lot down there. I still don't know why her parents never helped her; I'm sure they're separated, because why didn't they look after her when her guardian died last year? The divorce isn't through yet; Constance cryptically said she could get one on three different counts. Poor Constance! And yet do you know she looks magnificent; even more proud than before, and she holds her head very erect as if to say "I'm Constance and don't you ever forget it." I asked her why she came back here and she said simply "it's home". She asked a lot about you. To be frank she said: "How is the pixilated old loon?" She is fond of you, I think. Now she's getting a job at the Brewery as a secretary; she's acquired shorthand. Oh but Benny, she would have made a wonderful scientist, what a criminal waste!

April 19th 1947

Benny my darling:

. . . Nylons—what a heavenly present! You know really you shouldn't, you don't earn so much—7/3 a day isn't it? but what a thrill to receive them—I shall keep them and wear them the first day you're home. . . . Benny what do you think, Ken Heppel's father is going to buy the garage. As you know the owner died recently and Mr. Heppel has managed to raise an overdraft from the local bank, plus some small savings and a private loan from Sir Keith M. . . . I wonder what he'll be like as a capitalist? Even stranger, Ken wrote to Tess the other day saying he'd like to run it. You may think this an odd decision for such an idealist as Ken, but in fact I'm sure it's merely that he's utterly unambitious in a material sense and this will prove an unspectacular way of earning his bread and butter while he works at politics, which as you know is his first love. My God though, what an uphill struggle he's got to swing the Cressbrook Valley—it's been solidly and you could almost say manically Tory since the Reform Bill . . . still if anyone could do it Ken will. . . . I find it a bit ironic, do you remember that "garage proprietor" was one of his key words of contempt? "What will the garage proprietors of England say about *that*?"

Tess says one day they're going to build an entirely modern house on Cromwell Hill and it'll just have one huge piece of glass all along one wall so that they can look right down the Cressbrook Valley. . . . Benny I do envy them. . . . I've just bought a rather zippy new pair of slacks which I think even you, reactionary though you are about women's dress, will love. They're a crazy colour, not exactly mauve but a sort of wine colour if you can imagine such a thing. . . .

May 15th 1947

Benny my darling:

. . . Tess and Ken were married today, and although as you know I disapprove intensely of the hocus-pocus, well, when it came to the point I rather enjoyed it. I meant to be strong-willed about taking part, but when Tess asked me to be a bridesmaid how could I refuse? Joanna was the other one and I must say Tess looked lovely. Milo was best man and need I tell you, it took Ken all his time to get Milo ready! Even I, sophisticated old cynic that I am, felt a bit tearful.

Tess had been hoarding her coupons for ages and bought a gorgeous wedding dress—heavy creamy satin with long tight sleeves and a train. Her headdress was a tiny coronet of pearls and Mrs. Johnston lent her own lace veil.

As for the bridesmaids! Our dresses were both the same—a lovely soft, pale apricot colour with heart-shaped necklines and very tight waistlines (I could hardly breathe) and romantically full skirts. Milo gave us both pearl necklaces as our bridesmaid's presents. It was the first time for ages that I felt really grand and not in the least "utility".

We drank quite a lot of Champagne *chez* Johnston afterwards and there was dancing; you can imagine how lonely I felt when that well-worn but splendid old radiogram of theirs began to thump out "Perfidia". . . . Oh and Benny, another wonderful thing, Aelfric came down specially for the wedding and he and Constance took one look at each other and that was that for the rest of the evening. Poor old Aelfric, I don't know whether Ilex pushed him too hard, but he hasn't been at all on form and they're rather worried whether he's going to get much of a degree at all this June. He looks so painfully shy and sort of *taut*. Isn't it odd; I don't believe Constance so much as looked at Aelfric before, but now they're both a bit lost and they seem to find consolation in each other. . . . Benny it's only a matter of weeks now before you're home again and sometimes I find it all quite terrifying. But it will work out for us, you'll see. . . .

Benny my darling:

. . . It's spring at long last, that terrible winter is over. I've just had another of your delicious letters, you know as I read them I can hear you talking to me. This evening I walked alone up to our secret view and remembered the first day you took me there . . . now it's only a few weeks before you'll take me there again. Marvellous news about Constance—Aelfric asked her to go up to Oxford for a Commem Ball. As you know he's poor as a churchmouse, but he'd saved up some money just for this last fling by working on the land in the vacations. Constance watched the Eights from the college barge, she was quite a sensation at the Ball. One awful little squirt, an old Etonian, even proposed to her! She's softened a little and responding, I think, to the security of being among her friends again. Felix was here on leave looking even more dissolutely dashing than ever and what do you think? He saw Tony Hammond! He went into a record shop in Oxford Street and there was Tony *serving behind the counter*!

Of course they went and had a drink together and Tony rather made light of his job; he said it was temporary while he was waiting to hear from the B.B.C.; but Felix didn't believe it. After all, it's two full years since Tony left Cambridge, the brightest of our hopes, and what has he done? Not much apparently. He worked for a while in an art gallery in Paris, and got rather seriously involved with a married woman, and had to leave in a hurry. He went down to Spain and earned a very little teaching English, then he got a job on a yacht at Monte Carlo with some rich Greek. But what's it all for? What is his real strength? I could never make out whether he wanted to be Prime Minister or Poet Laureate or whether perhaps he didn't just want to drift along with the current. Oh he still plays that trumpet, by the way, twice a week in a small club. He's got a one-room flat in Cromwell Road. Felix says darkly that he believes Tony is paying a lot of attention to a German starlet of nineteen who's over here making a film. He is, Felix adds, wildly attractive in an unwashed way. Poor Tony!

July 7th 1947

Benny my darling . . .

. . . Rupert called tonight. What a character! My mother quite swooned though my father was less rhapsodical. He told me all about you, says you're the sweetest man he's ever met and quite unspoiled by living with *him* all the time. He brought your present for me—it was perfect, how did you develop such marvellous taste? I hope you haven't been talking to any strange women. . . . My mother admired it particularly and I shall be wearing it on my finger the day I meet you. Rupert stayed to dinner and told us about a plan you had to go into a partnership together—you as the technical man and he as the salesman—in the record business. It sounds terrific fun Benny, and perhaps I can be your receptionist; I'll wear a pair of severe hornrimmed glasses and frighten undesirable callers away. . . . But you will take your degree first won't you? Otherwise you'll always regret it. Of course I can understand you want to start earning money, so that we can marry soon, but we've all the time in the world and no one can take us away from each other. . . .

. . . I've had a long rambling letter from Tony Hammond. I don't know what to make of it, truly, it reads as if it's been written by a maniac. I hope he's going to be all right. Isn't it odd how the people one thought most of when very young usually come to a sticky end?

It's late Benny, and I must be up early tomorrow, I have a class at nine in Shallerton. I'm enjoying painting enormously and when you come home you shall be my first professional commission. The fee will be one of your kisses, the highest fee ever paid for a work of art. . . .

July 20th 1947

Benny my darling:

. . . Ilex left today and we all had to go to the gala farewell. You have to hand it to him, his public relations department is remarkable. He had the Minister down and half the county. The Minister said the Aylsbourn experiment would set the pattern for the British education in the next half century etc. etc. It appears that Ilex has produced—at any rate on paper—the best scholarship results (allowing for our small size) in England. And now he's off to be a high-powered university professor in California. Dear Ilex! He was (as usual) quite tearful when people said all these nice things about him. There's a new man coming to take over, from Lancashire, a rather bleak scientist, the first we've had in charge at Aylsbourn. Poor Mr. Johnston has been passed over. . . . Yet another crazy card today from Tony; you must try to see him when you're home; it's only a few days now . . .

15th August 1947

Benny my darling:

. . . These last few days are the worst of all. *Please* come home soon, I'm so lost and miserable without you. Any day now I'm expecting a letter to say you're on the way. I do hope you can fiddle a plane, surely the R.A.F. can do that for you after keeping you from me for nearly three years. For all I know you may have sailed or already be somewhere in the sky, flying towards me at three hundred miles per hour. . . . I must sound quite daft, but I sometimes go out and look up into the sky to see if it has any hint of you, but it's always inscrutable. . . .

23rd August 1947

Benny my darling:

 . . . Still no word from you and I'm getting so frightened. It's like calling out in the dark when you're small and afraid, and no one being there to reply. Do you know how many letters we've exchanged while you've been away? Nearly three hundred— I counted them the other night. . . .

24th August 1947

Benny my darling:

 . . . Please come home quickly. I need you desperately. Only you can give me the sense of security and the sanity and the love I need. Please come home quickly. . . .

X

The night, now that Benedict was saying goodbye to it, the Mediterranean night was one thing he would regret; its air clear as the Cressbrook and frigidaire-chilled; its sky like ace-black steel etched out with a billion silver-nitrate needle-points. He watched the waves sliding by below, mesmerised; indigo and creamy lace with, at night, a flash of phosphorescence on the edge.

In the early hours of the Wednesday, exactly a week after they had set sail, they passed Gibraltar and softly turned northward past the vivid bare Red Cheddar cliffs of St. Vincent. They looked, Benedict thought, like a foretaste of England; it might almost have been a piece of Devon; Torbay for instance, on a summer morning. He sighed. It was best not to think about it, to let the mind run free. . . . He had sent his last letter to Laura, number three hundred and twelve, and down in the hold of the ship were his homecoming presents to her; lengths of dress material from Alexandria, negro carvings from Nairobi, Israeli jewellery from Ramat Gan, an Italian handbag from Eritrea.

On Thursday morning they sailed purposefully up the coast of Portugal and the sea was still marvellously calm until they turned into the Bay; then it roughened as if by reflex action and the wind turned cold as the Cavendish Laboratory. A sister ship passed, southward bound, and they all crowded to the rail, glad to have even a fleeting contact with fellow-men on the unheeding sea. Benedict couldn't sleep that night; they were due in next day.

But Friday morning came at last and in disbelief he watched the termite life along the docks as they edged gently up South-ampton Estuary. And now he was only thirty miles from home.

When his name was boomed over the tannoy an iron-fisted fear seized his heart; he ran to the signals room and ripped the telegram open with shaking fingers. It was from Rupert: GO TO THE SOUTH DOCK GARAGE AT ONCE WHERE YOU WILL HEAR SOMETHING TO YOUR ADVANTAGE. That was a typical communication trust Rupert; he'd probably arranged a crate of Margrave bitter. Or was it possible that Laura—but no; he'd written to say specially she wasn't to come; there would be all the drear formalities of disembarkation and form-filling and he wanted to be alone with her when they met. When they met at her parent's house in Aylsbourn. Especially as her parents were in Italy.

He got to the garage by nine. Rupert had certainly arranged a surprise; a note in his own hand which said: "My dear Benny, Knowing how struck you are on this girl I thought it would be nice for you to have this car for your leave. Don't worry, I didn't steal it; I bought it, or rather put down thirty quid on it and the rest on the never-never. . . . I've gone to Paris with a bit of crackling; it's yours till Friday fortnight—make the best of it!"

It was an M.G.—Rupert knew it was Benny's favourite car; he would not have put it past the old reprobate to have bought it just for that reason; to give his friend this special pleasure.

He stowed his luggage in the back, buttoned up his civilian overcoat, wrapped a thick woollen R.A.F. scarf round his neck, and let in the clutch with a sigh of unalloyed happiness.

The roads were strange at first; narrow and twisting and left-orientated; but his heart raced as he saw the familiar signs of home approaching: the Margrave Beer advertisements, the Southern Region stations, the Wessex buses, the corn stooks, the elegaic scent of hay, the scars of white chalk on the low rolling downs, the sight of the most crystalline water in the world as he swept over a bridge and saw the Cressbrook rippling underneath; and then, quicker and quicker, the sights and sounds and smells of home—the names of the villages: Bales Whitney and Ashdale and the green signpost which said Public Footpath to Welcaster; then with a suddenness in which he seemed to be drowning, Brewery Hill; to the right the High Street, Brewers Lane to the left and at last the little road up to the Mill House.

He pulled up gently outside. He was home.

The house was in darkness. Evidently she had gone out somewhere; no one expected him till tomorrow. What would Laura say when she saw him? Would the shock be too great? Should he go down to the "Wheatsheaf" and ring her from there, deceiving her for a moment into thinking he was still in Southampton? And then gently revealing to her that he was only a stone's throw away from her, twenty seconds if he ran, his feet four inches above the Aylsbourn earth? . . .

He lay forward over the wheel and closed his eyes. He was entirely content. There would be no more waiting after this. He was home at Laura's door, the M.G. oiled and tuned and

215

ready to carry them away together where nobody would ever find them and where they would make love as no two young people had ever made love before. Soon he dozed. But through his imagination, mescalin-bright with love, there ran an unrelated jumble of ideas and phrases and snatches of song, a long disordered shorthand, a broken-up code, a key to his young life: I'll be seeing you, In all the old familiar places . . . Get those arms up in the air, Benedict, Keep them *up* . . . Well hit, Benny, we've got time for another . . . Adeste fideles, laeti triumphantes, adeste, adeste . . . where all the dark and white folks meet, Basin Street, land of dreams . . . when I consider how my light is spent, ere half my days in this dark world and wide . . . the best this country has to give, Benny, and then to learn to give it back again . . . hold me tighter, Benny, I won't bite . . . oh Benny, I'm so afraid, the world's such a big place and we're so alone . . . you lovely bastards, we're going to win today . . . arrogance, definitely, and then appetite . . . I'm bursting to do some Roman history with you; anyone here ever read a book called *I Claudius*? No, well . . . Dear chums, as it is my custom to commence with the most important item, I'll give you a list of what I've eaten . . . when they begin the Beguine . . . Quis multa gracilis te puer in rosa perfusus liquidis urget . . . Oh Benny that was the very first time . . . for me too . . . I'm sure my life will be very unhappy . . . I love beautiful things, trees, water, flowers, scents, sounds, colours, I hate ugly things . . . alpha minus query minus . . . he's very well *made*, all legs at the moment, but the head is very fine . . . to you my heart cries out Perfidia . . . when I'm married I shall expect my husband to have a horse and car . . . Benny, why are you so sweet to me? . . . I'll be seeing you in all the old familiar places . . . the children's carousel, the chestnut tree, the wishing well . . . two whole volumetrics, oxalic and H_2O_2 with $KMNO_4$ . . . Constance, please, isn't there anything we can do? . . . all dreams have to end, Benny, as you'll find out one day . . . it's the manure, the malt, the hay, the river, the wood, all trees breathe, they give off a sort of sweetness when they're heavy with fruit . . . lay your sleeping head my love, human on my faithless arm . . . promise me, when you come home . . . that old pub at the source of the Cressbrook—remember—and we shall make love properly as no two people ever did before . . . sweet slob, dear old butch, darling boy, dear cadet Benedict it is indeed a most unhappy duty . . . he used to go round secretly

putting an extra polish on our shoes . . . and I shut myself in
my bedroom and sobbed my heart out, for I felt as if I'd lost a
little bit of you . . . shoes five and a half, stockings nine and a
half, vital statistics . . . I'll be seeing you in all the old familiar
places . . . Hello, Benny . . . Hello, Benny . . . Hello, Benny . . .
Hello, Benny . . . Hello, Benny.

"Hello, Benny."

He opened his eyes, then shut them quickly. It was light; the
early morning sun was in the sky. The face that stared so intently
down at him was familiar; those mild old blue eyes, that slightly
sawny weather-beaten old working-class face. . . .

"Hello, Benny. You remember me don't you? It's Mrs.
Duncher."

"Hello, Mrs. Duncher. What are you doing?"

"I'm on my way to work. But what are you doing?"

"I'm waiting for Laura. She doesn't expect me till today. I
must have dropped off to sleep. It doesn't matter. It passed the
time."

Mrs. Duncher was staring at him as if he were a phantom.

"But didn't you know, Benny?"

"Know what?"

She turned her head away because there are moments when
one human being should not look at another.

"She went away with Tony Hammond yesterday. He's been
here for the last ten days, seeing her every day. They—they were
married by special licence yesterday."

Mrs. Duncher, as she said this, had unknowingly shut her eyes
tight, as if to help her not see anything. In a little while she
slowly opened them again. Then she cried, "Benny!" And again
in compassion and fear, "Benny! Benny! Benny!"

XI

(a)

"But P.J., if I may say so with respect, you're just not with it. You're out on Cloud Nine. This is the twentieth century—remember?"

Sammy Spiral faced his managing director across the desk angrily. He was a long stringbean of a youth whose gaberdine coat had no reveres, and whose khaki-drill trousers were of the tightest possible diameter consonant with getting his feet into them. He wore a pair of dove-grey suède shoes, a thin hand-knitted wool tie, horizontally striped, and a coffee-coloured silk shirt. His thick, short hair was brushed forward over his forehead so that he resembled a moody young centurion. He had an I.Q of 150 and dirty finger-nails. He looked like a man who played a far-out tenor sax in a cool jazz cellar, or a beatnik, or a recent product of Cambridge University. As it happened he was all three.

He had come down just three years ago and chosen to work at Diskon after going for sixty-four interviews; after resisting all the enticements that Shell, I.C.I., Unilever, Hedley's, the Metal Box Company, Granada Television, and J. Walter Thompson could offer him. Something about the Diskon set-up had intrigued him; it was not a giant outfit, but pretty swinging and on the way up quick. He had been pleased by the note Diskon had sent through the Appointments Committee: "We are looking for a young man with a first or 2.1 in economics who combines ineluctable ambition with natural arrogance. We don't give a damn what school he went to or what games he plays. He must have a real passion for modern jazz, since it is this department of our business that he will have to develop: he must dig Gillespie, Monk, Coleman, Hayes, Harriott and Dankworth. He must develop a passion for selling records to the highly intelligent and progressive people who enjoy cool jazz; that is young professional people in the 25-35 bracket. He must be prepared to work with passion all the hours God sends and in return will not be expected to clock in or call anybody sir. He will start at £800, will hit £3,000 at thirty, after which it will be up to him."

This specification sounded as if it had been drawn up in heaven by the Archangel Gabriel with Samuel H. Spiral's names inscribed on it in letters of fire. Sammy's ambition was to go places but quick. He had no doubt, not a sliver of doubt, that he and his friends would be running England well on the right side of forty. Diskon sounded exactly the kind of outfit that would fall into his unmanicured but eagerly outstretched hand one day. After all, P. J. Benedict, the gaffer, though only ten years his senior, was a doomy old nut who once or twice had talked about jagging it in; if he ever did, Sammy Spiral was waiting with itching heels in the wings. Also, in fits and starts, he rather liked P.J., as everybody called him. Not today though. He looked at the old geyser with displeasure. He saw a tall, slightly stooping man of thirty-four with very large eloquent brown eyes and a moon-like face with unfashionably long hair curling a little over his ears. He was a pretty odd nut to have built up a business like this, Sammy reflected. But then, after all, P.J. had the reputation of being the most ruthless bastard in a fairly cut-throat business. Actually, on closer acquaintance, Sammy had decided that ruthless was the wrong word; P.J. had made good *because he didn't give a damn*; he had no emotions at all and worked with a continuous, cold fury. Sammy was no sentimentalist, as God well knew, but he couldn't quite see P.J.'s angle. What was it all for? He didn't seem to have any material ambition and he certainly didn't have any restless friends with whom he felt a compulsive necessity to keep up as Sammy did; in fact the very few times he'd seen friends of P.J.'s in the office he'd been struck by their peasant-like qualities. P.J. had no family to work for, no wife, no children, not even any parents. He wasn't interested in politics even though he went without much enthusiasm through the liberal motions. It just didn't figure. However, he was enjoying his job at Diskon and only occasionally did he feel a stab of irritation. Like now.

"Even in the twenty-first century I doubt if there'll be any future for fiddling the books," Benedict replied. "There'll be room for people like you in one of those therapeutic rest-homes that will replace prisons if the Howard League get their way."

"It's not fiddling, P.J. All we have to do is stick a simple little label on the consignments saying second-hand and we save ourselves thirty-three and a third per cent tax."

"The only drawback would seem to be that the consignments are not second-hand. When I last saw them, the discs looked kind of brand-new to my jaundiced old eye."

"But P.J., how are we going to compete? You know some of our new competitors are doing this all the time."

"We shall compete by selling better records with twice the energy and ten times the imagination."

"But nobody will ever *know*, P.J."

"I will know. And you will know."

"What possible harm will it do?"

"It will harm you and it will harm me."

"Look, P.J., I know you think I'm just an immoral young layabout. That's not so, you know. I'm as involved in morality as you are. But I'm interested in things that *really* matter. I was out in Algeria with the rebels, you know that."

"What is the good of bringing aid to the Algerian rebels—though I applaud it—if you swindle your own people with your other hand?"

"What do you mean swindle? It's only the *government*."

"Would you walk into a post office and lift a hundred pounds worth of notes from the till?"

"That's a false analogy, P.J. You have to live inside the contemporary ethical climate. You know that everyone tries to do the government for all they're worth."

"Do they? All the clergymen and schoolteachers and people on small pensions? Would your father try to do the government?"

"You know perfectly well he can't. He's just a minor civil servant. Anyway, he wouldn't have the enterprise. That's why he never got any further."

"But would he, if he had your opportunity?"

Sammy hesitated. "No. That's why I despise him."

"And that's why you despise me?"

"No, don't misunderstand me, P.J. You've done a great job with Diskon. But it seems to me you're fighting with one hand tied behind your back if you don't meet your rivals on equal terms."

"We shall still be expanding when those of our rivals who stick second-hand labels on new consignments are languishing in Pentonville," Benedict said. Then he added pleasantly, "And to bring this discussion to an amicable close, let me give you my word of honour, Sammy, that if you try it on you will be thrown out of here the very same day with one week's money. You get the idea?"

Sammy snapped his fingers in sudden inspiration. "I've got it, P.J.," he said. "You've given yourself away. It's that word honour. That's what's got you by the short and curly. You're still in the grip of an outmoded and discarded concept. Why, it's a word that's not even used seriously any more. I can't think of a single serious semantic use for it. Where did you pick the concept up?"

He had forgotten his anger; P.J.s threat had run off him like water off a duck's back. But he was genuinely curious about his last question.

Benedict smiled at Sammy with affection.

"I think I picked it up in another century," he said, "from some despicable old nut. Maybe even my father. You'll just have to ride along with our Dickensian concepts if you want to stay here, Sammy. Now which is it to be—the new labels or a week's money?"

Sammy uncurled slowly from the armchair. "The new labels," he said resignedly, "and don't come bollocking me when you see the next quarterly returns."

"They will be fifteen per cent up on this quarter," said Benedict easily, "or you will get that swift kick in the arse for which you have been so eloquently pleading. Oh and Sammy . . ."

Sammy turned. "Yes, P.J.?"

"Come to dinner tonight. You've got a girl friend, haven't you?"

"Sure, I have a chick. What do you think I am, made out of cement?"

"All right, bring her too. It's 223a Upper Brook Street. Seven-thirty."

"Black tie, P.J.?"

"No. Just a tie, if it's not too much bother. Send in Mr. Weston as you go out will you?"

(b)

Felix had acquired at least one unpleasant trait from his father, Benedict reflected: a passion for black suède shoes. He glanced down at Felix's feet with disapproval. Otherwise, the picture was much as he had imagined it. Felix wore a grey flannel suit and a bow tie. He was still very lean and now in

221

maturity good-looking so that he would notice in a busy street; too good-looking, you wouldn't trust him further than you could throw him. Benedict noticed with a sharp sense of shock that there were one or two hints of grey in Felix's glossy black hair; they were the same age—with very nearly half their days run through. And those talents which are death to hide: what had they done with them? It didn't really matter, it was strangely comforting to see Felix again. He shook hands warmly.

"Now then, Felix, what'll you drink?"

"What have you got?"

"Everything: scotch, gin, vodka, sherry, tomato juice. . . ."

"I'll take a scotch please. On the rocks if you can. Thanks."

"Cheers."

"Cheers."

There was a silence. Then Benedict said:

"I've ordered a special lunch for you today, Felix. I tried to imagine what you'd like best. Finally I settled on a rough paté, some pheasant with game chips and all the usual trimmings, mille feuilles, and some Stilton. I've got out some Mouton Rothschild in your honour. I hope you've acquired a taste for château-bottled claret?"

"I can take it or leave it, Benny. But today I'll certainly take it."

"I hope you can drink seven glasses."

"Seven?"

"Yes. I make it a rule only to drink one at lunch."

"I'll drink six if you'll drink two."

"All right; it's a deal. Now then—ah here comes that paté, let's sit down—tell me all about yourself. What have you been doing since we last met?"

Felix sighed. "My dear Benny, what a question. It would take me a year to tell you. But I could just pick out the highlights for you if you really wish."

"Go on."

Felix considered. Studying his face closely, Benedict noted with compassion that there were new lines in it he had never seen before; normally, he reflected, time paints in its greasepaint so slowly, that one doesn't notice. This was quite startling; just as if the Felix he had last set eyes on had disappeared for five minutes and come back in the disguise of the man he would be in fifteen years.

At length Felix decided how he would start.

"You know, Benny, there was always one writer I admired more than all the rest put together."

"Stendhal?"

"You've got a good memory. The great ambition of my adolescence was to follow in the footsteps of the young Stendhal —to be a writer of comedies and a seducer of women. It seemed in my first innocence a perfect career for me." He frowned. "Unhappily I found the second half of the project all too easy. The first half proved much more difficult."

"I thought you had decided to stay in the Army?"

"Yes, that was my idea at one point. But it grew so deadly boring, Benny. You've no idea what life in a peace-time officers' mess can be like."

"I don't even know what a wartime officers' mess is like."

"Oh no, of course you didn't get a commission, did you? Anyway, I realised I was learning nothing, not developing as a writer must. If you could have seen some of the officers' wives I was compelled to seduce to while away the tedium!" He made a grimace of disgust to remember. "Anyway, I came out, went to Cambridge, then in 1950 did all sorts of odd jobs. I was a Rolls-Royce salesman and a steward on the Queen Elizabeth, a trainee welder at Waterloo Station, a bookmaker's runner and even briefly a television announcer. But you know, it's a myth that a writer must have a multiplicity of jobs; what he must have is a clear eye and a sharp ear in the situation he happens to find himself; it might be Lloyds Bank or the Prudential, but there'll be material even in unrewarding places like that."

"Why didn't you write about us—I mean your friends?"

Felix waved the question contemptuously aside. "Have some sense, Benny. What in the name of heaven would I find to say about our peasant lives together? Why, the most interesting character in a novel like that would be me, and God knows I'm dull enough!" He was rather tickled at the thought.

"Yes, I suppose that's right. So what did you do?"

"Travelled. My trust, you see, fell in at twenty-one so I could do more or less what I liked. I went to the United States and lived in Manhattan, in Greenwich Village for a while."

"How was that?"

"Oh lots of fun—but not much material. You see, everyone seemed to behave in such closely predictable patterns. You know

223

I've kept a notebook ever since I was a boy. Well, I meant to use it only to record those snatches of dialogue, ideas, expressions, hints, moods, subtleties, which would be significant one day, would throw a strong light into the personalities I was describing. But I got nothing to record. Oh, I had some fun among the beats. There was one I was particularly fond of. His name was Zubinsky, and he read poetry in one of those beat cafés while someone played a cool guitar. I lived in his pad a while. He was a proper comedian. Always some new joke. He used to send his girl-friend in to my room every morning with the early-morning coffee. She was Javanese, and gorgeous."

"I can't see anything particularly funny in that."

"Yes, but absolutely starkers old chap. Not a stitch on. It was a bit of a facer first thing in the morning, even to a hardened campaigner like me."

"I get the joke now."

"Anyway, in the end even Zubinsky got boring and I decided to head west: Chicago, Detroit, Minnesota, and across the Rockies to San Francisco. That was beautiful, Benny, one of the two places in the world I could happily live in."

"The other?"

"Haifa. They've a lot in common, believe it or not. Anyway I taught in California for a bit—you know I got a degree in English eventually? It was only a third, but in California that puts you in the Leavis bracket. I even played some small parts in those canned TV films they make in Los Angeles now. But I had to get out of L.A. in the end. It became quite intolerable."

"What did?"

Felix's dark face gleamed with malicious pleasure.

"You mean you don't know? My dear Benny, L.A. is run by queers. You go to a party and you have to declare your interest before a girl will take any interest in *you*. You get girls coming up and saying, 'Are you a man?' You know the first time it happened I was eating a canapé and I nearly choked."

"I bet you did."

"Mind you I made some good friends out there in California. The beauty of the place is that you can make a packet with hardly more trouble than it takes to lift a peach from a tree. Why, I met a character out in Hollywood one night who'd just got bored with the rain in New York one day in 1948 and said to himself, 'Aw. hell, let's go west'."

"The slogan of the good American since the beginning of history."

"Yes. Anyway, he went. And today that fellow owns an electronics works, a laundry, a restaurant, a concession to import Mercedes cars and an art gallery. Just because it rained!"

"What about your writing?"

Felix looked almost—though it wasn't a word you could really use about him—crestfallen.

"I don't know, Benny; everything I wrote was opaque. You know writing is an odd talent. Not everybody thinks he can play a piano or paint a masterpiece. But everybody is taught to write in the literal sense, and therefore everyone feels he can be a writer. Look at the bloody generals," he added gloomily. "You know, Benny" he went on, "there are some writers who put words down on a piece of paper and they leap right off again. They write half a line and summon a character into your room. They can make you feel a woman's scent or the beer on a man's breath when there's no one there but you. But it's a bloody rare and precious gift. There's one young American writer can do it. I read a page of his and put my pen down in despair. His name is Philip Roth and he's only about twenty-nine; five years younger than us, Benny.

"Sometimes, you know, Benny, I really felt I was swinging. I'd sit down and I'd feel in a good mood and I'd say to myself: today I'm going to write the arse off all those other hacks, today's my day. And I'd write all day like crazy and go to bed not knowing if I mightn't have put down something fresh-minted like a 1960 half-crown. And then in the morning I'd wake up and read what I'd written and it would be flat, Benny, flat and lifeless as cold porridge.

"Finally I realised something. I've always resisted your all-or-nothing-at-all theory of life. But it began to dawn on me that nothing else but everything would do in this racket. I remembered reading a remark by that Russian writer, you know, *Not By Bread Alone*——"

"Dudintsev?"

"Yes. Dudintsev was quoted as saying that he'd given his whole strength to that book. Now at first that seems preposterous, a typical piece of Slav sentiment. And yet now I'm convinced that nothing less will ever do. It's a bit like taking up religion or romantic love; it's all or nothing at all. And I decided my trouble was I wasn't really prepared to pay quite such a heavy price."

"So you published nothing."

"Oh yes, under another name. Just to make quite sure it wasn't masochism, that I hadn't got a masterpiece on my hands. I hadn't. All three books sank without trace. They sold about two thousand copies each; the critics ignored them, not that that matters, though. I only wanted three friends and one girl to say yes to my book, Benny, and I'd have been happy. Three friends and a girl; all the rest is meaningless to me. But they never did."

"I'm a bit surprised that you mention a girl. Surely not one special girl?"

Felix looked a trifle shifty. "No, not really. Whatever was on the cards at the time. What a frightful bore all that bed jag is, Benny! You know I've tried all colours, white and black and coffee——"

"Some took it like the host, some like a toffee."

Felix looked genuinely surprised for a moment. "You know I was doing that sub-consciously. Good for you, Benny. I didn't know you kept up with the O.K. versifiers still."

"Felix, almost any modern poetry could be applied to you. As you were talking I kept thinking of that other one—what is it?—oh yes, something about he ran through women like a child through growing hay, looking for a lost toy whose capture might atone for his own guilt and the cosmic disarray."

"That's good," said Felix with his dark and slightly evil grin, "the cosmic disarray. But I don't believe I've ever been guilty of guilt, if you follow me."

"You just want to be left alone."

"Yes. Leave me easy, leave me alone. You see, Benny, I never expected anything out of life. Therefore I'm not disappointed. You, on the contrary, are always full of hope. Therefore you must be vulnerable always, for ever being hurt and disenchanted."

"You're wrong, Felix. I haven't had any real hope for the best part of fifteen years now, since the year I last saw you."

"Benny, I don't often say I'm sorry. But I'm sorry about what I said on the rock. There was no need to make it worse than it had to be anyway. You know, there wasn't a word of truth in what I was saying. Poor Laura was perfectly innocent at Torquay, in fact I'm prepared to take money that when she ran off with that bastard Hammond she was *vierge du corps*. No, promiscuity wasn't her kick at all; it's just that"—he groped for the expression—"she was made for disaster. She was made to be snatched away. She was predestined to unhappiness. Remember, in the war, how people used to resign themselves to the possibility of death? They'd say: there's nothing I can do if it's got my number written on it. Well, that was Laura's misfortune. The good Lord wrote Tony Hammond's number on her when he slid her down the chute into the world."

"You know she writes to me each year on my birthday?"

"You don't say! Where are they?"

"She never puts an address. The letters are posted in central London."

"What on earth does she say?"

"Always the same. Just wishes me a happy birthday, says she reads about me from time to time and is glad I'm doing well, hopes I'm happy, and that's it."

"Nothing about Hammond?"

"Nothing."

There was a pause while Benedict poured out the last of the wine and they both lit cigars.

"Now tell me about our other old buddies, Benny. You know I never keep in touch. What's Milo doing?"

"He's a scientist. He's working on some diabolical new rocket in Applestreet New Town."

"Isn't that the monstrosity they've built in the Cressbrook Valley?"

"That's it. He's very respectably married by the way, to a brisk, sensible nurse he met at a dance, and they have two small girls."

"I hope the poor little bitches don't look like Milo."

"They don't look like anything very much. I haven't seen him for some time, only when he comes up to London, usually on his way through to Woomera."

"He's on the up and up, the old human slide-rule?"

"Oh yes. He'll soon have his C.B.E. and he'll get his K. before he's forty-five. He'll be Sir Milo all right. Not that he gives a jot one way or the other."

"And Ken Heppel?"

"They run the local garage. It's a big business nowadays. They're among the most prosperous people in the town. They're supposed to have a dream-house on Cromwell Hill, but I've never seen it."

"You've never gone back?"

"No."

"Isn't that a bit melodramatic?"

"Just common sense. I tried it once, but when I was getting near I began to tremble so much—as if I'd got a shock—that I couldn't drive. I had to turn back."

Benedict paused and turned a troubling thought over in his mind.

"Do you know something, Felix?" he said at length. "Seeing you has done something quite dramatic for me. You seem—if you'll forgive the extravagance—to have broken the spell. I believe I could go back again now. No"—now he was certain—"it's not a question of could. I will go back. I'm determined to see what's happened to everybody. To hell with whether it's a mistake. I'll go late—after dinner tonight. I'll damned well stay there until I've sorted it all out. God, you know something? Felix, you've broken the spell."

"Poor old Benny. So you're what a psychosomatic syndrome looks like."

"That reminds me: Constance is still in Aylsbourn. She married Aelfric Gates—remember?—he's an assistant manager at the Brewery now. Something went wrong with him at Oxford; I never quite found out what. Anyway, he has a reasonable sort of future. You know old Keith Margrave died and one of the big breweries bought his business up. Of course the sentimentalists complained; but it means more chance for Aelfric. It also means I can buy Margrave bitter anywhere in London now."

"But now what about yourself, Benny, how did you come to encumber your sensitive spirit with all this success?"

"Oh it was just that I had no other interests in life. Anyone with a little intelligence and no other interest in life can make a pile these days if he wants to, Felix. Mind you I was lucky in my partner—he's a chap called Rupert Ripley, the best salesman in Greater London—and of course we got in at the bottom of the market, just before the rocket went up. It was quite fun in the early days. I didn't bother about a degree you know. . . ."

"Why not?"

"Oh I couldn't face it at that stage. I wanted to get stuck into something that would take up seventeen hours of each day. And this business certainly did. We started with a capital of twenty-one hundred pounds—all the money my father left me, a bit Margrave was decent enough to give me, and Rupert's gratuity.

We started off in a basement in Praed Street. Gosh, it was fun."

Benedict looked excited in a way he had been careful not to do for thirteen long years. "We started as a record club, making under a hundred copies of each record. The first discs, I remember, were fifteen shillings. We made them of plastic, not shellac, because that was too expensive. We bought an American recording instrument for £140 and cut our first concert in Birmingham Town Hall. That was in 1948. We made a loss of fourteen pounds in our first year. And now we have a turnover of £460,000."

"Do you realise, Benny, that if you'd been such a fool as to marry Laura, you'd probably be a BBC engineer by this time, making seven hundred and forty a year?"

"I expect you're right. Anyway, I'm entirely indifferent to that side of it. It's just something I'm grateful to, that's all, for using up all my energy and giving me no time to think."

There was a long silence. Each was lost in his own thoughts. In the end Benedict said: "Felix, did you tell me the other night what you are in now—export, is it?"

"Yes. I have a small shipping business in the City. That's not ships you understand—we're agents."

"Isn't that rather dull?"

"Monumentally dull. But then you know, Benny, I think I'm basically rather a dull fellow."

"What nonsense you do talk still, Felix."

"It's true. I go in at nine-thirty, I make a few calls, have lunch at Pimms, ring a few people up, sign some letters, and get back to my flat in Belsize Park. In the evening we go to the local cinema."

"We?"

Felix looked shifty again.

"Yes. Joanna and I."

"Not our Joanna?"

"I'm afraid so. Well, you know, Benny, I was always fascinated by women older than myself."

"But she's only a year older than you!"

"Yes. Well, I don't know. I looked her up when I got out of the Army. It was strange, but she seemed quite refreshing after all those awful colonels' wives. I didn't have to make any sort of effort, you see. She knew what an utter shit I was from the word go. Mind you, I gave her an awful time. She was only just getting over that frightful man and I was the first friendly face she'd seen

229

in London for years. She cut herself off from her family you see, just wouldn't see them. I behaved in a despicable way, Benny. I used to use her flat as a base for my operations. Sometimes I didn't come back for weeks on end. Usually she'd throw the G.P.O. directories at me, sometimes all four, but she always took me back in."

"What was the point? Why didn't you go and live in Dolphin Square or any other of those big anonymous blocks where you could have done whatever you liked without all those tiresome scenes?"

"I dunno. It was pleasant to have someone to talk to with no artifice, no mask to the face."

"It never occurred to you to offer to marry her, I suppose?"

"Benny, have a heart. Who'd marry *me*? Actually, in a moment of gin-soaked depression I did once make her a mean sort of offer, which she declined."

"What offer?"

"I said I could give her ten years' love."

"Ten years *what*?" Benedict interjected sharply. The great debate was resumed after thirteen years and he was rather enjoying it.

"Ah yes. Our semantic disagreement. I used the word love, Benny, as a convenient emotional shorthand. She knew what I meant all right, even if she wouldn't admit it to herself. I meant: I desire you sufficiently and sufficiently often to overcome the tedium of your breakfast face and the boredom of your small talk and the slightly emetic distaste I get when you squirt deodorant under your arms. Isn't that all it means?"

Benedict beamed with pleasure. "I can't tell you how happy I am to see you again, Felix," he said. "You know, growing up spoils some people. But nothing will ever erode your particular and unique charm."

"Who was right about life, Benny? You or me?"

"We were both right. And both wrong. You know, Felix, I can see an even more horrifying fate looming ahead for you, Stendhal reincarnated, Henri Beyle of Belsize Park, writer of comedies and seducer of women."

"What fate?"

"I'm very much afraid that one day you will get up and steel yourself with a triple shot of gin and put on your best suit and take Joanna off in a new hat with a veil to the Register Office.

And having married her in three minutes flat you'll both go and get sloshed at the Salisbury, and you will both have got what you deserve."

"What did Joanna do to deserve me?"

"I think suffering was necessary to her, as disaster was to Laura. And you were destined to be the instrument to inflict it."

"It's not quite as desperate as all that, Benny. Sometimes we get rather soppy about each other, bring each other home ridiculous little presents, and laugh like young. You know all that stuff people go through." He paused and there was a long silence. He seemed to be struggling with a new and unfamiliar concept.

"You know what, Benny, you may be right. After all, marriage is about the only kick I haven't tried. It'll be a new sensation, and there aren't so many left."

"Mightn't it be that it would be good for Joanna? Or would that be pushing logic too far?"

"Benny, after what she's put me through, she doesn't deserve to be happy." He added absently: "The long, miserable, jug-eared, ugly, half-baked bitch."

"Felix, you've given yourself away. I never thought to hear you use so many loving words about a woman in one sentence."

There was another long silence. They puffed reflectively at their cigars. At length Felix said:

"All right, Benny. I've told you all. Now it's your turn. There's one old friend of ours you haven't mentioned yet. Someone important. Hadn't you better own up?"

"Yes," said Benedict. "I'll own up."

"HELLO, BENNY."

Benedict groaned and turned over. He couldn't think where
he was; he felt as if he had been hit very hard on the head. It
wasn't like coming back to the world after sleep; it was as he
imagined it must be to come out of a long marijuana dream or
maybe a nine-hour operation. He felt as if he had been a long way
away. But it was no good shutting his eyes again; you had to come
round in the end; after a long dream you had to face the grey
world as best you could.

Arabella was sitting beside his bed. No, that was wrong. It
wasn't Arabella he had come to see, it was——

Then he began to remember, and he closed his eyes again.

In a minute, though, he opened them again in sharp curiosity.
God damn, it *was* Arabella! And this room looked a little familiar,
like a room lived in during a previous incarnation. Then he
recognised it under the new paint; it was Felix's room. What in
the name of heaven . . . ?

"Don't talk, Benny. Just rest. You've been asleep a long time—
nearly twenty-four hours."

"Arabella—what am I doing here?"

"Mrs. Duncher rang me up, when you passed out, from the
nearest call-box. I got round to you in our car in five minutes
and we got you here between us and put you to bed. Dr. Anderson came and gave you something to make you sleep. He thinks
you've got a virus infection, probably something you picked up
abroad. Also, he said you showed symptoms of shock. So it was
bed for you, Benny, with a sleeping pill, and a week before you
get up."

"Arabella—I must have been dreaming. I had the most
awful——"

Arabella gently shook her head. "I'm afraid you didn't dream
it, Benny. It's true. She's gone. But don't think about it. Go back
to sleep. Here, the doctor said you must take this."

He drank without resistance; he didn't care. And it was the
next day—two days since he had first seen England again—before

he awoke. Arabella was at his bedside again. She wore a house-coat and was stirring something seriously in a toothglass. He watched her through half-closed eyelids, pretending to be still asleep; she hadn't changed much. He had forgotten her high cheekbones and slight slant of her eyes; maybe she had a little Eastern blood in her. He'd never thought of that before. At last she noticed him.

"Good morning, Benny. Do you feel as if you're coming back to us now?"

"Yes, thank you, I feel fine now."

"There are a lot of presents for you from your friends. Look at those heavenly yellow roses. Tess sent them. And the books are from Ken. Milo, need I say, sent the grapes. No doubt he'll be round to eat them soon."

Benedict tried to sit up in his panic, found he was not so strong as he thought, and fell back again. "Arabella," he pleaded desperately. "Please don't let anyone see me. Not even my friends. I've got to get out of here. . . ."

"You'll stay exactly where you are," she said firmly. "But I promise you faithfully I won't let anyone see you if you'd prefer that."

He lay back, relieved. Somehow he had to pull himself together again, start the long, painful job of picking up the pathetic, shattered little pieces of his life.

"Here," Arabella said, "drink this."

"What is it?"

"Never mind what it is. It'll be good for you. Take it."

He was glad to be told what to do, and he obeyed her. Soon he had dozed off again. It was afternoon before he felt able to talk. Arabella brought him some soup and a glass of red wine.

"Drink this, Benny. You haven't eaten for nearly two days. We'll soon fatten you up again."

"Arabella, this is awfully good of you. I hope Gerard doesn't mind."

"He's in Czechoslovakia, attending some Iron Curtain trade fair. Mrs. Duncher's moved in to help me look after my two boys."

"Two boys?"

"Tim and you. He's seven now, you know. He keeps wanting to come and see you. I've promised to let him when you're a bit better."

233

"I'd like to see him. But I can't impose on you, Arabella, I must get up. . . ."

"The doctor says you will stay in bed for another five full days. And that means right here. Even then he thinks you should take it easy for another week. The Johnstons will want to have you then, they've been most anxious about you."

"I couldn't talk to anyone at the moment, Arabella. If I really must stay in bed, please let me stay here out of everyone's way."

"That's just what I'm telling you to do. Now do you want to sit up and read a paper?"

"I'd rather just talk to you."

She sat on the bed and said: "Now, Benny, let's talk. Tell me all your adventures while you've been away from us."

For a while they avoided the subject that was first in both their minds. At length it was Arabella who mentioned it first: "Benny, I know there's not much one can say to help. But you mustn't feel bitter about Laura. She is the one who will suffer most because of this."

"I don't feel bitter. To tell you the truth I don't feel anything. I still don't believe it."

He thought for a while. Then he said: "And yet, you know, if I search my mind ruthlessly, I believe right back, deep inside, I always knew this or something like this would happen. I had always been afraid of it sub-consciously."

"I expect you're wondering how she could have said the things she did—at least the things I imagine she said—if she didn't love you. But Benny, if you will forgive a perfectly extraordinary statement, I'm sure she did love you. She would have loved you for a long time, maybe always, in a gentle way, if it hadn't been for Tony. And what she feels for Tony is not, in my dictionary, love. I don't know if this has ever been explained. Let me give you an example of what I mean. When Masha went to Trigorin, was that *love*? I don't think so. It was compulsion. Does the fish love the hook? There is just no alternative; for some women a man says come with me and she has to go; it's inevitable as death; it's beyond logic or reason or argument or ethics. It's just that Hammond and she were predestined for each other and, I believe, for each other's destruction. I'm afraid I've explained that very badly, but I do believe it with all my heart."

"I suppose," Benedict said with a touch of bitterness, "it was the same predestination that drove you and Tony together."

She flushed under the insult.

"No, Benny, you know that's not so. I turned to Tony in despair when I realised that Gerard and I were through."

"You were through as long ago as that?"

"Oh but of course, didn't you know? The first time he was unfaithful to me I thought it didn't matter; but it did, like the little worm you can hardly see that eventually eats out the whole heart of the apple. He had mistresses even when we were married; he never gave them up."

"What sort of people?"

"Any sort—barmaids, waitresses. He wasn't fussy; on the contrary." She shivered to remember. "I've never hated anyone quite the way I hate him."

"Then why——?"

"Why stay with him? Oh the usual thing, I don't have any money of my own now, and Tim's all I've got. I must stick it out, at any rate till Tim is older and we can get a proper financial settlement."

"What was Tony really like?"

She smiled and there was tenderness in her face even after the passage of five years, when she thought of him. "Oh he was so sweet, Benny. I suppose you're feeling he must be an absolute ruffian to take Laura away. It's not so. First, I don't suppose he quite understood the depth of your relationship, but even if he had, he couldn't have helped himself. He's not really bad, you see. Just—somehow put together the wrong way—like a marvellous and powerful engine with the controls all set in reverse."

There was silence in Felix's room. Then she hesitated and decided to go on.

"He was just what I was waiting for. I *was* waiting for someone you see. I'm not ashamed to admit it now. He was so—pretty. I was afraid you'd take him away from me." (Benedict never understood that remark.) "I couldn't believe it when I first saw him, that men could still look like that. I grew up in Paris, you see, where my father owned some hotels. He had quite a lot of money once, but it all went on women. He was a brilliant man— imagine an *Englishman* beating the French at the hotel business —but he made a complete mess of his personal life. In the end I grew to hate him—yet it's his type I'm still drawn to physically." She smiled. "He was married four times. I literally had to

235

'trnoduce him to the son of his first marriage. I was the child of his fourth. My mother was a dancer. I don't mean a ballerina, I mean a dancer in a *boite*. She died and soon after, so did he, but fortunately there was enough money for my education. I went away to a convent and to a finishing school in Lucerne, a very smart one where all the girls were daughters of ambassadors or viscounts. That was *fun*, Benny—I had no worries or thoughts for the future; just hours of gossip and lessons in what to wear and what to say and what makes a beautiful picture."

"You learned a lot there, Arabella; I've never heard anybody talk quite like you."

"Oh, but I learned—from the other girls let me say—to talk *franchement*; life's too short for subterfuge, for us to hide behind our inhibitions. Anyway, then the finishing school ended, and I went to live in Paris. I was supposed to be studying music. But in fact I was having a whale of a time." She smiled, and Benedict saw suddenly how men could be deflected by a woman's smile. "You know, Benny, at one time the idea of being a very grand and famous courtesan seemed quite attractive to me. There were so many men in Paris before the war who had yachts and smelt delicious."

"I remember you telling us about this subject when we had tea in this room."

"Yes I remember. It was a wicked thing for me to tell you, but you must remember, I was in a pretty desperate state."

"You looked perfectly—serene—to us."

"That only shows how little a boy sees. But though I should never have said such an outrageous thing to you, Benny, it happens to be true. You won't read this in *Woman's Own*, but it's frightfully important for a man to have a *sympathique* smell."

"What else?"

She looked at him, studied his face carefully, then made a decision. "You think you're old enough now for the advanced course? You know, I believe you are, Benny. What's more, I think this is just the time for me to give it to you. I've got to get your poor old feet back on terra firma."

She took a breath, and pursed her lips gravely while she organised her thoughts. Then she began to talk without the slightest sign of inhibition or self-consciousness, straight from the heart, straight from her experience; *franchement*.

. . . "For me Benny, it's the most important thing in the world.

It's metaphysics; it's the only way of breaking out of the solitariness we each inhabit. It's crucifixion, yet it's liberation. I suppose you must know that poem of John Donne's—it's very famous—how does it go?—oh yes, something about lovers' souls descending to affections and to faculties—'Which sense may reach and apprehend, Else a great Prince in prison lies'."

"It's a marvellous poem. But tell me, what else is important in a man?"

"He must be good and heavy. You have to feel there is no escape. But please don't imagine that just physical details are the only important consideration. Making love, to a woman, you see is at least three-quarters intellectual; she can start to make love one night, and finish the next. Women are very secret people, haven't you noticed? There was always something very delightful for me in meeting my father for a terrifically respectable lunch at the Ritz—for he always cosseted me, however badly he behaved to his various wives—after having made love all the night before, and knowing one would make love again that very evening. Are you shocked Benny?"

"Not yet, I'm afraid."

"I must try harder." She reflected, and her face was suffused with the intensity of emotions recalled from another life. "The little intricacies are never recorded, Benny; the wonderful shock of discovery; the astonishment at seeing the hair on a man's stomach turn suddenly as your eye travels down his body, from black to a glorious red—I mean it's so *surprising*. But the detail I love best is the hair just behind a man's ears and on his neck. Don't ask me why, it's always been my special thing. Oh and another point, the hair must be soft, and yet springy. It must be resistant to a woman's touch, and have a life of its own."

There was another pause. Then she said tantalisingly: "I think that will do for lesson one, Benny. Go to sleep and I'll give you lesson two tomorrow afternoon."

The next day they were quite alone: Mrs. Duncher had gone to Winchester for the day and Tim was at school. Arabelle brought up lunch for them both on a tray and a bottle of wine. When they had finished she lit a cigarette and smiled with provoking innocence at him.

"Well, Benny," she said. "Do you want to hear lesson two?"

"Yes, please."

She considered. "It's hard to know where to begin. But this is the essence of the thing, I think. To know somebody in bed is really the only real way to know them; the Bible gets it right as usual. It's not love, but it's the sealing-wax of love; the thing is not completed until it's been sealed in bed."

"You told us once that love was rare."

"Yes, I mean that. But I'll accept passion. Passion is pure and good. What I am against with all my heart is the mechanical habitual act."

"Do you think it's true that it means more to a woman?"

"Not always—generally though. A woman, you see, doesn't *have* an erotic experience. She *is* an erotic experience."

"Do you think it's better for the woman than the man?"

"How do I know, Benny? But do you remember that old myth about the Greek God who turned into a woman? He was asked how the two experiences compared and he said for the woman it was ten times better. I will say this; for me, it couldn't be better than it is."

"You told me some fascinating stuff yesterday about the details that appealed to you. Are there any more?"

She thought. "I'll tell you a nice thing about a man. That's the exact point where his shirt disappears under his belt. Now isn't that ridiculous? Also, the smell of a man's shirt—when he's got it on of course—is specially nice. Some women get a kick out of men's socks——"

"Arabella, you're joking!"

"No I'm not. It's really quite astonishing what tricks the life force will play to get us into bed. Think of a girl's legs in a swimming costume. You don't think twice about them, do you? But if you see four inches of stocking above the knee, you think you're seeing something madly exciting."

"Yes I see that. But *socks* . . ."

"Benny, I'm perfectly serious. Some girls get a kick out of a pair of rumpled socks, out of watching a man's ankles move on the clutch and the accelerator as he drives a car. Oh . . ."

"Yes?"

"That reminds me. One of the sexiest things I ever experienced in my life. This is good, Benny. One day when I was only eighteen, I went to a marvellous ball outside Paris. I was driven out there one summer evening by a Frenchman of forty-six who had a red Alfa-Romeo. We did a hundred miles an hour all the way. I was wearing a white dress and I had been given scent, almost for the first time I think. I'd only just escaped from the convent. Anyway, it was something to do with the contrast between the fragility of my new white dress and the virility—*the power*—of all that speed. You know that Frenchman could have had me there and then if only he'd known."

"What, in the car?"

"Certainly. A car is both an awful and at the same time an exciting place for a woman. Normally she likes space and leisure to make love. She doesn't like those quick furtive smash-and-grab affairs. But there is this side to a car—it can sometimes powerfully convey the sensation of being ravished; and I needn't tell you how primitively exciting that is to a woman."

"But you can't——"

"No—of course you can't take her by force. But I think you'll find that if you take a woman by absolute gentleness, mixed up with moments of—well—brutality only just contained, you'll find you've aroused an erotic force in her you may not be able to cope with."

"And what else should you do to reach this kind of . . .?"

She smiled. "One thing above all, Benny. One thing the Catholic church understands to perfection. Did you ever realise, Benny, that the Catholic secret is its instinctive knowledge and understanding of sex? That's what it's about really; you know all that Bride of Christ stuff? No, what I was going to say was that the church understands the importance of abstinence. The French have a saying, 'Il n'est sauce que l'appetit.' God how true that is of making love! That's why," she added thoughtfully, "that I was so glad to have been brought up in a convent. You came to it fresh; you miss all those grubby little adventures of adolescence. For the same reason naval marriages are usually happy. They're apart for months at a time and then, Christ Almighty!—when they're together again . . ."

"I remember a man saying something rather direct to me about that once, Arabella, but it seemed true. He said that after a long abstinence it felt as if your spine was being shaken right out of your body."

Arabella laughed. "My dear Benny! You're not quite so innocent as you look. That's marvellous and it's right. Now I shall bore you with all these theoretical lectures soon. It's time

239

you registered for one or two practical lessons. From now on, Benny, you're on your own. . . ."

Odd, Benedict thought afterwards, how sentences are said in an ordinary way, and you receive them in your brain, and you allot them an ordinary importance and it's not for minutes or days or sometimes years after that you realise their true importance. Her last sentence was like that; an ordinary flat, English sentence, which he heard, and understood, and was about to discard again; when, in an instant he seemed to be struck, as if physically, by its significance. It was just as you might take a piece of shot silk in the hand, and it would look an ordinary green, and then as you turned it in the light it would suddenly become gold. The words echoed through his head over and over again, getting louder each time, till they seemed to explode inside him:

Now you're on your own. Now you're on your own. Now you're on your own.

What did those simple five words remind him of? Oh yes: of a different world, the innocent world in which he'd grown up, into which the first hints of love, the first tangential whispered invitations had insinuated themselves in sentences of similar simplicity and apparent guilelessness; What are you waiting for, Benny?—Yes that night in Tessa's room. And again: Will you be able to live on Platonic love for ever, Benny?—And again: Benny why have you never . . .?

She was staring at him in amusement: "Why, whatever is the matter, Benny? You've gone quite pale."

He swallowed. "It's nothing. I——"

But it isn't nothing, Benny. Say it to yourself softly again: Now you're on your own. What does that mean, Benny? You know no woman ever says yes, not just like that. Doesn't it mean—what are you waiting for, Benny?

It's three o'clock, Benny, in the afternoon, and Mrs. Duncher has gone to Winchester for the day. Tim won't be home from school till half-past four. The door's shut, Benny, you're alone in Felix's room with Arabella. Now you're on your own. What are you waiting for, Benny?

He tried to speak, but there was no voice left in his throat to speak with. And as Arabella looked down at him a miraculous thing happened; the smile very slowly melted away from her face and the room was suddenly full, not of ordinary silence, but an oppressive absence of sound, like the interval between a sliver of lightning and the following crack of thunder. While this was happening, Benny saw that Arabella realised what she had said; perhaps what had really happened was that she had known subconsciously what she meant all the time, but had not admitted it inside herself.

Now you're on your own. What are you waiting for, Benny?

He reached out his hand and laid it gently on hers. She had a small hand. His fingers were shaking so much that it was almost comic. But she had on her face now the intensely serious expression he had seen once before, the set and grave expression that Laura had worn that first time at the secret view. For, after all, it was a serious thing for a woman to embark on. . . .

Her fingers closed, gently but quite deliberately, round his.

The first emotion he could disentangle from the great new orchestration of his senses was a most curious access of pity. For how defenceless, he always reflected afterwards, when it comes to the heart of the matter, a woman is! How little and childlike she seems, when all her defences are removed, when her clothes, guardians of her public *persona*, make only a little tumbled silken citadel on the floor! Now that he saw Arabella properly, for the first time, saw her as she would only reveal herself for the act of birth, the act of love, the act of death, he felt for her only a compassion so overwhelming that it seemed for a moment to overwhelm even his need. But very soon she saw to it that his pity was usurped by a desire that was steel-hard; her peripatetic fingers slid over him without fuss, without hurry, and without shame. They moved over his back and through his hair, her nails sinking softly into his flesh; her tongue, her teeth, her lips flirted gently with his. She smelt a little of cigarettes and wine and scent; her lipstick was slightly smeared and her hair scattered over the pillow; knees and tresses folded to slip and ripple idly. With soft playfulness she led him into the act of love, revealing in every gentle movement the sophistication of her erotic ideas and the variety of her experience. But now a new emotion seemed to be strangling him: a sharp sense of surprise that even those unexpected and asymmetric patterns in his desire found an exact and answering analogue in her own. Still he held back, a little shy and unreleased. She too seemed untroubled yet by any thrusting sense of urgency; the rigour with which they could still contain their sensual play seemed only to accentuate their delight.

She made love with allusive and tangential skill, enticing him to try new ways of pleasing her, coaxing and refining his first amateur researches with infinite and loving care. She offered herself to him with deliberate coquetry. Then, in a very little while he felt her arms tighten round his neck and he realised that she had reached, with great delicacy and elegance, a first quiet peristalsis. She sighed and lay back in his arms, lovely in the first fulfilment of her passion, but even now solicitous not to precipitate his own enormous longing. At length, however, she began to entice him again along the swift-rising curve of their shared and needle-sharp pleasure. Now her hospitality had a new urgency: she moaned and rolled her head from side to side in delicious agony at the sweet rut. The broken words of love with which they had initiated their miraculous congress blurred and dissolved into wordless sounds wrenched from them by pure desire. Soon it became clear that they must come to the end of the beautiful matter. Now they had thrown all intellectual restraint aside and were at last free to reveal in the sensual riot. Her libido was ferocious; she had the wild strength of a velvet tiger maddened by an unknown hunger. This then, must be that strange moment of hate between a man and a woman when they are still separate, before they blend in the final moment of truth. This must be that last knowledge, that exquisite crystallisation; this was what it meant, in the biblical sense, to know a woman; this must be it. For a moment the blindness induced by their ecstasy seemed to lift and through a mist he saw Arabella transfixed, transformed, set free. Though the boundaries between thought and speech seemed to have dissolved away long ago, so that he no longer knew one from the other, yet some huge sub-conscious force must have thrown the frenzied question up to the surface of his mind and given it utterance: Is it now, Arabella, is it this is it this is it this? Finally, through everything, as the light was fading and despite the terrible and marvellous sensation of drowning and melting and dying he heard her say: Yes, Benny.

Yes Yes.

Yes. Yes. Yes. Yes. Yes. Yes. Yes. Yes.

Oh Yes Yes. . . . Yes Yes. . . . Yes Yes

Yes.

XIII

"Yes," said Sammy Spiral, undoing his thin knitted tie, "it was quite a swinging affair."

"Oh Sammy, I wish you'd stop using all that jazz slang. It's all right when we're at the Flamengo but it doesn't sound right coming from a young executive."

"Hoity-toity! Who's been out to dinner with the boss? Who tried to prove she wasn't a common little slut by putting on a hyper-refined accent?" He did a mincing imitation: "Yes, P.J. No, P.J. Oo, you are *clever*, P.J."

Jackie ripped off her stockings angrily. Really, sometimes she wanted to throw things at Sammy. Sometimes, as a matter of fact, she did. But the trouble was, she couldn't help adoring him. She had loved him from that first moment he'd walked into the record shop six months ago to try and buy a new Ornette Coleman; they didn't have it in stock but they'd got into conversation and found they both dug the same music, so what more natural than that Sammy should ask her to come jiving one evening at The Marquee? Since that evening they hadn't looked back; with the wild abandon of espresso-age children they had leaped into bed at once and would soon be coming up for what Sammy wittily called their seven-month itch. She had moved out of her Y.W.C.A. hostel on the pretence that she was going to share a flat with a friend; so indeed she was, but the friend was Samuel H. Spiral, who would not have met with the unqualified approval of the Y.W.

Sammy had rented a grubby flat in Camden Town; he did most of his entertaining at lunch-time and believed in going out at night. Like all his contemporaries, he had no intention of getting mixed up with an intelligent girl who'd give out with Sartre and all that gear. He had lost no time in acquiring this cute little scrubber. She was no trouble, didn't argue, loved him dearly, and thought he was the cleverest young man in England. What more could a nut want? Only, like all chicks, there was a snag somewhere. Now this chick had met P.J. she had suddenly gone all broody. A very unpleasant fear crossed his mind: surely she wasn't expecting to *marry* him? But if not, why all this jazz about the disc-biz; why had she spent so much time yacking to P.J.'s chick? Come to think of it, how *about* that? So P.J. had a chick after all. . . .

"Well," he said, doing up his pyjamas, "they say still waters run deep. Did you dig the gaffer's chick?"

"Sammy, unless you stop using that ridiculous language I'll go and sleep on the settee. Honest I will. A boy with a brain like yours and you have to talk that rubbish."

"Aw belt up, willya?" He climbed wearily into bed.

"I thought she was perfectly sweet."

"Oh did you now?" He had put on his posh voice again. "How frightfully decent of you."

"I suppose you'll grow up one day. Why don't you try and study P.J. a bit more? He has charming manners."

"Look here, dearie, will you leave me to manage my own affairs? P.J. is a doomy old goon like I told you. He's in Cloudsville. He's just not with it."

"Then how do you explain this smashing business he's built up?"

But Sammy was not listening. He had been thinking.

"You know what, Jackie?" he said. "I think I've got the answer. P.J. must have been brain-washed at some point. He told me once he was on an intelligence jag in the war. What happened, the Russkis must have got him, taken his brain out, unscrewed the parts, then put it all back the wrong way round."

"He looks quite normal to me—no." She checked herself. "There *is* something, Sammy. But it's not what you say. There's something about his eyes."

"Or maybe," Sammy said thoughtfully, "he's been psychoanalysed. They sometimes get that very simple, broken-down look when they've had a couple of years of it at twenty quid a week."

"No," said Jackie definitely. "I'll tell you what it is. Some time, he's been horribly badly hurt. That's what his eyes say."

"Aw don't talk such crap," Sammy said, yawning. "I know that old geyser. He's hard as nails. Insults, set-backs, disappointments—they all bounce off him like peas off a Centurion tank."

"Yes, but how long have you known him?"

"Three years."

"This must have happened a long time ago. Maybe around

244

when I was born. Maybe it was some wartime romance that went wrong!"

"Maybe it's just this chick he has in tow. She must be pushing forty hard; she must have been around a while."

"She told me they've been together now for thirteen years—ever since her little boy went away to a boarding school."

"We've been tergither nah fer thirteen years," sang Sammy irreverently. "And it don't seem a die too much. Thère haint a lidy lerhivin in the land. As I'd swop for my dear old——"

"Belt up will you, nut?" she pleaded. "You're not a patch on Peter Sellers."

"So why doesn't he marry the chick and get it over? He doesn't have a gig with any other scrubber does he?"

"No. She obviously can't marry him; maybe because she's already married and her husband won't divorce her. Did you see—she was wearing a wedding ring? Anyway," she added, "what does it matter to a mature, sophisticated woman like that? She's got P.J. for keeps—what does she need to tie him down for?"

"Ah," said Sammy, yawning horribly, "that's the sort of language I love to hear. How right you are, dearie! Why should a pure and honest love be fouled by the bourgeois stigmata of slavery? A woman after my own heart."

"They can't get married. We can."

"Yeah. But we won't."

"We'll see about that. Tell me, Sammy, what did P.J. say to you when we went out for coffee?"

"He told a couple of really fruity stories. Ooh, real lush they were."

"Don't lie to me, Samuel Spiral. I know he wanted to tell you something. Arabella told me he has some big business deal on."

"Yeah. Well, since you seem to know all about it, there's no need for me to tell you, is there?"

"That's it," she snapped with finality. She picked up her pillow and swung her legs out of the bed. Sammy just managed to catch the back of her nightdress.

"Come back, you lousy slut. I'll tell you."

She got back into bed, triumphant. She had Sammy on toast when it came to the point!

"Well, dearie," said Sammy, "it seems that the gaffer has decided to sell out the biz. Or to put it more precisely, to establish

245

a charitable trust which will own it. He'll draw a rentier income and an old geyser called Grumman who's failed to make good at the Bar will be administrator of the trust. It makes no difference to my side of the business; we still have to *earn* the money. It gives me a bit more chance, with P.J. out of the line, that's all."

"Who'll take over?"

"Rupert—a man after my own heart."

"But, Sammy, that wasn't the theory you had last time we talked; you said something about a public company."

"Yeah, that was the buzz, especially when he called in this old nut Grumman. But come to think of it, why should he need Grumman to float an issue? All he'd have to do if that's the scheme would be to work through a stockbroker or maybe an issuing house"—Sammy was interested in what he was saying now; the idiom had evaporated for a second—"sell off maybe twenty-five per cent of his shares at around par and probably pay ten per cent on around fifty-five thousand profit."

"You know, I don't understand all that gear, Sammy. The main fact is that P.J. wants to quit."

"Yep. He says he wants time to do a spot of thinking. Maybe take his chick round the world. Funny, in a way—whenever I got sick of working seventeen hours a day and complained, he used to tell me that was all he was in business for."

"She said a funny thing to me. She said, 'I believe at long last he's coming back to earth.' "

"Like I told you, he's on Cloud Nine."

"No, Sammy, there's more to it than that. He's a strange fish. And yet I'm sure they're very happy together."

"Yep," said Sammy. "They seem to make like young."

"Sammy."

"Yes?"

"P.J. must like you to tell you all this."

"The old geyser does give me a wintry smile from year to year. I'll be quite sorry to see him go. Still, all the quicker for me."

"Sammy, I wish you could love me like that."

"Oh but I do."

"Put your arms round me and swear to it on your honour."

"On my *what*?"

"You heard me, Sammy."

He hesitated. The first part of her instruction was one that was uppermost in his mind; it was hard not to obey. As for the second, well, in his weird and ragged moral code, you didn't tell a chick a thing like that unless you meant it. Of course it didn't really matter, it was just a semantic haggle, but there was a little, almost invisible seed of goodness in Sammy which he had probably inherited from the old cube who was his father. So at length he did as he was told and added:

"Sometimes I get to feeling I want to come back home and forget everything and just curl up with a certain slut."

It was not a very high-flown declaration of love but Jackie instinctively knew it would do. "Oh Sammy," she said "I do love you so."

Samuel H. Spiral, he said to himself, you're heading for very big trouble indeed.

(*a*)

"THE ONLY THING I can't forgive," Benedict said, "is the detergent foam in the Cressbrook."

He had been staying with Tess and Ken for two days now; he had spent them wandering dream-locked about the Valley.

Tess smiled indulgently at him over the breakfast table. They were alone; Ken had already gone down to the garage. "Benny, if you could have forgiven *that*, we would never have forgiven *you*. But Ken's fighting it for all he's worth. He spends such a lot of time trying to make the Cressbrook Valley a better place to live in. He always says that if some stiffnecked old Victorians hadn't fought and sweated and worried their guts out for us, we wouldn't have had the chance to grow up as human beings; we'd still be vegetables living off the land; so what are we doing for our children and for theirs?"

Benedict let his eyes wander round the room; over the piles of *Encounter* back numbers, the Art Treasures Book Club volumes, the Contemporary Fiction books, the hi-fi, the stereo, the long rack of gay record sleeves, and then, through the enormous glass window at the view, a view which would make him drunk to live with.

"You know, Tess," he said, "you are the only girl from all our gang who just met and fell in love without complications. You had none of the heartaches and betrayals that all the other girls had to go through."

Tessa seemed to look at him oddly for a second. Then she said quickly: "Here you are, Benny—your favourite—mushrooms."

"Good heavens, Tess, how on earth did you remember?"

"Oh I remember. Make the most of them. They're getting rare. The new fertilisers they put on the fields destroy them."

"I hope somebody benefits from my loss. I could easily develop into an old Blimp, bellyaching at every step forward and regretting the end of the days when you could get a servant for thirty shillings a week. The only snag with that world was that we were the servants."

"No, you couldn't be a Blimp, Benny. Not you. You don't love people and places uncritically; you love them warts and all."

"I don't know. I'm afraid I invest all my friends with qualities they don't have. I think of them all as a hundred and ten per cent of what they really are."

"For a woman, that's a very agreeable trait."

"Maybe. But as I get older, I find my feet are coming slowly back to earth again. I no longer run along four inches above the ground."

There was a silence between them. Then Tess said: "Who are you going to see today, Benny? You've so many friends to catch up with, and since that paragraph in the *Journal* yesterday you'll find people will be ringing up all the time. You must make a programme."

"First," said Benny, "I'm going to see an old lady that I never knew at all well. It's funny how, when you're young, old people are so tiresome. But now they have a restful quality. I think first, this morning, I'll go and call on Lady Margrave."

(b)

Inside the Brewer's House there was the same stillness that Benny remembered from childhood; an overpowering calm in which the tick-tock of the grandfather clock seemed to be counting away the seconds left till Doomsday.

Lady Margrave came out herself into the hall to greet him. She was nearly seventy now, and she walked with a stick. But she was still courageous in her elegance; her skirt was fashionably short and there was blue rinse in her hair; her face had new lines in it but was still kind and good to see again. She held out her hand.

"Benny, my dear boy! This is a most wonderful surprise." She led him into the drawing-room. "Come and sit next to me. I want to hear all your news. How long is it since we met?"

He was still surprised to hear the Edwardian clarity of her vowels; she was the only woman in a ten-mile radius who still pronounced girl "gel".

"It's thirteen years, I'm afraid, Lady M." The familiar abbreviation came back naturally.

"Is it really? And you've done frightfully well in those years, so I read. Congratulations, Benny. Poor Keith would have been

249

so proud of you. He always wanted you to come into the Brewery, you know."

"I was extremely sorry to hear he'd died, Lady M."

"Thank you, Benny. But these things must come to us all in time. We must just ask God's grace to help us bear it." There was pain in her old face for a moment; but it passed and she smiled at him.

"Now what else, Benny. Are you married yet?"

"I'm afraid not, Lady M."

"You mean that scoundrel Weston persists in his cruelty?" (All Aylsbourn knew the story.) "Poor Arabella! Never mind, she must know you would never leave her. And though one should never wish harm to a fellow human-being, one must face the fact that Weston won't be with us for ever. He's sixty-seven now, you know, and crippled with arthritis. His heart is none too sound either, I hear." She tried to suppress the unchristian relish in her voice.

"I hope you're in good health, Lady M. You look wonderful."

"Oh thank you, yes, Benny; thank God, I'm still sound in wind and limb. There's life in the old gel yet. I have a companion, you know, my old friend Doris Maddocks, so I always have someone to talk to when I'm lonely."

"Not——?"

"Yes, Miss Maddocks, Keith's old secretary. Why do you look so surprised?" She laid a hand rather saucily on his. Then she added: "Oh, if you mean about Doris being sweet on Keith, why I knew all about that." She sighed and glanced up at a faintly bovine portrait of Sir Keith above the fireplace. He wore his I Zingari cap. The artist had caught the mottled tones in his indulgent middle-aged face perfectly.

"Poor Keith! He was such a dear, but rather dense I'm afraid. Poor Doris loved him devotedly for twenty years and he didn't even notice. You must think it a little strange that we live here together. Well, you know, women do not have the same fierce jealousies as men. Or, if they do, they become resigned to them. You see, Benny, Doris and I have much in common." She smiled. "We both loved the same man. I happened to be lucky to be first, that's all. We often talk about him. We are good friends."

"I can't imagine, Lady M., how a man could have someone in love with him all those years and never notice."

"Can't you, Benny? But you see, Keith wasn't as clever as

some of you young fellows. He didn't know as much about women as you do nowadays."

"I suppose so. Tell me, how is the Brewery?"

"I seldom go in now, Benny. It's most efficiently run from London, and apart from attending the annual directors' luncheon —they let me stay on the board for old time's sake—and drawing my dividends, I know little about it."

"Do they still have the big cricket match against Hampshire?"

"Heavens, yes. The only difference is, now the men have to pay for their own beer. Don't think I'm criticising, Benny. In our day it was a different relationship. It was largesse we were offer-ing. Wages were pitiful—often three pounds a week or less. Now these chaps have their own cars and can afford to buy their own beer. But tell me, why don't you play next summer? You're a shareholder still, aren't you?"

"Yes but——"

"Then you must play, Benny. I insist. You used to be such an elegant bat. I used to keep the score for all Keith's games and I know a good bat when I see one. Promise me you'll play?"

"You tempt me, Lady M. May I think about it and let you know? I haven't even held a bat for about fifteen years."

"I shan't take no for an answer. Now tell me about all your other young friends. I do hope they are enjoying them-selves now."

"What exactly do you mean, Lady M.?"

"I always felt so sorry for you young people during the war. No lights, no clothes, not much to eat, no parties, no fun. Look at the young people nowadays with their coffee bars and scooters and such elegant clothes specially designed for them and all these newspaper articles. I mean they're so much in everybody's thoughts. No one ever had time for you young things during the war; we had so much else on our minds."

"You know, I never thought of it that way, Lady M."

(c)

"Yes, Benny," said Mr. Johnston, "there've been a lot of changes."

They sat on the old stools, side by side, in the physics labor-atory. Benedict studied Mr. Johnston with interest. He realised with a shock that he was nowhere near as old as he had supposed; he might be fifty-five now, and apart from a thinning out of the

251

hair on top of his strangely turnip-shaped head, he looked no different.

"We've got six hundred and fifty here now," he went on. "A hundred in the senior school alone—we call it the sixth now; seventy-five doing science, fifteen modern subjects, and the rest arts."

"A hundred," said Benedict in disbelief, "but the whole school wasn't much bigger than that in my day."

"Yes, well, everyone stays at school now. And we have this big influx from Applestreet New Town. Have you seen the New School yet? No? well let's walk up there."

They strolled slowly out of the school and up Windmill Hill. Benny stopped as they turned the corner. For where the footpath had once led to his secret view—their secret view—there was now a massive modern building: steel, glass, concrete stretching away in smooth planes and long perspectives. It was a beautiful building. They had built it right over the place where he and Laura . . .

"You've got to admit," said Mr. Johnston, "that it's a decided improvement. Yes, very pretty. And you should see the new laboratories—finest in England. They don't have anything better at Winchester I can tell you that."

"Who chose this place?"

"The architect. A bright young man from London. He walked up the hill and he stopped there and he said, that's it."

"What a splendid architect he must be. So all the children can see right to Oakhanger from their windows."

"Yes. Mind you, I don't know how many of them appreciate it."

"Tell me, Mr. Johnston," Benedict burst out without considering, "why did you come to live here? Couldn't you have been a research scientist?"

Mr. Johnston considered. "I'll tell you," he said. "I was driving along here with Milly in my bull-nosed Morris in—maybe 1926. And we stopped here and had a picnic up on the side of the Downs. And I looked down on the little place and I said, Johnston, this will do for you. A research scientist? You would really have preferred to see me grinding away in some dreary laboratory every day instead of doing the most exciting job there is—opening up the minds of the young to all the astonishing possibilities there are in the world? If I'd got to the top of the tree and made my three thousand or whatever, I'd only have come back here. I'd have suffocated in the town. Here I'm my

252

own master and in the morning when I wake up I can hear the Cressbrook from my bedroom window. No, I'm doing what I want to do."

"Wouldn't you have liked to have been headmaster?" Mr. Johnston shook his head vehemently. "Certainly not, Benny. Then I wouldn't have been able to teach, which is all I ever wanted to do. I'm second in command here now and that's good enough for me."

"Do you have any really bright boys or girls at the moment?"

"Only boys, Benny. Didn't you know they've split the school in two. The girls are going to a new school at Applestreet."

"How do you feel about that?"

"I don't know. The educationists are all for segregation. They say it's more efficient. I suppose it's true that a boy might get eight 'O' levels instead of nine if he's only with other boys." He grinned. "You'll remember, Benny, that girls can be a distraction. On the other hand, I find boys and girls together easier to teach. It was more fun. They seemed more alive. Still, that's what the educationists have done, and we have to carry out their ideas as best we can."

"What's your new head like?"

"Leftmarker? Good chap. Nice, efficient Newcastle lad who got a first in chemistry at Cambridge. That's another thing, Benny, it's getting more competitive all the time. All the old staff have been superseded by younger, brighter people. You see, it's not just the public schools who're having to struggle for places at university now. We, the old grammar schools, are having to fight like mad too—against them, against the new big secondary school, against each other. Yes, Leftmarker's all right. And Ilex's influence is still strong here, you know. We built a new wing with some money he wangled out of a Californian trust for us. But if you want my honest opinion, the finest head this school ever had is Macpherson."

"How do you mean—*is*?"

"He's still alive. Didn't you know?"

"But he can't be. He was very old when he retired."

"He was sixty-seven. Now he's eighty-five."

"But he had a weak heart."

"He still does. But the life-force is strange, you know. It will burn for a very long time if you turn the lamp down low."

"But," Benny cried out in horror, "when I left here he was——"

253

"Blind? He's still blind."

"You mean," said Benny, but really to himself, "that all these years I have been eaten up by my own small troubles, he has been sitting alone in the dark."

(d)

"You won't stay too long will you, sir," said Macpherson's housekeeper. "He's a very old gentleman and we have to preserve his strength."

He was sitting in the corner when Benedict came in, out of the light; it was immaterial. In old age his skin had taken on a strange, luminous quality and the flesh seemed to have sunk a little on the bones. The hands were scrubbed as pure as a surgeon's, and the finger-nails had the extra cleanness that only very old people can achieve. It was impossible to know that he was blind except by the slightly uncertain way he held out his hand.

"Well, Benny, my boy," he said. "They tell me you're a very distinguished young man these days."

The voice was higher than Benedict remembered it, high and lighter; there was not much left of the beautiful bass he remembered.

"I've made a lot of money, that's all, sir. I'm not particularly proud of the way I've made it."

"Why ever not, Benny? Ye know Johnson's remark—yes of course you do, so I won't trouble with it. I take it that you are *innocently* employed?"

"Oh it's not crooked, sir. We make gramophone records."

"Do ye now? Well they are one of the great solaces of my old age. Did ye realise they've recorded many of the great English poets and novelists now?"

"It's not our line, sir, but I did know. May I hear one?"

"Of course." The old man reached out and began to wind an old clockwork gramophone beside him. Benny intervened. "Here, let me do that, sir."

"Thank you, Benny. Please play a little of the Thomas Hardy, will you?"

Benedict put it on. The recording was all right, but the reproduction seemed dreadfully thin and scratchy to his experienced ears.

"Ay it's a great blessing. And then sometimes, once or twice a year maybe, an old pupil comes and reads a little to me. That's a most refreshing change."

"Perhaps I could read something to you now, sir, if you'd like that."

"Of course, Benny. Please help yourself from my bookcase."

He took down at random the *Oxford Book of English Mystical Poetry* and read a poem by George Herbert. Macpherson chuckled with pleasure as he ended.

"That's good, Benny. 'Cabinet of pleasure' is felicitous. The poem is well made, Benny. Ye know in my part of Scotland they still use the old, archaic word for a poet—they call him a maker. It's apt. But I mustn't start boring you with a lesson. Why don't you read me something more up to date—ye used to enjoy modern poetry if I recall rightly. There's a book somewhere there"—he indicated the shelf—"sent to me by one old pupil for my birthday. I've not been able to get anyone to read it to me yet."

Benedict searched the shelves and found a new volume of Dylan Thomas.

"I think I've got it, sir."

"Ay. Then go ahead, Benny."

He opened it at random and began to read:

> "*Do not go gentle into that good night,*
> *Old age should burn and rave at close of day;*
> *Rage——*"

Macpherson waited with the marvellous patience of the very old. The room was very still.

"Go on, Benny. Those are good lines."

"I'm sorry, sir. I'll begin again."

When he had concluded, Macpherson considered for a moment. Then he passed judgement.

"The poem is very fine, Benny, by any critical yardstick at all. It will last. But ye know, one can tell it was written by a very young man."

"How, sir?"

"Because of his impatience and anger at death. When ye get to ripe old age like me—as I hope ye will—ye'll find it's not so bad as you think. Old age has many compensations, Benny. There's no more striving, no more broken hearts. Ye have time to think. And ye'll realise what a comedy it all is. Then maybe in the evenings there'll be a new record of Bach to play before you drop off to sleep. There are many worse fates, Benny. I'm quite content. . . ."

On his way along the High Street he stopped at the Post Office and wrote a card to Sammy Spiral:

Would you please: a. ring our technical department and say I want our best two men to report to me here on Monday. I'm sending on a list of the equipment they'll need.

      b. get me a complete and up-to-date list of all spoken prose and poetry now on record and tape.

      c. get me a complete list of the best new recordings in the entire Bach repertoire.

Thank you

    P.J.

He then sauntered up to the market square to have tea at Miller's.

But Miller's wasn't there. Instead, a green neon light said Gino's. Behind its gleaming chrome Gaggia espresso machine, were waitresses briskly serving plates of apfelstrudel, spaghetti bolognese, wienerschnitzel and ravioli. And, of course, coffee.

He pushed open the door, a little unsure of himself, and took a seat by himself in a corner.

He had been sitting there for only a few minutes when a young man who had been watching him from the other side of the room got up and crossed over. He was dressed with casual elegance in a grey flannel suit, cream shirt, and college tie.

"Excuse me, sir," he said politely, "but aren't you Mr. Benedict?"

"Yes. I'm afraid——" The young face was absurdly familiar. It was a dark, humorous face, with incipient black rings under slightly slanting eyes. "Good heavens! You must be Timothy."

"Good shot, sir."

"Well come and sit down. And for heaven's sake don't call me sir, it makes me feel so old. Call me Benny."

"Certainly. Tell me, how is"—He used the Christian name with the easy familiarity of a child whose parents have been long parted—"how is Arabella?"

"Oh, she's absolutely fine. She'll be mad to have missed you. Why don't you ever come up to the flat?"

Arabella had adopted a policy of always taking Timothy to

their cottage by the sea in her turns to have him during the holidays; she had deliberately kept him away from Benedict, not wanting to complicate either of their lives.

"I'd like to very much. I have to go back to Oxford in a few days; perhaps I could call in on the way."

"We'd love that, Timothy. It's quite central and you can entertain your friends. I'm supposed to have one of the biggest record collections in London, and there's plenty of jazz too if you like that sort of thing."

"Of course I do. Thanks very much. And tell me, how is my brother?" He deliberately seemed to want to avoid saying half-brother.

"Felix? He's in great form. We had lunch together just the other day."

"I'd like to see him again. We haven't met since I was at school. He turned up a few weeks before I left, gave me a tenner and some good, if rather cynical, advice, and pushed off again."

"Which school?"

"Winchester. My father got fed up with Aylsbourn after Ilex left. Also, he's not very happy at the way Felix has turned out."

"What sort of advice did Felix give you?"

"Oh it was a sort of Polonius speech brought up to date."

"Tell me."

"Let me see—oh yes—he said on no account to marry till I was fifty."

"Ah. It used to be forty. He's raised his sights as he's got older. And yet somehow I think his bachelor days are coming to an end. What else did he say?"

"He said always to live a thousand a year above my income. And to stick to English mistresses. He said it was a bit like choosing cheese; when you're young you rush for all those exciting French and Italian things, but as you grow older you realise that the English ones are, in a subtle way, quite the best in the world."

"Unexpected patriotism—from Felix."

"He said that of course if I could find a Chinese mistress for my old age that would be ideal. Oh, and he was very interesting about friends. He said to give all Americans a wide berth, except New Yorkers, all athletes, and all politicians. Otherwise, he said, I'd die early of boredom."

"Dear Felix! He doesn't change much."

"He was particularly adamant about the politicians."

"Did he say who you *should* cultivate?"

"Yes. He said to make my friends among Jews, Catholics, and queers. Jews, because they understand music. Catholics because they understand drink. Queers because they understand women. And all three because they understand money. As he put it himself—what else is there?"

"Felix is unique. You should see more of him; cultivate him. I'm sure you'll like him. I'll give you his address."

"That's awfully kind. Yes, I'd like that. I very much enjoyed our last meeting."

There was a pause. Then Benedict said:

"How old are you, Timothy?"

"I'm twenty—just starting my third year at Oxford."

"My God I remember you being born. That dates me, doesn't it?"

"But you're not so old, Benny."

"I'm thirty-four; but you make me feel a hundred and four."

"But how absurd of you. We talk the same language."

"The trouble is, we *nearly* do. When you speak to someone thirty years older, you don't bother to try to communicate. But with someone only half a generation away, the language is tantalisingly similar; it's just been put through a scrambler, so one doesn't *quite* understand it."

"It's the war which produces this curious gap; I can't even remember it."

"I suppose you can't. And you can't remember a world where there was no nuclear fission. That's the main difference. The thirties were dreadful. They had a bleak, mean quality: it was Hitler's decade; we had Jarrow and Jessie Matthews and the sort of interior decoration you see in the Trocadero—and we knew the war was coming, even though we were only children. But there wasn't this all-pervasive sense of doom you get now with the bomb."

"But you see, Benny, I've never known any other world. Therefore I have no sense of loss. O.K., so the bomb goes off. So we die. But we die anyway. We're all in the condemned cell."

"True. Another funny thing, though, Tim, before the war the sun seemed hotter. It's an illusion of course, you have only to look up the records. But my God it *seemed* hotter."

"It couldn't have been hotter than the summer of 1959."

"That was dreadful, Tim; it was unnatural. I had a crawling

258

feeling down my spine every day; to tell you the honest truth, I really thought it had something to do with the Bomb."

Tim laughed: "I can't win. All right, what about books. Shall I tell you whom I like?"

"Yes, please."

He considered: "Capote, Kerouac, Vailland and Roth among the new boys. Otherwise the usual names: Hemingway, Koestler, Huxley.

"What about the angries? Don't you dig them?"

Tim made a contemptuous gesture. "They give me a pain in the belly. Their values are so parochial. What does it matter whether people eat their peas off a knife or not? The main thing is, we've all got knives; we've all got peas." He leaned forward. "We're the world's aristocrats, Benny. Yes every one of us, even Jimmy Porter and Jim Dixon. All this manufactured social indignation must strike the average Asian as a sort of neurotic internecine squabble between pampered courtiers. The rabble are howling for bread outside." He glared out of the window and gave a wave of recognition. "Take our old Mrs. Duncher who's coming in to see us now, for example. She packs away as much food in a day as the average Chinese peasant does in a week."

Mrs. Duncher came over to the table and Benny got up to shake hands with her. "Well, Benny," she said, "it must be thirteen years since I last saw you."

"I wish I could say I'd weathered as well as you, Mrs. D. Won't you join us? Tim and I are just comparing life now with before the war."

"Thanks, I will. Oh there's no doubt about it. It's much better now. Look at this wonderful New Town. My son Joe can make fifteen quid a week easily. Before the war he'd have been lucky to make three."

"You don't think the New Town may be spoiling the country-side?"

"Spoil it? Who cares? What ever good has the countryside ever done for the likes of us? No, let's fill up all the fields with New Towns I say."

Tim got up. "Please excuse me, Mrs. Duncher," he said courteously, "but as you know, I always ring my girl-friend at noon each day. Our love affair is rather intense at the moment."

"Off you go, dear, and enjoy yourself," said Mrs. Duncher

259

expansively. She watched his slim figure disappear with pro-prietorial affection.

"Such a charming young fellow," she said. "Much more easy-going than his brother, though they're both lovely boys. I feel so sorry for this young one," she confided "What with his father getting worse and worse and no mother—if you'll pardon me saying so."

"That's all right, Mrs. D."

"It's a shame," went on Mrs. D. to no one in particular. Then leaning forward she added: "And him illegitimate too, poor little mite."

"I beg your pardon?"

"Didn't you know, sir? It's my belief that Mr. Weston and her was never married. I once chided her for not wearing a ring, said it wasn't proper. And she laughed and said: 'Mrs. D. it's much worse than you think. As a good old-fashioned communist, Mr. Weston doesn't even believe in holy wedlock. I'm a kept woman and I rather enjoy it.' Yes, I rather enjoy it, those were her very words."

"Are you sure of this, Mrs. D.?"

Her simple peasant's face took on a new look of apprehension.

"Now don't you dare tell on me, sir. I've always been too scared to mention it, only it just slipped out then."

"I promise not to mention your name, Mrs. D. But you know, you've just given me some quite marvellous news."

(f)

"*One* two three and *one* two three and *one* two three dee dah dee dee. . . ."

Through the open window Benedict heard the patient voice chanting above the excruciating sounds of children's violins practising a minuet. It was a familiar voice; he remembered the first day he had heard it: "Anybody here read *I Claudius*? Well, we'll start with that. . . ."

Martin Hennessy had not changed much. His boyish, curly hair was a little sparser and he wore glasses. But still he exuded that unqualified enthusiasm which had always swept every problem away in front of him like a powerful snow-plough.

As he entered the music room in the Civic College at Apple-street New Town, Hennessy began yet again: "Now then, every-body, *one* two three and *one* two three and . . ."

It was evening; the little group of violinists was bunched together in a pool of light. Hennessy played too, rocking gently back and fro in time with the music, entirely absorbed by the back-breaking pleasure of his task.

He jumped up when he saw Benedict. "My *dear* Benny," he cried, "what a surprise." Then to the children: "All right, that'll do for this evening. Be here again tomorrow, and remember it's only a week now to the concert."

They sat side by side in the music room among the discarded music scores. Hennessy's slightly fishlike face sparkled with genuine excitement. His blue eyes seemed slightly more protrusive than ever, and his thick lips glistened with saliva. I suppose, thought Benedict, that if I'd met him for the first time today I'd have written him off as a complete prune.

"Well, Martin," he said, "this is the last place I'd expected to to find you."

"Really, Benny? Why ever do you say that?"

"I had a feeling that you'd be headmaster of some famous school by this time, or a university administrator like Ilex, or maybe that you'd be a Labour M.P. . . . ."

He realised this must sound condescending and stopped. But Hennessy only laughed."

"Gracious me, Benny, what a boring fate you saw ahead for me. No, I came into this business, believe it or not, with a passionate urge to teach. Of course, some of that early enthusiasm got rubbed off by the attrition of many brutal small boys, but some will always remain. And here in Applestreet I do the most exciting teaching there is."

He leaned forwards in his enthusiasm. "Here, Benny, in this rather grandly titled Civic College, I deal simply with boys and girls aged between fifteen and eighteen who have come on from the execrated secondary modern schools. They are, in other words, the detritus of our educational system; the people who simply hadn't got the brains to pass the eleven plus."

He beamed. "In two years we put them through their 'O' level and the best of them get seven subjects. Among two hundred we get about five—only five—who fail to pass in anything. And every one of these children, Benny, is a failure on arriving here!

"The third year, we put them in for 'A' level—one, two or three subjects. Some of them go on to the university—people who couldn't pass their eleven plus remember—and many go into the civil service, teaching, engineering, the church. Now, Benny, don't you think that's more exciting than working up a lot of young smoothies with IQs of 140 for Oxford scholarships?"

"Yes, I can see that, Martin. But I don't see how you do it."

"Remember first that the children who come here all *want* to learn. They realise they've missed something. Many of them are simply late developers. Our job is to open up their minds to what they're missing. To do that, you really have to enter into their world a hundred per cent. For example, recently I learned to jive, just to see what it was like. Even though I'm nearly fifty, Benny, I enjoyed it. I cut out those Pfeiffer cartoons and stick them on their notice board. At first they thought they were half-witted; now they lap them up. I take them to France for their holidays; thirty of us in a bus at fourteen pounds each. I take them up to town to see 'West Side Story'. And in between, Benny, I teach them history."

"I hadn't looked at it like that. I suppose that's why you left Aylsbourn?"

Hennessy's face clouded. "Not really, Benny. I was extremely happy there. But I'm afraid Ilex and I didn't see eye to eye."

"He was too ambitious for you?"

"Benny, the school—no the actual human beings in that school—were just cannon-fodder for his campaigns. They were instruments of his ambition. He was the most unscrupulous man I've ever come across."

"Ironic, really, when you think of all that's been written of the Aylsbourn Experiment."

"Experiment my foot! It was a disgrace. You see, Benny, Ilex bent all you young people to fit his strategy. It didn't matter what you *wanted* to do, or what you would be *happiest* doing. Look at poor Aelfric Gates—one of the cleverest boys I ever taught. He should be a scientist now, not an under-manager in a brewery!"

"I never understood quite why he failed."

"He failed, Benny, because he'd lost his faith. You know I was taking him for his scholarship?"

"Yes, I remember."

"Well, just before the examination—only two nights before if I recall rightly—Ilex took me on one side and said in that chummy way of his—'My dear Martin, I want you to give Aelfric one last cram.' Of course I was keen, so I said yes, I would. Then he said —and I always remember this—'I should give him a thorough run-through on the effect of bank rate on unemployment in the 1832 to 1845 period. And then do go very carefully into the Trevelyan Report and Civil Service Reform.' "

"Well, I don't quite see what's wrong with——"

"Hennessy held a hand up dramatically: "Benny, *both those questions were in the paper when Aelfric turned it over two days later.*"

"You mean——?"

"I mean that Ilex committed a deliberate and calculated fraud. With two out of four questions served on a plate, Aelfric sailed through. Well, he would have anyway. But he never forgot. He knew, you see. He was never quite the same again. It took the heart right out of him."

(g)

"Yes," said Milo, "it's a very beautiful piece of machinery. We're going to call it 'Mac the Knife'."

They were sitting at Milo's dining-room table in his trim semi-detached house in Applestreet New Town. On the table there stood a number of bottles of Margrave Extra. Milo's wife sat in her chair by the fire, knitting briskly. She did not appear to be listening. She was a pleasant-looking girl of about twenty-five who wore a twin set and a pair of slippers.

Milo looked very little changed. His spectacular bent nose still dominated his homely face, and his ears still protruded at right angles. His always sparse hair was now thinning out rapidly, and, like Hennessy, he had taken to spectacles. There were a pair of large horn-rimmed glasses perched on his nose as he talked.

Mac the Knife was a horrifying rocket; an oil picture of it hung over Milo's fireplace. "Yes," Milo added, "my chaps gave me that painting as a wedding present. Rather imaginative of them, don't you think?"

"Staggering," said Benedict. He could hardly take his eyes off Milo's brain-child. Then a question occurred to him.

"What exactly is it *for*?" he asked.

"It's a ground-to-air rocket, designed to intercept aircraft. I was out in Woomera testing it earlier this year. It's fabulous. Do you realise," Milo said with pride, "that if it came to a show-down we could now guarantee to knock one hundred per cent of enemy aircraft out of the air with this? It's got a brain inside that makes it keep going till it homes in its target. It can't miss."

"But," said Benedict, "we all know that the next war will be fought rocket against rocket. Can you guarantee to knock a hundred per cent of their *rockets* out of the sky?"

"Not yet. But as soon as we detect the enemy rockets coming up over the horizon, we shall send up our own interceptor missiles and they will work out which way the enemy rockets are coming even as they're taking off. The aim will be to get them into the same piece of sky as the opposing rockets at the same time, and then create one vast nuclear explosion in the stratosphere which will blow their rockets and ours to kingdom come. Of course, some are bound to get through."

"Milo, you're not serious about this?"

"Of course I'm serious. Can you think of any better idea?"

"Throw the whole damned lot into the sea."

"Ah, yes, unilateral disarmament. Well, I'm not a politician, Benny. My job is to make rockets, not decide how to use them."

"But doesn't it ever worry you? I mean the thought of all that waste? Because if it *doesn't* go off you've spent your whole professional life on nothing, and if it *does* go off you won't even survive to enjoy the excitement of seeing your charming monster in action."

"On the other hand," Milo said, "the very fact that we're making our rocket may stop them using theirs."

"Tell me," Benedict said, "what your working day is like, Milo."

"Sure. Well, I get to the works at eight twenty-five."

"Not eight twenty-four or twenty-six?"

"No, eight twenty-five. That's when everyone else starts, and I have to be there too. I work through till five twenty-five with an hour for lunch in the work's canteen. Of course, if there's a flap on I may stay late. And I always have these"—he indicated a mound of scientific papers on the sideboard—" to read as homework. I've picked up German and Russian so that I can keep up with as many of their technical journals as I can."

"But what *do* you do during your day?"

"Well, we have a big programme, you see. Each of these things costs two million pounds. It takes hundreds of electronics engineers to produce each one. It has a quarter of a million parts and nineteen thousand valves. Any of those can go wrong. My job is to jolly the chaps along, and keep the programme up to schedule."

"Do you ever fall behind?"

Milo looked a little crestfallen.

"I'm afraid so. We're running about two and a half years behind now. It's not our fault. It's the bloody government. They keep changing their minds about our allocation. The fact is, Mac the Knife will be obsolete by the time it's delivered to the R.A.F." He sighed. "It's a great pity because it really is a beautiful rocket."

"What do you do when you're not working?"

"Not much. Joan and I watch the television most evenings. Do you ever see that fellow Tony Hancock? He absolutely slays me. Then on Saturdays we go shopping in Applestreet, and on Sundays I play golf. I read the *Sunday Times*, of course, and that takes me most of the week."

"What about holidays?"

"Oh we generally get in the old Ford Consul and head for the coast. Anywhere where there are some good golf courses."

"Tell me, Milo, do you ever see any of our other friends?"

"No," said Milo. "Oh, I did see Doreen Pepper once. It was in one of those Soho strip joints. She's some sort of manageress, in charge of the girls' morals and all that stuff. Her, her, her." Milo gave his dirtiest chuckle. "Can you imagine the old Pepper-pot in charge of anybody's *morals*?"

"You didn't tell me about this, dear," said his wife. She did not look up from her knitting.

Milo peered at her over his horn-rimmed glasses. "Didn't I, dear?" he said mildly. "Well, don't distress yourself. I have to entertain these visiting American scientists, you know, and that's their idea of an evening's fun."

"Did she recognise you?" Benedict asked.

"Of course. She said: 'Hello, Milo, old fruit.' "

"And what did you say?"

"I said: 'Hello, Pepperpot. Fancy seeing you here.' "

"And what did she say?"

"She said: "I might say the same about you.' "

"And that was all?"

"Of course it was all. What do you take me for, a playboy?" He poured out more Margrave Extra.

(h)

"Trust you, Benny, to arrive at the worst possible moment."
Constance stood in the doorway, her face flushed from the

stove, a print apron over her old tweed skirt; she wore a powder blue jumper with the sleeves pushed up to the elbows and her hair was a little untidy. To Benedict she looked, as she always did, enchanting; proud and beautiful as ever, her head held very high and her eyes looking straight into his with mocking challenge in them.

"Constance, I do apologise; it was a wild impulse, I should have rung you up first."

"Come in, Benny. I'm only teasing you. It's wonderful to see your moonstruck old mug again. I read that you were in town and we were going to invite you. I'm just making cakes for my children; they have a party after school this afternoon. If you don't mind the mess you can come and sit in the kitchen."

But of course there was no mess in the kitchen; it gleamed with the same stainless efficiency that had once distinguished her small corner of the laboratory, and Benedict felt again a sense of regret that this splendid intelligence could not have been given space and time to flower. He sat down at the kitchen table.

"Now if you'll excuse me going on working; I'd like to hear all your news from the beginning. First though, how is Arabella?"

"She's fine, thanks."

"Why didn't you bring her with you?"

"She didn't want to come this time. She will, you'll see."

"How long is it since I last saw you, Benny?"

"Believe it or not, sixteen years."

"Sixteen years—I was only a child then. Have I altered very much, Benny?"

"Not to me. I am astonished to see how little you've changed."

It was true; there were one or two very small lines round her eyes that had not been there before and her face was more mature now; sixteen years of living, suffering, loving had touched, but not harmed her; she seemed softer now, fulfilled by —or resigned to—the ordinary cares of house and family.

"You look very grand, Benny. I bet that suit cost a packet."

"Yes, too much. I waste a lot of money. But I've never cared tuppence about it."

"You're just at your best now. Men are ripening all the time until they're forty. In their twenties they should be left strictly alone."

"But women are best in their thirties, too, Constance."

266

"No, Benny," she sighed. "Thirty is the great turning-point. After that, you can only take consolation in watching your children's faces change each day."

"You have two children, don't you, Constance?"

"Yes. Johnny is eleven and Kate is ten. I'd better find some pictures."

She went and searched in her handbag, and produced a small leather folder. Inside were two photographs: one of a girl with already, if only incipiently, her mother's marvellous expression of disdain in her face, the other of a delicately good-looking boy; he looked as if the demands of his intelligence might one day put stresses on his physique. Benedict stared at the pictures in disbelief.

"Constance, in a few years they'll be as old as we were when we first met. Yet now they just seem like children!"

"We were only children."

"But the things we thought and felt!"

"They think and feel them too."

"And what about Aelfric: how is he?"

"Aelfric is fine. He quite enjoys his work at the Brewery, but it's just a job to him. He should really have been a research physicist. He might have done something wonderful."

"So might you, Constance."

"No. I was just a little above the average. Oh, I would have got a degree, and maybe toiled away in a laboratory for a while, but in the end I'd have married some spotty chemist and started rearing children; all that's happened is that I've had them earlier; which, as they said in Ten Sixty-Six and All That, is a Good Thing. An intelligent woman is always in an impossible predicament."

"You can't sell me that one, Constance; you desperately wanted to go to a university. I never understood why you didn't go."

"That's a long story, Benny. Here"—she poured him out a cup of coffee, then one for herself. She sat down at the other end of the table and looked at him for a moment. Then she smiled. "You know it *is* good to see you, you old loon." Another, more troubling thought passed through her mind, and her smile faded. She put a hand instinctively to her hair. "I must look an awful sight. Why do you do these things to me, Benny?"

"I'll tell you the truth, Constance. I wanted to catch you

unexpectedly; I wanted to see you as you really are in your ordinary everyday life. I'm sorry if I've annoyed you."

She shook her head, smiling at him. "You could never annoy me, Benny. You're incapable of hurting anybody."

"You should tell that to the people in my office."

There was a silence. Then she said: "You'd like to know why I never took up my scholarship?"

"I'd be fascinated."

"Then I'll tell you. The first thing you must realise, Benny, is that I was born, as they say, on the wrong side of the blanket. I'm illegitimate."

"You don't know who your parents were?"

"Not so fast. I was adopted when I was a baby by the Hayleys. They were good, God-fearing, simple people, and I owe them nothing but gratitude. They're both dead now, you know."

"I didn't realise."

"One of the rules of adoption is that the real parents must give up all claim to the child. They must promise never to see it. When you think it over that makes sense."

"Yes, otherwise the child never knows who it belongs to."

"Exactly. I used to get Christmas presents from my mother when I was a little girl, though I didn't know where they came from. I never really bothered very much about it till I was about eighteen. Then one day I found my birth certificate in a desk. It gave my mother's name—Pickering is her name by the way—and an address. I wrote there—a very guarded letter, not even saying who I was. I didn't want to upset her, or even enter her life again if she didn't want it."

"And she replied?"

"Yes; Can you imagine it, Benny? We met on St. Pancras Station. We recognised each other at once. It was—well it was wordless."

"What was she like?"

"I think you would have said that she was a highly intelligent woman, Benny, and I thought she was quite beautiful. She was only thirty-seven."

"About our age now."

"Yes. She was a nurse, and she'd fallen in love with a man she was looking after in a private clinic. It wasn't till after I was on the way that he told her he was already married. She tried to keep me, but it wasn't so easy in those days, Benny. She worked in a textile mill for tenpence an hour; in the end her health gave up and I had to be adopted."

"Christ, it sounds like something out of Dickens."

"But it *really happened*, Benny. It happened to your old girl-friend Constance."

"And when you found your mother?"

She shrugged, but there was distress still in her cool and lovely face. "I won't harrow you with the details. She was still desperately poor and, Benny, she was dying. How in the name of heaven could I go to Somerville knowing that? All I felt was an anger so cold and passionate that I'd have killed my father if I could."

"Why didn't he help?"

"He did what was expected of him. The Hayleys had a regular cheque each month from him for my upkeep and education. Mind you, they were always very frugal people. The reason my skirts were always so short Benny, had nothing to do with fashion. It was simply that I wore them and wore them until I'd grown right out of them.

"I don't think my mother ever let my father know what happened to her. Anyway, she had a little fun in the last few months of her life. I took her abroad, to Switzerland and Italy, and she loved that. Of course she was upset about my first marriage, but that was inevitable really. I just ran into the first friendly arms I could find."

"What about your father, Constance? Did you ever see him?"

She raised her chin a fraction higher, and stared Benedict proudly in the eyes.

"I don't have to see him, Benny," she said. "I can read about him in the papers almost any day of the week."

"You mean—he's famous?"

"Yes. If you'll forgive me, I think I ought to keep his secret."

"Do you still hate him?"

"No. It was just one of those things. My mother should have asked for help; she was too proud, so he never really knew. I I shall tell my children who he is one day; and they will be proud too."

When Benedict left, a long time later, when they had discussed all their other friends and laughed a lot and sometimes fallen silent, and then talked in snatches and laughed some more, he kissed Constance on the cheek.

269

"Oh Benny," she said. "That's not how you used to kiss me. You see how old we're both getting."

"You know, Constance," he said. "May I confess something to you? I realise now that, mixed up with everything else, I was a little in love with you."

"But Benny," she said, "surely you realised. We were all a little bit in love with each other."

Her lovely face haunted him as he walked slowly along the High Street.

Now I know, he thought to himself, why she always held her head so high.

"Mr. and Mrs. Tony Hammond," said the name-plate.
Benedict rang the bell and waited. Life teemed in the street all
round him; small rosy children played hop-scotch and a rag-
and-bone man shouted his sad needs as he rolled by in his horse-
drawn cart.

It was a basement flat in Pimlico; once no doubt a prosperous
merchant's flat, but now divided and subdivided into apartments;
and the names of all the inmates were grubbily inscribed on
cards beside the many front door bells. Benedict was no longer
afraid; he felt no emotion except a vague curiosity. Constance had
given him the address; she had always got on well with Laura and
occasionally they exchanged letters. It was a piece of information
he could easily have dug out for himself if he had ever cared; but
he had never cared.

Laura herself opened the door and when she saw Benedict
standing there she showed no surprise. She said simply: "Hello,
Benny."

"You recognised me after such a long time?"

"Of course. I always knew you would come one day."

She led him into the flat. It smelt faintly of unwashed children.
There was a pram in the hall.

The living-room was spacious but rather dark. The September
light streamed in from one large basement window let in at the
front. Benedict could see the sky only when he had taken a seat
in the only armchair; it was a perfect autumn afternoon and the
air had a tint of kodachrome blue in it. The sun on the bare
solitary lilac tree and the wall in the front garden was the colour
of gold: not mustard or primrose or copper or egg-yolk but like
gold bullion melted down and sprayed on every branch and brick.

Laura sat at first on a small stool in the shadow; then as if to
show she was not frightened to be seen, she moved forward a
little, and the flood of liquid golden bullion caught and drowned
her face in light, making Benny—even after so long—catch his
breath.

She was thin, this was his first impression; she had lost the pleasing shapeliness of her girlhood and even her cheeks were a little hollowed, throwing into dramatic relief those still-miraculous green eyes. Her skin was still pale but overlaid now with a dull crimson flush. Her nose still had its little arrogant tilt and her hair, though shorter, was still held in an Alice band. Her wrists were fragile and her hands, though still well kept, with the nails cut square, were red with housework. She wore a full red skirt, a simple white shirt and sandals. She wore no make-up; so that she looked younger than her thirty-six years; hardly more than twenty-five until you noticed the lines round mouth and eyes.

She opened a box of cigarettes and offered them.

"Thank you," he said, "I don't."

She lit one herself and drew in the first lungful of smoke with a sense of necessity that told Benedict a lot about the last thirteen years; she had never smoked before.

"Well, Benny," she said, "how did you find where we lived?"

"Constance told me. I was down there for a few days."

"Constance!" She said it softly with recalled affection. "How is she, Benny? God, it seems such a long time ago!"

"She's extremely well and as far as I can see quite unchanged. You know she has two children now?"

"Oh yes. I even have their photographs. They're very sweet."

"Tell me about yourself, Laura. What have you been doing all these years? And how is Tony?"

She looked away. "Benny," she said, "why do you want to know?"

"Do I have to tell you?"

She shook her head slowly. "No," she said. "No. I understand. But it's such a long story, Benny."

"Tell me just a little, then."

She thought for a while. "It's no good my trying to say any-thing now about what happened between us, Benny. Any words of mine would be so inadequate that they would sound insulting. In any case I have no reasonable explanation to give you. But I will just say that I am sorry—sorry in a way I can never convey to you."

"Don't say that, Laura. I've thought about it a lot, and I think I do understand; a bit at any rate."

She tried to remember. "Believe me, Benny, there was nothing between Tony and me in those days—nothing that is, except a curious tension. If there was anything between us, it was like an invisible piece of fine wire looped round us both. Neither of us knew exactly what it was, and we never discussed it. But we both sensed that there was something."

"This was right from the word go?"

"Right from the word go—from the first day you saw us."

"Ah," said Benny, but it was more like a sigh than a word. "So I was right after all."

"If you were, you were the only one that knew it for sure. He went away in 1942 and—apart from maybe an odd, neutral card at Christmas or birthdays—I had no more contact with him. You knew, I suppose, that he failed to get a degree?"

"No, I didn't realise that."

"Heaven only knows how he managed that. He wasn't lazy, and he had an unusually perceptive intelligence—you know that, Benny. It was just that—well, he seemed set on hurting himself. Then came those awful itinerant jobs in which he thought he was opening up his personality to new shapes and sounds and colours and scents. But of course he was doing nothing of the sort. He was just drifting."

"Did he never have a clear idea what he wanted to do?"

"No—did any of us?"

"Milo, I think."

She shrugged it off. "Well Tony didn't. The long curve downward had begun before he even left the Cressbrook Valley. He began to write to me again early in 1947. Benny, I know by any accepted standard of morality I should have told you at once; but how could I? And what would it have done to you—longing as you were for me—just as I longed for you? At first his letters were short, jocular, friendly. Gradually though, they grew more frenetic and neurotic. Benny"—she was remembering and her hands knotted and unknotted her handkerchief—"they were terrible letters. They terrified me, each one—*because I knew I had to read them. And because I knew a long way down that they were summonses, just like summonses which lead a man to prison. Summonses to which there is no alternative; no payment that will amend or lighten the punishment.*"

"Truly, Laura, I can understand something of what it was like. I promise you."

"Then he turned up. I'd told him, of course, that you would be home soon and this seemed to drive him crazy. He turned up in Aylsbourn. One day"—she bit her handkerchief and her small

273

sink-red fingers were trembling—"he was waiting for me at the bottom of the lane. Oh Benny, if I could have jumped on a plane and come to you, escaped, everything would have been all right."

"I'm afraid it would never have been all right, Laura."

"But that was what I desperately wanted to do. Of course my parents at first thought I was crazy; naturally they could hardly approve of Tony after what had happened between him and Arabella, but—well they didn't disapprove. They were quite fond of him, and he had no parents of his own"—she paused. "You know, I suppose, that they both died—within a year of each other?"

"Yes, I heard."

"Anyway, they saw the danger within—within two or three days. Oh Benny, it was terrible in a way I can't put in words. There was no hope for me. I was in a cage, and only Tony had the key. But he wanted me in that cage, and so he threw the key away. I'm talking nonsense, I'm afraid."

"No."

"It got worse each day, the nearer to the day you were due. And, Benny—believe me—I was so longing for you to come home, even in the middle of all this—do I sound like a lying dirty little whore?—or can you believe such an improbable thing?"

"I can believe it."

"Then—then he asked me to marry him. He said that once you got back he would never ask me again; I had to decide then. Benny, I swear to you that as I said yes—while I was actually saying it, my whole body was revolting and struggling against it, and do you know, Benny, truly I was sick when I got home. I just was sick, or in plain words I vomited; I seemed to be sicking up my heart and soul and all my self-respect."

She was not actually crying as she told Benedict this, but her voice was shaking and it seemed she had difficulty in breathing. He waited till she could go on again.

"So we were married—in a Register Office—with a couple of his boozy pals as witnesses. And I got tight, Benny—it was the only thing I could do—and we passed the night of our—our 'honeymoon' "—she used the word in quotation marks—"at the Strand Palace. When I woke up in the morning I was calling out your name. He's never forgotten that."

"I heard you call."

She seemed not to take this in. She was trying to control herself so that she could go on.

"He was working as a barman at the time. He used to come in tight—oh, he lost that job, like all the other jobs—and we used to fight. But I mean fight—nails and teeth and even fists. Benny, did you ever see a play called *Look Back In Anger*?"

"Of course, Laura."

"What did you think of it?"

"I thought what a marvellous talent, but somehow pointing the wrong way."

"But Benny, it's the greatest play ever written. Every word of it was true. It was us, Benny. He even blows his trumpet like that man in the play."

"He still plays?"

"That's how we live, Benny. He could never keep a job—but he could play jazz. He formed a group called the Ravers. They're not very great, but they make a living. They play in the South London dance halls and a few river pubs. He's come up with the boom—even bad jazz pays well now—and we often make fifty pounds a week. It's not money we're short of"—her voice broke. "It's freedom from each other."

"Has he ever gone away?"

"Has he ever gone away?" she echoed bitterly. "Do you know, Benny, his manager calculates he's had between two hundred and three hundred women—usually in shop doorways or in the back of his car?"

"*What?*"

"Benny, you can't imagine what it's like. The other day I got so crazy I put my hand through a window, I was trying to commit suicide, I think. Here"—she held out one of her small hands and he saw the new scar. It would be there for life. "And do you know what he did? He said, 'Two can play at that game.' And then he smashed his hand through the broken glass as well." She put one of her little clenched fists in her mouth and bit it hard as if to try to believe it. "Sometimes I ask him why he can't think of a quick way to commit suicide; not this slow way."

"Laura, why does he do this?"

"Why, Benny, why? Do you think I haven't asked myself this thousands of times? But I think I know why now." She took a deep breath. "It's because he's so full of life. Benny, if you'll forgive a rather crude expression, sometimes the life seems to be

275

overflowing out of him, its pressed in so hard, out of his mouth, his ears, his eyes. . . . He doesn't exactly mean to be bad, you see, he was just given too much life and it spills out of him all wrong. I knew a woman once, Benny; I met her in hospital— yes, I've been there a few times, but I won't depress you with it —who had a most horrible illness. She would conceive a baby, only it wasn't a baby; it was all the raw material growing and spawning inside her and making nothing that anyone could ever look at. And that's what it is with Tony: it's teeming inside him and he can't cope with it; he doesn't know what to do. He drinks, he has women, he takes drugs, anything to reach a kind of clarity. He never gets it. And I'm part of his life-sentence, Benny. He can't do without me. Can you imagine, after all we've done to each other we sometimes go to bed"—and now she was sobbing— "and we make love as no two people ever made love before."

Now it was Benedict's turn to look away. Eventually her sobs died away and she put her hand pathetically out towards him. Reluctantly he took it.

"Benny," she said. "I've just realised what I've said."

"It's all right."

"I can't hurt you any more, can I? I couldn't if I tried."

"Tell me, Laura, isn't there any good side to all this? Aren't you ever happy?"

"Oh sometimes, for a little while. Sometimes he even brings me home something. And of course we have the children."

"You have *children*?"

"Yes. Four. And, Benny, do you know what this terrible surplus life in him has done? As if to make it up, it's given us the four most beautiful children you ever saw in your life. I know I'm their mother, but it's not just maternal pride. People stop and stare at them in the streets."

"How old are they?"

"Mike is eleven, Louise is seven, Angela is five, and Pete is one. I'd like more, but the doctors said I'd die for sure if I had another. They're beautiful children, Benny, you should wait and see them come home from school."

"Laura, not now. I don't think I'd like to today."

He got up slowly. Over the fireplace, though hidden in the shadow, was a painting in oil. As he came closer, he saw that it was of Tony Hammond.

"That was painted last year. It's by Carlo Rewson, his best

276

friend. He's mad, everyone knows that, but God he's a marvellous painter."

Benedict studied the picture with interest. It had a ferocity about it that was a little unnerving; the colours seemed to have been hurled on to the canvas and the face that now stared out at him conveyed an impression of super-reality. The painting spoke about its subject in a way that no photograph could ever begin to do. Hammond looked—well it was an odd word to use, but to Benedict he looked—possessed. There was still beauty in the curious wedge-shaped face, but the eyes behind the thick glasses were frightening: they seemed to stare out of the picture with the hopelessness of a soul in Bedlam. Rewson had painted Hammond with his battered yellow trumpet raised to his lips, and so powerful was the painter's talent that you could almost hear him hitting one of his high notes.

"Tell me, Laura," he asked with interest, "does he really play so badly? I always thought he was wonderful."

She went to a long cabinet that lay along the wall, and turned a switch. "He made this tape the other day," she said. "Judge for yourself."

Benedict felt his skin crawl at the first note of the trumpet. It was exactly the sound that had first thrilled him over twenty years ago. But as he listened, he realised with astonishment that the sound Hammond was making was appalling; he had not moved on one iota from that day in 1939. His timing was ragged, his tone poor and his ideas naïve.

"He was sloshed that night," she said. "Some people think jazzmen play better when they're a bit high." She shook her head. "They have to think it out and orchestrate; and the farther out they are the more thought they need to put into it."

"Still, the kids love it, I expect."

"Oh yes—but all they want is a good old thump, thump, thump to jive to. Now listen"—she manipulated the knobs and the tape raced forward—"here's the one you always used to love, Benny."

She turned up the volume and Benny started—so taut had his nerves become—at the flood of sound. It was the Original Dixieland Onestep, the tune Tony Hammond had played on the night of the second great football game, and as Benedict heard it he felt the old delight leap up in him again. And this time Hammond seemed to be inspired; his tone was urgent and driving and full of joy. Laura and Benedict stood looking at each other as the magnificent sound pounded and pulsed through the shivering basement room. When it was over she snapped the switch off.

"That's all, Benny," she said. "That's all he'll ever do now. And he could already do that when we were all children, growing up together."

XVI

ARABELLA WAS SITTING at her desk, writing a letter. He was touched, as he always was, to see that she was wearing her glasses. She was, like all women, resentful at having to wear them at all, and tried never to do so when Benedict was there. She took them off as he came up behind and kissed her.

"Hello, Benny darling. Did you have a wonderful time?"

"Wonderful. But I wish you'd come. I met Tim."

"Oh, then I am sorry. How was he?"

"Diabolically good-looking—all that buccaneering Felix stuff crossed with your slightly mysterious Oriental look."

"Benny, you're quite ridiculous. Who else did you see?"

"Oh everybody. Constance, and Milo's father, and Tess and Ken send their love of course; and I went over to Applestreet to see Milo and Martin Hennessy. . . . But who else do you think I've seen?"

"There are so many people you might have met, Benny. Tell me."

"Laura."

Arabella turned round quickly.

"And?"

"It was just as I expected."

"They're unhappy?"

"Dreadfully. They live in a squalid basement in Pimlico."

"I suppose you felt you'd got to help them?" There was a bitter note in her voice. "You feel you have to help every lame dog over the stile, even the ones that have bitten you."

"No. I can't help them. They don't need money. All they really need is someone with a pair of pliers to cut an invisible wire."

"You're talking nonsense as usual, Benny."

"I'm sorry. Oh and I saw Lady M. She said I should play for the Brewery team next summer. And you know what, Arabella? I went to see the estate agent. I suddenly thought how marvellous if we could get a house in the Cressbrook Valley. Maybe we could even find one where it ran through the bottom of the garden so that . . ."

279

Arabella's face had grown serious. "Benny," she said, "I want you to sit down and listen carefully. For thirteen years— thirteen wonderful years—I've lived with you and tried to help you do whatever you wanted."

"Of course, Arabella. You know how I feel about . . ."

"But you are not going to live in the Cressbrook Valley."

"Why not?"

"Because for you, it would be a disaster. You'd never do another thing. You'd sit on all the local fatstock committees and judge baby competitions, and become a J.P. Benny, you'd be quite appalling as a squire."

"I assure you, the picture you paint sounds grisly to me too."

"Yes, but you'd get talked into it. I can see you, Governor of your old school, Lord Lieutenant of the County, Master of the Hunt, Conservative M.P. for the Cressbrook Division . . ."

"Not on your life!"

"All right. Let's leave that for a moment. The next point is that you are not going to turn the business into a charitable trust so that you can sit and dream all day and salve your conscience by remote control. That's too easy, Benny. You will keep the business. If you really have this masochistic desire to give something back—I'm pulling your leg now, Benny, so don't look so crestfallen; you know how I feel about that—but frankly you've got to do it some much harder way. You've got to stay in the rat-race. Also, you will keep the business because I am an extravagant slut and I want you to marry me."

"Yes, I was coming to that. Why in hell's name didn't you tell me . . ."

"Because, Benny, in the first place I wasn't sure about you. No, don't look so hurt. You're such an idealist, and you fell in love so deeply when you were very young, that I wondered if you'd ever get over it. I know we've been very happy and that in a quiet way I've helped."

"Arabella, don't be ridiculous. If it hadn't been for you . . ."

"There'd have been somebody else to bring you slowly back to earth. You know something, Benny; you used to say that you felt as if you were running along with your feet four inches above the ground. Well, now you're coming very gently back to earth. The spell is breaking. Only promise me you'll always stay a quarter of an inch above sea level. You've acquired some arrogance. You have the greatest appetite for life of any man I've ever met. And you have a very pleasing smell. I have, therefore, decided to marry you. I always wanted to have a chance to ask a man that and now I have."

"You know perfectly well, Arabella, I'd have married you years ago if I'd known . . ."

"Benny, I didn't want your chivalry or your charity. I didn't want you till you were looking at me straight and cold and clear and saying to yourself: she's a raddled old bag of forty, six years older than me, and she's been around a bit but I'll have the old slut all the same."

"That's not quite how I see it."

"Well that's how I see it."

"I can't understand why no one ever told me you weren't married to Weston."

"You'd have found out if you'd ever gone back to Aylsbourn. And as soon as you did, Mrs. D. told you. Similarly, if Felix had ever come home, we'd have told him. Before, he was too young. We arrived from our honeymoon when the poor little fellow was only twelve and trying so hard to adjust to a new mother. We didn't—I didn't—want to give him an added problem to struggle with. Anyway, enough of these squalid recriminations. Is it yes or no?"

"It's yes."

"Good. One other point. I want to have your child, Benny. I always have. More than one, if there's time."

"I'll see what I can do. And now I'm going to give you one or two orders."

"Yes, my lord." She got out a pad to write them down. It was a harmless game they played.

"Lay in twelve dozen bottles of the dryest champagne you can find—Bollinger or Krug I should think."

"Yes, my lord."

"Get the grub from Fortnums and see they include vol-au-vents made with Cressbrook mushrooms."

"Yes, my lord."

"Go to Victor Siebel tomorrow about your dress."

"Yes, my lord."

"Send invitations first to our personal friends. Mr. and Mrs. Kenneth Heppel. Mr. and Mrs. Aelfric Gates. Tell her I shan't take no for an answer. Mr. and Mrs. Milo Johnston. Mr. and Mrs. Henry Johnston. Mr. Felix Weston and Miss Joanna

Johnston. I'll tell you all about that later. Squadron-Leader Rupert Ripley and friend. Tell him she'd better be presentable, this time—we're getting respectable in our old age. Mr. Samuel H. Spiral and Miss Jackie Mason. Tell him if he doesn't bring her he's fired. Mr. Timothy Weston and friend. Mr. and Mrs. Martin Hennessy. Lady M. and Miss M. Oh and Mrs. D. of course. . . . I'll think of some more later."

"Yes, my lord."

"Book us in at that hotel at Portofino. You know, where we had that other honeymoon."

"Yes, my lord."

"And come here."

"Yes, my lord."

XVII

KEN HEPPEL AND Tessa sat in front of the fire. He was reading Alan Sillitoe's latest novel; she was sewing. It was Tessa who broke the silence first.

"Darling?"

"Yes."

"I can't help thinking about Benny."

"What about him?"

"Well it's so long since he was last in the Cressbrook Valley. Thirteen years at least. Why do you think he came back?"

"Because seeing Felix again seemed to liberate all his old inhibitions. He was bound to come back one day, but there had to be some moment which would tip the scales. Felix provided it."

"What does Benny really believe in?"

"That's simple. Benny is a man haunted by the incorruptible. He is out of phase with his time. He happens to believe in a heresy and a blasphemy. His heresy is that to live is sweet. His blasphemy is to claim that life is good."

"What's strange about that?"

"How can a man like that be in gear with the world nowadays? Of course he's doing better than most people; in fact he's made a great material fortune, and that, I suppose, is the index of success in 1960. He's made it from his own disillusion. He's made a quarter of a million, Tess, in a fit of absent-mindedness."

"How has he done it, though? I mean he used to be so gentle and unaggressive."

"He's done it because—leaving aside his natural intelligence, which thousands of other men have—he never gave a damn whether he made a packet or lost it. Consequently, the world being what it is and the genuine competition pretty thin, he made it."

"He didn't care?"

"No, he didn't care. He was trying to forget what he had lost. Remember, he had no orthodox religious faith, only the ordinary humanist's belief in men and women."

283

"But, even I know, darling, that that's a pretty reckless belief to stake your life on."

"I know. But he did. He never understood why those who lost their trust in God should also lose their trust in people. In fact Benny works on the reverse theory: that if there is nothing else then we are of infinite importance to each other. And that all of us, therefore, should live as if this were so."

"But he was disappointed in his belief?"

"Yes, and it hurt him more than anyone has ever understood. Yet, you know, I believe he accepted all the time, a long way inside, that he would have to be disenchanted."

"Had to be?"

"Yes, you see he really is no Pangloss. He doesn't see life in perfect perspectives and glossy colours. On the contrary, he loves it unaffectedly, warts and all, as a man may still love a woman after seeing her face each day for fifty years. If you put Benny to the stake and called on him to recant, he would still cry out that life was good as they cut the hot entrails out of him."

"But is Benny's view so unusual?"

"No! the longer I live the more I see that the world is entirely a subjective illusion. And our view of it is entirely independent of our circumstances; we find it heaven or hell because of the way we are made, the disposition of our hormones, our genes, our glands. Some of us were born rich and despise life; others as poor as church-mice love it all the way. Felix's father has a hundred thousand, yet Felix despises life, I was always in favour of life, even when my father had only three pounds a week."

"This is where he always disagreed with Felix."

"Yes; I've listened to the debate between Benny and Felix for nearly fifteen years now; neither is right, neither is wrong. But both views should be heard and understood. Benny's view is out of favour."

"But what exactly *is* Benny's view? I mean in a nutshell, so that I can understand it?"

"Benny divides people into two simple categories: the life-enhancers and the life-diminishers; he is a believer in the first, a leader of the pro-life party."

"Yes, I've heard Laura use that phrase."

"That doesn't mean he accepts things as unmovable. He's a radical; he's grasped that the only way to preserve a country's true essence—or a man's—is to carry that essence onwards in changing material forms from one generation to the next. Radicals seek to preserve the best by continously altering the outward forms; conservatives destroy the best by a rigid adherence to the external shape of a civilisation at the expense of its true inner meaning."

"You make it sound rather complicated, darling."

"O.K. Let me put it more simply: see what happens to a ship when the wheel is held straight. To keep it on course you have to keep swinging the wheel."

"You may be right. But that doesn't sound like the Benny I know."

But Kenneth wasn't listening to her now. He was on his favourite theme. "Benny argues," he went on, "that we are living on a spiritual island; all our most talented young men are firing their beautiful, white-hot bullets out to sea at the traditional enemies, while the real enemies are creeping up behind us; or are already inside the barricades. He argues that far more fortresses have fallen through treachery inside than ever did from exterior assault."

"You're serious about him being a radical?"

"Yes. Today's young angries are the true conservatives; they are not against the Establishment, only against not being in it themselves. Otherwise, when they want to launch an assault, why do they choose the most boring Aunt Sallies in the world: God, the Government, the Middle classes, parents—traditional chopping blocks of the young since the beginning of human history?"

"Benny has different causes?"

"Yes, Benny on the other hand, has chosen something really unpopular to champion; something that genuinely puts him in the world's pillory. You know we've cleaned up some of our four-letter words recently, washed their faces and restored them to respectable use again. But can you imagine anyone taking Benny's four-letter word seriously?"

Tessa, the girl who, as Benny thought, was the only one of all his friends who had never been tormented by love unreturned; who, as he believed, had only loved once, said: "Even I know which word that is, darling."

"Remember the story of his examination fiasco? He wrote down his entire faith in his own four-letter word that morning."

"Does he have any other key words which he lives by?"

"Yes, an even more ridiculous one: honour. Turn it over in

285

your mind; can you think of a single serious use to which it could now be put? We've not only scrubbed it clean, which was necessary; we've scrubbed it away. No one can get up and use that word now, except as a joke, without being howled down; it has *no serious meaning*."

"But there must have been something wrong with the word or we wouldn't have had to treat it so drastically."

"Yes. Of course it had to be cleaned and overhauled. Maybe it should be put back into the machinery of our civilisation in a different gearing or fitting or angle. But it must go in somewhere; I mean people have got to live in a certain moral framework, however sophisticated, or we really are finished."

"You're beginning to talk in riddles, darling. But I think I understand. Benny came to see us because he's trying to get his bearings back, to decide what he can do next; what he can give back."

"Yes. That's exactly it. Take a humdrum thing like the question of his business. He thought of giving it up. But he's going to carry on with it; it would have been too easy to opt out. He's going to marry Arabella—and about time. He'll probably have children, and later they'll come into the business."

"But there's only one business in which he's really interested, darling, and that's the business of loving."

Kenneth Heppel looked at his wife with new interest. "You know, my dear," he said with genuine affection, "you're not half so silly as some people think."

"Tell me, Ken," she said without seeming to notice, "what was it that Benny found so strange about the air here? It's good, I know, but there's nothing unique about it, is there?"

"Good heavens no. Benny, you see, is a romantic. He has a way of bending the world to fit his view of it. The paradox is that this makes it no more or less valid than anyone else's view. There is no objective world: only our own conception of it. I can see the world quite easily through Benny's eyes if I try; on other days I see it the way Felix does."

"What was it, though, about the air?"

"The beech-trees. I'm convinced that's all it was. They have a special fragrance. It's been noted in the local histories for four hundred years now. You'll find references to our 'delicate sweet air" in one of the Elizabethan poets."

"So that's all it was."

286

"That's all. Everything is amenable to reason; there's a rational explanation for everything. We live in the age of the picaresque hero and the positivist philosopher; we must do without our illusions. There's no magic in the world, except what we put into it.

And that," he concluded, "is all there is to it."

Tessa went and looked out of the window.

Date Due

Lightning Source UK Ltd.
Milton Keynes UK
UKHW022141060223
416587UK00005B/102

STONE
AND A
HARD PLACE

R.L. KING

MAGESPACE
PRESS

To Dan, once again

ACKNOWLEDGMENTS

A lot of people helped me out on my quest to finish this book, and I want to thank them here. First as always, thanks to Dan Nitschke, my spousal unit, best friend, and first audience. He puts up with a lot from an obsessed writer, he's my most vocal cheering section and inspiration during writerly funks, and I'm grateful for all of it. Additional thanks go to Mike Brodu, my "picky beta reader," for finding plot holes and providing general encouragement; to my editor, John Helfers, for making the book better with his comments and suggestions for moving things around; to Glendon at Street-light Graphics for the awesome cover, ebook formatting, and other assorted nifty bits; to the folks from the South Bay Writers critique group who found other errors; and to the readers of my Facebook author page for encouragement, kind words, and patience.

CONTENTS

| PROLOGUE

Adelaide Bonham was convinced that her house hated her.

She clutched her heavy comforter tighter around her bony shoulders, but it didn't help. Mainly because it hadn't been the sudden wave of cold rolling through her bedroom that caused the shaking in her wrinkled hands.

Not entirely, anyway.

The first time she'd heard the voices, a couple of weeks ago, she thought it was the workmen. The house and its grounds were so vast that there were always workers around, doing some task or another: repairing, cleaning, landscaping. She thought it was odd that they were still there so late in the day, but there'd been enough exceptions over the years that she didn't worry about it. She mentioned the voices to Iona in passing, then promptly forgot about them. Despite her love for thrillers and cozy murder mysteries, Adelaide Bonham wasn't a woman prone to flights of fancy or unreasonable fears.

The second time she heard the voices, about a week later, she didn't tell anyone. She had a good reason: at eighty-nine years old, she was well aware that anything out of the ordinary she claimed she saw or heard would be instantly attributed to that dismissive diagnosis of senior citizens everywhere: *her mind's starting to go, poor dear.*

Adelaide was certain her mind was not starting to go. Sure, she might have her occasional bout of forgetfulness, but everybody had those. Even Iona, who was young enough to be her own daughter, sometimes forgot where she'd left her reading glasses or the day's newspaper. The modern world simply moved at a faster pace than it had in Adelaide's youth, and it was inevitable that things sometimes slipped through the cracks.

Nonetheless, the night she heard the murmuring while seated in her favorite chair in the upstairs library, she'd simply buzzed Iona and told her she was tired and wanted to go to bed. She watched the nurse's face carefully when she came in, but saw no sign that Iona had heard anything.

The voices kept whispering and murmuring, however, a far-off conversation too indistinct to follow as Iona pushed her out of the room in her wheelchair. Adelaide didn't look back.

Tonight, she'd gone to bed early, but not to sleep. One of her most cherished pleasures these days was curling up in her big bed under her heavy covers, turning on the cheery lamp on her nightstand, and cracking open her latest mystery novel. Iona made sure to keep her well supplied, and though she'd had to switch over to the large-print versions in the last few years, she'd never lost the almost childlike feeling of anticipation whenever she opened a new one. Diving into another beloved world of murder, mayhem, and the amateur sleuths caught in the middle allowed her to forget, if only for a little while, that it had been a very long time since she was young. Sometimes, as she was dropping off to sleep, she fantasized about what it might be like to have a mystery of her own to solve. She didn't tell Iona about this, either. Some fantasies were better kept to yourself.

Tonight was one of the best kind for mystery-reading: cold and cloudy, with rain pelting a comforting cadence down on the roof. Adelaide loved the rain, at least when she was inside the house. There were few things that made her feel safer and more secure than being warm and dry and bundled up in the midst of a rainstorm. The wilder, the better.

She was deep into the latest exploits of James Qwilleran and his delightful mystery-solving cats when it hit her.

The sudden, inexplicable feeling of being an unwelcome intruder in her own home.

There were no words to the feeling, only impressions. But the impressions were clear enough:

Hatred.

Loathing.

Adelaide sat up, her book slipping from her hands. "Is—is someone there?" Her voice came out as a quavering whisper.

Get out.

You are not wanted here.

Go, while you still can.

Then the wave of cold, like someone had opened a freezer and allowed a slow current of frigid air to creep across the floor.

Adelaide's heart pounded. She clutched her comforter and glanced toward the window. She was sure the heavy drapes were closed, and Iona never opened the windows.

The murmuring voices began again.

Adelaide remained there, her comforter pulled up under her chin, her eyes wide, her breath coming in short, sharp gasps. She half-expected to see the little puffs of air as they escaped her lips, like you saw when you were outside in the morning chill, but she didn't.

What was happening?

Get out...

"Who's there?" she whispered. Her terrified gaze darted around the room, but despite the fact that her vision wasn't what it once was, she didn't think anything was moving.

She didn't want to do it. She resisted it as long as she could. But as she sat there in her little pool of light, straining to make out what the ghostly voices were saying, her courage finally broke. She scooted over to the edge of the bed and scrabbled at the nightstand for the call button that would summon Iona.

As she waited for the nurse to arrive, Adelaide wasn't sure which thought frightened her more: that she was imagining the voices and the cold waves and the feelings of dread...or that she wasn't.

| CHAPTER ONE

Alastair Stone suspected the Universe was conspiring against his desire to keep the two sides of his life separate.

That suspicion was confirmed the moment he picked up the phone (*who the hell is calling at three bloody thirty in the morning?*) and heard Walter Yarborough's voice on the other end.

"Alastair. I'm terribly sorry to bother you, but I'm in a bit of a jam. I need a favor."

Stone glanced at the other side of the bed. Megan Whitney, assistant professor of English literature and magically oblivious girlfriend, was stirring from deep slumber. He willed her not to wake up. It would make a lot of things easier.

Easier. That was amusing.

"Alastair…?" She rolled over, voice fuzzy. "Who's that?"

"Nobody." Then, to Yarborough: "Just—hold on a minute. Can't talk here."

"Can't talk to who?" Megan muttered.

"Nobody. Go back to sleep." He patted her shoulder, already swinging around to a sitting position. He stuck the phone between his ear and his shoulder and tried to shrug into his robe without dropping it. He could have taken the call here, but that would be a bad idea. Whatever Walter wanted to talk about, the odds were high it would be something Stone wouldn't want to explain to Megan in the morning.

"Where are you going?" she asked. She was still mostly asleep; her arm flopped across his half of the bed as if expecting to find him there.

"Loo," he said, hurrying out. "Back soon. Just go back to sleep." He closed the door behind him and headed down the hall to his study. He closed that door, too.

"All right, Walter," he said, not caring that he was failing utterly to keep the annoyed growl out of his voice. At this time of the night, "coherent" was about the best Walter could expect. "Pleasant" was pushing it, and "cheerful" was right out. "What is it that couldn't wait until a reasonable hour?"

To his credit, Yarborough got it right away. "Oh, bugger—I forgot about the time difference, didn't I?"

"Well, I'm up now," Stone said, his tone dark.

"All right, then. I'm sorry to ask, Alastair, but I don't know anyone else in the area who can do it. There's a boy—his name is Ethan Penrose. Lives with his mother in San Jose. He just turned eighteen, and I was planning on taking him on as an apprentice. He was due to come over here next month."

Stone's eyes narrowed. "And—?"

"And—well, plans have changed. His mother's taken ill. Some kind of heart issue. It came on suddenly, and it's quite serious. Understandably, he doesn't want to leave her and come over right now. Even taking the portal across, it'd still be a long trip up here to Leeds from London."

Even half-awake, Stone was already seeing where this was going. "Walter—"

"I know. I know. You've always said you didn't want an apprentice yet. But you're a brilliant teacher. We both know that. He's a good lad—you'd like him. And it wouldn't have to be permanent. Just for a year or so. I'm sad to say it sounds like his mother isn't doing well at all."

"Why doesn't he just wait until she's better, then? Shouldn't he be taking care of her, not off somewhere learning magic?"

"She's got a nurse staying there who takes care of her, but the unfortunate truth is that she might not *get* better. Even though he's helping out where he can, he's an eighteen-year-old boy. He loves his mother, but he's got nothing else in his life. He hasn't even applied to university, because he thought he'd be too busy with his apprenticeship. His mother only recently told him about the fact that he's got the Talent at all. Everything's been a bit of a shock to him these past couple of months."

"Where's the father in this equation?" Stone leaned back in his desk chair and swiped his hand through his dark, unruly hair. "If the kid is a mage, then the father—"

"His father died when Ethan was very young. We were friends for a long time—I met him back when I was living in New York. That's why I was originally supposed to take the boy on. His mother and I have pretty much assumed that's the way it would go for years."

Stone paused, his gaze traversing the bookshelves, wooden desk, ratty leather armchair, and other fixtures of his study. The shelves were lined with row after row of books, from old moth-eaten tomes with bindings that barely held together to modern paperbacks, interspersed with skulls, bits of feathers, stone statuettes, and other eclectic objects he'd picked up over the years in his travels. "Walter—" he began after a long pause. "I—"

"Will you at least give it a try, Alastair?" It was odd hearing a pleading note in Walter's usually staid and confident voice. "That's all I ask. Just meet with him. Talk to him. See if you get on. If there are any expenses involved, I'll take care of them. And since he's local, he wouldn't have to live with you or anything." A pause, and then: "I know how much you enjoy teaching. Wouldn't it be a nice change of pace to teach *real* magic for a while in addition to all that 'Occult Studies' rubbish you feed those kids at Stanford?"

Stone closed his eyes and sighed. The sad thing was, Walter was right. Taking on an apprentice was something almost every mage did eventually—it was the sort of "pay it forward" system that kept the magical society running smoothly. You learned the Art from your master, and then later on you turned around and taught it to the next generation of students. At thirty-one, he was already overdue to take his turn, especially given how young he himself had been when he'd begun his own apprenticeship. He'd been putting it off for all these years not so much because of the teaching part—he loved teaching, and was damned good at it—but mainly because he didn't want his life disrupted by the responsibility the whole business would require. But—

His mind was already betraying him, spinning off lesson plans in the background and prioritizing magical techniques according to importance and level of difficulty. "Fine, Walter," he said at last, resigned. "I'll meet him. But that's all I'm promising. If he ends up being an entitled little toe-rag, all bets are off."

"Wouldn't have expected anything else," Yarborough said, sounding satisfied. He gave Stone the boy's address and telephone number. "Just give him a call when you're ready to get started. I'll call him and tell him to expect you—and warn him about you," he added with a chuckle. "And—thank you, Alastair. It'll mean a lot to him, and to me."

"Next time, thank me by not calling me in the middle of the bloody night," Stone grumbled.

He hoped Megan would write the whole thing off as a dream, but as she was getting dressed the next morning, she asked, "Who called last night? Is everything all right?"

"Fine," he assured her. "Just a—erm—distant relative from back home. Always did have a hell of a time remembering there's an eight-hour time difference."

She regarded him as she buttoned her jacket. It wasn't hard to tell she didn't entirely believe him. But then again, he hadn't fallen for her because she was stupid. "That's it?"

He shrugged. "Actually, it's a bit more than that." If he was going to continue seeing Megan—and he had no intention of stopping any time soon, since she possessed the rare quality of being satisfied with the level of commitment at which they were currently operating and showing no signs of wanting to increase it—he'd have to come up with some sort of cover story to explain Ethan. "He's asked me to...look out for a young cousin of mine over here. Sort of a mentor thing. His mum is ill, and he's having some trouble coping. So you might see him around here fairly often."

"I never pegged you for the Big Brother type," she said with a wicked smile.

"Yes, well—it would seem I'm overdue, then, aren't I?"

| CHAPTER TWO

Stone had a light class load that day, so he used one of his breaks to call the number Walter had given him. He spoke with Ethan's mother, and even over the phone line he could hear the weariness weighing down her voice. She was pleased to hear from him, though, and invited him over for dinner that evening to meet Ethan. "If you don't mind pizza," she said. "I'm afraid I'm not doing much cooking these days."

He showed up promptly at six o'clock. It was shaping up to be a drizzly, overcast evening, and it took him a while to find the right apartment among the maze of buildings that made up most of the block where Ethan and his mother lived. He glanced around as he walked, pulling up the collar of his black wool overcoat and wishing he hadn't left his umbrella in the car. Almost unconsciously, he slowed his normal brisk walk to a more sedate pace.

Do I really want to do this? He couldn't back out of at least meeting the kid—not after he'd promised Walter he would. But after—he wasn't sure. Taking on an apprentice wasn't the sort of thing one did without a lot of thought. Even if it were for only a year (and Stone had no illusions about the fact that Walter was expecting that if he and the boy hit it off, the apprenticeship would last much longer) it still meant giving up a lot of the freedom and mobility he'd become accustomed to. It was the same reason he hadn't asked Megan to move in; fond as he was of her, he was sure they probably wouldn't be coming up on six months of mutually pleasurable association if he had. There were certain things Alastair Stone required for proper functioning, and one of them was his own space. Megan was the same way, which is why they'd made it this far.

Ah, well. At least he wouldn't have to give the kid room and board. That was something.

The Penroses' door was on the second floor, up a steep stairway. His knock was answered almost instantly.

For a moment the two of them just stood there, taking each other's measure. Then the slim, blond boy spoke: "You must be Dr. Stone."

"Well, I'm fresh out of pizza, so I must be," Stone agreed. He flashed his best engaging grin; the one that put his first-year Occult Studies students at ease when he started discussing ghoulies and ghosties and things that ripped out your innards and wrapped them around your neck in the night.

The boy just nodded, then stepped aside and waved Stone inside. "Hope you didn't have too much trouble finding the place. It's kind of a rabbit warren around here. I'm Ethan, by the way, but I guess you already knew that." He indicated the space down the hall with a vague nod. "C'mon in. The pizza's here already, and Mom's in the living room."

Stone trailed behind him, frowning. He was usually pretty good at reading people, but Ethan Penrose wasn't sending off the kinds of signals he'd expect to see from a kid who was excited about finally starting on the path to becoming a mage.

"Hi there," another voice said as they entered the small living room. "Ethan, where are your manners? Take Dr. Stone's coat."

Ethan's mother reclined on a large overstuffed sofa, propped up on two big pillows and covered with a blue blanket. She waved him toward a chair across from the couch. The coffee table in the middle contained a large pizza box and a stack of plates. "Have a seat. I'll put the boy to work and then you two can pig out and chat."

Stone handed his overcoat to Ethan and settled into the offered seat. He didn't need to study Mrs. Penrose to see that her health wasn't at all good. She was pale under what once had been a good tan, her short blonde hair hung limp around her face, and he could see she'd lost a lot of weight in a short time. Still, her eyes crinkled with good humor; she watched Ethan fondly as he hung up Stone's coat, then brought out glasses and ice from the kitchen and set his mother up with a slice and some soda. "Dig in," she said when everyone was seated. "And don't mind me. I know what's going on, but this is your show tonight."

Ethan had perched on the other end of his mother's couch, watching Stone with wary eagerness. When it became clear he wasn't going to speak first, Stone broke the silence. "So—why don't you start out by telling me what you know, and what sort of arrangement you had with Walter."

Ethan shrugged. "He's an old friend of my dad's. I always knew my dad had some sort of—weird abilities. I don't remember him very well...I was only five when he died. But I do remember him doing things like making my toys fly around in my room, turning himself invisible, that kind of thing. He mostly did it to make me laugh."

"I see," Stone said, nodding. "And how long have you known that you also have these so-called 'weird abilities'—or at least the potential to learn them?"

"A year or so. I kinda hoped it might be true before that, but I didn't know for sure until then. Mom said I couldn't start studying until I finished high school. She said they didn't let you start too young."

"That's true," Stone admitted. "There's no hard and fast rule as far as age goes, but most of us won't take on apprentices younger than about seventeen or so. The magical community generally frowns on having children running around using powers before they're mature enough to control them. It's not only dangerous to the children and whoever comes into contact with them, but it puts the entire community in danger of discovery."

Ethan nodded. "Yeah, Mom was saying that there aren't that many mages around. I guess it could be kind of a pain to try to explain to a cop why you just turned somebody into a frog, huh?" For the first time, he smiled. It lit up his whole face. Stone reassessed his initial opinion about how excited the boy was about his future.

"Well," he said, chuckling, "most of us don't turn people into frogs. Transmutation of living matter is a bit beyond the standard skill set. But you've got the general idea. It's really more that we don't want to end up getting dissected by overeager government agencies who want to find out what makes us tick."

Ethan rubbed at his chin. "So—what *can* mages do, then? I thought the frog thing was sort of a classic."

Stone sighed in mock annoyance. "*One* bloody idiot sees an illusion spell and gets the wrong idea hundreds of years ago, and we're inextricably linked with amphibians for the rest of recorded time." He paused to take a bite of his pizza slice. "But at any rate—we're not there yet. I want to know about your arrangement with Walter. What has he told you about his plans for you?"

"Not that much, really. In a month, I was supposed to go to England and stay with him, but that fell through when Mom got sick. I didn't want to leave her alone for that long, you know?"

"Of course. Quite understandable."

"He said there's some kind of teleportation portal thingy that mages use to travel, and there's one near here and one in England, but it's still three or four hours away from Mr. Yarborough's place. That's just too far to be away right now." He glanced at his mother, and Stone didn't miss the concern in his tone.

"And you feel guilty about the fact that you still want to learn magic, don't you?" Stone asked gently. "Your loyalty to your mother is stronger, naturally, but that doesn't mean you weren't disappointed at losing the opportunity?"

Ethan's head came up quickly, his expression startled. But he nodded and became suddenly interested in his plate again. "Yeah," he said. "But I won't leave her," he added, louder.

"And you won't have to," Stone said. "If I agree to take you on, then you can study with me at my place in Palo Alto, and have plenty of time to be home and help your mum."

"What do I have to do, then?" The wariness was back in his eyes. "What kind of requirements do you have before you'll accept me?"

"Hell, I don't know. I'm making this up as I go along. I've only had a few days to get used to it myself." Stone smiled, but then he got more serious. "Tell me, Ethan, why do you want to learn magic?"

"Huh?"

He shrugged. "Just tell me what you want to get out of it. Why do you want to be a mage? It's not all beer and naked nymphs, you know. Well, actually, it's not *any* beer and naked nymphs. Mostly it's a lot of work. Hard work. It'll take you weeks before you can cast your first feeble little spell, and months before you even begin to get your mind around the basics. The whole apprenticeship process takes several years, and at the end of that you're essentially where you are now in your other life—a high school graduate. Which—no offense intended—means you don't really know much of anything useful yet. So, why do you want to do this?"

Ethan seemed to think about that a long time before he answered. Stone could see the mental wheels turning behind his gray eyes as he struggled to come up with the right answer—or the answer Stone wanted to hear. At last, he said, "Because it's what I was meant to do. My dad was a mage. Mom told me that magic usually goes by sex—fathers to sons and mothers to daughters. And it doesn't always do it, either. So I—feel like I've been given this awesome opportunity to do something that hardly anybody else can do. And I want to." He cast a nervous glance at Stone to see how his response was being received.

Stone considered it, pausing for another bite of pizza as he leaned back in his chair. "Not bad," he said at last. "Most guys your age think it'd be brilliant at helping them pick up women. And they're not too good about hiding it."

"Well, that wouldn't *hurt*," Ethan admitted, chancing a grin. "I mean, I'm not gonna turn it down or anything, if it happened."

"You won't have time for women," Stone said. "If you apprentice with me, you'll be so busy you'll think taking a double load at university will be a breeze by comparison. I'll tailor your training to let you do most of your study at home so you can be near your mum, but that just means you'll need to have more discipline, because you won't have me looming over you with a whip all the time."

"A whip?" Ethan's eyebrows came up.

Stone shrugged. "A metaphorical whip. But if you slack off, there'll be times you'll wish it was a real one." He leaned forward, his eyes narrowing. "Here's the bottom line, Ethan. You'll work, and work hard. If you want to be my apprentice, you'll have to agree to do what I tell you without question or complaint. Anything having to do with your magical education will be mine to control. You won't seek out supplemental training elsewhere if you think you're not moving fast enough. You'll read the books I give you to read, do the exercises I set you, and you'll put everything you have into the effort. I'm not a tyrant—I know your mum is going to be on your mind and I'll make allowances for that. But if you want to learn from me, you'll have to prove to me that you're worth my time. Do I make myself clear?"

He was pleased to see an *oh shit, what am I getting myself into?* look pass across Ethan's features. Sure, he'd laid it on a little thick, but he also meant every word of it. He still wasn't entirely sure he wanted to do this, but Ethan seemed earnest enough, if a little immature and preoccupied. Nothing like most of the kids who'd grown up knowing what they had waiting for them when they were old enough, impatient to get started and wanting to learn everything at once. This one might actually have potential—and more importantly, this one might not annoy him to the point where he'd end up calling the whole damned thing off after a month. He didn't change his expression; he just kept his gaze fixed on Ethan's face, waiting.

"Sounds like it'll be hard work, but worth it—if you really can do what you say you can." the boy said at last, a hint of a challenge in his voice. "So far, all I have is your word you can do magic. How about you show me some?"

"Ethan!" Mrs. Penrose sounded shocked. "That's not—"

Stone held up a hand. In truth, he'd been waiting for this. He'd have been disappointed if the kid hadn't insisted that he back up his claims: you didn't get far in magic by accepting things without question. "So, you want to see some magic, then?"

"Yeah. Let's see it."

Stone rose, trying not to grin. "Tell you what, I'll make you a wager." He put a fresh slice of pizza on a plate and picked it up. "See this? You've got two minutes to try to take it from me. If you can't, you'll agree to follow my instructions about your apprenticeship without question or argument."

Ethan narrowed his eyes, looking intrigued. "And what if I *can*?"

"I'll let you set your own magical curriculum," Stone said with a sly smile. "I'll teach you anything I know, in whatever order you like, without question. Fair enough?" He glanced at Mrs. Penrose; her eyes glittered with amusement.

The boy appeared to consider for a moment. "Deal!" he said, and lunged across the table toward Stone.

He was fast; Stone was faster. He took a step back, a faintly glowing bubble appearing around him. Ethan hit it and slid off, crashing to the floor.

The boy scrambled up, puffing as he tried to conceal his surprise. "Nice trick," he said, eyeing Stone. "Got more?"

The shield disappeared. "Of course I've got more." He made a mocking 'come on' gesture with his free hand. "Have another go. I won't even use the shield again. Need to keep this interesting, after all."

Ethan didn't attack right away this time. He stood back, still panting a little, watching Stone. Then he feinted to one side and dived low, going for the mage's legs.

The lights went out, followed by a loud crash as Ethan once again hit the floor empty-handed. "What the hell—?"

"You didn't think I'd make it easy, did you?" Stone raised a hand and summoned a light spell around it, illuminating the room more thoroughly than the single pole lamp had. "You're running out of time, Ethan. Best to start thinking outside the box." He gestured again, switching the lamp back on and dropping the light spell. He was showing off, and he knew it. It wasn't often that he got the chance nowadays.

He held out the plate, waggling it a little. "Come on. It's right here. Take it. Think about all the things I could teach you, if you can just—"

Ethan moved before he finished speaking. Snatching a metal horse figurine from the coffee table, he flung it at Stone's head, then followed it with a roar and another lunge at his midsection.

Stone didn't flinch. He waved a hand in an almost languid gesture, stopping the figurine in midair a foot from his face. He pointed his other hand at Ethan. The boy yelped and backpedaled as an invisible force shoved him backward and down onto the couch next to his mother. The horse figurine landed neatly and gently in his lap.

"Enough?" Stone asked. The pizza slice on its plate floated with mocking calm next to him.

Ethan struggled to rise, but the unseen force held him in place. His face reddened. "Yeah," he said through gritted teeth. "Enough."

Stone grinned, dropping the spell holding the boy down. "Right, then." Unable to resist a grand finale (it was *so* rare he got to let loose like this—it was considered tacky in magical circles), he switched off the pole lamp again, summoned an invisibility spell, and wreathed his body in crackling blue eldritch lightning. When he turned the light back on, he was sitting in the chair he'd vacated, calmly taking a bite from his slice of pizza.

"So," he said after swallowing, "I trust my qualifications are acceptable?"

If Ethan's eyes had gotten any bigger, they might have fallen right out of his head. He nodded. "Uh…yeah. Yeah."

Mrs. Penrose laughed. "You did ask him to show you what he could do."

Ethan didn't answer for a long time. He looked first at Stone, then at his mother. "So…what do you think?" he asked her. His tone suggested he wasn't asking for her permission, but for her counsel. Making her part of the decision.

She smiled a wan but proud smile. "It's up to you, kiddo. I know you've got it in you, but it sounds like you're going to have to work your butt off to get it. Are you ready for that?"

"If you need a bit of time to think about it, you can give me a call tomorrow," Stone said. "It's not the sort of commitment one should make lightly. Sleep on it, if you like. Give me an answer in the morning. Or next week. I'm not in any hurry."

But Ethan shook his head. "I don't need to think it over, Dr. Stone. This is what I want to do. I accept your conditions. Will you train me?"

Stone nodded briskly. "All right, you've got yourself a teacher." Rising from his chair, he pulled out a business card, scribbled his home address and phone number on it, and passed it to Ethan. "I expect you at my place next Monday afternoon, three o'clock. That'll give me some time to prepare a few lessons ahead. Don't be late. Oh! And—" He glanced around until he spotted his overcoat hanging on the hall tree near the door. He gestured, and a small red book sailed from an inner pocket and landed next to Ethan. "Read this by then. It'll give you a little grounding, so I won't have to trot out the whole tiresome intro lecture."

For only the second time that night, Ethan's thin face lit with a smile. "Thanks, Dr. Stone. I won't let you down."

"See that you don't." But Stone returned the smile. Maybe this would work out after all.

To his surprise, Mrs. Penrose got up and accompanied Stone to the door, motioning for Ethan to stay put. She gave Stone a faint, tired smile. "I'm so glad you've agreed to take him on, Dr. Stone. He's a good kid, but he just needs a little guidance. Things haven't been great for him, losing his father so young and now...this." She spread her hands, indicating herself.

Stone nodded. "I'm sure we'll do fine."

Her smile grew wistful. "I miss Matthew terribly, even after all these years. He used to show me the most amazing things. I wish you could have met him—I think you'd have liked him. He loved magic so much. I'm sure he was looking forward to seeing if Ethan would have it too, so he could teach him." She shivered and looked away. "I...I hope you won't take this the wrong way, but the magic isn't the only reason I'm glad you've agreed to this."

"Oh?"

She glanced toward the living room, where Ethan still sat. "Ever since Matthew died, it's just been Ethan and me. We do all right, but I...I think it will be good for him to have a man in his life. Sort of...a father figure."

Stone didn't answer right away. He didn't want to tell her that he was hardly father-figure material; this didn't seem the right time. "I'll—do my best, Mrs. Penrose. I wasn't kidding about the amount of work I'll be expecting of him, though. He won't have time to get into trouble."

She chuckled. "That's what I was hoping for. It's been the two of us for too long. He needs someone else around to give him something else to care about. Especially since there's a good chance I might—" She trailed off, but her meaning was obvious.

Stone saw no reply that wasn't either dismissive or patronizing, so instead he said, "I'll make a mage of him, Mrs. Penrose, if he's willing to work. You have my word on that."

"Good." She swallowed. "I know you will, Dr. Stone. I know you'll do well by him. Walter speaks very highly of you. He says you're probably the best teacher Ethan could have. I know he's in good hands."

After Stone left, Ethan waited for his mother to return to the living room. He still held the book Stone had given him, and idly began flipping through it.

"So…?" his mother asked, resuming her seat on the couch and gathering her blanket around her "What do you think?"

He didn't answer right away. For several moments he continued leafing through the book. It was old, bound in leather, with heavy, deckle-edged pages and old-fashioned print. Along with the text, there were many diagrams, depicting circles with odd sigils and symbols around them, old-style drawings of naked humans engaging in various magical acts (this gave him a moment of panic: *nobody does magic in the nude, do they?*), and elaborate mystical formulas that looked like the world's weirdest math problems. He looked up at his mother. "Do you think I'll be able to do this? To do—the kind of stuff he did?"

She smiled. "Your father did. And Dr. Stone seems to think you can."

"What did you think of him?"

"Dr. Stone? He seemed very…focused. And a lot younger than I thought he'd be," she added after a moment's consideration.

"Yeah…" Ethan had spoken with Walter Yarborough on the phone a couple of days ago to get some idea what to expect. He recalled Yarborough's words about Stone: *he's bloody clever, eccen-*

tric as hell, and the best mage of his generation that I know. But even with that, the mage had been nothing like Ethan had expected.

He'd only met Yarborough himself once, a few years ago. The older man was every bit your typical stodgy British stereotype: salt-and-pepper hair, impressive paunch, big moustache, gray tweed suit that had gone out of style long before Ethan was born, clothes and fingers festooned with strange pins, rings, and amulets. Maybe not exactly mage-looking, but definitely in the ballpark. And definitely fatherly—if not even grandfatherly—in his demeanor.

Stone, on the other hand, was—for lack of a better word—*cool*. How many mages wore a long black overcoat, jeans, and a Queen T-shirt? Yeah, okay, it was a geeky kind of cool, but Ethan understood that all too well, since it was the only kind he himself could reasonably aspire to. He gave a short laugh. "Mr. Yarborough said he'd be hard to deal with. Said he's moody and—how did he put it?—'doesn't suffer fools gladly,' but if I can keep up with him, he'll make me into a good mage."

"That's what you want, isn't it?" Mom asked. She pulled up her blanket a little more, even though the room wasn't at all chilly.

"I'll probably piss him off."

She gave him a fond smile. "You might—but I think your natural charm will win him over."

Ethan ducked his head, looking away. She was his mother so she had to say things like that, but he didn't think he possessed very much in the way of natural charm. He didn't think anybody else he knew thought so, either. "Well, I'll work hard anyway. I want this, Mom. I really do." He closed the book, got up, and bent to kiss his mother good night. "I'll see you tomorrow."

I'm going to be a mage. The thought settled in his brain as he headed down the hall toward his bedroom. In the back of his mind he was already doing the things Stone had showed him. Before he knew it he'd be casting spells, slinging magical energy, and never having to worry about anyone disrespecting him again. It was going to be great. He could get along with anybody for that kind of pay-off.

| CHAPTER THREE

S tone spent his next few evenings and the breaks between his Occult Studies courses preparing lessons for Ethan. He called Yarborough (making sure to conveniently "forget" about the time zone difference) to let him know he'd agreed to take the boy on, and Yarborough had been so grateful he hadn't even complained about being roused from a sound sleep.

Sunday night he took Megan out to Emilio's, a little hole-in-the-wall Italian restaurant in Los Gatos they'd discovered a couple months ago. "What's the occasion?" she asked while they dawdled over after-dinner drinks.

"Been neglecting you, haven't I?"

She grinned. "You do that all the time. You must be feeling guilty about something else. I can always tell. Wait, don't tell me—it's your Little Brother, isn't it? You've bonded, and you're planning to adopt him."

"You've found me out." He finished his drink and set the glass down next to hers. "You're half right, actually. It *is* about Ethan. I'm going to be working with him for a while. Doing some—tutoring to help him catch up with schoolwork he's missed. Mostly in the afternoons, so you shouldn't see much of him, but I figured I should warn you in case you drop by and find a strange young man hanging around my townhouse."

She nodded. "Just as long as you haven't found yourself—what do you Brits call it?—a bit on the side? I don't share. Not even if he's smoking hot and built like Brad Pitt."

He chuckled. "I'm all yours, my dear. You're already more than I can handle."

Megan rolled her eyes. "So what's he like, this kid? Sounds like he's had some trouble."

"He's a bit adrift, I think. His mum fell ill rather suddenly, so not only is he dealing with all that, but all his plans got buggered up, and he's had to scramble to figure out what he wants to do with himself."

"I take it his dad's out of the picture?"

"Died when he was a child."

"Poor kid. Well, I hope you can do something for him. Let me know if there's any way I can help out with anything."

He grinned wickedly. "Well—I think I can handle his stress. Think you can handle mine?"

"How about we go back to your place and find out?"

Ethan was waiting on the doorstep of Stone's townhouse when he pulled his black Jaguar into the garage Monday afternoon. "How long have you been here?" Stone asked as he came around to let him in.

Ethan shrugged. "Not too long." He wore jeans and a Cyber-pope T-shirt, and carried a backpack slung over one shoulder. "I wasn't sure how hard it would be to find the place. Mom's letting me use the car since she doesn't drive anymore."

"Good, good." Stone waved him in. Inside was a short hallway with a staircase on the left and rooms opening out on three sides. "Today we'll get started in my study upstairs, since we won't be doing any of the practical stuff that might get messy yet. Did you read that book I gave you?"

"Yeah."

"And?" Stone asked, glancing back over his shoulder as he mounted the stairs.

"Kinda dry, but interesting, I guess. I didn't know mages had been around for so long."

Stone chuckled. "*Dry* is a good way to put it. *Bloody boring* is even better. I'll be honest with you—the whole history end of the magic thing was never one of my favorite topics. I'm much more interested in the here and now—magical artifacts, rituals, spellcast-ing—*using* magic." He pushed the door open. "Have a seat there on the couch."

Ethan did as he was told, glancing with interest at the large, old-fashioned wheeled blackboard wedged between an ancient leather chair and one of the walls of books. Nothing was currently written on it.

"So," Stone said, leaning against the edge of his desk. "Before we get into anything too deeply, a few questions. How's your mum, by the way?"

"Not so good." Ethan sighed. "She almost had to go to the hos-pital this weekend, but Mrs. Hooper—that's her nurse—was able to get her settled down." He looked up at Stone, an odd light in his eyes. "Dr. Stone, can magic...heal people?"

"Ethan—" Pause, then softly: "No. Not the way you think. There are mages who can heal injuries, if they catch them soon enough. But we can't do anything about disease."

"So there's no—like—alchemy? Magic potions?" It was clear he'd had this on his mind for some time. His tone clutched at any-thing he could grab.

Stone shook his head. "No, not really. Not the way you're thinking, anyway. There are some of us who dabble in that sort of thing, but I can't think of anyone off the top of my head who has anything approaching expertise nowadays. And even then, most magical concoctions are more for dealing with things like increased concentration and minor injuries. They wouldn't work on some-thing as serious as whatever your mum's got." He regarded the slump-shouldered boy for a moment, then added, "I'm sorry, Ethan."

"No, it's okay. I just—" He looked up, steeling his expression. "Let's just get started, okay?"

"All right, let's. I need to set you up with some more books to take home, so—" Glancing around the room, he directed one hand at one shelf and the other at another, gesturing as if conducting an unseen orchestra. One by one, three books sailed from their places, glided across the room, and settled neatly on the couch next to the wide-eyed Ethan. "There you go. The first one is an intro text—I'll give you a bit of the intro today, but that's more in depth. The second is theory. It won't make much sense to you now, but just start familiarizing yourself with the concepts and terminology. And that third one there, the small one, is sort of an exercise book. Formulae and such. Lots of math. That one's a stretch—if you're feeling ambitious, read the theory book and the formulae in the exercises and see what you can come up with. I don't expect much from you yet, but it'll be nice to see what you do with it."

Ethan seemed to only have heard about a third of what Stone had said. "I still can't quite believe I'm…gonna learn to do that," he said in a hushed tone, waving his hand around to indicate the path the books had taken.

Stone grinned. "That and a lot more, if you listen to me and keep up with your studies. But I'll reiterate: we aren't going too fast in the beginning. I want you to have a good grounding in theory before you start doing the more interesting bits. It's sort of like learning to play sport: you have to build up your muscles before you get started, or you'll hurt yourself and set back your progress. You might learn faster from another teacher—a lot of them are rather slapdash nowadays, sad to say—but you won't learn more thoroughly. So be patient. This is a journey, not a destination. Got it?"

"Yeah." He glanced up. "I don't have to call you 'sir' or anything, do I?"

"You do, and I *will* turn you into a frog," Stone said. "Now, then. Sit back, stop thinking about levitating young ladies' skirts up, and start listening."

"I wasn't—"

"You will." Perching back on the edge of his desk, he asked, "So—do you know what the difference is between black magic and white magic?"

"I—uh—White magic is good, and black magic is evil, right?"

"Sort of. Though 'good' and 'evil' are pretty simplistic terms when it comes to magic. It's entirely possible to do 'good' things with black magic, and 'evil' things with white magic."

"It is?" Ethan was clearly confused.

"Very much so. This is an important distinction—probably one of the most important you'll learn." Almost unconsciously, he got up and began pacing around the room. "The difference between the two is how they're powered. Tell me: if you wanted to zap someone with a lightning bolt, would you use black or white magic?"

"I'm gonna get to zap people with lightning bolts?"

"Stay focused," Stone ordered. "Answer the question."

"Uh—black magic, I guess."

"Wrong answer. It was a trick question. You can zap someone with a lightning bolt using either type."

"So—I'll be able to do both?"

"You will—but you won't want to. Not for long. Not unless you want to give yourself over to black magic in fairly short order, in which case tell me now so we can call this whole thing off before we get too far in."

"Why won't I want to?"

"Because," Stone said, walking over to lean on his desk, "White magic is powered with your own energies, and with specially designed items that you construct to contain and store those energies. At its best, it's more subtle than black magic, more permanent, and much more powerful in most areas. If you want to build a magical portal, or put a permanent enchantment on a place or a person, you'd use white magic."

Ethan nodded, taking it in. "Should I be taking notes or something?"

"Not yet. I'll drill this bit into your head so much that you won't be able to forget it. This is fundamental stuff."

"Okay, so—what about black magic?"

"Black magic is powered by the energy from others. It's ultimately a very selfish, very visceral form of magic. Its power lies mostly in more transient sorts of spells, like those you would cast in a magical battle."

"But—wouldn't I want to—"

"Get into a magical battle?" Stone raised an eyebrow. "So—when was the last time you were in a physical fight?"

Ethan shrugged. "It's been a while," he mumbled. "And I didn't start 'em."

"Precisely. Ever shot someone with a gun? Stabbed anyone?"

"No!" He sounded shocked.

Stone nodded. "Well, there you go, then. Magic is *dangerous*, especially the kind designed to injure living things. You know how when you start to learn martial arts, they tell you all that rubbish about your body becoming a lethal weapon? That you should only use it in self-defense? Well, with magic, it's true. And it's damned important that you realize it as soon as possible. I'm not going to teach you those kinds of spells—not anytime soon, anyway. Certainly not during the first couple of years of your apprenticeship. By then you might well be back with Walter, and it'll be up to him to decide whether he wants to. If you come along well in your studies, I *might* end up showing you something nonlethal that you can use to defend yourself should the need arise. But the point is, magic isn't about hurting people. Not for white mages."

"So, you're a white mage, then?"

"I'm—sort of pale gray. It's hard to actually practice magic and stay completely white. But that's the other thing you're going to need to know—black magic is addictive. It's like smoking, or drugs, or liquor: the more you use it, the more you want to. I'll tell you right up front that black magic feels *good* to cast. There's a rush to it. But the problem is, you get to where you need more and more of that rush to get the same feeling. And every time you use others to gain power, you—" he cast about for the right words, "—well, 'corrupt your soul' isn't quite right, but you get the idea. You make it so it's harder and harder to do white magic, and eventually you can't do it at all." He fixed his gaze on Ethan. "So, I'm telling you right now—don't let yourself be tempted. That's why we're taking this slow. Unless you plan on making a career as a serial killer, everything you should want to do with magic, you'll be able to do with the white variety. Understood?"

"Yeah. Except the part about—what did you mean when you said that you 'power white magic with your own energy, and black magic with others'? How does that work?"

"Just like it sounds. Think of it this way: white magic is like running a race. When you're done you're tired, but you've accomplished something on your own. Black magic is like having someone carry you on their back and run the race for you. You still get the same result, but instead of you getting tired, the other person does."

Ethan's eyes widened. "So you mean—you *literally* take power from other people? Like—you drain their energy?" He shuddered. "That sounds like something out of a horror movie."

"And it is, essentially," Stone agreed. "Some black mages have hangers-on that agree to supply them with power in exchange for—well, whatever. Money, influence, sex, whatever they want. Those mages are at what I call the 'dark gray' end of the spectrum. As long as they don't do any permanent harm to their 'batteries' and the fools are willing, then there's really not much that can be said about it."

"That's—disgusting." Ethan leaned forward on the couch, staring at Stone. "People actually *let* them do that? Doesn't it hurt?"

"It tires them out for a while—how much depends on how powerful the spell is. Sometimes it kills them, if the mage loses control. That doesn't happen often with willing participants, but I've heard of cases where it did."

"And so, white mages do this to themselves? So you get tired when you cast spells? That doesn't seem very useful, either."

"White magic isn't really designed for casting quick harsh spells. We focus more on longer-term things, rituals, permanent enchantments, that sort of thing. But we can do it if we need to. And if we know ahead of time that we might need to, we can build items that will help take up some of the heavy lifting. But if you're caught unawares, yes, you'll have to watch yourself and make every spell count, because you won't be able to cast many before you exhaust yourself." Stone pushed himself off the desk. "But look at you—your eyes are glazing over. Don't hesitate to tell me that I'm boring the socks off you. I've been told that I love the sound of my own voice, and I can't really put up much of a defense."

Ethan chuckled. "No, it's fine. It's just a lot to take in, is all."

"Best to get used to it. Before we're done, I'll be filling you so full of information that you'll be dreaming in magical formulae."

| CHAPTER FOUR

tone was in his office at Stanford late one afternoon a couple of weeks later when there was a knock on his door. He glanced up, curious. This wasn't during his normal office hours, and the building that housed his office was far enough off the beaten track—Occult Studies wasn't exactly a prestigious subject around these hallowed halls—that people didn't drop by without a reason. "Come in," he called, pushing aside the stack of student essays he was reading.

The figure that shoved open the door wasn't a student. "Hey there, you old fraud," he called, erupting into the small space like a tousle-headed force of nature. "Long time no see!"

Stone grinned. "Tommy! How are you?"

Professor Thomas "Tommy" Langley taught Medieval History (which meant he had digs in an only marginally nicer end of campus than Stone did). He was a little older than Stone, about twice his width, and often joined him on sporadic weekend pub-crawling excursions. Stone hadn't seen him in a few weeks though, and figured he must be busy with his course load.

Langley shrugged, dropping down into one of the chairs in front of the desk. "Can't complain. You?"

"Wondering what you're doing here, actually," Stone said. "It can't be that you want to invite me out drinking, because you'd call for that. It would take something much more important for you to actually drag your carcass up here in person."

"Can't I just have missed you?" His grin got bigger. "I mean, come on, Al—you know I've always had a thing for tall, skinny English guys."

Stone glared. "Damn it, don't call me 'Al'." Sighing, he slumped back in his seat. "So, really—what are you doing here? You *didn't* drag yourself all the way up here just to invite me pub-crawling, did you?"

Langley shook his head. "Nope. Believe it or not, I've got a problem that demands your uniquely strange set of skills."

"And what set of skills would that be?" Stone asked with a raised eyebrow.

"You know—the way you're always going on about all that spooky stuff." Langley wiggled his fingers in "ghostly" emphasis.

"'That spooky stuff' is kind of what I do here," Stone reminded him, wondering where this was going.

"Exactly. Which means you've got *expertise*. That's important."

"Why is that important?" Stone spaced the words out slowly.

Langley spread his hands. "Okay. So I've got this aunt. She's almost ninety. Rich as Midas. Lives in an ancient, enormous house way up in the Los Gatos hills with her caretaker lady and seven or eight part-time staff. I visit her a few times a year. She's sweet as they come, but—well—a little dotty, if you know what I mean."

"If she's almost ninety, she's earned the right to be a little dotty." Stone shrugged. "But I don't see—" His eyes widened. "Tommy—you don't want me to frighten her, do you? Because I'm not exactly in the business of—"

"Don't be an idiot." Langley's tone was indignant. "I'm quite fond of the old lady. I don't give a damn that she's rich—it's not like I'd have any chance of inheriting anyway, and even if I did, it wouldn't matter."

Stone had to allow that that was probably true. Aside from a voracious appetite and a fondness for good beer, Tommy Langley had never shown any inclination toward greed. "All right, then, what *do* you want?"

Langley picked up a weathered statuette from Stone's desk and toyed with it. "Well—she's convinced herself that something's going on in her house. Something... supernatural."

"Supernatural?" Stone frowned. "What, did she think she saw a ghost or something?"

He shrugged. "She can't explain it. She says she hears things in the middle of the night sometimes, and that the house has developed a—her words—'chilly feeling.' Naturally, the caretaker lady and the rest of the staff think it's all in her head, but they humor her because she pays them a lot of money. It was actually the caretaker who called me about it. She's worried."

"Worried about what? It's probably just the house settling. Old ladies get cold easily. P'raps she should just turn up the heat a bit and—"

Langley shook his head. "You're probably right, but she won't hear any of that. She's convinced something's going on."

"So, what do you want me to do about it?"

"Well—I thought it might help if you went with me and talked to her a little."

"Me? Why the hell would she believe some stranger off the street?"

"Because it's your field. You know about the occult. You can go on about all that weird shit like you know what you're talking about. I think she'd believe you if you told her there was nothing going on."

Stone pondered. This was the first time in years that anyone had asked him to do anything in a professional capacity, aside from delivering occasional papers at very strange conferences. "Tommy, I teach Occult Studies. I'm not an occult investigator. The whole business is rubbish anyway. Half my students are goths trying to get into each other's pants, and the other half are horror writers looking for material."

"*I* know that. And *you* know that. But Aunt Adelaide doesn't know that. She hasn't got a clue that there's even a difference between what you do and somebody who runs around hunting ghosts. Besides, *she* doesn't think it's rubbish. She still has an astrologer who comes by a couple of times a year to do her charts and read her tea leaves or whatever the hell they do. She *believes*. Also," he added with a grin, "You turn on that British charm of yours, and you'll have her eating out of your hand before you know it. Everybody knows all women are suckers for British accents. That's why you've got a hot girlfriend, while I stay home at night watching *Seinfeld* reruns with my dog."

Stone's eyebrow crept up again. "Well, if you put it that way, how can I decline?"

Langley's grin widened. He levered himself up out of the chair. "Excellent. I'll owe you one for this."

"You certainly will. And don't think I'll forget it, either."

Megan was amused by the whole thing, but declined to come along when invited. "I'd probably burst out laughing when you started talking about all that occult bullshit like you actually took it seriously," she said, grinning.

"Yes, well, *I* might have trouble with that myself," Stone admitted. He was wandering around his townhouse, hunting for items that might look sufficiently convincing as the tools of an occult investigator. So far he'd gathered a couple of old meters that lit up but didn't otherwise work, the skull of something that might have been a ferret, a handful of feathers attached to a leather strap, a set of ancient, oversized headphones, and a microphone that he'd connected to one of the meters. He'd stowed all of this in an impressive-looking, cracked leather satchel that he'd dug up in the attic. "Might take Ethan along, though—he's into that sort of thing. He might find it interesting. I can pass him off as my assistant or something."

"A regular little Scooby gang, you three," she said with a chuckle. "All you need is a Great Dane and a green van."

"She'll have to settle for an overweight pug and a black Jaguar," Stone said, distracted as he tossed items out of an old chest. Emerging with an odd-looking pair of goggles with purple lenses, he tossed them in the bag along with the rest.

"Yeah, like you'd let Tommy bring old Charlemagne anywhere near your car."

"Point," he admitted. "Scooby-free, then."

Ethan, as Stone had guessed, was eager to come along on the mission. "What do I have to do?" he asked. "I don't know anything about pretending to be a ghostbuster."

Stone shoved a notebook into his hand. "Just—scribble something down whenever I say anything that sounds important," he said.

"So, it's basically just like being your apprentice," Ethan said with a grin.

"Silence, insolent pup," Stone growled.

They picked up Langley at his place in San Jose after dinner that Friday evening so they could drive up to Los Gatos together.

Stone introduced him to Ethan. "Every proper occult investigator needs an assistant," he said. "Hope your aunt won't mind. Oh, and that said—" He pulled the old satchel from his shoulder and handed it to Ethan. "Make yourself useful, assistant."

"Yes, master," Ethan said in his best 'Igor' voice.

Langley looked Stone up and down under the porch lamp's glow, taking in his tweed jacket with suede elbow patches, argyle sweater vest, old-style overcoat draped over one arm, skinny black tie, and crazier than usual hair. "You really went all out, didn't you? Where'd you find that get-up—Doctor Who's garage sale?"

"What, you expected me to show up in jeans and a Pink Floyd T-shirt? We're putting on a show here—let's do it right. Do I look sufficiently eccentric?"

"You look like a raving nutball. The hair's a particularly nice touch. All you need is some round, wire-rimmed glasses and a lab coat. And wait a minute—that sunken-eyed thing you've got going on: did you stay awake for three days, or are you wearing *makeup?*"

"Borrowed it from Megan—just a bit to finish off the look. What do you think? Am I convincing?"

"You're gonna scare the crap out of her. Better not forget the charm. Remember, we want to reassure her, not give her a heart attack."

| CHAPTER FIVE

L angley hadn't been exaggerating when he'd said his aunt's house was 'way up in the Los Gatos hills.' Los Gatos was a tony little village a few miles from San Jose that was home to many of the area's more affluent residents. Affording even the more modest homes in its vicinity required a healthy household income, but the hills that surrounded the town were dotted with the mansions and estates of the truly wealthy. Stone, directing the Jaguar around yet another sharp inclined curve, glanced at Langley. "You weren't kidding about her being loaded, then."

"Nope. Her husband was some kind of industrial magnate type. Died years ago, she never remarried, so she's sitting on some pretty serious bank accounts. That's part of why I want to get this handled quietly—if it got out, she'd be hip-deep in quacks who'd feed her a line about hauntings and infestations and separate her from a hefty chunk of her cash."

"As opposed to the quacks who want to help her," Stone said with a wry grin.

"Exactly. Slow down—we're getting close. The turnoff's right up ahead here."

Even with Langley pointing the way, Stone almost missed it in the darkness. He had to turn the wheel sharply when he spotted the narrow dirt road, and it took them nearly five minutes to wend their way through the open gate and carefully up toward the house. "Wow," said Ethan from the back seat.

"Pretty impressive, huh?" Langley agreed. "Old, too. It's one of the oldest houses in the area."

The house was indeed impressive. Though it was hard to see it clearly with only the perimeter lights and the cozy glow from the windows for illumination, they could tell it was three stories tall, built in a solid, old-fashioned style, and well-preserved.

As they all got out of the car and stood staring up at it, the door opened. "Hello?" came a female voice from a shadowy figure in the doorway. "Tommy, is that you?"

"Yep, it's me." Langley waved at Stone and Ethan to follow him to where a heavyset, smiling Asian woman of about sixty waited for them. "Guys, this is Iona Li. She's a nurse. She's been friends with Aunt Adelaide for years, and takes care of her. Iona, this is Dr. Alastair Stone, the—occult investigator, and his assistant, Ethan."

Stone bowed slightly. "Pleasure," he said with his best charming smile.

Iona motioned them in. "Mrs. Bonham has been waiting for you. She's very excited to have someone come around who can explain what's causing her...odd feelings." She exchanged a glance with Tommy, and Stone realized she was in on the ruse as well.

She led them down a wood-paneled hallway, lined with paintings that were quite probably Aunt Adelaide's forebears, into a large but cozy sitting room full of antique furniture, opulent but somewhat dusty oriental rugs, and lamps with fussy shades. The whole room looked like it hadn't been updated in at least seventy-five years, and practically screamed "rich old lady."

"Hello!" a quavery, cheery voice called from near the heavy drapes covering the front picture window. They'd almost missed her sitting there in the chair: a thin and birdlike old woman with fluffy white hair and a city map's worth of lines and creases on her face. Her bright blue eyes lit up her narrow face as she waved to the newcomers. "Please, come in. I hope you don't mind if I don't get up."

"Hello, Aunt Adelaide," Langley said, moving to approach her and motioning for Stone and Ethan to follow. "How've you been?" He leaned down to plant a kiss on her wrinkled cheek.

"I'm eighty-nine," she said, chuckling. "I'm still alive, so about as well as can be expected, all things considered." Her gaze settled on Stone and her smile widened. "Well. You're quite a looker, aren't you? You're a friend of Tommy's?"

Stone was only taken aback for a second, then he returned her smile. "It's a pleasure to meet you, Mrs. Bonham. I've heard so much about you. I'm Alastair Stone. This is my—assistant, Ethan Penrose."

"Oh, yes!" She made a tiny little jerk, and Stone could almost see the light bulb go off over her head. "You're the young man who's going to figure out what's going on with my house. He didn't tell me you were English. I *love* Englishmen. I could listen to you talk all day."

Langley flashed him a triumphant *See? I told you so!* look.

"Yes, well—suppose we get started. I don't want to disturb your home for too long."

She waved him off. "You needn't worry about that. I'm sort of a night owl. And I'm used to having people trooping through the house. We've always got little projects going on around here. Had the windows done last year, and the young men doing the earth-quake inspection in the summer—"

Stone nodded, remembering the moderate shaker that had hit the area earlier that year. Megan, a lifelong California native, had been amused at how much it had unnerved him. "You should see what a *big* one is like," she'd teased when he'd had trouble getting back to sleep. "I don't even notice them anymore unless they knock me out of bed."

"Old house," Langley said. "They had to do the inspection to make sure there wasn't any damage, but Aunt Adelaide's right: this place is built like a fortress."

Stone perched on the edge of a floral-print couch covered in doilies. "All right, then: before I set off to look around, suppose I start by asking you exactly what's been going on?"

Adelaide shivered and drew her jacket tighter around herself. "I know Iona and the others think I'm getting balmy in my old age, but I know better. I might be old, but there's nothing wrong with my mind. And I *felt* it. I *heard* it."

"Felt and heard what, Mrs. Bonham?"

She took a deep breath and shivered again. "I hear—voices, sometimes, when I'm in bed. Late at night. They—they *whisper*."

"Can you understand what they're saying?"

"No," she said, shaking her head. "I'm not even sure they're speaking English, honestly."

"All right," Stone said. "And what did you feel?"

"Cold. Like there's a draft in the house, only it feels like it's going right through my clothes and into my *soul*." Her round, frightened eyes came up. "Is any of this making any sense to you, Dr. Stone? Have you ever encountered anything like it before? I keep thinking that I've somehow angered a spirit or something, though I can't imagine how I might have done that."

When Stone answered after a pause, his tone was careful. "Mrs. Bonham—you say you felt a draft. Please, I don't intend any offense, but I have to explore all the angles: are you sure you *didn't* just feel a draft? This is an old house, after all—"

"No, no," she insisted. Again she shook her head, more emphatically this time. "It wasn't a *real* draft. For one thing, Tommy is right: this place might be old, but it's like me. It's solid. The only way there could have been a draft was if Iona had left a window open. And since *she's* the one who gets cold, she doesn't even open the windows. We have central air in most of the house, so we don't need to. Plus, as I said, we had the windows replaced recently."

"All right..." Stone glanced over and was pleased to see Ethan busily scribbling in his notebook. "Anything else you want to tell me before I go have a look around?"

"Well—" She shifted in her chair.

"Come on, now," he said with an encouraging smile. "I can't help you if you don't tell me everything."

She was silent for several seconds, clearly trying to decide whether she wanted to say more. Then she motioned him closer. When he leaned in, she spoke under her breath: "I didn't even tell Tommy about this. I thought he'd just laugh at me. But sometimes I get the feeling that there's something—*wrong*—in the house. Something...*evil*, even. Please don't laugh."

Stone didn't laugh. In fact, he was beginning to wonder if the old girl hadn't picked up on something that the others were too brain-blind to notice. It wasn't common for mundanes with an interest in the supernatural to pick up garbled signals from the real thing, like radios badly tuned to a distant station, but he'd seen it happen before.

He gently patted her liver-spotted hand. "Don't you worry, Mrs. Bonham. If there's something here, I'll find it. And if I don't find anything, then I'll be reasonably certain that there's nothing to find. That sort of feeling can come from all sorts of things. Even we occult investigators—the ones who are any good, anyway—start by looking for ordinary, normal reasons for strange manifestations. For example, I once read about a family who moved into a new house and one of the kids started feeling constantly on edge and stressed. Turned out he was just sensitive to the subsonic frequency from a nearby electrical transformer."

"Maybe that's it," Langley agreed, clearly glad to have a straw to grasp at.

"I don't even know if there are any transformers near here, "Adelaide said. "Do you, Tommy?"

"No idea. But we could check tomorrow."

Stone rose. "Come on, Ethan. Bring the bag and let's have a look around. Mrs. Bonham, if you could spare Tommy, I'd like him to come along as well. I don't like wandering about in people's private spaces without a guide."

"You go ahead," Iona Li said, moving over next to Adelaide. "I was about to get Adelaide's evening cup of tea ready, anyway."

"And my show is on soon," the old lady said with a twinkle in her eye. "I do hate to miss my murder mysteries. Tommy can show you where we'll be when you're done. Take your time, Dr. Stone. I promise, you won't be keeping me awake past my bedtime."

Stone motioned for Ethan and Langley to follow him back into the hallway, but stopped halfway to the door. "One more question if I may, Mrs. Bonham."

"Of course, dear."

"Was there anywhere in particular in the house where you experienced these odd feelings? You said you heard voices in your bedroom, but what about the drafts?"

"Upstairs mostly, in the east wing and that hallway," she said. "I have a lovely library sitting room where I used to like to read, but I don't like to go up there any more now."

"Thank you. We'll check it out."

In the hall, Stone gathered Langley and Ethan into a small huddle. "All right," he said. "If Aunt Adelaide isn't going to be accompanying us, and she's the only one not in on what we're doing, we can skip all the toys in the bag. But Tommy, if you could show me her bedroom and this library—it makes sense to start where she says she notices it most."

"Wait a sec," Langley protested. "I thought we were just going to wander around up there for a while, and then come back down and tell her nothing's up. Do we actually have to go anywhere in particular?"

Stone shrugged. "Let's make it look realistic. Besides, what's to say we won't find a perfectly normal, non-supernatural explanation?" Truth be told, he wanted to check out his hypothesis that the old lady was picking up vibes from somewhere, but he didn't think telling Langley that would get him anything but laughed at. He glanced sideways at Ethan, who looked intrigued by the whole thing.

"Fine. C'mon—the main stairway's this way."

Stone and Ethan followed Langley down the hallway and into a wide open hall; on the other side was an elaborately carved stairway. "How does she make it up all those stairs?" Ethan asked.

"She doesn't. There's an elevator. But it's easier for us to take them. Let's go to her bedroom first."

Adelaide's bedroom was on the second floor, at the end of a wide hallway lined with more family portraits, landscapes, and pastoral scenes. Langley pushed the door open and stepped aside to let them in.

As Stone expected, it was your classic 'rich old lady' bedroom: heavy drapes, brocade bedspread, elaborately carved antique furniture. The only things that didn't fit the decorating scheme were a couple of pill bottles on the nightstand and a small oxygen tank in a rack next to the right side of the bed. A large-print paperback copy of *The Cat Who Brought Down the House* lay open next to the pill bottles. The drapes were closed. The whole place smelled vaguely musty, with a floral overlay.

Langley came in last and plopped himself down in a chair, looking skeptical. "You wander around all you want with your magnifying glass and your magic deerstalker hat. Me, I'm gonna take a load off."

Stone got right to it, pacing the room and reaching out with his magical senses to see if anything caught his notice. Nothing did—of course, he was doing his best to be subtle about the whole thing so Langley wouldn't ask uncomfortable questions. His examination of the bedroom, which included getting down to look under the bed and tapping on various walls, lasted about ten minutes. Then he disappeared momentarily into the bathroom and emerged only a minute or so later. Ethan trailed him, looking like he wasn't sure what he was supposed to be doing.

"Anything?" Langley asked, sounding bored.

"Not a thing," Stone said. "If she's hearing voices, they're not coming from in here."

"Or—you know—there aren't any."

"That too. All right—take me to the east wing."

Langley seemed eager to get out of this all too intimate space of his old aunt's. "This way." This time he took the lead, with Stone following. Ethan once again brought up the rear.

No doubt about it—the house was vast. It took them several minutes to get to the third floor and find their way down another wide painting-lined hallway to the library. "Why does she stay in this place?" Stone asked. He himself was no stranger to large houses, being the owner of a decaying old manor back home in England that he could barely afford to keep one step ahead of collapse, but this one made his place look like a three-bedroom in the suburbs. "Obviously she's got the money to keep it up, but wouldn't it be more comfortable for her if she didn't have to lay in supplies to make the trip from the bedroom to the kitchen?"

Langley chuckled. "Iona adores her, and if she needs to go anywhere she gets pushed around in a fancy wheelchair. Plus, she absolutely refuses to move out. She says she's got too many good memories here, and she'll leave when they wheel her out in a casket."

"I guess nobody does stubborn as well as a rich old lady," Stone conceded, following Langley inside. "This is the—"

A wave of lightheaded weakness struck him from nowhere. He swayed, reaching for something to grab as he felt himself toppling over.

| CHAPTER SIX

It was a cliché to refer to someone moving through a space 'like they owned it,' but in the case of the individuals currently holding court at a goth/industrial club called Will to Power in San Francisco, it was true.

They called themselves The Three, and while they didn't actually own the club or have any idea who did, the manner in which they prowled and stalked its darkened spaces had a way of convincing others to get out of their way—even those who had never encountered them before. More than one hapless club patron, withering under the combined force of their gazes until sufficiently unnerved to give up a desirable table or cede prime real estate on one of the dance floors, was convinced they were vampires. Those who knew better than to believe in such nonsense just rationalized things by deciding that it wasn't a good idea to mess with all three of them at once. Since they were rarely seen far from each other's proximity, that was a reasonable precaution.

Currently, The Three lounged at an out-of-the-way table near one of the club's black-painted walls, watching the ebb and flow of the club-goers and listening to the pounding beat of the band currently on stage. The band was a quartet called IED, and they were doing a good job of living up to their name. The wall of sound was so loud that it was difficult to hear oneself think, let alone carry on a conversation.

For now The Three were silent, acknowledging with a kind of regal grace those who waved or nodded at them as they went by. Most people just avoided them with the same kind of instinct that kept them away from poisonous spiders and large snakes, but in any evening's crowd there were always those who wanted to curry favor. The Three found this sort of thing amusing. They accepted the free drinks and other small courtesies that came their way with haughty disdain, and if anyone noticed that they never provided anything in return beyond a brief acknowledgment of the giver's existence, they weren't brave enough to bring it up.

Ten minutes later, IED finished their set. The frontman yelled something into the mic that might have been that they were going to take a break, then all four hurried off stage and the DJs immediately filled the silence with more pounding music. This was somewhat quieter, though—at least enough that The Three could hear each other without resorting to the indignity of having to shout.

"I'm bored." Oliver Hargrave said, downing the rest of his drink. His handsome features dripped with contempt. "Let's ditch this fuckin' place."

Trin Blackburn reached out her hand and stroked down his chest with one long black-painted nail. The finger didn't stop until it had moved below the table and lingered suggestively over the bulge in his fashionably tight jeans. "Patience," was all she said. "I like these guys. I want to hear their next set."

Across from them, Miguel Torres smirked. "Get a room, you two." He glanced up, waved lazily, and immediately another beer appeared in front of him. His own gaze followed the leather-clad ass of the slender, pale young man who'd delivered it.

The Three were not vampires—not in the classic, bite-the-neck-and-drink-the-blood sense, anyway. They'd arrived in San Francisco a year or so ago, blowing in from some unknown location. They never talked about their past, nor what made them decide to move from one big city to another. They attended all the right parties, and were fixtures at all the right clubs, their unerring instincts steering them away from one venue right before it fell out of favor and toward another at the beginning of its rise. If it occurred to them that their interest in a particular club or crowd might contribute toward the ascendance of its star, they didn't say anything about it. They simply took it as their due.

For the most part, all three of them liked Will to Power. They'd been coming here for longer than any of the other clubs they frequented, long after they'd have given up any other venue as "old news." There was something about the raw vibe here that turned them on—a constant level of energy that went beyond what they might encounter from the typical dance club.

This made it a great place to hunt.

Not that they had to, of course. Their prey came to them and willingly—if unknowingly—gave them what they sought. After a night here, they never lacked the energy they needed to power the spells and the dark rituals that they performed in the small hours of the mornings after most of the city had closed briefly down to prepare for the next morning.

All it ever took was a smile, a gesture, a quirked eyebrow. There was never a shortage of willing participants. And if these participants walked away from their encounters feeling a little woozy and disoriented—well, that was simply the alcohol, and the afterglow of having been noticed by the Beautiful People.

That was what kept them coming back.

The Three weren't here to hunt for any particular purpose tonight—they didn't have anything planned that required them to take on extra energy to power it. That didn't really matter, though, since it had long ago become a habit that they indulged on all of their nightly adventures. Why should they be without power, even if they didn't specifically need it, when there were so many eager batteries around to provide it?

Trin and Oliver watched, amused, as Miguel rose, grinned at them, and moved over toward where the slender waiter stood near the bar. He himself stalked rather than merely walked, every step broadcasting supreme confidence and sensuality. It wasn't that he was overly handsome—in fact, next to the blond Adonis that was Oliver, Miguel had the look of someone with an eclectic collection of perfect features assembled from several different contributors. They didn't quite go together properly and, taken as a whole, gave him a predatory and more than a bit creepy look—until he smiled. There were very few people, men or women, who could resist the effect of Miguel Torres' smile at full wattage.

The waiter was not one of them. Trin and Oliver continued to watch as Miguel initiated a conversation, and only a couple minutes later the two young men had slipped off into a shadowy corner. Only because they knew what to look for could they tell that the waiter's slumping posture was not due solely to Miguel's charisma.

"I'll be back," Trin said, running the side of her hand along Oliver's jawline. "You stay here like a good boy, yes?"

"Wherever would I go?" he asked, turning his head to nibble on her finger.

She had barely moved out of sight when a woman detached herself from the crowd where she had obviously been waiting and dropped down into the vacated seat next to Oliver. "Hi there," she said with a sensuous, alcohol-fueled smile.

Oliver regarded her without reply. He'd seen her around the club on more than one occasion; she was hard to miss in her slinky red dress that left little to the imagination, bright red lips, and over-teased bleach-blonde hair. Her entire look was at odds with the club's punk/goth/industrial aesthetic, but he figured she must have gotten in by bribing one of the doormen in her own special way.

"Don't have much to say, huh?" Her voice slurred more than a bit, her blue eyes glittering. Oliver revised his estimate: more than just alcohol was in play here. This woman was blasted off her ass. She reached out and mirrored Trin's gesture—or would have, if he hadn't pulled back. Oliver didn't like it when people touched him without permission. People other than Trin, anyway. Not that Trin cared much about things like permission.

"Something wrong?" she purred. "I'm Angelique, by the way." She rolled the name off her tongue in a desperate but mostly unsuccessful attempt to sound sophisticated and French. "And you are—?"

"Not interested," he said, sliding his chair away. If she kept it up much longer, he might consider using her for a little power top-up, but drunken chicks trying way too hard weren't his type.

She glared. "What are you, a fag or something?"

Oliver chuckled. "Nah." He nodded at the bar, where Miguel and the waiter were still feeling each other up. "My friend's the fag. I just have standards."

"Standards?" She rolled her eyes. "You mean that skinny bitch you were with? You can do better, baby, trust me." Once more she reached out, this time aiming at his chest in its skintight black T-shirt.

"Problem here, Oliver?"

Both of them looked up. Trin stood there, arms crossed over her chest, looking both imperious and amused.

Oliver grinned. "Nah, no problem. This lady just—got lost or something. I think she thought I was somebody else."

"Ah." Trin nodded. She turned to Angelique. "Well, that's a pretty good idea, actually. So get lost."

Angelique glared at her. For a moment Oliver thought she might go all spitting-cat and take a swing at Trin, but instead she just rose and leaned down low over Oliver so he had an unobstructed view of her impressively augmented cleavage. Then she produced a pen from her tiny handbag and, taking her time as if oblivious to Trin's glare, jotted her phone number on a napkin, kissed it to make a moist red impression, and pressed it into Oliver's hand. "Call me when you get tired of Bitchy-Poo here," she said, then tottered off unsteadily into the crowd in search of easier prey.

Trin resumed her seat, watching Angelique go. "Did you at least make her pay for her nerve?" She made a careless gesture at the other woman, who suddenly tripped, pitching forward with a shriek into the arms of two drunken young men. Trin smirked.

Oliver shook his head. "Didn't want to touch her," he said as Miguel arrived back at the table and sat down. Oliver picked up the napkin with two fingers and looked at it. "She dotted her *i* with a heart. How fuckin' sad is that?"

He made as if to toss it away, but Trin plucked it out of his hand and examined it. "Hmm…" Then she smiled a most unwholesome smile as she tucked it into her leather jacket. "I think we can have some fun with this. You two game?"

Miguel chuckled. "Trin, honey, remind me never to get on your bad side."

| CHAPTER SEVEN

L angley spun as Stone stopped speaking, his eyes getting big. "Hey, you okay?" he demanded. He grabbed Stone's arm to stop him from falling, and led him to a chair. "Sit down before you keel over."

Ethan, looking as weirded out as Langley, clutched the bag as he hung back and waited to see what was happening.

Stone didn't answer right away. His forehead was dotted with beads of sweat and his breath had quickened as if he had just exerted himself. He swiped a hand through his hair and just sat there for a moment, getting himself together.

Langley squatted down next to him, worried. "What's going on? You all right?"

Stone nodded. "I—I don't know what that was. Could I trouble you for a glass of water?"

"Uh—sure. I'll be right back." Langley hurried out.

When the two of them were alone, Stone turned to Ethan. "Do you feel that?" he asked. His voice held a strange edge.

Ethan frowned. "Feel what?"

"You *don't* feel it?"

"I don't feel anything. What's going on? Are you sure you're okay?"

Stone took a couple more deep breaths. "There's definitely something going on in here, and Aunt Adelaide is definitely *not* barmy. I can't believe you don't notice it."

Ethan turned away, looking around the room. After a moment he shook his head. "Sorry, Dr. Stone. Maybe I'm just not far enough along in my—"

Langley picked that moment to come back in. He carried a glass full of water, which he handed to Stone. "You look like you just saw a ghost," he said, still worried. "You—ah—*didn't,* did you?"

"Of course not. Must have been—something I ate." Stone paused to down half the glass of water in one go. "That's better. Thank you."

"You want to keep this up? Maybe we should just go back down and—"

"No, I want to have a look around now that we're here. Don't worry—I'll be fine." He got up, tested his balance, and stood for a moment just looking around. He had to be careful not to let on to Langley yet—at least not until he figured out how to do it without giving away his secret—but this whole business was spooking him far more than he was showing.

The moment he'd walked into the library, Stone had been hit with a wave of what he could only describe as cold hatred mixed with a kind of unwholesome longing. Something in this house didn't want him to be here—probably didn't want *any* of them to be here—but most of them were too hopelessly mundane to pick up the signals. Aunt Adelaide had probably only gotten a fraction of it, and it had been sufficient to scare her into calling in a stranger to investigate. What was odd was that Ethan hadn't noticed it either. The boy's progress in learning magic hadn't been spectacular so far, but he'd mastered the basics of magical sight over the last couple of weeks, at least.

Stone turned back to his friends. Langley and Ethan watched him warily, like they expected him to go green and bolt out of the room any second. Waving them off, he took a deep breath and began pacing around as he had in Adelaide's bedroom. This time

Ethan didn't follow him, instead choosing to remain near Langley. The boy's gaze followed Stone, but his mind appeared far away.

After a few minutes passed and Stone hadn't had a repeat of his strange attack, Langley appeared to relax. He sat down in the chair Stone had vacated and leaned back. It was obvious he thought this whole business was a waste of time, but he was willing to humor his friend.

"Dr. Stone?"

Stone paused in his examination of a bookshelf as Ethan spoke. "Yes?"

"I—need to use the restroom. Is it okay?"

"Of course. Tommy, where is—?"

Langley waved toward the closed door. "It's a bit of a hike, but you can't miss it. Down the hall, take your first right, then it's three doors down. I left the door open when I got the water, so you should be able to find it with no problem."

"Thanks." Ethan set the satchel full of bogus 'occult investigation' gear on the floor next to Langley's chair and headed out of the room, and Stone resumed his pacing.

"You're just putting on a show for the kid, right?" Langley said, the light finally dawning.

"What?"

"You know—all this pacing around and poking at things. You're trying to impress him. Is he one of your students?"

"Sort of," Stone admitted. "He's—the son of an old friend. He's interested in my field, so I thought he might enjoy seeing a bit of it in action."

"Did you fake the dizzy spell too? For dramatic effect?"

Stone sighed, coming back over. "Tommy—" He almost said more, but this simply wasn't the time. All he knew was that he would need to come back here, this time with some *real* detection gear, if he was going to find out anything definitive. And for that to happen, he had to be very careful what he said to Langley. "I didn't fake the dizzy spell," he said at last. "I told you, I think something I ate disagreed with me. But let me finish this, all right? Then we can get out of here."

"Sure, sure." Langley plucked a random book off a nearby shelf and leaned back in his chair. "Just call me when you're done communing with the spooks."

Out in the hall, Ethan moved quickly. His path was purposeful, but he felt oddly detached, like he was watching his body from somewhere up above it. It wasn't as if he wasn't in control of his actions, but rather that he was proceeding according to some directive that he didn't even understand.

He hurried down the hall, but instead of making the first right as Langley had indicated, he continued in a straight line. He moved unerringly, even as he entered a part of the house that they had not passed through to reach the library. He—or some part of him, at least—knew exactly where he was headed.

At the end of the hall was a small, unassuming door. He reached for the knob, knowing it would be unlocked, and slipped through, closing it behind him. His fingers found the light switch like he had lived here all his life, his feet mounting the narrow wooden staircase with complete confidence.

At the top of the stairway was another door, also unlocked. He emerged into a vast, dark space, illuminated only by the moonlight coming in through the skylights high above. All around him rose the bulky, covered forms of furniture and other stored items, with the smell of dust and long disuse hovering heavily in the air. Ethan didn't look down, only peripherally noticing the puffs of dust raised by his sure steps across the space. Even though his mind wasn't truly here, a corner of it knew that he didn't have long before he'd be missed. He'd have to do this fast.

Operating on unseen instructions, he shoved aside a large, sheet-covered object to reveal a taller, narrower one behind it, a few feet out from a wall. He crouched, grabbing the bottom of the sheet

R. L. KING

and whipping it free to reveal a mirror, taller than he was and surrounded by an ornately carved wooden frame. Then he backed up a few feet and waited, staring into its depths as if he expected to see something other than his own reflection in its milky, grime-encrusted surface.

When the glow appeared, he was not surprised, nor was he frightened. He waited in silence, unmoving. After a few moments passed, he nodded.

By the time he descended the stairs and reached the familiar hallway leading back to the library, he couldn't remember what he was doing there. *Must have taken a wrong turn,* he figured, hurrying back to where he'd left the others.

Stone was just finishing his inspection of the library's bookshelves when Ethan hurried back into the room, puffing. The mage raised an eyebrow. "Took you a while, Ethan. You all right?"

"Little upset stomach," he said with a self-conscious grin. "Plus I missed the first right, so I kinda got lost and had to backtrack a little."

"Yeah, that happens a lot," Langley said, nodding. "First few times I was here I could barely find my way back to the main part of the house without a trail of breadcrumbs and a Sherpa." He glanced at Stone. "So—have you seen enough? Are you ready to go? It *is* getting kind of late."

Stone paused in the middle of the room, took one last look around, and then nodded. "I think so," he said. "For now, anyway."

"For now?" Langley was confused. "What's that mean?"

"Tell you later. Don't worry, I won't frighten Aunt Adelaide. You're right—she really is a delightful old lady."

Seemingly mollified, Langley led them out of the room and back down the two flights of stairs. Instead of going to the sitting room where they'd all talked before, he led them in the opposite direction toward a cozy little room with an overstuffed couch and chair, both aimed at a surprisingly small, antiquated television set. Aunt Adelaide and Iona Li sat at opposite ends of the couch, watching *Murder, She Wrote.*

They both looked up as the three came in. "Well," Adelaide said with a smile, "did you find anything, dear?"

Stone paused, his mind whirling as it considered and discarded responses. If he told the old lady the truth—even a fraction of it—he would probably give her quite a scare. And for what? It wasn't like she was going to leave the house in any case, and so far whatever was there hadn't done her any harm, beyond making her uneasy. But if he told her he hadn't found anything and the place was clean, not only would he forfeit any chance to get back into the house for a more thorough investigation later, but as a mage he couldn't bring himself to leave these people exposed to potential danger without at least warning them that it might exist.

The old lady watched him with an expectant expression. "Well—" he said at last, "—I didn't find anything conclusive." That much was true. He knew there was *something* there, but he had no idea what it was.

Ignoring Langley's *what the hell?* glare, he continued, "It's probably nothing, but I can't be completely sure without a bit more examination, and for that I'll need some more equipment. It's up to you—like I said, it's probably nothing. But—" He spread his hands.

Now Iona was looking at him with suspicion as well. Obviously, Langley and she were both trying to figure out why he'd chosen to deviate from the agreed-upon game plan.

Adelaide, however, was contemplative. Her round glasses shone as she shifted her gaze between her nephew, her friend, and the odd stranger she'd invited into her home. "I know you two think I'm crazy," she said at last. "I don't blame you—I'd think I was crazy too, if I didn't know for sure that I'd seen and felt what I did. And I know you probably brought this nice young man along to assure me that everything was fine." She settled on Stone. "*Are you really an occult investigator at all, Dr. Stone?*"

Langley and Iona exchanged glances. *Busted!*

But Stone was unperturbed. He came around in front of the couch, careful not to block the ladies' view of the TV, crouched down, and met Adelaide's eyes. "I'm a professor of Occult Studies at Stanford," he told her. "That's where I know Tommy from. I'm not an occult investigator *per se,* but I do have a fairly extensive knowledge of the occult and the supernatural."

"Are you—sensitive?" she asked.

"If you mean do I notice things that others might not, then yes. Mostly because I know what to look for."

Behind the couch, Langley and Iona let their breaths out simultaneously. At least it was no longer looking like Aunt Adelaide would chuck the lot of them out of the house for trying to put one over on her. The old dear was sharper than either of them had given her credit for.

Adelaide considered. "Did you feel what I felt, up there in the library? Did you hear anything in the bedroom?"

"I didn't hear anything." Again, the truth was the best course when he could employ it. That would make the half-truths and outright lies he'd have to tell go down easier. "And, as for the library—I think there could be something there. I didn't feel a draft, though, or a sense of coldness. It was more subtle than that. And again, it might well be nothing."

"But it might be something."

"It—might," Stone admitted, acutely aware of Langley's and Iona's eyes on him.

"Then you're welcome to come back and check further," Adelaide said with a nod. "If Tommy trusts you, then I trust you. What do you charge for your services, by the way?"

Stone looked startled. "Mrs. Bonham—"

"Adelaide, please, dear. If we're going to be friends, let's not be so formal."

"Adelaide, then. And of course I wouldn't dream of charging you anything." He deployed the charming grin. "As you said—

we're friends. I'm happy to help." Pulling a card from his pocket, he handed it to her with a slight bow. "Don't hesitate to call if you discover anything else."

"Oh, you're sweet. That's so kind of you." She smiled at him, tucking the card away in her own pocket, and turned back toward the television. "I think it'll have to be another time, though. It's getting late, and I do so want to find out who killed poor Mr. Chalmers. Give me a call when you want to come back."

"What the hell was all that about?" Langley demanded when they were back in the Jaguar and heading back down the twisting road toward Los Gatos. "You were supposed to tell her everything was *fine*. Why did you—"

"Because it wasn't," Stone said flatly.

"What do you mean, it wasn't?"

"There's something going on in that house. I don't know what it is. I don't know whether it's supernatural or mundane. But I do know it's there. And I'd like to figure out what it is."

Langley let out a loud sigh. "Look," he said, clearly trying to keep the frustration out of his voice. "This isn't what I brought you up there for. She's a sweet old lady, and she's really suggestible about that kind of thing. If I'd thought you were going to fill her head with all this horseshit about evil spirits—"

"I didn't say a word about 'evil spirits,' Tommy, nor will I." Stone still refused to get defensive. "Look yourself. I know how you feel about her. I understand. I liked her the moment I met her. I think she's a lot more clever and a lot less dotty than you give her credit for, and I respect her enough to believe her when she claims to have heard something. And now you've given me a puzzle, and as long as she's willing to go on with it, I'm not giving up until I solve it."

Another loud sigh. "I forgot about that," Langley said, resigned. "You and your damned puzzles. Are you sure you didn't have cats in your family tree somewhere? This curiosity thing of yours is going to get you in trouble one of these days."

They continued bickering the rest of the way down the hill. Neither of them paid more than a passing glance toward Ethan, who hadn't spoken since they'd left Adelaide's house and who now sat silently in the back seat.

They reached San Jose, and Stone dropped Langley off at his house. "At least promise me this," Langley said as he got out. "If you want to go up there again, call me first and let me go along. Okay?"

Stone shrugged. "Sure, if that's what you want. You'll probably find my next steps pretty boring, though. I intend to get hold of some actual equipment that works and see if I can pick up any readings. That kind of thing can take hours, and usually turns up no usable results."

"That's okay. I'll bring a book. I know you mean well, Alastair, but a lot of the stuff you spend your days with your nose buried in is pretty freaky for your average everyday citizen. I just want to make sure you don't end up giving her a heart attack with something you think is perfectly normal."

Back in the car, with Ethan now riding shotgun, Stone glanced over at him. "You've been quiet tonight. Anything wrong?"

Ethan shook his head. "No, not really. Like I said, kind of an upset stomach."

"You're sure that's all it is? I still find it hard to believe that you didn't feel anything in that library. I haven't felt something that strong in quite some time."

"What do you think it is?"

Stone took a deep breath and let it out. "I have no idea. Whatever it is, I don't think it's centered on the library. The feeling was strong, but diffuse. It's clearly connected with the house somehow, but it seems odd that she'd only start picking up on it now. That either means it's only recently arrived, it's been there all along and something or someone's disturbed it, or something's changed with Adelaide to make her notice it now when she never did before. Or possibly that it's been gathering power, and only now has enough to be able to affect things around it."

"Any guesses about which?"

"Not yet. Like I told Tommy, I want to get in there and get a better look. Which means I'm going to have to come up with some more convincing looking data-gathering gear, so he can amuse himself watching the lights flash and the meters move around while I'm actually getting a look at things magically." He shrugged. "Anyway, none of this is helping you with your lessons. Let me drop you off at your place so you can get some rest, and we'll get back to it tomorrow if you're feeling up to it."

"Sounds good."

Stone glanced sideways at him, but didn't reply.

| CHAPTER EIGHT

T he walls in the attic of the abandoned house that The Three used as their ritual space were painted black, dotted here and there with magical sigils spray-painted like graffiti. They had long since cleared the uneven wooden floor of debris and moved in the larger gear they needed for their activities. They didn't worry about anyone getting in and disturbing it. Not only had they gone to the significant extra effort of weaving spells and wards around the place that prevented anyone but the most persistent fellow mage from finding it, but if anyone *had* managed to break in, the enchantments would trap them in place until such time as The Three could make use of them. It was kind of like a bonus.

It was three a.m. on a rainy night. The door flew open and Oliver entered first, dripping, carrying a smaller box stacked on top of a larger one. Miguel came in behind him bearing a pizza box. Trin, of course, carried nothing. She never did.

Oliver set the smaller box down and pulled out various bottles of liquor, a baggie of pot, and some rolling papers, setting them down on a nearby table. The larger box he placed in the middle of the floor. The three of them chattered on about their evening at a particularly good party, performing their jobs without needing to discuss them.

For a while they just talked, eating pizza, passing a joint around, and downing shots of the liquor. Finally at about three-thirty, Trin pulled something from her pocket. "Okay. Ready to send that bitch a little fun?" She waved the lipsticked napkin that Angelique had given Oliver back at Will to Power.

Miguel grinned. "What do you have planned?"

"We could make all her hair fall out," Oliver suggested.

Trin glared at him. "The problem with you, Oliver, is that you don't think big enough."

He frowned. "You're not gonna kill her just for being a skank, are you?" He appeared mostly unfazed by the idea, as if he were merely bringing up another suggestion.

"Oh, no. I thought maybe we could set her house on fire or something. Or blow up her car, if she's got one."

"Nice," Miguel said, nodding. "Or maybe give her an uncontrollable case of the shits. Less conspicuous, but a lot more embarrassing."

"Hmm..." Trin considered that. "Not a bad idea, but a little juvenile. And the fire's going to be tough in this rain. I've got it: let's flood her out. She'd better hope she can use those implants as flotation devices."

The other two recognized the finality in her tone, and didn't bother suggesting anything else. Oliver picked up the large box and began passing out various pieces of ritual material, and The Three set to work customizing the magic circle they'd painted on the floor. As before, they moved as a single entity and without words, each one knowing his or her role in the ritual so well that they didn't need to consult.

When the circle was complete, the candles were lit, and the foul-smelling incense was burning in the brazier in the center, Trin flipped on a small radio in the corner. An eerie instrumental metal tune wafted over the attic, loud enough to be heard, but not loud enough to disturb them. She nodded to the others, and each stepped to their appointed place inside the circle.

Oliver pulled a small knife from his pocket and waved it over the brazier, then used it to make small nicks in both of his palms.

He handed it to Miguel, who did the same thing and gave it to Trin. Nicking her own palms, she set it aside and the three of them clasped hands around the circle. They could each feel the magic already forming, a low current of energy passing between and around them. They had hunted well tonight at the party, drawing energy from many of its guests—including one man Miguel had left stuporous and barely breathing in a back bedroom. They felt flush with power, eager to release it now.

They had done variations on the same ritual many times—it didn't pay to piss off The Three, because they truly enjoyed the process of revenge. They hadn't killed anyone—yet—but they had discussed the possibility, and considered that it might be something they wanted to try if the perceived slight was sufficient.

Trin, as always, took the lead, beginning a low chant that the other two took up. Their eyes were closed, their nerves singing with the power they were building between them. They writhed and swayed, punctuating the chant with moans of ecstasy as the power rose higher, joining their individual auras together into a coherent and more potent whole. If anyone had been watching them from the outside, their first thought would not have been of a magical ritual, but of an orgy. The energy around them was becoming visible now, tracings of magical power around their bodies, their hands, the circle.

Trin shifted her focus for a moment, the napkin rising up from her pocket and moving into the center of the circle. It hovered over the brazier and then settled into it, the flames licking and dancing as they ignited and began to devour the tiny bit of paper. Preparing to send the spell on its way, she gathered the energies from her two companions, wove them into the pattern of the spell, and then joined it with the bit of Angelique from the napkin.

Together, the fragments of energy formed a reddish cord that snaked up through the house's roof. The Three followed it, their own consciousnesses riding along to its termination point.

It didn't take long—after all, it wasn't like Angelique the bar skank had any magical protections. In less than a minute, the cord dropped down into a small, unremarkable apartment on the second floor of a three-story building. Most of it was nearly indistinguishable, lifeless to magical sight, but a glowing form was curled up in what looked like a bed in one of the small rooms.

"Bonus," Miguel murmured. "Maybe her neighbors will blame her for flooding them out."

"Shh," Trin said, concentrating. "Help me with this."

Neither one of the guys had to ask for details. They focused together, feeding power into the reddish cord, directing it, shaping it to their will. It didn't take much effort at all to find the water pipe leading to the bathroom and warp it until it snapped. They felt rather than saw the liquid spewing out inside the wall; though they couldn't see each other's grins, they all felt the squeezes of their hands.

"One more, to be sure," Trin said. She moved her focus, and the other two followed.

In the kitchen, they opted to plug the sink and turn the tap on full blast. They remained there until the sink filled and began to overflow, then went back to check their handiwork upstairs. It would take a while before the water seeped out through the walls, but it would be at least a few hours before anyone in the building awakened. By then, the water would have done its job. It was more subtle than The Three's usual plans, but subtlety was good sometimes.

Angelique needed to learn some subtlety anyway.

They returned at the same time, breaking contact and stepping out of the circle. None of them looked tired or spent from the ritual. That was what the power they'd stolen earlier tonight was for: so they didn't have to be. Tiring oneself out doing magic was for weaklings who didn't have the will to claim the power all around them, ripe for the plucking.

Trin began rolling a joint. "That *was* fun," she said. "But we need to start thinking bigger. Maybe we'll kill the next one. You guys up for it?"

Miguel shrugged. "Sure." His satisfied smile was chilling. "After all, it's not like anyone's ever gonna catch us at it."

| CHAPTER NINE

Stone wondered if Ethan wasn't going to show up for his next lesson. It was already quarter after three, and there was no sign of the boy. Maybe he really *had* had an upset stomach last night, but it wasn't like him not to call. Stone thought he'd done a pretty good job of impressing on Ethan the importance of being reliable.

Last night had been odd on many levels. Aside from whatever was going on inside Aunt Adelaide's mansion—which was quite enough oddness for anyone—Ethan's behavior had set off warning bells somewhere deep in Stone's mind. Not serious ones, just the kind that made him notice the fact that the boy had been acting strangely ever since he'd returned from the bathroom. Ethan had never exactly been a chatterbox, but to remain almost completely silent for the better part of two hours wasn't like him either.

Okay, so if he really *had* had a stomach bug, he might have been embarrassed about stinking up a rich old lady's bathroom full of potpourri and little cat figurines. Teenagers were like that, getting inappropriately embarrassed over the most trivial things. But something told Stone that this wasn't the case this time. He wondered if Ethan *had* felt something in the house, and either didn't want to admit it for whatever reason, or else didn't even realize that his strange behavior had been brought on by forces he didn't quite grasp. That had happened to Stone himself when he was an apprentice, similar to the story he'd told Langley about the child and the electrical transformer—except that in his case it had been the floating miasma of negative magical energy hovering around an old, abandoned graveyard back in England. It had turned out that a particularly nasty spirit had taken up residence in a crumbling mausoleum, and the mages he'd been with had quite a time dealing with it. He himself had been mostly useless, watching wide-eyed as they'd done battle with it, and eventually sent it back where it had come from.

That was one thing Stone had learned in his over fifteen years of practicing the Art—no two people responded to it the same way. Sure, there were the basics and the commonalities, but every individual approached it from their own perspective, bringing with them all the baggage and detritus that their psyches had accumulated throughout their lives. That was why there were no magic schools, and why those like Stone who possessed both magical talent and the knack for teaching were in such demand: magic was very much a one-on-one kind of process, and the master-apprentice system, as archaic as it was nowadays, remained the best way to impart knowledge from one generation to the next.

He pushed aside the drapes to look out the front window of his townhouse. Past the small, well-kept yard, the tree-lined street was quiet and empty. Maybe Ethan had car trouble on the way over, or—

He was about to let the drapes fall back and make a phone call to Ethan's mother when he spotted the familiar blue four-door flying around the corner at significantly over the speed limit. It pulled into his driveway and Ethan tumbled out, snatching his backpack and running to the house.

Stone waited for him in the open front doorway. "I'm sorry," Ethan puffed. "I know I'm late, but Mom had another attack, and I had to help Mrs. Hooper get her to bed. Thought I could still make it in time, but—"

Ah. Of course. He stepped aside and motioned the boy in. "How is she doing?"

Ethan sighed, his shoulders slumping. "Not so good," he said in a dead tone. "She's getting worse. She might have to go to the hospital."

"Sit down." Stone waved him toward one of the stools at the breakfast bar and began putting together a glass of iced tea. He set it in front of Ethan and leaned on the counter. "I'm sorry to hear that. Are you sure you should be here? If you—"

"No, it's okay for now." Ethan shook his head. "She's sleeping, and Mrs. Hooper said she probably would be for a few hours. She's better off with her than me anyway, since she at least knows what she's doing." His tone sounded bitter.

Stone watched him for a few moments while he drank his tea. He almost said something else about Ethan's home situation, but decided there really wasn't anything he could say that wouldn't sound like a platitude. Instead, he ventured, "Ethan—if you're sure you're all right being here today, I wanted to discuss something with you before we start."

"Uh—sure. What is it?" His gaze came up from where he'd been staring into his glass.

"It's about what happened last night."

"What about it?"

Stone watched him carefully as he spoke. "Are you quite sure that you didn't feel anything last night? Nothing at all?"

"I already told you I didn't." He looked a little defensive. "You don't think I'm lying to you, do you?"

"No..." He kept his tone even and non-confrontational. "But I wonder if perhaps you might have felt something and not even re-alized it."

"How could that be?"

"Well, you said you had an upset stomach. That's one of the ways magic can affect someone who's sensitive to it and doesn't know what he's experiencing. Similar to Mrs. Bonham's chills."

Ethan thought about that. "Well, then, I dunno. Maybe I *did* feel something. But I sure didn't notice it."

"I take it your stomach problems are sorted?"

"Yeah, I felt better in the morning." A pause, and then: "Are we going back up there?"

"To Mrs. Bonham's?"

He nodded.

"Why, do you want to?"

"I dunno," Ethan said with a shrug. "I just thought maybe if you went, I could go along—you know, to see if I feel something this time. Now you've got me curious. I don't like thinking that something's affecting me and I don't even realize it."

Stone pushed himself off the counter. "I'll think about it. But for now, come with me. We're already half an hour late starting your lesson, and I want to try you on something new today."

Instead of heading for the stairway leading up toward the study, Stone moved toward the back of the house and opened a door on another stairway downward. Ethan looked confused. "Where are we going? Aren't we—"

"Today I thought we'd get in a little lab work," Stone said, motioning him ahead. "Which means I really don't want Mrs. Olivera discovering us in the middle of casting a spell." Mrs. Olivera was Stone's part-time cook/housekeeper; Ethan had met her briefly last week, when Stone had introduced him as a distant cousin.

Ethan's eyes widened. "We're actually going to do real magic?"

"Maybe. That all depends on you." He switched on the light, illuminating a large open basement with concrete walls and a few scattered rugs on the floor. Pushed back against the walls were various work tables and bookcases, a ratty old couch, and two large chalkboards, one of which Ethan recognized from upstairs. In the center of the room was a small table with two chairs facing each other and a thick candle in a holder in the middle.

"Sit down," Stone said, indicating the table. He headed to one of the worktables and puttered around for a moment. After a couple of minutes he returned with something in a small silk bag, which he tossed on the table. It clinked as if it contained pieces of metal. With two quick gestures, he lit the candle and turned off the overhead light, leaving the candle as the room's only illumination, and sat down opposite Ethan. The candlelight flickered in his glittering, unblinking eyes. "All right, then," he said softly. "Let's see how you do with this."

Picking up the silk bag, he withdrew a small coin, which he tossed on the table between them. "Levitate that," he ordered.

Ethan's eyes widened. "What?"

"You heard me."

"But—how—"

"You've been reading the books I told you to read, haven't you?"

"Yes, but—"

"It's all there, if you were able to put it together. Go ahead—try it. I want to see what happens." He made a languid gesture and the coin slid across the table and came to rest on Ethan's side.

Ethan looked at him for a moment, then dropped his gaze down to the coin. Stone doubted it was a type the boy had ever seen before—it was neither American nor British, and had an odd portrait on it, of something that didn't quite look human. Ethan stared at it, clearly willing it to rise up off the table. After several seconds, however, it remained resolutely immobile.

He took a deep breath, squared his shoulders, and squinted at the coin. When it still didn't move after nearly a minute, he raised his hands and put his fingers to his temples.

Stone rolled his eyes. "You look like a telepath in a bad movie," he teased.

"Well, how am I supposed to do it, then?" Ethan grumbled, glaring. "You're supposed to be teaching me how, not just giving me books and saying 'go!'"

"I wanted to see how much you got out of the books," Stone said, unperturbed. "It's all right, though—honestly, I would have been surprised if you'd been able to do it this soon and with no guidance." He fixed his eyes on the coin, and it rose smoothly off the table and returned to his hand. "Magic," he said, in the tone of a lecture, switching his focus to Ethan, "or at least the variety I practice and you'll be practicing soon enough, is all about the will."

"The will?"

Stone nodded. "What our abilities allow us to do—what the average mundane person wouldn't be able to do even with all the magical knowledge in existence at his command—is to impose our will upon the world, and make it do our bidding. Now, that sounds pretty grandiose, and in some ways it is. But in the main, all it means is that we can make things happen with our minds. The stronger the mind, and the will behind it, the stronger the magic. That's the other reason why I'm so concerned about your distractions. I know that some of them aren't your fault, but it's hard enough to teach willpower to someone your age without having the extra difficulty that comes from your mind being fragmented over other things."

"You mean that being worried about Mom is making it harder for me to learn?"

"Quite probably, and I'm not at all surprised. It's always harder to learn anything when your mind isn't fully engaged. But as I said before—I knew that was a factor when I took you on, and I'm prepared to work around it. All it means is that our progress might be a bit slower than it otherwise would have been. But you'll get there, I promise." He quirked a tiny grin. "I've never lost a student yet." Tossing the coin back on the table, he magically nudged it back over in front of Ethan, then got up and went to the chalkboard. He drew a complicated pattern and then stepped back, illuminating a glow around his hand to make reading it easier. "Do you remember this?"

Ethan studied it a moment, then nodded. "It was in the workbook."

"Right. And do you see how it relates to what you're trying to do there?"

Again he studied it, eyes narrowing. "I—think so. I'm—changing the properties of the air. Or gravity. Or something like that."

"Good. What you want to do is impose this pattern over the small space where the coin is, then use your will to grab hold of the coin and raise it up in the air."

"You make it sound so easy," Ethan said with a sigh.

"It *is* easy—once you know how to do it. It's like riding a bicycle, or learning to see those 3D pictures that always give me a frightful headache. Takes a while to get your mind around it, but at some point it just snaps into place, and you wonder how you ever managed not to see what was staring you right in the face." He came back over and sat down opposite Ethan. "The thing you need to always remember, though, is that your brain isn't like everyone else's. The thing that makes you a mage is what makes it possible for you to do this. The first time is always the hardest, because you have to *believe*. Our kind of magic isn't about faith—it's about knowledge and study and discipline. But even here, you have to take that first leap of faith and *believe* that you're capable of doing this. I'm telling you that you are, and I know what I'm talking about. So if you can't believe in yourself yet, believe in me. All right? Now—try it again. Picture the pattern, make it real in your mind, and then impose it on the coin."

Ethan took a deep breath and leaned over the table again. Glancing at the chalkboard, he stared back at the coin. His breath came faster, he gritted his teeth, and small droplets of sweat popped out on his forehead. For a moment Stone thought that nothing was going to happen, but then after several moments the coin rattled against the table and moved an inch to the right.

Ethan was so surprised he let his concentration slip and the coin stopped. "Did I do that?" he demanded. "Was that me?"

"All you," Stone assured him, amused.

"No, seriously. You're not messing with me, are you? Because that would be—"

"Ethan. That was you. All you. Now that you've got the trick—do it again." Stone tilted his chair back, arms crossed over his chest, watching the boy with the same pride he always experienced upon seeing a new mage actually harness the Talent for the first time. He remembered his own first time, many years ago: the sense of accomplishment that was so strong it was almost tangible. It had been one of the best feelings he'd ever experienced in his life. It was better than sex, though he'd never tell Megan that. It was why he loved teaching so much.

"Go on." He nodded at the coin. "You've got the pattern now. Let me see you lift it right up off the table."

Once again, Ethan hunched over the table, grabbing hold of it with both hands. He took a couple of deep breaths as if preparing to heft a heavy weight, then leaned in and glared at the coin.

It moved sooner this time, shifting over to the left about two inches.

"Now lift it up," Stone murmured. "It's the same pattern—just go up instead of over. The air can hold it up as easily as the table can, if you force it to."

The coin rattled. It shifted crazily back and forth. And then, after several more seconds, it rose two inches off the table and hovered there.

"Hold it there..." Stone ordered, still keeping his voice low and even. "Long as you can, now..."

For a second it seemed as if Ethan had startled himself sufficiently that he would lose his concentration again; the coin pitched and yawed, spinning a couple of times in the air before he got hold of it again. He was already sweating, his hands shaking as they gripped the edge of the table. Stone watched impassively, offering no further comment.

After nearly two minutes, Ethan let out his breath in an explosive blast and slumped; the coin clattered back to the table.

"Well done," Stone said, smiling. "Very well done for a first time."

Ethan was puffing like he'd just sprinted two or three laps around the block, but his face split in a big grin. "I—did it!"

"You did indeed."

He leaned back, still puffing and sweating. "But—is it supposed to be that *hard*?" Picking up the coin, he turned it over. "This thing—it weighs nothing, but I feel like I'm gonna puke."

"It will get easier. You've just asked your brain to do something it's never done before. It's like exercising any muscle: you have to work at it." He gestured and the light came back on. Blowing out the candle, he stood up. "And that's your homework for next time: I want you to go home and practice what you've learned. Stay with light things: coins, pencils, that sort of thing. I don't want you to try anything heavier than that for now. What I do want you to do is practice your control. See how high you can make it float. Try moving it around the room. See how long you can hold it in one place. If you get too tired, stop and rest. Once you demonstrate proper control over a small object, we'll move on to something larger. Rest a bit for now, and we'll try it a few more times to get you used to the feeling."

"So, how large can you do?" Ethan asked, shoving his sweaty hair off his forehead.

"Me personally, or mages in general?"

He shrugged. "Either one."

"How much do you weigh?" Grinning, he waved a hand and Ethan rose up, chair and all, and floated in midair. When the boy scrambled to hang on and nearly toppled to the floor, Stone lowered the chair gently back down.

Ethan stared at him, eyes wide, mouth hanging open. "That's—that's—"

Stone shrugged. "You have to understand, I don't go around levitating things just to see if I can. But I think if I had to and was properly prepared, I might be able to lift a small car. Briefly, anyway. I couldn't fling it around like Superman or anything, at least not without putting myself in hospital for a week."

"And how good is that? Compared to other mages, I mean?"

"Ethan," he said with a chuckle, "It's not a contest. We don't have the Magical Olympics or anything. We—" He stopped as a red light over the door flashed. "Phone's ringing," he said. "Excuse me a moment." He headed upstairs.

After a few moments, he reappeared in the doorway. "It's for you."

The boy hurried up the stairs, took the phone, and listened a moment, his expression growing concerned. "Okay, thanks," he said in a monotone. "I'll be there as soon as I can." He handed the phone back to Stone and just stood there.

"What's happened?" Stone asked gently. "Your mum—"

"She's in the hospital," Ethan said in the same dead tone without looking at him. "They took her off in an ambulance. I need to get over there. They're saying it's really bad this time."

| CHAPTER TEN

When The Three went clubbing again a few days after flooding Angelique's apartment, they had no particular plan in mind. Plans were boring. It was much better to go where the night took them, making their decisions based on the situations that presented themselves. That way, they never had to miss an opportunity.

They might even have passed the evening pleasantly: a few drinks, some good music, maybe a little weed to loosen them up. They might not have decided to kill anyone after all. They didn't do everything they talked about—not even everything Trin talked about. Oliver and Miguel half-expected her to forget about the whole thing.

She almost did, too, until she overheard some drunken douchebag at the bar bragging to his friends about how he was going to get "that fag" out in the parking lot and "fuck him up."

Trin didn't mind people calling Miguel a fag—hell, *she* called him a fag. Miguel called *himself* a fag half the time. The chance that mere words would arouse her ire depended entirely on her current mental state, and tonight she was feeling pretty good. But threatening any of The Three, even when the threat came from someone who was obviously so wasted he probably couldn't get out of his own way, was an entirely different matter.

It didn't take her long, after the guy's friends had departed to chat up women in other parts of the club, to slink up and convince him to buy her a drink. Once she had him believing she thought he was the hottest thing in the club—pathetically easy, given his wasted state—it took even less time to slip the clasp on his expensive watch and drop it into her pocket. Then she flashed him her best seductive smile and excused herself to the ladies' room to freshen up.

Miguel, Oliver, and she were in their SUV and halfway back to their ritual space by the time he figured out she wasn't coming back.

"So, you really want to do this?" Oliver asked an hour later while putting the finishing touches on their circle. It had taken a little longer this time: Trin insisted that everything had to be just right. The odds of anyone tracing the magic back to them were low, but the precautions only added a few minutes to the setup time.

"Why—you wussing out?" Trin asked.

"Nah. Just gettin' tired." He took another pull on his joint. "I could sleep for a week."

"You can sleep when we're done," Miguel said, plucking the joint from his fingers. "I still think we should've just ashed the guy back at the club. All that wasted energy."

"I want to try this ritual," Trin said. "It's a new one I found. Supposed to kill without a trace. Might be useful if we ever want to make somebody disappear long-distance."

"Eh, whatever," Oliver said. "Let's get it over with. I wanna crash."

They took their positions around the circle. They had augmented its basic structure with a fair bit of extra detail, most of which Trin had copied from a book while Miguel and Oliver stood back, passed the joint between them, and watched.

"Okay," she finally said. "This one's a little deeper than the usual stuff, so don't lose focus. I don't want to get my brain fried because you two chucklefucks are stoned off your asses."

"We got this," Miguel assured her. "Come on, let's do it."

Trin propped the book open on a stand next to her position, then took the douchebag's watch from her pocket and placed it on a small table in the center of the circle. Each of The Three did as they'd done the previous time, nicking their palms and then clasping hands to initiate the contact. The power began building almost instantly, rising to a low humming thrum as Trin consulted the book and recited the words of the incantation in a low, steady voice. All of them noticed that the power flow was different this time: less electric, more primal. It passed through their bodies, gaining potency as it went.

Trin kept chanting for several more minutes, then gripped Miguel's and Oliver's hands. "Okay," she said. "Ready to send the energy. This is where we have to really focus. Concentrate on the watch, and we'll—"

Something happened.

One moment they were all standing, hands clasped around the circle, the energy zipping and twisting between them like a mad thing straining to be released, and then the next moment they were—somewhere else.

They all felt the shift. The glowing tendrils of power disappeared, the black walls and brazier and spray-painted sigils replaced by something deep, earthy, and unwell. It was as if they were standing in a damp cave, suffused with the smell of a thousand rotting corpses.

Something spoke in their minds.

"Spoke" wasn't quite right, though, because there were no words. Whatever it was, it communicated by images, by nuance, by suggestion. It reached into their minds one by one and hovered there, sifting and examining what it found with the clinical detachment of a scientist. And it told them things.

The Three didn't try to fight it, or to break the circle. Partly they were afraid to: whatever this was, they'd never experienced anything like it in all the times they had performed these rituals.

They weren't sure what would happen if they tried to interrupt it—or even if they could. But mostly it was because whatever this thing was, this formless, powerful thing paging through their minds and their experiences—somewhere deep within them, they understood it. They understood what it wanted, and they understood what it could offer them if they helped it to achieve its goals.

They had no idea how long they stood there, hands locked together, legs shaking, eyes clenched shut. As the thing became more familiar with their minds, as its alien thought processes slowly meshed with theirs, its communications became clearer: still not words, but the images and concepts grew incrementally more lucid. It showed them four, repeatedly, intertwined with a mélange of others: a large house, a nondescript apartment building, a blond teenage boy, and a slim, dark-haired man.

At first they were confused, and sent that back to it; they had never seen the buildings, the boy, nor the man before, nor did they have any idea what the thing wanted with them. They could sense its frustration at their inability to understand it, but also a deep, abiding patience. It had time.

Now that it had made contact with someone it could communicate with, it had all the time in the world.

CHAPTER ELEVEN

As much as Stone hadn't been sure he'd wanted to take on an apprentice, he found to his surprise that he was missing the time he'd been spending with Ethan.

It had been three days since the boy had hurried out of the house, scared that if he didn't get there soon enough, his mother might die, and he wouldn't get to say goodbye. He'd politely declined Stone's offer to drive him to the hospital and raced to his car, leaving at the same high rate of speed at which he'd arrived.

He'd called back a day later with news: his mother wasn't dead, and they'd managed to stabilize her to the point where she most likely would survive this episode. Things were still very touchy, though, and she would have to remain in the hospital for the next couple of weeks at least. Ethan had apologized, but told Stone that there was no way he was going to be able to make it up to Palo Alto for a while. He promised to keep up his studies and practice the levitation spell, but that was the best he could do.

What could Stone say? "No, you're my apprentice now and damn your mother's precarious health, I want you here promptly at three o'clock"? Yeah, no. Instead, he told Ethan to keep him posted and not to hesitate to call if he needed anything and gone back to splitting his time between his job and Megan.

"You seem distracted," she said a couple of nights after Ethan had called. "Something wrong?"

He reminded himself again that her quick and perceptive mind was a big part of what was appealing about her in the first place. "Just a bit concerned about Ethan, I suppose."

"Why?"

"His mum's taken a bad turn, so he's spending most of his time at the hospital with her."

"What's wrong with that?"

"Nothing's wrong with that. I'm just concerned about him. She's not doing well. If she dies, then he's not going to know what to do with himself."

She moved in closer, snuggling her head against his shoulder. "You were enjoying that mentor thing, weren't you? You're missing it."

He shrugged. "Perhaps I am." That wasn't quite it, but of course he couldn't tell her that. In truth, the time he'd been spending teaching Ethan had made him realize just how little effort he'd been spending actually *doing* magic lately, as opposed to studying it and reading about it. And realizing that made him also remember how much he loved doing magic.

"Well," she said gently, "He's going to need you if…something happens to his mother."

He lay there, staring up at the darkened ceiling and not answering, for several minutes. Finally, he said, "I think I'll give Tommy a call tomorrow."

"Tommy Langley?" She seemed startled by the abrupt change of subject. "Why?"

Again he shrugged. "I want to have another look at his aunt's house. This is as good a time as any. It'll give me something to do."

"You want to go back there? I thought you were just supposed to tell her that everything was fine and there was nothing haunting her towel closet or whatever." She rolled over to face him, her eyes getting big. "Alastair. You're not telling me you *believe* that nonsense, are you? You don't really think something weird's going on in that house?"

"I don't know what I believe," he said, a little defensive now. "Who's to say there aren't things going on out there that we don't understand?"

She rolled her eyes. "You're starting to believe your own course descriptions. I knew it would happen eventually."

"Look," he said. "You don't have to go. You don't have to be involved with it at all. I'll just nip out there with Tommy for a couple of hours, have a look around, and then come back and we can go check out that new sushi place you found. All right?"

"Bribes," she said, snuggling back into his shoulder. "Hey, if you want to be a nutcase on your own time, that's none of my business. Just don't ask *me* to believe it."

"Fair enough," he agreed.

Langley, as Stone expected, was reluctant to sanction another expedition to Adelaide's house. "I still think this whole thing is all in your head," he said when Stone showed up at his office the next day. "You and Aunt Adelaide are feeding on each other with your stories. Hell, maybe you just want to impress her. I dunno. But I don't believe in spooks, and I thought you didn't either."

"I just want to have another look," he said, neatly sidestepping the issue of spooks. "That's all. I promise not to tell Aunt Adelaide anything frightening. I just want to see if what I felt there the other night is still there, or if I was just tired."

Langley sighed. "I don't like it, Alastair. I'd really rather you didn't. It's just—weird."

Stone stood and began pacing in front of his friend's desk. "Listen, Tommy. First of all, you have my word that I have nothing but your aunt's best interests in mind. I shouldn't even have to tell you that, should I? How long have we known each other? Do you honestly think I'd do anything to purposely frighten an 89-year-old woman?"

"Of course not," Langley said, not looking at him. "But you know as well as I do that you get kind of—well, okay, *strange*—about this sort of stuff sometimes. I've seen you do it before. I know you don't believe all the hooey about the occult, but—" His eyes came up, and he was frowning. "But shit—you told her you were 'sensitive.' You said you could feel the same kind of stuff she was feeling. So you lied to her so she wouldn't bust you for being a bogus occult investigator."

"I didn't lie to her, Tommy." Stone dropped back down into the chair. This wasn't going to be easy—he'd have to be very careful about what he said next. Sometimes he wished he could just tell the world that he was a genuine, real-deal mage. It would make things easier in situations like this. A lot tougher in most others, though, which is why he kept his mouth shut.

"What do you mean, you didn't lie? Are you trying to tell me you *are* 'sensitive'? Whatever the hell that even means?"

"I'm trying to tell you that there's a reason I chose the field I did, and it wasn't just because I wanted to write bad horror novels and impress goth women."

"So you believe in this stuff? Ghosts and werewolves and vampires and all that shit? You told me it was all 'rubbish.' That was exactly your word. So did you lie to *me?*"

"No. I've never met a ghost, a werewolf, or a vampire." That much was true. "But I *do* believe that there are forces in the world that we humans don't understand yet. And I believe that they can affect people who are sensitive to them. I think your aunt is one of those people."

Langley sighed, putting his face in his hands and shaking his head. "Alastair...sometimes I wish I'd gone looking for drinking buddies in the Physics department or something. You're a hard guy to be friends with sometimes."

"Let me remind you," Stone pointed out, "that *you* called *me* about this, and you did it precisely *because* of my area of expertise. Why not let me finish what I started? I'm not going to hurt your aunt. If anything, I might be able to get to the bottom of the problem so she doesn't have to deal with it anymore. Or at least give her a different perspective so it doesn't frighten her."

For several seconds Langley didn't respond. Then he looked up and rolled his eyes. "Okay. One more trip? That's it? Do you promise?"

"Well, that will be up to Aunt Adelaide, won't it?" At Langley's glare, he added, "All right, fine, then. One more trip. If I don't find anything definitive, I'll just tell her it was a false reading and we'll go on our way. All right?"

Langley looked at Stone like he was trying to figure out what his angle was. Finally he dropped his hands to his desk. "Fine. I'll give her a call. You want to go tonight?"

"The sooner we go, the sooner we can get it over with."

This time, instead of one satchel full of bogus gear, Stone showed up with the satchel and a pair of boxes in the trunk of the Jaguar. He had also ditched the "crazy occult investigator" outfit for jeans and a Who concert T-shirt under his ubiquitous black wool overcoat. At Langley's raised eyebrow he pointed out, "She already knows I'm not a real investigator. Might as well be comfortable."

"So what's in the trunk, then?"

"A few bits of measuring equipment I borrowed from a friend." That wasn't true. He'd actually made an afternoon trip to the Weird Stuff Warehouse in Sunnyvale and picked up a selection of things with interesting meters and flashing lights.

"What about your assistant?"

"He—won't be joining us today. He has other commitments."

"Lucky him."

Aunt Adelaide was happy to see them, insisting that they sit down and chat for a few minutes over a cup of tea. "Are you still experiencing the strange feelings?" Stone asked.

She nodded, fear showing in her eyes. "Not so much the voices now, but I still don't like going into that library. What are you going to do tonight?"

"Just a bit more checking with some new equipment I've brought along. You're welcome to watch, if you like."

She shook her head. "No, thank you. If you don't mind, I'll just stay down here." She shivered a little in emphasis.

Pressing Langley into service to help carry boxes (they took the elevator this time), Stone set off for the third floor. He kept his senses open all the way up this time, focusing on anything that seemed out of the ordinary. Now that he knew what he was looking for, there was no question in his mind that it was here. What "it" was, however, was another matter completely. He had no idea, probably wouldn't have much chance of finding out without doing an actual ritual, and he didn't think his odds of getting one of those past Langley were too good. All he could tell with his limited ability to probe the area was that it was most likely malevolent, and it was probably a good deal more powerful than it was letting on. In fact, if anything it seemed less potent than before. *It's hiding,* he thought. *It knows I'm here and it knows I can find it, so it's trying to make that difficult.*

"Hey!" Langley's voice broke in on his musings. "Did you hear me?"

"What? Erm—no. What did you say again?"

"How long do you think this is going to take?"

"No idea. Depends on if I find anything." He took the lead this time, heading for the library. Before entering, he made a quick gesture hidden by his body and felt a shield settle over his mind. He couldn't shield himself completely—not if he wanted to pick anything up—but at least it should keep him from keeling over in a faint if the thing decided to pull any of its tricks.

Langley set down the boxes and moved over to the chair he'd sat in before. "You don't need any help, do you?"

"No, you're fine." Quickly, Stone opened the boxes and made a show of setting up his "detection gear" as quickly as he could. He plugged it in and switched on the various pieces, pleased to see that they were performing as he expected them to.

Langley looked up with interest, examining the flashing lights and meters. "That stuff is going to help you find the evil boogeyman?" he asked in the same sort of tone he'd use to converse with a four-year-old about Santa Claus.

"Hope so." Stone continued to focus on watching the meters until he heard Langley pick up his book and settle back in his chair. Then he closed his eyes and cleared his mind, reaching out with his senses.

Even without the extra effort he could feel it in here; stronger than outside, but not as strong as before. He was almost certain this wasn't where it lived, though. It was in the house somewhere, or perhaps on the grounds nearby, its power emanating outward. But what *was* it? Why was it trying to hide from him? If he was going to find it, he'd have to—

From far off came a distant popping sound, followed by a scream.

Immediately, Stone snapped his senses back and whirled. "What was that?"

"Downstairs!" Langley was already pulling himself out of the chair. Before he'd made it up, though, Stone was out of the room and moving fast, taking the stairs downward two at a time at breakneck speed.

He skidded to a stop when he reached the ground floor. "Adelaide?" he yelled. "Iona? Are you all right?"

"In here!" Iona called from the direction of the TV room. Langley had reached the top of the second-floor stairs now, huffing badly.

Stone didn't wait for him. He ran into the room and stopped, taking in the scene.

Adelaide sat on a chair near the doorway, shaking, her face in her hands. Iona hovered over her, her head swiveling back and forth between the doorway and the television set.

The television tube had exploded. Shards of glass and metal covered the rug, the coffee table, and glimmered on the couch where Adelaide and Iona had been sitting. "What—" Stone began.

Langley came barreling up behind him. "What happened?" he demanded. Then he got a look over Stone's shoulder. "Holy shit! Aunt Adelaide!" He shoved past Stone in the doorway and crunched his way over to his aunt.

"It—we were just sitting here watching it. Iona was just helping me to the bathroom, and as we were leaving the room it—*exploded,*" Adelaide said, her voice shaking.

"It was horrible," Iona agreed. Tears streamed down her face. "Thank God we'd gotten up when we did, or—"

"Are you hurt?" Stone asked. He moved over to the television set, which was still sparking, and surreptitiously used magic to pull the plug from the wall. He didn't see any blood on either of the two women.

"No—we were far enough away that none of the glass hit us. But look at the floor!"

Langley looked frazzled. "Oh, man," he breathed. "If you had been sitting here in front of this—that's it, Aunt Adelaide. You're getting a modern TV, and that's all there is to it. You could have been killed!" He took her arm and helped her up. "Come on—let's go sit in the other room. You shouldn't be tracking this glass and stuff around."

Adelaide allowed Langley to lead her out of the room, with Iona trailing behind them. "Coming?" he asked over his shoulder to Stone.

"In a minute," Stone replied, distracted. When the three of them had gone, he squatted down and took a closer look at the destroyed television, once again reaching out with his magical senses. He had a suspicion: the explosion had occurred just as he had begun ranging out to try to pinpoint the location of the entity in the house. The entity that didn't want to be found. That was too much of a coincidence to *be* a coincidence.

It didn't take long. "There you are, you bastard," he murmured in triumph. It couldn't completely hide its traces from someone with his power, and now there was no doubt in his mind: the entity, whatever it was, knew he was here and didn't want him to find it. And it was willing to put people in danger to prevent that.

He sighed, rising up from his crouch. This was going to make things even more difficult. Before tonight, he'd suspected it was here and didn't know it was dangerous. Now he knew it was both here and willing to hurt the residents of the house. Preoccupied, he headed back out to where the others had gathered in the sitting room.

"—should probably have an electrician over to look at the wiring," Langley was saying. "But I'm guessing that ancient TV you've had practically since I was a kid finally gave up the ghost and blew."

"Probably," Adelaide conceded. She looked less shaken now, though Iona was still trembling. The old lady looked up as Stone came in. "Are you all right, Dr. Stone? You look...odd."

Langley shot him a warning look from behind his aunt, and he nodded. "I'm fine."

"I think we should clear out and leave you two alone," Langley said. "Promise me you won't go back in that room until you've had somebody in there to clean up the mess and haul the TV away, all right?"

Iona nodded. "Don't worry, we won't. I'll have Maurice and Cory come clean it up tomorrow. They're the handyman and one of the landscapers," she added to Stone.

Langley, apparently assured that his aunt and Iona had recovered from their shocks, shepherded Stone upstairs to gather his gear. Stone followed willingly, but slowly. "What's up?" Langley asked him. "You look like you're a million miles away."

Stone shook his head. "Nothing. I'm—fine." His mind was moving fast, trying to figure out a way that he could get himself invited back to the house without either pissing Langley off for breaking his promise or unnecessarily frightening Adelaide. It was getting more imperative now since the entity, whatever it was, had shown that it was willing to do more than just sit back and bide its time.

But, he rationalized while disconnecting the meters and stowed them back in the boxes, *maybe I'm the reason it did what it did. It was afraid I was going to find it so it did something to cause a distraction. If I weren't here—*

He slung the strap of the leather satchel over his shoulder. He knew it didn't work that way. If there was something here and it was trying to make contact, it wasn't going to give up. Even if it was willing to wait for now, eventually it would get impatient. If it was gathering power, it would soon grow potent enough that it could do more than frighten mildly sensitive old ladies. He couldn't let that happen, but for now he was fresh out of acceptable ideas.

Back in the car, after they'd bade the ladies good night and put the boxes in the trunk, Langley glanced over at him. "That was damned weird," he said. "I've never even heard of a TV blowing like that. Not even one that old."

"Did you ever think perhaps it wasn't the TV?" Stone asked carefully, eyes on the road.

"What do you mean by that? Of course it was the TV. You saw the mess all over the—wait a minute..." He shifted in his seat to glare at Stone. "Are you trying to tell me you think this had something to do with all that bullshit you were doing upstairs?"

Stone shrugged. "I'm not saying that. I'm just saying that the possibility exists. I was—getting some good readings when your aunt screamed down there."

Langley let his breath out in a long loud blast. When he spoke again, his voice held a dangerous edge. "Alastair—you promised. You are *done* with this. There are no spooks in Aunt Adelaide's house, and I'm not going to let you keep scaring her because you've got some wild idea that there are. You got it?"

"Yeah," he said, unwilling to fight about it right now. "I've got it."

They made the rest of the trip down the hill to Los Gatos in uncomfortable, stony silence.

| CHAPTER TWELVE

E than shoved the cart up and down the supermarket aisles, his head down and his feet shuffling. Occasionally he'd pause, consult his scrawled list, and toss some item into its basket. He'd been doing this for the last half hour, and had only worked his way through half the list.

Part of this was because his mind wasn't even close to being here. His body moved by rote but his thoughts whirled, chewing with relentless tenacity over the same topics. He wished he could just make them shut up for a while.

Nothing was going right. It had been a week and a half since they'd taken his mother to the hospital and she was still there. He visited her every day, spending hours sitting next to her bed, making small talk when she was lucid, trying to reassure her that everything would be fine and she'd be back home soon. Even though he couldn't bring himself to believe it anymore.

When the hospital people or his mother finally kicked him out and ordered him to go home and get some rest, he'd just collapse in front of the television set, turn on something mindless, and spend his evenings in a half-stupor without the motivation to get up and do anything. Every time he thought it might be a good idea to do something other than sit on the couch, his brain steadfastly refused to cooperate. His life had become a groove worn between the apartment and the hospital.

He'd thought about calling Stone a couple times, but decided not to. Stone was a strange guy—Ethan couldn't decide whether the mage gave a damn about him as a person or not, or whether he was even supposed to. Ethan was his apprentice; that just meant that Stone was responsible for his magical training. He hadn't signed on to be some kind of father figure or somebody Ethan could dump his load of emotional baggage on. Alastair Stone didn't seem to have a lot of patience with emotional baggage. For that matter, Ethan couldn't really picture him as anyone's father.

Stone had actually called twice, but Ethan let the calls go to the answering machine and deliberately waited until he knew the mage would be at Stanford before returning them, so he could leave a vague "I'm fine, I'll let you know when Mom's doing better" message and not have to talk to him. He didn't know exactly why he didn't want to talk to Stone, but he didn't. Brains were funny like that—sometimes you just knew you were doing something that didn't make sense, but you did it anyway.

He *had* spent quite a bit of time practicing the levitation spell. In fact, aside from visiting his mother and vegging in front of the TV, the spell was the only thing that motivated him. He had not yet gotten over the fact that he, Ethan Penrose, childhood beloved of bullies everywhere, was now capable of making coins and pencils hover in the air with the power of his mind.

It wasn't just coins and pencils, either. He had started out following Stone's directive, lining up bits of change, paper clips, pens and pencils, and other light items on the coffee table in the living room. He practiced visualizing the pattern as Stone had taught him, imposing it on the world in the area occupied by the item, and lifting it up. When he'd gotten to where he could do that, he practiced moving it around until he could make it zip around the room and settle back down in front of him.

He couldn't believe how *tiring* it was, though. Whenever he finished a session of practice he felt like he'd just spent two hours pumping iron at the gym. Or, more correctly, how he imagined someone must feel after doing that. Ethan had nothing but contempt for the kinds of people who spent their time at gyms lifting weights. He wondered how Stone was able to do the spell so effortlessly—was it just practice? Experience? It did seem to get a little less exhausting as he went on, but not much.

Midway through the previous week, his impatience had gotten the better of him and he'd started trying larger objects: first one of his mom's pill bottles, then a paperback book, and finally the smallest of the collection of magical tomes Stone had lent him. He'd quickly discovered that the heavier the object was, the more energy he had to expend to make it do his bidding. His first attempt at lifting the magic book had left him bathed in sweat, nauseated, wilted into the couch cushions like he was trying to become part of them. Was this *ever* going to be easy?

And Stone had said that if he had to, he could lift a small car? Either he was lying, or he was a hell of a lot more powerful mage than he was owning up to. Ethan wasn't sure which, and he wasn't sure whether the thought of his being that powerful pleased him (because having a powerful teacher was a good thing) or frightened him (because the consequences for any screw-ups could be dire indeed). In any case, Stone did seem to be holding up his end of the bargain: Ethan was now capable of performing magic, albeit in a very limited manner. He wanted more, though, and he didn't think Stone would have too much patience with that attitude. He wondered if all apprentices were like him: impatient, dazzled by the potential of what they'd be able to do someday, and chafing at having to wait months, possibly years, before they'd be able to even start thinking of themselves as real mages.

Ah, well. It wasn't like he had a choice. He could read the books Stone gave him and try to learn what they taught, but he didn't exactly know where to go to buy more magic books, and he doubted that there were any other mages in the phone book he could call for some supplemental training. He was at the mercy of Stone's schedule, and that was all there was to it. But until his mother was stable and able to come home, it wouldn't do him any good to get back into the habit of studying regularly with Stone. That was just a reality he'd have to accept. Maybe it was the universe's way of teaching him patience.

He'd finally broken away from his grueling schedule of visiting the hospital, sleeping in front of the TV, and levitating objects around the room when he'd hauled himself up to get something to eat and found the cupboards and fridge nearly bare. When Mom had been home Mrs. Hooper had taken care of most of the shopping, with Ethan being sent out to pick up occasional one-off items, but now that Mom was in the hospital, there was no need for the caregiver to be here. That left things up to him. Fortunately Mom had left a credit card that he could use for groceries and household emergencies, so he'd taken a fast shower, thrown on some clean clothes, and set off for the supermarket. And that was why he was walking around in a half-stupor, trying to track down the items on his list and get back home in case the hospital called.

"Hey! Watch where you're going!"

Ethan was startled out of his fog by a sharp female voice. He looked up quickly: a woman a few years older than he was had ducked down and was in the process of picking up several cans that had scattered when he'd apparently hit her with his cart.

"I'm sorry!" he said quickly, moving to help her gather her stuff. "Oh, wow, I'm so sorry. I wasn't looking at all. I—"

She balanced three of the cans on top of each other and rose, flashing him a grin. "Don't worry about it," she assured him, reaching out to take the two that he'd picked up. "Should have gotten a basket." She was tall and slim, dressed in tight, artfully ripped jeans and a T-shirt from a band Ethan had never heard of. Her dark-red hair was cut short, her makeup in an understated punk style.

Ethan sighed. "I really am sorry."

"Hey, it's okay," she said. "Seriously, no big deal." She looked him up and down with appraising eyes. "Have I seen you around here before? You look familiar."

"Uh—" For a moment, he literally couldn't think of anything to say. It was like the gear that connected his brain to his mouth slipped, and his thoughts were spinning their wheels. "Maybe," he finally said, mentally kicking himself. *Smooth. Real smooth.* She had a series of intricate tattoos on her forearms, and her fingernails were painted a deep blood red.

"I don't bite," she said, laughing. "I promise. Not unless you want me to, anyway."

He laughed a little, hoping he didn't sound forced. She was *very* attractive.

"You know, I'm sure I've seen you around here before," she said. "I'm good with faces. My name's Trina, by the way."

"I'm—uh—Ethan." *How can you forget your own name?* "Ethan Penrose. I guess you might have seen me. I don't live too far from here."

"Ethan Penrose. Why does that name sound familiar?" She considered for a moment, then shook her head. "I can't remember. I'd swear I've heard it before." She shuffled the five cans in her hands when one started to slide off.

"Hey," Ethan said quickly, recovering his manners and indicating his cart. "Why don't you put that stuff in here for a minute and I'll go get you a basket? That's the least I could do after I tried to murder you with my cart."

"Sure," she said. "Thanks."

He returned after a moment, doing his best not to run. "You know what?" she asked as she retrieved her items from the cart and stacked them in the basket. "I notice you don't have anything frozen in there. There's a Peet's a couple of doors down from here. Want to go get a cup of coffee or something? I'm still convinced I recognize your name from somewhere, and I want a little more time to try to figure it out." She punctuated her words with a smile that made something deep inside of him feel very pleased with itself.

He tried not to stare. This woman—this attractive, sexy, older woman who clearly had no idea the effect she was having on him—actually wanted to have coffee with him? She didn't want to get away from his geeky, awkward self as fast as she could? "Uh—sure. Yeah. That'd be cool," he said before she could change her mind and realize who she was talking to. "I'm almost done here. I'll just finish up, and—"

"Sure thing," she said, smiling wider. "Tell you what—I'll just go pay for my stuff and stash it in my car, then go over there and wait for you." She reached out with one red-nailed hand and touched his arm briefly. "See you soon, Ethan Penrose."

He waited for her to disappear around the end of an aisle before he let all the air out of his lungs in a rush, gripping the cart's handle for support. He had no idea what that had been, but he wasn't going to argue with it. It had taken him half an hour to finish the first half of the list—he did the second half in five minutes. Hurrying to the checkout line he let his thoughts spin off freely, weaving all sorts of scenarios. Some of them even seemed plausible.

He stowed the groceries in the trunk of his mother's car and forced himself to walk nonchalantly down to the coffee shop, in case she was watching out the window. He half expected that she wouldn't even be there—girls had pulled that one on him a few times during his early years in high school—but no, there she was, sitting in a secluded corner. She waved as he came in and motioned him over.

He looked around, seeing but not really noticing the other patrons: a woman with a laptop computer, an older man reading a newspaper, and two young men a little older than he was, seated on the opposite side of the room. Ethan dropped down in another chair opposite Trina.

"Hold on," she said. "Let me get us something." She headed off and returned in a few moments with a couple of steaming cups of coffee. Once she'd settled back in, she smiled at him. "So—I've still been trying to figure out where I know you from. I don't think we went to school together—I'd remember you, I think." She tilted her head. "How old are you, anyway? Twenty or so?"

"Yeah. Twenty. Almost twenty-one." It slipped out before his mental censors could amend it.

She nodded, sipping her coffee. "Wait, I know. Maybe it was at a club. What kind of music are you into?"

Ethan had never been to a club in his life, but he wasn't about to admit it. Instead he shrugged, trying to look nonchalant. "I like lots of stuff. Punk, metal—" He glanced at her T-shirt. "Those guys local?"

She looked down. "Oh, IED? They're based up in the City. Ever been to Will to Power?"

"Nah." He decided to risk a little bit of the truth. "My mom's sick, so I mostly stay down here and help take care of her when she needs it."

"Aww, that's nice," she said. "Nothing serious, I hope."

He didn't answer. Instead, he took a sip of coffee and caught himself once again looking at the tattoos on her forearms. They were very intricate and the more he looked at them, the more he couldn't shake the nagging feeling that he'd seen them, or something like them, somewhere before.

"See something you like?" she asked wryly.

"Oh!" His eyes came up and he chuckled, suddenly more self-conscious than before. "I'm sorry. I—uh—that's some awesome ink you've got there."

She grinned. "Yeah, isn't it? The artist did a great job. Hurt like a bitch, though, and he had a hell of a time getting them right."

And then, suddenly, he realized why the tattoos looked familiar.

He'd seen versions of some of them in the magic books Stone had given him to read.

Something must have changed in his expression because Trina frowned. "You okay, Ethan? You look strange, all of a sudden."

He swallowed and shook his head, trying to figure out a way to bring up what was on his mind without sounding like a total idiot if he was wrong. "I'm—yeah, I'm fine." After a moment, he nodded toward the tattoos and asked, "What do they mean? If it's okay to ask, I mean. If they're personal—"

She smiled. "Well, they are personal, but I don't mind if you ask. They're magical symbols." Her green, unblinking eyes met his.

"Magical."

"Yep."

He forced himself to grin. "So—are you, like, a witch or something?"

Her expression didn't change. "Yep." She nodded. "You can leave if you want. I won't mind. Sometimes it puts people off. Or else they don't believe me. I get that a lot."

Ethan didn't leave, though. Instead, he reached down and fumbled in his backpack. He still had one of Stone's books inside, along with a sweatshirt and some notebooks. Not sure he really should be doing what he was doing, he pulled it out of the pack and set it on the table next to his coffee cup. He didn't say anything.

Trina looked at the book, then at Ethan. Her expression was neutral, revealing nothing of what she was thinking. She indicated the book with a head motion. "Mind if I—?"

"G-go ahead." Ethan felt strange, almost disassociated from himself. He felt like he was standing on the edge of a precipice or in an open doorway, and that his next actions, whatever they ended up being, would be some of the most important he'd ever take in his life. *Be careful,* a little voice told him. *Don't let this get away from you.*

Smiling encouragement, she glanced around to make sure nobody was watching, then made a small gesture and the book floated up into her hands. She leaned back in her chair and paged through it, occasionally nodding or murmuring something to herself that Ethan couldn't hear. Ethan watched her, sitting stiffly forward, scared of what she might say. She'd just proven it—she wasn't lying about being magical. He suspected she'd done that on purpose, to put him at ease. It wasn't working too well.

After several minutes, she set the book back down on the table. "Well," she said with an odd, faraway smile. "I guess that explains where I might have heard of you."

"Really?" He was surprised. "How—"

"You're an apprentice, aren't you?"

Ethan swallowed. He was wishing now that he had never run his cart into this very attractive young woman. This was all moving way too fast. "I'm not sure I should be—"

She laughed. "Don't worry about it, Ethan. I won't tell anyone. Why would I? It sounds like you and I are the same."

"You're an apprentice, too?" He looked up at her. She seemed too old, and far too sure of herself to be at the same stage of her training as he was.

"Well, I didn't mean it like that," she said. "I'm not, not anymore. I just meant that we're both students of the Art. Not that many of us around—it's good to find each other, right?"

"I'm not sure—" he began. He took a deep breath. "I'm not sure I'm supposed to be telling anyone."

"Why not?" Her laugh was amused. "I mean, of course we're not supposed to tell anyone who isn't one of us, but what's the harm in meeting others? Doesn't it feel lonely sometimes, being the only one? Only having your master to talk to?"

He had to nod. He couldn't even talk about magic with his mother, not really. It wasn't just that she was so sick that he didn't want to bother her with it—it was that he didn't feel like he could really explain it to her even if she was healthy and wanted to hear it. And aside from her, there was only Stone. "I—Yeah. Sometimes it does."

"Mind if I ask who your master is?" She was still looking neutrally interested, like she was enjoying having a chance to chat with someone who shared her favorite subjects.

He hesitated.

"Wow, you *are* a newbie, aren't you?" Again she laughed, but this time it held the tiniest hint of mocking. "Don't worry, Ethan. Seriously. It sounds like whoever he—or she—is, they've got you pretty worried about giving anything away. You don't have to tell me if you don't want to."

Suddenly Ethan felt stupid and embarrassed. Here he was, talking to the only other mage he'd ever met in his life besides Stone and his father long ago, and he was acting like a frightened five-year-old. "He—his name's Alastair Stone," he said, his voice taking on a little defiance. "He lives up in Palo Alto."

She considered. "Stone. Hmm...sounds familiar. Oh, right: British guy? Early thirties? Tall, thin, dark hair? Kinda hot in a geeky way?"

Something burned a little inside Ethan when she said 'kinda hot,' but he shoved it down and nodded. "That's him, yeah. Do you know him?"

"Know of him. Never met him. We don't exactly travel in the same circles. I can see why you're so scared of letting anything slip, though." She tossed the book back on the table.

"Why's that?" Ethan finished up his coffee and stowed the book in his pack.

She shrugged. "Stone's kind of old school. He's young, but he was trained by the old guard, and it shows. He's actually a pretty big deal power-wise, but you'd never know it since he kinda does his own thing. Don't tell me," she added, grinning. "He gets all authoritarian and gives you these big lectures about what you are and aren't supposed to do, and tells you it'll take you years to get through your apprenticeship."

Ethan nodded, torn between how great Trina's tight T-shirt looked as she breathed and not wanting to say anything against Stone. "Yeah, kinda. But he's a good teacher," he added quickly.

"Oh, I'm sure he is. I've heard he's a fantastic teacher. And if you can stand working with him until he decides you're done, he'll probably teach you some great stuff." She smiled and glanced at her watch. "Hey, listen, Ethan, I've gotta get going, but I'd like to get together again if that's okay with you."

He nodded. "That'd be cool," he agreed. He was relieved that she wasn't talking about Stone anymore, but also didn't want their conversation to end.

"Tell you what—there's a little thing at the Darkwave in Sunnyvale this Friday night. I'm gonna be there with some friends. You want to join us? It's 18+ so it's okay that you're not 21 yet."

Ethan forced himself not to sound too eager. This was the first time in his life that anybody had invited him to this sort of event. He thought briefly of his mother, but it would be at night—visiting hours would be over anyway. She'd probably be happy that he was finally getting himself a social life. "Yeah," he said. "I'd like that." Pause, and then: "Are your friends—"

She grinned. "Yep. So you'll have a chance to meet some more of us, if you want." She reached in her small leather bag, pulled out a card, and wrote a time and an address on the back next to the words *Nightmare Room.* "Here's where the party is. Starts at 10, but things don't really get going until midnight. If you have any trouble getting in, just tell 'em you're with me." She handed him the card, brushing his fingertips with hers. "I really hope to see you there, Ethan. Oh—" she added, getting up. "One more thing."

He was studying the card and trying to hold on to the tingle in his fingers where she'd touched him. "What's that?"

For the first time she hesitated, looking nervous. "I hate to say this because I don't want to encourage you to do anything you're not comfortable with, but—would it be okay if you didn't mention to Dr. Stone that we met? Like I said, he's pretty old school, and I'm not sure he'd approve of you meeting other mages this early in your training. I really don't want him showing up at my place going all Wrath of God on me for messing with his apprentice, or telling you he doesn't want us getting together anymore." She rolled her eyes. "Trust me—from what I've heard, the guy might seem nice enough, but you don't want to piss him off. And I'd feel pretty guilty if he decided to cut you loose because you're not lockstepping along with his rules."

Ethan nodded. "I won't tell him." He felt weird about that—keeping secrets from his master this early in his training didn't seem like the right thing to do—but Stone didn't have to know *everything* about his life. It wasn't like Trina was going to be teaching him any magic or anything like that. They were just going to hang out, talk a little, and maybe he'd get somebody else's perspective on the way things worked in the magical realm. Hell, Stone had even mentioned that most people who were Talented knew about it when they were a lot younger than he was, and that probably meant that by the time they started their apprenticeships, they knew a lot more general stuff about the arcane than he did. So, what would be the harm?

"Great," she said. Damn, but she had a nice smile. She leaned down and brushed a kiss on the top of his head. "See you Friday, then. I think you and my other friends will get along great."

And then she was gone, leaving Ethan to sit in his chair and watch the door where she'd exited. His thoughts were already far away, though. He didn't even notice anything odd when the two young men—one blond, one dark-haired—got up and left the coffee shop a couple of minutes later. And it was several minutes after that when he remembered that he had a trunk full of groceries he really needed to get home.

Oliver was laughing his ass off as The Three drove north toward San Francisco. "You played that kid like a rented violin," he told Trin from the driver's seat.

"I wonder if he's even been that close to a girl before," Miguel said from the back. "Shit, I feel bad for the coffee shop guy, having to clean up all the drool around his chair after he leaves."

"Now, now," Trin said with a wicked grin. "He's a nice boy. I just showed him a little attention, is all." She stared out the window, thinking. "It'll be a little harder than I thought, though: I didn't know his master was Alastair Stone."

"So?" Miguel asked.

She shrugged. "Stone's a strange one. He's an academic, mostly. Keeps to himself, but he's got a reputation for being smart and good at reading people. Not to mention dangerous as fuck if you get him pissed off. We'll have to be careful. The kid said he wouldn't mention us to him, but he's weak. If Stone catches on that something's up, he'll have it out of the kid in five minutes. And then we could be in trouble if we haven't gotten what we need from him yet."

Oliver made a contemptuous noise. "C'mon, Trin. No way Stone could stand up to all three of us. He's a white mage, right? That means he'll suck in a fight. We'd wipe up the floor with him."

"Maybe, but I'd rather not have to," she said. "Not directly, anyway. We can't be involved personally. But it would be better if Ethan didn't talk to him before Friday. Let me talk to a couple of people, and see what they can do for us to make that happen. Sometimes the mundane way is the best way of dealing with this sort of thing."

| CHAPTER THIRTEEN

Stone was working late in his office on Thursday night. His course on Modern Occult Practices was particularly popular with the horror-writer set, which meant that any essays he assigned usually came back with far more detail than he'd asked for—or really wanted to read. He liked their enthusiasm, but always had to allow extra time for grading their essays.

He leaned back in his chair after finishing up one particularly purple specimen, raising his arms in a stretch and luxuriating in the satisfying *pops* up and down his back. A glance at the clock told him it was already after eight: he'd been here, hunched over his desk, for more than three hours following his last class of the day.

There were still at least ten more essays to go; if he did them tonight he wouldn't get out of here for at least another couple of hours, and he'd half-promised Megan that he'd take her out to dinner. They hadn't seen each other for a few days, since preparing upcoming final exams for their respective courses had taken up most of their time. Right now, Stone wasn't missing his time with Ethan; if he'd had the boy's magic lessons in addition to his course load, even the few hours of sleep per night that he'd been getting lately would become a luxury. He wasn't exactly *glad* that Ethan hadn't called, but he hadn't done anything about it from his end, either.

Sighing, he ran a hand through his hair, a habitual gesture that tended to make the front of it perpetually stick up in random, untidy spikes, and rose from the chair. "Tomorrow," he muttered, gathering the ungraded essays, stuffing them in a folder, and filing them in his desk. The graded ones went into a different folder in the same drawer. Then he picked up the phone and tried Megan's office on campus. She wasn't there.

"Well, at least *somebody* has the sense to leave work at a proper time," he continued under his breath, hanging up and dialing her home number. She didn't answer there either, but that didn't surprise him: she was probably on her way home or stopping to run errands. He left a message telling her he was leaving and that he'd pick her up in an hour, then shrugged into his overcoat, picked up his briefcase, and locked his office door behind him.

The building was deserted, as was the area around it, but this didn't concern Stone. In the distance, he could see the pinprick lights of students' bicycles as they rode by, heading toward the more central areas of the campus, along with the occasional car's headlights filtering between the trees and the buildings. The ancient, ivy-covered building housing his office was about as far as it could be from the middle of campus and still be part of Stanford proper—it amused him more than offended him that Occult Studies was one of a number of small fringe programs that didn't get much respect next to their more prestigious counterparts in the sciences, arts, and medicine.

After all, he'd known the way things were when he'd accepted the associate professor post in the department two years ago—which had brought the number of faculty members associated with it to exactly three. The other two were a stodgy old woman named Edwina Mortensen, who'd been threatening to retire for the last several years, and a failed horror author named MacKenzie Hubbard, who did as little as possible while using his free periods to pound out more unsalable prose. Neither of them thought much of Stone, who had come in and revitalized the department with his youth and charismatic lecturing style to the point where enrollments were actually up. The program was, for the first time in its history, not living in perpetual fear of landing on the chopping block next time there were budget cuts.

Stone exited the building and headed for his car. There was a parking lot closer to his building, but he chose to park the Jaguar in one a couple of blocks further away due to the fact that he didn't like leaving it under trees and dealing with the leaves and bird droppings he'd find on it every day.

The lot wasn't quite deserted; there were still quite a few evening courses that hadn't let out yet. The Jaguar was right where he'd left it, three spaces down from the nearest overhead light. He was already going over possibilities for restaurants to suggest to Megan when he drew close to it and noticed that its rear driver's-side tire had gone flat.

"Oh, bugger," he muttered, dropping his briefcase and leaning down to examine it more closely. He—or rather his mechanic—kept the car in good repair, and there was certainly no reason why the tire should have died on its own. He must have run over a nail or something.

Frustrated, he bent over more, wondering if he should risk a light spell to see if he could spot the damage. He also wondered if he should try to change the tire on his own or if he'd need to trudge back up to his office and call Campus Services to come and do it for him. Either way, this was definitely going to make getting home on time to have dinner with Megan problematic.

He was so preoccupied with his thoughts that he didn't hear the silent figures approaching him until they were upon him. One grabbed the back of his collar and pulled him upright, while another—dark, shadowy, and masked—drove a meaty fist into his stomach and doubled him back over.

He dropped to his knees, all the air forced out of him by the punch. He tried to form the pattern for a spell, but his attackers didn't let up long enough to allow it. The one that had hold of his collar let go, instead grabbing his arm and yanking him back up to a standing position, locking it behind his back in an iron grip. The other thug gave him a couple more shots to the gut followed by a cross to the jaw. The first attacker released his arm and he staggered back, slammed into the Jaguar, and fell to the ground. Lights danced in front of his vision; he could feel himself starting to black out. Again he tried to form a spell, but again his head lit up with pain and the pattern skittered away, eluding him. With no other ideas presenting themselves, he drew his legs up into him and tried to protect his head with his arms. He hoped that whatever they wanted, it wasn't to kill him, since he couldn't see any way he could stop them.

The two were silent and efficient in their work. Stone heard nothing but their breathing as they snapped three hard kicks into his ribs, then one to his head that he was able to deflect most of by shifting position at the last minute. He heard a moan, and realized it was coming from him. A far-off voice yelled something that sounded like "Hey!" Hands fumbled in his coat, and then the sound of running feet.

He tried to force himself out of his fetal position, to fling a spell at the retreating attackers, but the pain was coming from everywhere at once, and only got worse when he moved. *I wonder where the voice came from...*was his last thought before he passed out.

He opened his eyes to find two blurred, worried-looking faces hovering over him. "Oh, God," one of them breathed. Female. "He's awake. Stay still, sir. We don't know how bad you're hurt. Paul's gone off to call an ambulance."

He was still on his side, still tightly pulled up in the fetal ball. He tasted hot blood and felt small rocks from the parking lot cutting into his cheek. A crumpled candy wrapper lay a few inches from his face. He tried to say something, but it came out as an inarticulate groan.

"Please don't move," another voice urged. Male this time. Young. They both sounded like students, and both sounded scared. "Help's coming soon."

Ignoring them both, Stone gritted his teeth and tried to straighten his legs. Big mistake. His entire midsection burst with pain, as if someone had lit him on fire. A weak little scream forced itself out between his teeth as he rolled himself onto his back, eyes clamped shut.

"Here, hold on—" The female student's voice shook. She fumbled for a moment and then there was something soft under his head. "Better?"

He nodded, not trusting his voice. Lying still now, he tried to take inventory past the layers of cotton wool that were packing his brain. His stomach hurt, and he was vaguely nauseated. The back of his head throbbed, a dull, digging ache that hurt like the world's worst migraine. His jaw stung, and he still tasted blood. And worst of all, his lower ribs felt like each one was traced with its own personal line of white-hot fire. Might be cracked, but he was afraid to move any more to check.

The female student put a warm hand on his forehead, shoving his damp hair back. "What's your name, sir?"

He had to give that some thought. "S...Stone."

"Do you teach here? We couldn't find your ID..."

Stone opened his eyes. The female student was crouched next to him, while the male was upright, keeping watch—either for the ambulance, or to make sure that the thugs weren't coming back. "I—" He nodded. "Y-yes." He waved vaguely and immediately regretted it.

"Please, you shouldn't talk anymore. Just lie still."

"Listen—" he whispered. When the girl leaned in, he continued, "Call—call Megan. Megan—Whitney. English... department. Tell her...I'll—be late." Then the cotton wool finally closed in, and he didn't get to find out whether she'd gotten the message correct.

| CHAPTER FOURTEEN

hen Stone dragged himself back up to consciousness, the students were gone. He was lying on a narrow bed with rails that was surrounded by a fabric curtain and lit with harsh fluorescents. Beyond it were the sounds of hurried footsteps and busy people calling to each other. There was a chair next to the bed, and sitting in the chair was— "Megan."

She looked up, startled, from the magazine she was paging through. Relief washed over her face. "Alastair. My God, what happened? Someone called me—" She reached out and gently clutched one of his hands. "They said someone beat you up in the parking lot at your office."

He nodded. Risking the pain, he pulled himself up slightly so he could get a look at himself. His shirt was gone, the lower part of his ribs wrapped in heavy white tape. An IV tube snaked from his arm up to a plastic bag of clear liquid. Reaching up with his other hand, he felt the back of his head: no bandage there.

"You've got a nasty lump back there," she said. "I should let the doctor give you the details, but it sounds like you got lucky. Two cracked ribs on your right side, but nothing badly broken, and they don't think you have any internal injuries. Possible mild concussion. They said they want to keep you overnight for observation."

"Sorry..." he murmured, trying for a smile. "Guess I'll have to—give you a rain check on dinner, won't I?" He looked around.

"What time is it?" He tried to make his voice sound stronger, but it came out as a weak croak.

"About ten. I got the call from some girl—a student. I guess she must have found my number somewhere. She said she and her friends came upon you getting beaten up by two thugs next to your car. Can you tell me what happened?"

He looked around. Wherever he was, it didn't look like a hospital room. "Where is this?" His voice sounded a little stronger now, but putting any volume behind it hurt.

"Emergency room," she told him. "The doctor should be in soon to talk to you. Once he figured out you weren't in any danger, he went off to deal with other patients." She squeezed his hand. "Do you have any idea why someone would beat you up?"

He shrugged, which also hurt. He could already tell this was going to be inconvenient. "No idea. Robbery, possibly? Did they take my wallet? I vaguely remember someone feeling around in my coat before I passed out."

"I think they must have—they didn't find it on you when they took your clothes." She sighed. "Did you get a look at them?"

He thought about that, trying to picture them. "No. Never saw one of them, and the other one was wearing a mask. All I saw was that he was big—heavier than I am, but not as tall. Not much help, I'm afraid."

"I'm sure the police will want to talk to you when you're feeling better, but for now try to get some rest, okay? How do you feel?"

"Ghastly. Why haven't they given me any of the good drugs? I thought that was the whole point of hospitals."

"I think they wanted to make sure they weren't masking any pain that they needed to pay attention to." She squeezed his hand again.

He nodded. "I really appreciate your coming, Megan, but you should go home now. I'll be all right. There's no point in you sitting here watching me lie around in bed, and I don't fancy worrying about you being out late when there are dangerous sorts running loose." He gave her a pained smile. "Don't worry about me. Really, I'll be fine. I'm tougher than I look."

"That wouldn't be difficult," she said, chuckling, leaning down brush a kiss on his lips. Then she grew serious again. "I hope they catch the guys who did this soon. I'd hate to think they're running around campus and this might happen again."

As Megan had predicted, they kept Stone overnight at the hospital for observation to make sure that his minor concussion wasn't anything more serious. The fact that he didn't protest would have told anyone who knew him that he wasn't feeling well at all, because he normally hated anything to do with doctors or hospitals.

A young policeman showed up in the morning to take his statement about what had happened. The campus police had recovered his wallet not far from where the Jaguar was parked; it was missing the cash and his credit cards, but fortunately they'd left his driver's license. He told the cop what he knew, which wasn't much.

The doctor finally sprung him around noon on Friday. Megan took time off from her classes to pick him up and take him back to his townhouse. She found him in his hospital room, standing in the bathroom clad only in jeans and examining the blossoming collection of bruises on his chest, abdomen, and chin in the mirror. "They already took off the rib wrap?" she asked.

"Apparently they don't do that anymore. Something about pneumonia."

"You look a lot better than last night, even with the bruises."

"That's because they've got me dosed up on so many painkillers that you could hit me with a baseball bat and I wouldn't notice." He grinned, a little glassy-eyed. "And I've got a prescription for more."

"Oh, nice. Well, let's get you home and you can spend some quality time resting. No argument. And no baseball bats."

"Yes, ma'am," he said. She helped him get dressed, and he followed her slowly out to her car. "Where's the Jaguar, by the way?"

"At your place. They fixed the tire and dropped it off over there this morning. Oh—you might be interested to know that you didn't run over anything. Somebody let the air out of it."

He frowned. "Which means they were lying in wait for me. Odd..." He filed that thought away for the moment as the nurse came in with his discharge papers.

Megan took him home and hovered over him until he was safely in bed. Mrs. Olivera, who was there cleaning the place, promised to check in on him periodically. "I'm not a bloody invalid," he protested, glaring at both of them. "Both of you—I appreciate your concern. I really do. But I'd appreciate it even more now if you'd both just clear out and leave me to recuperate in peace."

Megan kissed his forehead. "I'm going now, but if you're a good little boy and listen to Mrs. Olivera, I might bring you some ice cream tonight."

"Off you go," he ordered, making a 'shooing' motion.

Once he was alone, the first thing Stone did was call Ethan. The boy wasn't home, but he left a message on his machine asking about his mother and informing him that it would be at least Monday before he could get back to any further magic lessons Ethan might want to restart. Then he lay back on the pillows in frustration.

Alastair Stone was a terrible patient. He hated inactivity more than almost anything else, and the thought of being stuck in bed for even the next day or two annoyed him. Another thing that annoyed him was how easily he'd been jumped. No two ways about it: he simply hadn't been paying attention.

And worse, he hadn't been prepared. If he'd been in any kind of magical fighting trim, he could have summoned up a shield and a stun spell, and had the two attackers laid out on the pavement before they'd done more than hit him once. Instead, he'd let himself be a victim. Indirectly, in Stone's somewhat skewed way of looking at the world, this made his injuries his own damned fault. Which meant that they didn't deserve coddling when there were things to be done.

Frowning, he sat up, testing his ribs. They didn't hurt much right now, due to the pain pills, and neither did the rest of him. The doctor had told him that moving around wouldn't do him any harm as long as he didn't overdo it, though it would be better if he'd just rest for at least the first day.

The hell with that.

He got out of bed, pulled on jeans and his favorite Pink Floyd T-shirt, and headed slowly downstairs. In all likelihood he wouldn't ever be attacked again, but if he was, he was bloody well going to be ready for it.

Managing to avoid Mrs. Olivera as he worked his way down toward his basement workroom, he closed and locked the door behind him. Yes, it was a little dangerous if something went wrong and he passed out again, but he always kept this room locked. Wouldn't do to have one's housekeeper—or one's girlfriend—finding one's magical sanctum. Far too many messy questions to answer.

Moving slowly, he gathered the items he'd need, glad that he'd stocked up a few weeks ago. Practicing magic while in the grip of powerful painkillers was one thing, but he thought if he tried to leave the house and drive, Mrs. Olivera would wrestle him to the floor and sit on him until he saw sense. The thought amused him as he dumped the items on the table in the middle of the room and set about his work.

CHAPTER FIFTEEN

It was eleven-thirty on Friday night. Ethan looked at his watch again to verify it. Was this late enough, or should he wait until midnight?

He was sitting in his car a couple of blocks down from Dark-wave. The club took up an entire block of Murphy Street in Sunnyvale, which was a small street mostly full of ethnic restaurants and smaller dance clubs. He'd driven past it and could already hear the pounding beat coming from inside. Several knots of people, dressed in everything from ripped jeans to leathers to sleek suits, miniskirts, and slinky gowns, lounged around outside, smoking and chatting.

If it hadn't been for the memory of Trina's dazzling green eyes and the way she'd smiled at him when she'd given him the card with the information about the party, Ethan would have just driven on past and back home. This wasn't his kind of place. Sure, he desperately *wanted* it to be, but all through high school he had steadfastly lacked whatever gene was necessary to understand the vagaries of the cool kids. Even when he tried to get the latest hot fashion item, listen to the latest hot band, or otherwise poke hopefully at the edges of that rarefied territory, it always seemed like he was a week late and everyone else had moved on. The cool kids didn't exactly bother him about it—by high school he'd grown sufficiently and was attractive enough that he didn't fit in with the habitually bullied, either—but sometimes he thought what they did was even worse. They pretty much ignored him.

He was halfway convinced that when he arrived inside, Trina and whatever mage friends she'd promised to bring along wouldn't be there. Sure, she'd showed up at the coffee shop, but this was different. Girls—*women*—like her weren't into guys like him. That was just the way of the world.

He'd never know if he didn't try, though. The worst that could happen would be that he'd have to hang out there by himself for a while before heading home. He might even meet somebody else. He really did need a social life, even if it didn't involve other mages. He'd been thinking about that a lot today as he sat on the couch watching a mindless game show after visiting his mother at the hospital. She was doing a little better, but the earliest she might be able to come home was next week. Aside from her, his only regular contact with other people was Stone, and he wasn't exactly best-buddy material.

He'd heard the phone ring today, and listened as Stone left the message saying he wouldn't be available until Monday. He'd sounded oddly strained—sick, maybe. Ethan wasn't sure he was glad about it because it meant he didn't have to keep putting the mage off, or resentful because Stone was supposed to be teaching him magic. Never mind the fact that he himself was the one who'd been slowing things down.

He sighed, getting out of the car. He checked himself in the side mirror: black IED T-shirt he'd picked up at Paramount Imports, the trendiest jeans he owned, hair artfully mussed. It was the best he could do. He hoped it was enough not to get him laughed out of the place.

As he walked up, Ethan felt the eyes of the lurkers outside on him, scrutinizing, evaluating, judging. They didn't say anything, though—at least nothing he could hear. The doorman didn't look twice at him, just took his cover charge, checked his ID, said "Have fun," and motioned him inside.

Inside, the music was even louder. It pounded all around him, getting into his bones and making him feel alive. He didn't know the band, but he didn't care. Ducking off into an alcove, he consulted the card Trina had given him. In her offhand scrawl was a name: "Nightmare Room." He glanced around, but didn't see anything by that name, so he moved further into the club.

The place was packed now, writhing bodies on the dance floor mingling effortlessly with the knots of people on the sidelines drinking, talking, and soaking up the music. The band on stage pumped out the decibels with enthusiasm, their lead singer running all over the stage and occasionally diving into the crowd. When this happened, a cheer went up and hands shuttled him back to the edge of the stage, ripping at his clothes and screaming their approval.

Ethan headed to the bar. It took him a while to get the attention of the attractive female bartender, but finally she smiled at him. "Sorry, honey," she said, pointing at his arm. "No wristband, no alcohol. Club policy."

"What?" He hadn't even been thinking about alcohol, so her words confused him for a moment. "Oh—no. I don't want a drink. I'm trying to find the Nightmare Room."

"The what?" A cheer had gone up again as the singer had tossed himself once more into the crowd.

"The Nightmare Room!" he yelled.

"Oh." She pointed toward some stairs on the far side of the room. "It's up there. Invitation only, though."

He grinned at her. "I've got an invitation." *I hope.*

She flashed him a dazzling smile and a thumbs-up, then went back to her duties.

Doubt rose within him as he mounted the stairs. He was certain he was about to be humiliated. At the top were double doors painted black and festooned with frightening figures in fluorescent paint that glowed under the club's black lights. Two large men in matching suits lounged on either side of the doors. When they saw Ethan, they looked at each other and smirked. "Back downstairs, kid," one of them said, pointing back the way Ethan had come. "Invitation only up here."

Here goes nothing. "I'm with Trina's group," he said, injecting as much confidence as he could into his words. "My name's Ethan Penrose." Calling on the memory of his elation when he realized he really was a mage, he met the speaker's gaze with a steady one of his own and waited.

The two bouncers glanced at each other. "Yeah, right," said one, but the other held up a "wait here" hand and slipped inside.

After a moment he came back, looking stunned. "Damned if he isn't," he muttered. Ethan had to read lips to get it, but he grinned as the other one, looking equally flummoxed, opened the door and motioned him inside.

The Nightmare Room was much smaller than the one downstairs, and once the door was shut, almost all of the sound from there was blocked, replaced by the beat of another band Ethan could see on a stage at the other end of the room. This music wasn't pounding or loud; it was eerie, atmospheric, and downright creepy. Ethan loved it. Feeling much more confident now, he glanced around taking in the scene and looking for Trina.

The room was dotted with tiny tables only big enough for two people—three if they were very friendly. Opposite the band was a small bar manned by a slender young man in a black suit. There was sort of a dance floor in the middle, but nobody was dancing; the closest was that a few couples, both opposite sex and same, stood around with their arms draped over each other, swaying in time with the strange rhythm of the music. Ethan wondered how many mages there were in here.

Then he spotted Trina. She was sitting at a table at the edge of the room, lounging in her chair like she owned the place, and flanked by two young men, one blond and one dark. All three were dressed in black; leather and ripped denim and hints of velvet and silk. Even fashion-blind Ethan could tell that they weren't following trends here, they were setting them. A flash of jealousy rippled through his mind at the sight of the men—he wondered if they were the "friends" she'd spoken of, and realized that subconsciously he'd just assumed they'd be female.

She spotted him and grinned, motioning him over. She said something to the blond man, who got up, grabbed a chair from another table, and plopped it down. He and the dark-haired man pushed their chairs back to make room; Trina herself didn't move.

"Hey," she greeted. "I hoped you'd make it. Was beginning to wonder. The door guys give you any trouble?" It was still a little hard to hear in here, but much better than downstairs.

"Nah," Ethan said, trying his best to sound nonchalant.

"Excellent." She indicated first the blond man, then the dark-haired one. "These are my friends, Oliver and Miguel. Guys, this is Ethan, the one I was telling you about. He's one of us."

Oliver nodded to him. "Another one, huh? Cool. Not many of us around the area." He motioned at the chair. "Take a load off."

Miguel looked him up and down as he settled into it. "Hey," was all he said.

Trina raised a hand, and in a few moments a cocktail waitress in a leather miniskirt and bustier came over with a tray, setting drinks down in front of each of them. "You do drink, don't you, Ethan?" she asked.

"Uh—" He glanced at their arms. None of them were wearing the wristbands from downstairs. "Sure," he said, a little defiantly. "Thanks." Picking up the glass, he took a sip. It was spicy, and had an odd aftertaste.

"So," she continued to the other two. "Ethan's an apprentice. Yeah, I miss those times. Pain in the ass, but looking back it was a helluva trip, having all that potential and knowing what you were gonna be able to do."

Miguel nodded. "You got that right." Addressing Ethan, he said, "So, what are you learning? How long have you been at it?" He threw back half his drink and fixed him with a snaky smile.

"Still pretty new," Ethan admitted. "My—um—master likes to take things slow." The word sounded so strange, so old-fashioned.

Miguel raised an eyebrow. "Really? So do I. Maybe I should hook up with him sometime." Trina shot him a look, but he just grinned.

"Don't worry," Trina said. "It might seem slow now, but before long you'll be doing things you never believed were possible. That's what rocks so much about magic. There's really no limit to what you can do—well, no limit except your own will, and how far you want to take it."

"We could help you with that, you know," Miguel said, watching the band.

"You—can?"

He shrugged. "Sure. We could show you a few things. That's the way it is with mages. We learn from each other."

Ethan hid his nervousness under taking another sip of his drink. What had Stone told him about seeking out supplemental instruction? He'd made a huge point back at the beginning about setting the pace, and Ethan would just have to live with that. "I—" He took a deep breath. "I probably shouldn't. I'm not really supposed to be studying anything outside of what Dr. Stone's teaching me."

Oliver snorted. "Yeah, of course not. He'd say that, wouldn't he? He just wants to control you, man. They're all like that, the old guard. They want to keep everything under wraps. They don't even understand the way magic can sing if you let it."

"He's not old," Ethan protested, nettled. "He just wants to make sure I learn it right."

"Yeah, c'mon, Ol," Trina said, giving Ethan an encouraging smile. "Don't try to mess with his training. That's not cool. It's up to him what he wants to do."

"Yeah, okay," Oliver conceded. "Sorry, man."

They fell silent for a while, listening to the music and watching the writhing bodies. Miguel got up at one point and said something to a slim man in a tank top and tight jeans, and a couple of minutes later the two of them were draped over each other, swaying on the dance floor. The sight of them drained a little bit of Ethan's jealousy away.

Oliver caught him looking. "Miguel's a slut," he said. "What can I say?"

Ethan didn't know how to respond to that, so he just shrugged and smiled. He was hoping that Trina would ask him to dance—there was no way on Earth he was brave enough yet to ask her—but she seemed content to just lean back and watch the room. Occasionally little groups of people would filter by their table and greet her and Oliver like they were some kind of royalty. They even smiled at Ethan, and he realized that somehow he'd finally managed to work himself into the circle of people who were genuinely cool—even if he was only a little way in. It was better than he'd ever done before.

"Are there…a lot of mages here?" he asked, leaning in closer so no one outside their table would hear.

Trina shook her head. "Not really. A lot of wannabes, but I haven't seen any others with the real deal, besides us."

He nodded. "Dr. Stone said we're pretty rare." It felt good to say *we*.

"That's why we've gotta stick together," she said, smiling at him.

Ethan couldn't help smiling back. Something about her eyes and the way she looked at him just turned his insides to jelly. He glanced down and realized he'd finished his drink without even noticing.

"So, I take it you didn't have any trouble getting away?" she asked as Miguel came back to his seat. "Didn't you say your mom was sick or something?"

"She's in the hospital," he said. "There's nobody home but me right now. And she wants me to get out and have fun."

Trina nodded. "What about Dr. Stone? Did you have to clear it with him?"

"Nah." Ethan shook his head. "I think he might be sick or something, too. My lesson schedule's been spotty because of my mom, but he called this afternoon and said we wouldn't be starting again until Monday at the earliest. He sounded kind of weird on the message. I didn't tell him I was going out tonight."

"Way to go," Oliver said, exchanging a glance with Miguel. "Just because he's your teacher doesn't mean he runs your life."

"Yeah," Ethan agreed. "Yeah. He doesn't." He accepted another drink from the leather-clad cocktail waitress and smiled.

CHAPTER SIXTEEN

Stone didn't remember falling asleep—or maybe passing out—on the old leather sofa in his basement sanctum, but the pounding on the door snapped him out of an uneasy dream of blood and screams and something about a carnivorous house eating a television set. The first thing he realized when he awoke was that he was face down, with one leg hanging off the edge of the couch and his foot dragging on the floor. The second thing he realized was that every part of his body was screaming at him.

"Bugger..." he muttered, glancing at the clock. After seven. He'd missed his next dose of painkillers by nearly three hours.

The door pounded again. "Alastair?" Megan. "Are you down there?"

"In a minute," he tried to call, but it came out as a feeble croak.

This was not going to end well.

He reached down, put his hand on the floor, and tried to push himself up, but the only thing he succeeded in doing was to set off some sort of large-scale explosion centering around his cracked ribs. Clamping his teeth around a shriek of pain, he rolled over and landed on his back on the floor. It was a very good thing that this was one of the spots where he'd covered the concrete with a rug, and another that the old couch was so saggy that he didn't have far to fall. Even so, his ribs throbbed anew.

He lay there, panting, and considered his next options. Some- how, he was going to have to get up, stagger across the room, and drag himself up the stairs, all before Megan freaked out and called the fire department to break the door down.

Wait, wait, he told himself. *She doesn't know you're down here.*

Where the hell else would I be? The car's still here—she's not going to be thick enough to think I just nipped out for a walk.

Why had he given her a key to the place, again?

He was wasting time. Gritting his teeth, he reminded himself that this whole thing was his fault, and if he hadn't been such a lazy mage he wouldn't have gotten himself hurt in the first place. Pain wasn't a valid excuse when it was your own doing.

He crawled over to the table, every movement feeling like someone was stabbing him in the side. When he got there he grabbed the edge and hauled himself to a kneeling position. At least his knees were all right. That was something.

With some satisfaction and very little memory of having finished them, he noticed several objects laid out on the table: a half-dozen crystals, a ring with a blocky purple stone, and a necklace with a pendant in the shape of a miniature felinoid skull with horns. He shifted his sight a bit (which caused his already pounding head to throb warningly) and noted that all of them glowed with power like tiny suns. At least he'd done what he'd come down here to do in the first place. It was probably why he felt even worse than he should—infusing focus objects with power took a lot out of him—but at least he'd taken the first concrete steps toward making sure that he'd be ready if somebody tried to jump him again.

The thought gave him a bit more energy. By sheer effort of will, he pulled himself to his feet, swaying back and forth like a drunken toddler. Fighting down a wave of nausea and dizziness, he began moving toward the stairs.

"Alastair, are you down there?" Megan's voice sounded far away: the door was quite thick on purpose, bound with metal on the inside. The fire department, should she decide to call them, would be in for quite a surprise if they tried to knock it down.

Gathering all his strength, he called, "Coming!" He hoped she heard him, because he wasn't going to be able to do that again. He'd nearly shouted himself off his feet, and there were still the stairs to deal with.

You never truly think about how hard it is to climb a simple flight of stairs until various parts of your body are registering their protests in ways that are impossible to ignore. Stone gripped the railing and used his arms to drag himself up one step at a time, pausing on every third to get his breath back. That was another thing about cracked ribs: it hurt to breathe. By the time he made it to the top he was swaying again, blinking back the gray fog settling around his head. He grabbed the doorknob, yanked the door toward him, staggered out and closed it behind him before Megan could do more than stare at him in shock. Then he took two more steps forward, tripped, and barely caught himself before his full weight fell into her arms. "Evening," he managed, trying to summon up a cheery smile.

Megan caught him and held him up long enough to hustle him over to a chair. Her expression warred between anger and worry in equal measure. "Alastair—what the—?" Pausing to compose herself for a moment, she continued, "What the *hell* were you thinking, locking yourself down there? What were you even *doing* down there? In the basement?"

He leaned forward, letting his head drop into his hands. "Don't shout, Megan," he slurred. "I'm—sorry. Lost track of time."

She sighed, a long-suffering sound that anybody who spent more than a casual amount of time with Stone was very familiar with. "How long were you down there?"

He considered shrugging, decided that wasn't smart, and rolled his head back and forth in his hands. "I don't know—fell asleep. Three-four hours or so, I think." In the vague periphery of his senses, an interesting aroma wandered by. Food of some sort. He realized he hadn't eaten since this morning, and he was ravenous. "Something smells good..."

"I brought Chinese. Figured you wouldn't want to go out. But I'm wondering now if I should be taking you back to the hospital." She made a move like she was going to smack him in the head. "God, you're such an idiot sometimes. You couldn't have just stayed in bed like a good boy?"

He shook his head. "I'm a bad boy, Megan," he muttered. "You can spank me later—might be fun. Right now, though, be a love and bring me my happy pills from upstairs, will you? Then I'll be delighted to join you for Chinese food and bad television."

Half an hour later, the painkillers had kicked in, and Stone was feeling significantly better. He sat slouched into one side of the overstuffed sofa in the living room, poking at a carton of kung pao chicken with chopsticks and paying no attention to whatever terrible rom-com Megan had found to watch. She wasn't paying any attention to it either. She fished her briefcase from off the floor, dug in it, and tossed something in his lap. "Saw that today. Thought you'd like a copy for posterity."

It was the *Stanford Daily*, the campus newspaper. Unfolding it he saw his own face, taken from his university ID card, staring at him from beneath the headline *"Professor Attacked, Robbed in Campus Parking Lot."* He skimmed the article: the details were sparse, and neither the campus police nor the Palo Alto department had managed to catch the attackers yet. The article urged students and faculty to be cautious when walking on campus after dark, and to use the buddy system whenever possible or call for an escort. He tossed it back at Megan. "At least they spelled my name right."

"The whole thing makes me nervous," she said, clutching it. "Thinking there are thugs wandering around campus—a couple of my colleagues are scared to walk to their cars now."

Stone leaned back, trying to remember something that had caught his interest before. The medication fogged his mental processes a bit, but he almost had it. Something relevant to what she was saying—

Then he remembered. "Megan—you said something about the air being let out of my tire, didn't you?"

She nodded. "That's what they told me, yeah. Why?"

"Maybe nothing," he said slowly, pondering. "But I'm just paranoid enough to wonder if p'raps they were after me specifically."

She stared at him, chopsticks full of chow mein hovering halfway between her carton and her mouth. "Why would you say that? Why would anyone want to beat you up? You don't have any enemies you haven't told me about, do you?"

If only you knew. "It just seems odd that they'd do that rather than just jumping me. There *were* two of them, and at least the one I saw was bigger than I was. They wouldn't have had any trouble with me if they'd attacked, rather than risking being seen messing about with my car. I'm not exactly that imposing." Physically, anyway. Unless they knew he was more than he appeared to be, and they wanted to make sure they got their hits in before he could fight back.

"But I don't get it. What would they gain by it? What would make you a better target than someone else?"

He shrugged. It didn't hurt, which was nice. He decided that he really liked his happy pills, and wouldn't forget to take them again no matter how preoccupied he got. "No idea. P'raps the combination of driving a nice car and parking in a remote area made them think I'd be easy money. There are plenty of people around there who drive nicer cars than I do, but most of them park them in more populated lots." Of course this wasn't what he really believed, but once again he had to come up with a plausible explanation that would satisfy Megan.

"Maybe so," she said, but she didn't sound like she believed it either. "Oh—one other thing, before I forget. Tommy Langley was asking about you. I saw him at the cafeteria today. He said to tell you he hopes you heal up quick so your little group can all go out and get drunk again soon." She rolled her eyes, clearly indicating her opinion of this activity.

"I'll get right on that," he assured her.

They settled back, ostensibly to watch the movie, but Stone's mind was actually far away. Megan's mention of Langley had sent it off in a different direction, reminding him of what had been going on up at Adelaide Bonham's mansion. He wondered if she'd had any more incidents, and remembered that even if she had, his promise to Langley effectively prevented him from investigating them. His foggy brain then served up the absurd possibility that the thing in her house and what had happened to him could be linked, but the thought almost made him chuckle aloud. As far as he'd ever seen, frightening entities hiding in dusty old mansions didn't hire thugs to beat up mages, no matter how powerful they might be otherwise.

As he felt himself beginning to doze off against the soft cushions, he didn't fight it. His last waking thoughts were that he was going to have to find another way to find out about Adelaide's house, and somehow figure out who had jumped him. And why.

And, just as a stray side thought, he wondered what Ethan was doing with his Friday night, and hoped his apprentice was having a more exciting time than he was.

| CHAPTER SEVENTEEN

Ethan wasn't at all sure he was doing the right thing, but at that moment he didn't care.

His head rested against the window in the back seat of a black SUV. Miguel was next to him, and in the front were Trina in the shotgun seat and Oliver driving. It was two a.m., and the music blasting from the SUV's top-end stereo system mixed with the air coming in from the open front window to drive off the worst effects of the three shots of liquor he'd consumed back at the club.

About an hour ago, Trina had looked around the Nightmare Room and abruptly announced, "This place is a snooze. Let's get out of here."

Ethan, his lifetime of geekiness convincing him they were about to ditch him, felt a moment of panic, but then Trina smiled at him. "You want to see a real club, Ethan?"

"Er—"

"Yeah, none of this suburban crap," Oliver agreed.

"Come on," Miguel urged. "Live a little. Get out from under old Stone's boot."

One look into his mocking eyes, combined with the liquor, sealed the deal. "Yeah," he said firmly. "Yeah, I would. Let's go."

He wondered where they were taking him, and how he was going to get home, since he'd left his car parked down the street from Darkwave. But part of him didn't care about that, either. For once in his life, he was going to actually do something spontaneous. If that meant having to catch BART back and use some of his savings to get a cab ride the rest of the way, then so be it. It wasn't like he had anything else to spend it on.

His mother didn't have to know, and neither did Stone.

The SUV flew up Highway 280, making good time in the sparse traffic. At first he thought they were going to Palo Alto, but they flashed by all the exits for that town and continued north. "So—" he ventured, "—where *are* we going? That club you mentioned up in San Francisco?"

Trina shrugged. "Maybe. Getting kind of tired of that place, too." She grinned, twisting in her seat to fix him with her captivating green gaze. "Hey, I know."

"What?" Oliver glanced sideways for a second, then turned back to watch the road.

"Screw clubs. I'm sick of them anyway. Same old boring grind. Why don't we show Ethan some real magic?"

Ethan stiffened, his eyes widening. Going to clubs with these people was one thing, but he'd given his word to Stone that he wouldn't get involved with any other magic. "Um—" he started, but they ignored him.

"Great idea," Miguel said, turning his electric grin on Ethan. "Give you some idea of what you'll be able to do someday."

"I don't think—"

"Jeez, Ethan, you worry more than anybody I've ever met," Trina said. She was still smiling and there was a fondness in her tone, but also an edge of impatience, like she was growing tired of his constant hesitation. "It's not like we'd ask you to join in or anything. I doubt you're far enough along that you could anyway. We just want to show you what it looks like. Even Stone couldn't object to that, could he? Most apprentices have seen all kinds of magic by the time they start their training. I know I did. Didn't you?"

"Not—really," he admitted. "I kinda found out about it late." His insides squirmed at her tone. Taking a deep breath, he said, "I just don't want to get in trouble with Dr. Stone. If he kicks me out and says he won't train me, then—"

"Look," Miguel said. "First, he doesn't have to find out if you don't tell him. Mages can't read minds. If he tries to tell you he can, he's full of shit. And second, we're not gonna be doing anything wrong. Like Trin said, you're not gonna be *doing* any magic. Just *watching* it."

"Come on, dude," Oliver urged. "It'll blow you away. Trust me. We can do some pretty cool shit when we get going. Don't you want to see what you'll be able to do someday?"

Ethan considered. His mind was in turmoil: on the one hand, he was scared to death that Stone would somehow find out what he'd been up to and terminate his apprenticeship. That would effectively mean the end of his magical training, since even if Walter Yarborough agreed to go back to the original deal, there was no way Ethan was going to go that far away from Mom when she was so sick. On the other, maybe Miguel was right: it wasn't like he was going to be performing any actual magic. And Stone didn't have to find out. Ethan wasn't going to see him until Monday at the earliest anyway, so even if he ended up with a hangover, he'd have the weekend to recover from it.

And then there was Trina—or Trin, as her friends apparently called her.

He wondered if he'd ever be close enough to her to call her Trin.

She was smiling at him now, her eyes full of encouragement and mischief and—something else? No, that part was all in his mind. It had to be. She couldn't be looking at him that way. But that was okay. The possibility that it might happen someday wasn't as completely remote as it had been earlier that day.

Take a chance, a little voice in the back of his head said. *You'll end up kicking yourself if you don't.*

"Let's do it," he said, grinning.

Trina nodded approvingly. "Good deal."

They drove into the heart of San Francisco, and after a time Oliver parked the SUV in front of what looked like a rotting, abandoned house. Ethan said nothing, but once again he was beginning to rethink his agreement.

"It doesn't look like much," Miguel said, apparently picking up on his apprehension, "but wait till you see what we've done with the place."

They led him upstairs to the attic and he stared at their ritual area: at the black painted walls, the graffiti-style magical sigils, the circle laid out on the floor. "What do you think?" Trin asked.

"Cool," Ethan said, and he meant it. This was *much* cooler than Stone's basement.

"C'mon," Oliver said. "Let's get started." Instead of grabbing ritual materials, though, he picked up a bottle of tequila from a rickety table and took a swig, then offered it to Trin. They passed it around; Ethan didn't really want to drink more, but he wasn't about to turn them down. When they finished the bottle they began constructing the circle. By that time, Ethan was feeling quite the buzz.

When the circle was complete, the three of them took their places, leaving a fourth place for him. "Okay," Trin said. "Here's the deal. We all join hands, and we'll start building up power. You don't need to do anything yet except watch us magically and see what we're doing. Once you think you have a handle on it, just see if you can step into the flow and channel some of the power yourself. If that works, you'll feel it. Then concentrate on feeding more power in, adding to what's already there. Think you can do that?"

"I can do it," he said. "But—you said I wasn't going to be doing any magic."

"This isn't really doing magic," Trin said, waving a dismissive hand. "You aren't going to be controlling anything, just helping us deal with the power. Simple stuff. Think you can handle it?"

Ethan swallowed. He had no idea if he could, but Trin's tone of challenge made him game to try. The alcohol was giving him courage. He nodded. "Yeah. I can handle it."

"Good. Let's get started, then." She held out her hand for Ethan to take it. He did, and grasped Miguel's on the other side. Slowly, the three of them began to chant, and Ethan shifted to magical sight. He could see the pattern already beginning to grow, very simple and rudimentary at first, but taking on power and complexity as he watched them weave bits of themselves into its structure. It took him a while, but eventually he thought he grasped what they were trying to do, and gently reached out to take part of it and begin weaving his own power into the tapestry.

"Good, good," Trina murmured, nodding. "Just keep that up, and when you're in, start feeding power in."

Ethan did as he was told. The pattern continued to build until it became a thing of beauty, complex and mathematical like some kind of perfect equation. He almost lost control of his part of it when he grew enraptured with just watching the way it moved and shifted as the participants made small adjustments to variables. He'd always loved math in school and had been good at it—this was like math made tangible.

"Careful, Ethan," Trin said, smiling. "You're starting to lose it. Don't stare at the pretty lights. *Be* the pretty lights."

He snapped his attention back and fell once more into the pattern. He let it sing through him until at long last the others began to draw back, slowly dismantling it until it faded to nothingness. Oddly, he was sad watching it go.

"So, what'd you think of that?" Trin asked.

"That was—the most amazing thing I've ever seen," he said, and he meant it. He wondered if Stone was ever going to show him things like that, or if he even *could* without more mages to participate.

"Yeah, we get that a lot," she said, amused. Oliver was already fetching another bottle of liquor, and Miguel was digging some pot and rolling papers out of a cigar box. "C'mon. Sit down and we'll just talk for a while. Takes some time to come down off a magical high like that. Let's go for something a little more conventional."

They all settled back and began passing around the bottle and the joint. Ethan was hesitant at first, but after sharing that amazing ritual with these three, he felt a kind of oneness with them. He didn't want to be excluded from their group. He barely noticed or cared that when the bottle went around, the other three were actually drinking very little, and hardly touching the joint at all. Eventually, Miguel and Oliver got up and drifted out of the room, leaving him alone with Trin.

She lounged back on the pile of pillows they'd scattered on the floor, reaching out to run her nail gently down Ethan's cheek. "Pretty fucking amazing night, huh?"

"Totally," he agreed, lying back next to her. His mind floated on a cloud; he felt like when he spoke, his voice was coming from another place.

"I'm really glad we could share that with you. I love seeing new mages discover things." She rolled over on her back, staring up at the ceiling. "I hope you can come back and do it again."

"Oh, yeah..." he whispered. "I really want to do that."

"Great," she said, smiling. She paused for a long time, and then said softly, "Hey, Ethan?"

"Yeah?"

"I was wondering if maybe you could tell me something."

"Anything."

She reached over and stroked his chest with her fingernail. "I heard that Dr. Stone is doing something at this old house down by where you live. Do you know anything about that?"

Ethan shrugged. "Sure."

"You do?"

"Yeah. I've been there," he said proudly.

"Really? That's great. So what's the deal with it?"

A little suspicion poked its way up through his alcohol- and marijuana-fueled fog. "Why?"

She kissed the tip of his nose. "No real reason. It just sounded cool, is all. A haunted house."

He grinned. "Don't know if it's haunted. There's something in there, though. Something big, Dr. Stone says."

"Does he know what?"

"Not yet. He's trying to find it."

"But he hasn't yet?"

"Not yet..."

She nodded. "Just curious—where is this house?"

"It's in Los Gatos. Up in the hills...it's really big. Huge," he added with a big, goofy grin. He could feel himself beginning to float off on a brightly colored cloud with Trina's face on it. "Really huge...with these old ladies. Nice old ladies..."

"That's great, Ethan. Thanks. It sounds like it's a pretty cool place." She stroked his hair. "You go on to sleep now. I'll wake you up when it's time to go back."

"Okay..." he whispered. His words were slurred now. "You know what? I really like you, Trina..."

"I like you too, Ethan. Now go to sleep."

He slipped into deep slumber, the big, goofy grin still plastered on his face.

| CHAPTER EIGHTEEN

S tone couldn't get Adelaide Bonham and her haunted house out of his mind.

He woke up the next morning stretched out on the couch with a blanket over him. Megan was gone, but she'd left a note saying to call if he needed her, the Chinese leftovers were in the fridge, and thanks for a night of torrid and acrobatic passion which he probably didn't remember a bit of. He chuckled and pocketed the note.

After a breakfast of painkillers and cold kung pao chicken, he dragged himself upstairs for a shower and a change of clothes, then went down to the basement and retrieved the items he'd built yesterday. He donned the ring and the amulet, stuffing the feline skull under his shirt, then stuck a couple of the crystals in his pocket and left the rest on the kitchen table. At least if anyone tried to jump him again, he'd have a fighting chance of showing them the error of their ways. Of course, even without the focus objects, he didn't think they'd catch him by surprise again. Laziness about the world around him was a luxury he could no longer afford.

He lowered himself into the nearest chair, and tried to figure out what to do next. It was Saturday, so he had no classes. It was nearly eleven o'clock—he supposed he could call Megan, but decided not to. Like him, she needed her alone time, and he didn't want her to feel obligated to hover over him like a protective mother bear. He was actually feeling better today, especially after the shower—he'd only taken one pain pill. He thought he'd even be all right to drive, should he have anywhere to go.

One thing was sure: he couldn't go back to Adelaide's house. Not if he wanted to keep his friendship with Langley. It wasn't like the two of them were best buddies or anything, but Stone did like him enough that if he was going to break a promise, he'd need a better reason than 'there's something there, and it might be dangerous.' He wasn't even completely certain that the entity had been behind the TV explosion, but if someone had offered to bet him, he would have taken it.

If he couldn't go to the house, he'd have to come up with some other angle to pursue. He leaned back in the chair and thought about it, halfway wishing that Ethan was there to bounce ideas off. The boy might not be far along in his magical training yet, but he was smart and picked things up quickly, and Stone did his best thinking when he had an audience to lecture to.

He thought about the entity—the spirit, or ghost, or whatever it was. Why was it there? He'd suggested some ideas while talking to Ethan at the house itself: that it had always been there, gaining power; that something had happened to "awaken" it; that it was newly arrived. He didn't think the latter was true—things that powerful tended to put down roots and associate themselves with particular areas, buildings, or people. But if it had been there all along, then why was it only now causing trouble? How long had it been there? The house was very old, Langley had said: one of the oldest in the area. Had it been there since the house was built?

"Hmm..." he said aloud. If it *had* been there that long, maybe it had caused trouble before. Some similar spirits waxed and waned in their power, going dormant for many years before waking up again. Maybe this was one of those. The next step, then, was to find out more about the history of the house.

Fortunately, he had one of the best sources around for such things, easily available to him. Pleased to finally have a plan, he first drove to Green Library on the Stanford campus. After an hour of digging, he determined that what he wanted wasn't there. The house was in Los Gatos, so perhaps the library there was more likely to have the information he sought.

The Los Gatos library did have some documents about the Bonham house. He had to ask the librarian to get hold of them, but she set him up with a couple of large bound books full of early newspapers, a box of microfiche reels, and a small stack of books chronicling the history of the town.

He left two hours later, his notebook full of scribblings that he'd jotted down while reading through the books and periodicals. None of it was much help, though: the house had been built in the early part of the century by the father of Edgar Bonham, Adelaide's late husband. The elder Bonham had been a wealthy steel magnate, and had built the house as a gift for his beloved wife, who was sickly and couldn't take the climate back East. As far as Stone could determine, the house didn't have any kind of checkered past: he couldn't find accounts of any murders or other crimes in or near it, and by all accounts Edgar Bonham Sr. had doted on his wife and she on him. He had died in the mid-1920s, and she'd followed almost ten years later. Edgar Jr. had been their only child.

This was interesting in a general sort of way, but it wasn't giving him what he was looking for. He drove back to Palo Alto with a sense of frustration—he wasn't sure what he'd been expecting to find, but he'd hoped that whatever it was, it would be sufficiently compelling to convince Tommy Langley to let him go up there again. Good as the information he'd found was, it wasn't going to get him his wish.

He'd made it as far as Mountain View driving back up 280 when he realized there was one more place he could check. Mentally he almost kicked himself for not thinking of it before, or actually first. He sighed: he'd been out of the game too long, spending most of his time lately playing Occult Studies professor, and too little staying connected with the magical community around the Bay Area.

That was going to have to change, and no time like the present for it to start.

The only thing that East Palo Alto shared with its high-class sister city was part of its name. It was mainly a working-class town, but parts were becoming increasingly rundown, vacant, and in the process of being overrun by the sort of people that the police worked hard to keep out of Palo Alto, and the law-abiding, working-class majority in EPA worked hard to keep out of their neighborhoods. Stone never felt particularly comfortable driving through it, but the place he was headed was smack in the middle of one of the town's worst business districts. If he wanted the information, he'd have to go where it was.

Parking the Jaguar, he glanced around to make sure no one was obviously watching, then summoned a small enchantment around the car to make it blend in with its surroundings. The eyes of anyone who wasn't specifically looking for it would just slide over it like it wasn't even there, or see it as the sort of car that routinely parked in the neighborhood. He'd have to make this quick: the initial enchantment wouldn't last long unless he spent some effort shoring it up.

There were few active businesses or shops on this street; most of them were closed, their doors boarded up, their windows covered with graffiti-strewn sheets of plywood and stout bars. He headed directly for a small, nondescript door between two defunct shops: a liquor store and a purveyor of adult novelties, both of them awash in trash and gang symbols. The door itself was not marked; in fact, Stone knew that it held a more permanent version of the same enchantment that he'd put on his car. He knew this because he'd put it there, several months ago. That was the only reason he could see the door without uttering the passphrase that the establishment's other customers would need to get past the blending spell. Opening the door, he slipped inside and quickly shut it behind him.

Inside, things looked significantly more upscale, if still a little threadbare. There was a carpeted stairway leading down and ending in another closed door; this one had a small bell hanging next to it with a dark red silken pull. Stone took the stairs slowly, favoring his ribs even though they didn't hurt at the moment. When he reached the bottom, he tugged once on the pull, causing the bell to jangle an odd note, and then waited.

He hadn't been here for quite some time. In fact, the last time he *had* been here was to renew the enchantment on the door. It was a favor to the shop's proprietor, in exchange for some help the man had given him in the past. The place didn't exactly make him nervous, but it did make him more watchful than usual. No sense taking chances.

The door swung open on a room that looked like a turn-of-the-century shop, all dark, soft carpet, glass cases, and wooden fixtures and shelves. The chandeliers hanging from the ceiling were lit with actual candles, adding a flickering eeriness to a place that was already strange enough as it was. Stone strode past the shelves full of old books, bones, desiccated animal parts, and similar objects without really seeing them. They weren't what he was here for.

At the back of the store was an old-fashioned roll top desk, and sitting at the desk was a man. He rose and bowed as Stone drew closer. "Well. Alastair Stone. It *has* been a while. To what do I owe the pleasure? Surely the door—" He got a good look at Stone and his eyebrows rose just a bit, but he did not ask.

"Hello, Stefan. How are you?"

Stefan Kolinsky was somewhere indeterminately between fifty and sixty-five. He was a tall man, almost as tall as Stone, but more powerfully built, with dark hair swept up from a high forehead, glittering dark eyes, and a hawk-like profile. He wore a tailored black suit, somewhat old-fashioned of cut, without a wrinkle in it. Kolinsky was one of the few people around who could make Stone feel almost chronically underdressed, even though he'd been told that he actually cleaned up quite nicely on the rare occasions when he had to attend something formal.

"I am well, thank you." Kolinsky's voice was soft, with just a hint of an unidentifiable accent. "But may I ask why you've come? I suspect that you aren't here to peruse my wares." He looked rueful.

"Not today, no." Stone glanced around the shop, making sure they were alone.

"Pity," Kolinsky said, shaking his head. "One day I hope that you will see the error of your ways, and realize how much you choose to limit yourself."

Stone raised an eyebrow. "I thought you'd given up on that by now." Their words had the feel of familiar banter, like they were getting something out of the way before getting down to business. It wasn't far from the truth. Stone didn't exactly *like* Stefan Kolinsky, but he did respect him. He couldn't help it, since the man was one of the finest magical minds on this side of the country. It was merely inconvenient that he played for the other team. As long as you kept a close eye on him and were very careful about the favors you asked, he could be a valuable source of information about all sorts of interesting things that most white mages wouldn't go near.

Kolinsky chuckled. "Never." Tilting his head, he looked Stone up and down. "What's happened to you, old friend? You don't look—well."

"My own fault," Stone said, shrugging. "Possibly related to why I'm here, but I doubt it. I'll get right to it, if you don't mind, so I don't have to go back out and hide the car again. When are you going to get better premises, by the way?"

"This place suits me," he said serenely.

"If you say so. Anyway—I'm looking for information about an old house. Probably nothing you'd have anything on, but I figured if you can't put your finger on anything interesting, it probably isn't there to find."

"Indeed." Kolinsky's eyebrows rose like the ears of a dog who's been offered an enticing scent. "Any particular old house?" He gestured, sliding another chair over next to the desk, and motioned for Stone to sit down.

Stone smiled. This was the reason he kept coming back to old Stefan. Not because his magic was as black as his suit. Not because he ran the only place south of San Francisco and north of Los Angeles where you could buy some of the more exotic of the items on his shelves (including the ones in the back that only the most select of customers ever got to see). No, it was because in addition to being a purveyor of things dark and arcane, he was also a formidable magical historian with a particular interest in the Bay Area. If it had to do with magic and had happened around here in the last two hundred years, odds were that Stefan Kolinsky could lay hands on some documentation about it. Or at minimum, he could come up with some pretty reliable rumors.

"It's in Los Gatos, up in the hills," he began. He told Kolinsky about the house, about Aunt Adelaide's strange feelings, and about his own first impressions and subsequent suspicion that whatever was there, it was trying to hide from him. "I'm thinking that p'raps it's been there a while," he finished, "and possibly either gaining enough power to be troublesome, or else it's coming into a potent period after a long dormancy. Either way, I need to know anything I can about what it might be, and whether it's been seen before."

Kolinsky thought about that, leaning back in his chair and steepling his fingers. "Why not simply go there again and find out for yourself?" he asked at last. "I am certain that you have the means to perform a ritual that would locate it and more precisely identify its nature."

Stone blew air through his teeth. "Well, there's the rub," he said. He told him about Tommy and his determination that Aunt Adelaide wasn't to be frightened by what he called 'that fake occult bullshit.'

"Then it will be on him if something should happen to his aunt," Kolinsky said, his tone revealing no emotion. "Why does this become your problem?"

"Because I don't want to see a charming old lady hurt because her nephew's mind is hopelessly stuck in the mundane," Stone said. "That, and—"

Kolinsky smiled a snakelike smile. "That, and your curiosity is eating you alive. You want desperately to know what this thing is, what it can do, and how to get rid of it."

Stone had long ago accepted that putting one over on Stefan Kolinsky was only somewhat easier than pushing liquid uphill. "Well—yes, if you want the truth of it. I like Adelaide, and I don't want to see anything happen to her. But this is big, Stefan. Whatever it is, it's powerful and it's growing. And I want to find it."

He nodded as if that had been obvious. "I will see what I can do, then. Unfortunately, I won't be able to give you the results of my research until at least Monday. I was preparing to close the shop when you came in—I have out of town business that will take me away from the area for most of the weekend."

Stone studied him silently. "Stefan—"

"No, no, Alastair. It's true. You don't fully trust me, and I understand. But you should know me well enough to know that I have no interest in searching out your little problem ahead of you, fascinating though it might be. I am content to discover the information in my own ways, and share what I find with you. For the standard arrangement, of course." He cocked an eyebrow at Stone.

Stone nodded. There was no way around it, and he knew Kolinsky was right. That was a good portion of the reason why he valued his relationship with the black mage as much as he did: Kolinsky was like a spider, sitting back and watching what went on at all the far-flung reaches of his web. But Stone had never known him to do anything with the knowledge, unless it affected him directly. He seemed, as far as Stone could tell, content to merely collect information and hoard it like a dragon sitting on a pile of gold. And he could be persuaded to part with bits of it for a price. "Standard arrangement, then."

Kolinsky's smile widened. "Excellent. Contact me on Monday and I'll tell you what I've found out. This one will be intriguing, I think—it will require me to dig up some reference material that I haven't looked at in a very long time." He stood, politely indicating that the meeting was over. "It's good to see you, Alastair. I hope you're feeling better soon, and I hope I'll be able to find something to interest you."

CHAPTER NINETEEN

Ethan jerked awake to the sound of someone rapping on his car window. He jumped, nearly hitting his head on the roof, and his eyes widened when he saw the helmeted, sunglassed head of a motorcycle cop peering in at him. He rolled the window down, hoping he didn't look as bleary as he felt. "Uh—good morning, officer."

The officer nodded, his expression stern. Ethan could see his own haggard face reflected in his mirrorshades. "What are you doing here, kid?"

"I—uh—" For a moment he didn't remember. He'd been in San Francisco with Trina and the others. How had he gotten back here? But then a vague memory resurfaced of jostling along in the back seat of their black SUV. They must have brought him back to his car. "I—was at the club last night, and I stayed pretty late. Realized I was too tired to drive home, so I figured I'd sleep it off to be safe."

"Are you drunk, son?"

"No, sir." He hoped he wasn't, anyway. The clock on the dashboard said 8:07—that should have been enough time for it to get out of his system. He hoped.

The cop made him get out of the car, dig out his ID and registration, and take a breathalyzer test. "Okay," he said at last, grudgingly after he'd taken down all the information. "You can go.

I don't believe you that you weren't drinking, but I can't prove it, so you're on your way. Just don't let me catch you again, got it?"

"Yes, sir."

Ethan got out of there fast (well, as fast as he dared) as soon as the cop rode off. He pulled into the parking lot of a fast-food joint and checked to make sure he still had his cash, then went inside for a big cup of coffee and an unhealthy breakfast.

As the coffee seeped into him and brought him back to some semblance of coherence, he looked out the window and let his mind drift over the events of the previous night. His emotions were in turmoil: he was still terrified that Stone would somehow find out what he'd been up to and kick him out on the street, but he also felt energized at the taste of what it felt like to do real magic. He wasn't sure why Trina and the others had been interested in the old house in Los Gatos, but it didn't matter to him if they knew. That was Stone's thing, not his.

Something in the back of his mind, maybe his conscience, was appalled at the way his attitude was developing. Stone had never been anything but fair to him. Sure, he was a taskmaster and a little hard to get close to, but that wasn't anything personal. As far as Ethan was concerned Stone was doing a great (if somewhat slow) job of teaching him magic, and he had no doubt that if he kept up his own end of the bargain, he'd come out of this as a damned good mage.

But Trina and her friends—they were different. Walter Yarborough had told him that Alastair Stone was one of the most powerful mages he knew, but Ethan had a hard time believing it. Thus far, he hadn't shown Ethan that he was capable of much more than levitating a few small things around the room, going invisible, and turning lights on and off. And he was so—what was the word—*blasé* about it! He just acted like a normal kind of guy his age who was a little eccentric. Trina, Oliver, and Miguel, on the other hand, practically *exuded* power. He hadn't missed how they strode around the club like they considered everyone else in it their inferiors, or their subjects. People respected them, looked up to them, cared about their opinions. They didn't spend their time hanging out in an old house with dusty books and a musty old basement—they got out there in the world and made things *happen.*

That, and he couldn't get it out of his head the way Trina had looked at him several times last night. He didn't think she'd seen him looking, but she was watching him like—well, like she wanted him.

Geeky, skinny him.

He slugged down some more coffee, ashamed of himself. This was crazy, and he knew it. He'd agreed to be Stone's apprentice, to follow his rules about magic. And he'd already broken his promise because he'd been dazzled by three flashy young mages who seemed to want him to be part of their group. The best thing he could do right now was to drive up to Stone's place, admit to what he'd done, and ask forgiveness.

Naturally, he had no intention of doing that. Mr. Yarborough had said that Stone didn't have any patience for that kind of thing. What if he admitted what he did and Stone *still* told him to get lost?

No, he'd just have to be good from now on, that was all. He'd call Stone back on Monday, tell him he was ready to get back to his lessons, and put this behind him. No more magic with Trina and the others.

But, he thought as he finished the coffee and prepared to leave, there was no harm in just *seeing* them, right? Maybe just talking with Trina, if she wanted to get together again?

He hoped she wanted to get together again. Even though he was sure he was wrong about how she'd looked at him—it was always possible he'd been right, and more than talking would be involved.

The Three met at their San Francisco ritual space on Saturday evening around five o'clock. From the look of them, they hadn't dragged themselves out of bed much earlier than that. "So, what's the plan?" Oliver asked, lounging in an old chair and popping a beer. "I take it you got enough from the twerp to tell you where we need to go?"

"Fuck, that kid's annoying," Miguel complained. Affecting a childish voice, he singsonged, "*Oh, should I take a chance? Should I be doing this? What will Stone think? I need a new diaper!*" He dropped a leg over the arm of another chair and slouched into it sideways. "We better get this done quick—I don't think I can stand being around him much longer without smacking him in the head."

Trin chuckled appreciatively. "Come on, he's not *that* bad. We need to take this slow. I think we got him drunk enough that he won't remember exactly what he told us, which is good. But if we're going to do what we need to do, we might need to go down there a couple of times. I want to know more about what we're up against before we do it for real. We'll only get one chance."

"What about Stone?" Oliver asked. "He gonna be a problem?"

She shook her head. "Shouldn't be. I heard back from my guys, and they worked him over pretty good Thursday night—put him in the hospital, they said. Remember how the kid said he sounded sick on the phone? Even if he's home, with any luck he'll be curled up with his blanket and slippers and out of our hair for the weekend."

"Okay, so where are we going? And when?" Miguel asked.

"Tonight. The house is in Los Gatos, up in the hills. The kid said there's just a couple of old ladies who live there, and some gardeners and stuff that might be around."

"We gonna have to go in?" Oliver took another swig of his beer.

"Not yet. Tonight's just recon. We can set up a circle outside on the grounds and try to get in touch with it from there." She smiled an unwholesome smile. "You guys were there when it contacted us. It wants to use us. But we've got other plans."

Miguel matched her smile. "I don't much like being used. Unless he's gorgeous and has a big—"

"Yeah, yeah," Oliver interrupted. "We're not gonna fuck the thing, Mig. I don't care how hot it is."

"Well, maybe we are, metaphorically," Trin said, her eyes sparkling in the same way that was so successful at curdling Ethan's hormones. "That's why we need to be careful. It's powerful, but I think if we do it right, the relationship's going to end up a little different than it expects."

| CHAPTER TWENTY

Stone had finally gotten comfortable. It was late—had to be well after midnight—and the combination of a recent pain pill, a soft, comfortable bed, and Megan's warm presence lying next to him were coming together quite nicely to drive off all his stray thoughts about pain and Ethan and Stefan Kolinsky and why anyone would want to attack him in a parking lot. He lay on his back, Megan's arm draped over his chest and her head snuggled into the crook of his arm, dozing. Things were good.

He'd gotten home around five o'clock to find her message on his machine wondering where he'd gone. After calling her back and assuring her that he was quite capable of driving, he felt better, and he'd just had some errands to run, he'd smoothed over the last of her concern by proposing that she choose what she wanted to do with the evening, and he'd go along with it.

She had shown up two hours later with a couple of bags of groceries, a bottle of good wine, and her usual teasing remarks about his appalling lack of cooking skills and the fact that he never had anything decent to eat in his townhouse unless it was one of Mrs. Olivera's nights to cook. "I'm going to make you dinner," she said. "And you're just going to sit back, relax, and stop stressing your body out instead of acting like you're eighteen and can heal overnight."

"Yes, ma'am," he'd said meekly. "You know, I could get to like this whole 'being waited on' thing."

"Well, don't get too attached to it. You still owe me dinner from Thursday night, remember."

She'd whipped up a quick but tasty pasta dish and they'd taken their time over it, sipping wine and chatting about completely mundane subjects for the next couple of hours. He'd insisted on taking care of the dishes, after which they'd retired to the dimly lit living room for some soft music and no television.

"See?" she'd said, leaned back comfortably against him. "This is nice. No essays to read, no students, no skulls or little old ladies or parking-lot thugs."

"Mmm," he'd agreed. "Quite nice. You're turning me domestic, my dear."

She snorted. "Yeah, right. Next stop: white picket fence and 2.5 adorable children. And a Labrador retriever."

"How about one adorable child and 2.5 Labrador retrievers? Or better yet: just the picket fence?"

One thing had led to another and they'd ended up in the bedroom, and despite the fact that they'd had to be more careful than usual because of his injuries, they'd managed to have an enjoyable evening. Stone had dropped off to sleep contented, for the first time in days not feeling like something was hanging over his head. He slipped in and out of deep restful sleep, his racing mind finally slowing down while Megan slumbered on next to him.

The phone rang.

"Bloody hell!" he whispered, jerking fully awake and wincing as his injured ribs protested. Megan stirred as he quickly rolled over and tried to snatch it up before it rang again. According to the clock on the nightstand, it was 1:32 a.m. "Walter, if this is you again—" he muttered into the phone.

"Dr. Stone?"

The voice was trembling, female, and sounded terrified. It took him a moment to identify it. He stared as Megan stirred again, draping her arm back over him. "Mrs.—Bonham?"

Whoever was on the other end sounded like they were on the verge of hysteria. "Dr. Stone, is that you?"

"It's me, Mrs. Bonham. What's wrong? Is something wrong?" He sat up a little, propping himself up on his pillows. Megan's arm slid down over his stomach, but he didn't even notice that she was there.

"Something's here," she quavered. "Something's...happening."

He was fully awake now. Carefully, he moved Megan's arm and sat on the edge of the bed. "Calm down, Mrs. Bonham, please. I'll help you if I can, but you have to tell me what's happening."

"I don't *know*," she sobbed. "It's like the whole house hates me. Noises—cold winds—things slamming—"

"Is Iona there? Can you put her on for a moment?"

There was a shuffling sound and then a different voice spoke, sounding almost as frightened as Adelaide Bonham had. "Dr. Stone? This is Iona."

He took a deep breath. "Iona. What's going on? Is Mrs. Bonham—"

"She's not imagining things," the woman said. In addition to sounding frightened, she sounded like she couldn't believe what was going on. "I can hear them too. The noises. The feelings. It's horrible, Dr. Stone. Something's going on."

Another deep breath. "All right. All right. Er—listen to me. Ask Mrs. Bonham—if there's a place in the house where she feels particularly safe or comfortable, go there. Lock yourselves in if you can, and wait. I'll be there as soon as I can."

Shuffling sound, and Adelaide was back on. "Should I call Tommy too?"

"No. No, just do as I said. Go to where you feel safest and wait. I'll get there as fast as I can." He was already getting up, painfully pulling on his clothes as he held the cordless receiver between his head and shoulder. He broke the connection and dropped the receiver on the bed.

"Alastair?" Megan's voice sounded muzzy from sleep. "What's going on—? Was that the phone?"

"Go back to sleep," he murmured, shrugging a sweater on over his T-shirt. "I have to go out for a bit. I'll be back soon." He sat down on the bed and hurriedly began pulling on socks and shoes.

"You have to go out?" She was more awake now. "Wait a minute. What time is it?"

"It's late. Shh. Go back to sleep. I'll be back before you know it." *I hope.*

"Where are you going?" She rolled over on her back, staring at him. "You can't go out now. It's the middle of the night!"

He didn't have time for this. Leaning over, he kissed her warm forehead. "I'm sorry, Megan, but I have to go. Go back to sleep, and I'll be here when you wake up in the morning." Before she could protest he hurried out the door. He heard her calling to him as he reached the top of the stairs, but he didn't pause.

Breathing hard, acutely aware of how long it would take him to drive from Palo Alto to Los Gatos even at this hour when there would be next to no traffic, he forced himself to pause when he reached the ground floor. He took a quick inventory and hurried downstairs to his basement sanctum, donning the ring and amulet and stuffing all of the crystals in his pocket. He'd need all the power he could get if something big was happening down there, and after the last couple of days, his personal power level wasn't at its highest. Next he found a bag on a shelf and began tossing various candles, jars of sand, incense sticks and other ritual materials into it. He had no idea if he'd need them or even have a chance to use them, but better safe than sorry.

Back upstairs his gaze fell on the bottle of pain pills by the sink. He snatched it up and stuck it in his pocket, but didn't take one now. He couldn't afford to dull his senses; he'd just have to deal with the pain unless it got so bad it was causing its own problems.

He grabbed his black overcoat and threw it on, then hurried out through the garage door. A couple of minutes later he was on the road heading toward 280, his mind thrumming with possibilities about what could be going on. He wished he'd thought of consulting Stefan Kolinsky earlier—if the man could have come up with anything, he might have a better idea what he was dealing with. He hated going in blind.

It was about twenty-five miles from Palo Alto to Los Gatos, not counting the smaller roads that went up into the hills. He opened up the car on the freeway as much as he dared—getting pulled over now would slow him down more than if he just drove the speed limit. All the while his brain continued to spin horrific scenarios of some potent, malevolent force having its way with the two helpless women trapped inside the house.

Why had it chosen to make its move tonight? There was nothing mystically significant about the time period—it was merely a cold, slightly foggy night in early December, no different from any other. He couldn't imagine how Adelaide or Iona could have done anything to provoke it—the only thing he figured was that perhaps he'd been right that it had been gaining power on its own and had finally hit the tipping point when it could affect the material world in a more direct way.

That was bad news, especially since he had no idea what it was, and thus no idea how to fight it.

Bugger Tommy and his mundanity, anyway! If he hadn't been so insistent that Aunt Adelaide not be frightened by what he believed to be bogus concerns, Stone could have done more tests, and maybe taken more of the thing's measure before it became too dangerous.

Ah, well. No point in focusing on that now. He just hoped he'd be able to keep his promise to Megan and be back by the time she woke up the next morning.

Or that he'd at least be alive by the next morning.

It was close to two-thirty when he slewed the Jaguar right onto the turnoff leading up to the house. He couldn't see anything in the distance: no pyrotechnic lightshows or anything as blatant as that.

This wasn't necessarily comforting, though: a lot of magical entities were quite a bit more subtle. He pulled the car over for a moment and stopped, leaning over the steering wheel and closing his eyes, willing up his mental defenses to their maximum. It would take a bit of his energy to sustain them, but if this was one of the more subtle variety of mystical baddies, he'd be grateful he'd taken the effort later.

Continuing up the road he reached the gate. It was closed. *Damn. Forgot to tell them to open it before they hid.* He jumped out of the car, leaving it running, and tried to open it.

It was locked up tight. Of course it was. A cold, biting wind sliced through his coat.

With a sigh he went back to the car, pulled it off to the side, and gathered up his gear from inside. He hadn't wanted to waste magical energy yet, but he was going to have to get over that gate and there was no way he was going to climb it. He didn't know how long the fence around the place extended, and he didn't have time to find out.

He slung his bag over his shoulder, focused his will, and levitated himself up and over, dropping down neatly on the other side. That spell came easily for him, fortunately, so he was barely breathing hard when he touched down. Ahead, he could see the bulk of the house rising up like a dark presence all its own, lit only by its perimeter lights. No cheery inside lamps now. He wondered where Adelaide and Iona had chosen to hide, and hoped they'd chosen wisely.

He kept to the side of the road as he moved up toward the house, reaching out with his magical senses to see if he could get any more information about the entity before he had to go inside. Immediately he picked something up—it was all around him. The thing was agitated. But the strange thing was, it didn't seem any more potent or powerful than it had the first time Stone had touched it back when he and Tommy had made their first visit.

Odd, he thought. *Almost like something's disturbing it.*

There was also something else—something he couldn't quite put his finger on. A trace of a different sort of magic in the air. Less powerful, more focused.

More familiar.

Was there another mage here?

No, that was absurd. What would another mage be doing out here in the middle of nowhere on a night like this? He checked again, and the odd trace was gone. He pulled up the collar of his overcoat against the wind and resumed his trudge toward the house. When he got there, he pounded on the door. "Mrs. Bonham!" he yelled, wondering if she'd even hear him from inside the vast house. "Iona! It's Alastair Stone! Open the door!" His voice was nearly carried off by the rushing wind.

Nothing happened. He stood there, hands in his pockets, teeth gritted, glancing constantly around him as if expecting something to sneak up on him, for nearly five minutes. He was beginning to wonder if he'd have to try getting in through one of the windows when the door opened. A wide-eyed Iona was on the other side, dressed in robe and slippers, her dark hair in disarray. "Oh! Dr. Stone. Thank God you're here! Come in, come in!" She grabbed his arm and tugged him inside, then slammed the door shut behind him and locked it. She was breathing like she'd just run two circuits around the grounds.

Stone's gaze took in the entry chamber. Nothing looked out of the ordinary here. "Iona. Are you all right? Where's Mrs. Bonham?"

"Come with me." She led him out of the room and down a long hall to what looked like a smallish office. Unlike the rest of the house which showed strong leanings toward Adelaide Bonham's old-lady decorating tastes, this one had a distinct masculine feel, with paneled walls, shelves lined with old books, and even a couple stuffed deer heads. The furniture was heavy wood and leather, overstuffed and comfortable in a functional way, and another door led to a tiny bathroom at the far end. The room had no windows, and only a single exit door. Iona waved Stone through it, and then closed it after a quick peek outside to make sure nothing was following them.

Adelaide was perched on one end of a brown couch, clutching a handkerchief and trembling in her quilted pale-blue dressing gown and slippers. She looked up as he entered and tears sprang to her eyes. "Oh, Dr. Stone. I'm so sorry to drag you out of your bed at such an hour—and what happened to your face?"

He crouched in front of her, taking her hand reassuringly. "Think nothing of it, Mrs. Bonham. I'm fine. Now, tell me—what's gotten you so frightened?"

She didn't have to tell him, though. As she drew breath to answer the house made a sudden loud creaking sound, low and rumbling and sustained from somewhere deep in its bowels. This was followed by the sharp slams of several doors opening and closing and then a low, agonized moan. Adelaide and Iona made little screams and clutched at each other, trembling.

"Oh, dear God," Iona whispered. "What is it? *What is it?*"

Stone was not trembling. The initial creak had startled him, but when it continued to draw out he pulled himself to his full height, shifting his perceptions over to get a better look. He stood there, jaw set and grim thousand-yard stare fixed somewhere out beyond the confines of the house, for almost a minute after the moan died out.

The two women looked at him, for a moment appearing almost as frightened of him as they were of what the house was doing. "Dr...Stone?" Adelaide ventured at last.

He shook his head quickly as if clearing it, and his gaze switched back to the here and now. "Sorry," he said. He let his breath out and sat down in a nearby chair. His mind was still far away, but he forced himself to focus on the two ladies. "Just—trying to figure out where that was coming from."

"What was it?" Iona asked, voice shaking.

Stone took a deep breath. Here was when things were going to get interesting. "I don't know what it is yet. I'll need to do more tests to find out. But whatever it is, it's somewhere inside the house."

Iona and Adelaide exchanged terrified looks. "In the *house?*" Adelaide echoed. She looked around like she expected to see something come crashing through the closed doors.

"Yes. How long as it been doing this? Is that what frightened you initially?"

Adelaide nodded, eyes wide. "Y-yes. It started a couple of hours ago—not long before I called you. I had just gone to bed about half an hour before that, and so had Iona. Her bedroom is near mine so I can call her if I need her for anything. And then suddenly the house just started doing—*that.*" She waved her hands around to encompass what had just occurred.

"That...but nothing else?" Stone asked. "Nothing flying around, or breaking? Nothing like when your television set exploded?"

Iona shook her head. "Not unless all that crashing was things falling off shelves or something. But nothing dangerous around us. Right, Adelaide?"

Again, the old lady nodded. "No, just very, very frightening." Her pleading gaze fell back on Stone. "Dr. Stone, please tell me you can help us with this. Because if you can't—"

Stone patted her arm. "Don't worry, Mrs. Bonham. I think I can help you. But what I want you to do for now is to stay put in here—is this the place you feel safest in the house?"

"Yes—it used to be my Edgar's little study. Where he went when he wanted to just get away from the world for a while. We used to spend a lot of time in here, just the two of us. That's why I never changed the furnishings or anything."

Stone nodded, most of her words beyond 'yes' not even registering as his mind continued working through possible causes and solutions. "All right, then—stay here, and don't come out until I either come back or it's morning. Can you do that for me? I won't be as effective if I have to worry about you two out and about."

Adelaide reached out and took his hand, holding it between her two cold ones. "Are—are you going to be safe, Dr. Stone? If something happens to you—"

He patted her hand, exuding a confidence he didn't entirely feel. "I'll be fine. I promise. You just stay here and I'll be back as soon as I can. Oh…would you trust me with a key to the house?" he added. "If I have to go outside, I don't want to leave the door unlocked or ask you to come and let me in again."

"Of course." She nodded to Iona, who pulled a key on a smiley-face fob from a nearby drawer and handed it to him.

"All right, then," he said with a slightly manic grin, squaring his shoulders. "Time to go find out what this thing is, what it wants, and why it's being so rude."

| CHAPTER TWENTY-ONE

F ar out on the spacious grounds surrounding Adelaide's house, hidden from view by the thick growth of trees, The Three continued their magical ritual.

They'd been at it for nearly two hours now; this was no simple symbolic-link ritual like the ones they often did to get back at hapless club patrons for minor slights. This one had the potential to go horribly awry if they didn't pay careful attention to what they were doing. They didn't want to get this wrong, so they'd taken extra time to set up their circle.

After all, it wasn't like anyone was going to come out here and catch them at it.

They'd had a bit of trouble finding the place, since Ethan's directions hadn't been precise, and he hadn't remembered the house number. Miguel, who excelled at that sort of thing, had hunted it down using the old woman's name, and they'd pored through the Thomas Guide for the area until they'd identified the twisty little road that led to the place. Thwarted by the locked gate (they could probably have used magic to break the lock, but they didn't want to draw any attention to themselves), they'd driven a few yards off the road, hidden their vehicle, and levitated themselves over.

Once they located the house proper, it was an easy matter to head out into the woods, find a suitable clearing, and set up the materials they would need. So far they hadn't heard anything out here but the wind and a few small animals, but they had set a couple of magical warning devices thirty yards or so away, one toward the house and one in the direction of the road; if anyone blundered near, they'd know about it and could take appropriate action.

The Three stood inside the circle they'd made, hands clasped, each concentrating on his or her specific task. Individually none of them was highly accomplished at this sort of thing, but to their fortune, magical rituals' power multiplied significantly depending on the number of people involved in casting them—and when you added that to the fact that they'd worked together for so long that they could practically read each other's thoughts, it meant that their individual deficiencies in skill were largely negated by the sheer amount of power and focus they could bring to the table when working together.

They had tried to anticipate any potential difficulties in casting the circle and performing the ritual: things like bringing along tall enclosures for the candles to shield them from the wind, and a larger barrier to put around the brazier in the center for the same reason. They had each provided a bit of blood to fuel the casting (usually one contribution was sufficient for their minor rituals) and had made a point to stop by a nightclub for an hour or two earlier that night to top up their power so they would be at their strongest.

All of this, when it came down to it, was because they were afraid. They'd never admit it, of course: The Three never admitted to being afraid of anything. But when the entity, whatever it was, had taken control of their previous ritual, transported them to a different location in magical space, and imposed its images and impressions upon their minds, they realized that they were dealing with a being of vast power—and one that had far more experience manipulating arcane forces than they did.

And it wanted out.

That's what it had told them. It was imprisoned. Though the bars of its confinement were beginning to slip enough that it could communicate with those who were sensitive to the vibrations of the supernatural world, it was impatient. It didn't want to wait any longer. The blond boy knew where it was held, but he didn't have the power to release it. The dark-haired man had the power, but he was wily and dangerous, and difficult to tempt. And so it had reached out to The Three, with promises of power and forbidden knowledge if they could aid it in breaking free of its prison. They had listened to its offer and agreed to help.

And then the ritual had ended, and The Three, as they were inclined to do, began to wonder if there might be a way that they could turn this situation more to their own advantage. The entity (they had no idea yet what else to call it) had been imprisoned: that meant that someone had imprisoned it. And if it could be imprisoned, perhaps it could be bound.

The ritual tonight was not designed to bind it: in fact, if all went as they planned, it wouldn't even notice what they were doing. Although The Three were young, and impatient for results themselves, even they wouldn't attempt to harness power of this thing's level without some serious advance reconnaissance. It would be equivalent to trying to disarm a powerful bomb while possessing neither schematics nor even a basic understanding of what kind of bomb they were working on. In other words: very bad idea.

The reason they were here tonight, then, was to perform that reconnaissance. Their aim, should they pull off the ritual successfully, was to get a better idea of what kind of magical thing they were dealing with, and what kind of power level it had. Was it a spirit, a physical being with magical powers, an extradimensional entity of some sort—or something they'd never even seen before? If it turned out to be any of the first three, they had a chance of being able to deal with it. They didn't have the knowledge now, but part of Miguel's most valuable contribution to their little cabal was his unsurpassed skills at research, surveillance, and other similar things he called "magical spy stuff" (which often included stalking, but that wasn't relevant to the subject at hand).

So far, the casting was going well. It had taken them over an hour to set up the circle, and once they joined hands and began channeling their power into a shared spell, they found what they were seeking nearly immediately. There *was* something there, and it was somewhere inside the house. They did their best to be subtle, to search around the edges of its consciousness without alerting it to their presence. As far as they could tell, its "mind" (or whatever you called it in the case of an entity like this) seemed to be elsewhere, or disassociated—as if it were asleep and dreaming. They got too close a couple of times and felt it stir, reaching out to try to find them, but they pulled back and held off their continued search until it had quieted once again. It wasn't the kind of work they enjoyed doing: all three of them preferred their magic faster, more visceral, and more immediately gratifying, but so far this seemed to be working as they hoped.

They didn't have much left to do tonight—maybe another half an hour's work at most plus whatever time it took to dismantle the circle. If they were successful, they could then go back home, do their research, and prepare a trap. Sure, they would "help" the entity break free of its prison—but it didn't have to know that they were preparing another, even more permanent, one for it to occupy.

| CHAPTER TWENTY-TWO

S tone buttoned up his overcoat. The wind was picking up, whistling through the trees and slicing at him, even through the coat's thick wool. His ribs were beginning to ache again, and he wondered if he should take another pain pill.

Not yet. Not until I find out more about this thing.

He'd quickly determined that if he was to have a hope of triangulating on the thing inside the house, he'd have to start outside. The mansion was simply too large, with too many haphazard passageways and long corridors—it was like trying to find something in the middle of a maze, and he didn't have time to keep backtracking every time he chose the wrong path. Outside, he could figure out the general part of the house where it was located, then try to home in more carefully inside without having to explore the entire place.

It was almost three o'clock now. The fog obscured the moon, so there wasn't much light once he got out past the boundaries illuminated by the perimeter lighting; he summoned a small light spell centered around his hand and held it up to show him the way. He'd have to move out some distance if he wanted to do this quickly.

Keeping his magical senses open, he left the lighted area and headed out into the forest. It was hard to track the creature and walk through the uneven terrain at the same time; twice he almost tripped over a root or branch and had to shift back to mundane vision to avoid it. Even so, though, he could still sense the entity. It was stronger now, but still diffuse. He couldn't explain why; the best way he would describe it if asked was that it felt like only a subset of a greater whole was actually here—but that a significant part of it existed somewhere else. As he had inside the house on the first night, he sensed both a deep, abiding hatred and a longing for something, but he wasn't sure for what.

He moved further out, keeping his little light spell glowing on his hand. It wasn't much help, as it only lit an area three feet or so in diameter around him, but it was better than nothing and if he moved slowly he could watch both the mundane and the magical worlds without too much fear of catching his foot on something.

He was getting closer; he could feel it.

The Three were jolted out of their concentration by the sound of their magical alarm going off. "What the—" Miguel began, looking around.

"Fuck! Somebody's out here?" Oliver, too, began swiveling his head to try to spot the intruder.

"Damn it, hold it together, you two." Trin's voice sounded strained as her companions let their grips slip on their parts of the pattern and she struggled to pick it up. "Miguel, go check it out. Oliver and I can hold this for a few minutes. But make it fast. We don't have time to start over." Her green eyes met his. "If you find somebody out there, take 'em out, then get back here quick."

"With pleasure," Miguel said, grinning. He paused, closing his eyes and carefully taking himself out of the pattern the three of them were weaving, waiting until Trin and Oliver had picked up the threads before stepping out of the circle. Once his eyes had adjusted to the darkness, he faded into the forest, pulling a spell around him to obscure him from the view of anyone who might be nearby. He found a spot away from the circle, hid behind a tree and waited. His hands hummed with power, itching to release it on whatever unfortunate fool had blundered into their business.

It was only a minute or so before he saw the light approaching. Someone was definitely coming. He glanced back over toward the circle: he could barely see its flickering candles through the trees, but only because he knew what he was looking for and where to look. Would the intruder spot it as well? He waited.

The intruder approached closer. A tall, thin, dark-haired man dressed in some kind of long coat, he held a flashlight in his hand, and—

Wait a minute.

Miguel strained to get a better view.

That wasn't a flashlight.

His breathing quickened a bit, more from excitement than fear.

There was another mage out there.

He forced himself to be patient, to wait for the man to approach closer. He didn't have a lot of time to wait, but he wanted to be sure what he was dealing with. If this had been a mundane intruder, there would be no defense. He could just hit him with something that would be certain to take him down. But with a mage, there was always the element of uncertainty. He'd probably only get one chance, so he'd have to make it count. For now, he focused on keeping his blending spell up and watched as the mage moved into his line of sight.

Miguel had never seen Alastair Stone before, but he'd heard Trin's description. He stared. Could it be? How could Stone be here? He thought Trin had said her thugs had put him in the hospital, but he seemed to be moving fine, if a bit slowly. He held his light spell in front of him and stepped gingerly over fallen roots and branches, all the while heading in the general direction of The Three's circle. Had he seen it?

Miguel grinned. It didn't matter. In a couple of minutes it would be all over.

Stone continued picking his way through the uneven terrain, trying to watch both directly in front of him and out into the forest at once. He was still getting closer; he sensed a significant source of magical energy up ahead somewhere now. He hoped he could find it soon, as the cold was really starting to seep in through his overcoat and do a number on his ribs. Once he'd identified the location, he could go back inside. Magically it might not be safer, but at least it would be warmer, and he wouldn't have to keep moving around so much.

He was looking toward the house, trying to spot the source, when something caught his attention from the corner of his eye, further out in the forest. "Odd..." he murmured. There shouldn't be anything out there—he was sure whatever he was looking for was coming from the house.

Still, he was nothing if not thorough. Stopping, he focused his attention on the direction where he thought he'd seen something. For a moment there was nothing, but then he picked out several tiny glows down close to the ground. And—

Magical energy.

The same magical energy he'd noticed a trace of before.

Bugger! There's another mage here!

And then something bright lanced out of nowhere and slammed into him, driving out all further thought.

❖

Got him!

It took all his self-control for Miguel not to whoop aloud in triumph when his concussive blast hit Stone square in the chest and blew him backward out of sight. So much for the so-called "powerful" mage. He might be powerful, but by The Three's standards he was old—old and slow.

Miguel wondered if he'd killed him. He listened for a moment, heard no sound, and thought about going after him, to finish the job. But Trin had said to come back quickly, or there was a risk that their whole ritual would fail. Much as he hated it, he knew that was more important. With one last glance back toward where Stone had gone flying, he grinned again and loped off back toward the circle.

❖

Stone couldn't think straight.

He'd blacked out for a moment, but when he came to, every nerve in the core of his body was on fire. His ribs felt like someone had snapped them. What the hell *was* that?

He thanked whatever gods or lucky stars looked out for him that he'd spotted the movement behind the tree just quickly enough to get a shield up, or he'd probably be dead now. With no time to react it hadn't been much of a shield, but at least it had soaked the worst of the damage when his body had slammed hard into a tree. Still, he was afraid he might have collected a couple more cracked ribs for his trouble.

Concussion blast, he thought grimly, struggling to his knees. That wasn't the kind of magic every mage knew—not by a long shot. There was no prohibition about mages learning combat spells, nor was there any governing council or other body that dictated what they could and couldn't do or learn. But he was the only white mage he knew who even bothered with that sort of thing. Combat magic was very difficult stuff for white mages, due to the way it was powered, just like long-term enchantments were difficult for black mages.

Which meant that he was most likely dealing with a black mage.

He was disgusted with himself for taking so long to arrive at that conclusion. He couldn't afford to be out of it now. Quickly he glanced around to make sure that whoever it was, he or she wasn't now sneaking up on him and preparing to deliver the final blow.

With effort he re-established his shield, stronger this time, using one of his crystals to power it. They wouldn't catch him by surprise this time.

He grabbed the tree and dragged himself up the rest of the way. His chest and sides were on fire. He thought about taking one or two of the pain pills in his pocket, but decided against it. The pain was bad enough, but a dulled brain when going against a black mage would be worse. If the mage wasn't coming after him, it had to mean one—or possibly both—of two things: that they thought they'd killed Stone or incapacitated him, or that they had more pressing things they had to deal with.

The lights.

Whatever was going on, they were the key.

Slowly, carefully, Stone began moving in the direction where he'd seen the lights. He didn't use his own light spell this time, fearful that the other mage would spot it. He didn't want to take another hit, even with his shield up. Still, he had to hurry: the small crystal wouldn't power the shield spell for long. He wove a blending spell, using another crystal to power it, then moved forward again, hoping that the mage wouldn't hear him huffing like a freight train as he crept through the forest. He was having a hard time getting a deep breath. One way or another he was going to have to deal with this soon, because before long he wouldn't be able to.

Miguel reached the circle, grin still fixed on his face, and stood waiting at its edge.

Trin, face focused on her task, shifted concentration a bit to provide an opening for him to re-enter. "Did you find anything?"

Miguel stepped back in, joined hands with Trin and Oliver, and picked up his part of the pattern before he replied. "It was Stone," he said.

"Fuck!" Oliver breathed, glancing out as if expecting him to be standing there.

"Don't worry. I took him out." Miguel sounded pleased with himself.

"How—" Trin began.

"He didn't even see me coming. I might have killed him, even."

"You're not sure?"

"You said come back fast. We can check after. I don't think he'll bother us, though."

Trin wasn't so sure. "Let's wrap this up," she said. "If he's still out there somewhere and you didn't kill him, I want to be out of here before he wakes up."

This was just getting worse and worse.

Stone stood behind a tree, shield and blending spells still up, watching the magical circle.

There were three of them.

Not just one. Three.

And what the hell were they doing?

They stood in a circle, hands clasped, and with his magical sight Stone could see that they were calling up a significant amount of power—but *why?*

He stayed quiet, trying to still his breathing so they wouldn't hear him, but they seemed completely occupied by what they were doing. He recalled the ruined beacon he'd passed (how had he missed it the first time?) that had probably alerted them to his presence in the first place—whatever they were trying to accomplish here, they didn't want anyone to see it.

Were they somehow responsible for what was going on in the house?

He studied them. The woman looked vaguely familiar: tall, dark red hair, tattooed forearms. He didn't think he'd ever met her, but he'd seen her in some context before. He recognized the circle construct, though: the three of them were definitely black mages. This was an odd ritual for their type to be doing—spells like the concussion blast were much more their style. This ritual didn't even look like it was designed to hurt anyone. Instead, it appeared to be set up to study something. But what—

And then he understood.

They were doing the same thing he was: trying to figure out what was in the house. The tendrils of magic that carefully, subtly (since when were black mages that young subtle? Stone had never met one who was) creeping out and toward the house had been designed and constructed to gather information.

But why? How did they even know about the thing? Had Adelaide Bonham contacted someone else before she'd talked to him? Had Tommy told someone? Had they just somehow picked up on the magical emanations coming from the house and followed them back to their source?

He didn't have time to worry about it now. The ritual was reaching its climax, and if he didn't do something soon, they'd get what they wanted. If they then tried to come after him after they finished, he wasn't sure he'd be able to fight them off.

Or worse—if they tried to go after the ladies in the house, so they'd have the place to themselves without interference—

Stone gritted his teeth. He wasn't going to let that happen. This wasn't subtle and it was going to hurt like hell, but it had to be done. Gathering energy around him, pulling in the power from another of his crystals, the ring, and the amulet, he held it in place and waited. He still had two crystals in reserve, but if what he was trying to do failed, he'd need them to defend himself.

The trio of mages in the circle were chanting now, something low and guttural and not in any language Stone was familiar enough with to understand. They raised their hands and turned as one toward the direction of the house, their voices rising to a crescendo. Off in the distance a rumble came from the house.

Stone pulled a deep, shuddering breath, pointed his hands, and let loose with a column of magical energy that slammed down into the middle of the circle like a glowing hammer. The brazier went out, and one by one the candles' enclosures popped and died. Screams echoed from the three mages as they were assaulted physically and mentally by feedback from the ritual's abrupt destruction. One, a blond man, clutched his head and dropped like his strings had been cut. The other two staggered, flailing their arms and yelling out curses and cries of pain.

"Fuck!" yelled the dark-haired young man. "It's Stone! Get him!"

Stone stared. *They know who I am?* This had just gotten even more interesting. But he didn't have time to think about it now: even with his focus objects helping him, that spell had been a huge expenditure of energy. He could feel grayness closing around his mind and deliberately twisted his body to light up his ribs again. Bright pain lanced through him, but his head cleared instantly. *Can't let them see weakness.* He steeled himself, trying to draw more power to him from his remaining crystals.

But the woman, it seemed, was wiser than the man. "No. Take Ol and let's go!" She leaned down and hefted the unconscious (or worse) blond man's shoulders and glared out into the woods. "This isn't over, Stone! You're a dead man!" She flung a random bolt of magical energy in his direction, then said something to her other friend. He picked up the blond man's feet, and together they moved off into the forest with their burden.

Stone let them go. He didn't have much more in the tank, and if he went after them and cornered them he might not be able to handle what they threw at him. He waited several minutes, doing his best to get his breath, then moved forward with the blending spell still up to examine the smoking remains of the three mages' circle.

It was completely destroyed, blasted and dead. He was actually a little amazed by how much power he'd managed to pump into that spell, but it had done its job. It was impossible to even tell what the circle's purpose had been, and its power had faded to nothing. He reached out and tried to touch the house again; its energies had gone back to what he'd noticed before: still there, but calm and un-ruffled. Resting, perhaps.

Waiting.

His right arm clutched around his middle, hunched over like an old man, he staggered back up toward the house. He fell to his knees twice but kept going, driven on by sheer force of will. He couldn't pass out here on the grounds. Adelaide and Iona were counting on him.

They were waiting for him, huddled on the couch together with big round terrified eyes as he opened the door to Edgar's study. When they got a look at him they both gasped. "Oh my God," Iona exclaimed, getting up to hurry to him. "Dr. Stone!"

He let her help him to a chair, dropping into it on the last of his energy. For a moment he just sat there with his eyes closed, struggling to get a deep breath.

"I'm going to call an ambulance," Iona stated, moving toward the phone.

Stone shook his head. "No…" he whispered. "I'll—be all right."

"But you're *bleeding!*" Adelaide protested.

That was news. He reached up and touched his face, feeling wetness around his nose and mouth. His fingers came away red. "It's all right," he said, trying but not succeeding to make his voice louder. Nosebleeds and such were the unfortunate side effects of channeling too much magical energy at once. Normally he would have been fine with the focus objects doing the heavy lifting, but his body was so exhausted that even they hadn't been enough. "Just a—tissue or something, if you'd be so kind. I'll be fine." He coughed a couple of times, which was a mistake. He hoped none of the blood was coming from that instead of simple magical exhaustion.

Iona looked at him fearfully. "Dr. Stone—is it safe to leave the room?"

"Did you find—" Adelaide began.

"I think so," he said, nodding. "It's—still here, but I don't think it was the problem tonight. Not—directly, anyway." It was so hard to talk, to form coherent thoughts around the grayness.

Iona disappeared into the little bathroom and returned with two wet washcloths. Refusing to listen to his protests, she used one to wipe the blood from his face, then urged him to lean back in the chair and put the other one on his forehead. "How's that?" she asked, all nurse now.

"Better. Very nice. Thank you."

Adelaide scooted over closer to Stone's chair and put her hand on his arm. "Dr. Stone—what did you mean by 'not directly'?"

He didn't answer for a long time, trying to gather his thoughts together sufficiently that he didn't say anything he'd have to explain—or regret—later. "There—is something in the house," he murmured. "It's—potentially powerful, and potentially dangerous. But it's—still weak now. Dormant. I think it's—trying to draw power."

"Power...for what?"

"Don't know yet. I found some other ma—people—on your grounds. They were—trying to do the same thing I was. Find out about whatever it was and what it could do."

"Other people?" Iona was confused. "At this time of night?"

"Tell me—" Stone whispered, still looking at Adelaide. "Did the house—shift, or moan, or whatever, about twenty minutes ago? Like it had before?"

The two women both nodded. "It did. But then it just—stopped."

Stone grunted wearily.

"You know why, don't you?" Adelaide asked.

He nodded. "These—people—were...well, let's just say they were disturbing it as they tried to find out about it. Sort of like—poking it with a stick."

"What—what happened to them?" Adelaide glanced toward the door. "Are they gone?"

"For now, yes. I don't know if they'll come back. I don't know what they wanted from it." He reached up and rubbed the washcloth around on his forehead, closing his eyes. "It might be best if you hired on a bit more temporary security, though, just to be safe."

Adelaide was silent. When Stone opened his eyes to see why, he discovered she was staring at him with an odd expression. "Dr. Stone—do you mind if I ask you a question?"

He shrugged, just a little. "Go ahead."

"What...*are* you, exactly? You're more than just a professor at Stanford, aren't you?"

Now they were both staring at him. He took a ragged breath and let it out slowly. "It's—hard to explain," he said at last. "But yes. I am."

"It *is* real, isn't it? The supernatural? This thing that's in my house? And you...*deal* with this kind of thing, don't you?"

He gave her a small, pained smile. "I try to."

She squeezed his hand again. "I won't ask you to tell me your secrets. I'm grateful to have you on our side, whatever you are." Pause, and then her voice took on a tentative, frightened edge. "Do you—do you think this thing will stay dormant? If these people are gone, I mean? Before tonight, I was the only one who noticed it— well, except for you, of course. Do you think that will stay true?"

Stone frowned. "What are you getting at, Mrs. Bonham?" He could tell from her tone that there was something she wasn't saying.

She and Iona exchanged glances. "Well..." she said, "It's just that—I've got a very important event that's supposed to be happening here next week. And it's too late to cancel it."

Stone closed his eyes. "Event? What kind of event?"

When she spoke after a moment's pause, she sounded like a schoolgirl preparing to deliver a bad report card to a stern father. "It's...a charity function. A ball. I donate a great deal of money to charity every year, and we have the ball here each year around this time. It's got a Christmas theme." When Stone didn't say anything she pressed on: "We raise money for homeless and abused children,

Dr. Stone. The ball and the silent auction generate considerable amounts of money for the charities. It would be a terrible blow if we had to cancel this late."

"Why didn't you tell me this before?" Stone asked without opening his eyes. He realized that the question sounded abrupt and somewhat harsh, but he felt terrible and his sense of tact, even in the face of kindly old ladies, was getting a bit frayed around the edges.

"Well...it didn't really seem relevant at the time," she said. She scooted a little farther away from him on the couch as if afraid he might snap at her. "I mean—everyone was telling me that all of this was in my head, and no one believed me. I thought—well, maybe there was a chance that they were right."

He sighed. "And you can't reschedule it? Change the venue? Anything?"

She shook her head. "Not this late, I'm afraid. The invitations are all sent out, and this time of year everything's all booked up. We've already taken in thousands in pledges."

Stone didn't answer.

Tears sprang to her eyes. "I'll cancel it if you tell me it's not safe, but the children—"

He sighed again, scrubbing at his hair. Nothing was ever easy. "How late can you cancel it, if you have to?"

"Uh—I suppose up until the day before, though that would obviously not be desirable since people travel to attend."

"And it's in a week?"

"A week from last night, yes." She watched him, her expression intent, hopeful, and frightened.

At last he nodded. "All right, then. I've got about five days to figure out what the hell this thing is and deal with it." He started to get up, but his ribs were having none of it. He fell back in the chair with grumble of frustration. "I'll start tomorrow."

| CHAPTER TWENTY-THREE

"Fuck, fuck, *fuck!*" Miguel was practically yelling out the open window as he drove the black SUV at breakneck speed up 280 toward San Francisco.

Trin, in the back seat with Oliver's head in her lap, glared at him. "Shut up, Mig. We'll get through this. And Stone's going to pay." She looked down. Oliver was still unconscious, his complexion gray and clammy. He rolled his head back and forth in her lap, muttering something she couldn't understand.

"Damn fucking straight he'll pay," Miguel agreed. "Soon as we get Oliver someplace where he can get some help, I'm going back down there and—"

"No, you're not." Trin's eyes were hard. "We're sticking with the plan. We didn't get everything we could from the ritual, but we got enough to start with, and we're not going to lose our one chance because you want revenge. What you're going to do is what you're good at—research. You know where the house is now, and you know what we got from tonight. Take that and see what you can come up with."

"But Stone—"

"Don't worry. We'll deal with him once we've got that thing under control. And besides, I don't think he got a good look at us. We can use that. I think I'm going to give little Ethan another call soon, and see what we can do for each other."

When Stone arrived home at a little after eleven on Sunday morning, Megan was gone. She'd left him a note asking him to give her a call when he got in; the wording was more abrupt and chilly than her usual chatty style.

All he wanted to do right now was go upstairs, crawl into bed, and sleep for another seven or eight hours, but he couldn't do that. He didn't have time.

Iona had insisted on letting her check him over after he'd nearly passed out in the chair. She'd found the cracked ribs—he'd been right, he now had another one in the back to add to the two in the front he'd started with—but he'd convinced her that the injuries had all come from the incident at Stanford. That had been the first either she or Adelaide had heard about that, and he managed to deflect them from too much further inquiry by giving them the short version of what had happened. Then he'd feigned exhaustion (it hadn't taken much feigning) and Iona had hustled him off to a spare bedroom to sleep for a few hours before she let him go. He slipped himself a pain pill when she wasn't looking and managed to sleep from around four until eight.

Before he'd left he'd had the presence of mind to ask Adelaide if she had any books, diaries, newspaper clippings, or anything similar about the history of the house; she'd said she thought there might be some old things in the attic but obviously she couldn't look for them herself and she wouldn't ask Iona to go up there, but he was welcome to do so himself as long as he wasn't afraid of spiders. He thanked her and told her he'd be back to do just that. He also asked her to try to remember anything she could about the house: anything her late husband had told her, family anecdotes, anything at all. She promised she would.

Finally, he'd asked her not to mention the events of the previous night to anyone, including Tommy and the rest of her staff, and to make sure she hired her supplemental security people from a reputable agency. "Do you think those horrible people will come back?" she'd asked, fearful.

"I don't know. I hope not. But let's be safe, shall we?"

Home now, Stone showered, changed clothes, and contemplated his next move. He could go back to Adelaide's and hunt through her attic, but he decided to leave that for tomorrow after he saw what Stefan Kolinsky managed to come up with. He had another question for Stefan tomorrow as well: whether he might have some idea who the three young black mages were. There weren't that many mages of any moral persuasion in the Bay Area—possibly a couple dozen if you stretched the definition hard—and old Stefan had his finger on the pulse of the black-magic scene far more than Stone himself did. But he couldn't do that until tomorrow.

He called Megan; she wasn't home, so he left a message that he was fine, apologized for disappearing on her, and told her he'd try calling back later. He also said that he quite understood if she didn't want to see him today. He hung up the phone, stared at it for a moment, then picked it up and punched in Ethan's number.

He expected the machine to pick it up and was surprised when it was answered on the third ring. "Hello?"

"Ethan. It's Alastair Stone. How are you?"

There was a long pause. "Uh, hi, Dr. Stone. I'm fine. How are you?"

It wasn't at all hard to tell from the boy's tone that Stone's had not been the call he'd been expecting. "Much better, thank you. How's your mum doing?"

"Still not so good. She's still in the hospital, and they don't know when she'll be able to come home."

"I'm sorry to hear that. If there's anything I can do—"

"Thanks, I appreciate it. But I'm fine. Really. Getting along okay." Pause, and then: "Did you need something, Dr. Stone?"

"No—Just checking in to see if you might want to be getting back to your lessons tomorrow. No rush—if we wait too long we might need to go back over a few things, but that's easily done. Have you been practicing your levitation spell?"

"Yeah. I'm getting pretty good at it." He sounded proud of himself. "Uh—sure, we can start up again tomorrow. Mom's bad, but they tell me she's pretty stable right now. I can work lessons around visiting hours, if that's okay."

"Of course. Just let me know when you can be here, and I'll arrange it."

"I will. I'll call you tomorrow. Uh—I have to go now, though. I'm making lunch and I think something's starting to boil over."

"By all means, then. Take care, Ethan. I'll wait to hear from you."

Ethan sighed and hung up the phone. He wouldn't have answered it if he'd known it was Stone—for whatever reason that he still couldn't quite articulate, he still didn't want to talk to the mage. He felt stupid, though: *Yeah, sure. She's gonna call you. Dream on, geek-boy. You probably made a fool of yourself Saturday night and you're lucky they even bothered dragging your sorry ass back to your car. You'll probably never hear from her again. I bet they're all laughing at you.*

Even with all of that, he was reluctant to leave the house to go visit his mother, which made him feel even more guilty. She was asleep when he arrived and he didn't wake her—she was asleep a lot lately. Part of him wanted desperately for her to wake up, to be her old self again, so he could confide all this to her. A near lifetime of being all each other had made her unusually adept at sorting out Ethan's snarled emotions, his moods, his confusion about wanting to do the right thing but always managing to screw it up somehow.

He thought about Stone as he sat there next to her, listening to the beeping of the machines and the low distant murmur of nurses' and doctors' and visitors' conversations. Maybe he *could* talk to Stone about all of this. The mage had been a teenage boy once—

maybe he'd understand, if Ethan just gave him a chance. After all, that was part of taking an apprentice: you took responsibility for more than just their magical development. A lot of apprentices, even nowadays, went as far as to move in with their masters to make the teaching relationship more convenient, especially if the apprentice didn't have a job or another place to live. That implied a certain amount of pseudo-parental guidance. Hell, the man was a professor in his other life—he must have at least some experience dealing with young people.

Just tell him everything, said a voice in the back of his head that sounded uncomfortably like his mother's. *Just tell him about Trina and going to San Francisco and watching the magical ritual. Tell him you got caught up in the moment and you won't do it again. That's all it'll take. He might yell at you a little, but then he'll forgive you and forget about it and you can move on.*

That was, he realized abruptly there in the hospital, why he was so reluctant to go back and resume his magical training.

I don't deserve it. I lied to him, I didn't follow his rules—and he's going to know right away as soon as he sees me. And all because I couldn't stop thinking about Trina and the way she looked at me. Some things are just more important than that. I mean, seriously, you're gonna give up the chance at learning magic because you can't stop thinking with your dick?

He sat up straighter, gently taking his mother's hand. "I've gotta tell him, Mom," he whispered. Standing, he leaned over and kissed her warm forehead, pushing her hair off her face. "I'll be back tomorrow. I love you."

He felt like a load had been lifted from his mind as he drove home. He still didn't know if it was the best decision he could make, but he knew it was the right one. He'd call Stone as soon as he got in—maybe even meet with him tonight, if he was willing.

He shoved his way into the apartment, tossed his backpack on the sofa, and headed straight for the phone. He wanted to do this before he lost his nerve.

The red light on the answering machine was blinking.

He almost—almost—didn't listen to it. *Don't do it. Call Dr. Stone first. Set up the meeting, so you can't get out of it. That way, even if she—*

He punched the button.

"*Ethan? It's me. You there? Pick up if you are, okay? No? Okay, well, I just wanted to say I had a great time on Friday night—I hope you did, too. I'd like to see you again, if you want. Tonight, maybe? Don't worry—nothing you're uncomfortable with. I just thought we could talk a little. If you want to, meet me at Printer's Inc. on Castro in Mountain View tonight at eight. I've got an errand I need to run down that way anyway. I'll wait till nine. Hope you get this and I see you there. Bye!*"

Ethan swallowed. She sounded so animated, so happy. Like she was actually looking *forward* to meeting him. Maybe he'd completely misjudged what had happened Friday night.

I should call Dr. Stone.

He sat there, staring at the phone for a long time and not moving, his mind in turmoil. *I should call him, and I should just not show up tonight.*

But she was going to come all the way down from San Francisco just to see him. How rude would it be for him not to even show up?

Damn damn damn! Why did this all have to be so *complicated?*

You could call him and tell him, but say that you're just going to meet her to be polite. That you're going to tell her you can't see her anymore.

He *was* going to do that, wasn't he?

"Arrgh!" he growled aloud, flinging his backpack across the room where it slammed into a wall.

Look, said the voice, reasonably. *You're going to see Dr. Stone tomorrow. You're planning to tell him everything, right? So why not just wait until then? Go meet with Trina tonight, see what she wants, and then you can tell her that Stone doesn't want you hanging out with her anymore. He doesn't have to know you were going to tell him today. He won't know unless you tell him. Remember, Miguel said mages can't read minds?*

He fell back against the couch. He had to admit that did sound like a reasonable course of action, and it still meant that he would tell Stone.

Just tomorrow instead of today.

CHAPTER TWENTY-FOUR

Stone tried calling Megan early Sunday evening. This time she answered.

"Alastair. I got your message. Are you okay?"

"I'm fine. Are you still speaking to me?"

There was a pause. "I don't know yet." She sounded more resigned than angry, though.

"Want to go get something to eat? I still owe you a dinner."

"Sure. Nothing too fancy, though. I think we need to talk about this a little more."

They didn't say too much over dinner, which was at a quaint little bistro in downtown Palo Alto. Stone asked neutral questions about Megan's day, and she answered them just as neutrally. He felt like he was picking his way through a field of eggs filled with poisonous spiders. Finally she looked at him over her wineglass. "What's going on, Alastair?"

He raised an eyebrow. "What?"

She shook her head. "Something's going on—it has been for a while now, but I can't figure out what it is. I'm feeling like there's part of your life that you've walled off from me and won't let me near."

Stone sighed. This conversation was inevitable at some point in all of his relationships; it was the reason his last three girlfriends had decided to pursue other interests. It was always cordial and they always remained friends, but the results, up until now, had been predictable. Usually it had happened sooner, though: his previous record since moving to the Bay Area from his home in Surrey had been four months. "Megan—"

She held up a hand. "No, Alastair. Let me say this. I've been thinking about it all day." She paused, taking a sip of wine. "Look—I know what you're like. I know you've got your own things going on, and you're not the type to be joined at the hip with anybody. I'm that way, too. That's why we get along so well. But—" Another deep breath. "I hate feeling like you've got this—I don't know, almost like a secret life that I don't know anything about. If you were anyone else, I'd think you were running around on me."

"I'm not sure whether to be flattered or insulted," Stone murmured.

She gave him a look he couldn't quite pin down, but he shut up nonetheless. "I don't think that. But what I *do* think is that I'm concerned about some of the things around you. Like the fact that your basement is locked up, and you won't ever let me see what's in there."

He was silent. There wasn't anything he could say that would make things anything but worse. Instead, he waited, watching her with a neutral expression.

Finally, she said, "I just don't know what to think about that. I mean, yeah, it's possible you're a serial killer or a vampire or something and you're using the basement to stash bodies, but that's really kind of crazy. The thing is, I can't really think of anything it could be that's not—*wrong.*" She looked at him. "Why else would you keep it such a secret? I don't want to intrude on your privacy. But I can't help but think that one day the police are going to show up with a camera crew and they'll find—something horrible down there."

"Always the quiet ones," he agreed. Then, before she could glare at him, he waved it off. "Megan, listen. I know you don't believe me and there's no way I can prove it to you, but there's nothing nefarious going on in my basement. No bodies, no enormous pornography stash, no smuggled illegal contraband or clandestine collections of Barbie dolls and stuffed animals."

"Can you tell me *anything* about it? Anything at all?"

He thought about it for a moment. "It's—sort of a workroom. A laboratory."

"Oh, God..." A little color drained from her face. "Alastair, are you cooking drugs down there?"

"No!" His answer was instant and shocked. "Is that what you think?"

"I don't know *what* to think! And then last night, you got that phone call and left in the middle of the night—are you in trouble? Are you mixed up with organized crime or something? Is that why you thought those guys who beat you up were after you specifically?"

He glanced around to see if anyone else was paying attention to them, then reached out and touched her arm. "Megan. This is all fairly absurd, but if it will make you feel any better: I give you my word that I'm not involved in organized crime, I'm not brewing drugs or any other illegal substance—in fact, I give you my word I'm not doing anything illegal down there." That much was true. How could magic be illegal if nobody in mainstream society even knew enough about it to make laws?

She sighed, looking down at her hands. "Where did you go last night? Can you tell me that?"

"I went to Los Gatos. To Tommy's aunt's place."

Her eyes came up: she was clearly surprised, both that she'd gotten an answer at all and that it wasn't anything close to what she expected. "The old lady in the mansion?"

He nodded.

"But—why?"

"I'd given her my card—told her to call me if anything strange happened."

"At one thirty in the morning?"

"Well," he said, quirking a smile, "I didn't exactly put a time boundary on it."

"What—did she want?"

"She was frightened. She heard odd noises in the house, and she wanted me to check them out."

"At one thirty. In the morning." She poured herself another glass of wine. "So—did you find out what was causing them?"

"Sort of. I'll be needing to go up there again. Possibly several times in the next few days. She's got some sort of huge charity thing happening soon, and she wants to make sure this is sorted before then. I told her I'd help her."

She looked at him like she wasn't sure he wasn't putting her on. "Alastair...I know she believes in this occult stuff, but—*you* don't. You're humoring her, I get it. She sounds like a nice old lady. But to spend this much time—Does Tommy know about this?"

"Not about last night. And I'd prefer it remain that way."

"You're not going to tell him?"

"Not yet, no."

She frowned. "But—is that right? She's an old lady. He's her relative. You're just his friend that he called in to convince her that her house wasn't haunted." Tilting her head, she said, "He's going to be pissed when he finds out, you know."

"I'll have to take that chance," he said. He leaned forward. "Megan, here's the bottom line: I like what we have. I hope you do, too. I'd be very happy if it continued. But if we're going to have anything together, you're going to have to trust me on some things. There are parts of my life I can't share with you. I promise you, none of them are illegal, or nefarious, or harmful. They shouldn't affect you at all, beyond the occasional late-night phone call. But they're things I've made commitments to long before I met you. All I can do is ask you to understand that, and outside of it, I'll do my best to make you happy."

She looked down into her wineglass, for a long time, then back up. The candlelight flickered in her eyes as she met his. "Nothing illegal. Nothing dangerous?"

He shrugged minimally with a rueful smile. "Nothing illegal. I can't promise the other bit, though. Not completely. All I can promise is that I'll be as careful as I can."

She continued to watch him, unblinking. "I've got it. You're in the CIA. Or—no, wait—you're *Batman*."

He chuckled, feeling the ice finally breaking and the spider-filled eggs beginning to recede. "You've figured it out, my dear. Always knew you were brilliant. Why do you think I insist on doing my own laundry?"

"Mrs. Olivera does your laundry," she pointed out. "Hmm...maybe I'll bribe her to look for gray and black tights."

"Hey, If that's what you're into, I'm willing to give it a go."

She shook her head, her face getting serious again. "All right, Alastair. I'll give you the benefit of the doubt. I like what we have too, and I don't want to be one of those women who drives a man off by being too suspicious. But just be aware that this is bothering me, this not knowing. I'll deal with it, but I won't like it."

"That's about the best I can hope for," he said softly. He reached out and took her hand. "You're really quite amazing, Megan. Did you know that?"

"I did, yeah." She smiled. "Come on—let's go back to my place tonight. That way I won't be tempted to drug you and pick the lock to your secret basement lab while you're sleeping. Unless you're worried that the old lady is going to call you back again."

"Just this once, let's live dangerously."

| CHAPTER TWENTY-FIVE

Trin was waiting for Ethan when he arrived at Printer's Inc. She was sitting at a table in the back with a cup of coffee, leafing through a book. She smiled as he approached. "Hey," she said. "I was afraid you might not come." She waved him to the chair across from her.

He sat down, smiling back. The book she was reading, he could see now, was called *Magick in Theory and Practice.* She grinned when she caught him looking at it. "Crowley had the right idea," she said, tossing it aside. "But he didn't take it far enough. I think he felt inadequate that he didn't really have the Power. You want something? Cup of coffee?"

He shook his head. "Thanks, I'm fine."

"'Kay, cool." She sipped her coffee. "Glad you could join in with us on Saturday. That was pretty awesome, wasn't it? One of our better ones, actually. I hope you got something out of it."

"I did," he said, remembering how it had felt to have the magic coursing through him, even with the small role he'd had in the ritual. It was like being truly alive for the first time in his life. "It was great. I hope I'll get to do more stuff like that with Dr. Stone."

"Oh, you will," she said. "He'll show you the ritual stuff. That's pretty standard for most teachers, because you use it so often for so many things. But it's always better with more people. They feed on each other, pump in more energy—when you get enough people all on the same magical wavelength, it's like a big old mystical orgy."

She grinned at him, her eyebrows raising suggestively. Her eyes were very green and very beautiful.

Ethan swallowed. *Tell her now. Tell her you can't see her anymore.* "So, uh—what brings you all the way down here? Seems like a long drive just to have coffee."

She shrugged. "I wanted to see you. You kind of remind me of myself when I was an apprentice. You know—impatient. Always wanting more."

"I shouldn't be that way," he said.

"Why not? Mages should always seek knowledge and new techniques and new ways to use their powers. That's what we're all about." She leaned back and crossed one leg over her knee. She was wearing very tight, very ripped jeans. "But that's okay if you don't want to talk about magic. Like I said before, I don't want to get you in any trouble."

Tell her, said the voice in his head. *Tell her that you've got to go. She just gave you an out—use it.*

He snorted. "Don't worry about it. I *do* want to know more. That was incredible on Saturday night. It'll be hard to go back to levitating coins and stuff after that."

"Well," she said, rubbing the back of her head with her hand as if thinking something over, "You know, there's really no reason why you can't. I don't want to get you in trouble, but if you really want to range out a little bit, expand your horizons—we might be able to help you out with that. Dr. Stone wouldn't even have to know about it. But only if you want it," she added hastily. "There's no way I'm going to get between a master and his apprentice unless he asks for it."

"We?" he asked. "You and Miguel and Oliver?"

"Yeah. We've been working together for a long time now. But I'll be honest with you—we might have room for one more in our circle, once you're up to speed. You did a really good job helping us channel the power the other night—I can already tell you've got the talent for it. You just need the training."

"I don't know," he said, looking down. *Stop it, you idiot. Stop looking at her. Just tell her and get out of here before you end up in big trouble.* "You guys seem to have a pretty good group going. You and Oliver—"

She laughed. "Oliver and me? Seriously, you thought that? Oliver's a good fuck, that's all. Pure animal attraction. And Miguel—well, if you didn't already figure out that he's into outies, not innies, then you weren't paying attention."

"Well, yeah," he admitted. "Hard to miss."

"Besides," she said, reaching out to run a black-polished nail down his forearm, "You're not one of those jealous types, are you, Ethan?"

"Nah," he said, too quickly. Somewhere down below the level of the table, his body was making itself very distracting. *Did she really say that? I didn't just hear what I wanted to hear?*

"Hey," she said, "You know—you could really help us out, if you wanted to."

"Me? How?" Despite his hormonal flip-flops, his suspicion ramped up a bit.

"Well, we've been working on a new ritual for a while now, but Oliver got sick yesterday and he can't do much until he's better. Don't know if Dr. Stone told you this yet, but it gets a lot harder to channel magic when you're sick or hurt. Something about the body pathways or some shit like that. I don't care about the details—if I wanted to study anatomy I'd be a doctor instead of a mage. All I know is that it doesn't work right."

"Sick? What's wrong with him?"

She shrugged. "Bad cold or something. He'll be fine, but he's too sick to sling the spells. We could use somebody to stand in for him for a couple of days if you're interested. Otherwise we'll have to wait till he's back. And before you say anything about not knowing enough," she added, holding up a hand to forestall him, "It's okay. You don't have to know a lot. Miguel and I can handle the detailed stuff. We just need you to help channel the power, like you did the other night. Think you can do that?"

Damn it, you idiot, tell her you can't. You're gonna go talk to Dr. Stone tomorrow. Don't make this worse! "Uh—sure. Depending on when, though."

"Tomorrow night? You can take BART up—we're not far from the station." She smiled encouragingly. "Up to you, Ethan. I'm not going to force you. But I think you'll really like it. And really get something out of it."

He almost said no. He almost got up and walked out. But then he got another look at her—her eyes, her smile, her body—"Sure. Sounds like fun."

Her smile turned to a grin. "Excellent." She stroked his arm again, her fingers lingering. "I knew I could count on you, Ethan." She stood up, and he thought she was going to leave. Instead, she said with a look of mischief and something more, "C'mon. I know a much better place to hang out than here." Pause: "If you want to."

"Yeah," he said, getting up. "I want to."

| CHAPTER TWENTY-SIX

S tone showed up to teach his Monday morning class, but persuaded old Hubbard to take the afternoon one so he'd have more time to work on Adelaide's house problem. His students all looked surprised; by now everyone had heard what had happened to him on Thursday night, and they were eyeing him like they expected him to fold up and collapse in the middle of the lecture. He assured them that he was alive, well, and fully functional, and pissed them all off by dropping a last-minute pop quiz on them near the end of the hour before reminding them of the finals schedule for the rest of the week.

He waited until lunchtime to call Stefan Kolinsky. He even answered the phone, which was rare. "Ah, yes," the black mage said. "Come over whenever you like. I've unearthed some very interesting information for you. Have you had lunch? There's a little place over on University I've been wanting to try..."

Of course Stone bought lunch, and of course Kolinsky let him. Kolinsky was clearly amused by making him wait for the information, but Stone did nothing to show his impatience. He made small talk and entertained Kolinsky with anecdotes about his Occult Studies students, not even fidgeting when the man decided he simply had to have one more glass of the excellent wine before they left. That was just the way he was, and there was no point in trying to change him.

It wasn't until they were back at his East Palo Alto shop that he smiled at Stone across his old roll top desk. "Well, Alastair, I must tell you, you gave me quite an interesting research project. As I said, I had to dig back through some reference material that I haven't looked at for many years. So I thank you for that."

Stone waited, leaned back in his chair. He was fairly certain at this point that Kolinsky had found something good: the more he stalled, the better the data he'd come up with. Usually.

Kolinsky reached into a cubby on his desk and pulled out a yellowed sheaf of papers, which he spread out on the clear surface in front of him. "Your house was built near the turn of the twentieth century, 1901 to be precise, by a man named Edgar Bonham, Sr." He glanced up to see if Stone showed any recognition.

"That would be Adelaide's husband's father, most likely," he said. "She mentioned that her husband's name was Edgar, but even given that he died many years ago, the ages would still be wrong for it to be him."

Kolinsky nodded, making a note on a small pad. "Edgar Bonham, Sr. was an extremely wealthy man. His main business was steel, but he had his fingers in many pies: railroads, heavy industry, mining, that sort of thing. He was mostly a silent partner, which is why his name isn't as well-known as some of the other industrial magnates of the era." He looked through his sheaf of papers, extracted one, and held it out.

Stone took it and examined it. It was a wedding announcement. "Edgar married—Amelia Hastings, two years before the house was completed."

"Yes." Kolinsky took back the clipping and returned it to the stack. "Miss Hastings was apparently a rare beauty and quite sought after. Edgar won her hand and took her back with him to his home in Boston, but it quickly became apparent that the Eastern climate didn't agree with her. She was always frail, but the winters and the pollution were simply too much for her. When she became increasingly more ill and at one point almost died, Edgar set out to build her a magnificent home in a climate more fitting to her constitution."

Stone nodded. "All right—that explains why they came out here. But so far I'm not getting anything out of the ordinary from this."

"And you won't, until many years have passed," Kolinsky said. He clucked in mock admonishment. "So impatient, Alastair. Let me tell the story. You know I'm a showman at heart."

"Forgive me," Stone said. "Take your time, Stefan. I've got nowhere to be for a while."

"Thank you. So—the house was magnificent, yes, and Edgar's money guaranteed that it was built as quickly as it could be. It was smaller than it is now—they added on to it many times during their marriage. Amelia flourished in the California climate, and by all accounts their time together was a very happy one. They had one child, a son, but it was a difficult birth and Amelia was not able to have any more children after that. She was heartbroken, but she still had Edgar and now she had her son as well, so her life was good."

He riffled through the stack of papers again and took out a clipping, which he passed to Stone. "A few years after that, however, more tragedy struck for the family."

Stone examined the clipping. It was an obituary: Edgar Sr. had been the victim of a freak accident at the age of 56, when an open car he was driving was hit by lightning during a storm. He looked up at Kolinsky. "He died young."

"Yes. And this is where things begin to get interesting." Once again, he returned the clipping to the stack, then put the stack aside and pulled out a large, leather-bound book. "As I'm sure you're aware given your line of work, many people—especially upper class people—have been interested in the supernatural over the years. They stage séances, consult mediums and Ouija boards, have their tarot or tea leaves or astrological charts read, all in the service of things like divining their futures, coercing the objects of their affection to reciprocate their feelings, attempting to contact dead loved ones, and so forth."

Stone nodded. He taught a whole course on the occult in modern America and Europe. "It was mostly fake, though—sometimes a real mage would get down on his or her luck and resort to that sort of thing, but usually it was charlatans trying to make money from gullible people."

"Indeed," Kolinsky agreed. "But as you said, not always. Amelia Bonham had always had an interest in the spirit world and the supernatural, from the time she was a child, but everything I can find prior to her husband's death indicated that she considered it merely a diversion, something to have fun with at parties and use to entertain her friends. There's no indication that she believed in any of it."

"That changed after her husband died?" Stone was beginning to get the first faint glimmering of an idea where this was going.

"Yes. She was utterly distraught at Edgar's death, to the point where her friends and the servants began to think it would drive her mad. But then she found a purpose: she began reaching out to spiritualists and mediums in hope of finding someone who could help her contact her husband from beyond the grave. She refused to admit he was gone, and became obsessed with communicating with him."

Stone nodded. "Let me guess—she actually managed to find herself someone who wasn't a charlatan."

"A woman named Selena Darklight—or at least that was what she called herself; her real name was apparently Mara Jones—contacted Amelia and told her that she might be able to help her." He looked up at Stone. "Now, I'll bet you can figure out where this went next."

"They set up some sort of ritual to attempt to contact Edgar's spirit?" Stone shrugged. "It wouldn't work, though, even if this Selena Darklight *was* the real thing. You can't contact dead loved ones using magic. It's not possible."

"Well," Kolinsky said with a little nod of agreement, "That is, of course, true. But Amelia didn't know that—and Selena, despite being a *bona fide* mage, wasn't exactly the most ethical person around. That, and she needed money. But you haven't heard the best part of the whole thing."

"And that is—?"

Kolinsky opened the leather book to a page he'd marked with a red silk ribbon. "This isn't widely known at all—this is the part I had to dig through a lot of dusty piles of books to find, so I hope you appreciate it—but it seems that Amelia was one of us as well. Or at least had the potential to be."

Stone stared. "Amelia was a mage?"

"Yes. And Selena saw that potential in her. Naturally, since she knew that it wasn't possible to contact Edgar's spirit *per se,* it was in her best interest to do all she could to extend the duration of their association as long as she could. And so she told Amelia about her potential and offered to train her. She convinced her that she'd have a much better chance of contacting Edgar directly than through a medium."

"And hoped that in the meantime she could figure out some way of faking the contact," Stone added.

"Exactly. Amelia proved to be a very quick and motivated study—naturally she had to keep her activities secret from everyone, but the house was large enough by then that it wasn't difficult to do so. And as time passed, Amelia became an extremely talented black mage, with a strong specialization in rituals and spirit summoning."

"Wait," Stone said. "Don't tell me, let me guess: Selena figured out a way to summon something up and pass it off as Edgar."

Kolinsky raised an eyebrow and frowned. "Don't get ahead of me, Alastair, though you are somewhat close to the truth. Because you see, Selena had plans. For many years she had sought to summon a particular spirit—you might even call it a demon, if you were inclined toward that sort of thing—and to harness it to her will. She was wise enough, though, to know that she didn't possess sufficient power to do it herself, even though she knew its true name. Training Amelia at last gave her another potent mage to add to the casting. She arranged to have several other, less powerful mages—former students of hers—arrive, and Amelia thought they would at last be joining together to summoning Edgar's spirit back into our world."

Stone leaned forward, his gaze locked on Kolinsky.

"Things—didn't go as well as Selena had hoped," Kolinsky said. "This was the other part that was very difficult to find, mainly because most of the principals died that night."

"Indeed..." Stone murmured.

"They attempted the summoning, but somehow lost control of it. My sources don't say why—perhaps the demon had grown in power since Selena had last touched it, or perhaps someone in the circle lost their nerve. I don't know."

"Or perhaps Amelia was brighter than Selena gave her credit for, and realized that the ritual wasn't what it had been billed as," Stone said.

Kolinsky nodded. "Or that. But at any rate, they managed to open a gateway to its home, and to bring it over—but Selena couldn't control it. My sources don't report specifically what happened to it, but when it was all over, everyone but Amelia had disappeared."

"Disappeared?" Stone frowned. "Back into the demon's home dimension?"

"Probably. The only one left to tell the tale was Amelia, and she wasn't talking at the time. When the servants found her, she was wandering the halls of the house, speaking in gibberish. She was sent to an asylum for several years, where she later died. The account I've given you comes from one of the nurses there, who wrote down some of the things she said when she became a bit more lucid. The nurse didn't believe them, of course, but she thought they were entertaining, and perhaps she could write them up as a story someday."

For a long time, Stone was silent, staring at nothing. Finally, he said, "So—what do you think happened to the demon?"

"The question is—what do *you* think?" Kolinsky asked. "You're the one who's been to the house."

"I think it's still there," he said in a monotone.

"Indeed?"

He nodded. "That's got to be it. I felt something—very powerful, very malevolent, the first time I was out there, but then the next time it was less so. I think it's hiding from me." He got up and began pacing. "Stefan—you know more about summoning rituals than I do. Could it still be there? If Selena's ritual had gone awry, would it have been easier for them to—contain it somehow—than to send it back?"

"Yes, of course," Kolinsky said. He swiveled his chair around to watch Stone. "Are you saying that you think they imprisoned it in the house for all these years?"

"It's the only thing that makes sense," Stone pointed out. "I doubt old Adelaide and Iona are out there summoning demons in between episodes of *Murder, She Wrote*. If it's been there all this time, p'raps something's happened to weaken its prison. Or else it's just weakening on its own, after all these years."

Kolinsky pondered. "So what do you propose to do about it, then? I have great respect for your abilities, Alastair, but I don't think you're strong enough to send something that powerful back on your own. Especially not when you aren't at your best due to your injuries."

"I know," Stone muttered. "I know. But I have to do something."

"I think the best you can hope for is to fortify its prison again, long enough for you to buy some time and possibly enlist some help. You're going to need a powerful circle to send it back, I think. Unless—"

"Unless what?" Stone's gaze came up quickly.

"Well…" Kolinsky said, "unless you can somehow get hold of its true name. Then you might have a chance, given that it's already partially imprisoned. You wouldn't have to fight all of it—merely close the door between the dimensions, and shut the part of it that's here it back in its own domain with the rest of it."

Stone shook his head. "And finding that is about as likely as my being crowned King of England. I don't suppose you have any reference books lying about that might contain that kind of information?"

"I fear not, Your Majesty," Kolinsky said with a rueful smile. "In any case, I don't envy you your task, Alastair. I wish you luck and success, but I don't envy you."

"I don't suppose you'd be willing to help?" Stone asked, raising an eyebrow.

"Alas, no. My forte is research, not action. I'll leave that for younger—and braver—mages than I."

Stone didn't even try to argue with him, since he'd already known the answer. At least old Stefan was honest. "All right, then: just a couple of other questions, and then I'll leave you to whatever it is you were doing."

Kolinsky inclined his head.

"If I'm right—if this thing *is* imprisoned and its prison is starting to fray, how fast do you think that will happen? And will having a lot of mundane people in proximity to it cause the process to accelerate?"

"Ah," Kolinsky said, smiling a little. "Of course. I hadn't put it together until you said that. The charity ball."

"How did you know about that?"

"I received an invitation. Naturally I declined, but—"

"Well?"

He shrugged one shoulder. "I couldn't say. It's possible that if it senses all that energy nearby it might redouble its efforts to break through, but it's also possible that if it wants to break through surreptitiously, it might go quiet while the house is heavily occupied. Or, it might simply continue as before."

"So in other words, you have no idea."

"I believe that's what I said, yes."

Stone sighed. "All right. Thank you, Stefan. I owe you a big one for this. I'm sure you'll come up with some creative way to collect, but I'd ask that you wait until after next week. I think I'm going to have plenty to occupy my mind until then."

"Of course. It was a pleasure, as always." He made a little half-bow in his chair.

Stone had made it halfway across the room toward the door when he remembered something. "Oh—Stefan?"

"Yes?"

"One more thing. Sorry, but I'd forgotten about it in the middle of all the rest of this." He turned and came back over. "I know you're fairly familiar with the—er—darker side of the magical community. I'm wondering if perhaps you might be able to help me identify some of them."

Kolinsky tilted his head. "Identify?"

"Long story. There were three of them. They were working together—all of them fairly young. Two men and a woman. I didn't get a good look at them, but they seemed to know who I was."

"Well, you *are* one of the more accomplished practitioners in the area." Kolinsky said with an arch little smile. "Any particular reason you want to know about them?"

"They tried to kill me Saturday night. And they're interested in the house. I have no idea how they might have found out about the demon, but I caught them outside with a circle, trying to contact it."

"Interesting..." Kolinsky thought about it for a moment, then quirked an eyebrow at Stone. "This is, of course, a separate arrangement?"

"Of course."

Kolinsky pondered. "I don't know their names, but I think I've heard of them. If they're the same ones you're referring to, they arrived in the area a couple of years ago. I believe they're based out of San Francisco, and they spend much of their time there, which is why I don't have more to give you." He looked disapproving. "They're arrogant, hedonistic, lacking in discipline—nothing to speak of separately, but they have an unusual rapport that makes them dangerous when together. I believe they refer to themselves as The Trio, or The Three, or some ridiculous thing like that."

"The Three." Ah, youth and their pretentiousness. "Are you sure you don't have names?"

"Sorry," Kolinsky said. "The only other thing I can tell you is to be careful. As I said, separately they aren't that formidable, but from what little I've heard, they have few qualms about causing injury to get what they want."

Stone nodded. "I intend to. And if you *do* happen to find out anything else, please give me a call. Remember, if I'm dead I won't be able to repay you for your help. Unless you've need of some slightly beat-up body parts for reagents."

Kolinsky's only reply was a sly smile.

| CHAPTER TWENTY-SEVEN

Stone arrived home around two-thirty, still thinking over everything Kolinsky had told him. It all seemed absurd, but he couldn't afford to treat it that way. Whatever was in Adelaide's house, whether it be spirit, demon, or something else, it was dangerous. If nothing else, he'd have to see about temporarily reinforcing its prison in the short term. He wanted nothing more than to call Adelaide and tell her to cancel her charity ball, but that would be taking the easy way out. He still had time to do this.

First he had to find the thing, though. That was going to be the hard part.

He glanced at his answering machine: no flashing light. That meant that Ethan hadn't called to tell him when he could come over. He didn't expect to hear from Megan, as she was working, and her last class didn't finish until six o'clock.

He wanted to go to Adelaide's house and search through her attic, though at this point he didn't think he'd find out anything that Kolinsky hadn't already given him. He might even be able to spend some time poking around looking for the spirit (he refused to call it a demon—even things most people called demons were merely some kind of nasty spirit from another plane of existence). Before he could do that, though, he had to find out what was up with Ethan. He was a little annoyed that the boy hadn't called him already, even if it was just to tell him he couldn't make it for whatever reason. Picking up the phone, he punched in Ethan's number and wondered if he'd get the machine again.

He didn't: it was picked up on the second ring. "Hello?" The voice sounded a bit breathless.

"Ethan. Alastair Stone."

Pause. "Hi, Dr. Stone." Another pause. "Oh, man, I was supposed to call you. I'm sorry! I—was down visiting Mom, then I got in the middle of some stuff and lost track of the time."

Stone had seen less evasiveness in antelope trying to avoid becoming lion chow. "Ethan, if you'd rather not come up for your lesson—"

"Oh, no, of course I want to. I can come right now if you want."

"Why don't you do that, then?" He went over the timetable mentally: it would take Ethan about half an hour to get to his house. If the lesson lasted an hour, he'd still have time to get down to Adelaide's before it was too late. "I'll see you in a bit."

A little more than a half-hour later, Ethan's little blue car pulled into the driveway. Stone watched him come up the walk with a slight frown. He looked different somehow, but Stone couldn't quite put his finger on how. Something about the way he carried himself.

Once inside, Ethan was again quick to apologize. "I want you to know I'm really sorry for the last few days. It's been crazy with Mom, and—hey, what happened to you?"

Stone raised a questioning eyebrow.

"Your chin's all bruised, and you're walking funny. What happened?"

He waved it off. "Nothing to worry about. I'm fine. Now, then. Come with me. I'd like to talk with you before we go downstairs and you show me how well you've been working on that levitation spell."

Ethan seemed reluctant, but he followed along to the sitting room and sat down on the overstuffed couch where Stone indicated. Stone himself sat in his usual chair. He leaned forward and silently studied the boy for several seconds.

Ethan was clearly trying not to squirm under his scrutiny. "Uh—what is it?" he finally asked.

"I don't know." Stone replied slowly. "Something's changed about you, and I can't decide what it is."

"Changed?"

He nodded. "You seem—different." His gaze sharpened. "Ethan, are you sure you're being completely honest with me? I get the feeling that you might be holding something back."

Ethan met his gaze. "Different? I don't know what you mean, Dr. Stone. Different like how?"

"I don't know. I can't quite identify it. But I'm usually fairly good at reading these kinds of things, and I can't shake the feeling that you're hiding something from me." Absurdly, he was taken back to the conversation with Megan just last night. Now he was on the other side. His sympathy for what his girlfriend was experiencing went up a notch. "What have you been doing with all this time you've been at home?"

"Spending time at the hospital visiting Mom, like I told you. And practicing the levitation spell. I guess maybe I did go a little further than you told me to, but I got tired of lifting coins."

"Oh?"

Ethan nodded. "Yeah. I can do books now. Just one at a time and just small ones, but I'm getting pretty good at it."

"Excellent. You'll have to show me. But that's for later. Listen, Ethan. I told you when I first agreed to take you on that you were going to have to make it worth my while. That you'd have to agree to follow my orders as far as magical training went, and work as hard as you could. You remember that, don't you?"

"Sure. And I have been." Just the tiniest hint of something defiant touched his tone.

"Have you?" Stone's expression was neutral.

"Sure I have!" His voice rose a little. "Look, Dr. Stone, I'm sorry if I'm not the perfect apprentice. I don't even know what that is. But I've been pretty stressed out lately with Mom being so sick. I'm trying to do the best I can, but—"

Stone held up his hand, still expressionless. "Ethan, stop. I'm not saying that you're not doing a good job, given the circumstances you have to deal with. It's just that—I feel as if you've been avoiding me these past few days, and I want to know why. I don't think it's entirely because of your mother. Am I wrong?"

Ethan didn't answer for a long time. "No," he finally said. "You aren't wrong."

"Why, then?"

"I don't *know*," he said. "Everything's crazy. I want to learn magic, but there's so much going on that I have to do at home, and—"

"And?"

He looked down at his lap. "And nothing. I've just been having trouble concentrating."

Stone sighed. "All right, Ethan. All right. We'll play it your way for now. If you don't want to tell me, you don't have to. I want you to know this, though: I'm happy to teach you magic. I like teaching. I like helping the next generation of new mages learn. But I won't stand for being lied to or deceived. I'm not one of those hidebound old fossils who insists on absolute obedience. These are new times, and things have changed from the way they were when I was an apprentice. But one thing hasn't changed: I expect you to work, and I expect you to take this seriously. As long as whatever extracurricular activities you've got going on that you aren't telling me about don't interfere with your studies, then fine. Do what you want. I don't care. But if they do—"

"They won't," Ethan said, sounding defensive again. He looked up from his lap. "Let's go downstairs, Dr. Stone. Let me show you what I've been doing. Then you can decide for yourself whether I've been following your lesson plan."

Reluctantly, Stone motioned him up and led him down to the basement. He settled himself in a chair, tilted it back on two legs, and nodded at the boy. "All right—show me."

Ethan watched him for a moment, then reached in his back-pack and pulled out the book he'd been practicing on. He set it down on the table, focused his concentration, and the book rose up from the table and began a slow, meandering circle around the room. It bobbled a couple of times and slowed down halfway through, but for the most part it maintained a smooth path.

Stone watched it go, saying nothing until Ethan, puffing, dropped it gently back down on the table. Then he nodded. "Very well done, Ethan. Very well done indeed. I hadn't expected you to get that far yet."

Ethan grinned, and for a moment whatever oddness Stone had been trying to identify in him disappeared, replaced by honest pride. "Thanks. It's one of the things I've been frustrated about, not having anything new to practice. I got tired of doing coins, so I started on bigger things. I hope that's okay."

"It's fine. You did a good job." Stone leaned forward, the chair coming down with a *clunk*. "And I think that kind of performance does deserve a reward, so I'm going to give you something new to focus on."

"Yeah?"

"Yes." Stone glanced at his watch. This was going to take long-er than an hour, but Ethan had earned it. "I think it's time for your first lesson in circle-casting."

Ethan brightened. "Cool."

"I'm just going to show you a very simple one today, and then I'll give you a couple of books to take home and read. Do you have a place at your apartment large enough to draw a circle four feet or so in diameter and safe to burn candles?"

"I—guess in the kitchen, I could. At least while Mom isn't home. After that I'm not sure."

"Well, once your mum is home, you can do them here for the time being, until we find you a better location." Stone prowled around the room as he talked, pulling boxes off shelves and amassing a small pile of things on one of the worktables. "Do you know anything about circles? I don't think there was much in the books I've given you so far, was there?"

"Not a lot," he said. "A little in the intro text. You make them with candles and chalk and sand and stuff, right?"

"Sometimes. Except for very specific exceptions, what you use to make them isn't as important as the power and intent you infuse into them. In essence, a circle is simply a barrier to keep things in— or out—while you're working magic. They're a way to concentrate your energy and channel it in specific ways, but your own willpower and control are still the most important parts of the process." He picked up some of the items and moved to the large, open area in the room. "Come over here and watch what I do."

Ethan did as he was told, dragging his chair over.

Stone didn't take a lot of time building the circle, since it didn't need to contain or keep out anything harmful. He drew the circle itself with sand, then sketched in a pattern in the middle with colored chalk and anchored its edges with candles. "This is Circle 101," he said. "It's the equivalent of using child's building blocks to build a house. But shift over and watch with your magical senses while I power it." He waited until he thought Ethan had complied, then stepped into the circle and completed the circuit. Dim lines of power flared between its end points, illuminating the pattern. "See?"

"Cool," Ethan said, leaning forward in his chair.

"Now come over here and step inside with me. Be careful not to smudge the chalk lines or disturb the sand. That's the first thing you need to learn about circles, especially when you're depending on them—don't do *anything* to tamper with their structural integrity. At best you'll get a bugger of a headache. At worst, something might eat you, or suck you into another dimension somewhere. That's never convenient."

Carefully, Ethan got up and stepped into the circle, watching where he put his feet. It wasn't a very big circle, and the position put him uncomfortably close to Stone. "Uh..."

"Yes, I don't like it any more than you do," Stone said. "Let's make this quick. Just watch what I do, and see if you can get enough from it to duplicate it yourself." He stepped back, putting as much distance as he could between himself and Ethan, and Ethan did the same. Stone closed his eyes and began murmuring under his breath.

His eyes were closed, but Stone's magical senses were well aware of what was going on. He continued to murmur, gathering energy to him and shaping it into a pattern. He was planning to show Ethan a simple sending spell, one of the easier rituals to re-create.

Suddenly, though, he felt a shift in the pattern. Refocusing his senses, he almost took a physical step back in shock when he saw what was happening.

Ethan had picked up part of the pattern and was holding it in place, feeding more power into it.

How the *hell* was he doing that?

Stone cracked open an eye to look at the boy with normal sight. Ethan was standing there, his own eyes closed, his face looking like he was putting out some effort, but not an unusual amount. He held the pattern steady without even seeming to realize he was doing it. He was even supplying some of his own power to it.

Without letting on that he'd seen anything, Stone continued with the ritual as if Ethan wasn't participating. He completed the pattern, held it for a few seconds, and then let it go. "All right," he said," stepping out of the circle. "Did you get that?"

"I—think so," Ethan said. "I saw what you did. I'm not sure I can do it myself, though."

"Give it a try. That's all I expect right now. Once you get the basics down, there are all kinds of things you can do with a ritual like that. Let me get that book for you, and then I'll let you go for today. I'll also give you some basic ritual materials, though as I said, it's not really important that you use anything specific for one this simple. What I want you to do for homework is read the book, attempt to recreate the circle, and use it to send a communication to me stating that you've done it. The book will give you the details on how to do that. And I want to see you back here on Wednesday afternoon. Call me if you can't make it, but unless your mum is having trouble or you're ill yourself, I expect you here. All right?"

Ethan nodded. "I'll be here. Thanks, Dr. Stone." He gathered up his backpack and put the book he'd been levitating back inside.

Stone gave him a small box of ritual materials and the book he'd referred to, then saw him out, bid him good afternoon, and closed the door behind him. Only then did he let his shoulders slump. He leaned against the inside of the front door, letting his breath out.

Something was definitely going on with Ethan. Something he didn't want Stone to know about. And something that had to do with magic. It was the only way he could have learned to do what he'd done.

Somebody else had showed him how.

He'd been thinking the boy had perhaps found a girlfriend, or was spending time with friends from school instead of doing his lessons. But if he was getting magical instruction from another source—

Stone sighed. Another problem he didn't have time for. Why did everything have to happen at once?

CHAPTER TWENTY-EIGHT

Miguel had spent most of the day doing research, tracking down information about Adelaide Bonham's house and what might be in it. He didn't often admit to it because he thought it made him look like a geek, but he was very good at this job. Usually he used it to find out details about the marks that Trin had set her sights on—things like where they lived, what their habits were, and so forth, so The Three wouldn't have to waste power and time on doing it the magical way. He had a harder time with this one, however. By the time the early evening rolled around, all he'd been able to track down was the historical information about the house, Edgar Sr., Amelia, and the birth of Edgar Jr.

"Sorry," he told Trin when she asked him how things were going. "Nothing about whatever it is that's down there. The best I could get was that the woman Amelia might have been involved with the occult, but lots of people were back in those days. Most of them were fakes. She probably was, too."

Trin frowned. "I wonder if Stone found out any more," she muttered. "We can't have him getting ahead of us on this."

Miguel shrugged. "We could just hit him again. If he's dead, he can't go after us."

"No," she said, shaking her head. "Too dangerous. He's bad news, and he's gonna be harder than ever to surprise now that he's got his full defenses up and knows somebody's after him. Look what he did to Oliver. We still don't know when he'll be okay."

They'd taken Oliver to a hospital when he hadn't responded by the time they reached San Francisco, and he was still there, in some kind of half-awake, half-comatose state. The doctors weren't sure what was wrong with him; they suspected drugs, but they couldn't find any evidence that he'd taken any.

"We can't just let him get away with fucking Oliver up like that," Miguel protested.

Trin's eyes narrowed. "Trust me, Stone's gonna regret ever messing with us. But not yet. Let's wait till he's not expecting it. We've got more important things to do now."

"What about the kid?" Miguel asked. "Did you fuck him yet?"

She smiled, and it wasn't a pleasant sight. "I fucked his brains out last night. He wouldn't say a word against me if you put a gun to his head."

"So use that," he said. "Get him to tell you what's up with Stone. He's his apprentice—he's gotta know something. Maybe Stone's found out more than we have, and he's told the kid about it, or he can ask."

"Not a bad idea," she said, nodding. "I'll have to handle it right, but if I promise him another night like last night and toss in a little subtle magic, I could probably get him to hand over his mother to me." She ran a hand down the back of her head, smoothing her hair. "He's coming up here tonight to help us out with some of the ritual stuff. Let's see about building some bits into it that'll help us work on him some more. The more I think about it, the more I think he's going to end up being the key to this."

"Oh, one more thing," Miguel said. "Don't know if it's relevant or not, but I found another bit of info about that house. There's going to be a humongous charity thing of some sort there this Saturday night. All kinds of rich stuck-up types drinking too much and giving money to orphan baby seals or something. I don't know the details. But it's gonna be at the house."

"Hmm..." Trin thought about that. "This Saturday?"

"Yeah."

"Interesting. Let me work on that. It might be just the break we need."

Stone called Adelaide, and asked if he could come to the house that night.

"Of course," she said. "You don't have to ask. Just come down whenever you have time."

He also left a message for Megan that he would be going down there, and probably would be there for most of the evening. He didn't really want to go spend all that time puttering around the house and grounds, and possibly the attic, but he was running out of days. It was already Monday evening and he only had four more days to do something he had no idea if he could do. That, and deal with those three mages if they turned up again, and figure out what the hell was up with Ethan.

Nothing like a having full plate. At least he wouldn't be bored.

He grabbed a quick dinner on the way down, and arrived at the house a little before seven. It was already dark, and a light rain was falling. Great. On top of everything else, he'd track mud all over everything.

This time, he took the time to set up a simple circle in front of the house before he even went in, searching for any sign of The Three. He found none, which he supposed was one good thing.

Iona came out while he was finishing up. "Dr. Stone? Is that you? What are you doing?"

"Just checking something," he assured her, picking up the circle components. "Nothing to worry about."

"Well, come in out of the rain." She took his arm and hustled him inside.

Adelaide was waiting in the sitting room. "What are you going to do tonight?"

"Spend some more time looking for where this thing is, mostly," he told her as Iona deftly slid him out of his overcoat and hung it by the fire to dry, then steered him toward a chair. "If you're feeling it in the library, then odds are it's somewhere on that side of the house. Does your attic extend across the entire place?"

"Yes," she said, "but it's divided into smaller sections if I remember correctly. I haven't been up there in probably twenty years. It's all full of old trunks and clothes and furniture and dust and spiders. I'm not even sure it's safe up there, to be honest. Promise me you'll be careful if you go."

"What about a basement? Have you got one of those?"

"Same thing," she said. "Very big, divided up into sections, and full of old furniture and other things like that."

"Part of it's more accessible than the rest," Iona added. "There's a big larder down there where we keep large nonperishable food and serving items we use for the various functions we hold here, and a large wine cellar. Those are the only parts I've ever seen. The rest of it is locked off. Do you even have the key, Adelaide?"

"I'm not sure," she said, looking fretful. "I don't think anyone's even looked for it there since those young men were here inspecting for earthquake damage a few months ago. They never did end up going down there. Are you going to need to go down, Dr. Stone?"

"Probably," he said. "I can—er—deal with the lock if you can't find the key, but my way will be rather permanent."

"Permanent?"

"You'll need a new lock, is what I mean."

Iona stared at him, eyes wide, but didn't comment.

"Well," Adelaide said, "If that's what you need to do. I haven't the faintest idea where the key is."

Stone nodded. "No more incidents since Saturday night?"

"Nothing," Iona said. She hesitated, then asked, "Do you think—well, is there any chance that whatever it is, it's—gone?"

"Unfortunately not," Stone said. "I can still feel it. It's still here. But don't you worry. I'll deal with it." He spoke with more confidence than he felt. Then, to Adelaide: "Did you happen to remember any of the historical information I asked you to think about?"

"I'm sorry," she said. "I didn't. It's all been so long ago—" She spread her hands. "Like I said before, if there's anything to find, it's probably in the attic. I'm sure there are trunks and boxes full of old papers up there. But finding them is going to be hard, especially on such short notice. There's *so* much junk up there..."

"Don't worry," Stone said, getting up and hefting his bag full of paraphernalia. "I'll get to the attic soon, but I want to start with the basement. If you'll just show me the way to get down there, I'll get started so I can be out of here before it gets too late."

Iona took him out of the sitting room, through the big main room, and down a couple of hallways to a part of the house he hadn't seen yet. "This is the kitchen," she said, leading him through a pair of double doors into a large, gleaming area full of long counters and expensive appliances. She pointed to another set of doors. "Through there is the main dining room, and beyond that is the grand ballroom where the charity event will be. But we're going this way."

Continuing through the kitchen, she went through a single door on the far side and out into a hallway that was much more utilitarian than anything Stone had seen so far. "This part of the house is where a lot of the service work is done: laundry, dishwashing, and so on—most of it when we have functions. There are other ways to get to the basement, but this one is the most convenient, and the only one that leads to the parts that are easily accessible."

Stone nodded, just following along. A year or so ago, he'd visited the Winchester Mystery House in San Jose with a former girlfriend who'd wanted to see the Halloween flashlight tour (a visit he preferred to think about as rarely as possible, as it had led directly to another ex-relationship), and been impressed and a little amazed by the size and haphazard construction of the vast house. Adelaide's place, while laid out with more logic and far less insanity, certainly rivaled it for sheer size.

Iona opened one more door and led him down a stairway to a hall with several other doors. She pointed to the one at the end. "That's the one you want. Like I said before, it's locked. I'm sure if we looked around long enough we could find the key, but unless you've got some sort of skeleton key..."

"I'll take care of it," he assured her. "Go on back to Adelaide. You needn't accompany me—I'll be fine on my own."

She looked dubious, but finally nodded. "Good luck, Dr. Stone. And be careful. If nothing else, there are rats and spiders down here. Maybe even bats!"

He smiled. "I've dealt with far worse than rats and spiders, Iona. Don't worry."

She gave him one last odd, frightened look, then turned and headed back toward the main part of the house.

When she was gone, he turned his attention to the door. As he suspected there wasn't much to it; it only took a small spell to break its flimsy lock. He pushed it open and walked inside.

It was very dark in here. He looked around for a light switch and found one, but when he flipped it, nothing happened. This time, though, he'd come prepared: from his bag he pulled a large flashlight and snapped it on. He could have used his light spell, but he didn't want to waste energy to power it. If he found what he was looking for, he might need all the energy he could summon to deal with it.

He moved down the hallway, the flashlight casting eerie shadows on the stained, unpainted walls. There was nothing elegant or opulent about this part of the house: it looked weathered and sinister. Stone suspected it had not been updated since the days when it had first been built.

It was cold down here, too. He shivered; he was wearing a sweater over his T-shirt, but he wished he'd remembered to reclaim his overcoat. The cold was making his ribs ache more than usual. Too late to worry about it now, though.

He moved further in. The hallway ended in a t-intersection; he shined the flashlight down both directions, then reached out with his magical senses to try to get a feel for which way he should go. The feeling was vague and diffuse; still, though, he sensed something else—brief flutters of activity. Was it asleep? Was it watching him from somewhere while trying to keep hidden? He put a bit more focus into his search, and was rewarded with what he thought was the correct direction: to the right. He was getting closer. The feelings were definitely stronger down here. He rounded the corner and continued on, moving slowly.

No doubt about it, this place was creepy. It was mostly silent, but every couple of minutes something would creak ominously off in the distance. Stone was sure the creaks were simply the house settling, but as he moved further away from the door leading upward, they became correspondingly more eerie. Couple that with the faint distant skitterings of rats, and most sane people would have given up the mission and headed back for the light already.

Stone wasn't most sane people.

Still, he found himself wishing that he could have brought Ethan along. If nothing else, it would have given him the chance to talk to the boy, to find out what he was up to. Or even to talk to him about anything. After all Stone had seen in his magical career, it wasn't easy to frighten him, but even then he wasn't fond of the overly dark and creepy.

There were occasional doors along the hallway he was following now. He ignored most of them because his magical senses were telling him what he sought was still ahead, but a couple times he tested them and, when he found them unlocked, shoved them open for a quick look inside. In both cases they led to small rooms packed full of the large bulky shapes of covered furniture. The moldy, musty odor that rolled out of each was nearly visible in the chilly air, and in the second one, a large, furry form darted out through the doorway, scampered over Stone's right foot, and disappeared into the darkness ahead. He didn't open any more doors after that. He did notice that the hallway was sloping subtly downward as he continued forward.

After what seemed like a very long time, but in actuality was probably only about five minutes, the hallway opened up. Stone paused at the entrance, panning the flashlight back and forth to get a better look before he stepped out into the space.

The area was huge, a wide open expanse of concrete floor surrounded by more towering, shadowy forms of shrouded furniture, building materials, and rusty old gardening items. The ceiling here was higher too, rising about fifteen feet up. From where he was standing, Stone couldn't see any other doors leading out, but it would be easy to hide them in the midst of all this clutter.

He took a couple more steps in, then stopped. "Anyone there?" he called. His voice sounded dead, muffled against the decaying cloth covering the furniture. It didn't echo at all. High above him, he thought he heard the flutter of wings beating—the bats Iona had spoken of. Looking around, he tried to spot them; if they were here, they had to have some way to get out, but given that the floor was covered in dust but no bat droppings, he suspected he—and Iona— were just imagining them.

"All right," he muttered to himself, just to hear some sound. "Let's get on with this." Moving to the center of the open area, he closed his eyes and reached out again with his magical senses. The feeling of the thing was very strong here—he was close, and it couldn't fully hide itself from him anymore. "Where are you...?" he whispered. "You know I'm going to find you, so why don't we just get it over with?"

The room creaked ominously, and a couple of the cloth-shrouded towers of piled furniture swayed back and forth.

"Oh, that's the way you want to play it, then, is it?" Stone hurried back over to the safety of the entrance and watched the room to see if the swaying got any worse. If that thing dropped an armoire on him, by the time anyone was brave enough to come down here and find him, there'd be nothing left but bones and a few shreds of clothing. Just to be safe, he put up a physical shield and powered it with one of his remaining crystals. It wouldn't be strong enough to stop anything seriously heavy, but if they were stacking things that heavy that high up, then more was wrong here than just demons in the basement.

Staying close to one side, and glancing up every few seconds to make sure nothing was about to fall on him, Stone crept forward and explored the room, magical senses at the ready. He'd been right: there were small walkways between the piles, radiating out toward the edges of the room. Some were blocked by items that had already fallen, probably many years ago or during the recent earthquake. The creaking wasn't repeated.

He wondered how long it had been since anyone *had* been down here. Had it been back in the days of Edgar Sr.? Had the disastrous ritual that had taken the lives of Selena Darklight and her students, along with Amelia Bonham's sanity, been the last time anyone had ventured down? It seemed unlikely, but the items here easily looked like they could have lain undisturbed for all those years. The musty smell of a long-unaired space was getting stronger; Stone wondered briefly if the air was even safe, but decided it must be if the rats were getting in and out. Even so, he wished he'd brought a scarf or a mask or something to avoid having to breathe the dust he was sending up with every footstep. Bad idea of breathing all that dust notwithstanding, his ribs weren't going to stand for too many coughing fits.

"Remind me again why I'm doing this?" he muttered aloud. He could have been back home, sharing a good dinner and a lovely evening with Megan. "Because I'm an idiot, that's why," he answered himself, and moved forward again.

The feeling was growing stronger as he approached the back of the room, farthest away from where he'd entered it. He stood for a moment staring down one of the narrow walkways through the junk, focusing his senses.

Whatever it was, it was in this direction.

Making sure his shield was at full strength, he crept down the walkway. He had to pick his way over a smashed dresser and the remains of a player piano that disgorged a family of mice as he stepped past it. He shone the flashlight up ahead, wondering what he'd find when he reached the other side.

It was a dead end.

The way was blocked by a large bookcase, full of moldy old tomes and stacked with yellowing newspapers. He stopped, frustration growing. The feeling was so strong here—perhaps the next walkway over might be the one, but—

Wait…

He glanced behind him to make sure no one—or nothing—was approaching, then brought the flashlight in closer and examined the bookcase in more detail. He stepped back and looked at the floor: it was covered in the same layer of dust that the rest of the basement was, but he could just see faint, semicircular tracks that indicated that something had been moved here, though not recently. Setting down the flashlight, he moved his hands around the edges of the bookshelf, then skimmed his gaze over the titles of the books. Most of them were boring: old encyclopedia volumes, classics from the early part of the century and similarly unexciting books. But on a lower shelf a leatherbound tome caught his eye. Its title was in a language he didn't recognize, a series of squiggly lines that made him uncomfortable to look directly at it for long.

He paused a moment, then hooked his finger on top of the book and tugged.

The bookshelf swung out, rusted hinges protesting with every inch. Stone grabbed hold and pulled harder. It wanted to swing shut again, so he forced it open, grabbed his flashlight, and slid through. As soon as he let go of it, it immediately slammed shut behind him.

He spun and pushed at it, and was relieved to discover that he could still shove it open. It hadn't locked behind him. Stone let his breath out slowly and just stood there for a moment, getting his bearings.

"Well," he murmured. "*This* looks promising."

| CHAPTER TWENTY-NINE

He stood in a large room, though not nearly as large as the one he'd just left. This one, however, was not piled high with the cast-offs and detritus of the house's former residents.

Instead, the floor was empty, except for a large, permanent ritual circle that had been built directly into it, laid out using different colored stone and tracings of gold and silver metal. Stone examined it carefully, shining his light around its entire border. It was one of the most complex circles of its type he'd seen in many years, certainly more complex than anything he'd used in his work recently. This was the kind of circle you used to do big things: summon or control powerful entities, send spells at large numbers of people at once, or perform the kinds of transformations that nobody did anymore because they were so difficult and costly. It was also the kind that you didn't use alone. He estimated that the ritual that would need a circle this complicated would require a minimum of four people to power and direct it.

He was pretty sure he'd found the site of Selena Darklight's disastrous summoning attempt.

Dragging his attention away from the circle itself, he looked around the room. There were no bones or bodies, but he could see dark patches on the floor and the walls that, even covered in a layer of dust, looked very much like old, long-dried blood. Great chunks had been ripped out of the wood paneling that covered a couple walls. On the far side of the room was an oversized, wooden armoire. Its doors were closed, but didn't quite meet in the middle. Tables and bookshelves lined one side of the room, all stacked haphazardly with dusty tomes and piles of yellowed papers covered in diagrams and cramped writing. On the other side were a series of rotting, empty wine racks, attesting to what this room's original purpose must have been before Amelia and Selena Darklight appropriated it for their own use.

Stone's curiosity was on fire: if the books and other materials were what he thought they were, he'd just found a treasure trove of magical information. He could easily spend many days or weeks down here, studying them one by one. There was no time for that now, though. He could practically feel the energy of the creature straining against its bonds; it knew he was here, and he knew that it could well be in the same room with him, half-shifted between dimensions, invisible even to his magical senses. In order to see it, he'd have to set up a ritual of his own. And if he could see it, he hoped he could set up wards or other protective enchantments that would keep it contained temporarily—at least until after Adelaide's party—to give him more time to see what he could do about it more permanently.

Picking up his bag, which he'd left just inside the room's bookcase entrance, he began pulling out items and placing them on a nearby table. He'd have to make his own circle; there was no way he could or would use the existing one without further study. He glanced at his watch: a little after 8 p.m. If he was lucky, he could finish this up in a couple of hours and be home by 11:00.

He carefully constructed his circle behind the larger one, making sure every bit was secure, that there were no gaps, and he hadn't skipped anything or written any of the sigils incorrectly. He felt a buzzing in his head now, almost like a low-grade background count of distracting energy. It didn't quite hurt, but it did make it difficult to concentrate on what he was doing.

It's fighting me.

Despite the cold down here, he was getting warm from the effort of setting up the circle. He stripped off his sweater and tossed it on the table, leaving just his black T-shirt. That was better. His body couldn't decide whether it should shiver or perspire, so it did a bit of both. He pushed his damp hair off his forehead and stood back to inspect his handiwork.

The circle, which had taken him about an hour to construct, looked sound to both his mundane and magical senses. It was about six feet across and glowed with power, easily contained within its confines.

No point in waiting any longer.

Stone took a few deep breaths, stretched, and stepped into the circle. He felt its protective enchantments weaving around him, creating a barrier between him and whatever might be out there. Inside the circle, the irritating hum faded away to the faintest of sounds. He closed his eyes, centered himself, and reached out.

His senses were drawn to the armoire at the end of the room. With the altered perceptions that were heightened by the circle's power, he saw a crack in the door where an unwholesome sort of light shone out. It crept around the edges of the doors, testing the boundaries, trying to find a way to force them open further. He also saw that the armoire was more than just an armoire: powerful enchantments still surrounded it, wrapping it in nearly unbreakable mystical chains.

Nearly unbreakable.

He nudged his perception open a bit more, probing for information. *What are you?*

He didn't expect to get an answer, but his mind was suddenly flooded with images that flew by too fast for him to make sense of them. Gritting his teeth, he tried to slow them down or, barring that, to pick out individual frames.

—A large room.—

—A hellish domain seething with creeping, crawling creatures.—

—Magical sigils spinning in a mad circle.—

—Several robe-clad people standing in a circle, hands clasped.—

—A desperate attempt to stop something, to slow it, to send it back.—

—Darkness.—

—A vast rumbling as the earth moved.—

—A tiny crack in the structural integrity of the prison that held something back.—

Stone probed further. He didn't think he'd be able to get it to reveal its name, even imprisoned as it was. He felt it probing back, poking around the edges of his mind, trying to gain any knowledge it could of him—who he was, why he was there, whether he could be persuaded or coerced to help it. And all the while, he felt the sheer malevolence of it.

This thing could not be allowed to get free.

Once, a long time ago, he'd seen a poster depicting the side view of an iceberg—the part that emerged above the level of the sea was only the tiniest fraction of the vast bulk floating below the water line. He couldn't get a good look at the thing from here, not without a much more complicated ritual and probably at least two more participants, but he could tell that the part of it that was emerging into their plane of existence was a similarly small fraction. If the whole thing were allowed to come through, the entire area—and perhaps much more—would be in peril.

He couldn't allow that.

But how the hell was he going to stop it?

A whole ritual group, led by a woman who was probably every bit the practitioner he was, and assisted by another powerful mage and several lesser ones, hadn't been able to do more than imprison it temporarily. And they had *had* its name. All he had was his resolve, his experience, and a body in no shape to be throwing around forces anywhere near potent enough to deal with something like this.

He couldn't send it back—not yet, at least. But he could do his best to reinforce its prison. Gathering his strength, he began weaving patterns and enchantments, taking cues from those that were already there, and interweaving his own with them in much the same way that one braids a series of thin ropes together to form a stronger one. He knew it wouldn't hold for long, but if he could stay its momentum long enough to gather some more mages, then maybe it would be enough. He could call Walter Yarborough, and a few others he knew—

The crack was widening. The light around him was changing.

The world shifted.

He still stood in the center of the same room, though it didn't look the same now. His circle was gone.

The room was lit by candles in sconces along both of the long walls, as well as a large brazier in the middle. Flames licked up from the brazier, creating a strange-smelling, cloying, purple smoke that wound up to the stone ceiling and then dissipated.

Stone looked around. The dust, the smell of mold and disuse, were gone. Everything in the room looked new and fresh, including the paneled walls (now blood free) and the brilliant circle in its center. Several robed and hooded figures—a quick count revealed seven—stood swaying inside the circle; six arrayed around its inside perimeter, their hands clasped and energy coursing between them. The seventh figure stood in the center, hood lowered, gathering the energy flowing from the points around the diameter and weaving the separate threads into a powerful whole that glowed like a small sun. Stone had to squint as he looked at it, but he could tell the level of power it contained was immense. Certainly far more powerful than anything he could call up on his own.

He stepped forward. The circle occupants didn't appear to notice him, or if they did, they didn't react. They continued swaying and chanting, feeding power to the tall, olive-skinned woman in the middle. The woman herself was turned away from him, focused on the other end of the room.

Stone followed her gaze—the armoire was there, looking solid and substantial, but its doors were open. More light, as brilliant as that inside the circle, but an unhealthy red-purple, shone from inside, illuminating the entire end of the room in its eerie glow.

The woman in the center of the circle chanted loudly, her body writhing with either ecstasy or agony—it was hard to tell which. Stone edged farther forward, his gaze never leaving the group in case they noticed him, and saw sweat streaming down her face. He couldn't make out any specifics in her chant, though he struggled to pick out anything intelligible.

And then something burst through the armoire's doors, pouring out into the room. For a moment Stone just stared, unable to believe what he was witnessing. A series of—things—boiled out through the opening, moving toward the circle. The creatures were humanoid, barely, made of tentacles and flayed flesh and great glowing greenish eyes. The sounds they made weren't anything close to human, and each time they moved, it sounded like flesh being ripped from bones. Behind them, dark slime trails stretched back to the armoire.

They surged toward the circle.

One by one, the six participants around the edges became aware of them, shifting position, crying out in alarm. The woman in the middle yelled out an order and directed some of the power she was handling toward the first couple of creatures. They screamed and exploded in sprays of ichor.

The other creatures were not idle, though. Two of them reached the circle; they grabbed the two closest figures and pulled, seemingly unaffected by the circle's protective power. Stone watched in horror as the creatures yanked the hooded figures out of the circle and began devouring them, accompanied by screams and great wet rending sounds.

The others screamed too, but the woman in the center barked a command. The remaining four figures around the outside quickly moved to clasp hands, while the center woman adjusted her chant.

The power coursing around the circle changed, and the light at the center shifted from bright white to a deep red. She yelled something, and directed the red light toward the armoire.

Something else was coming through.

Something big.

The four remaining participants looked as if they might panic at any moment and flee, but they held it together for now. Stone had to summon rarely tapped reserves of will to do the same, and he still wasn't sure how long he could do it. His heart pounded; his mind screamed for him to run, to flee, to get himself away from this thing as fast as he could, before it pushed itself through into the light. He had trained most of his life to deal with things that shouldn't exist, but this—this was an entirely new level. He was reminded suddenly of the H. P. Lovecraft stories he used to read back in his University days. Whatever this was, he'd never seen anything even remotely like it...and he was becoming more and more sure that he didn't want to.

Stone forced himself to move around the rear of the circle, wondering if the creatures could see him, wondering if he could help. He saw now that they had changed their tactics, and were attempting to seal the armoire gateway. He knew he couldn't join the circle: he wasn't sure how the creatures had gotten their two terrified victims out without breaking it, but he had no confidence that he could do the same if he tried to step in. Instead, he focused on one of the creatures and flung a concussion spell. The creature was knocked off its feet (or tentacles) and sailed back toward the armoire opening.

The circle participants paid him no attention, but unfortunately, the other creatures did. More were coming through now, and the ones that were already here changed direction to head toward Stone. Inside the circle, the four remaining edges and the woman at the center continued their chanting. The armoire door was closing, but slowly.

Stone took two steps backward and summoned a shield spell. It came up around him just as the first creature reached him. He had a better look now and wished he hadn't: the thing had two long arms ending in wicked, clawed hands. It shambled like a zombie, ichor drooling from its open mouth.

It reared back and swiped at him. His shield flared red, but the attack didn't get through. Stone backed off another step. *The shield won't hold long. Those things are bloody strong.* He risked a glance at the armoire again: the doors were nearly closed, but more creatures had gotten through. They were heading for the circle.

Another creature took a swing at him. The shield blocked it again, but even as it did, it flared a second time and went down. Hastily-constructed shields like that weren't designed to fend off more than one or two attacks before they failed. Stone backed off again, but found his back against the far wall.

The creatures moved in closer. He could smell them now: wet and moldy and impossibly disgusting, like a dead, gassy body found floating in a hot, fetid swamp. Gritting his teeth against his rising gorge, Stone blew another creature back with a concussive blast.

The woman's voice rose in triumph, and he spared another glance over: the armoire was nearly closed now. She directed the red light, and two more of the creatures flew back through the tiny opening, flailing their strange arms. There were only a few left now.

Stone couldn't look anymore, though: two more of the monsters had reached him. He struggled to erect another barrier, but before he could manage it, the closer of the two swung at him. Its claws were like a sloth's: long and wicked, extending out past the end of its hands for several inches. His feint to the left was too slow: the claws raked across his chest and abdomen, shredding his T-shirt and leaving bloody trails. He cried out and flung himself sideways, heedless of the pain. Beyond him, he could hear the shrieks of the circle participants as the creatures went after them. The entire room smelled of rot, blood, and terror.

Barely able to get a breath, Stone threw another concussive blast at the closer of the two creatures. His head pounded with the effort, but he knew he couldn't hold back this time. If he didn't get out of here, he would be dead.

The other creature, however, had other plans. It fell on top of him, raking its claws across his arms, his chest, his legs. Beyond coherent thought now, he screamed, trying to shove it away. It was far too heavy for that, though, and in any case he had no strength left.

It grabbed his arm and began dragging him back toward the armoire. He felt his shoulder pop out of its socket, and new waves of agony washed over him.

"*NO!*" he cried feebly, struggling to break free. The creature's claws sunk into his arm as it dragged him toward the opening with relentless strength. His last conscious thought as he finally blacked out was to wonder if anyone would ever find his body.

| CHAPTER THIRTY

The first thing Stone noticed when he awoke was that he was chilled to the bone. He lay on his back on a surface of cold stone, crumpled like a broken doll, every muscle shivering, despite his efforts to quiet them. Fearful of what he might find, he opened his eyes.

He was in total darkness, so thick that he couldn't hope to pierce it. He heard no sounds at all: no screams, no skittering of rats or flapping of bats, no ripping-skin-on-bone sounds from the horrific creatures that had poured through the armoire's open door. The only thing he could hear was the ragged sound of his own breath as it wheezed in his throat.

He coughed, and must have passed out again from the pain. After a few moments—or perhaps it was a few hours, he had no way of knowing—he struggled again to consciousness. This time he didn't try to move, doing his best to take inventory from a still position.

Why am I not dead? Those things ripped me up—

Very carefully, still shivering and miserable, he moved his arms to his stomach. He was terrified of what he would find there.

There was no crust of dried blood, no sudden flare of agony. His thin T-shirt had ridden up when he'd fallen; he shoved it up the rest of the way and probed the skin of his chest and stomach with tentative fingers. He was whole and unslashed. He pulled the shirt back down, though it did nothing to alleviate the bitter cold.

What the hell—?

He lay there, listening. Still no sound, but he smelled the musty, dusty odor of the room he was in. He realized why it was dark: *The flashlight's batteries died. How long have I been out?*

Convinced now that whatever grievous injuries the creatures had inflicted had somehow only been in his mind, he dragged himself up to a seated position. His ribs still burned and he was unable to stop shivering, but aside from that he seemed to be mostly unhurt. He risked a light spell.

He was sitting on the stone floor of the circle room. The armoire was still there, still slightly cracked open, but a quick look with his magical senses confirmed that he had managed to supplement the protective wards around it before things had gone south. He was fairly certain that as long as no one tampered with it, it would hold long enough Adelaide's charity ball to go off safely. Still, complete certainty was a luxury you didn't get very often with this kind of magic.

He struggled up to his feet. His legs felt like limp rubber, his whole body weak, as if he'd exerted himself too hard for too long without a break. His head throbbed from the strain of channeling too much magical energy, and he tasted the sharp tang of blood, probably from another nosebleed. He staggered over to the table where he'd left his sweater, and shrugged into it. That was a little better; at least the shivering abated somewhat. Then he glanced at his watch: he'd started the ritual around 9, and it was a little after 10:30 now. He'd been unconscious for about an hour.

Gripping the table, he fought to understand what had happened. What had he seen? Had the creature showed him something? The night it was imprisoned, perhaps? Why? Had it wanted something from him, and he'd managed to fight it off?

He had no idea. Right now he didn't care very much, either. He still had a long way to go before he even reached the main part of the house, and he wasn't sure his legs were up to the task. He wanted nothing more than to lie back down and let the blackness have him again, but he couldn't do that. Not yet.

Somehow, he made it out of the hidden room (the bookshelf was a struggle: he'd never been the strongest of men physically, and right now he wouldn't bet on himself in a fight versus a reasonably robust kitten) and back through the enormous room full of piled-up furniture. There was no creaking or swaying now: either the thing was truly locked back away, albeit temporarily, or it had expended enough energy in putting on its little stage show that it was resting. Either way, Stone slowly headed back, retracing his steps until he reached the stairway to the service area, and the door where he'd broken the lock what seemed like a very long time ago.

Barely on his feet now, he moved down the hallway, back through the kitchen, and continued until he reached the main part of the house. He didn't know where Adelaide and Iona were, but if they were still awake he guessed they were probably in the sitting room, especially if she'd had a new television delivered by then. As he drew closer, he was rewarded by the sound of the TV and of faint voices coming from the room. Holding on to the open door-frame, he called, "Mrs. Bonham—?"

She turned, and her eyes widened as she got a look at him. After a second, Iona turned too. "Oh, dear God, Dr. Stone! What happened?" She got up and hustled over to grab his arm.

"I'm—I'm all right," he mumbled. "Just—tired."

"You're white as a ghost, and covered in blood worse than the other night!" she protested, steering him toward a chair. Adelaide moved closer, her blue eyes huge with fear. She was about to say something when another voice came through the open door where Stone had just come in.

"Alastair? What the *hell* are you doing here?"

Stone sagged in the chair even as he turned toward the new voice. He already knew who it was, though.

Tommy Langley stood in the doorway, his face dark with anger.

Stone closed his eyes. It hadn't been his night thus far—why start now? "Tommy." His voice sounded infinitely weary.

Langley stumped up and stood over him. "What the hell—" he started to repeat, then got a good look at Stone. "What happened to you?"

Iona had left the room and now returned with a washcloth, which she used to mop Stone's face. "Leave him alone, Tommy." To Stone, she said, "Dr. Stone, what happened? Your nose is bleeding again. And you're so pale...I should call someone—"

He put a limp hand on her arm—he couldn't summon the energy to fight her. "No...it's fine. Really. Just—so tired..."

Adelaide just stared at him, eyes big in her pale face. "Dr. Stone—" she ventured, very tentatively. "Did you find—?"

He nodded.

"Is it—"

He struggled to open his eyes. "I think—you'll be all right. For now." His words came out on little rushes of air, barely audible. "It isn't gone, but it's—contained."

"Then—we can have the ball? It's...safe?"

"I want to come back again tomorrow—do a few more checks—but I think so."

"Wait a minute," Langley protested. "You're not coming back. You're not even supposed to be here *now*. I don't know what's going on here, but you promised me you wouldn't do this. You gave me your *word,* Alastair. You—"

Stone wasn't sure how it happened, but sitting there in that chair, exhausted to the bone, ribs aflame with pain and barely able to draw a full breath, something snapped inside him.

He couldn't do this anymore.

Who cared if anyone knew? What difference did it make? Why was he making all this effort to keep what he did a secret when all they wanted to do was hinder everything he tried?

Gritting his teeth, he struggled to his feet and glared at Langley. "Shut up, Tommy," he growled.

"What?" Langley's eyes got big and he took a step back. This dead-pale, bloodstreaked madman wasn't the cheerily sarcastic Alastair Stone he went drinking with on Friday nights in Palo Alto. "You can't—"

"I can and I will." Stone's anger, his rage and frustration at his inability to fully deal with the situation and the ignorant mundanes who kept getting in his way, gave him energy. He took another step forward, and Langley took another one back.

Adelaide made a little moan of fear, but both men ignored her.

"Listen—" Langley began, his own anger rising.

"No. *You* listen." Stone's voice wasn't loud—in fact, Langley had to watch him closely to make out all of it—but there was something in it, a quality of authority and cold steel that drew Langley up short. "I'm bloody tired of trying to keep you happy in your ignorance, Tommy. I won't do it anymore. I can't. Not now."

"What are you talking about? Sit down before you fall down."

Instead, Stone took another step forward. He had a good four inches of height on Langley and used it to his advantage, looming over the shorter man like some kind of bloody, avenging spirit. His eyes locked onto Langley's. "What you want doesn't matter, Tommy. Not a bit. Not anymore."

"Wait a minute—"

"Shut *up.*" He paused, getting his breath. The anger-fueled energy was still there, but it wouldn't last long. "You're going to listen to me now, Tommy. Not another word. Your aunt is in danger. This *house* is in danger. There's something here that needs dealing with, and I'm going to deal with it. Somehow. And you're bloody well not going to get in my way while I do it."

Langley stared at him. "You're *crazy,* Alastair. You're insane, and you've got my aunt scared to—"

"You think I'm a fake?" Stone growled, gritting his teeth again, his eyes blazing. "You think I'm a charlatan, and all of this is a sham?" He pointed his hand at Langley and, still not blinking, sent him reeling backward onto a large couch a few feet behind him.

Adelaide and Iona both yelped in surprise.

Stone ignored them, moving implacably forward until he towered over the terrified Langley again. "I'm not a fake, Tommy. I'm the real deal, and the danger here is real, too. I'm not going to let some hidebound mundane with no imagination drive me off. I plan to see to it that this lady and her home are safe, as long as it's in my power to do it. Do I make myself clear?" The last sentence came out like spaced bullets from a gun. He held up his hand, letting blue energy crackle around it. Lightning danced in the dim light.

Langley stared at it, transfixed. He shoved himself back on the couch, clearly trying to put as much space between himself and Stone as he could. "What—*are* you?" he whispered.

But before Stone could answer, Adelaide did. Her voice trembled, but her words were clear. "He's a friend, Tommy. He's a good man, and he's helping us. I know you don't believe, but I've *seen*. So has Iona."

Next to her, Iona nodded. She, too, was trembling.

Langley's gaze darted back and forth between Stone and his aunt, settling once again on the mage. "You—"

"She's right, Tommy." Stone was swaying now, the power going out of his voice. The lighting around his hand fizzled and died. His outburst spent, his energy was draining away like water, and his exhaustion was coming back and bringing friends. "This is—too big for you to stop now. Just—either help me, or get the hell out of my way." His legs buckled and he dropped, slumping across the other end of the couch from where Langley was cowering.

"Oh, God," Iona breathed. "Dr. Stone, let me call someone—"

He wasn't quite out, and he struggled to stay focused against the rising tide of grayness creeping inexorably across his brain. "No…Just—let me use your spare bedroom again. I'll be—all right—in a few hours." He wasn't even sure if he was actually speaking the words or just thinking them.

The last thing he remembered before the grayness finally won was Iona's stern voice ordering, "You heard him, Tommy—make yourself useful and take him to the bedroom."

| CHAPTER THIRTY-ONE

E than rested his head against the window in the BART train, looking out at the rain.

It was nine o'clock on Monday night. He wore a heavy parka, and his ubiquitous backpack rested on the seat next to him. On top of it was a slip of paper containing the directions Trina had given him for the club where they'd start the night. He'd already visited his mother today—she'd been a little more awake, so he told her that his magic studies were going well, and that he'd met a woman he liked and who liked him. She could do little more than smile at him and weakly squeeze his hand, but he could tell she was happy for him. He'd kissed her forehead and left with a feeling that if his mother approved, things must be okay.

His mind drifted back to his last night with Trina. It was doing that a lot lately. So much, in fact, that he'd started wearing baggier pants in addition to carrying his backpack to use for cover if need be. It was an occasionally embarrassing side effect, but he wouldn't have traded the experience for anything in the world.

He hadn't told her he was a virgin, but he suspected she'd known anyway. She didn't tease or laugh at him—she was incredible. That was all he could say. He couldn't even be jealous about the fact that she'd certainly done this many, many times before. All those times didn't matter now. She was doing it with *him*. And the twinkle in her eyes, the curve of her smile, the way her body responded to his told him that she liked it. She'd used her hands, her body, her mouth to drive him to levels of ecstasy that he didn't think it was possible for a human being to experience. She only let him have a little alcohol beforehand ("Don't want to dull your senses," she'd said with a grin) and afterward she lay stretched out naked next to him on the pillows, quite unselfconsciously, and shared a joint with him. They lay there for what seemed like hours, just listening to her odd, spooky music and watching the candles flicker. He didn't remember much about the trip home, because the theater of his mind insisted on playing back every detail over and over, so they would be seared indelibly into his consciousness forever. He didn't ever want to forget that night.

And now maybe tonight, after he helped them out with their ritual—maybe he and Trina could do it again.

He slumped a little against the window when he thought about the ritual. He didn't want to think too much about it, because it made him feel guilty. He'd even been defensive with Stone this afternoon, and he knew that was dangerous. Stone had seen something—he knew it. But how much? Ethan thought he might have managed to deflect some of Stone's suspicions by showing him how well he'd done with his levitation spell, but this was different. The other night had been a one-off—he hadn't expected to be doing anything more than watching the last ritual, and had been surprised and nervous when they'd pulled him into it. This time he was going to San Francisco to meet up with Trina and her friends for the express purpose of doing another ritual. And this time they actually needed his help with it.

He let his breath out. *I shouldn't do this. I should turn around and go home. He's going to find out. And if he does, he'll kick me out.*

But...

If he didn't go, then he wouldn't have a chance of another night—maybe many more nights—with Trina. His mind spun myriad exciting possibilities: perhaps she'd like him enough that she'd give up her other lovers and hook up with him exclusively. Maybe he'd even think about moving up to SF after Mom got better. Maybe he could move in with Trina. She had mentioned that they might have another spot open in their circle—

Really, why did he have to learn from Stone at all anymore?

The thought shocked him, in the way new thoughts that hadn't ever occurred to you before tended to do. He hadn't even ever considered that option.

Did he have to learn from Stone? He was a mage. He had the stuff; he'd proven that. He could learn from anybody. Sure, the original plan had been that he'd apprentice for Walter Yarborough in England, but Yarborough was an old family friend. A friend of his dad's. Who was Stone? A friend of Yarborough's, sure, but Ethan had no particular obligation to him. Did he even *want* to learn magic in Stone's old-school, rigorous, and discipline-heavy style? Trina and her friends were powerful, respected mages—and they had *fun* with their magic. They used it to help them, to get what they wanted, to revel in the power flowing through them and what it could do for them. For Stone, it seemed like some kind of—*responsibility.*

For Trina's friends, it was a tool. A game. A weapon, even.

Ethan wasn't quite ready to explore such a subversive line of thought. He realized he didn't have to, though. Not yet. If he could keep his extracurricular activities from Stone, then he might be able to live his "double life" long enough to figure out what he really wanted to do. If he could learn from both Stone *and* Trina's group, that would give him a leg up on his magical education. Trina already knew about Stone, and didn't care. If he could keep Stone from knowing about Trina, then—

He smiled. He could do this. And then he wouldn't have to give up his nights with Trina.

After what he'd experienced the other night, he was pretty sure if Stone ordered him to stop seeing her, he'd just tell him to go to hell and that would be the end of it.

The train clattered to a stop at his station, and he hefted his backpack and exited with several other people. He barely even noticed the pouring rain.

The club where Trina had told him to meet her was two blocks from the station. By the time he reached it, his whole body was damp and chilled, even through his parka. He paid the cover at the door, checked his coat and backpack, and headed in to look for her. Even then, after all this time, he still experienced a quick panic that she'd stood him up. Some old habits died hard, and some corner of the back of his mind still saw himself as the awkward geek that girls wanted nothing to do with.

But no, there she was, right where she said she'd be. There was a small knot of guys around her who appeared to be trying to get her attention, but when she saw Ethan she waved them off and motioned him over. "Hey," she said with her ubiquitous grin. "You look like something the cat dragged in." There was no malice or teasing in her words, though.

"It's a little damp out there," he admitted, sitting down.

She smiled. "We'll warm you up, don't worry."

"Where's Miguel?" he asked, looking around.

"He had some other guys—er—things to do for a while," she said, shrugging. "He'll be around for the ritual."

"How's Oliver? Still sick?"

"He's a little better, but still piled up under about nine blankets and bitching that he needs more Kleenex." She snorted. "Guys are such fucking babies when they're sick."

"It's because we like it when hot girls take care of us," Ethan said without thinking. It just sort of popped out; he followed it with a sheepish, apologetic grin.

She just laughed. "Yeah, ain't that the truth? But c'mon—do I look like Florence fucking Nightingale?" She waved at the bar and after a moment drinks appeared for both of them. She scooted her chair a little closer to his. "So," she said, "You ready for this?"

Ethan noticed that, whenever he was with Trina, nobody seemed to care that he was obviously underage. He picked up his drink and took a sip. "I'm ready," he said.

"No guilt about what Stone might think?"

He shook his head. "I don't care what he thinks. He won't find out anyway."

"That's the spirit!" she said, smiling and touching his arm. "You've already come so far, Ethan. It's kind of cool to watch. I hate seeing mages being slowed down by the old guys' stupid rules. Let them take it slow and easy. The power's there to grab—why not grab it and make it your bitch?"

They sat in silence for quite some time, sipping their drinks and listening to the pounding beat of the music. It was a small club and the band wasn't very good, but they were loud and the crowd seemed to appreciate them. Eventually Trina leaned back, stretching in a most alluring manner and looking Ethan up and down. "So, I want to show you something before the ritual tonight. Something that'll help you. You game?"

"Sure."

"Not even going to ask me what it is?"

"I don't care," he said with a grin.

Her eyes sparkled; she reached out and ran a hand gently down the side of his face, smiling when he shivered. "You know, Ethan, when I first met you I wasn't sure about you. But you're all right." She cocked her head toward the crowd. "Okay, so I'm going to go dance with a guy. Don't get jealous—it's part of what I want to show you. Just shift to magical senses and watch what I do, okay?"

He nodded, and she got up, heading out to the dance floor. It only took her a few seconds to cull a young man from the group, slipping her arms around his neck and leaning in close to him. Ethan fought down a wave of jealousy, but did as he was told, watching them closely with magical senses.

His eyes widened as some sort of energy began to swirl around them, focused around the man's head. It was almost like it was rising from him, glowing brighter than his dull yellow aura. Everybody had an aura, he knew: the more powerfully magical you were, the brighter it glowed unless you did something to hide it. Stone had showed him this during their lessons early on, and since then he often amused himself looking at them when he was bored. Most normal people's were fairly dull, only flaring brightly when they were agitated or emotionally charged. Colors varied all over the rainbow: Ethan's own aura glowed pale yellow, while Stone's, when he wasn't hiding it, was a brilliant purple tinged with gold. Trina's was a strong, clear red.

Right now, as Ethan watched, Trina's aura seemed to flow out and engulf the man's head and shoulders. He slumped into her, resting his head on her shoulder as they continued to dance, and she kissed the top of his head. After a few seconds, she gently pushed him away. He swayed on his feet for a moment, and then tottered off into the crowd. Ethan noticed that his dull yellow aura seemed even duller than before, while Trina's blazed correspondingly brighter. Her smile was electric as she returned to their table and sat down. "So? Did you see it?"

He stared at her. "What did you do?" For a moment, he almost forgot that this woman had the power to completely curdle his hormones with a smile.

"I just borrowed a little of his power. Nothing to worry about. He'll be tired for a couple of hours, but it'll come back. It's just like he did some exercise. He'll think he drank too much and partied too hard."

"And you—"

"I'll have a little extra something to use for the ritual," she told him. She leaned forward, pulling him in with one hand on the back of his head and kissing him, hard. Her other hand caressed his chest through his T-shirt.

"It's wonderful, Ethan," she murmured, pulling back a little. "It really is. You don't have to try it if you don't want to, but why not? I promise it doesn't hurt them, and they don't even need the power, don't even know they have it. Why let it go to waste?" She moved in for another kiss, her tongue probing insistently into his mouth.

Trembling, every nerve ending on fire, Ethan fought warring instincts. How could he have been so stupid? Stone had told him about black mages—how they stole power from others to fuel their work. How had he not realized that was what Trina was?

*But still...*said a little voice that was having a hard time getting past his rising physical excitement as Trina's hand on his chest worked its way slowly downward. *Is it really so bad? The guy's still fine. He's still dancing, even. She didn't hurt him.* "Mmm..." he began.

Trina withdrew her tongue just enough so he could speak. "Hmm?"

"You...you took energy from him, but it didn't hurt him."

"Nope," she agreed, her hand reaching for the waistband of his jeans. "He's just fine. And he'll feel completely normal in a couple of hours."

"You're a black mage." His voice held no accusation or judgment; he was merely stating a fact. Sort of like "You're a woman," or "You look amazing in that outfit."

"I don't like those distinctions," she said, dismissive. Under the table, her hand went lower until she gently grasped him and began a slow massage. "Those are for old people like Stone. Or did he tell you that black mages were *eeeeevil?*" She drew out the word, dripping with sarcasm. "That we eat kittens for breakfast and rape baby seals and want to take over the world?"

Damn, but it was hard to think with her hand probing his lap. He hoped she'd never stop. "No..." he said, sounding muddy and slurred. "He didn't say that."

"I'm surprised. What *did* he say?"

Ethan shrugged, but it turned into a squirm as her grip tightened just a little. Oh, God, it felt good. He was glad that the club was barely lit and the table was between them and the rest of the crowd. "He—he said it's about how it's powered. That...black mages can do good things, and white mages can do bad things."

"Really? He's more open-minded than I thought." She smiled. "But it doesn't matter. He's right, you know. It's not about morality. It's all about power, and whether you're willing to take it. It's about how far you're willing to go to get what you want." She tightened her grip again ever so slightly and grinned as he writhed under her touch. "You like that, Ethan? Does that feel good?"

"Oh, yeah..." he whispered.

She gave him one more stroke and then pulled back; he slumped back into his chair like he couldn't get up if he wanted to. "I'm glad..." she murmured. "More where that came from, later, after the ritual. I'd just skip it and we could go now, but I promised Miguel."

"Mmm, no, it's okay..." His voice was still slurred. "Oh, God, Trina...that felt so good..."

She stroked the side of his face. "You know, Ethan...my friends call me Trin. Now—you want to try my little trick?"

All he could do was nod.

| CHAPTER THIRTY-TWO

S tone stood in the middle of a long room lit by flickering candles in sconces. Dressed only in a thin, hooded robe, he shivered against the frigid cold as the red light at the far end disgorged creatures one after another. They marched toward him, inexorably; he tried to move, to run, but his bare feet were rooted to the floor. His brain struggled to remember the formula for a spell, but the knowledge skittered maddeningly away. The things grew closer, closer, reaching out their hideous long-clawed hands—

"Dr. Stone! Wake up!" An urgent voice cut into the creatures' gibbering advance. Stone gasped and opened his eyes.

Iona leaned over him, backlit in her quilted bathrobe, looking worried. She put her hand on his forehead. "Are you all right? You were having some sort of nightmare."

For a moment, he had no idea where he was. Then, through the vague haze of grayness, he remembered Tommy half-guiding, half-carrying him to the elevator and installing him in the same guest bedroom where he'd slept off the effects of the fatigue last time he'd been here.

"I-Iona?" he muttered. "What time is it?" He sat up, flinging off the covers, heedless of the pain in his ribs, and realized he was clad in nothing but his shorts. "Iona!" he protested, yanking the covers back up.

"Oh, don't be silly," she said, waving him off. "I needed to check you over for injuries and clean you up a bit. I'm a registered nurse, remember? You haven't got anything I haven't seen a thousand times before. Now—are you all right? How do you feel?"

Stone took inventory. His headache was gone, as was the grayness. The fatigue was still there, but at a fraction of its former intensity. All that was left was the pain in his ribs. "Not—bad, all things considered," he said. "What time is it?"

"About two-thirty. Adelaide's gone to bed, and Tommy went home. He wants to talk to you when you're feeling better, though. He said he'd call you later today."

"Great," he muttered. *Just what I need—another round with Tommy.* Realizing that Iona was right about his misplaced prudishness, he pushed aside the covers again and sat up. "Where are my clothes? I need to be getting home."

"You won't leave this late, will you? You're welcome to spend the night and leave in the morning if you like."

"No, I really need to get home. I'll come back tomorrow." His mind went over the events of the evening, checking to make sure he hadn't overlooked anything. "I'll want to take another look at what I did to make sure it really is as safe as it's likely to get, and I also want to look in the attic."

"Of course," she said. She pointed over to a chair next to the bed. "Your clothes are there. But are you sure you won't reconsider? You were in pretty bad shape. The blood—"

He shook his head. "It's nothing serious. Looks worse than it is. It happens when I overdo it, sometimes. Seriously, it was mostly just exhaustion, and most of that's gone. I still have a lot to do, and I need to pick up some things from home before I do it." He got up and began pulling on his jeans, T-shirt, and sweater.

Iona didn't watch him dress, but she obviously had something on her mind. "Dr. Stone…"

"Yes?"

She looked at him, silent for a long moment. Finally, she said, "What—what's really going on? What is it that you do? What did you do down there, and how do you know it's going to work?"

He took a deep breath. "It isn't going to work for very long. What I did amounts to nailing plywood over an open doorway to keep a tiger out. It's going to get through eventually—I can only hope that the plywood holds it off long enough to come up with a more permanent solution."

"And this—tiger—what is it?"

He sat back down on the edge of the bed and pulled on his socks and shoes. "Iona, I'm not sure you really want to know."

"It's something horrible, isn't it?"

He nodded. "Yes."

"And—how did it get down there in the first place?"

"It's a long story. I'll tell you, but not now. After this whole thing is over, I'll tell you. But I really think that you and Adelaide should consider going somewhere else for a while after your event is over. I'm not at all comfortable with your even letting it go on, but I understand the impact if you cancel it, and I think I've held off the problem long enough that things should be fine."

She pondered that for a few moments. "Why are you doing this?"

"Hmm?" He finished tying his shoes and stood. "Have you got my coat, by the way?"

"It's out front. I'll get it before you leave. But I really want to know: why are you doing this? It's obviously dangerous for you— you've already been injured trying to fight whatever it is down there. You barely know us. Why would you put yourself at risk?"

He gave her an odd smile. "Honestly, Iona, I don't know. I'm never been particularly chivalrous, so the 'save the damsel in distress' thing doesn't tend to work on me. P'raps it's just that I like puzzles, and this is quite an intriguing one. Well, that, and I've grown fond of you and Adelaide. I don't want to see you hurt. You didn't do anything to deserve this—you're just in the wrong place at the wrong time."

She nodded slowly. "Well, I'm glad you're here, for whatever reason."

He tipped an imaginary hat to her and headed for the door, but stopped before he reached it. "Ah, that reminds me—when you get a chance, please talk to Adelaide. I'll be needing an invitation to the event. I want to be there to keep an eye on things, just in case our basement-dwelling beastie gets up to more mischief than expected. Besides, it'll give me an excuse to get my tuxedo cleaned."

| CHAPTER THIRTY-THREE

E than was pretty sure that if he felt any better than he did right now, he'd have to check and make sure he hadn't died and gone to his own personal vision of Heaven.

It was very late. He lay next to Trina (*Trin,* he reminded himself) in her bed. Both of them were naked and spent; Trin had spent the last hour showing him several different ways she knew to blow his mind and thoroughly pickle his hormones. The only reason they were taking a break now was because after two times, he'd been unable to rouse himself for a third without a pause to recharge. She dozed now, her arm draped possessively across his chest.

He went over the last several hours. The evening had been quite an education—far more, his traitorous brain acknowledged, than almost anything Alastair Stone had taught him as of yet. He had broad new horizons to explore, and many decisions he'd have to make.

He had tried Trin's trick of siphoning energy from another person, and it had been amazing. He chose a girl and asked her to dance, then did his best to duplicate what Trin had done with the man. She'd given him some pointers beforehand, warning him to be careful and not to take too much, no matter how good it felt. "We don't want to kill anybody," she warned. "And we don't want people to get suspicious. Just take a little from each person, so they feel tired. There's no way they can trace that back to us."

And so he did. His arms around the girl, he'd reached out with his magical senses and engulfed her aura with his own, feeling her life energy flowing into him. He stopped probably too soon, worried that he would hurt her, and she'd just sagged a little in his arms, giggling about having drunk too much. Ethan, meanwhile, felt like his nerve endings were on fire—a good kind of fire that burned away any dullness or pain or uncertainty. He'd felt *alive* with power.

When he'd returned to Trin's table, she was grinning at him. "Way to go!" she said, stroking his arm. "Very nice for a first time! You could have taken a bit more, but better to go easy while you get a feel for it."

"That was *incredible*," he agreed. "And we can power our spells that way? We don't have to get tired?" He remembered his first few attempts at levitating the coin, where he'd felt like he'd run a marathon at the end. Was that how Stone and other white mages like him did magic? It seemed so limited. Even with the power objects, you still had to use your own power to infuse them. It made you vulnerable.

Ethan was tired of being vulnerable.

"That's right," she said. "Why waste our own energy when there's so much out there just ripe and ready for the taking? Like I said, they'll never miss it."

They each repeated the performance twice more before they left the club for The Three's ritual space. It wasn't far from the club, so they walked. "What are we doing tonight?" Ethan asked. "What's this ritual about?"

"It's just something we've been working on, to gather detailed information about a subject. It's really Miguel's thing—he loves all that research shit, mostly because it helps him stalk all his slutty boyfriends—but sometimes it's useful to know things about people. If you know things, you can use them. Remember that."

He nodded. She leaned in and kissed him, giving him a taste of what was to come later.

The ritual, aided by the power he'd claimed from the other clubgoers, had been a tremendous rush. Miguel had been waiting for them, and already had the circle halfway set up and ready. Trin helped him finish it, and then the two of them had given Ethan instructions on what they wanted him to do. Mostly it was like the other night: help hold the pattern steady and feed power into the circle, but they taught him the incantation they would be using and told him he would be joining in. "Just watch how we set it up," Trin told him, squeezing his arm encouragingly. "You'll see where there's a break in the pattern that we leave for you. Just weave yourself in. It'll be more obvious when you see it."

She was right, it had. He had little trouble doing what he was asked to do, and the extra power he was wielding sang through his body like a drug. Rather than feeling spent and nauseated when at last they unclasped their hands, he felt like he could go out and run around the block a couple of times.

He stared at Trin. "I didn't know it could be like this," he breathed.

"Old Stone was holding out on you," Miguel teased. "He didn't tell you how awesome it is, did he?"

"He—said it was a rush. But a dangerous one. Addictive."

Trin laughed. "Only addictive if you care about doing weak versions of magic. Otherwise, it's the only way to go."

Miguel had left shortly after that, and Trin had set about taking Ethan on a journey he would never forget. He shifted a little under her arm now, letting out a long sigh of utter contentment.

She roused from her light doze. "Ready to go again?"

"Not quite yet," he said. "Soon."

"Ah, youth." She stroked his chest. "So much energy." Rolling over on her back, she put her hands up behind her head, seemingly oblivious to the show she was putting on. "Ethan, can I ask you something?"

"Anything."

"What are you going to do about Stone?"

"What do you mean, what am I going to do about him?"

She shrugged. "I saw the way you were tonight. It was like you were born for this. I'll have to talk it over with Miguel and Oliver when he's feeling better, but I'm pretty sure we do have a spot for you in our circle, if you want it."

He stared at her. "Really?"

"Yeah. We might not be classically trained mages or any-thing—" Her voice clearly demonstrated her contempt for the concept. "—but we've got a good thing going here, and having an-other mage in our group will make us even stronger, so we can do bigger stuff. Plus," she added, rolling on her side and letting her hand trail down his chest and abdomen and disappear beneath the covers, "that way I can keep you around more."

He shivered at her touch. "I'd like that," he said. He paused. "But the thing is, with my mother sick—I can't really leave her."

"You wouldn't have to leave her," Trin said. "We only do ritu-als a couple of nights a week, unless we've got something special going on. You could come up for those, and sometimes I could come down there. You could show me the South Bay. Maybe even introduce me to Mom."

He nodded, not allowing his mind to engage in any further speculation. This was already better than he'd dared to hope. "I was thinking—" he said.

"Yes?" Her hand continued its wanderings, and she took hold of his with her other one and encouraged it to do some wanderings of its own.

"Well—I thought maybe I could keep things up with Dr. Stone for a while, too. You know—not tell him about this yet."

Her smile was sly. "You want to keep learning from him and us, too. You're devious, Ethan. I like that."

"Well, you did say knowledge is good."

"It is. And more is better."

"He won't be able to tell, will he?" Ethan suddenly looked nervous. "I mean, by just looking at me with magical sight? He can't see that I've been doing—"

She shook her head. "As long as you don't do anything 'dark' around him, he won't be able to tell. At least not for a while. Don't *worry,* Ethan," she teased. "Everything's gonna be fine."

He nodded, his smile a little goofy. "Yeah, it is."

"Hey, listen," she said, gently stroking him in an effort to get things going again, "You know, if you're going to stick with Stone for a while, maybe you can help us out, too, if you wanted to."

"Yeah?"

She nodded. "I don't know if you remember the other night— you were pretty drunk—but I was asking you some questions about that old house in Los Gatos that Stone was interested in."

"Yeah, I remember that. Some old lady, and there's something going on in her house."

"Do you know anything else about it?"

"Like what?" He shivered, feeling himself begin to stir again.

"I don't know. I'm just kind of interested in it, and I was hoping you might know some more."

"Not really. I went with him that first night we looked around, but I haven't been back since."

She nodded. "Do you think you could—" her hand moved expertly "—find out a little more?"

He shivered again, looking confused. "You want to know about the house?"

"I want to know what Stone knows about it," she said. "Can you get him to tell you? From everything I've heard about him, if you get him into lecture mode he'll talk your ear off about whatever he's got a hard-on about at the time. Just see if you can get him talking, then come back and tell me what he says."

She smiled as her efforts down below the covers began to bear fruit. "Mmm, speaking of hard-ons, there we go. Do you think you could do that for me, Ethan? And don't let on about why you want to know, of course."

He nodded, not trusting himself to speak. "Yeah," he grunted. "Yeah, I can do that."

"You're fantastic, Ethan," she said, green eyes twinkling invitingly as she moved in for round three.

| CHAPTER THIRTY-FOUR

Stone got home around four a.m. and was pleased to see that there weren't any messages on his answering machine. That probably meant that Megan had been busy and hadn't tried to call him, which meant he didn't have to explain to her what he'd been doing out all night. He fell onto his bed without bothering to take off anything but his shoes and slept nightmare-free until around eight.

He thought about not going up to campus, but this was the last week before the Christmas break, and he remembered that his Occult in Europe and America final was today. Maybe he'd see about finding Tommy and figuring out where they stood, then head back up to Adelaide's house after lunch. He wanted to verify that the reinforcements he'd put up around the demon's prison were holding and would likely continue to do so; if they were solid, he planned to spend some time examining the books in the ritual room, and then head upstairs to tackle the attic.

Mrs. Olivera was due to come in today and clean the place; he plunged deep into his walk-in closet and found his tuxedo, which he took downstairs and left her a note asking her to take to be dry-cleaned. He hadn't worn it in at least a year—not since he'd attended another charity shindig for the University in the company of his girlfriend at the time. At least he didn't have to worry that it wouldn't fit: he'd always been one of those types that couldn't gain weight if he tried. Right now he was glad about that, since his usual form of exercise, long-distance running up at the Stanford campus, was pretty much out of the question until his ribs healed fully. With just a hint of vanity, he regretted that he wasn't planning to invite Megan to accompany him to the ball, for her own safety in case anything went wrong. More than one former girlfriend had told him he looked quite dashing in formal dress. Ah, well—he wasn't going to be there to enjoy the festivities anyway.

The final went well; all he had to do was sit at the front of the room and read the paper with his feet up on the desk while the students toiled away on his rigorous essay questions. When the last student dropped her paper on his desk and left, he headed back up to his office and found a message: Tommy Langley wanted to see him, if he had time. He'd be in his office until noon.

Sighing, Stone set off toward the other side of campus. The weather was drizzly and overcast, not quite willing to commit to rain in earnest, but not ruling it out either. He pulled up his overcoat collar and made sure his simple shield spell was in place. He doubted anyone would try jumping him in broad daylight, but he wasn't taking chances.

He saw the light through the open door of Langley's office before he got there, then paused in the doorway a moment. Unlike Stone's office, which looked like he bought all his decorations at "Creepy Shit R Us," Langley's was full of old Stanford sports memorabilia, piles of history books, and a large neon sign from one of the local craft breweries.

Langley himself was sitting behind his desk, going through a stack of what looked like essays. "Tommy," Stone said softly in greeting.

Langley looked up, startled. "Hey. Uh—you look a lot better today."

He nodded. "May I come in?"

"Uh—Yeah, sure. Just toss that stuff on the other chair. It's not important." There was an odd edge in Langley's voice, almost like nervousness. Or fear.

Stone closed the door behind him, then shifted a pile of papers to the second guest chair and sat down. For a moment he watched Langley without speaking.

Langley shifted nervously in his chair. "Alastair, I—" He blew his breath out. "I don't even know where to start. I don't know what to say to you."

"You're afraid I'm going to send you flying across the room again. Or worse."

"What the hell *are* you?" Langley blurted, unable to conceal his fear. "I thought you were just a guy who taught a quack subject about spooks and things that go bump in the night. But—"

"But," Stone said softly without moving, "things really *do* go bump in the night, sometimes."

"How did you do that, last night? How did you make me—"

Stone dropped his gaze into his lap. *Here goes.* "I wasn't kidding about being the real thing."

"The real—*what,* though?"

"Magic is real, Tommy. And I'm a mage."

Langley stared at him. He didn't blink. Then he shook his head back and forth, raising his hands in a defiant denial. "No way. I'm sorry, Alastair, but that's bullshit. There isn't any such thing as magic, or mages, or witches, or ghosts, or any of that fairy-tale shit. I don't know what I saw last night, but—"

Stone was watching him closely, though, and he could already see Langley's resolve was cracking. He was saying the words, but he didn't believe them. "You saw what you saw, Tommy. Watch." He raised his hand, and several items from Langley's desk rose up, flew around the office, and settled back into their places.

Langley didn't quite scream, but he did shove his chair rapidly away until he smacked it into the rear wall of his small office. "Holy *crap!* What the *fuck?*"

"I didn't want to tell you. It's not something I spread around. But what's going on is bigger than what I want now. It's bigger than what you want. That thing in your aunt's house is real, and it's dangerous. It has to be dealt with. I was serious when I said I don't have the time or the energy to indulge your skepticism now. This is too important. I have to make you see."

Stone almost felt sorry for Langley: watching him, he saw a man who was being forced to come to terms far too quickly with the idea that several fundamental tenets on which he'd based his life were wrong. That couldn't be easy for anyone. Under normal circumstances he'd have been more understanding, tried to help Langley accept the truth slowly. But these weren't normal circumstances, and there was no time for gentleness. "Here's the bottom line, Tommy: you don't have to get involved. You don't have to help. You don't even have to believe. All you have to do is stay out of my way. I'm sorry I had to break my promise to you not to go to Adelaide's house again, but *she* called *me*."

Langley nodded, not looking at him. "I know. She told me, after—after you passed out last night. And Iona chewed me out good." His eyes came up. "Listen, Alastair: I'm sorry that I—"

Stone waved him off. "Don't worry about it. No apology needed. I just need you to know—and I know you're not going to like this, but that isn't relevant at the moment—that you aren't going to stop me. I'll do whatever I need to do to get this sorted."

For a very long time, Langley said nothing. He stared down at the mess on his desk, shuffled a few papers around and squared them up into a stack, and rearranged several pens into a line. Then, without looking up, he said in a barely audible voice, "I want to help."

Stone wasn't sure he'd heard him correctly. "What?"

Langley looked up, meeting Stone's gaze. "I said, I want to help."

"Tommy—"

"Look," he said, his voice laced with stubbornness. "She's my aunt. She's family. I love her. If she's in trouble and there's something that can be done about it, I want to be involved."

Stone closed his eyes for a moment. "You can't, Tommy," he said softly. "There's nothing you can do. Dealing with this takes abilities you just don't have."

"No." Langley shook his head. "There *are* things I can do. If nothing else, I can lug jars of Eye of Newt or whatever around for you, so you can make with the hocus-pocus." He let his breath out. "I don't want to believe any of this. I really don't. Magic is—it's for kids' stories. It's not something *real*. But if Aunt Adelaide and Iona are in trouble, and I have to believe in magic in order to help them deal with it, then make with the fairy dust and let's get to it."

Stone stared at him, making no attempt to hide his amazement and respect for Langley. This kind of thing simply didn't happen, in his experience. Usually, on the rare occasions where a mage had to reveal him- or herself to a mundane in times of emergency, the mundane either shut down completely and refused to acknowledge that anything was happening, or ran out of the room and found excuses to avoid the mage—usually permanently. Stone had seen more than his share of friendships end over most mundanes' inability to accept what was going on right under their noses. "Tommy—"

"No. No more chit-chat. There's stuff to be done. Just tell me what you want me to do, and I'll do it. Once we get through this, then maybe we can talk more. Right now, if I keep talking I'm gonna run outta this room and straight to the guys in the white coats." He squared his shoulders and stood up. "So what's the plan, Mandrake?"

Stone had to smile at that. "Sit down, Tommy. And if you've got a tuxedo, make sure it's clean and you can still button it over that vast gut of yours. You're coming to the ball."

Langley grinned, even though his eyes were still fearful. "Aww, Al. I thought you'd never ask. But you'd better bring me a nice corsage. Green, to match my eyes. And I'm warning you now—I never put out on the first date."

Stone was still amazed when he thought about it later that afternoon. He was back at Adelaide's house, pleased to see that she'd taken his advice and hired some security people. They prowled around the house in official-looking jackets and sunglasses (the rain had finally stopped for now, bringing with it a rare and welcome sunny day) and even stopped him and checked his ID before letting him past.

His plan was to spend the first part of the afternoon in the ritual room in the basement, double-checking his reinforcement of the demon's prison and adding to it if necessary, and going through the stack of books and papers in the vain hope that somebody might have written down its true name somewhere. Honestly he didn't expect to find that, but his fingers itched to open the tomes and explore the mysteries inside. He was already formulating a plan to ask Adelaide if he could buy the collection from her once all this unpleasantness had been dealt with. He suspected she'd let him have it cheap, if she charged him at all, but he didn't care what she asked—he would pay it. As far as he was concerned, these books were priceless.

He was thinking about Tommy when he pushed aside the bookcase and entered the room. The man had frankly astonished him. From hidebound mundane to willing (albeit reluctant) assistant in such a short time—that showed the kind of mental fortitude that Stone didn't often see. Although, he acknowledged, Adelaide had it, too. Maybe it ran in the family. He just hoped it didn't end up getting Tommy killed.

The armoire looked as he'd left it; shifting to magical sight, he saw that the additional bonds he'd added were holding. Nothing was showing any signs of fraying. He decided he'd come back every day until Saturday, or at least as often as he could manage it, to ensure that was still true. He knew the hard work wasn't going to start until after the charity ball, but he could worry about that later.

His only concern right now was that the event went off without turning into a massacre.

He sighed, setting up the lamp he'd brought along with his flashlight and switching it on. He knew he shouldn't be allowing this. He should have told Adelaide to just cancel the ball. Okay, it would mean losing a big pile of money for the orphans and the homeless, but was that worse than a houseful of dead people if that thing got out and ran amok?

He had no illusions about his abilities, nor any false modesty. He was good. Damned good, in fact. One of the best, when he was in top form. But he wasn't in top form now—nowhere close. Even if he were uninjured, he was out of practice. And even then, his best would be barely more than a fly trying to stop a freight train if that thing got loose. If he had its name, he might—*might*—have a chance of sending it back. Without it—well, he just had to hope that the plywood he'd put up would be sufficient to hold off the tiger.

He gathered up the books and piled them on the table along with the stacks of papers. He'd just glance through them at first to figure out if any of them jumped out at him, and then—

—The dull pain in his ribs finally made itself sufficiently annoying that Stone looked up from his studies. Startled, he realized that the lamp's light was dimming as its battery died. *Bugger. Lost track of time.* He glanced at his watch: it was already eight o'clock. He'd gotten here at three.

Stretching, he heard several things pop, and his ribs twinged again. His shoulders ached from hunching over tomes filled with faded and hard to read text. He'd managed to get through quite a few of the books by skimming their contents, though he wanted nothing more than to dive back in and read them in depth. They covered several esoteric aspects of summoning, including several that were uncomfortably dark in their origins. As far as he could tell, though, there was nothing about this particular demon, and certainly nothing that might be a clue as to its name. The papers, which had been apparently written by Selena Darklight, showed ritual diagrams, incantations, and notes on things she planned to work on in the future, but once again no names. Had she even written it down at all? Perhaps she'd thought it was too dangerous to do more than just hold it in her own head.

He ran a hand through his hair and stood up. He'd planned on heading up to the attic tonight, but he was tired and sore and very hungry. A quick glance at the demon's prison revealed that nothing had changed. *I'll just come back tomorrow,* he decided. *Do the attic then. Maybe I can even bring Ethan up here to help me search, if he's free.*

That decided, he packed up his gear and left. Behind him, the eerie light behind the armoire's skewed doors shifted a bit, following his progress until the door closed behind him.

| CHAPTER THIRTY-FIVE

Stone more than half-expected Ethan to come up with an excuse for not showing up for his lesson Wednesday afternoon, and was surprised when the blue car pulled into his driveway promptly at three o'clock. "I take it your mum's doing all right," he said when the boy came in.

"She's stable," Ethan said. "Still bad, but at least she's not getting any worse for the moment."

Stone nodded. "Any luck with the circle yet?"

"I didn't get a chance to try it yet. Yesterday I spent most of the day at the hospital. I was planning on working on it this weekend, if that's okay."

"That's fine. Actually—come up to my study. I want to talk to you about something."

Ethan looked nervous, but followed. He sat down on the couch and tossed his backpack down next to him. "About what?"

"I'd like your help, if you have the time."

"My help? With what?"

"You remember old Adelaide Bonham and her house in Los Gatos, right?"

"Yeah, sure."

"Well, I'm still dealing with some trouble down there, and I'm running out of time. She's having a big charity ball this Saturday night and I'd like to get some things done before then. Unfortunately what I want to do involves poking around in an enormous dusty attic looking for some bits of information. It'll go a lot faster if I can get your help. If your mum can spare you, of course."

"Uh—yeah, sure, I can do that. When, though?"

"How about tomorrow afternoon? We'll head up there around this time and with any luck we can find something useful. I'd also like you to attend the ball itself if you can. Having an assistant with magical ability will be invaluable, even if all you do is keep watch with your magical senses. Do you think you might be able to do that?"

Ethan nodded. "Sure. Would I need a suit or something?"

"Rent a tuxedo, and send me the bill."

"Okay." Ethan paused. "Dr. Stone—what's going on down there? Did you ever find out?"

"Yes. There's some sort of nasty spirit, or demon, or whatever you want to call it, imprisoned in the house's basement. How it got there is a long story—I'll tell you tomorrow, when I show you where it is. It'll be easier to understand with context."

"And the stuff you're looking for is related to dealing with it? How does that work?"

"Quite likely it doesn't. I found some books and papers in the basement, but they don't seem to be related to what's imprisoned there. I'm hoping we might find more in the attic, p'raps packed away in a trunk or an old bookcase or something. What I really want to find is the spirit's true name, but I doubt anyone wrote that down."

"Its true name?"

Stone nodded. "That's the best way to deal with spirits—sometimes the *only* way. If you know a spirit's true name, you have a lot of power over it. You can imprison it, enslave it, or send it back to where it came from. You hope, anyway. There's still the matter of pitting your power and will against its—they don't exactly want to go along with what you have planned, and they'll fight you every step of the way. In this case, all I'm hoping to do is send the bit of it that's in our dimension back home with the rest of it, and close the opening between the two." He raised an eyebrow. "That's *all*. I make it sound like that will be easy. It won't. But at least we won't have to deal with the whole thing."

"So—only part of it is here?"

"Yes, or we wouldn't have a prayer of doing this. The people who imprisoned it did a good job, but their efforts are slipping after all these years. The prison is failing, and some of it is bleeding through."

Ethan nodded, taking it all in. "I'll do what I can to help," he said. "I—"

Downstairs, the doorbell rang. "Excuse me a moment," Stone said, and headed out of the room.

It was Megan. "Hey," she said. "I was in the area, so I thought I'd stop by and see if you wanted to do something tonight." She glanced past him. "Oh, I didn't realize you had company."

Stone turned around. Ethan had drifted out of the room and stood at the top of the stairs, watching them. "It's just Ethan." To the boy, he said, "I really don't have that much more prepared for you today, Ethan, if you want to take off early. Come back tomorrow and we'll go down to Adelaide's. And don't forget to see to that tuxedo."

Ethan nodded, coming down the stairs. "What time do you want me there on Saturday? What time does the ball start?"

"I think it starts at seven; be there at six so we can decide on our plans."

"You got it." He nodded goodbye to Megan, waved at Stone, and headed out the door.

She closed it behind her. "Ball? What ball?"

"Just a little thing Adelaide's having down at her house on Saturday night," Stone said, trying to sound like it was the most uninteresting thing in the world.

"Are you going to a party? And you didn't ask me to go with you?" Megan didn't look angry, but she did look a little hurt.

"I'm not going to have fun, Megan. I'm going to work. This is part of what I'm doing to help Adelaide with her house problem. Ethan's going to be assisting me."

"Still," she said, reaching out to stroke his jawline. "I heard you say 'tuxedo.' Are you going to be wearing a tuxedo?"

Stone could see there was no easy way to get out of this. "Yes. I'm going to be wearing a tuxedo."

"I've never seen you in a tuxedo. I want to." She grinned. "Between the accent and the tux, you'll be irresistible. Besides, it'll give me an excuse to break out the sexy black dress I bought a couple of months ago and haven't had a chance to wear yet. And even better, for one time since we met I might actually be able to see the front of your hair laying down like a normal person's." She reached out and ruffled it, making it worse. "So—am I coming with you to the ball, or are things going to get ugly? And by *things,* I mean a certain Dr. Stone's love life?" Her eyes twinkled to take the sting from her words. "Seriously, Alastair, is there any reason we can't go together?"

"I suppose not," he said, still reluctant. "Though I won't have a lot of time for dancing and whatnot. As I said, I'll actually be working. Keeping an eye on things."

"In case the ghost or whatever it is decides to disrupt the party?"

"Something like that, yes."

"I'll watch out for ghosts," she promised. "And I'm sure I can find *somebody* to dance with if you're not around. Tommy Langley, maybe. Now—how about you let me treat you to dinner for a change? You need a break. You can go back to ghostbusting tomorrow. Fair enough?"

"Fair enough," he agreed.

He tried to forget about the horror in Adelaide's basement and focus on enjoying a pleasant evening with Megan. They had dinner at a new restaurant in Saratoga, then went to see a movie that both of them had expressed interest in and hadn't gotten around to yet.

They ended up back at Stone's place a little after eleven, and shortly after midnight they were both asleep, snuggled close together under the covers.

❖

"...*I'm going to kill you...*" said a voice in the darkness.

Stone stirred, opened his eyes. He was still where he thought he was, Megan's cheek warm against his bare chest, his arm draped protectively over her back. He listened for a moment, then shook his head. He must have imagined it. Or maybe it was the wind. He glanced at the clock on the nightstand: 1:42 a.m.

Megan muttered something and snuggled closer to him, and he settled back.

"...*I'm going to kill you, and everyone you ever cared about. As soon as I am free, I will rip their entrails from their bodies...*"

His eyes flew open again. He sat up a little, looking around, then shifted to magical sight. Nothing was out of the ordinary on either the mundane or the magical plane. "Who's there?" he whispered, not wanting to wake Megan.

"...*I will flay your skin from your body, and boil your eyeballs until they pop. You will beg for death...*"

Stone looked around, trying to identify the source of the voice. At first he saw nothing, but then a faint light caught the corner of his eye. He turned.

There was a crack in the door to his walk-in closet. A thin line of unhealthy-looking greenish light shone from it, creeping out into the room.

And the line was getting thicker.

Stone sat up the rest of the way, carefully moving Megan's arm. She murmured something, rolled over, and began to snore softly.

The greenish light crept inexorably closer, but that wasn't the only thing going on in the room. As he watched, horrified, the dresser drawers slid open one by one and glutinous tendrils oozed from them, flailing as they reached toward the floor.

The bed began to shake. For a moment Stone thought they were having another earthquake, but the other furniture wasn't moving. The bed rocked back and forth, then bucked a few inches forward. Next to him Megan slept on, oblivious. Soft, mocking laughter echoed through the room.

Once again shifting to magical sight, Stone nearly cried out in surprise as the entire room lit up with magically active energy. The ooze coming from the dresser glowed with a reddish aura, and the entire floor under the bed flared a sickly, radioactive green. Something wet and dark trickled down the walls on all four sides, puddling on the floor and creeping toward the bed.

They had to get out of here! He prodded Megan's shoulder, but she just mumbled something about it not being a school day and shoved him away. "Megan! You have to get up!" he urged.

Something dropped onto his head.

That time he did cry out, reaching up to claw at it with both hands. It was soft and yielding, and everywhere it touched, it left burning trails behind it. "Megan!" he yelled. *"Wake up!"*

The bedroom door flew open with such force that it slammed into the wall behind it. Stone, kneeling on the bed and still flailing at whatever was on his head, stared in horror.

The creatures from Adelaide's basement ritual room had found him. They were flowing through the door, shambling one after the other, their wicked sloth claws reaching for him. He tried to gather the energy to throw a spell, but the oozing thing on his head dropped down over his eyes, probing its ropy tendrils into his nose, his mouth, his ears—

He tried to scream and a tentacle plunged down his throat. Another one reached down further and wrapped around his neck, and a third gripped his shoulders, shaking him—

"Alastair! Wake up! Oh, God, please, you have to wake up!"

He snapped awake. For a moment he had no idea where he was, where the creatures had gone or even why he was still alive. The room lights were on. There were no creatures, no ichor, nothing dripping down the walls. He was kneeling in the middle of the bed, drenched in sweat, his arms up as if trying to ward something off.

Megan knelt in front of him, her eyes wild with terror, her hands gripping his shoulders. "Alastair? What are you doing?" she demanded. Her voice pitched high and bright, radiating fear.

For a moment he just stayed there like that, his breathing coming so hard and fast that his ribs shrieked in protest. "Megan—"

"It's okay. It's okay. You're all right. It was just—some kind of bad dream." Her voice shook; he could hear her trying hard not to sob.

She reached out, trying to pull him into a hug, but the memory of the slimy thing shoving a tentacle down his throat caused his gorge to rise and he knew he was going to be sick. He shoved her away and dashed for the bathroom, barely making it in time. When he finished he just slumped over the bowl, shaking, shoulders heaving, deciding that maybe death might not be such a horrible thing after all, compared to this.

And then Megan was there kneeling next to him, putting a gentle arm around him. "You okay?" she asked softly.

"Don't—don't touch me, Megan," he muttered, miserable. "'M disgusting." He reached up without raising his head and flopped his hand around until he found the flusher.

"Oh, I've seen a lot worse in college," she assured him, brushing his hair back from where it was plastered to his forehead. "Let me get you a glass of water."

She got up long enough to get him one, then dropped back down next to him. "Come on, honey, drink this. It'll make you feel better." Putting her arm back around him, she tried again to pull him into a comforting embrace.

This time he let her. He took the glass and drank down the water. "Thank you..." he whispered, lowering his head until his face was buried in her shoulder. They sat there on the floor like that for a long time, and Megan held him and stroked his back until he stopped shaking. When he at last looked up at her, a little color had come back into his face.

"What—*was* that?" she asked, clearly afraid that even asking might set him off again. "A nightmare? I've never seen one so bad. I've never seen you even have one before."

He shook his head. "It was—a nightmare, yes. But—I think there was more to it than that."

"More to it?"

He nodded. "I—had a similar one the other night, at Adelaide's place. Not as bad, though." He sighed and dragged himself slowly up to his feet. "Let me take a shower, Megan. I feel ghastly."

She looked uncertain. "We're not in any kind of danger, are we?"

"No." *Not yet.* "Go on—get back in bed. No need for you to be cold. I'll be in shortly."

It was obvious she didn't want to go, but she took one last look at him, nodded, and left the bathroom.

Stone stood for a moment gripping the sink, staring at his sunken-eyed, corpse-pale reflection in the mirror. What the hell was that thing *doing?* How could it reach out to him from such a distance? If it could do that, then it had to be even more powerful than he'd feared.

He met his reflection's eyes. Standing there at nearly two in the morning, bruised and sweating and tired in both his mind and his body, he wondered how he ever thought he was going to be able to fight this thing.

I don't really have a choice, though, do I? If I don't do it, who will?

He pushed off the sink and turned on the shower. He didn't have an answer for that question. He might be able to call in some other mages—doubtful on such short notice, even with the portals—but so few of them nowadays were equipped to deal with these kinds of threats. There were still a fair number in this country, in England, in Europe, but most of them never pursued the Art this far anymore. It just took too much effort, too much time to really get good at it, and most of them would never even come near the kinds of threats that required Stone's level of magical ability to combat. Most of them contented themselves with learning a few techniques, enough to make their lives easier, and let it go at that. He'd be sending them to their deaths if he asked them to fight something like this with no preparation. "You're a dinosaur," he told his reflection, then got into the shower.

Megan was waiting for him when he came out, towel wrapped around his waist and damp hair sticking up in all directions. "Better?" she asked.

"Much." He noticed that she must have gone downstairs, because there was the most beautiful bottle of Scotch in the world sitting on the nightstand. "Ah, Megan, you *are* brilliant."

"Thought you might like that." She poured him a glass and handed it over.

He drank it down, reveling in the feeling of the burning liquid as it warmed him all the way down. "Just what the doctor ordered," he said with a satisfied sigh, crawling back into bed and tossing the towel on the floor. He turned to her and gave her a tired smile. "Thank you, Megan. For everything."

She tousled his hair. "Now you have to take me to that party, you know. You owe me one for tonight. Just because you don't have long hair to hold doesn't mean it's not the same idea."

He nodded, realizing that it didn't matter anyway. He wasn't keeping her safe by refusing to take her to the ball. If that thing in Adelaide's basement got out, she wouldn't be safe wherever she was. What had it said? *"I'll kill everyone you ever cared about."* Better to keep her close by, where he could keep an eye on her. "I'd be honored. You might even convince me to dance."

"Let's not go *too* far," she said, reaching over to shut off the light. "You sure you're going to be okay?"

"I'll be fine." He leaned over and kissed her. "Go back to sleep. I promise not to scare you again."

"See that you don't," she murmured, moving over to snuggle close to him. He stroked her hair gently until she dropped off to sleep a few minutes later.

He himself lay awake for the remainder of the night.

| CHAPTER THIRTY-SIX

S tone picked up Ethan in San Jose on Thursday afternoon. He only had one final to administer that day, so they got an early start. They boy climbed into the Jaguar's front seat and tossed his ubiquitous backpack in the back.

"So, ghost hunting again," he said as Stone drove off.

"Nothing so exciting, I'm afraid," he said. "Mostly information hunting today. But I do want to show you where the spirit is imprisoned, in case I need to send you down there on Saturday. That, and I want to reinforce my defenses again."

Ethan nodded and settled back, appearing deep in thought. Stone glanced at him a couple of times as he drove, still convinced that something was going on with him that he was keeping secret. He wanted to ask about it, but right now he didn't have the time or the energy to deal with the inevitable defensiveness it would cause.

He was still curious about where Ethan had learned the trick with the circle, but it wasn't like it was anything particularly impressive or dangerous. It was a simple technique taught to every student of circle-casting. In fact it was possible—not likely, but possible—that Ethan had just picked it up instinctively on his own. Stone himself hadn't, but he'd known a couple of mages who had an inherent affinity for circles and were able to do things like that even before being taught. Maybe that was where Ethan's talent lay. He made a mental note to investigate it further after Saturday, but for now it had to be a lower priority.

They reached Adelaide's house around 1:30. Again, Stone had to show his ID to the patrolling security guard, and introduced Ethan as his assistant. The guard waved them through, and before long they were sitting in Adelaide's living room with cups of hot coffee delivered by Iona.

"I know you want to get right to it," Adelaide said, "But I just wanted to tell you how grateful I am that you're doing this for us, Dr. Stone. It means so much to me. This is a horrible thing, but I have every confidence that you'll be able to take care of it."

"You have more confidence than I do, Adelaide," Stone said. "But I'll do my best to make sure that your party isn't disturbed by anything supernatural."

They got away as soon as they politely could, and Stone led Ethan down to the basement. The boy looked around nervously as they went through the room with the towering stacks of furniture. "This stuff looks like it could fall on us any minute."

Stone nodded. "Yes, and I think has done in the past," he added, indicating the ruined player piano. "I wish I'd taught you a shield, but there's no helping it now. Just look sharp and keep your wits about you. I'm hoping that I've got that thing locked up tight enough that it won't be able to pull off any more shenanigans, but never take that for granted."

He pulled open the secret bookcase door and motioned Ethan inside. For a moment the boy could do nothing but stare. "Wow," he breathed. "That is some circle."

"It is indeed. You need a big circle to deal with a big spirit like this. But we don't have time to stay here and study it—the attic calls. Just take a look at the creature's prison magically, and watch while I add a few touches to the barriers I've put up."

Ethan did as he was told. After Stone finished, he followed him back out of the room and Stone slid the heavy door shut behind them.

Upstairs, they found Adelaide again: she was in the sitting room with Iona, watching a soap opera. "Sorry to interrupt," he said from the doorway, "but can you show us how to get into the attic?"

"Of course," Iona said with a small shudder. "I'm glad it's you and not me going up there, though. There are all sorts of nasty things. I hate spiders. Please be careful."

She took them up to the third floor, down a side hall to a nondescript door. "It's up there," she said. "You should be able to reach the whole thing—it's mostly a big open space, with a few smaller areas. I don't know if the furniture and stuff have shifted around, though. You might have trouble getting through some of it."

"Do the lights work?" Stone asked, eyeing the bag of gear Ethan was carrying, which included two heavy-duty flashlights and a lamp.

"They should."

Well, that was something. "All right, then. Let's go." He opened the door and mounted the narrow staircase. Ethan followed him.

At the top was another door. Stone shoved it open and stepped into the attic, moving aside to let Ethan in. They stood near a wall; Stone hunted around until he found a light switch and flipped it. To his surprise, several naked bulbs high overhead blazed to life. It wasn't much light for such a large space and it created more eerie shadows than illuminated areas, but at least they could see where they were going.

"Hold on to that bag," Stone ordered. "You'll need the lights when we separate to search. If the overheads go out, I can make my own light if I need to. That's another thing I have to teach you soon," he added as an afterthought, his mind already on the task ahead.

He began walking forward, then stopped. "That's odd…"

"What?"

Stone pointed at the floor. "There's a lot of dust up here. But look there—looks like recent footprints. Somebody's been up here, and not too long ago. Wonder who it was."

Ethan shrugged. "Maybe one of the workmen?"

"Probably," Stone agreed. "I doubt Iona would come up here, and in any case those are definitely a man's prints. Come on—let's see where they go."

They followed the footprints, which were quite easy to see in the thick dust. They didn't go far: they'd only walked for a couple of minutes before the prints veered off to the right and stopped at the end of a jumbled pile of random furniture. A large, wooden-framed mirror stood there next to the crumpled form of the sheet that had obviously covered it until recently.

Stone stopped, examining the mirror. "Not dusty," he said. "Whoever was up here, it was definitely recent, and it looks like they pulled the cover off this. I wonder why."

"Dunno," Ethan said. "Maybe they were looking for stuff to sell, and thought it was something else?"

Stone leaned in for a closer look. "There doesn't seem to be anything odd about this..." He shifted to magical senses. "Interesting..."

"Interesting?"

He nodded. "There are traces of magical energy around it. Very faint, but they're there."

"Are mirrors magical?" Ethan asked.

"Not inherently. I've seen a couple of enchanted ones, but this one doesn't seem to be enchanted...just seems like something magical might have occurred near it recently." He looked down at the footprints again, then shook his head. "Another mystery I'd like to get to the bottom of, but it'll have to wait until later. We need to get on with this."

He turned back around and shooed Ethan out to the main aisleway. "All right," he said, glancing around. "You go left, I'll go right. Look for bookcases, chests, anything that might contain books or papers or anything like that. Use your magical sight, but unless it's got words on it or it's glowing with magic, I'm not interested in it. If you see anything that looks likely, grab it if you can, otherwise mark where it was and come find me. All right?"

Ethan nodded. "Okay. Anything specific I'm looking for?"

"If you find anything with the name 'Selena Darklight' on it or anything that looks like it might be the name of that thing downstairs, call me right away. Other than that, just use your discretion. You know what magical texts look like. We don't have time for a thorough search, so we'll have to do what we can. Meet me back here in a couple of hours and we'll decide what to do from there."

Ethan hefted his backpack over his shoulder, picked up the bag Stone had given him, and set off. It was cold up here; he was glad he'd worn his parka. He hoped he would be able to find something—ideally he would run across something that he could show Stone along with information he could take back to Trin.

He had no idea what she and the others wanted to do with the thing downstairs; in fact, the thought made him a little nervous. From what Stone was saying, it sounded like whatever it was, it was incredibly powerful. Did they want to try to control it? He didn't think they'd be interested in sending it back; that didn't seem like their style. But he wondered if they had any idea how powerful it was. Even the small glimpse he'd gotten today had shown him it wasn't something to be trifled with. Did Trin and her friends have the power to deal with it? Stone was powerful and he obviously was concerned about being able to handle it—that's why he kept adding bits to its prison like a desperate homeowner nailing up new scraps of wood over his window.

He remembered what Trin had told him, though, about how she and Miguel and Oliver were good at joining their power together and making things happen. Individually they might not be as strong as Stone, but together? Besides, it wouldn't just be the three of them. He'd be there, too. He wouldn't be much help yet, but every little bit added to the shared power.

Picking his way over bits of broken furniture, rusting toys, and piles of ancient, yellowing magazines, he wondered if he was even going to have a chance to find anything. The attic was huge, and there was *so* much junk up here! Who let stuff accumulate like this? It wasn't like they were ever going to use it again.

He turned back to see if he could still spot Stone. He wasn't sure, but he thought he saw the mage's light spell bobbing away from him, far off in the distance. He hoped Stone wouldn't find the information first—if it was even here to find.

Time passed, and he grew increasingly discouraged. He'd poked through the drawers in dusty dressers, opened chests, examined bookcases, pulled apart piles of haphazard, broken objects, looked inside armoires, and even gone through a pile of brittle movie magazines he found in a corner. He'd encountered countless spiders, mice (and evidence of where mice had been), the skeletons of three small creatures that might have been large rats or small raccoons, and more dust than he wanted to see again for the rest of his life. He'd resorted to pulling up his T-shirt to cover his mouth and nose to keep from breaking out in coughing fits. A couple of times from far off in the distance he heard Stone coughing as well.

He glanced at his watch: almost 4:00. It was getting close to Stone's two-hour mark, but he'd almost reached the end of a pile of junk and he wanted to finish checking it. He knew he'd have to head back soon: evening visiting hours at the hospital started at 5:30, and he wanted to see his mother that evening. For him to have time to get home, clean up, and get to the hospital, he'd have to leave no later than 4:30. He stepped up his pace, tossing aside junk until his arms grew sore, but found nothing. Sighing, he ran a hand through his hair in an unconscious imitation of Stone's habitual gesture.

He'd have to accept it: maybe there was just nothing here to find. Disheartened, he trudged back toward where he and Stone had first separated.

Idly as he got closer, he thought of the footprints again, wondering where they'd come from. They seemed oddly familiar somehow, but he had no idea why. He'd certainly never been up here before; he'd remember if he had. But there was something about that mirror—

And then a thought came to him. The kind of thought that made you smack your head and go, "Of *course!*"

His breath quickened, as did his pace. He had about ten minutes before Stone was due back at the rendezvous point. Would it be enough time?

Arriving back at the footprints, he followed them to the mirror. It was taller than he was, intricately carved and very fancy. It also looked quite heavy. It hadn't even occurred to Stone to try to move it. But what if—

He took hold of one side of it and pulled.

Nothing happened.

Disappointment washed over him. He'd been so sure! He moved over, took hold of the other side, and pulled again.

The mirror swung toward him.

Ethan grinned. "Yes!" he whispered, pumping his fist. Quickly he slipped behind it and pulled it back to its original position.

There was no secret room here, no fancy ritual circle or anything like that. Just a continuation of the same pathway through the junk. But at the end of it, his gaze immediately fell on a small stack of books and papers piled in an untidy heap on the floor. He hurried over and dropped to his knees, picking up the first book and examining it.

It was small, the size of a diary, bound in cracked red leather. There was some kind of strange sigil on the front of it, and a lock holding it shut. He turned it sideways, and on the edge of the pages he could see something written. Pulling his flashlight close, he shone it down and was rewarded by the initials "S. D."

Selena Darklight!

It was all Ethan could do not to whoop in elation. He turned to make sure Stone wasn't coming up behind him, then stashed the little book in the inner pocket of his parka. He was sure Trin would very much like to see it. And she would be very happy with him for delivering it.

Quickly he turned his attention to the other books and papers. There weren't many papers; they contained diagrams of circles and densely packed handwritten text that was nearly impossible to read. None of the rest of the books looked like diaries: they were all large, thick, leatherbound tomes, and all of them had the look of magic to them. He picked up a couple and riffled through their pages. They looked very old, but professionally printed, not written in someone's hand. He couldn't make out much of what they were about because they weren't written in English, but by the diagrams it seemed like they had something to do with summoning. Unfortunately, all but two of them were too big to fit in his backpack. He stuffed those two in along with the papers, but there wasn't anything he could do about the rest of them.

"Ethan?"

It was Stone, and he was very close. Ethan's gaze darted around, but he didn't see any way to get out of here unseen and hide his find from the mage. Instead, since there was no way he could take the rest of the books to Trin, he decided to try to allay some of Stone's suspicions about him. "Over here, Dr. Stone! I found something!"

"Where are you?" He was closer now: he sounded like he was near the point where they'd separated.

"Behind the mirror! I found some books here!"

He could hear Stone's footsteps hurrying toward him. In a moment, the mirror swung open and the mage appeared, grime-streaked, sweating and flustered. "Bloody hell!" he swore. "You mean it was right here all along?"

Ethan grinned. "I guess it was," he said, pointing at the books.

"How did you find them?" Stone dropped to his knees and picked up one of the books, paging through it as Ethan had.

"I thought about the footprints," he said. "I figured maybe if there was nothing special about the mirror, maybe there was something behind it."

Stone let out a long sigh. "I must be tired," he said. "Either that, or I'm an idiot. Well done, Ethan. I'm glad *one* of us is thinking, at least."

Even knowing what he was planning to do, Ethan felt a swell of pride at Stone's words. He really did like and respect the mage, he realized—he just didn't agree with his method of teaching. He glanced at his watch again. "Uh—Dr. Stone?"

Stone was still focused on the books, looking through one after the other. He didn't look up. "Yes?"

"I—kinda need to get going. I want to go see Mom tonight, and visiting hours start pretty soon."

Stone shut the book he was examining, and began gathering up the rest of them. "Yes, of course. Sorry. Here—help me with these. I'll take them home tonight and look them over. Hopefully there's something useful in here somewhere."

Ethan helped him pick up the rest of the books, and together they carried them back downstairs. Adelaide and Iona were still in the sitting room watching television. Iona looked up as they came in. "Oh!" she called. "You two are a mess! I hope you found what you were looking for."

Stone nodded. "I hope so, too. Adelaide—is it all right if I take these books with me? I'll bring them back when I'm finished."

"You keep them, Dr. Stone. I have no use for them. Are they what you were hoping to find?"

"Not sure yet. I'll find out tonight. But it's quite possible."

They said their goodbyes and headed out. "Home, or straight to the hospital?" Stone asked as they exited back onto the winding road toward Los Gatos.

"Home," he said. "I gotta clean up a bit. Thanks, Dr. Stone."

"Thank *you*," he said. "Good job finding that hiding place. Give my best to your mum. I should come and see her sometime soon—tell her how well you're doing with your studies."

Ethan grinned. "Yeah, but maybe not tonight," he said, looking Stone over. "What did you do, take a dust bath?"

"Damn close," he muttered. "Got a bit overzealous in my search there toward the end."

By the time Stone dropped Ethan off at his apartment building, it was already nearly 5:30. Ethan hurried inside, tossed his backpack and parka on his bed, and dug fresh clothes out of his pile of clean laundry. He'd have preferred to have a shower, but he didn't want to be late. He hoped Mom was doing better today—maybe even well enough that they could talk. He had a lot he wanted to talk to her about.

He threw on jeans, T-shirt, and hooded sweatshirt, ran a comb through his hair, and headed straight back out. Less than five minutes later he was on the road, and fifteen minutes after that he reached the hospital. On a whim, he stopped at the gift shop on the first floor and bought a bouquet of flowers. His mother had never been much of a flower type, but he figured they'd brighten up her room and give her something nice to look at when she was awake. Then he took the elevator up to the fourth floor where her room was.

He knew something was wrong when Matilda, the desk nurse for this shift, spotted him and rose from her chair. "Ethan," she said softly.

"Hi Matilda," he greeted, waving the flowers. "How's Mom doing? Is she awake?"

Her dark eyes met his, and she came out around the desk. "Ethan, I'm sorry. We've been trying to reach you. We called your place, but there was no answer. You didn't get the message to call us?"

His blood froze. "What's—going on?"

She reached out and gently took his arm. "I'm so sorry to have to tell you this, Ethan. Your mother passed away about an hour ago."

| CHAPTER THIRTY-SEVEN

The Three were three again, and Trin for one was glad. She would never have told him, but she'd actually been concerned that Oliver would succumb to whatever Stone had hit him with back at the old woman's house. Not that she loved him or anything—in truth, Trin didn't love anything but herself, and power—but she'd gotten used to having him around. He was like a comfortable old shoe that she liked to slip into when she needed a good fuck. In any case, he blew the doors off that geeky little virgin Ethan, sex-wise. She consoled herself that she'd only have to deal with the kid for one more day, and then it would be over. If she played her cards right, she might not even have to fuck him again. It was getting harder to pretend she was enjoying it.

They picked Oliver up at the hospital Friday morning. "About fuckin' time they let me out," he complained, climbing into the SUV. "They wanted to keep me an extra day because they still can't figure out what the hell was wrong with me. I got *this* close to telling them that some asshole mage whacked me with a magic sledgehammer, and that I just needed to sleep it off." He leaned back in his seat. "I need real food. No more hospital shit. And you guys need to tell me what I've missed."

They stopped at a favorite diner near their ritual space. Oliver ordered the biggest breakfast they had and demolished it while Trin explained what had happened over the last few days.

"Lemme get this straight," he said through a mouthful of pancakes. "This twerp Ethan's gonna try to grill Stone for information about whatever's in the house, and we're gonna get whatever he's got to tell us and get him to let us in for this ball thing on Saturday night so we can find it. I take it that's why you guys haven't killed Stone yet?"

"We'll kill him once we get what we're after," Trin said.

"But how are we gonna do that?" Oliver asked, shoveling in another mouthful. "Do we even know how to control whatever this is? Do you really think the kid is gonna be able to get enough info out of Stone so we can do it? He seems like kind of a fail to me. You're putting that much trust in him not fucking up?"

Miguel smiled; a nearby waitress got a look at the smile and quickly found somewhere else to be. "Nah, Oliver. See, if he doesn't come up with the name, we've got a Plan B."

"We do?"

He nodded. "Yeah. I've been doing some research on this place, and also on enslaving big spirits. It's best if you have their true name, but there's another way to do it, too."

"Yeah?" Oliver looked mildly interested, but still more interested in his breakfast. "What's that?"

"Human life force. Like the kind you get from a ritual sacrifice."

That was enough to bring Oliver up out of his pancakes. "You're shittin' me."

"Nope," Trin said, looking satisfied. "And not any old human sacrifice, either. You get the best power when you use somebody who *has* power. Like a mage."

Oliver stared at her. "We're gonna sacrifice *Stone?*"

She shook her head. "Believe me, I'd love nothing more than to slice that bastard open and watch him bleed, but it's too dangerous. Too much chance he'd get lucky and fuck us up. No, I was thinking of a little more—*inexperienced* mage."

"One that has such a puppy-love crush on Trin that he'd walk into a woodchipper if she told him to," Miguel added with a nasty grin. "Especially if she fucked him before he stepped in."

Oliver grinned. "Ah, okay. I get it now. And if he does come up with the name?"

Trin shrugged. "We might sacrifice him anyway, just for extra insurance. We need to get rid of him somehow, because if I have to fake being hot for him more than another day or two, I'm gonna hurl. Oh—that reminds me. I should call him today. Make sure everything's set, find out what he knows, and figure out the plan for getting us in. I hope you guys have decent suits."

Thursday night and all of Friday passed as a blur of indistinct images for Ethan. He remained at the hospital until late Thursday night, answering questions, signing papers, and talking to a kindly counselor that Matilda found for him. He didn't even remember what he said or what he signed. He stumbled home and fell into bed, sobbing and exhausted.

Friday morning he briefly thought about calling Stone, but decided not to. He didn't know what the mage would say: whether he'd insist on coming down and helping Ethan deal with things, or whether he'd offer perfunctory condolences but be so distracted by the business at Adelaide's that he'd remain distanced from the situation. Either way, Ethan didn't think he could stand it.

The hospital had introduced him to a woman who would help guide him through the process, and he was grateful for that because he was mostly numb. He didn't have any relatives that he knew of; it had pretty much always been just his mom and himself since his father had died. He supposed he could contact Walter Yarborough, but it hardly seemed right to drag him all the way over here from England just to hold Ethan's hand. He was eighteen now—an adult. He should be able to deal with this.

But not too many eighteen-year-olds had to navigate the confusing seas of administering their mother's last wishes and making sure that things like funeral arrangements and burial details were taken care of.

The woman from the hospital, Mrs. Jackson, probably got him through the day. She gently explained what needed to be done, told him he didn't need to make every decision right now, and helped him make the ones he did have to make. He drifted through the day on a fog of confusion and grief, signing where they told him to sign and going where they told him to go, and didn't arrive back home at the apartment until after eight o'clock that night. He threw himself down on the couch, wishing he had a big bottle of something alcoholic to help dull the pain. Once again, he thought about calling Stone. At least the mage might take pity on him and buy him a bottle of booze.

His answering-machine light was blinking. *Blink-blink. Blink-blink.* Two messages.

He thought about not playing them. He'd already listened to the one from yesterday from the hospital, the carefully professional voice of Matilda the nurse letting him know that he should go there as soon as he got the message. These two were new. He didn't want to listen to anybody right now.

He dragged himself over to the machine. Better to get it over with. He stabbed the button.

"Ethan? Stone here. I forgot to ask you if you wanted us to pick you up for tomorrow night, or if you'll be driving yourself. Let me know when you can. Give your mum my best when you see her."

Hot tears formed, and he angrily forced them back, clutching one of the couch pillows so hard he nearly split it. *He doesn't know,* he reminded himself. *Nobody's told him yet.*

A beep sounded, and then the second message. "Ethan? It's Trin. You there?" Pause. "Okay. Well, I was just wondering if you found out anything about that stuff we talked about. Give me a call tonight whenever you get home, 'kay? Can't wait to see you tomorrow. Bye!"

He slumped back into the couch cushions. He hadn't even thought about Trin all day. He wasn't sure he wanted to call her now, but he supposed he should let her know what was going on. He didn't know if he could bring himself to even go to the ball tomorrow night. The last thing he wanted was to put on a monkey suit and stand around in the middle of a bunch of old rich people pretending to have a good time. Stone would understand, he was sure. And as for Trin—she could just come by tomorrow and pick up the stuff he had for her. He didn't even want to go outside.

He picked up the phone and punched in her number. She answered on the third ring. "Hello?" She sounded distracted.

"Trin?"

"Is that you, Ethan? You sound weird." There was a muffled sound in the background.

"You left a message," he said. "I'm calling back."

"Oh. Uh—right. So, did you find anything?"

"Yeah. I got you some stuff. We found it up in the attic. And I saw the thing in the basement." In a monotone, he described what he remembered, including the existing prison, Stone's efforts to reinforce it, and the massive summoning circle in the basement room.

"That's great!" she said. "You're awesome, Ethan. So when can I see you so I can get the stuff? We need some time to look it over before the party. You *can* get us in, right?"

He paused. "Trin...I don't think I'm going to the party."

Now it was her turn to pause. "What do you mean, you're not going?"

"I—" He waited to make sure he could keep his voice from betraying him. "My mom died yesterday, Trin."

"Oh, man..." There was a long pause, and some muffled sounds in the background again. "I'm sorry, Ethan. Really, I am."

He nodded, even though she couldn't see that. "Thanks. I just—don't think I can go, you know? I still need to call Dr. Stone and tell him I'm not gonna be there to help him."

"Ethan..." Her voice sounded careful. "We really kinda need you there. We planned the ritual with four. If you're not there, we can't do it. I'm really really sorry to ask you—I feel like the world's biggest heartless bitch for asking right now. But—is there any way you could come for even a little while? We can probably figure out how to get inside on our own, but we can't do this without you. And we won't have another chance."

"I don't know—"

"Look," she said softly. "I know this is horrible for you. I'm so sorry. If you can just help us out for a little while, we'll go somewhere after and hang out. Just the two of us. We'll just talk, if that's all you feel up to. You really should be talking to somebody about this, Ethan. I take it Stone's being his usual hard-ass self?"

"I...dunno. I didn't tell him about it yet."

"Well, don't worry about it. I'll help you, Ethan. What are friends for? We can talk all night if you want to. But if you could just do this one little thing for me—"

He sighed. Right now his libido, which usually did his thinking for him when Trin was around, was silent. But the kind tone in her voice did reach him. "Okay," he said. "I'll come for a while, and let you in. I'll bring the stuff, too. I think it'll be helpful."

"Great," she said. "Thanks, Ethan. Really. And if there's anything I can do to help you out, just let me know, okay?"

"I will. Thanks."

He hung up the phone and stared at it for a long time before he finally fell asleep.

| CHAPTER THIRTY-EIGHT

Stone spent the rest of Thursday evening and all day Friday studying the books Ethan had found, and powering up as many magical focus objects as he could. He knew he had to be careful: every bit of his power that he put into them was that much less he'd have to draw from within himself, so he'd have to make sure he had time to recharge before the ball. It wasn't helping that he hadn't slept after Wednesday's nightmare, and barely at all on Thursday night. He didn't tell Megan how much the nightmare had affected him—especially since it was the second one he'd had in less than a week. He wondered if he'd even be able to fall asleep before he was so exhausted that his body just took matters into its own hands. He didn't have time for rest this weekend anyway.

Megan had a couple of finals on Friday, so he had the day to himself. The books, unfortunately, turned out to be mostly useless for what he needed, though they were fascinating magical texts in their own right. One in particular, bound in brown leather with a red gem on the cover, was unusually potent and contained detailed information about how to summon several different types of powerful and useful creatures. Of course the book practically reeked of black magic, but that was where Stone had gotten most of his "pale gray" distinction: if it had to do with magic, it was like catnip for him. He didn't care if it was good, evil, or somewhere in between— he wanted to know its secrets. And besides, there was a big difference between knowing *how* to perform a particular technique and actually *doing* it. That was why he was pale gray instead of dark gray: because he didn't have any particular lust for power beyond what he could get from white magic techniques. He just wanted to be able to recognize the others, and understand the mechanics and philosophy behind them.

He caught himself wondering idly how much old Stefan Kolinsky would offer for these books, but immediately dismissed the thought. Sure, it would make things easier, since he'd probably take them in payment for his last bit of very useful help instead of some of the more...*interesting* means of repayment he usually came up with, but Stone wasn't ready to let them go just yet. Maybe, if he was able to get his hands on the ones from the basement summoning room, he might offer a couple of them to the black mage. But that would come later.

Mrs. Olivera showed up at midday with his tuxedo, which she'd picked up from the cleaners, and stuck around to make him lunch when she saw that he'd gotten so busy with his research that he'd forgotten to eat. She shook her head in mock maternal concern. "You should marry that woman, Dr. Stone," she told him. "You need somebody to look after you."

He chuckled. "Come on, Mrs. Olivera. You know better than that. We'd drive each other mad if we got married. I'm too much of a hermit for that much togetherness. Besides, what makes you think she'd even have me? I'm not exactly the world's best catch, am I?"

"I think you sell yourself short," she said, but let it go at that. She'd learned long ago to leave him alone when he got like this. It was easier for both of them that way.

By the evening, he'd managed to get through all the books with at least enough comprehension to tell that they didn't contain the true name of the thing in Adelaide's basement and probably wouldn't be any help in dealing with it. He had just called Ethan and left a message asking whether he wanted to be picked up tomorrow night when the phone rang.

It was Tommy Langley. "Hey," he said. "A couple of the other guys and I were gonna go out and have a few drinks. Thought you might like to join us. You know—get your mind off all this heavy hocus-pocus shit for a while and talk about boring stuff like the old days."

He almost said no, but realized that his only real alternative was to crawl into bed and probably not sleep. At least if he got drunk enough, he might not have the nightmare. "All right, Tommy," he agreed. "That sounds like just the thing."

And it was. They met at a little pub where they usually got started, and Stone bought the first round. The "other guys" were three fellow professors, one from the Computer Science department, one from Mechanical Engineering, and the third from Journalism. They were all around Stone's age, give or take a few years, and their interests were eclectic enough that even when drunk they were full of fascinating stories and anecdotes.

It felt good to be back together with them again—to be normal, even if it was just for an evening. Every once in a while—not that often, admittedly—Stone caught himself wondering what his life would have been like if he *hadn't* been born with the potential to be a mage, and raised among those who had the ability to recognize and nurture that potential. Sometimes he felt like his life had been mapped out for him from the time he was a small child, and occasionally he resented it. Sometimes he just wanted to be mundane, with no idea what kinds of things were out there in the world, right beyond the edge of where those who didn't have the Talent could see them. At times like that, blissful ignorance seemed like a pretty damned good idea.

The feeling never lasted long, though. He loved magic, loved using his will and his training to shape and control the world around him, even in his own small way. He knew it was an occupational hazard of mages, and worse among those at higher power levels: they often succumbed to arrogance about their own abilities, believing that there was nothing out there that they couldn't handle. Though he had succumbed himself on more than one occasion, Stone usually knew better. That's why he had accepted Langley's invitation: he just wanted to forget about it all for a night, before it all came crashing back down on him tomorrow. There was a very real possibility that he might not survive the weekend—that was a good enough excuse to get roaring drunk the night before. Hey, it worked for the Vikings.

He'd lost track of how many Guinnesses he'd downed when Langley took him aside for a private chat—not that it mattered, since the other members of their group were busy entertaining each other with a raucous tale involving (as near as Stone could pick out of their slurred delivery) a naked woman, a rabbi, and three goats.

"You never did tell me what you wanted me to do tomorrow night," Langley said with a goofy grin. "You want me to—punch that ghost a good one in the nose?" He pantomimed this activity, flailing his fists around so wildly that Stone had to lean back and nearly lost his balance on his chair.

"It's not a ghost. And I'll—figure it out as we go along," he said, righting himself.

"What—you don't have a plan?"

"Not really." Stone finished his pint and contemplated whether he wanted another. "Hoping nothing happens at all. Probably won't. We'll just have a nice night with your aunt and a bunch of elderly rich people."

Langley nodded, suddenly looking melancholy. "I'm scared, Alastair. I want to help you, but I'm scared."

Stone nodded. "So am I, Tommy."

"You are?" His look of surprise was almost comical. "But you're Mandrake the Magician. Master of the Mystic Arts, or whatever."

"No." Stone shook his head. "I'm just a poor sod who's out of his league. And I'm afraid that if I bugger this up, people will die."

"You're serious." Langley leaned in close. "Die?"

"Die, Tommy," Stone said softly. His pleasant buzz was threatening to morph, as it sometimes did when he got drunk while in the wrong frame of mind, into a black depression. "Not too late for you to back out, you know."

"For you, either. You could still just tell them to cancel it. Aunt Adelaide would do it, if you said so. She's pretty impressed with you."

He shook his head, staring down into his empty glass. "Too late now for that. I think it'll be all right." He rubbed at his eyes. "Ignore me, Tommy. I get like this sometimes. Just tired, I guess."

Langley patted his arm. "It's okay. Come on, have another drink and forget about it for a while."

"No, I think I'll be heading home," he said, dragging himself to his feet. "Got a lot to do tomorrow, and I'm already going to be wasting half the morning fighting off a hangover."

Shortly after that, he sat in the back of the cab heading back to his house, window rolled down, deep in thought. Even through the fog of alcohol, he couldn't help thinking there was something he'd forgotten. Some factor in all this that he wasn't including in his plans.

And as the cab stopped in front of his townhouse and he got out and paid the driver, he suspected that, whatever it was, he was going to regret not remembering it.

| CHAPTER THIRTY-NINE

By the time Stone dragged himself out of bed slightly before noon on Saturday, Ethan still hadn't called back. He tried again. To his annoyance, he got the machine. He'd swear that boy was avoiding him. "Ethan, this is Stone," he growled. "I really need you to call me back and—"

The phone picked up. "Hi, Dr. Stone."

Stone frowned. Ethan's voice sounded very strange. Colorless. Though he supposed he shouldn't talk: his own probably sounded like someone had run his throat through a cheese grater. "Are you all right, Ethan? You sound odd." There was a very long pause on the other end. "Ethan—are you still there?"

"I...uh...yeah. My—mom died, Dr. Stone."

For a moment Stone was speechless. If someone had asked him to list the top ten things he thought the boy might say, that wouldn't even have made the list. "Ethan, I'm so sorry," he said at last, dully. "When?"

Another long pause. "Thursday afternoon. I—found out when I got to the hospital. She was—already gone by the time I got there."

Stone closed his eyes and bowed his head. Ethan's mother had died while he'd had the boy poking around through rubbish in an attic, chasing some obsession that he had no right to even involve him in. "Why didn't you tell me?" he asked, his tone gentle. "Have you been all alone down there?"

"No—the people from the hospital have been helping me out. Helping me deal with stuff that needs to be done. I'm—okay."

You don't sound *okay.* "Do you want me to come down there? I could help you—"

"No, it's okay. Thanks, but I'll be all right. Yesterday was kind of rough, but today's a little better. I—kinda guess I knew this was coming."

"That doesn't make it any easier, though, I know." Stone sighed. "If there's anything I can do—anything at all—don't hesitate to call me. You shouldn't be handling this sort of thing alone."

"Thanks, Dr. Stone. I appreciate it."

"I mean it. Any time of the day or night. You take care of yourself, Ethan. Don't worry about anything else until you're feeling up to it again."

"Oh—right—you wanted to know if I needed you to pick me up for tonight. You don't have to. I can drive myself."

Stone stared at the phone. "Ethan, you don't have to come tonight. I wouldn't expect you to—"

"No, it's fine. I want to. It'll—take my mind off things. I kinda want the excuse to get out of the house for a while. If it's still okay, I mean."

"It's—of course it is. If that's really what you want to do. Please don't feel any obligation. I can handle it without you if you'd rather not—"

"I'll be there," Ethan said. "Six o'clock. See you then."

Stone hung up the phone and slumped back onto the bed. Guilt clawed at him: if he hadn't insisted that Ethan help him hunt through Adelaide's attic, he could at least have been there with his mother when she'd died. *Bloody brilliant job I've done, helping him deal with anything. No wonder half the time it seems like he doesn't even want to talk to me. I don't blame him.*

Despite the fact that he had a lot of things he needed to do before that evening, he couldn't bring himself to rise from the bed. He lay there, half dressed and face down in the pillows, for nearly an hour before he could rouse himself sufficiently to get up.

When he arrived at Adelaide's house a little after two o'clock, the place was teeming with activity. There were so many cars, catering trucks, and other vehicles scattered haphazardly around the front part of the grounds that he had to park the Jaguar halfway up the driveway and walk to the house.

He found Adelaide in the living room, seated comfortably with Iona on a couch, dealing with a stream of service personnel flowing in and out. She smiled when she saw him. "Well, hello, Dr. Stone!" she called, waving. "You're a bit early for the festivities."

"Just thought I'd do a last-minute check on things downstairs," he told her. "To be sure—well, as sure as I can be."

She nodded. "Of course, go right ahead. And when you're done, come back. I want to have George—he's sort of the stage manager of our little event here—show you around so you'll know where everything will be, in case you need something tonight."

Stone noticed that she looked radiantly happy and more energetic than she had in a long time. Obviously this party, and the money it would bring for her charities, meant a lot to her, and he planned to do everything he could to make sure things went off without any trouble. He slipped out and headed down to the basement, negotiating the maze of hallways and furniture until he reached the summoning room.

This whole situation was a new one to his experience, which was part of why he was being so careful with it. He'd never seen such a powerful spirit, demon, or whatever this thing was imprisoned between two dimensions. He couldn't be completely sure that it wasn't just biding its time, pretending to be more weakened and confined than it was, just waiting for the best moment to spring free, and that was the nagging worry that wouldn't leave him alone. Beyond trying to contact it and dominate its mind sufficiently to compel it to tell him—something he had absolutely no desire to attempt—he'd just have to trust that the measures he'd taken would be sufficient. He knew the hard work would begin after the party was over, but right now he was only allowing himself to think one day at a time. He'd keep the charity ball and its guests safe, and after that, perhaps he could call in some help and see if between himself and some of the other mages he knew, they might be able to send this thing back permanently to where it belonged.

He spent about half an hour prowling around the room, magical senses on full alert, checking and reinforcing his defenses. He realized that what he was doing was the mystic equivalent of building a fort out of random two-by-fours and pieces of corrugated metal, but elegance wasn't something he had time for right now.

The spirit, for its part, was silent. He could feel its presence, but it seemed to be dormant at the moment. Maybe reaching out and giving him nightmares strong enough to make him physically ill was taxing to it in its half-present state. "You just stay asleep," he murmured to it as he put the finishing touches on his reinforcements. "We'll talk again tomorrow, after all these people are safe in their homes."

Back upstairs, he found Adelaide again and was introduced to George Fayette, a tall, stoop-shouldered older man with an easy smile and dark, lively eyes. "George is the president of our foundation," Adelaide told Stone. "He's in charge tonight. I just provide the place for us to hold the ball."

Stone noticed that she introduced him to George as "a friend of my nephew's, who's doing some consulting work for us." *Yes, well, 'consulting mage and banisher of extradimensional horrors' might be a bit much,* he decided wryly. Besides, he hadn't banished anything yet.

He followed George around the lower floor of the house as the other man pointed out the grand ballroom where the party would be held, where the bandstand and the bar and the tables would be (a crowd of people were busy setting up all three as they went through), where the guests' coats would be stored, the location of the items up for auction, and the bathrooms that would be in use for the ball. Then George took him into the dining room and kitchen ("We won't be having a full dinner, of course—just various cookies, candies, hors-d'oeuvres, eggnog, that sort of thing"). Stone had seen most of these areas of the house, of course, but George's tour gave him a good idea of the logistics of the party, where the guests would be and where they wouldn't be, and ways he could get around without anyone noticing if he needed to.

"So," George said as he took Stone back to Adelaide when the tour was over, "What sort of consulting do you do, Dr. Stone?"

Stone shrugged. "Oh, little of this, little of that," he said. "Sort of—unconventional security."

George tilted his head. "Unconventional? We've got a full security force tonight, to keep an eye on the guests and make sure no one who isn't invited gets in. We wouldn't want anyone's jewelry or purses stolen while they're having a good time."

"I'm here more in an—advisory capacity," Stone said. "Ah, and here we are back where we started. Thank you so much for the tour, George." He shook the man's hand and made his exit before he'd have to answer any more questions.

It was now almost four o'clock. He was supposed to pick up Megan at 5:30, which meant he'd have to hurry if he didn't want to be late. He said his goodbyes to Adelaide and Iona, and told them he'd be back later.

CHAPTER FORTY

S tone knocked on Megan's door promptly at 5:30. When she answered it, all he could do was stare.

"You look—amazing," he said. And she did. She was a lot like him: she preferred casual clothes, but she could dress up with the best of them when she wanted. Her dress, black and shimmery, clung to her like a second skin, and she wore her stiletto heels with the same confidence as her usual sensible slip-ons. Her hair, usually worn long, was swept up in a graceful, elegant up-do that framed her face beautifully. "And you're ready on time, too," he added. "That makes you truly a rarity among women."

She smiled, motioning him in. "Flatterer. You look pretty damn sexy yourself. If I'd known you looked that good in a tux, I'd have gotten you to take me to more formal affairs. Shame about the hair, though," she added with a grin.

"Hey, I tried," he protested. He had, too; it was just that his hair was every bit as stubborn as he was, and he felt that plastering it down too forcefully made him look like a nerd. "If you're ready, though, we'd best be going—I don't want to be late."

"Well, early," she pointed out. "But I'm not complaining." She grabbed her little bag and wrap from a table near the door, then locked it behind her. "Are we picking up Ethan?" she asked as they drove off.

He shook his head, looking troubled. "No. He's going to get up there himself." He paused. "Megan—I called him this morning. His mum died Thursday afternoon."

Her eyes widened. "What? Oh, no. That's horrible."

He nodded. "He didn't even tell me until I called him to find out if he wanted me to pick him up."

"Why not?"

"I don't know." He sighed.

"You're not making him go to this thing tonight, are you?"

"No. I told him I didn't expect him to. I offered to help with anything he needed, but he said he was fine and that he wanted to come. Said it would take his mind off things."

She glanced over at him. His eyes were fixed on the road ahead, his jaw set. "You're feeling guilty about something, aren't you?"

He continued to watch the road. A light rain was falling, and the oncoming headlights made dazzling patterns in the droplets on the windshield. "He...wasn't with her when she died. Because of me."

"Because of you? What do you mean?"

"I had him up at Adelaide's place searching through her attic with me for some information I wanted to find." He spoke softly, his jaw still set tight.

She touched his arm. "Alastair, that wasn't your fault. You didn't know."

"No," he said. "I didn't. But I did know she was ill."

She sighed, as if knowing there was nothing she could say that would change his mind. Instead, she just squeezed his arm and said, "I'm sorry."

He didn't reply.

The house was ablaze with festive lights that they could see from the road before they even reached the gate. They were still early, so they didn't have to wait in a line of cars, but a few other early birds were already showing up. Uniformed teenagers with lightsticks waved them in, and a valet took charge of the car near the door. Megan, who had never seen Adelaide's house before, gaped. "Wow," she said. "You didn't tell me your old lady lived in someplace *this* fancy."

"Normally it doesn't look quite this good," he told her, taking her arm and escorting her up the steps to the front door. There, he showed their invitation to the doorman and they were bowed inside. "They've fixed it up quite a bit for the party. I've never seen all these lights before."

"If I win the lottery, I'll buy a place like this," she said, stopping to gaze up in wonder at the twenty-foot-tall Christmas tree standing in the entry chamber. Another uniformed attendant took their coats and gave them claim checks. "And you can be my kept boy."

Complete with ravening demon imprisoned in the basement? "I'll take that deal," he said aloud with a wicked grin. "But trust me, you don't want a place like this."

Adelaide and Iona greeted them warmly from the dining room, where Stone introduced them to Megan. "You two make a lovely couple," Adelaide said with a smile. "I do hope you'll be able to enjoy yourselves tonight. Don't spend all your time working. There's no need, is there?"

"I just want to keep an eye on things," Stone said. "But don't worry. We'll make sure to enjoy your hospitality."

Tommy Langley came in then. Unlike Stone's tuxedo, his fit like a rental and looked a bit like he'd slept in it, but he grinned when he saw Stone and Megan. "Oh look, it's Beauty and the Beast. Good to see you, Megan. You look fantastic."

Stone raised an eyebrow. "Hey now—I thought I was your date for the evening, Tommy."

"I'll share you," Megan said, laughing. "But I get the first dance."

Ethan arrived a few minutes later, shown into the room by one of the uniformed guides. He looked sad and preoccupied, still wearing his parka and carrying his backpack over his rumpled tuxedo. "Hi, Dr. Stone." He waved in greeting to the others.

"Ethan, I was so sorry to hear about your mother," Megan said kindly, soft enough so only he and Stone could hear.

"Thanks," he mumbled without looking at her.

"Right, then," Stone said, realizing that the last thing Ethan wanted right now was to be reminded about what he wanted to forget. "Ethan, if you're feeling up to it, why don't we head off and check things out before too many people start arriving. You can leave your stuff there if you like."

Ethan nodded. "Sounds good."

"Check what out?" Megan asked.

"We won't be long," Stone assured her. "Just some of the work we're here to do. Back in fifteen minutes or so. Tommy, you'll keep Megan company, won't you?"

"With pleasure," Langley said, grinning. "Come on, Megan, I'll show you where the food and the bar are. Aunt Adelaide really went all out with the spread this year."

Stone led Ethan downstairs, through the basement to the summoning room. "I've already checked it once today—just wanted to get a last look. I'll probably come down again sometime tonight, but I want you to keep your eyes open—magical and mundane—and let me know if you see anything unusual, all right? Anything at all. If it looks odd, let me know right away."

Ethan shrugged out of his parka and backpack and tossed them in a corner. "I will, Dr. Stone."

Stone turned around, facing him. "Ethan," he said, his voice gentle, "You really don't need to be here if you don't want to. I hope you don't think I'm going to hold it against you or somehow think you've failed me if you'd rather be doing something else."

"No, really, it's fine," he said, still looking at the floor. His eyes looked haunted in his pale face. "There really isn't anything else I could be doing. I'd just be sitting home at the apartment. I've done enough of that already."

"All right, if you're sure," Stone said. "But you have to promise that if you need anything or if you change your mind, you'll let me know. If you want to leave, just tell me or leave word with someone before you go so I'll know not to look for you."

"I'll do that."

Stone nodded. "All right. Let's take a look around here, then, and get back upstairs before Megan comes looking for us."

Nothing had changed from the afternoon: the thing in the armoire still seemed to be sleeping, and all the reinforcements Stone had put into place were still undisturbed. He waved Ethan out, and they headed back up to the festivities.

By a little after seven o'clock, many of the guests had already arrived, and the areas designated for the ball were starting to feel comfortably crowded. Stone tracked Megan down and liberated her from Tommy, who was telling her a long-winded story about one of his students. They got drinks and circulated among the crowd.

"Have you noticed that we and Tommy are the youngest ones here?" Megan asked Stone after they'd made a slow circuit around the ballroom.

"By many years," Stone agreed. It was true: most of the party's guests were older, and many were quite elderly. The women all dripped with jewels that were almost certainly genuine, the men clad in classic, old-fashioned tuxedos and dinner jackets. There were a few younger guests, but even they were in their fifties.

"I guess those new computer billionaires I've been hearing about don't get invited to things like this," Megan said.

Stone raised an eyebrow. "Perhaps they were, and they just opted to make a donation. Seriously," he added, glancing around, "I don't think I'd be here if I wasn't working, would you?" The band, warming up on the little bandstand he'd watched the workmen erecting this afternoon, were limbering up big-band style instruments. Not an electric guitar in sight.

"Well, it *is* a little slow," she admitted. "Nice, though. Very old world." She smiled at him. "It's just nice being here with you, Alastair. We should do more formal things. It's fun to play dress-up sometimes. And maybe later we can play dress *down,*" she added with a suggestive grin.

"Ah, something to look forward to."

They continued circulating, sipping their drinks and greeting people as they went. As time went on and nothing horrible happened, Stone began to feel a bit more relaxed. Perhaps this evening would end up all right after all.

| CHAPTER FORTY-ONE

S ome distance off in the forest, The Three stood watching the
house.

"Look at all those fancy-ass cars," Oliver said. "This thing's bigger than I thought."

"That's good," Miguel said. "It'll make it easier for us to get in without being noticed."

"Ethan said to go around back," Trin said, pointing. "He said he'd meet us at eight near the back door on the west side of the house."

"He better be there," Oliver growled. "If he skips out on us—"

"He won't," Trin assured him. She began walking, careful not to trip over anything. "Damn these fucking shoes anyway."

All three were dressed in evening clothes; Trin even wore long opera gloves to cover up her distinctive tattoos. They planned to use their blending spell to get inside, but wanted to be careful in case anyone spotted them. Oliver carried a leather bag containing some notes, ritual materials, and other gear. It also contained rope and a long, wicked-looking knife in a leather sheath.

"You think the kid's come up with anything we can use?" Miguel asked.

Trin shrugged. "I don't care at this point. If we don't get its name, then we'll just go with our other plan. Either way, it should work out fine."

Oliver didn't look so sure about that, but he didn't voice his misgivings. In The Three, it never paid to go against what Trin had decided.

Inside, Ethan glanced at his watch. It was almost eight. *Almost time.*

He lurked near the buffet table, trying to be as unobtrusive as possible. A couple of the elderly people who'd come by had mistaken him for one of the caterers, and he was fine with that. If he could have blended into the walls he would have, but Stone hadn't taught him that spell yet.

He knew that once he let The Three into the house, there was no going back. This was his last chance to back out. Was this really what he wanted to do? Is this what his mother would have wanted? He feared his attraction to Trin was clouding his judgment. He really should just go to Stone right now, tell him everything, and then try to start fresh once he'd had some time to recover from his grief. The mage had been kind and sincerely concerned about him, both on the phone and in person. Ethan didn't doubt that both he and Megan genuinely wanted to help him.

But Trin did, too. She had also sounded shocked when he'd told her about Mom's death. He didn't resent the fact that she'd asked him to be here—he knew they needed him, and they wouldn't be able to do what they were planning without him. She'd offered to talk to him afterward, and maybe talking to someone closer to his own age might be preferable. Less lecture, more understanding.

He picked up a plate and put a couple of hors-d'oeuvres and a chicken wing on it, nibbling as he agonized over what he should do. Glancing around, he almost hoped to see Stone coming in looking for him, but the mage was nowhere to be seen.

Five to eight.

He had to go now if he was going.

He bit into some sort of little sandwich thing and chewed; it tasted like cardboard and his mouth was suddenly dry. He thought of Stone, then of Trin.

He set the plate down on a nearby table, and headed for the back part of the house.

❖

The Three had made it to the edge of the tree line at the back of the house, and now stood impatiently waiting, watching the door.

"The little twerp isn't coming," Miguel muttered.

"He'll be here," Trin said. "No way he's gonna let me down."

Oliver glanced around. "I hope they don't have security patrols out here. If we're spotted—"

"If we're spotted, we'll drain 'em and hide their clothes," Miguel said. His tone was matter-of-fact, like he was talking about what he wanted from the buffet. "Nobody'll find the ashes."

"We're pretty topped up already," Oliver pointed out. It had been a little early to go to a club for their usual shot of energy, so they'd hit a local mall and pulled power from the crowds of Christmas shoppers.

"We'll need all that for the ritual," Trina said. "Much as I like this sacrifice idea, it would be easier if we had—"

"Shh—look!" Miguel hissed, taking her arm and pointing.

The door was opening.

"That's it," Trin urged. "Go!"

Blending spell in place, they hurried across the open yard and slipped inside. Ethan stood there, looking breathless and miserable.

"Good job, Ethan," Trin said, squeezing his shoulder. "How are you doing?"

He shrugged. "I'm okay, I guess."

"Good. I'm really glad you decided to come help us out. This shouldn't take long at all, then we can leave and go find someplace more private to hang out."

Ethan nodded.

"Okay," she said. "Come on—let's get this over with. Can you show us the place?"

"Yeah. Come on—this way."

"Just act casual—nobody will pay attention to us as long as we don't go through any crowds."

Ethan tried not to look nervous as he led the three of them down the back hallways toward the kitchen. The sounds of the band and the low hubbub of people's conversations filtered in from not far off, and every time he turned a corner he expected to run into a knot of partygoers—or worse, Stone, who would probably see right through The Three's blending spell. Guilt racked him, and indecision. He still wasn't sure he was doing the right thing.

Too late to turn back now...

They reached the kitchen without incident; a couple individuals returning from the bathrooms passed them, but those people just went by with a nod to Ethan and no indication that they thought anything was odd.

"Be careful here," Ethan whispered to Trin. "The kitchen's busy tonight."

"Just keep going."

He led them through and down the hall toward the basement door. He lingered there for a moment until he was sure nobody was watching, then quickly opened it and waved them through. He slipped in behind them and closed the door.

Trin immediately summoned a light spell. "Ugh, no lights?"

"No, they don't work."

Oliver dug in his leather bag and came up with a flashlight. "How far is it?"

"Just follow me," Ethan said.

He'd only been down here a couple of times, but following his and Stone's footprints in the dust on the floor, he was able to navigate them down the hallways and through the big room full of stacked furniture. "Holy shit," Miguel breathed. "This old bat must be loaded. Look at the *size* of this place."

"Be careful," Ethan told them as he turned the corner to the narrow passage leading to the summoning room door. "That stuff's stacked pretty high. Don't bump anything."

Oliver looked up, nervous. "This shit isn't gonna fall on us, is it?"

"Hasn't yet," Ethan told him, picking his way over the corpse of the player piano. "But like I said, be careful." He pulled on the bookcase and it slid open. "In here."

They all crowded inside, with Ethan coming in last. He let the bookcase return to its closed position. "This is it."

His statement was unnecessary. They all stood there, taking in the huge circle set into the floor, the bookcases and tables, and the armoire at the end of the room.

Oliver pointed at the ornate piece of furniture. "That's what we're here for, isn't it?"

"Can't you tell?" Trin asked. She took a few steps closer, seemingly fascinated by the sight. She smiled, but it didn't come close to her eyes. "Sit tight," she told the thing in the armoire. "We're here to let you out, just like you wanted."

Behind her, Miguel smirked.

"Okay," she said. "Let's get this circle set up. Ethan, you said you had something for us?"

"Oh, right." He'd almost forgotten about the stuff in his backpack. He hurried over to it, dug out the books and papers he'd shoved into it, and offered them to her. "I haven't looked at them yet, but I hope they're what you wanted."

She took them, motioning for Oliver and Miguel to get to work setting up the circle. "Only one way to find out," she said. She took them over to one of the candles Miguel had lit along the wall and began examining them.

Ethan, unsure of what to do, just loitered near the circle and watched the two other guys work. They were setting up candles, incense burners, and small items that looked uncomfortably like dried body parts, every once in a while pausing to consult a sheaf of papers.

"It's great that this permanent circle is here," Miguel said. "It makes things a lot faster. Otherwise this would take us at least an hour to set up."

As it was, it only took about twenty minutes before they finished. There was a wide-open spot in the middle of the circle—the two of them cleared some books and papers off one of the tables, hefted it, and placed it there, parallel to the armoire.

"What's that for?" Ethan asked. He'd been amusing himself watching the room with his magical senses; the thing in the armoire seemed to be waking up and taking an interest in its surroundings now. The light coming out of the crack pulsed in anticipation.

"Just for putting some of the stuff we need for the ritual," Oliver told him. He moved over behind Ethan, toward the door. "Hey, Stone isn't going to show up down here, is he?"

"He's busy," Ethan said. "I don't think he'll be down for a while."

"We should be done by then. You getting anything out of that stuff, Trin?" Miguel asked. "We're about ready here."

She shook her head. "Nah, nothing. This is good stuff—I want to try some of these summonings later. But nothing about what we're doing here."

"Ah, well. Plan B, then," Miguel said. He didn't sound upset about it.

"What's Plan B?" Ethan asked. And then he noticed something else. "Hey, why are there only three spots in the ritual circle? I thought you said you needed—"

Oliver grabbed him from behind, pinning his arms behind his back.

"What the hell?" he yelled, struggling. "What are you guys doing?"

Miguel smiled. "Don't worry, kid—you're about to find out exactly what Plan B is." He reached into Oliver's leather bag and pulled out the rope and the knife.

Ethan struggled harder, his eyes wild, but Oliver was much stronger than he was. "Trin!" he yelled, his terrified gaze locking on her. "What's going on? Why are they doing this? Tell them to stop!"

She smiled. It wasn't the beautiful, twinkle-eyed smile that had so captivated Ethan's lust, but a snakelike grin more at home on Miguel's face. "Sorry, kiddo," she said, shaking her head. "I guess you picked the wrong side. But don't worry—you're going to be a big help for what we're doing tonight. A really big help. And hey, cheer up—before too long, you'll get to see your mommy again."

Ethan screamed, but now the other two were there. Oliver clamped a hand over his mouth and they hustled him forward, toward the prepared circle.

| CHAPTER FORTY-TWO

Upstairs, Stone glanced at his watch. 8:45. The party was in full swing now, with people dancing, standing in little groups chatting, getting tipsy, and generally having a good time. Truth be told, he felt a bit out of place among all these elderly revelers. Megan had convinced him to dance with her a couple of times, but even she was looking like she'd rather be somewhere else.

"What time is this over?" she asked him. "Isn't it getting close to bedtime for some of these folks?"

"No such luck," he said ruefully. "Adelaide told me that the auction doesn't even start until ten, and things don't wind down until after midnight." He glanced around. "Have you seen Ethan lately?"

She thought about it. "Not for a while," she admitted. "Though I haven't exactly been looking for him. What did you tell him to do?"

"Just to circulate and keep his eyes open." He sighed. "I should probably go check on him and make sure he's all right. Mind being on your own for a while?"

"Not a problem. I'll go see what they've got for the auction. Maybe I can get us a nice weekend in the Wine Country or something. Or dance with some guy old enough to be my grandfather."

Stone headed off. He had no idea where Ethan had gotten to, nor even where to start looking. He made a quick circuit around the ballroom, then checked the dining room. No sign of him. He looked outside where a small group of men and a couple of women were smoking cigarettes on the porch, but he wasn't there either. *He's probably in the bathroom or something,* he thought, though part of him wondered if the boy had just decided he couldn't handle the party anymore and taken off, possibly having left word with someone who hadn't made it back to Stone yet.

He went back inside and was moving back toward the hallway leading to the bathrooms when he saw Langley coming out. "Hey," Langley greeted. "Having fun? No spooks yet, I hope."

"No, no spooks. Have you seen Ethan recently?"

He shook his head. "No, but I'm not too surprised. There's a lot of people here."

"So he didn't tell you he was leaving or anything?"

"Nope." He tilted his head. "Why the concern? You think something's up with him?"

"His mother died a couple of days ago. He's rather distraught about it. I told him he didn't have to come, but he insisted. I want to make sure he's all right." A thought occurred to Stone. "Hmm..."

"What?"

"I wonder if he's gone down to the basement."

"Why would he do that?" Langley asked, perplexed. "There's nothing down there but spiders and—oh, shit," he added, eyes growing fearful as light dawned. "That's where it is, isn't it? The spook."

Stone nodded. "Yes. And he knows it. Perhaps he went down to check on it."

"Wait a minute," Langley began. "He's a—" he waggled his fingers, "—too?"

"He's my apprentice, yes." He paused, taking another look around. "I should go check on him, I suppose. I was planning to go down there to check on things at some point—this is as good a time as any."

"I'll go with you," Langley said.

"Tommy—"

"Hey, don't argue. I kinda want to see this spook anyway. And besides, no offense to Aunt Adelaide, but this party is a major snooze if you're under sixty. I could use the diversion."

Stone shrugged. "Sure, come along, then. But be careful. It's quite dark down there. Don't trip over anything."

He summoned a light spell (making Langley gape in awe) and headed down the stairs. When they got to the end of the first hallway, Langley asked, "How big *is* it down here, anyway? I've never actually been here. I took Aunt Adelaide's word for the spiders."

"It's big. Just stay close."

Langley did as he was told, sticking so close behind Stone and his light source that it wasn't long before it got annoying. "Back off a little, Tommy," he grumbled. "I keep thinking you're going to grab my arse."

"I told you I don't put out on the first date," he protested, but he did move back just a bit.

Before long they were standing in front of the bookcase. Stone motioned Langley back. "It's here?" he asked. "What is this, some kind of secret door?"

In answer, Stone slid it open and waved Langley in. Wide-eyed, he entered. "Holy shit..." he breathed.

Stone, thinking Langley was just referring to the room in general, squeezed in behind him. He froze as he took in the scene before them.

The Three were arrayed evenly around the big summoning circle, all focused on the armoire at the end of the room, where the thin crack had increased to nearly a foot wide. A roiling cloud of glowing energy swirled around the opening, probing outward. The Three were too far apart to clasp hands, but their arms were stretched out toward one another. With his magical sight, Stone saw shifting, reddish energy flowing around the outside of the circle, moving between them.

It was what was in the center that drew most of his attention, though. Lying spread-eagled, tied to a table that had been dragged into the circle, his chest bared, was Ethan. Blood shone on his side from a wound there, but he was still alive because he was writhing in pain. His eyes were clamped shut. The lines of pulsing reddish energy that ran between The Three also extended from each of them and into the center, where it converged on Ethan like eldritch wheel spokes, dancing around him as if looking for a way in.

The Three were all chanting something in the same unintelligible language and ignored the newcomers.

"Holy shit," Langley said again. "We have to help him!" He stepped toward the circle, but Stone grabbed his arm and yanked him back.

"No!" he snapped. "Don't break that circle, Tommy. If you do, you'll kill everyone inside it, and probably yourself as well."

"What do we do, then?" Langley's voice began to take on an edge of panic. "It looks like they're gonna—sacrifice him or something! And why aren't they noticing us?"

"They're focused," Stone muttered, thinking hard. His gaze fell on the books open on the table—books he hadn't seen before. "Stay here. Just—don't do anything for a minute. I need to think."

"But—"

"Stay *here,* Tommy," he ordered. He ran across the room and snatched the open book on the table, skimming over the information on the page, and then riffling through other pages near it. Every few seconds, he glanced up at the circle. The reddish energy was growing more distinct, the lines clearer and thicker. Stone was very much afraid he knew what was going to happen next. They had already opened the thing's prison—it was coming through. Their next step would be to try to bring it into the circle and control it. That was where Ethan came in. Stone berated himself for not seeing it before: it was the only other way that might allow them to deal with the spirit if they didn't have its true name: to kill a mage and generate sufficient power for their circle that they could wrestle it in by main force and subjugate it while it was still weakened from its trip through.

The frightening thing was, they had a chance of succeeding.

"Alastair, come on, hurry up! I gotta do *something*," Langley pleaded, continuing to stare at the circle. " We can't just let them kill that poor kid! What can I do?"

Stone was distracted, still paging through the book in the vain hope that he'd find something useful in it. "I don't *know*, Tommy," he growled. "If you want to help, find a way to disrupt that circle without breaking it."

Langley nodded. He looked around until he found a heavy stone gargoyle candle holder sitting on a nearby bookshelf. Shaking, he picked it up, hefted its weight, and then drew his arm back. His football days were long behind him, but he aimed at the head of the closest circle member—an athletic-looking blond man—and let fly.

Stone glanced up just as he did this, his eyes going wide with shock. "Tommy, *no*—!" he cried. He tried to summon a spell to grab the gargoyle and pull it back, but was too late.

The heavy projectile flew unerringly to its target, smashing into the back of Oliver's head with a sickening *thud*.

Several things happened nearly simultaneously at that point, so quickly that for a moment Stone could only stare in horror.

A bright light flared in the circle as the red energy conduit was disrupted. Oliver died instantly. He pitched forward, his arms and legs jerking as his body had not yet realized he was dead. His flailing right leg struck one of the thick black candles around the outside of the circle, sending it rolling off to the side of the room where it ignited a pile of papers and one of the wall tapestries. Dry and brittle, they flared up like kindling.

Oliver's body continued lurching forward, crashing into Ethan's table. The table, its rotting wood barely strong enough to hold Ethan's weight, collapsed to the floor. The reddish energy flared and died.

Miguel and Trin clutched their heads, fighting crushing psychic feedback. Both had but a second to erect their mental shields, and both had done so, but imperfectly. Miguel screamed, staggering around half-blind.

Trin, meanwhile, her eyes blazing with rage, recovered fastest. She pointed at Langley and snapped out an unintelligible command. The terrified professor lifted off his feet and flew toward her. She clamped her hand on his shoulder and locked her gaze on Stone.

Stone regained his wits just in time, and was able to raise his shield just as Trin screamed something and pointed at him. Langley's screams rose above hers as he bucked under Trin's touch as if she were running a strong electrical current through him. His scream pitched to a shrieking crescendo and then suddenly he was gone. His badly fitting tuxedo fluttered to the floor, along with a swirling pile of ashes.

"*Tommy!*" Stone cried, lunging forward despite knowing there was nothing he could do.

Trin's spell struck his barrier and pulverized it, sending him careening back into the wall. He slammed into it and fell to the floor, scrambling sideways, his whole body alight with pain. Her eyes wild with power now, Trin advanced on him, pressing the attack.

Stone wasn't giving up that easily, though—stunned as he was by Tommy's sudden and horrific death, he knew he couldn't let his guard down. If he did even for a second, he'd be dead.

Grateful for all the time he'd spent infusing his crystals and other power objects, he summoned a lightning bolt and directed it at Trin. She dived aside, and got her own shield up just in time, but the bolt flew past her and struck Miguel a glancing blow. He staggered again, swaying alarmingly close to the rising flames. Blinking sweat out of his eyes, Stone saw the opening in the armoire had grown wider, and the swirling mist a little more substantial.

It was coming. He had to finish this fast. He dragged himself back to his feet and faced Trin, breathing hard.

She laughed, still brimming with the power she'd sucked in from killing Langley. She pointed both hands at Stone and let loose with another concussion attack. "Die, you bastard!" she snapped. "I already killed your pet. Maybe I can use you in his place!"

Stone had once again barely managed to get his shield up, but the feedback from her spells made his head feel like it was splitting in two. "Not—yet—" he breathed, aiming his own concussion beam at her. This time it hit her, and he was rewarded with the sight of her being flung back and slammed into one of the bookcases. Her shield flared and died.

Neither of them noticed Miguel making his slow and painstaking way toward the door. He'd swiftly taken stock of the situation, and realized things were not looking good. Oliver was dead. The fire was rising. There was a very real possibility that Stone would beat Trin—even if Miguel stayed to help. But half-blinded, his head splitting from the circle's disruption, he was forced to be a realist. Realists survived—and Miguel was nothing if not a survivor.

With one last glance at the two combatants locked in their battle, he shoved open the bookcase door and slipped out.

| CHAPTER FORTY-THREE

U pstairs, Megan was beginning to wonder where Stone had gone. It had already been longer than fifteen minutes, and she was growing bored with listening to the enthusiastic war stories an old man in a plaid tie was trying to regale her with. Politely excusing herself, she hurried off, thinking she'd find Stone somewhere nearby.

She didn't see him anywhere, though: she didn't realize it, but she nearly retraced the steps he'd taken searching for Ethan: dining room, grand ballroom, outside smoking area, hallways leading to the bathrooms. A little concerned now, she ranged out further, taking another hallway that she didn't think was strictly part of the party area. *Maybe he found Ethan and they're having a talk,* she decided. If that were true, she'd just find them, verify that they were both all right, and then head back to the party and wait for them to rejoin it.

She kept waiting for a security guard to stop her, but none did. She guessed there probably weren't enough of them to cover the whole house, and in any case, she didn't think the elderly guests were much to worry about, security-risk wise. The worst that might happen was that one of them might get lost on the way to the bathroom, or maybe stroke out in the punch bowl.

She was about to turn around and go back the way she'd come when she smelled something unexpected. *Smoke? That's strange. Maybe I'm near where the smokers are—*

But she wasn't near the smokers. They were up at the front of the house, and she was somewhere in the middle. She moved back, following the smell until she saw something that made her gasp: wafting up from an ancient floor register were tendrils of foul-smelling black smoke. Not a lot, but she knew enough to know that this was not the cheery smoke from a fireplace—even if there had been a fireplace for it to be coming from.

"Oh my God," she whispered. For a second she froze, then she hurried back down the hallway and back into the party area. She grabbed the first blazer-clad security guard she could find. "Come on—you need to see this," she breathed.

He looked at her oddly: here was a pretty young woman in a tight dress and heels, looking like she'd just seen a ghost—or a murder. "What's the problem, ma'am?"

"I think there's a *fire,*" she whispered, not wanting to start a panic if she were somehow wrong. She grabbed his arm and tugged. "Come *on*—let me show you this!"

The man followed, his expression suggesting that he was humoring her. That lasted until he saw the smoke wafting up from the register. "Holy shit," he growled, stiffening. He turned back to Megan, already pulling his walkie-talkie from his belt. "Listen, lady—you need to get out of here. I'll call it in. We gotta start evacuating people. Oh, holy hell, this is gonna be a nightmare with all these old people."

"I'll help," she said. "I'll start getting people to leave, to go outside. I'll tell them there's a gas leak or something."

"Yeah, okay," he said, already focused on talking into his radio. He waved her off.

Megan hurried back toward the party, realizing as she did that she still hadn't found Stone or Ethan. She hoped very much that the fire and their disappearance weren't related.

Outside the summoning room, Miguel hurried as fast as he could down the aisle back toward the main large room. He was in full panic mode now—all he wanted to do was get out of here alive. The fire was already burning through the wooden wall of the summoning room, providing flickering light that made the shadowy piles of furniture loom eerily above him. He glanced upward—

—and tripped over a piece of the ruined player piano, falling forward. He tried to throw himself sideways, but in his disorientation he miscalculated: his reeling body slammed into a tall pile of stacked furniture. It swayed alarmingly, and then something large dislodged from the top and tumbled down, crashing onto Miguel's legs. He screamed as he felt bones break among the splintering wood, and a wave of agony washed over him. He went down and lay still.

Inside, Stone and Trin were still locked in their battle.

"Give it up, asshole," Trin growled. "You can't fight me. You're soft, like all your type. Can't handle the power."

She flung another bolt at him—his shields were weaker now, and most of it got through and smashed into his arm. He staggered back, falling over the top of another table.

Scrambling up, he didn't bother answering her. More than ever now, he knew he had to end this fast, before Trin killed him. She didn't have a chance of controlling that thing now if it came through—not by herself, and not in her weakened state. If he failed, all those people upstairs would die, and probably a lot more, too.

She was right about the combat-type spells: they weren't his specialty, and they were tiring him out fast. Instead, he went with his strength: telekinetically snatching up the same stone gargoyle that Langley had hit Oliver with, he flung it at her, putting all his will behind it.

She wasn't expecting that. It breached her shield and hit her leg hard, taking her down with a pained shriek. Stone struggled up again and tried to press the attack before she could get her bearings back.

Unfortunately for him, the power black mages drew when they killed their "batteries" was immense, and she still had quite a bit left. Without getting up, she put her two hands together, aimed them at Stone, and let fly with a spell that looked like a whirlwind full of tiny knives. It sliced through his shield, weakening considerably as it did, but what was left flayed at his body, opening up myriad small, bleeding slashes all over. He tried to ward them off, but couldn't concentrate enough to cast anything. He lurched backward, hit the wall, and slumped to the floor in a bloody heap. He lay unmoving as his consciousness faded.

Trin threw one last concussion blast at him, laughing as she watched his body jerk and writhe on the floor against the wall. Then she turned and quickly left the room.

Megan did the first thing she could think of: she found Adelaide. The old lady was holding court in the main ballroom near one of the large Christmas trees, laughing with some old friends while Iona stood beaming next to her.

Megan hurried up to her. "Mrs. Bonham?"

She smiled. "Oh. You're Dr. Stone's date, aren't you, dear? What was your name again? Mary? Margaret?"

"Megan," she said. She ducked down to whisper in the old woman's ear. "Mrs. Bonham, there's a problem. There's a fire somewhere down below. I've already told security, and they're calling in help, but we need to get everyone out of here quickly. It won't be safe much longer."

She glanced around, her eyes growing wide and fearful. "A—fire?"

Megan didn't have time to wait for it to sink in. She hurried over to the bandstand and snatched the microphone, startling the bandleader. "Ladies and gentlemen," she said, feeling herself shaking. "Please listen to me. We need everyone to exit the house and go outside onto the front lawn. There's been—a small kitchen fire, and we want to make sure everyone's safe. Please go now in an orderly fashion, and help those who can't make it on their own. Thank you." She handed the mic back to the bandleader and climbed back down off the stage.

There was a murmur of conversation among the guests, occasionally punctuated by a louder "Fire?" or "Fire!" Meanwhile the security force was coming in, attempting to usher people out of the ballroom and toward the front lawn. It was slow going; some guests didn't believe there really was a fire, and some couldn't move very fast. Others were already heading toward the door.

Megan looked around. Where was Stone? Where were Ethan, and Tommy? Suddenly everyone she knew had disappeared, and in the middle of a potential disaster. This didn't bode well.

Trin found Miguel outside the circle room, his legs crushed, moaning in agony. "Trin..." he whispered. "Help me. For God's sake, get me out of here..." He reached toward her.

She looked at him, then back at the fire. "Sorry, man. You're on your own." And then she was past him and away, running back past the growing flames toward the exit.

| CHAPTER FORTY-FOUR

O n the shattered table, lying under the dead weight of Oliver's body, Ethan regained consciousness. His whole body was in pain—he was pretty sure at least a couple bones were broken, and he'd lost a lot of blood. Struggling free of the bonds that no longer held him, he rolled Oliver's body off, trying not to scream with the effort. He looked around, coughing, struggling for breath. *Why is it so hot and smoky in here?*

Then he saw and heard the blazing fire, and it all came back to him.

Trin.

Trin had betrayed him. She'd intended to betray him all along.

And he'd fallen for it, because she'd smiled at him. Because she'd made him feel like he was worthwhile. Because he'd wanted so badly to believe it that he'd ignored everything else.

He looked around. The crack in the armoire's doors was nearly two feet wide now, the swirling mists almost reaching the edge of the circle. He had to do something.

But what?

He continued looking, and his gaze fell on the still form of Stone, lying broken and bleeding against the wall. Was he dead? Ethan couldn't tell. Painfully, he crawled toward him. Even if he was alive, though, what could he do now? He couldn't do a sacrifice, and he didn't have the spirit's name. There was no way he could—

And then he saw his parka, lying there on the floor close to Stone. And he remembered.

He hadn't given Trin all the books he'd brought. He'd forgotten he'd even put one in his coat, with all he'd been through in the last couple of days. The news about his mother had driven nearly everything out of his mind. But now, he remembered.

The diary.

Selena Darklight's diary.

If it was anywhere, it would be there.

He had to hurry.

He continued crawling toward the parka and Stone, aware of the spreading flames behind him and the ever-widening crack in the armoire door.

The evacuation was proceeding a little more effectively now that the house's smoke detectors had at last registered the fire and gone off. Megan joined the security guards in hustling the elderly guests outside, herding them out to the porch, where the more able-bodied among them helped the others into the yard. In the distance, she could hear the sirens of fire trucks approaching, but she knew it would take them a while to make it all the way up here.

Grimly, she realized she still hadn't seen Stone. Now she was beginning to worry in earnest: if he were here, he would be in the thick of the action, doing whatever he could to help out. The fact that she couldn't hear his distinctive British tones cutting through the panic, giving orders and hustling recalcitrant oldsters out the door, told her everything she needed to know.

He wasn't here.

But where *was* he?

R. L. KING

Ethan had the book. Clutching it in his trembling hand, fighting to stay awake, he dragged himself over to Stone and rolled him over on his back. The mage was unconscious, the white front of his tuxedo shirt shredded and soaked in blood. Ethan shook him. "Dr. Stone! Wake up! Please don't be dead!"

Stone moaned.

Ethan shook him again, harder. "Dr. Stone! Please, wake up!" Sweat ran down his face; the smoke was everywhere, darkness settling over his head like a warm, heavy animal. "Please! You have to wake up!"

Stone's eyes flickered open. He seemed to be having trouble focusing for a moment, then he saw Ethan. "E...Ethan..."

Tears streamed down Ethan's face. "Oh, God, Dr. Stone. I'm so sorry. I've been such an idiot, and now we're—"

"What—?" Stone tried to rise, but couldn't manage it.

Ethan held up the book. "Dr. Stone—this is Selena Darklight's diary. I found it the other day, in the attic. I was gonna give it to Trin, but I forgot I had it. You gotta take it, Dr. Stone. You gotta stop this thing. Look!" He pointed with great effort toward the armoire. "It's gonna get out...It's gonna—get—" His energy spent, he trailed off, slumping over.

Stone fought to make sense of what Ethan was saying. He forced himself to an elbow, focusing on what he had to do. He saw the thing in the armoire and stiffened.

He could suffer through his pain later. He could even die later. Later didn't matter. All that mattered was right now—and right now, he had to do this. He picked up the diary in a shaking hand and used a small spell to break its lock. Painfully, he began paging through it.

The crack in the armoire grew wider.

"...Give up, little worm. You will not stop me now. You have lost. You will die, and so will everyone you ever cared about..."

"Bugger off," Stone muttered, continuing to turn the pages.

The first of the fire trucks were arriving now. Small groups of shivering guests huddled together in the front yard, their eyes full of fear.

Megan was still inside. She was moving from person to person as they left the house, asking them if they'd seen anyone matching Stone's description, or Ethan's, or Langley's. Sometimes she got an affirmative, but it was a vague one: "Oh, yes, I think I saw him earlier tonight," or "Yes, he was in the ballroom when I got here." But nothing definitive. It was as if all three of them had vanished from the face of the earth.

She wondered if she should head upstairs and search for them.

Stone kept having to blink blood and sweat from his eyes as he struggled to read the blurry, cramped print in the diary. This was taking too long! Already the flames were growing so high that he wasn't sure he and Ethan could even get out safely anymore. If he didn't do something soon, none of this would matter. In frustration, he growled and gave the book a hard shake.

A piece of paper, possibly used as a bookmark, poked out from between two pages about three quarters of the way in. Breathing hard, Stone opened the book to the indicated page and shoved the bookmark aside.

On the page, written in thicker, embellished text, was a single word, surrounded by diagrams of magical circles. Even looking at the word made Stone uncomfortable.

The thing in the armoire made a low, rumbling warning sound, as if anticipating his next move.

"Yes..." Stone whispered in triumph. Gathering his will, he grabbed the edge of a nearby table and pulled himself up. He staggered to the center of the circle, leaving a trail of blood behind him. He opened the book and faced the armoire, and he began an incantation.

"*...No...*" whispered the thing in his head. "*...You will* not..."

The swirling mists, which had now reached the circle, solidified into tentacles with clawed appendages, raking at him. He held his ground, bellowing the incantation as loudly and forcefully as he could manage.

The creatures slashed at him, moving in. He reeled backward, fighting to hold his balance, barely remaining inside the circle as more and more forms boiled out of the armoire's opening. The horrific sloth-creatures came through, along with the sticky, searching tentacles from his bedroom. But there were more things too: things that he could barely look at, things that made his sanity recoil and begin to crack. His voice faltered, the incantation dying on his lips.

"*...You will fail, small one...*" the thing in his head said. "*...You have no hope. You cannot stem my power. You are too weak. I was old when your world was new. I will destroy you and everything you ever cared about...*"

The creatures were drawing closer now, moving around the circle, testing its boundaries. Stone was forced to divert energy to strengthen the wards around it, but knew he couldn't do that for long—his limited power had to go toward taking his best shot at sending the thing back before he simply collapsed, his formidable will no longer able to sustain his failing body. Already the grayness was closing around him, his legs beginning to buckle.

One of the creatures, a new one with wicked claws on the end of multiple whiplike tentacles, breached his shield and slashed at him, opening up a deep gash across his chest. He cried out, raising his hands to ward off the blows, clutching Selena Darklight's diary with all his will. If he dropped it now, he knew everything would be lost.

Faster than he could see, another tentacle lashed out and sliced through his hand with surgical precision. The diary, his severed fingers still attached to it, fluttered to the floor, landing in a puddle of blood. Stone screamed, dropping to his knees. Jamming his wounded hand under his opposite arm to try to stanch the bleeding, he lunged for the book with his good hand.

The creatures were getting through now. He couldn't hold the shield around the circle anymore. Had he broken it somehow? Smudged it when he'd fallen, or when he'd dropped the diary? It shouldn't work that way—either the shield was up, or it was down. He blinked blood from his eyes again, his gaze cutting madly around to locate the source of the breach as he scrambled for the diary.

"...*You will die, little mage...*" the thing's implacable voice spoke in his head. "...*You will die screaming in agony, and your power will feed my birth into this world...*"

"No!" Stone shouted. His eyes were nearly clamped shut now, sweat pouring from him, his hand fumbling for the diary. The heat from the fire seared him.

Something flashed in the corner of his vision. He braced himself for another creature, forcing his eyes back open. But it wasn't another creature. It was Ethan. The boy lunged forward with an inarticulate war cry. Stone tried to yell a warning, but his body wasn't responding properly to commands anymore.

The creatures tore Ethan to pieces in seconds.

Stone screamed again, trying to gather energy, to move forward, to do anything, but he could only watch in horror as the claws and tentacles snatched at the boy's shirt, his pants, his hair—and then slashed and pulled at his limbs until they tore free, spraying Stone with hot showers of blood and worse. The last expression he saw on Ethan's face was one of accusation. *Why don't you help me?*

"*Ethan!*" he shrieked. "*No! I can't—*" He watched helplessly as the boy's dismembered body crashed to the floor, his shredded white shirt drenched red on his torso, on his severed arms as they, too, moved of their own accord, and began crawling toward him. Stone felt his mind beginning to let go of the last of his sanity.

He couldn't do this.

The creature was right: he was too weak. This thing was eternal, ageless, immensely powerful—even at his best, there was no way he could fight it. How did he ever think he could—

Wait.

Something was wrong.

Something he desperately needed to notice.

His fogged brain struggled to latch on to it as the creatures continued to assault the circle. Not all of them were getting in, but he knew it was only a matter of seconds, as his will failed—

Think! Something—something about Ethan—

His blood-soaked shirt—his severed limbs—

And then he had it.

His mind flitted back to when he and Tommy had entered the room, when they'd found The Three's gruesome ritual laid out before them.

Ethan hadn't been *wearing* a shirt.

Ethan had been chained to the table, chest bared for Trin's knife to slash him, to spill his blood for the ritual. How could he be—

NO!

Stone spun, nearly upsetting his precarious balance again. The room shifted crazily, its angles somehow going *wrong.* Everything about this was wrong. Ethan, the room's strange geometry, his hand—

He looked down at the ruin of his hand, pulling it free from where he'd shoved it, bleeding, under his arm. For a moment he flinched, expecting to see severed, bloody stumps again.

His hand was there, whole and undamaged, still clutching Selena Darklight's diary as if letting it go would bring about the end of the world.

Because it might.

This was all wrong. His mind was playing tricks on him. This whole thing was like some kind of mad vision.

It was like some kind of—

—dream.

And then it was clear. All of it.

In a bolt of searing lucidity, he understood.

If anyone had been looking at Stone at that moment, they would have seen his expression change. Where before he had been beaten, demoralized, racked with pain, his face now took on a kind of fierce resolve. There was still pain there—he was dead pale, blood-soaked, grievously injured.

But now he *knew*.

All of this took place in the space of a few seconds. The knowledge, the rock-hard certainty slammed into him with the force of one of his own concussion blasts.

None of this was real.

This was simply a battle of wills, with the creature using everything at its disposal to try to divert his mind, to make him falter, to destroy his resolve because it could not yet destroy his body.

Not until it was through.

It was not going to *get* through.

He would see to that. Because what the creature didn't realize—couldn't realize, because all of the mages it had dealt with since it had touched this plane of existence had been black mages—was that when it came to willpower, white mages had it all over their darker counterparts. They had to—how else would they continually force themselves to take the more difficult path, to resist the temptation to seek the easy road to power?

Stone gritted his teeth, breathing hard, and forced himself upright. "I've got you, you bastard!" he cried. "Nice try, but you can stuff your illusions. They won't work on me anymore!"

A surge of energy ran through him. A glow suffused his body: he could see it radiating out from him as if he were some sort of beacon. But even as it did, he felt himself fading, his legs turning to jelly beneath him. For all his confidence, he still didn't know if he'd be able to do it—if his body would fail him before he could finish the job. He began the incantation again, pulling in all the power from all his remaining items, weaving it into his words, yelling them in defiance.

The claws and tentacles continued reaching for him, but he no longer noticed them. They were nothing more than smoke and mist, and no more dangerous. The only danger now was that he would be too weak to do what he had to do. He spat out the words of the incantation in a strong but shaking tone, speaking as fast as he dared.

And then, at last, it was time. This was it—either it would work, or it wouldn't. He wouldn't get another chance. As the thing screamed in his mind, thrashed at his body, tried with increasing desperation to breach his will, he threw back his head and barked out the last words into the mist: "Begone, foul thing!" And he followed it with the name from the book, praying that he was pronouncing it correctly.

He knew instantly that he had succeeded. The tentacles and creatures and apparitions drew back as if they'd contacted the burning sun, withdrawing into the armoire. A last scream rose, so loud and terrible and soul-searing that it could be heard throughout the entire area.

And then the armoire exploded. The weird, sickening light expanded and then contracted, and everything in it was sucked back into itself until it reached the size of a pinpoint and disappeared.

The room was silent except for Stone's labored breathing and the crackling of the rising flames.

And then there wasn't even that as he finally allowed himself to fall.

| CHAPTER FORTY-FIVE

than awoke. He didn't know how long he'd been out this
time, but his body seared with pain and everything was even
hotter than before. He could barely see anything through
the thick, acrid smoke filling the room.

What was happening?

Where was Stone?

Where was the thing in the armoire?

He rose up a little and looked around. The armoire was gone.
Stone lay in the middle of the circle, his limbs haphazardly splayed
out, a puddle of blood spreading beneath him. Around them, the
flames licked at the walls. It was getting hard to breathe.

He crawled over to Stone, checked him. Against all odds he
was alive, but not by much. His chest barely moved, and under the
streaks of blood on his face he wore a gray pallor.

Ethan took a deep breath. *He did it. He got rid of it.* He didn't
know how, but he didn't care. He just knew they had to get out of
here, and he had to be the one to get them out. If Stone could rouse
himself sufficiently to do what he'd done then he, Ethan, could do
no less.

He struggled up, grabbed Stone under his arms, and dragged
him toward the door. He was barely able to get him through it,
holding it open and pulling him through without allowing it to
close again. When they were out, he sat down again next to the
mage's body, puffing with exertion. He didn't know what to do.

The smoke wasn't as bad out here, but he knew how far it was back to the door—and once he got there, he'd have to deal with dragging Stone up a flight of treacherous stairs. Even if he could somehow manage it, Stone would never survive the trip.

I can't do this...

Wait.

He was a mage. Mages could lift things with their minds!

But I can't. I get tired lifting a book! How am I gonna lift him? He's bigger than I am!

He said he could lift a car if he had to. Maybe you can, too. You have to try, at least.

So he did. Focusing the last scraps of his willpower, he fixed his gaze on Stone and attempted to levitate him off the ground.

The mage's arm and part of his shoulder rose, then fell back again. Ethan's head lit up with pain.

I can't do this! I can't!

Nearby, a moan.

Ethan stiffened. "Dr. Stone?" But Stone was still unconscious. Besides, the mage was behind him, and the sound had come from in front of him.

He crawled forward. "Is—someone there?" he croaked.

"Help me..." came a weak voice.

Ethan crawled closer. Miguel lay there, buried under debris, pale and sweating. His legs had been crushed by a falling piece of furniture. "Ethan..." he begged. "Help me, man. Get me out of here."

Ethan looked at Miguel. He looked back at Stone.

He made his decision.

Reaching out, he leaned toward Miguel. "Give me your hand," he rasped.

Miguel reached out, wincing, and grasped Ethan's hand.

Ethan concentrated like he never had before, remembering the other night, remembering what Trin had told him.

Don't take too much, or you'll kill him.

By the time Miguel realized what was happening, he was too far gone to do anything about it. His weak scream as his body was consumed barely reached beyond the pile of furniture that had crushed him.

More fire trucks were arriving now, and they'd taken over the evacuation as they set about fighting the fire. The flames still weren't visible on the ground floor, but the smoke rose everywhere now. It was getting harder to see and harder to breathe.

Megan grabbed one of the firefighters as he was going in. "My friends are still in there," she said. "Please look for them. There are three of them. Two men around my age and a boy about eighteen. I can't find them anywhere."

He assured her that he would look, but then he was gone, into the swirling smoke.

Megan stood there, out of the doorway, and tried to decide what to do. *Think,* she ordered herself. *Where would they be?*

And then she knew. Of course. If the fire was in the basement, then that was where they had to be.

Would the firefighters even look for anyone down there?

She hurried back inside, hoping she wasn't making the biggest—and last—mistake of her life.

Ethan *brimmed* with power.

It wasn't that he didn't still feel the pain and the fear and the exhaustion. They were all still there, but they just didn't *matter* right now.

He felt like he could do *anything.*

He turned back toward Stone, who hadn't moved from where he'd left him. Focusing his mind again, he carefully formed the pattern and then fed it power from the vast reservoir he had at his command. Was this how Stone felt when he really got going? He decided that Stone couldn't possibly have ever felt this kind of power surging through him. It felt *wonderful.*

He sent the command. Stone's body rose and hovered there, about a foot off the ground.

Ethan began to move.

Megan blundered, coughing, through the antechamber, back toward the kitchen. She had a vague idea where she was going, but the smoke was getting thicker. She grabbed a decorative runner from one of the tables and put it up to her face to breathe through, kicking off her heels and crouching to stay low. Her eyes streamed. Around her, she could hear the voices of the firefighters as they called to each other, but she ignored them.

Down the hall, through the dining room, and then she reached the kitchen. She looked wildly around: the place looked eerie, deserted in the act of preparing more hors-d'oeuvres and plates of cookies as the chefs and caterers had evacuated.

Now that she was in the kitchen, she had no idea where to go next.

"Alastair!" she yelled in frustration, then a coughing fit seized her. "Ethan! Tommy! Where are you?"

A door on the far side of the room opened. She spun to face it, in time to see two bloody scarecrow figures shove themselves through. One collapsed on top of the other, and neither moved.

She raced over and dropped to her knees next to them. She could barely identify them through all the blood, but she realized in horror that Stone was on the bottom, and Ethan was lying across him.

"Oh my God..." she whispered. And then she screamed: "*Help! Please! Someone help me!*"

Ethan raised his head just a little and moaned.

"Don't talk," she urged. "Help's coming." She wondered if Stone was even alive, or if Ethan would be for long.

"Tell him..." Ethan whispered.

She leaned in close. "What? Tell him what, honey?" She brushed his bloody hair off his forehead.

"Tell him—I'm sorry I let him down," he whispered, and then his head fell on top of Stone.

| CHAPTER FORTY-SIX

Two Weeks Later

The basement lab was dark, except for a single candle guttering away on the table. There was a knock on the door. "You have a visitor…" Megan called softly.

"No," Stone said. "No visitors. Tell them to go away."

"I'll just…leave you two alone," she said, departing.

The deadbolt turned and the door opened. It closed again, then footsteps sounded on the stairs. "Alastair." The British-accented voice was familiar.

Slumped and shadowed, Stone had his back to the door, staring at the flickering candle. "I said I didn't want any visitors." His voice was colorless, monotone. Dead. The room smelled strongly of alcohol.

Walter Yarborough sat down on the ratty leather sofa. "Your lady friend let me in. She thought you might want to talk to me, since I've come all this way to see you."

"She was wrong."

Yarborough sighed. "I know it's been a rough couple of weeks for you, Alastair—"

Stone made a contemptuous sound, halfway between a mirthless laugh and a snort. "Who cares?"

"I do. You're an old friend. I want to help."

"Then go away, Walter. I don't need help. I don't need coddling, or kindness, or someone to hold my hand. I just want to be left alone."

Stone spun the chair around toward the sofa. He knew he was barely recognizable as himself: thinner, paler, his face all dark haunted eyes and wild hair and several days' worth of stubble. The bandages were gone for the most part—at least the visible ones—but the many small cuts and slashes were still evident on his face, neck, and arms.

"I didn't come here to coddle you, Alastair. I came to talk some sense into you. Because nobody else seems to be able to do that." He sounded stern but kind, like a loving father.

"I'd have thought you wouldn't want anything to do with me."

"Why is that?"

His eyes came up to meet Yarborough's. "I got your apprentice killed, Walter. You sent him to me, and I got him killed."

"You know," Yarborough said, meeting his gaze, "I still don't know what happened down there. Not exactly. You're the only one left who can tell me."

Stone turned his chair back around so he faced the candle. "Did you attend the memorials? The doctors wouldn't even let me out to do that."

"I did. Ethan and his mother—they had their services together. And I'm sure they would forgive you. Recovering from surgery is a valid excuse to miss an event."

Stone blew air through his teeth. "Walter, just go. Please. I want to be left alone."

"You can't hide forever, Alastair." He paused, and then: "Miss Whitney says you barely speak to her."

Shrug. "I didn't ask her to be here. She took that on herself."

"She cares about you. So do I. Why won't you let anyone care for you?"

Once again he spun to face Yarborough. His eyes were chilly. "I got my apprentice killed, Walter. I got my friend killed. I should have died myself. It's only because Megan had her wits about her that a whole houseful of people didn't die."

"I talked to Adelaide Bonham," he said softly. "She said she tried to contact you, but you wouldn't answer her calls. She also told me about what you did."

"What I did."

"She told me about the thing in her basement. It isn't there anymore."

"The bloody *house* isn't there anymore, Walter."

Yarborough shook his head. "Be honest with me: how bad was it? The—spirit, or demon, or whatever it was."

"Bad enough." He didn't look at Yarborough. "Truth is, I've never seen worse."

"And how many people would have died if you hadn't done what you did?"

Stone glared. "It doesn't *matter,* Walter."

"Because you think you killed Ethan."

"And Tommy."

Yarborough sighed. "Alastair, come back home with me. Back to England for a while. Get away from all of this. Bring Miss Whitney if you want to. Sitting here in your study drinking yourself to death isn't going to bring Ethan back. Or Tommy. And deciding you don't deserve to be alive because they aren't is just lazy thinking. It's not worthy of you."

Stone's gaze came up. "Is that what you believe I think?"

"It's pretty obvious. You've got a bad case of survivor's guilt, my friend."

Stone stared at the other mage for a long moment, then sighed, pondering. "P'raps…p'raps you're right. Maybe I do need a change of scenery. I haven't p'been home in a while."

Yarborough smiled just a bit. "That's more like the Alastair Stone I know." He rose, his expression growing serious again. "For what it's worth, I don't believe you got Ethan killed. I'm not stupid. I knew he'd be a handful when I put him in touch with you. Let me guess: he got himself involved in some things we'd both have disapproved of."

"It doesn't matter what he did. He saved my life, I know that. As far as I'm concerned, that's all I need to know. If I'd paid more attention to what was going on in his life, I might have been able to prevent some of what happened."

"Or you might not have," Yarborough said gently. "That's the trouble with apprentices—they have the unfortunate habit of being human. And you know as well as I do that any time you add humans to a situation, there's no way to know where or how it will end up. We're an unpredictable lot."

He paused, then came around behind Stone and put a gentle hand on his shoulder. "Remember, Alastair: when a master agrees to take on an apprentice, it's not only the apprentice who learns valuable lessons."

Stone looked up at him. His eyes were still haunted with guilt and pain, but something subtle in them had changed. "That's very profound, Walter," he murmured. "Did you get that in a fortune cookie?"

"*Magic for Dummies,*" he said mildly. "Now come on—when was the last time you had anything to eat, not counting alcohol?"

Stone thought. "Sometime—yesterday, I think. Megan tried this morning, but I haven't been much to live with lately."

"Come on, then—get yourself presentable, and let's go out for a nice steak, if you're feeling up to it. Just the three of us. Then we can talk about getting you back home where you belong for a while so you can recharge. And after that—I think you should look for another apprentice. I believe the expression is 'get back on the horse.'"

Stone shook his head, getting unsteadily to his feet. "I'll go out tonight, but I make no promises about the rest. And I'm done with apprentices."

"You say that now. We'll see. In any case, I think you owe Miss Whitney an apology for the way you've been treating her lately, don't you?"

"Yes, I think I do. It's a wonder she puts up with me, honestly."

Yarborough chuckled and headed upstairs. Stone paused for a long moment, gazing into the dying candle. Then he leaned down, blew it out, and followed his old friend up out of the lab.

Read on for a preview of

THE FORGOTTEN

Book 2 of the Alastair Stone Chronicles

Coming soon!

PROLOGUE |

In the darkness, Verity's eyes flew open.

Disoriented, she lay still for a moment, holding her breath. Around her there was no sound. The room was quiet and dark, the curtains still against the closed window, the soft glow of her alarm-clock face illuminating a few inches of her battered nightstand.

3:27 a.m.

She waited for several seconds, reaching out with all her senses. Something had awakened her. She didn't just wake up for no reason in the middle of the night. Was it the sound of one of the staff walking past the door? The closing door of one of the residents returning to his or her room after a trip to the bathroom? The blare of a too-loud radio or television in the far-off common room downstairs? She didn't think it was any of those. They were all normal sounds around here, part of the fabric of her existence. There was no reason why any of them would start affecting her differently now.

So what was it, then? A bad dream? God knew she had enough of those, but it still didn't seem right. Those kinds of dreams tended to jolt her awake in a cold sweat, the vestiges of whatever horror had sought to disturb her calm still alarmingly fresh in her mind.

She took a deep breath, rolling over and pulling the covers up so she could snuggle under them, cocoon-like. When she was a little girl back before things had all gone to hell, she used to think that nothing could hurt her as long as she was bundled up in her safe warm bed, the covers wrapped around her as tight as mummy wrappings. A lot had changed since those days, but the feeling still brought her comfort. *Okay,* she told herself. *Just go back to sleep. It'll be morning soon and you'll forget all about this.* To quiet her mind, she began to play an old game her brother had taught her many years ago: think of a category, then pick a random letter of the alphabet and try to think of something that fit the category. She usually fell back asleep before she hit ten letters.

Okay, she thought again. *Wild animals, and P. Possum. Q. Ugh, I hate Q. Oh, wait—quail! R: Raccoon. S, then—*

Scream.

She gasped, jerking fully awake. No mistake that time—she had heard it. It wasn't close, but it was there. The desperate, inarticulate scream of someone in terrible pain, or fear, or both. Somewhere inside the house. Downstairs, maybe?

For a moment she just lay there, trying to quiet her breathing, listening to see if the scream was repeated. It wasn't. She'd heard plenty of screams during her time here—everybody had. Kids were always coming down off something, having nightmares, detoxing. Hell, she'd produced a few of those screams herself, on some of her bad nights. That had been a while, though, thank goodness. Most of the residents here had been here for a while, and most of them had worked through most of their demons to the point where nights were usually pretty quiet. The worst she'd heard in the last month had been an argument between Ryan and Charles after Ryan had decided to blow off some assigned chores.

She took a deep breath. The easiest thing to do would be to just roll over, pull the covers over her head, and go back to sleep. Now that she knew what had awakened her, she could easily rationalize it as somebody having a bad night. It wasn't her concern. You learned early not to get too involved around here. Just focus on your own thing, and leave the rest of it to the staff. That's why they were here. Getting involved could get you in trouble, or worse. You just pretended you didn't see things, and pretty soon they went away. If you were lucky, anyway.

But yet something about that scream—it had sounded very young. Too young to be here. She knew everybody in this place, and the youngest resident was fourteen, three years younger than she was. That scream had not come from a fourteen-year-old. She would have bet a lot of money on that, if she had any. What a child was doing here, she had no idea.

Still trying to stay as silent as possible, she swung her legs free of the covers and sat on the edge of the bed. The wooden floor was cold under her bare feet—it would be winter soon and the air was full of a constant low-grade chill. They couldn't afford to run the heater all the time so they did what they could.

She didn't need to turn on a light—she knew every inch of this place like it was the home where she'd grown up. Quietly she padded across the room, pushed open her door—no locks here—and stepped out into the hallway. On either side of her were a row of closed doors; to her left a stairway led down to the kitchen, rec room, and other common areas. The hallway was deserted.

Still moving slowly and silently she crept toward the stairs, then stopped to listen. Nothing. The house was as still as she'd have expected it to be at nearly 3:30 in the morning.

It's not too late, she told herself. *You can just turn around and go back to bed. Nobody's seen you. You won't be in trouble.*

But the child—such pain for one so young. And the scream— why hadn't everyone heard it? Why weren't all the doors being flung open, people running out to see what was going on? She couldn't have been the only one who heard it.

They told her that she heard things—saw things—sometimes things that nobody else could hear or see. They tried to tell her that they weren't there, but she knew better. They were there, all right.

They were everywhere, all around. She even suspected that they were here, but she couldn't be sure. They hid their traces well. She had found evidence, almost like a leftover trail of body odor or perfume that remained in a room long after the person had left, but nothing definitive.

Nobody believed her, of course. She learned that a long time ago, and stopped saying anything about it. She'd been in places like this long enough to know how they worked. You kept your head down and your mouth shut, you did what you were told, and you tried to find ways to get by without attracting attention. She'd gotten good at that.

And now, if she kept up her current course, she could end up losing all the credit she'd built with the staff, all the trust she'd earned. It would be so easy to just turn around and go back to her room.

She thought of her brother then. She'd been close to him years ago, when she was a little girl and he was a teenager. She'd idolized him, loving the way he'd take on neighborhood bullies or barking dogs to protect her. He protected everybody. That was just the way he was. And she wanted to be just like him—a protector of the weak, not a coward who'd slink back to her safe warm bed at the slightest sign of danger. She'd never be able to live with herself if that child was injured.

She was at the bottom of the stairs before she realized that she'd been moving. Again she stopped; again she listened.

More silence. Had she just been hearing things? Had it just been the tail end of a particularly vivid dream, perhaps brought on by the cry of a bird outside her window? That was—

Wait.

What was that?

She froze, standing just inside the open entranceway that led to the kitchen and the dining room.

Had that been a whimper? The sound of someone desperately trying not to cry?

There it was again! It went on for a couple of seconds, then cut off abruptly as if purposely muffled. Then she heard the low rumble of a male voice.

It was coming from somewhere in the direction of the kitchen. She was sure of it. She was also sure that there was no way she could give up now. She had to know who this mysterious child was, and what this man was doing to him. The male voice hadn't been loud or distinct enough for her to recognize it, if she'd ever even heard it before.

Nearly tiptoeing now, knowing that if she made even the smallest of sounds she'd be discovered, she moved across the kitchen like a ghost in flannel skully pajamas. There wasn't much past this point: just the pantry closet and the door to the basement, which was always locked. She'd never been down there—when she'd asked, she was told they kept things like yard care items, cleaning chemicals, and other supplies there, and it was off limits to residents. She hadn't much cared; she had a normal amount of curiosity but wasn't in a big hurry to poke around a smelly, spidery basement.

Now, though, she noticed to her surprise that the basement door was open, just a bit. The tiniest crack of light poked out into the kitchen, softly illuminating a few of the blue and white floor tiles. And as she stopped near it to listen, she heard the whimper again.

It was definitely coming from down there.

She stopped, her breath coming a little faster. What was a distressed child doing in the basement with the weed whackers and the toilet cleaner? And what was a man doing down there with him? She couldn't think of any possible way that this could come out sounding good.

What to do, though? Should she call someone? Somewhere around the house at least one of the staff should be doing rounds soon; she could find them and bring them here. But what if they didn't believe her?

Or worse—what if they were somehow connected with whatever was going on?

She closed her eyes for a few seconds, willing her brain to calm down and let her think. Call the police? They'd never get here in time. Even that time when Johnny had ODed on some bad stuff he'd somehow gotten hold of and freaked out in the dining room, the cops had taken nearly twenty minutes to arrive. By that time Johnny had injured two residents and a staff member. So no, cops were out of the question.

Did she dare check it out on her own? Maybe if she sneaked down there—

Looking around the darkened kitchen she tried to find a weapon. The only light came from the tiny shaft from the basement door, the scant moonlight coming in from the window, and a small Mickey Mouse night-light plugged in near the toaster, but it was enough to show her that no weapons were forthcoming. Naturally they kept all the knives and other dangerous implements locked up. Even things like rolling pins were locked away out of reach.

She could sneak back to her bedroom and look for something there, or—

The child screamed again, loud and piercing. This time the scream started out with words: "*Nooo! Please...don't—*"

That was it. Tossing all caution away, she flung the door open and pounded down the wooden stairway, looking wildly around for the source of the scream—

—and stopped dead.

There were no yard-care implements here. No chemicals. No spiders.

There was only a featureless gray room with padded walls and a hard, concrete floor, illuminated by a bank of harsh fluorescent lights overhead.

In the middle of the room stood a man, his back to the stairway, holding on to a young boy perhaps nine years old. The man hadn't noticed her, the sound of her descent muffled by the child's screams. As she watched, shocked into immobility, the man laughed and touched the boy's forehead.

The boy screamed even louder this time, a sound of transcendent agony that rose to a shrieking crescendo and then abruptly stopped. For the space of barely a second the boy's eyes met hers over the man's shoulder—pleading with her to do something, anything—and then—

—he was gone.

Just like that, the space where he had stood was empty. There was nothing left but a faint smell of ozone in the air, a heap of disarrayed clothing, and a tiny charred pile of what looked like ashes at the man's feet.

"*NOOOOOOO!*" Her own scream, of defiance and shock and disbelief at what she'd just seen, was almost as loud as the boy's. She rushed forward, having no idea what she intended to do but not caring. She had to do something.

The man wheeled around, and she nearly stopped in her tracks again. His face was wild, almost inhuman in its ferocity. His eyes blazed with some weird inner light, and his mouth was stretched wide in a grin straight from the pits of Hell. He reached out toward her, his fingers seeking her.

"Go—AWAY!" she yelled. It was as if something alien had taken over her mind—she felt like whatever was happening, she was just along for the ride now. Instead of shrinking back from the madman lunging toward her, she held her ground. Clasping her hands together and pointing them at his head as if she were shooting an invisible pistol, she forced *out* with her mind. She felt something, some kind of power, emanate from her and contact the man. For a moment a nimbus of strange foggy light formed around him. He screamed, clutching his head and dropping to his knees.

She did step back now, staring at him as he writhed there, obviously engaged in some massive interior struggle. Then all the life went out of him and he dropped bonelessly to the floor. As she continued to watch, some sort of nebulous purplish...*thing*...wafted up out of his body and hovered for a moment in the air above him. It oriented itself, then shot toward her.

"NO!" she yelled again, and forced out with her mind as she had done before. She had no idea how she was doing this—it was instinctive, like breathing or crying. But it had its effect—the floating thing changed direction, darting around the room for several seconds and then heading straight up through the ceiling.

She didn't move for nearly a full minute. She stood there, rooted to the spot, her numb gaze taking in the room, the pile of ashes and clothes, the unconscious (*dead?*) man. The weird insane expression had left him; he looked now like nothing more than a nondescript middle-aged man in a suit.

When the compulsion to remain standing in one place left her, she did the only logical thing she could think of: she ran. Her only thought as she pelted up the stairs was to get away from the man, to find someone on the staff, to bring them down here and show them the man and explain to them about the ashes and the boy and—

—She flung herself out the door into the kitchen. She didn't see the shadowy figure standing there until she collided with it.